KILL HELL

A TRENT AND SINCLAIR MYSTERY

JANET PERIAT

BOOKS BY JANET PERIAT

How To Make Your Life Suck:
A Ten-Step Program in the Art of Self-Loathing

Confessions of a Pink-Haired Lunatic

Cinderolda

Caught

Payback

Kill Hell

Published 2019 by Madison Avenue Press

www.janetperiat.com

First Edition: 2019

ISBN 978-1-937813-08-6

Front Cover Art: Randall Cleveland

Book Cover Design: Frank Higgins

Editor: Amy Knupp

Formatting: The Formatting Fairies

For Anonymous
So all my friends can believe this book is dedicated to them

ACKNOWLEDGMENTS

This is the place where I normally thank all the people who helped me with the writing of the book. Here's my issue: during the writing of *Kill Hell*, I was accidentally poisoned with an anti-seizure medication at a hospital, had seizures and nearly died. No oxygen went to my brain during the seizures and I lost chunks of my memory. So I honestly have zero idea all the people who helped me write this thing. If you don't see your name here, please remind me and in future editions, I'll make sure your name is included.

So here are the people I remember who helped me: thanks to my critique groups, The Phoenixes: Ann Fischer, Anne Maragoni and Linda Hill, for all your amazing advice and insight on the book and The Armadillos: Linda Baxter, Teri Bradburn and Sueanne Snow, for your great guidance and help.

Thanks to my RWA friends, especially Karin Tabke for her kindness and guidance and Sharon Hamilton for her continuing inspiration.

Thanks to retired San Francisco Police Department's Sergeant Paul Maniscalco, for the police-y stuff.

Thanks to Delores De Alba, not only for keeping my head together, but for helping me build my more psychologically damaged characters.

I want to thank give a special thanks to Marianne Smith, who not only made me feel really good about my work, she helped me gain compassion for my damaged brain and life. Her constancy, kindness and tenderness during my ordeal have been instrumental in helping me make peace with my limitations and illness. I treasure our friendship and can't thank her enough for helping me heal when she was facing such huge challenges of her own. I hope she's still here by the time I get this book published. Girl, you'd better be waiting for me in The Light—with hot guys with six-pack abs, a bucket of ice-cold Heinekens and a chocolate buffet. Deal?

I want to thank Ginger Slonaker and Clare Wildenborg for being there for me when I was at my most screwed up and scared. Also thanks to my brothers from other mothers, Eison "Ike" Chan, Gus Gurevitch and Allyn Cook, for looking out for me after the accident and checking in so often.

Thanks to Rachel Lather for making me feel normal. Ceci Nunes for her limitless positivity. Huge shout-out to my Gavilan College Theater family. Another giant shout-out to my Gilroy High School friends, it's been awesome reconnecting with you all on Facebook, especially the Krahenbuhl brothers. Also a big shout-out to my UC Santa Cruz Theater friends, especially Sheryl Blanc Brog, Hillary Dimond Miller, Deborah Taylor and Cynthia Savage.

Thanks to Carol Little and Victoria Skinner for supporting my work by choosing my novels for your book clubs.

Thanks to Tina Bilan Skow and Jeanne Simari for making me feel so great about my writing.

Thanks to my neighbor, Paul Zawilski, for adopting Forrest and Malcolm, two of my favorite cat buddies. Since I can no longer have cats of my own due to allergies, I cherish their visits. (Addendum: RIP Malcolm, who was hit by a car late in 2015. I cried more over his death than most humans I've lost. I'll always remember and love him. He was a hell of a cat.) (Extra Addendum: The Zawilskis adopted another cat whom Forrest didn't like, so my beloved friend moved in with me. Big shout out to the Zawilskis for being so gracious about Forrest's choice.) (Extra Extra Addendum: I have a cat again! I love my little buddy! And he doesn't make me sneeze! Woo-hoo!)

A very giant, colossal thanks to my cousin, Diane Castle, who is always there for me. Love you more than you could know.

At the time of this writing, I'm still healing. Before the accident, I could write upwards of fourteen hours a day. For the first four months after the poisoning, I couldn't write at all. Then I could write for an hour. Then two hours. Now, I'm up to about four, five if I'm lucky, six if I'm having a spectacular day. Of course, what I wrote at first needed to be fixed. Luckily, I've finally healed enough to finish the book.

But it's been a long haul.

As it turns out, when you have brain damage, you can't tell you have brain damage. The only way you can tell is by the horrified expressions on your friends' faces when you attempt to communicate with them, and when you try to work things like an ATM machine or train ticket machine. It's like living in a Twilight Zone episode. You're locked inside your own version of reality, and don't realize it's changed until you try to interact with the outside world. And then you're totally shocked, appalled, and scared by the results.

My husband, Frank, and I were looking up at a bright, full moon one night in the backyard, about six months after the poisoning. I pointed upwards and said, "Moon." He looked at me like I had two heads. "What?" I asked. "I said 'moon.'" "Uh, no, you didn't," he replied. "You said, 'Maaaahh.'" And he proceeded to do an imitation of my empty-faced, vacant expression. "Oh. Crap."

Now six years later, I'm finally healed enough to realize what I lost. I see a giant difference between the way I was right after the accident and now, and I'm grateful for how much I've healed. But I'm still having major issues. The accident left me with chronic fatigue. I can't handle more than one or two short appointments a week. I just started to be able to go on short vacations, but they take extensive preparation and exhaust me. I rarely socialize, I don't attend concerts, weddings, or funerals. All plans are made with the contingency of a last-minute cancellation, depending on what energy I have that day. I used to be a fireball, now I'm a slug pretending to be a human being.

However, I am improving. My brain is firing much better these days. While I grieve for the loss of what I had, I celebrate what I have left, which is a beautiful, blessed life. I have enough food to eat (a little more than I need), a wonderful home, a great husband, and amazing friends. And I am especially grateful that the Story Factory in my brain still works, my only problem is the juice needed to fuel it.

So while I've spent much time over the past five years sitting in a recliner and staring into space, I've had a chance to examine my life, my choices, and my future plans. Before the accident, I was running at light speed without pause to stop and reflect, surrounded by abusive people who were using me. Once my illness rendered me unable to serve others, the unhealthy people abandoned me. While it completely freaked me out at the time—I was seriously screwed up and alone and scared when Frank was at work—in the end they did me a giant favor by revealing the truth of my old life. While I was dumped by the majority, I wasn't alone. Many wonderful people stepped forward and revealed themselves as true friends. I am grateful for each and every one.

But there was one person there for me the entire time. One person who never let me down. One person who held me when I was scared, one person who took care of me when there was no one else around. He showed me how to use public transportation when I lost my driver's license (licenses are revoked immediately in California following documented seizures), quietly reminded me of my friends' names when I'd forgotten them, and went to work every day to support me. Without my husband Frank, I have no idea where I'd be. I could not love him or thank him enough. During our thirty-one years together, he's always been a great husband, but in the past six years, he's transcended great, and is into Hella Amazing territory. You're the best, Frank, and I thank my lucky stars everyday that I found you. Love you, Big Guy.

CHAPTER 1

Helen "Hell" Trent gazed at the tall, dark-haired Adonis making her latte, wishing he were on the menu. *I'd like a Hunkachino with ripped abs and a nice, tight butt.* She tucked her skull-covered wallet into the inside pocket of her black leather jacket and ate a bite of currant scone. Mr. Beautiful's large, pale blue eyes met hers. Her heart stopped, and her body rushed with hormones. He handed her the latte, and his smile widened. Hell swallowed hard, returned the smile, and forced her legs to move. Tingling all over, she pushed open the glass door with her shoulder, walked out of Starbucks, and stopped on the corner of Seventeenth Avenue and El Camino Real.

Six lanes of Sunday morning traffic rushed by. Fairly light for the busy thoroughfare, but everyone still seemed obligated to go as fast as they could while disregarding as many traffic laws as possible. Drivers in the Bay Area—and San Mateo in particular—shared three things in common: they were all late, entitled, and cranky.

While she waited for the light and tried to think of an excuse to go back inside the coffee shop and ogle Mr. Beautiful, a cold breeze chilled her. She shivered. The clouds parted, and a stream of hot morning sunshine hit her. Hell's jacket and blue jeans trapped the welcome warmth. She couldn't wait for summer, when San Mateo temperatures were in the seventies instead of the current fifties.

A car backfired. The window directly behind her shattered.

Hell's body jerked, her heart rate skyrocketed, and her latte and scone flew out of her hands. She tried to catch her drink, but it smacked the pavement and exploded all over her black Converse high-tops. The scone bounced into traffic and was instantly flattened by a bus.

Why would the window shatter from just a loud noise? Still crouching, she turned to check out the damage. The car backfired again. Inside Starbucks, a light fixture exploded. Customers screamed and dove for cover.

Holy shit! It wasn't backfire; someone was shooting!

A blast of fight-or-flight juices amped her system, and she hit the ground. Her body on full alert, her limbs shaking, Hell searched the intersection. On the opposite side of the street, a guy in a ski mask driving a black sedan pointed a gun at her.

Popping sounds filled the air.

Screaming, she scrambled for cover behind a parked car. Pieces of stucco from the wall behind her rained down on the sidewalk. People yelled from inside the coffeehouse.

Her heartbeat wild, she leaned against the car and planned her escape route.

No more gunshots.

She got up on her knees and peered through the window of the car. Mr. Assassin's sedan screeched away.

She leapt to her feet and tried to read his license plate, but he was too far away. Black Honda Accord with California plates. Seventh generation produced between 2003-2005, before the triangular tail-lights of the 2006 and 2007 models.

The sedan took the Highway 92 exit west toward Half Moon Bay and disappeared.

Her body trembled uncontrollably. Sweat trickled down her neck, and her belly roiled with nausea. She whipped out her cell and called 911. Dispatch assured her that help was on its way.

Hell hung up the phone, and the truth hit her like an oncoming bullet train.

She'd been the target.

The threatening note taped to her door! *Stop fucking him, or I'll kill you, bitch.*

Tears stung her eyes, and she wrapped her arms around her body. "It wasn't a prank," she whispered.

Horrible. She'd only been shot at once before, but it was in a hail of bullets between two armed groups, not at her alone. Not that the instance hadn't been terrifying, but this was a bazillion times worse. This attack was *personal*.

Feeling vulnerable on the sidewalk with traffic whizzing past on El Camino, she walked down Seventeenth. She pushed past the throng of terrified customers streaming out of Starbucks and tucked herself against the wall of a bank.

But who the hell was "him" in the warning? She'd questioned all her ex-boyfriends and current lovers after she'd received the threat, but gotten no leads. The only boyfriend who hadn't gotten back to her was Marco Capasso, one of the more likely sources of the threat. Time to give him another call. Not that she relished the thought.

Still, she'd been seeing Marco for eleven years. They were anything but hot and heavy now. More like an old married couple who screwed once a year—despite her best efforts to avoid the asshole Mafia boss.

Maybe it was someone she'd put in prison. Greg Bawdon had been released recently. But he wouldn't taunt her by sending a note. He'd just track her down and shoot her.

Damn it, she needed help on this one. Joe would be there for her.

Her body went rigid. She couldn't reveal her whole list of lovers to the police! And not to an ex-boyfriend cop!

If her family found out... She shuddered and her limbs shook harder. Horrifying.

What about BC? She clapped her hands to her head. No one could find out about him. Her world would end. His world would end.

Sirens echoed from blocks away.

Hell hugged herself tightly. "Calm down, kid."

But how could the threat come from BC? He had so many girl-friends she was like an anchovy in a whole school. Besides, their liaisons were beyond discreet. More like black ops.

Still, she had to consider the possibility. BC was a rich, powerful man with more enemies than Obama. He was also the first new lover she'd taken on in the past two years, and she'd only been going out with him for a few months.

Her face burned, and her interior twisted. Only she could find someone more dangerous than a Mafia don. "This is what happens when you break your cardinal rules. No married men. No clients. No unethical, immoral, rich bastards. Damn it, you knew better."

Crap. Figured the best sex of her life would lead to her death.

Hell put on her hard face while she waited for the police to arrive, but all she wanted to do was go home, crawl in bed with Secret Teddy, and cry.

Monday, March 7, 2011, 10:32 a.m.

MATT SINCLAIR SAT AT HIS DESK AND STARED AT THE PHONE. TWISTING in his chair, he looked out his window at the empty parking lot. Day forty of his new business endeavor wasn't going so well. Neither had days one through thirty-nine.

He only had a month before his savings ran out. With Clint and Henry in college, Patty might never be able to quit her day job. His face went hot with shame.

His phone rang. He jerked, and his heart rate ratcheted high. A spark of hope lit in his gut. He reached for it when he heard his secretary's voice from the outer office.

"Sinclair Investigations, may I help you? Yes, Sergeant Piccolo, he's here."

Matt sunk into his seat, his shoulders slumping. Not a job. But at least Joe still talked to him. His ex-partner and the only cop at the station who believed that Matt had been framed. "I'll get it, Mindy, thanks." He picked up the phone. "Joe? What can I do for you?"

"Matty, howzit goin' there in your new business?"

"Great. Workin' hard. You know."

"Yeah, say, I got a favor to ask you."

"Uh-huh?"

"Pays."

Matt sat up in his chair and straightened his tie. "Huh...let me see. Might have some time this week. What's the case?"

"Possible attempted murder, woman's been getting death threats. We don't have the manpower to help her. You know with the budget cuts, if the vic don't bleed, we don't proceed."

"Yeah, understood. She a friend of yours?"

"Yeah..." Joe replied in a hesitant tone.

"Who is it?"

"Now look, Matty, she's a good person. She's helped me out a lot."

Already on the defensive? This sounded bad. "Who is it?"

"And she's scared. Of course, she won't let on. But I think someone really is tryin' to kill her. Actually surprised it hasn't happened before. But she's good people."

Matt closed his eyes, and his belly turned to fire. Who else would Joe defend like that? The woman needed a good defense. She was a scourge. No wonder someone was trying to kill her. "It's Hell Trent."

"Yeah."

"Well, I can solve the case right now. It's like *Murder on the Orient Express*; they all did it. All of her various lovers, all the people she put in jail, I'm sure they all gathered together for a Hell Hate Fest and are collectively trying to end her life and help make this Earth a better place. What really hurts me was that I wasn't invited to the party."

"Matt, don't talk about her like that."

"It's the truth. She's immoral, depraved, loud-mouthed, obnoxious—"

"Those are some of her best qualities."

"She's a disease on my new profession, Joe."

"She's also got work comin' out her ears. Ever since she cracked that Candler kidnapping case and brought Brittney home—"

Matt's jaw clenched and sweat dripped down his temple. His body turned into one giant ball of hate. He'd been on that case twenty-four hours a day for a solid week, and she'd waltzed in and broken it in a day.

"—she gets twenty calls a day. You don't think that if you hang out with her, and do good for her, she won't throw some of her leftovers your way?"

Matt's vision went blurry, and he gripped the phone hard. "I don't want her goddamned leftovers, I'm doing fine myself!"

"Let's see, you spent five grand settin' up that joint and have made, what? Seven hundred bucks in two months? Ain't gonna put the boys through college," he taunted in a singsong voice.

"I hate you." Matt should have never told him what he'd spent. Or earned.

"You won't. Not if I save your ass by hookin' you up with her."

"Have you forgotten that I was the one who put her in jail? Hell hates me."

"She needs you, Matty. She fired her secretary, and now the place looks like a total dump. She don't bill people, she don't answer calls, and now someone's tryin' to kill her."

"There isn't one person on this Earth I detest more."

"Okay, what do you hate more? Losin' your house, or swallowin' a little pride and helpin' out a friend of mine?"

"You have lousy taste in friends."

"You got that right."

Matt pursed his lips. "Does she know you're trying to send me over there?"

"She's, uh...warmin' up to the idea."

"No."

"Fine. I know Patty's dream is to work that lousy admin job for the rest of her life. She don't need to do those pretty tapestries. Kids can take a couple years off school, and work. They'll do great."

"Asshole." Matt slammed down the phone and glowered at his empty desk.

For the rest of the day, he muttered under his breath and snapped pencils in half.

His phone didn't ring once.

Tuesday, March 8, 2011, 10:01 a.m.

Swallowing hard, his temper barely in check, Matt strode into Helen Trent's outer office. Loud snoring filled the air. A desk piled high with unopened mail stood in one corner, and opposite, an open door to another room. The location of the snoring.

Matt walked to Hell's office doorway. Slumped in her chair behind a beat-up wooden desk, wearing a black leather jacket and jeans, Ms. Trent was sound asleep. Her worn, black, Converse high-tops perched on top of the desk, her long, skinny legs stretched out, her mouth was wide open.

A faint haze of marijuana smoke hung in the air.

His stomach churned like he'd eaten a couple of live alligators. His face flamed hot. He'd rather be boiled alive in a McDonald's fryer than help her, but this crazy degenerate might help make his mort-gage payment.

Matt stepped inside and scanned the room, disgusted. Piles of files were strewn about with no apparent order. A dying plant with-ered in the corner. A poster of Keith Richards hung on a light beige wall, his body covered in darts, only his face spared. A calendar on the wall behind her showed December of the previous year. A dirty window offered a view of a skinny leafless tree and a Dumpster.

Everywhere he looked, he saw failure. How could she solve her cases so fast? And why did people like her?

The phone rang in the outer office. The machine picked up. "Miss Trent, this is my fifth call to you. My name is Russell Hendrickson, and I represent the Hendrickson and Cleveland Law Firm. We are interested in hiring you on retainer. Please return my call as soon as possible so we may discuss our very generous offer." *Beep.*

The phone rang again. A woman wanted Hell to track her cheating husband.

Unreal.

He swung his attention to the miscreant behind the desk.

"What the hell are you staring at?" came her growl.

Dark, bloodshot eyes peered at him from beneath a tousled mop of short pink, brown, and gray hair. The nose was straight, the mouth full. If she wasn't scowling, she might be construed as pretty. While the bloom was off the rose—and today she looked all of her fifty-two years—Helen was a striking woman.

He despised every square inch of her. "Hello, Miss Trent."

"Detective Sinclair. Oh, wait, I mean, *Mr.* Sinclair. How the mighty have fallen," she drawled, her voice dripping with loathing.

His hands itched to strangle her. "I knew I shouldn't have come." He turned toward the door.

"You can't expect to work for me and not have me say some crap to you about our sordid past. I've spent quality time hating your guts."

He glanced back over his shoulder. "Ditto. And thanks for all the flat tires and graffiti on my house—"

"I only gave you one flat...tire. Oops." She sent him a contempt-filled grin.

His fists balled, and he faced her. "I don't care if I have to take my kids out of college, I'm not working for the likes of you. Joe is an idiot."

"Agreed. I told him the same thing. I said, 'I'm gonna know by the end of the day who's trying to kill me because it's gonna be Matt.' Or there will be some guy shootin' at me, and I'll be hiding, and you'll be jumpin' up and down, pointing at me. 'Over here! Here she is!' Holdin' me up like a human shield." She pantomimed the supposed actions.

He laughed, shocking himself. At least there were no pretenses between them.

She sent him a tired glare. "God knows how the fates conspired to put us in this situation, but here we are. You're available, and I can afford you. And I'm gonna take advantage of this little window of time while you're building your business. Because both of us know the only reason you're here is because you're desperate. Well, same goes for me."

All true. "So?"

"Here's the truth, Matt. I do hate you. A lot. I'm hiring you partly because I know how much being around me will torture you."

He snorted. "Miserable bitch."

Her bravado vanished. He saw shades of a normal woman his age in her face. Vulnerability appeared deep within her brown eyes. "I'm scared, Matt."

An overwhelming compulsion to protect her derailed his anger. His belly tightened. Unnerving reaction. He kept his face stern, gave her a brief nod, and sat down. So the witch had actual feelings. Still, he couldn't let her fear affect his decision to take the case. He had to keep in mind who she was and what she'd done to him.

Of course, he was apparently the only one in the world who didn't like her. Felons and cops alike treated her like a beloved celebrity. He doubted he'd ever feel anything for her except loathing, but maybe he could tolerate her long enough to solve the case and save her sorry ass.

But was saving her life the right thing to do?

The phone rang again, the caller with yet another job offer.

"Make no mistake, I haven't forgiven you." Her gaze glittered with malice, and her mouth went hard. "You took three months of my life away from me."

"You should have told me what you knew."

"Now you're in my game. How many jobs you think you'd get if you spilled your guts to the cops every time they asked, huh?"

The idea punched him hard, right across the jaw. He'd only just begun to grasp not having a steady paycheck. So many things he'd taken for granted. He hadn't been able to relate to her at all in that interrogation room. All he'd seen was an alien slut from Planet Depravity. A carbuncle on law enforcement's ass.

"I would have been ruined," she continued. "My clientele would have vanished. But, thankfully, it all turned out well for me. Because of that little stunt, and the Candler case, I get some righteous jobs."

"When you answer the phone."

Her brows wrinkled. "Yeah. Messin' up there. But that phone will not stop. I used to get two calls a day, which gave me enough work to make it. Now it's like, hell, all these people want me. Drives me nuts."

"Poor you."

"Yeah, I guess I shouldn't complain. I just hate disappointing people."

He lifted his chin. "I have a question. How did you get your PI license back? I know they revoked it when you were in jail. Felons can't have licenses."

She sent him a little smug smile. "I have low friends in high places."

Anger flared through him. This woman charmed her way through life with no regard to the laws she was supposedly helping to enforce. "Of course you do."

"And I have high friends in low places."

He smirked. "Ha."

"Look, Matt, I'll give you a shot here, but I don't like the way you look at me, I don't like the way you judge me, and to help me you'll have to know every niggling detail of my life."

"I realize that."

"My reputation is... I know what it is in your department. You spewed it at me for hours in that interrogation room."

"I won't apologize for that."

"I don't expect you to. But now you're working for me. And if you have an opinion, or judgment, keep it to yourself. I can't take it right now. I've never had someone try to kill me personally. Even the people I've put away mostly like me. I can't figure this out," she said, her gaze haunted.

His tight stomach loosened another notch, and his need to protect her grew stronger. He'd never seen her vulnerable before. It was like he was meeting a whole different woman. Only glimpses of that horrible, battle-worn bitch remained. "Let me help."

"Do you really charge five hundred a day plus expenses?"

"Yeah."

She took her feet off the desk, reached into her drawer, pulled out a small checkbook, and began writing a check. Almost all of her fingers were bandaged. From the age and wear on some of the Band-Aids, it was clear the wounds had happened at different times. What the hell was she doing to herself? She finished and handed him a colorful check.

Twenty-five hundred dollars written out on a SpongeBob SquarePants check. Rent plus utilities plus a few bucks for the secretary.

"What if we solve it fast?" he asked.

"That's yours to keep. Gotta keep those boys in college, don't you?"

Volcanic fire shocked his system and catapulted him from his chair. "I don't want your fucking charity." He threw the check onto her desk and challenged her with his posture and expression.

She rolled her eyes, but her emotions didn't rise to meet his. She sent him a weary, exasperated look. "Dude, you are such an idiot. Call the money an advance on your emotional trauma. Call it extra dangerous duty pay. Call it whatever you want, but don't let your children suffer—or me—because I said something wrong."

His muscles burned. He hated the mirror of his actions. He kept expecting her to attack him, and she wasn't. She was trying to hire him. His insides twisted hard. He hated depending on her, hated treating her like shit, and hated this whole situation.

He took a deep breath. "Okay." But he still didn't sit.

"And as ecstatic as it made me initially, what happened to you was really messed up. You did not deserve that at all. You were the most honest person on that force."

"Which is why they screwed me." He found himself sitting.

"Raw deal. Everyone knows it was a set-up. All my buddies in the station said you were a huge loss to the department. I can't believe they let that frame-up go down. Everyone knows you were innocent. Everyone."

Matt's opinion of her shifted on a dime. He thought she'd continue to rub his job loss in his face. That she'd believed he'd been on the take. But she meant what she said. The tension in his shoulders eased. "Thanks for that, Hell."

"I knew you were a good man, Matt. That's why it hurt so much when you attacked me. I know it was your job to break me, but once in a while, I still hear your voice in my head."

Matt lost his footing for a second. He'd never expected this level of honesty out of her; he'd had no idea she was capable. He smiled. "I didn't think you heard anything I said. Every time I got in your face, you sang 'Kumbaya.' Song stuck in my head for a week."

She finally cracked a smile. "Screwed myself, too. Didn't get that out of my head for a month."

He laughed. "And if you said, 'Come on, Matt, let's hug it out,' just one more time... I've never been that close to punching someone and not hit them."

She got a mischievous look on her face. "Gotta say it was fun pushing you back that day. And I pushed you with everything I had." Her smile faded, and her pain lines returned. "And then you put me in jail for three weeks. Then three more months."

"Hell, you were aiding and abetting a prime suspect in a murder trial. Damn right I sent you to jail."

"And damn right I protected Billie," she said, pointing a bandaged forefinger his way. "Last time she went to jail, she got gang-raped. Transgender people are targets. I wasn't going to let that happen to her again."

"That's beside the point. He was an ex-felon found at the crime scene with the murder weapon in his hand and plenty of motive."

"She was innocent."

"That's why I backed off eventually. Only reason you spent the extra three months in jail was because you talked back to the judge."

Her shoulders and eyebrows twitched. "She pissed me off."

"You probably wouldn't have even gotten jail time, you realize that? Then you start yelling, 'Bullshit. I call bullshit on these whole proceedings.'"

Hell laughed. "They *were* bullshit."

"You don't tell the judge that."

"Learned that lesson." She twisted in her chair.

He chuckled. "I couldn't believe it when you broke out with 'My Country,'Tis of Thee.' And sang it as the bailiffs carried you out of the courtroom."

While smiling, her attention dropped to her desktop. "That was, uh...unplanned."

"You hit all the notes," he offered.

She finally met his gaze, her dark brown eyes twinkling. "I was stoked when some of the court spectators started singing it with me."

"They all got thrown out, too. Damn, that was funny. Jesus, Hell."

She sighed heavily. "No one screws me better than I do."

And dead honest. He couldn't help but give her a couple more points for that. "So let's get to the case. Why don't you think the suspect they arrested—this Richard Tanner guy—is involved? He had the powder burns on his hands, gun in his trunk."

"Guy takes a lot of energy out on the firing range. But he wouldn't kill me. Not like him. Yes, he's a crazy Iraq war vet, and sleeping with him was a definite mistake. That's why I ended it after only two encounters. Yes, he stalked me. Yes, he doesn't sleep and has PTSD. But he's not the one. He isn't capable. That being said, I don't want to go see him alone."

"I heard he resisted arrest and punched the arresting officer."

"Yeah. Unfortunately."

"Doesn't he have a car like the one you saw?"

"Similar. But the year is off. Tanner's is a 2002; the black Honda I saw is a 2003. According to the cameras at the bank right there on El Camino and Borel. They also found a .38 at his place, and they're checking now to see if the ballistics match with the bullets recovered at the scene. They shouldn't. But if he used a different weapon or is covering his tracks, he could still be the one. I need to see him face-to-face. I'll be able to tell when I look him in the eye."

"So when do you want to go see him?"

"How about now? You busy?"

"Yeah. Workin' your case."

She stood and offered her hand. "Thanks, Matt. I know what it took for you to come here."

He reluctantly took hers. "Don't thank me until we catch the guy who's trying to kill you."

"Other than you," she said with a teasing smile.

"Other than me."

"You should drive."

"Yeah?"

"I'm super stoned."

"Hell, I don't want you smoking that shit around me."

She smirked. "Too bad. Besides, I'm medical. I'm not breaking the law."

Matt examined her. She didn't look sick. "You have cancer?"

"No. Depression. Especially when I run out of weed."

He chuckled before he could stop himself. "Bullshit."

"Truth. Pills didn't work for me. Weed does. Quiets the bad voices."

"I think you like being high and have found an excuse to smoke."

"Is that your professional opinion, Dr. Sinclair?"

He straightened his shoulders. "We're going to fight a lot."

"Yep." She flashed him a quick grin.

Didn't matter if she was charming and funny, he refused to like her. He wasn't going to fall under her spell. She was a depraved, old, teenage delinquent. Deserved to be in juvenile hall, not out solving crimes.

Hopefully, their liaison would be short. Hell Trent was nothing but a quick meal ticket. Period.

CHAPTER 2

TUESDAY, MARCH 8, 2011, 10:42 A.M.

Hell stepped out of her office building on Twenty-Fifth Avenue and checked everyone on the block for signs of danger. Usual suspects. Moms pushing strollers, rich ladies fresh from their yoga classes holding lattes, techie engineer nerds looking for an early lunch, and a few elderly San Mateo regulars in their giant boat-sized cars.

She climbed into Matt's Taurus and set her skull-covered backpack at her feet. Matt was already inside. For an asshole cop, he wasn't bad-looking. Square face with a full head of curly, sandy-brown hair streaked with gray, blue eyes that vacillated between kind and harsh, weathered, tanned face, wide nose broken at one time. Well groomed and clean shaven, with fairly even yet rugged features. He wore a dark blue suit jacket, light blue shirt with no tie and khaki dress slacks. He smelled like soap, and his nails were short and immaculate.

A little too immaculate. Just like his car.

Car was seven years old, but it looked showroom quality. Spotless. Surfaces polished with Armor All, windows so clean they looked open. Joe had told her about Matt's OCD tendencies. But she couldn't help admitting the car looked nice.

"Clean mats, Matt." She laughed.

He pursed his lips slightly.

"You'll get used to me."

"I hope not."

She laughed harder.

Directly in front of them, a young Asian couple checked out the menu in the window of Luceti's Italian restaurant. An overly skinny, middle-aged brunette woman wearing huge sunglasses and a black yoga outfit walked by carrying a yoga mat. Something about her was familiar. Probably a neighbor.

He made a face, then became serious. "I need to ask you a bunch of questions you probably won't want to answer."

Her neck and back tightened, and she started jiggling her leg. Why had she hired the one man in the universe who would judge her the most? Stupid self-destructive tendencies. "Hey, we've done this before. We'll be good at it," she tossed off cheerfully.

He rolled his eyes and started the car. "Joe told me that you got a threatening letter. What did it say and when can I see it?"

"It's at the police station, but I have copies. Damn, I should have shown you back in the office. I'm so blown away with you helping me, I got distracted. But I can't forget what it said."

He checked his mirrors and backed out of the parking space. "Which was?"

Her stomach contracted, and she dug her fingers into her knee. "*Stop fucking him or I'll kill you, bitch.*"

"Who's him?"

Hell couldn't help but give a chuckle. "Got me. 'Him' is a little vague. I was like, could you be a bit more specific? But initially I wrote it off to a crazy neighbor trying to intimidate me."

"Crazy neighbor?"

"Asshole next door." She waved her hand dismissively. "But he's too wimpy, and he was gone to LA this weekend. Too bad the cameras at the bank on El Camino revealed almost nothing but the make of the car. Angle showed the passenger side of the car but not the shooter, nor did it catch the license plate. All we got was a confirmation on the model. 2003 black Honda Accord."

"What did the note look like?"

"White twenty-pound stock, Times New Roman sixteen point, printed from a laser printer. No fingerprints."

He signaled for a right and stopped behind a line of waiting cars at the red light at the intersection of El Camino Real. "So aside from Tanner, what about your other lovers?"

She squirmed a bit and searched his face for signs of disgust. "You believe that rumor about my 'stable' of boys. Don't you? You sure did in the interrogation room."

Matt blushed, and his eyes widened for a split second, then he shrugged.

Great. Worst fear realized.

"I should have never slept with a cop. They get all obsessed on you and follow you around." She turned back to Matt, whose expression had returned to detached hard cop. "I love Joe, but I am discreet, Matt. My wild reputation—well, wild sex reputation—only exists in your old department."

A brief raise of his brows. "Really? None of your friends know?"

"No. Well, two of my closest girlfriends do, but even so, I don't give them the full count. What I'm doing is not socially acceptable, so I lie. My other friends and my whole family—except for one cousin— think I'm celibate."

Matt burst out laughing.

Hell tried not to join him, but it was funny. In a way. If you weren't her. "They do. I don't talk about my love life. No one knows."

The light changed, and he took a right onto El Camino. "Someone must have noticed you picking up guys," he said with a caustic undertone.

Gut punch. She hated this Slut Mirror. "I don't 'pick up' guys. I don't troll bars. I have used Match.com, but I mostly find my lovers through activities. Jase and I hike, Mike and I play Scrabble, Roman and I, uh, talk, and Dave's an old friend of Josh's. The other guys I met through jobs. I've been seeing all of them for at least four years, one guy for eleven." *Actually, two guys for eleven years, and one new guy, BC, but we're not talking about them until all other avenues have been exhausted.*

Matt did a double take. Her information was clearly not fitting his etched-in-stone opinion of her. "Huh."

She resisted the urge to slap him and forced herself to center. This jerk was her employee, and he needed to wake up and respect her, or she'd fire him. But to get his respect, she needed to earn it. She held herself taller in the seat. *Be in your corner.* "I don't throw myself at men, Matt. I try not to openly flirt; I find it demeaning. I choose my lovers carefully, and they are all nice men. Even if a few couldn't keep their damned mouths shut. So don't ask people in my circle about my sex life, okay? And especially not my family."

His shoulders relaxed, and he nodded. His brow still wrinkled slightly, but at least he seemed open to changing his opinion of her. "Okay. So, tell me about your lovers."

Hell took a deep breath and forced herself to calm. "Right now, I have seven: four men I see regularly, an East Coaster when he's in town—once or twice a year probably—and two European men I see about once a year, when they're over here on business. Basically, I have four regulars, and three guys I rarely see." Plus BC and Marco Capasso. Her insides roiled. She hated even thinking about them.

Still, she wished she could tell Matt about Capasso, but that would put the detective in too much danger. And BC? Just too humiliating. No way could she admit to sleeping with a married man when she couldn't even face it herself. Matt already thought she was a slut. If he found out she was willingly seeing BC, he'd be convinced she was a whore. Even though it was stupid not to tell him. She'd hired the guy to protect her, and she wasn't giving him all the information he needed. *Here, let me put a blindfold on you and tie your hands behind your back. Now figure out who's trying to kill me.* Shit. This was all so intolerable!

Matt took the right-lane exit off of El Camino for Hillsdale Avenue. When they got to the intersection, the light was green. He hung a left and headed toward the freeway. "Tell me about the regular guys."

The embarrassment burners in her face got set to high, and she resisted the urge to cool her cheeks with her palms. Didn't want to draw any unwanted attention to her reactions. "Dave, Roman, Mike, and Jase. Dave's a DJ in the City, Roman's a security specialist, Mike owns and operates a tattoo parlor in Redwood City, and Jase is a civil attorney. Jase lives in San Bruno, his office is in the City. Haven't seen him in three months or so." Or any of the others much. She'd been spending most of her free time with BC lately. Not that she'd intended to.

"Don't you worry about diseases?"

"Certainly. I shrink wrap my lovers in plastic and get tested quarterly. And I make them get tested and bring me the papers." Except for Marco. At least she'd managed to get him to wear a condom.

"They do it?"

"If they want to bonk me, they do. I don't need men; I like men. But I am incredibly choosy."

He snorted. "Seven is choosy?"

Nine. Nine is choosy. Hell kept eye contact to ensure she appeared truthful. "Yes. Believe it or not. I have no idea why, but I attract guys like catnip attracts cats. I know I look like an old, wrinkly lesbian, and I'm getting fat, but..." She shrugged. "Just happens."

Matt briefly glanced at her face, then her body. He gave an almost imperceptible nod and turned back to the traffic. "I'll need to talk to them all."

She inwardly smiled. Now not only was he starting to like her, he'd actually noticed her as an attractive woman. Too funny! "I have dissected their brains for information on their exes and current girlfriends, even though I don't sleep with them if they're in relationships. I don't believe in cheating." *Unless the guy is BC and is a tremendous lover and I have a stupid attack and keep trying to break up but can't seem to follow through.*

"Really?"

"Really. I never cheated on a spouse, and I don't sleep with duplicitous assholes." *Except two.* But Marco didn't count because she didn't want to be with him any longer.

Matt signaled for a right, took the exit ramp for 101 South, and merged onto the busy freeway. "Who's on your suspect list?"

Hell bit her lip. *Censor, censor, censor.* "Roman's out. He doesn't live in the Bay Area any longer, he's based in DC now and has no ties to anyone here but his Rampart Security coworkers. I see him a few times a year. And even though we spend a lot of time together when he's here, and we're pretty close, he has no exes in California. And I haven't seen him in six months. Last I heard, he was in Pakistan."

"I know Rampart. So Roman's a mercenary, right? Some special ops guy?"

"I don't ask what he does specifically. When I'm with him, I am not thinking about what he does for a living. Believe me. Like making love to a Greek statue come to life," she said, her voice heavy with lust and wonderment. She caught herself, and her face went hot again. "Sorry."

Matt pulled at his collar and swallowed. "What about Dave the DJ?"

She shrugged. "Girls get obsessed with him from time to time. But he sees so many women that I don't know why they'd single me out. Plus we're old friends. Known him for twenty-four years, been seeing him for eleven plus. Still, a night or two at his performances might settle that question." She ran her finger along a piece of trim on the Taurus's door. "Mike could be another source. He's had four wives and umpteen fiancées and girlfriends during our eight-year on-and-off-again affair. I'm his in-between-fiancées lover. But he is attracted to hotheads. His last two girls were totally crazy. I can't confirm their alibis yet. Mike said they're not capable, but he's a blind idiot when it comes to women."

Matt signaled, checked his mirrors, and changed lanes. "I thought you said the shooter was a male."

"I think he was. But honestly, all I saw was a ski mask and that fucking gun. There's still a possibility that the shooter was a woman. Especially because of the tone of that threatening note. Sounded like a jealous female to me. But it doesn't mean the woman who wanted me dead wouldn't have gotten some guy to do her dirty work."

"I'll want to interview all your lovers and their women."

Hell eased deeper into her seat and stretched out her legs. "Good, I'm afraid to see Mike's ladies alone. Same with this Tanner guy. He's the only man I've seen in the past year without a solid alibi for Sunday morning."

"The guy in custody. Wait. He's not a regular? He a once-a-year guy?"

"No, he was a two-time terrible mistake. He's not on the list. And he's totally insane. But like I said, I don't think he did it. I hope you'll be able to see something I'm missing, and we can either eliminate him or convict him." Hell absently picked at a loose edge of trim near the door handle.

"So how often do you see your regulars?"

"Depends on the dude. When Roman's in town, we see each other a lot. Like, most of the days he's here. We're almost like boyfriend and girlfriend. Then I don't see him or hear from him for four or five months to a year. Dave, about once a month or every two months. Mike, about two or three times a month—well, actually, lately he's been courting fiancée number ten, so we're kinda on hiatus. Still, she could be jealous. Need to check that out. There was some overlap between her and me. Jase and I saw each other a few times a month until he got too attached, and I've kind of backed off. See him about once a month now. Basically, I see them as often as I can without them getting possessive. I don't lead them on."

"Do they know about each other?"

"Not sure. But I am totally up front. I tell 'em everything right off the bat. I don't fall in love. I don't do romantic relationships. I'm not anyone's girlfriend. We don't spend the night—well, except for Roman. You don't drop by my house unexpectedly. You don't buy me gifts. You don't ask me about my personal life and other boyfriends. All I want is friendship, fun, and sex with no strings attached. I don't want feelings."

Matt sent her a get-real look. "Everyone has feelings, Hell."

"Not me. Too broken." The piece of door handle trim came off in her hand. She stifled a gasp, her heart thumping.

"I don't buy that."

She checked to see if Matt had seen what she'd done. Thankfully, his focus was on the traffic. She palmed the three-inch piece of trim. "Well, it's the truth. I'm done playing Hallmark fantasy games. All I deal with is reality."

"Didn't you love Josh?"

Dull, dark grief wrenched her insides, and she closed her fist, bending the small part of Matt's car interior. She quickly released her grip and tried to straighten out the plastic chunk with her fingers while keeping her focus out the front window. "He was the closest I've ever gotten."

"You still miss him?"

"More than anything." She doubted if she'd ever stop hurting.

"You loved him."

"Yeah. I don't know. I'd give anything to have him back. But ever since his death, I've done a lot of work on myself and finally uncovered the ugly truth: I'm broken."

"Can't you get fixed?"

"No. And not only am I broken and can't trust men, but I become a completely codependent dog in relationships and do everything for my guys. Their personal goddamned slave. And I'm done being some dude's bitch."

"*You?*"

"Matt, let go of everything you think you know about me." She started to gesture with her right hand, then realized that it held the door trim. Moving her hand down between the seat and the door, she kept her attention out the window so he wouldn't notice what she was doing. "My outward persona has little to do with who I am."

He looked over at her and blinked.

"So I finally figured out a way to get companionship without attachments, and that's what I do. I count on my girlfriends and family—well, some of the family—for my emotional needs, and have sex with my lovers, and never the twain shall meet." Hell felt around the side of the seat for a place to hide the trim.

"Sounds lonely."

"I've always been lonely. And I've never been lonelier than when I was in a bad marriage. Josh was okay, but Donny was a nightmare."

"Maybe if you talked to a clergy—"

"I don't believe in organized religion. But I'm okay with my life. I like it. I just don't talk about it." Her finger came upon a little opening in the carpet, and she slipped the door trim inside. A quick visual check revealed no sign of the car part. Relief washed over her, and she sighed. *Yes!* "But I'm actually very content. Well, all the way up until the point some asshole shot at me."

"If you were really okay with your choices, you wouldn't be hiding the behavior."

Hell heated with anger, made an exasperated noise, and, thankfully, was finally free to wave her hand around. "Are you out of your mind? Every single insult you threw at me in that interrogation room is what society thinks of women who sleep with more than one guy at a time. You have these thoughts and judgments, Matt, and you're the majority. Guys can have multiple lovers and be considered Don Juan. Women have multiple lovers, and we're whores, sluts, and dirt. Well, I'm not a slut or a whore or dirt. I've found a way to get my needs met with some very nice men—good friends—and my life is balanced. Or was. Now it's all blown to hell." She crossed her arms and frowned.

Matt drove, his face emotionless. She couldn't tell whether he was judging her or not.

Hell glared out the window at a big LED advertising video screen on a high-tech building. "Damn, this is super uncomfortable for me. I hate talking about this shit, especially to a good Catholic boy who's only slept with one woman. I know you think I'm a slut."

"No, I don't." He took the Veteran's Boulevard exit off of 101.

"It's okay, Matt. I'd rather have your honesty."

"I don't think you're a slut. I think you're still grieving for Josh. And have self-esteem issues, which prevent you from attracting the right sort of man."

Right on the former, wrong on the latter. Yet it was a relief to hear that he didn't think she was a whore. "I love your provincial thinking."

He made a face at her. "Okay, so can you write down the first and last names of the men you're seeing, and their addresses?"

They hit the red at the Whipple Avenue intersection.

"Last names?" She sent him an incredulous look.

His mouth dropped open. "You don't know their last names?"

Hell broke out in a wide smile. "Kidding."

Matt shook his head, and one side of his mouth briefly turned up.

"I have it all written down. Oh. In long hand. Another thing I forgot to do. I meant to type it out and give you a printout this morning, but I had a panic attack and didn't sleep last night. Finally passed out right before you arrived. I'll get it to you by tonight."

"Good."

Her phone buzzed in her pocket. "Someone's calling. Let me see who it is." She pulled out her iPhone. *Marco* read the screen. Her stomach convulsed, her shoulders hunched, and her brow furrowed to the point of pain. "Oh, shit," she muttered under her breath. All she wanted to do was hide. No way did she want to talk to him, but she had to eliminate him and his women from the list. "I have to take this."

"Okay," Matt said.

Traffic started to move, and he accelerated.

"Hey, how ya doin'?" she said into the phone, putting on her happy, upbeat tone. Had to always pretend she loved the guy. Only way to work him.

"Good to hear your voice, Hell," came his distinctive, gravelly, low-key voice.

"Me, too." *Not.*

"You have company?"

Hell glanced at Matt, who wore a frown for some reason. Probably traffic.

"Yeah."

"Okay. I'll make it short. I checked with all my contacts. It's not coming from anyone you've crossed who's part of my world. Has to be more personal. Look in your immediate circle, Hell. This has to be coming from close to you."

"Damn it. Thanks, I figured."

He tsked. "Told you too many boyfriends leads to too much trouble."

"Tell me about it."

"Wish I had time to make you mine for real, Hell. No one would touch a hair on your head."

Except you, you psycho creep. "Thanks, honey."

"I put out a warning, anyway. To leave you alone. And that I wanted to know who was after you. I'll let you know whatever I find out."

"You rock."

"What about the *billionaire*?"

Her back stiffened, and her fists clenched. She needed to handle this delicately. Couldn't show too much enthusiasm for BC, yet she couldn't lie. Marco still had her followed occasionally. "Don't think so, but I'm checking it out."

Unfortunate accident, running into BC and his wife on her last date with Marco a few months back. Had complicated matters considerably. The men had met previously at a museum fundraiser and were quite shocked to realize that they were both sleeping with her.

"So you're still seeing him?" There was a dark edge to his tone.

Please don't make this a problem.

"Yeah," she replied like she could care less. Had to downplay the BC thing. Besides, she was breaking up with him shortly.

"I thought I told you I didn't want you seeing him."

Her stomach hardened so fast acid went into her throat. She coughed and swallowed. "I know. Just sorta happened again."

She had to stand fast on this point and not give him an inch on this boundary. She'd told Marco in the beginning that if he wasn't exclusive with her, she'd never be exclusive with him. Thankfully, at the time, she hadn't known how crazy he was and had easily stood up to him. Good thing he'd been attracted to her defiance and sass. Too bad his attraction to her attitude hadn't lasted.

"Dangerous guy, Hell. I told you that."

"And I'm self-destructive, I told you that."

He snorted. "You sure this shooting doesn't have anything to do with him?"

"No."

"Hell, I told you this would happen. You have to get away from him."

"I have to find out who's trying to kill me first."

"Someone from his world."

Holy Christ. Capasso could have set up the whole thing to get her to dump BC. It was not beyond him to do that. This would be very, very bad.

But why would he have someone shoot at her? All he'd really have to do was forbid her to see BC, and there would be nothing she could do.

"Hell?"

"I'm here."

"I don't want you seeing him anymore."

And there was the order. Shit. "If you're right, then I have to see him to solve the case."

"I could solve your case with one bullet."

Adrenaline slammed her, and she almost cried out. She took a deep breath and forced her voice to stay calm. "And then what if it's not him, and they succeed? And he and I are dead, and you're in jail?"

"No, you're right. And I'm not going down for a billionaire asshole. He's got too many people. See, this is the problem, Hell. I can only protect you so far with that fuck. He owns the law, he makes laws, he could kill you and never get convicted for it."

"I've screwed over so many people it could be anyone."

"You're right. I shouldn't focus on that asshole. Not when you have so many other lovers. Jesus, Hell. I worry about you. I may have to figure something out so I can protect you better. My wife isn't going to last the year. Maybe you and I ought to think about getting more serious again. You drop your other guys, and we see each other more. I couldn't stand to lose you, baby."

Her blood went cold. She couldn't even stand to see him once a year. Any more often would be sheer torture. "Everything is fine. Please don't worry about all this."

"I miss you, baby. Why don't you come up to the City, and I'll take you out?"

Panic tightened her throat, and she rubbed it to ease the tension. Shit! "Love to, but right now I can't see anyone until I figure out who's trying to kill me."

"You know you're safe when you're with me."

Her mouth dropped open, and she almost laughed. Thank God she had the wherewithal to stop herself. "Let me put it this way: my mind isn't gonna be very focused until I solve this. I'm pretty scared."

"Sorry, baby. I'll do what I can on this end."

"Thanks." *Now can I go?* "Hopefully, this will be over quick. I'll keep you in the loop."

"Good. I really like the idea of seeing you more often. Like we used to."

Her jaw clamped, and she held herself so tightly she could barely breathe. "I'd like that." Her stomach burned from being so knotted.

"Take it easy, baby. I'll be in touch. Love you."

"Love you, too." The lie came easily.

Thrilled the conversation was over, she hung up, shuddered, and rubbed her arms. What an ordeal! After letting out a giant sigh of relief, she suddenly realized that they were parked in the garage for the county jail, and she'd missed the whole ride from Whipple Avenue.

She turned to Matt, and all his attention was focused on her.

Her heart dropped into her stomach, and her alarms sounded. Son of a bitch!

"Who was that?" he demanded.

Holy crap. He'd probably heard the whole goddamned conversation. She'd been so focused on Capasso that she'd completely forgotten that she was sitting in a car with an ex-police detective. He couldn't have missed how sharply her reactions had contrasted with her words. All her body language screamed that she was terrified of whomever was on the other end of the line. What about all that stuff she'd said about dying and going to jail?

"No one important," she tossed off, and focused on putting away her phone.

He bored into her with his intense gaze. "Don't give me that. You said you loved him. You talked the guy out of killing someone."

"No, I didn't."

"Bullshit. Whoever he was, he completely freaked you out. You held that phone so hard your knuckles were white. Sweat beading on your upper lip. And if you'd wrapped your arms around yourself any farther, they would have gone around twice."

Hell wiped her mouth and looked at him like he was crazy. "Hello? Hot flashes?"

"You're a terrible liar, Hell. Could he be the one who's after you?"

"No." *Maybe, but what the hell can I do about it?* Still she couldn't picture Marco going to all the trouble of shooting at her just to get her away from BC. And it sounded like he hadn't known until right then that she was still seeing him.

But Marco was devious, and a criminal. He loved his Machiavellian games. The assailant hadn't hit her, just scared her. There would have been better places to shoot at her if they'd really wanted her dead. Maybe Marco was screwing with her.

Ugly thought.

Matt locked his full attention on her face. "Who is he?"

Her neck and shoulders tensed, and she stretched to cover her reaction. "Just a guy." She finally made eye contact. "No worries, Matt. I've already eliminated him. We should go in." She grabbed the door handle. Matt could not find out about her nasty relationship with Capasso. That's all she'd need.

He caught her by the arm. "Not so fast. He's obviously a lover. And you're obviously afraid of him. Yet you haven't mentioned him. How am I supposed to help you if you won't give me all the information? Especially about the people you're afraid of."

Her face went hot, but she wouldn't look at him. "I'm not afraid of him, and I'm giving you what you need. That guy isn't involved. I'm sorry I didn't mention him, Matt. I'm not trying to keep stuff from you. I'd just eliminated him, and since there are so many other suspects, I didn't want to waste our energy. I only have so much money to spend on this investigation. We should go inside; I told my police buddy that I'd be there by now."

Matt didn't move and continued to stare at her. "I saw the name on your phone. Marco."

Her stomach shrunk to the size of a pea. She had to force her body to relax. How many tells had she just telegraphed to the dude? "Yeah? So?" She tried not to, but turned away.

"About eight years ago, I saw your name on a classified report I wasn't supposed to see, linking you to a very high-level guy in organized crime in the City whose first name just happens to be Marco."

She almost puked, and swallowed hard. The car swirled around her. She gripped the door for support.

"That was Marco Capasso on the phone."

Every instinct told her to jump out of the car. She fought like hell to maintain a neutral expression, but by the way her face twitched, she knew she was blowing it.

"Hell, it's okay. You know the information is safe with me. But this is pretty significant. We need to talk about him. And your relationship with him."

Get it together, Trent! Since her reactions had been so strong, there was no use in lying. She just wouldn't volunteer any extra information. But she had to turn this around quickly. "Look, Matt, for your protection, we can't talk about him." *And mine.* "You need to forget that you ever heard that about me. Honestly."

"Well, I already know, so let's at least have a discussion about him, okay? You hired me to help you. A relationship with a Mafia boss is huge. And you know it. Would you drop it if the situation were reversed?"

Her throat went tight, and she clenched her fists. Cornered by logic. Crap. She swallowed and sighed heavily. "No. I wouldn't. He said the attack isn't coming from him or his people or his world. He doesn't lie to me. Besides, would he try to kill me? He wants me alive.

He likes screwing me. And we've been seeing each other for eleven years. Why would he suddenly start shooting at me now?" *To get you away from BC.*

But that made no sense. Capasso knew that if he really put his foot down, she'd obey him. While he'd strongly suggested she stop seeing BC in the past, this was the first time he'd issued a direct order.

Still, just to make sure, she'd have to talk to Death about looking into Capasso's whereabouts on that Sunday. No way could she enlist Matt's help. She'd already put him in too much danger just by hiring him.

Matt gave a slow nod. "Okay. So why'd you get involved with him in the first place? Didn't you know who he was?"

"No," she said a lot more defensively than she'd intended.

His brows came down hard. "You didn't? Where did you meet him?"

"At a club." She was careful to look Matt dead in the eye. "Dude, he's not the one after me. Let's concentrate on the real suspects."

"What makes you so sure? Guy's a damned Mafia boss. He deals in violence, intimidation, and lies. How do you know something didn't just set him off?"

She tried to hold back, but the answer burst from her. "If Marco wanted to kill me, he'd do it face-to-face. He'd want to hear my screams. He'd want watch the light dim from my eyes. He'd make damned sure that his face was the last I ever saw."

Great job at keeping your mouth shut, Trent.

Matt's eyes widened. "Jesus, Hell."

She turned away and stared at the dashboard. Damn it, she was better than this. That stupid gunshot had rattled her. She had to get control. Get her shields back up and keep them there. She couldn't trust Matt. He was there to help her solve the case, but he had no rights to delve into areas of her life where she didn't want him. And where he might get himself killed.

However, her unplanned response had answered one question: if Marco *was* behind her attack, he didn't want her dead. He just wanted her away from BC.

"Why do you still see him?"

Who does an eight-hundred-pound gorilla sleep with? Anyone he wants.

Come on, Trent! Act, baby, act! Finally, she felt her Lie Factory come back online. The tension in her back and shoulders eased, and she slid into character. "As odd as this sounds, I love him. Yes, he's a scary mofo at times—but not with me. Like I said, I've known him eleven bloody years. We're like an old married couple. And he's never hurt me." The lie came out nice and strong. "In fact, he's protected me on several occasions. Saved my ass, really." *Very nice, girlfriend. Nice authenticity to your tone.*

Matt nodded and sat back in his seat. He blinked, worked his mouth, then leveled his best detective stare at her. "You were scared to talk to him, Hell."

Her stomach caved in, but she made sure not a muscle of her face moved. She kept the eye contact even though all she wanted to do was look away. *Mix in as much truth as you can, and make it good.* "Yeah, I know I reacted weird." She tried to take on a confessional tone, yet tempered with a blasé attitude. "I was afraid he'd be mad at me. He's been wanting me to quit my business forever. This shooting freaked him out. I hate arguing with him. I mean, I only see the guy once a year, but all of a sudden he'll barge into my life and bug me. He thinks he's being protective, but he's just a pain in the ass." Partial truth.

Matt's face relaxed almost imperceptibly. "You only see him once a year?"

"Now. We used to see each other more often. In the beginning."

"You really love the guy?"

"Fell for him before I knew who he was. I didn't tell you about him because I've promised him that I won't tell anyone about us. For obvious reasons. And I was fairly sure the shooting had nothing to do with him." *But now I'm having some doubts.*

"Joe doesn't know about him."

"By the time I got mixed up with Joe, Marco and I were cooled off. Thank God, dude could have gotten himself killed. Marco didn't like that I went out with a cop. If he'd noticed Joe following him around, it wouldn't have been pretty. Thankfully, Marco found out after the fact."

"A Mafia don. Christ," Matt said, shaking his head.

"He's a kitten."

Matt laughed.

Hell got out of the car and tried to block the memory she kept locked away, hidden from the world. Her hands went clammy, and her heart rate shot up. The most horrible night of her life. His fists coming at her. That soulless look in his eye. Predatory, darker than black. Her weakness. Her inability to protect herself. The endless sex sessions afterwards to assuage *his* pain.

Yeah, a real *kitten*.

"Hell? You okay?"

Shit. She checked Matt, and all his focus was on her face. She sent him a grin. "Haven't slept or eaten much in the last two days," came out fast. And it was the truth. Ish. "Feelin' a mite poorly. After this, let's get something to eat, okay?" she said as brightly as she could.

"Okay." The look behind his eyes said he could smell something was off, but wasn't sure what it was. Yet.

She walked on, kicking herself hard. She needed to keep her mind on the case and keep Matt's formidable detective talents focused where she wanted them.

Shit. How many uncontrollable men did she need to control to solve this case?

Tuesday, March 8, 2011, 11:05 a.m.

HELL TURNED TO MATT RIGHT BEFORE THEY WALKED INTO THE visitors' room of the Maguire Correctional Facility, a.k.a. the San Mateo County Jail. "Okay, so we know for sure that the bullets from Tanner's .38 don't match the bullets in the walls of Starbucks, and the cops will be releasing him soon. But he could have another gun hidden somewhere. I really want to eliminate him before he gets out of here. You'll protect me if Tanner gets physical, right?"

"You bet."

"Good." Hell's tense muscles relaxed a bit.

He took her by the arm. "Hell, I know we've had our issues, but you've hired me. I'm here for you a hundred percent. Just tell me what you need."

She stared at him. She'd never heard those words from a man's lips in her life. From a solid man who meant it. She'd rarely been in the company of someone so healthy. It was weird and threw her off. "Okay, thanks."

"Why are you looking at me like that?" he asked.

"No reason." She turned away and walked ahead of him into the visitors' room.

Hell spotted Tanner at a table in the far corner. He looked demonic. His dark eyes wild, his black hair matted, the orange jumpsuit set off his pale, sweaty skin, which almost matched the gray paint of the walls. He hadn't eaten in God knew how long. He practically disappeared inside his prison uniform. Skinny, sickly, and crazy, he sat at the table, rocking slightly, clearly ready to pop.

She sat down opposite him, and her heart went out to him. "I'm so sorry about this, Tanner."

His face wrenched in pain. Tears formed in his eyes. "I didn't do it, Hell!"

"I know. The cops know. The bullets didn't match. A buddy just told me as we were walking in here."

"They didn't tell me that! Why am I in here?" His whole body shook.

"We just found out a minute ago. Your lawyer should be here soon."

"That asshole?" he scowled. "Court-appointed fuck."

"You're still here because you went ballistic on the cops when they came to question you. You're in here for assaulting an officer."

"They wouldn't listen to me."

"I know. Look, I'll do what I can to help you. But you have to help me."

Tanner jerked his head toward Matt and threw him a suspicious look. "Who's this guy?"

"A friend who's helping me figure out who's trying to kill me."

His skeletal face reddened and twisted, and he looked like he was about to burst into tears. "I'm not!"

She reached across the table and gripped his arm. "I know. I never suspected you. But I think someone might be trying to make us think it's you. I think someone might have tried to set you up for the shooting." She let go.

His eyes went wide. "Holy shit," he said in a small voice.

"I need to ask you some questions. I promise I will do what I can to get you out of here."

His expression still wary, his shoulders dropped a bit. Then he threw all his intensity at her. "I'm freakin' out, Hell. I can't take it in here. If I don't stop freaking out—and I can't stop freaking out—they'll send me to a mental hospital and drug me. I can't take that, Hell. I can't. I'll lose it. I *will* kill someone."

Hell looked around quickly to make sure none of the guards had heard him. "Calm down, Tanner, and please don't use that kind of language," she said in a hushed tone. "You know how paranoid the cops are. Do your breathing exercises. Have you called Freddy? Can he come down here?" Freddy had been his direct superior in Iraq, a local vet who'd been helping keep Tanner's head together.

His clouded expression turned stormier. He crossed his arms and looked at his lap. "Freddy's dead."

Hell gasped and clutched her chest. "*What?*"

Tanner nodded but didn't look up. "Killed himself two days ago," he muttered.

"Holy shit." Hell fought her overwhelming urge to get up and hold Tanner. She couldn't lead him on.

Tanner finally made eye contact. The agony in his dark eyes made her gut sear. "That only leaves me and two other guys from our squad still alive. Half died in fucking Iraq; the rest have killed themselves at home."

No words could possibly express her sorrow. "I'm so sorry. Freddy was a rock."

The Army vet's eyes went hard, and his jaw clamped. "No, he wasn't. Scary. I never saw that he was even more fucked up than me."

Hell shook her head and ran her hands through her hair. "Jesus, that's terrible."

Matt nudged her.

Right. They only had a few minutes. Not enough time to give Tanner the emotional support he needed, but so be it. "I'm sorry, but our time is short here, and I have to ask you some questions."

"It's okay. Go ahead." He seemed relieved they'd changed the subject.

"Has there been anything weird going on in your neighborhood? Anyone out of place? Did you see someone who didn't belong there? Anything out of the ordinary?"

He shook his head. "Mission is always out of the ordinary. No."

She touched his arm again. "Please. Calm down, and think. Anyone you noticed around your car. Anything different about your apartment. Any anomalies. Any strange person hanging around. Someone who didn't belong there. A car that didn't belong in the hood. The smallest detail could be the key."

His gaze darted around the table, and then his eyebrows rose. "Well, there was that weird old lady. Not old, old. Maybe ten years older than you. But weird."

"How weird? And where did you see her?"

"A bunch of places for about a week. Like, two weeks ago. I thought she was following me. But you know me, I'm paranoid, and I can't trust myself. So I just thought I was making things up to scare myself. But I did see her more than one place, like, for a week. She showed up at the coffee shop, I saw her walking by my car, and then she stood out on the sidewalk and stared up at my building. I swore she was looking into my window. Finally, I got freaked out enough that I went out to confront her. But by the time I got to the street, she was gone. And that's the last I saw of her."

Hell looked at Matt, who gave a nod, and then she turned back to Tanner. "Describe her."

"Chunky, short, old-lady clothes. You know, bad gray hair, a brown skirt, brown sweater, weird, like a textbook cartoon school librarian. Thick glasses."

Sounded like a novice PI who shopped at Bad Disguises R Us. "Did you see what she drove?"

"No. Only saw her on foot. Or, like, sitting in the corner of the coffee shop."

Hell checked Matt again. "Got all that?"

"I do."

She turned back to Tanner. "Have you noticed anything amiss in your house? Like, something moved? Signs anyone had broken in?"

His thick black brows drew together. "Well, come to think of it, right around the time that lady was hanging around, I was out, and my landlord said that my renter's insurance agent came by to talk to me."

"Renter's insurance agent?"

"Yeah, you were the one who talked me into getting renter's insurance."

"I did?"

"Yeah."

"But renter insurers normally don't send out agents," Matt said.

Hell nodded. "I think we'll go talk to your landlord and see if he can describe the agent."

Tanner burst into a hopeful smile. "So maybe I'm not paranoid?"

"No, you're paranoid, just not in this case."

"Holy shit! A real conspiracy? Really?" He seemed very excited about the idea.

"Yeah."

His smile faded. He put his hand to his forehead and rubbed it. "Wow, is this gonna fuck my head up."

"I'm so sorry, Tanner."

"It's okay, Hell. I mean, you almost got shot. I'm... That freaked me out when I heard that. Everyone loves you."

"Apparently not."

"I'd never hurt you."

"I know."

His craziness vanished, and he looked about ten years old. "I miss you, Hell." His need assaulted her.

Hell imagined a psychic shield between them. "Aren't you still seeing Jeannie?" she asked gently.

"Yeah." He glanced at his lap, then back at her. "But she isn't you."

With no tactful response handy, Hell stood. Tanner got teary, and his lower lip trembled. Her gut burned with guilt. She felt like she was abandoning a starving, beaten dog, but what could she do? Any comfort she'd give him would be misinterpreted.

Matt got to his feet, bumping her. She had to step back to avoid falling.

He caught her and steadied her. "Sorry."

When she checked back at Tanner, his expression had gone more neutral, his tears were gone, and he was standing.

It was then she realized that Matt had purposefully knocked into her to break the tension of the moment.

Good one, Matt.

Tanner quickly moved forward and hugged her.

Outmaneuvered, she hugged him back. "Take care of yourself."

He clung to her too hard, stinking of BO, cigarettes, and jail. She tried to push away, but he held her fast.

Matt pulled Hell away from Tanner. "Hell, guard's signaling us."

Thanks, Matt.

Tanner folded his arms, and his pain lines went deep. "You'll make sure they get me out of here, right?"

"You bet."

He gave her a weak smile. "Thanks, Hell."

Matt nodded at Tanner, took her by the shoulders, moved her in front of him, and pushed her forward, then followed her out.

She was freaked out by the Tanner meeting, but so happy she'd hired Matt. She hadn't felt this safe in a long time. When was the last time a man had protected her? Josh. And before him, no one. Especially not Dadzilla.

As soon as they cleared the doors, Matt whistled. "Wow. Kid has an unhealthy attachment to you, Hell."

"Problem with sleeping with young men, some of them get a weird mother fixation on you and become super dependent. Especially kids who've had their minds destroyed by war. Damn, I need some weed."

"Not in my car."

"Then we'll stop in a few blocks. I'm not smoking in front of the police station."

"I thought you were legal," he said in a snide tone.

"I am. But I don't want to put them in the position of having to check my ID."

"Can't you wait?"

"No."

"Christ. Where was Tanner deployed?"

They reached the car, and Matt unlocked the doors. She climbed inside.

Matt got into the driver's seat.

"Iraq," Hell said. She gestured with a bandaged thumb over her shoulder toward the jail. "His squad got hit hard. Front lines stuff. But Freddy, that tears me up. Freddy was his immediate superior. Really was a father figure to the guys who were left. Kept them all together. And then he goes and kills himself." Her body went hard and hot, and she punched her palm. "Fuck. I hate George Bush and Obama for sending our good boys over there to die, all in the name of corporate profits for the military-industrial complex and the oil companies." She shook her head. "Don't get me started. I'm too angry about all this, and I have to focus." She rubbed her aching forehead.

Matt started up the car, pulled out, and drove out of the garage. "You believe his account of the librarian?"

"Yes. He's been trained to notice every detail of his environment to protect himself. Who would come after me and set up Tanner?"

"Someone smart. Our culprit is much more sophisticated than just a jealous, crazy lover gone bad. This person is manipulating the situation, planting evidence, giving us red herrings, which means they orchestrated your attack down to the smallest detail. They probably hired the bad PI—that librarian—and she could have shot at you. We still don't know how she figures in the scheme. I believe the culprit is either someone close to you who wants to hurt you or a criminal related to an old case or someone smart you crossed seeking revenge. Like maybe one of the deadbeat dads you tracked down."

Her mind tinged with darkness, and her stomach roiled. "Great. That only encompasses about three thousand, four hundred, and fifty-seven people."

Matt stopped at a light. "Or Tanner could have hallucinated the librarian if he's that strung out. And just because the bullets don't match doesn't mean anything. Tanner could have ditched the gun. But I honestly picked up no malice on his behalf. He really was looking to you for emotional support. Still, we need to keep him on the list."

"Agreed. But what's with the librarian? Has to be a bad disguise, right? No one looks like a freakin' librarian, especially not librarians. Damn, I have these librarian girlfriends who go to the Exotic Erotic Ball and they—Never mind. But don't you think that's weird that someone would be that noticeable?"

"Nothing's weird when you're that crazy. But if she is real, she wanted to be seen. Hanging out in the City in an old-lady outfit? Stick out like a sore thumb."

Hell's brow hurt from furrowing so hard. None of this made sense. "Yeah. Why would she want to be seen? Intimidation?"

He shrugged. "All I can think."

Traffic began moving, and Matt accelerated. By the precise way he applied the gas, Hell barely moved back in her seat. While good for his passengers, Hell betted his anal tendencies annoyed the crap out of his wife.

She twisted her mouth to one side. "My gut says Tanner didn't shoot at me, but I have to be objective and look at the evidence. He had the means, the motive, and the opportunity. And the stressor. Freddy kept him sane. Thanks for diffusing that situation so elegantly when Tanner was just about to freak out on me, by the way, with that well-timed bump. And for yanking me away from his bear-trap embrace."

Matt gave an almost imperceptible nod, but his eyes took on a shine. "You're welcome. Yeah, he's unstable. And as I've learned time and time again, unstable people are capable of anything. Especially military-trained people with PTSD."

A cold shiver went down her back. She rubbed her arms. "I suppose. Damn, I hope not. He's the first mistake I've made with a lover." *Other than Capasso.* "Tanner caught me at a weak moment, and I read his energy wrong. He was the first new lover I'd taken on in three years. And damn, he gave me enough hints. When I look back, I really felt I owed him something for going to Iraq and almost getting killed. And he was hot. And bathed then. Was not this crazy. I feel sorry for him, but I'm kinda afraid of him now."

Matt clapped her on the shoulder. "Don't worry, Hell. We'll figure it out and keep you safe."

Hell looked at his hand and then at him. "Do you realize you just touched me?"

He took his hand away like he'd been burned, and examined it. "Do I need disinfectant?"

She laughed. "Probably. Okay, pull over here in the Grocery Outlet parking lot."

"I don't like this, Hell." But he signaled and pulled into the lot.

"Too bad. Keeps me sane and focused. Works better than Prozac or Wellbutrin or Paxil, or any pills I've tried."

He parked the car. "Really?"

"Yes. I'd rather not smoke it, but if I don't, my head will explode. And you don't want my brains all over the immaculate interior of your sedan, do you? I'll be right back."

He made a loud, irritated noise.

She stepped out of the car and took a cursory glance around the quarter-full parking lot. An elderly lady with a white bubble hairdo slowly pushed a cart toward the entrance to the store, a good twenty-five yards away from her. No one else was in the lot.

Hell withdrew her wooden, one-hitter pipe kit and slid open the top. A cigarette-shaped, one-hit pipe popped up. She pulled out the metal cylinder and ground the bowl-end into the pot-filled chamber of the kit. After checking to make sure she got the perfect-sized amount, she stuck the fake cigarette in her mouth and lit it. The heavenly scent of smoke filled her lungs and nostrils, rejuvenating her body. She held in the lungful, then blew out a stream. One more hit, and the load was gone.

Warmth and relief spread through her mind and limbs. Her stomach relaxed. The tension in her shoulders eased. Back to normal.

She popped a stick of peppermint sugarless gum in her mouth and climbed back inside Matt's car.

He made a pruney-lipped, disapproving face. "I can't see how that crap helps you."

"You aren't me, and you don't have to cope with my brain."

"How long have you been using that stuff?"

"Since I was sixteen."

"That's a long time to be smoking."

"Tell me about it. But it's the only thing that helps with the PTSD."

"You have PTSD."

"Yes." *And we're all done with that conversation.*

He waited, but when she didn't continue, he turned over the engine. "Okay, so we're headed to Dave's studio in San Francisco?"

"Yeah."

"How about a stop at In-N-Out on Veteran's first?"

"Perfect."

Her train of thought derailed and fuzzed out. Problem with weed, it gave her peace of mind and took away a piece of her mind at the same time. She prayed that sometime in the future, she wouldn't need it.

But if people kept shooting at her, that day would never come.

CHAPTER 3

TUESDAY, MARCH 8, 2011, 2:24 P.M.

After they left Jase's place in the San Bruno hills and returned to the car, Matt sent her a sharp look. "Okay, I really want to know who this mysterious church lady slash librarian is."

Hell gave a shudder. "Yeah. Creeps me out. I'm gonna canvass my hood tomorrow and see if anyone has seen her. I know I haven't. I would have noticed. At least it proves that Tanner wasn't hallucinating her."

Matt referred to his pocket notepad. "So she followed Tanner, and according to the description of his landlord, impersonated an insurance agent to get access to his apartment. Jase saw her at his work and outside his condo. Dave saw her in a coffee shop, watching him, and at the music store. And Mike spotted her in front of his tattoo shop."

"Like you said, she clearly wants to be seen. She must be trying to intimidate them. Or me. But then why did she want direct access to Tanner's apartment? She could have easily gotten caught. Why are you gonna let people see you if you're planning on breaking into their pad?"

Matt's brow furrowed. "We need to get our hands on her and find out."

She shifted in her seat. "I still think she or he is wearing a bad disguise."

His gaze sharpened. "Him, huh?"

"Why not?" She gave a hand shrug. "Maybe it's some rookie PI who watched too many *Mission Impossible* episodes. Or *MacGyver*. I don't know, but we'll find them. Meanwhile, I gotta get Tanner out of jail. You think Joe can help?"

He shook his head. "No. Up to the courts. He's in the system now."

Hell scanned the condo complex parking area but wasn't paying attention to what she saw. "Shit."

Matt nodded at her and started the car. "Jase's still in love with you. You said his alibi checked out. You sure about that?"

Hell's stomach tightened. "Yeah." She rubbed the painful line between her eyes. "He was in Sacramento prosecuting a case. I drove by his house after I got out of the police station. He wasn't home. Checked with the neighbor who feeds his fish, and they told me he was in Sacramento for the previous two weeks. Then I called him to make sure."

"If you were that worried, you need to pay attention." He backed out and headed for the exit.

She waved a hand. "He has no history of violence or stalking his exes, but he has gotten weird and possessive with me. A few months ago, he lost it. Part of the reason I pulled back."

Matt turned onto the frontage road that led to 280.

Hell made an exasperated noise. "Moron was so worried I'd fall in love with him. He must have mentioned about a million times in the beginning of our affair that this was just sex, right? Idiot. Then he starts acting like a jealous husband. Spaz. Hot, but a total spaz. Only lover I've ever argued with."

His thick eyebrows went high. "He seemed pretty high-strung."

"Nice word for spaz." Hell stared out the front of Matt's car at the passing traffic while they sat at a red light. The 280 freeway loomed large above them to her right. She had an urge to smoke more weed. She pointed across the street. "Dude, can you pull over there at that little strip mall before we get on 280?"

His jaw tightened. "No."

She laughed. "C'mon, Matt. You don't want me smoking in your car, do you?"

"You are forbidden to smoke in my car," he pronounced, his gaze flaring.

She went into belly laughs. "The look on your face! Priceless! You kill me."

"Wish I could." Didn't look like he was joking.

"Matt, really. Would you stop me from taking a pill prescribed by a doctor? Would you be this angry if I popped a pill?"

His eyes narrowed, and his face went red. "No." He gripped the wheel until his knuckles turned white.

Apparently, he didn't think marijuana could ever be considered a legitimate medication. Too bad. His boiling-point expression was so funny she had to hold back more laughter. Didn't want to send him over the edge.

Seemed like it took all his strength, but he drove across the street and dutifully parked where she'd indicated. She stepped out of the car and gave a cursory glance at the street corner, the gas station across the street, and the small strip mall where they were parked to make sure no cops were around.

She filled the pipe, and an image of the librarian pumping gasoline popped in her head. Hell squinted at the gas station across the street. A short, squat woman in a dark brown skirt wearing glasses and a Stormtrooper-like helmet of gray hair stood beside a black Honda, screwing on the gas cap.

Hell's heart beat faster, and adrenaline fired through her. Holy shit! The goddamned librarian was pumping gasoline into a bloody black Honda! And a seventh- generation Accord at that!

Hell stuffed her pipe in her jacket and tore off across the street, running at full tilt.

The librarian walked around her car. As she opened her door, she glanced over at Hell and did a double take. Her mouth dropped open, and she leapt into the Honda.

Convicted! It was her!

Hell reached the woman's car just as it started to accelerate. She grabbed the driver's-side door handle and yanked the door open. "Stop the car!"

The woman scowled, reached out, and smashed down hard on Hell's arm, breaking her grip. Pain shot through her forearm.

Hell tried to grab the handle again, but the lunatic closed her door, screeched out of the parking lot, and launched into the street, narrowly missing a taxi. The yellow cab honked and swerved.

The librarian sped off toward 280.

"Hell, get in!"

Matt's car appeared next to her. She flung open the door, leapt in, and slammed it shut. He hit the gas, and the momentum pressed her back against the seat.

She grabbed the seat belt and buckled herself in.

His focus was sharp. He must have done this so many times it was probably like riding a bike for him. He shot her an irritated glance. "Why did you run across the street without telling me why and without giving me the option of joining you?"

"Sorry, not used to working with a partner, and I thought I could get to her in time."

"Reach under the seat and pull out the beacon, will ya?" He gestured toward the floorboards.

Hell did a double take. "You got a beacon?"

A little gleam appeared in his blue eyes. "You bet."

"That's illegal to use." She checked his expression to make sure he wasn't fooling.

"Fuck it. We need this woman." The cop was back, sans his black-and-white morals. Killer. Maybe he wasn't such a goody-goody after all.

"You rock." She fished out the light and stuck it on the roof. Magnet was so powerful she wasn't sure she'd be able to remove it later. She quickly plugged the end of the power cord into the cigarette lighter.

The librarian took the exit for 280 South.

Hell's heart raced, and sweat trickled between her breasts. "She must have been watching us at Jase's. But here's the bizarre thing, Matt, she's not wearing a disguise. That woman is really ugly."

He frowned. "Are you sure?"

"Yeah. Hideous. Really."

"Did you get her license plate?"

"Already memorized."

"Write it down."

"Good plan." She took out her notebook and scribbled down the plate. "Honda Accord, seventh generation: 2003, 4, or 5. I think it was a 2003, like the one the assailant who shot at me drove. Black, four door."

"How do you know the years?"

"Studied 'em."

Matt gave her another glance. She kept making notes. The plate number. She saw the woman's face in her mind. Mole on the left side of her chin. Fat, squatty, little nose. Thick salt-and-pepper eyebrows. Hirsute face. Brown eyes. Coke-bottle-thick glasses. Sneer. Thin lips. Gold bridge. Lots of dental work. Brownish teeth, and the car stank of full ashtray: smoker. Double chin. Maybe forty pounds overweight. Lesbian vibe. No make-up. No jewelry. No ring, so not married—huge shocker. Brown, knit, button-down sweater. Support hose. Boring brown shoes that looked a lot like oxfords. Dressed like she was eighty, but was probably in her late fifties.

Effin' freak. A librarian on steroids.

When Hell looked up, Matt was closing in on the woman's car.

Her heart sped up as she pointed out the window. "Pull up next to her. Let's see if we can get her to—"

The librarian slammed on her brakes. The rear of the black Honda got huge in the windshield.

Hell gasped, adrenaline swamping her body. "Watch out!"

Matt yelled and stomped on the brakes. Hell was flung forward, and the seat belt dug into her collarbone. Tires squealed. The back end of Matt's car slid out, but in a quick two moves, he'd regained control.

The librarian zoomed forward and veered into the slow lane, cutting off a Bug, which honked loudly.

Baring his teeth, he stepped on the gas. "Bitch!" His brows lay heavy over his flashing blue eyes as he pulled alongside the Honda.

Hell rolled down her window, hung out, and gestured sharply. "Pull over!"

The librarian lowered her window. The barrel of a handgun appeared, pointed right at Hell.

Her heart stopped. "Gun! Get down!" She ducked.

Matt hit the brakes again. The seat belt bit into her shoulder and chest. Horns blared.

"She's taking Trousdale!" he yelled.

"Follow her! I'll call the cops!" Breathing heavy, her pulse whooshing in her ears, Hell retrieved her iPhone from her pocket and called 911. "Dispatch?" Her hand shook so hard it was difficult to keep control over the cell. "I'm on 280 headed south at the Trousdale exit in Burlingame. The driver of a black Honda just pointed a gun at me. A black Honda Accord, year 2003, 4, or 5, license plate number: 5-Alpha Tango Charley 3-3-4. My name is Helen Trent. I'm a licensed private investigator. The Honda is leaving the freeway ahead of me and has just run a red light and is making a left, heading east."

Matt slowed, checked the Trousdale intersection quickly, and zipped through it, cutting off a gold sedan making a left onto 280. The driver honked and flipped them the bird.

The dispatch ordered her to get away from the car and informed her that she would alert the authorities.

"Yes, ma'am." Hell hung up and stuffed her phone back into her jacket pocket.

They drove under the freeway and quickly approached the 280 North on-ramp coming up on their left.

"She's getting back on the freeway, I know it," Matt said.

A huge eighteen-wheeler was headed toward them in the opposite lane.

"She won't make this light. I'll catch her," he said.

The librarian veered into the opposite lane, directly into the path of the semi.

Airhorns blasted the area.

Hell gasped.

"Holy shit!" Matt yelled. "She's gonna—"

The Honda disappeared into the bike lane on the other side of the semi, missing the front of the huge truck by inches.

Matt punched his steering wheel. "Damn it, she's getting away!"

Seemed like it took five minutes for the double tractor-trailer to pass.

"Come on, come on!" He bounced in place.

Since she'd been in his company, she'd never seen him glow like this. He might be angry and focused and completely in the job groove, but he was happy. He must be feeling like his old self.

Finally, the semi passed, and Matt zoomed onto the freeway entrance for 280 North.

As the car jetted forward, Hell braced herself and checked out the apartment complex to the right of the on-ramp.

A huge cloud of dust hung near the sign for the building. Landscaper was probably blowing the parking lot.

They sped forward, searching for the Honda. He accelerated quickly. Car had damned good pick up.

She scanned the six lanes of freeway traffic ahead but didn't see a black Honda.

After a few seconds, Matt said, "We should see her. She didn't get this much of a head start."

Hell spotted a black Honda far up ahead. "Is that her right up there?"

"No. A two-door."

All of a sudden, the realization hit her. "The cloud of dust! Shit!" She smacked her forehead. "Turn around, Matt, turn around!" She gestured violently.

"What?"

"I saw a freakin' cloud of dust right next to the intersection! The librarian off-roaded through the landscaping into that apartment complex!"

He did a double take. "Are you serious? Why didn't you say anything?"

"I thought someone was cleaning the parking lot."

"Shit." He hit the steering wheel and took the next exit. "Let's see if we can get lucky." He came to a red light and stopped. "No. *Fuck.*"

"Goddamn it. I let her get away!" She punched her palm.

"Neither of us expected her to be this crazy. A gun, and that *Bullit* car move she made in front of the semi? Whoever she is, she's nuts."

Sirens whined, and two CHPs flew by going south on 280. Looking for Miss Librarian, more than likely. A little late.

The light changed, and Matt got back onto the freeway, headed the opposite direction. "At least the cops are on it. Hopefully, they'll catch her. Hey, take off the beacon, will you? I don't want them to see that."

She reached up, and using quite a bit of strength, dislodged the flashing light and brought it inside. Nearly blinding herself.

Matt winced and quickly removed the cord from the cigarette lighter. "Jeez, Hell. You're supposed to unplug it first."

"I just realized that." She tucked the beacon under her seat, then withdrew her notebook and special Death phone from her skull-covered backpack.

"You have two cell phones?"

"This is a special phone. One use only."

"Huh?"

"Hold on." She punched a button with the preprogrammed number.

Death came online. "Hell, how is your sun shining today?" he said in his radio-announcer-on-helium voice. Death had spent a fair amount of time practicing to be a disc jockey, but his voice was too weird, and his interest in computers had superseded radio.

"Hi, baby. Got somethin' for ya."

"Figured you weren't calling me for my sparkling personality."

Hell grinned. "I'm always calling for that, Deathy. But this is a rush."

"Go ahead," he replied.

"Black Honda Accord. Year 2003, 4, or 5. Five-Alpha-Tango-Charley, 3-3-4."

"Yes. I have it. It's a 2003. Reported stolen three days ago in Sacramento."

"Shit, there goes that lead. Same year of the car of my shooter at Starbucks." She wrote *2003 Honda Accord* in her notebook under the librarian's information.

"What?" Matt asked.

"Stolen car," she said. "From Sacramento. She could be our shooter."

Matt gave a quick grimace. "Possible. But we could have used the lead on the car."

Death cleared his throat. "Would you like me to get you a printout and photos of all registered PIs in the Sacramento area?" he asked. "I can email that to you in an hour or so."

"I love you."

Matt stared at her.

She made a face. "I love Death, my computer dude, not you."

He seemed relieved.

"Awwww, I love you, too, Hell." She could hear the smile in Death's voice. "Who's with you?"

"You'd never believe it in a million years."

"Matthew Sinclair."

"How did you— Duh. I forgot." She'd just had Death do an in-depth report on Matt to help her make the decision to hire him.

"How is that going? Shall I destroy him for you?" he asked in a cheery tone.

She looked over at Matt. "No. I think he's nicer than we thought."

The ex-cop seemed extremely perturbed by her side of the conversation.

"Doubtful," Death said. "Here's something interesting. Your black

Honda received a parking ticket just two days ago in Belmont on El Camino. I'll email you the address."

A little flame of hope ignited in Hell. "That would be worth a look-see." If the librarian had gotten a parking ticket, it meant she'd spent some time in the area.

"Also, you asked me to check Capasso's whereabouts at the time of the shooting?"

"Yes?"

"He was at his house in Nob Hill."

"What about his people?"

"Two of his networks had no information about you. A third had some chatter, mostly it seems it regards tracking you."

"Shit." She sighed heavily. "That would be very bad."

"However, as I watch their other operations, especially regarding intimidation and threats, they seem to employ a large team for each activity. On that Sunday, there was a party with the majority of Capasso's people in attendance. That does not rule out subcontractors, of which their numbers are vast. But from the information that floated around the time of your shooting, it does not appear as if any known local criminal networks were involved in your attack."

"But Marco could have hired a subcontractor to intimidate me into stopping seeing Buh..." She almost said Brad! "Uh, my other men."

"I wish I knew for certain. I apologize. Capasso is very powerful, especially in the world of hacking. Even I was presented with many challenges penetrating his security. I will continue monitoring him, and I'll let you know the second anything new arises."

"Thanks, honey." Shit. She'd hoped to cross Capasso off her list.

"Would you care to stop by for a beverage later? The General should be here. I can meet you at our usual spot."

Her heart warmed at the affection in his voice. She missed him. "I'd love to. But I'm on the case."

"All righty, then. How many phones do you currently have? Are you using my rotating password protection program?"

She chuckled. "Yes, Dad. I'm using all your Internet condoms. And I have about five phones left."

"Excellent."

"Thanks, Deathy. If I have time to party, I'll drop you an email. If I don't make it, give my love to the General. Gotta go."

"Be seeing you, Hell." His usual sign-off from *The Prisoner*.

"You are Number Six," she said doing her imitation of Number One.

He chuckled and hung up.

Matt's attention went between her and the road. "Who was that?"

"My Internet oracle." Hell removed the SIM card and tossed it out the window onto the freeway. After pulling out the batteries, she wrapped a rubber band around the phone and tossed the batteries and cell back in the plastic bag.

Matt noted each and every one of her actions. "Death?"

"Uh-huh. Gave us a lead to follow up on if we strike out here." She stuffed the phone back in her backpack.

Matt's focus turned back to the traffic. "Good. Here's the exit. Let's go check out the apartment building." He took the exit, stopped, and made a left onto Trousdale.

Two cop cars were parked under the freeway. Another pulled in front of them, turning left onto Trousdale. But they'd clearly had no luck.

"Should we stop and tell them what I saw?" Hell asked.

Matt shook his head. "You saw a cloud of dust, Hell. Let's go see if we can get some concrete evidence before we alert the cops."

He drove down Trousdale and glanced at Hell. "That call from Death wasn't all good news. Who do you have to leave on the list? Capasso?"

"No." Hell scanned the area for the Honda.

"Hell, don't lie to me."

"Matt, he'd kill you. Without a thought. Without hesitation. You busted some of his guys and put one in jail. He isn't going to be happy when he finds out I've hired you."

Matt went a little pale and swallowed hard, then slammed on the brakes and turned, almost missing his left onto Hunt. "Am I in danger?"

"No, I wouldn't have hired you if I thought that was a possibility. He'll be pissed, but I'll be able to bullshit him into seeing my side. I'll tell him I hired you to degrade and humiliate you, and he'll go along with it."

"Go along. He has that much power over you?"

Hell looked away. "No, but I just try to avoid upsetting him."

"Why do you still see him? You can't love him."

She shrugged. "Matt, love is complicated, okay? You know that, too. I told you, I fell for him before I knew who he was. Now let's get back to what we're doing now, searching for that librarian bitch." She focused her attention out the windows.

"I'm going to want to talk about Capasso more, Hell."

"Fine, later." She checked the area carefully. But no sign of the Honda.

"I know she won't be here, but let's take a look."

Matt turned into the parking lot for the apartment building and drove to the very back.

Ahead of them, a large group of people stood at the edge of an expanse of lawn. They were all gesturing wildly and seemed quite upset.

"Let me guess, that's where the librarian drove through," Hell said.

"Let's see what the witnesses say."

He parked the car, and they got out.

Hell and Matt walked over to the excited group. A few of them were wearing workman's outfits and speaking Spanish. A tall, middle-aged, white lady in a suit with a skirt seemed to be in charge, maybe the manager, by the way she was interrogating the group. The rest of the people appeared to be residents, and a normal slice of the demographic of the Bay Area: professional Asians, Latinos, African-Americans, Indians, and whites in their twenties, thirties, and forties.

Beyond the group, in the large lawn, fresh, muddy, tire tracks grooved deep into the turf.

"She almost ran us over!" a young white woman in a red dress exclaimed to the group.

"Who's going to pay for this?" the tall manager woman demanded, pointing vehemently at the destroyed landscaping and lawn.

"Excuse me," Hell said loudly. "Did a black Honda come off-roading through here?"

The crowd swung their attention on her.

The young woman nodded emphatically. "Yes! Did you see it?"

"Yeah, earlier. Did you see where the car went?" Hell asked.

The young woman pointed behind them. "Out through the front."

Hell looked toward the entrance but couldn't see it well from where they stood. "Did you see if the car went left or right out of the parking lot?"

"No," the young white woman replied.

"Crap," Hell said to Matt.

A cute, black, thirty-something UPS driver walked up to the group. "Wilma, I have a delivery for the office, what— Wow, what happened to the lawn?" he asked and pointed to the damaged turf.

The tall woman, Wilma, replied heatedly, "Some nutcase flew up from Trousdale and carved themselves a new road through my land-scaping. The owners aren't going to like this. I told them they needed to extend the chain-link fence, but would they listen to me? No."

"You all sure the car was a black Honda?" Matt asked, his note-book out.

The group all nodded and voiced their agreement.

"Can you describe the driver?" Matt asked. "Which of you saw her?"

A young Indian woman raised her hand. "I was standing right here, about to get into my car when she came careening through those trees," she said, her eyes wide, pointing at the apartment building's sign on Trousdale. "I thought she'd stop, but she kept coming. Spinning the wheel, driving crazy, like she was in a movie. I ran back behind my car, and she drove right through here." She motioned from the edge of the lawn, across the sidewalk to the parking lot, and beyond. "Thankfully, no one was in the loading zone here."

"Did you get a good look at her?" Hell asked.

"Yes, seemed completely incongruent," the Indian girl said. "I thought it would be some young, crazy man, but it was an older lady. Long gray hair, brown suit, big glasses, and she looked mean. She looked like she was growling or something. Sneering. Scary. Looked completely crazy. I was so relieved when she drove past and kept going."

"Is there anything else you can tell us about the car or the woman?" Matt asked.

The Indian woman nodded. "Yes. I got part of the license plate. Um, 334 were the last numbers."

"Well, that answers that," Hell said.

"Who are you people?" Wilma asked, looking between Hell and Matt.

Hell stood tall. "I'm Helen Trent, this is Matt Sinclair. We're private investigators trying to get our hands on that lady."

"What did she do?" Wilma asked.

"For one, pulled a gun on us," Hell said.

"Did you call the police?" Wilma asked.

"Yeah," Hell replied.

"A gun?" the young Indian woman exclaimed. "What is with you Americans and your guns?"

"We're crazy and paranoid," Hell replied quickly. "Is there anything else you can tell us about the gray-haired lady or the car?"

The UPS driver snapped his fingers. "Hey, I just saw a weird old lady with gray hair, just back down the road. She was changing license plates on her black car, could have been a Honda. She was parked right in front of a house on Vallejo Drive, no more than a few minutes ago, my last delivery."

Hell's heart jumped.

"Where on Vallejo?" Matt demanded.

"Right by the corner of Vallejo and Conejo," the driver reported.

"Was she there when you left?" Matt asked.

The hot, black UPS dude nodded. "She was just getting back in her car."

Matt nudged Hell. "We need to go." He started jogging toward his car.

Hell followed. Over her shoulder, she said to Wilma, "If we find her we'll tell the cops what she did here so you can press charges."

Wilma brightened. "Good, thank you."

Hell and Matt hopped into his Taurus. Matt was out of the parking lot in a flash and headed down Vallejo.

"Shit, if we don't see her, we've lost the car," Hell said. "Damn it, who is this woman? She didn't steal the car; she stole the plates. And having extra license plates? Who besides me would have those?"

Matt did a double take. "You have extra license plates?"

"Yeah. Some fake ones for surveillance when I need them. But I don't use stolen plates, for God's sake. This chick must be an unlicensed, rogue PI. Or a hired gun."

They quickly reached the corner of Conejo and Vallejo. No sign of the Honda.

"Should we get out and check to see if she dropped anything out of her car?" Hell asked.

Matt gave a quick shake of his head. "I think we should keep going. We aren't far behind her. She's probably going to take Millbrae down to 101. Won't risk going back to 280."

"Okay, good. So if we can't find her, let's head to Belmont. Death said the librarian got a ticket just three days ago on El Camino."

"Worth a shot."

She scanned the area for the black Honda.

"So tell me how Death got his name," Matt said.

She snorted. "His other names weren't nearly as dramatic. I made him change it about twenty years ago. He used to be Rabbit. I was like, dude, no one is going to respect a bunny. Come up with something more ominous. Something really hacker-y. So then he went to Rabid. Which was much better. But it was still too close to Rabbit. We did tequila shots, bong hits, and, uh, some other stuff until we came up with Death. God, we laughed so hard that night."

Hell spotted a black Honda. Her heart beat faster. She was just about to tell Matt when she noticed it was a two-door. Shit. She tsked.

"So who is Death?"

"Friend." Lots of newer silver Hondas on the residential street, but no black older ones.

Matt leaned closer. "He a suspect?"

She shook her head. "No. He doesn't go out in public much."

"Oh." He relaxed back in his seat and stopped as they came to a stop sign.

Hell nodded. "Yeah. He's a little fringe-y. And very paranoid. And very on the FBI's Most Wanted List."

"*Right.*" He examined her a bit more closely and raised his eyebrows. "Really? What did he do?"

She shifted in her seat to get more comfortable, her focus sharp on the passing traffic and all the parked cars in the area. "You remember a few years back when the IRS website went down on April fifteenth and they had to extend the deadline for everyone by three days?"

"Let me guess. He was late on his taxes."

"No, I was," she said, laughing. A black Honda pulled up next to them, and her heart skipped a beat. Then her mood took a nosedive. Fat bald guy in the driver's seat. Bummer.

"He did that for you?" Matt demanded.

"Also to see if he could."

He rubbed the back of his neck. "Jesus."

Matt continued toward El Camino.

She checked every car in the area but saw no sign of the crazy librarian. "Now he works for many, many high-level people. But no one knows him."

"How do you know him?" Matt stopped at the light for El Camino.

Met him when I was ten. Grew up with him. Went to high school and college together. "Can't say."

"Will I ever meet him?"

"No one meets him. Ever. Especially not you."

Matt frowned. "Why not me?"

"You put me in jail."

He stared at her for a long second and then snapped his fingers. "Wait a minute. Right around then, all my credit cards got mysteriously cancelled." His eyebrows and lips flattened, and he glared at her.

The light changed, and he went through the intersection.

She sent him a sinister grin. "Let me put it this way, you are really lucky you have a wife and three great kids."

"You would have unleashed him on me?" His mouth curved downwards so far his lips almost touched his jaw.

Light turned green and Matt proceeded toward 101.

Hell scanned all the cars in the vicinity. "No. He would have done it all on his own. And he didn't care about your wife and kids. I had to give him a direct order not to hurt you. Mess with you, maybe, but nothing that would hurt your wife or kids."

"So I'm supposed to thank you?" His eyes narrowed as he went through an intersection on a green light.

Hell assumed her power pose. "Dude, if it weren't for me, you would not have your savings, that annuity at Bank of America, the timeshare in Lake Tahoe, your ski boat, your house on Monterey Avenue—"

Matt's face turned white. "How did you—"

"—or this car, and you'd be in jail for the rest of your life for embezzlement. Death can make anything happen to anyone. He has the power of God in this electronic age."

Sweat beaded on his forehead. "Are you serious? Christ, Hell. You know everything about me, don't you?"

"Just your financial holdings. And your GPA in college. And, uh... Yeah. Guess I do."

"Holy shit." Fear lines grooved deep in his rugged features. "So the government hasn't caught him, ever?" He signaled and took a right onto the South 101 freeway.

"Nope. Nobody screws with him. He's a legend. One of the most powerful hackers on the planet." Hell saw no sign of the black Honda anywhere on 101. Where was that bitch?

"People always make mistakes." Matt merged with the freeway traffic.

"Not Death. Never met anyone smarter. Nor more paranoid. Only thing that might get him is his preference for pharmaceuticals and speed."

"He's a drug addict?"

"User. Not as much as he used to. I was worried about him a few years ago and did an intervention. Found him arranging all his one thousand vintage action figures by size and color, his eyes as wide as saucers, his whole body shaking. He'd been up for a week and was totally bonkers. Absolutely convinced that the action figures had asked him to put them in order. Idiot. Luckily, he realized he was starting to crack up and got off the meth."

One side of Matt's mouth quirked, and he signaled and checked his mirrors to merge left. "So does Death live with his mother in the basement?"

"No. She lives in the basement, he lives upstairs. Kidding. Actually, I don't know where he lives for my protection and his. I'm beginning to think the librarian lost us, Matt. Let's go to the address on El Camino in Belmont. Right off of Ralston."

Matt moved into one of the middle lanes and turned off his blinker. "Okay. Wait. You don't know where Death lives?"

"Safer for him and me." Truth. He always met her and then brought her to where he lived so he could sneak her past security. Last place was a secret area of a large office building in Foster City. He'd found access to a huge enclosed space—an architectural anomaly in the structure—installed his own door, and moved in. He used their electricity, their computer mainframe, and no one ever caught on.

"Hell, eventually he'll make a mistake and—"

"Doubtful, since he no longer exists. When his parents died, he faked his own death. He uses aliases and has hundreds of personas—complete with birth certificates, credit cards, employment histories, education histories—that he rotates through. He doesn't have a giant ego, so he lets others take credit—and blame—for his work."

"Wow. So he gets you access to…"

"Any information I need. I just can't keep it for long. He always embeds his emails with self-destruct codes. So I can't use anything he obtains to build a court case. Can't use it to prove anything to anyone. He usually gives me info, and then I con a cop into looking it up for me if I need proof."

"Is he an old lover?"

"No. Even though he has offered on numerous occasions."

Matt chuckled. "Yet another man in your life."

"Yeah. I inspire a weird kind of loyalty in men, but I think it's only to my pussy. I'm not sure any of the guys in my life give a damn about the rest of me."

"They act like they do. Especially Jase."

She snorted. "Jase has attachment issues. But he's the same as the rest. All they care about is my box. I'm a big walking vagina."

Matt laughed. "Sorry, that's not funny."

"No, it's not. I need to do something about that. I'm getting sick of my life. I mean, I like sex. I don't feel disrespected, I just want more. I think I'm actually starting to crave a relationship. Which shocks me. And saddens me."

"Why?"

She pursed her lips and crossed her arms. "Because the men in my life aren't worth having a relationship with. Especially Jase. Nitpicky, anal-retentive, mercurial, critical dickhead. Almost everything I do bugs him: the way I take my wrappers off candy bars, the way I drive, the way I form words with my burps—he's constantly trying to change me."

"Why do you keep seeing him?"

Good question. "Because he's so bloody cute, and good in the sack. He loves to hike as much as I do. Still, I clearly need to clean house. Dump them all and start over. Maybe be celibate for—" She burst out laughing. "Oh, who am I kidding? I couldn't even get that sentence out. I love my boys." She sighed heavily. "I don't think I'm ever gonna be satisfied or happy. I wasn't super happy in a relationship, and I'm not super happy now. Maybe I'm doomed."

"I don't think so, Hell. I think you're on the verge of a life change."

She checked his expression. Earnest. Shrugging, she looked out the window at the passing traffic. "Well, I'm in the midst of a wake-up call, that's for sure." She glanced back at him. "But I don't know, Matty old boy. Every time I get any hope, someone comes along and nukes it."

"Don't predicate your future on your past."

She regarded him and raised one eyebrow. "Did you take a Wise Pill this morning?"

Matt grinned.

Tuesday, March 8, 2011, 3:34 p.m.

MATT PARKED ON EL CAMINO REAL WHERE THE LIBRARIAN GOT THE ticket. There were several cheap motels and small businesses in the vicinity.

After having no luck at the first three small motels and two businesses, they walked up to the office of the last motel on the block. And such a motel it was! The contrast between the three previous modest but clean motels and this horror-fest couldn't be more stark. The Rancho Belmont looked like it belonged in a movie about the Apocalypse. Hell half expected legions of serial killers to come out of the rooms holding bloody chainsaws and dragging dead bodies behind them. Creepy didn't even begin to cover it. She wanted to take a shower, and she hadn't even stepped foot inside.

They walked into the manager's office, which stank of cigarettes and Lysol spray. The carpeting was brown and greasy but at one time in its life had been green. Yellowing pictures of the Sierras and ski scenes hung on the smoke-stained walls. A shabby, faded, and stained avocado-green couch adorned with orange-gingham pillows sat in front of a dirty window. The manager was fat, had a bloated round face, puffy dark eyes, a bulbous nose, and the red skin of an alcoholic. He also had the worst gray comb-over ever. Looked like John Belushi's ugly cousin. Dressed in a black wife-beater and jeans, he had a pelt of black and gray hair on his arms and shoulders. Super attractive.

He eyed the two of them and sent Matt a lascivious grin. "Want a room for you and the lady?"

Matt's eyes bugged out. He gasped in horror and clutched his chest. "Good God, no."

Hell burst out laughing. Matt's face turned neon red. He coughed and loosened his collar. He sent her a sheepish look, and then his gaze hollowed like he'd just faced his own death.

She couldn't help but be slightly insulted. The thought of sleeping with her terrified him that much? What? Like she was a succubus who would suck out his soul through his dick?

Matt cleared his throat, stood tall, and faced the manager. "Have you seen a woman about five-five with long gray hair—"

"Like a helmet of hair," Hell broke in. "Coke-bottle-thick glasses, dresses like a librarian or church lady, and drives a black Honda."

"I might know somethin'." His eyes narrowed, and he got a smug tilt to his head.

Matt leaned forward, all squared shoulders. "Now look here, buddy, we don't have time for your games."

Hell took a fifty out of her pocket and tossed it on the counter.

Matt glared at her.

"No worries, Matt. Dude has to make a living. You think he wants to work here?"

The fat pustule of a human snatched the money off the counter as fast as a lizard catching a fly with its tongue. "Yeah. She's right."

"So you see her?" Matt demanded.

The oily creep eyed Matt in an unfriendly way, then turned his chins away and spoke to Hell. "Checked out yesterday but said she might be comin' back. Wanted to know about rooms next week. I told her, honey, we always got openings. Last time we were full was back when old Charley ran the place in the sixties. When the Peninsula rich would come here for their afternoon fun."

"What can you tell us about her?" Hell asked.

"Freak. Picky," he spat with his lip curled. "Like she expected the

Taj Mahal. I told her, lady, you want amenities, go to a real hotel. A real bitch, that one."

"Can I see her sign-in card?"

"Yeah, okay."

He fiddled around and withdrew a smudged index card.

Betty Fortune, San Jose.

Right. She and Matt exchanged knowing glances.

Hell turned back to Mr. Disgusting. He reeked of old alcohol, old man, and sweat. She took a slight step backward. "That's it?"

Indignant, he held his mouth in a superior pose. "She paid in cash. I didn't need to know more."

"That's not her name."

Mr. Greasy shrugged. "I didn't think so, either. She had a medical ID bracelet that said her name was Jones and she was a diabetic."

She snorted. "Jones? For real?"

"Yeah. I thought it was funny. See I got one, too." He held up his hairy wrist adorned with a silver medical bracelet. "That's why I noticed. And we had us a little chat about our disease."

"Did she say what she was doing here?" Matt asked.

"Working. On some important job for someone important, she said. Like she was somethin' special."

Hell nodded at the creepazoid. "Did she say who?"

He tapped his mouth with two cigarette-stained fingers. "No, only that they were rich. Blonde lady came by to see her. But she drove a black Honda, too, so she ain't that rich. If that was her client."

Matt frowned. "Two black Hondas?"

"Yeah."

"Around the same year?" Hell asked.

"Looked like it. Thought it was weird they drove the same car."

Hell took out her notebook and fished out a pen from her front pocket. "What did the blonde look like?"

He straightened his back and set his crossed arms on top of his enormous belly. "I don't know. Tall, skinny, wore big sunglasses and a baseball cap with her pony tail comin' out the back. Wearing one of them tight yogurt outfits you see on late-night TV commercials. You know, selling exercises, but, really, they're selling sex." He sent them a salacious smile.

Hell fought a shiver, and her brows wrinkled to the point of pain. "Yogurt?"

The repulsive man gestured, the folds of the flesh on his upper arms flapping. "You know, when ladies put their hands on the floor with their asses and tits hangin' out. All bent over like they want sex."

"Yoga?" she ventured.

He nodded, making his chins wag. "Yeah, yogurt." He made a grabbing motion and twisted his face into a lecherous grin. "Nice ass. A little too small for me, but round and tight."

A wave of nausea at the man's lewdness was cut short by a wallop of realization. Hell's heart and breathing stopped. Holy Christ. All of BC's lovers and his wife fit that description: Lindsay, Gwen, and Sherry.

Shit.

The threat was coming from BC.

Darkness claimed her mind, and she chewed her lower lip, her attention dropping to the threadbare carpeting. This could be bad. Very bad. Those ladies had unlimited bank accounts, were incredibly smart, and were all freakin' whack jobs.

All of whom exactly fit the description Matt had given earlier of their unsub.

Hell took a deep breath and focused on the disgusting pig. "Tell me about the interaction between the blonde and the ugly bitch."

"The blonde had to be her boss, because it was the only time Miss Jones didn't have her nose in the air. But that blonde lady sure did. Acted like she was the Queen of Sheba or something."

Double shit. Her mood plunged further. Again, the description fit all three. Out of all the people in her life, she would never have guessed that BC would put her in danger. Crazy.

Hell thanked the guy and followed Matt out to his car, her mind filled with dread. Those three females had the resources to make anything happen to anyone. It was amazing she was still alive.

"What?" he asked with a penetrating stare.

She broke out of her reverie and checked Matt. "What what?"

He looked right through her. Her belly dropped. Now she'd have to tell Matt everything. He really would think she was a whore after this. Her face warmed, and her stomach went cold.

"You took the news about the blonde lady pretty hard," he said in a knowing tone.

Her insides churning, she looked at the ground and kicked it. "Shit."

"You know who she was?"

She slowly nodded but couldn't look at him. "I'm fairly certain it was one of three people. But, hopefully, that means I'm being followed by them and not that they're trying to murder me—that is such a lie, Trent. Of course, they're trying to kill me. Goddamn, this isn't good."

"Who?"

Hell kneaded her hands together, her jitters rising fast. "Matt, I'm hungry. Let's stop by Whisper's Cafe on El Camino for an afternoon snack. It's a little past four. I don't want to spoil your dinner, but I need some food."

He eyed her and didn't make a move toward his car. "You have to level with me if I'm going to be any help to you."

"I know. I need food first."

He watched her for a long minute and finally said, "I could eat."

Ten minutes later, they were seated at one of Hell's favorite restaurants. Great salads, crepes, and sandwiches. Hell had the BLT with fruit salad, and Matt ordered a barbecued chicken salad. The waitress brought them their drinks, two iced teas.

"This seems unnatural," Hell said in a teasing tone.

"What?"

She quirked her mouth to the side. "Sharing a meal with you at a restaurant. The earlier burgers from In-N-Out in the car somehow didn't call attention to the fact that we were actually eating together."

He smirked.

She thought of the motel manager's mistaking them for lovers and chuckled.

"Okay, I'm waiting," Matt said with an expectant look on his face.

She stared at the wooden tabletop, and her stomach and shoulders tightened. Sighing, she finally made eye contact. "I don't want to withhold or lie to you again. I apologize. Given the tenuous nature of our alliance, I initially decided not to tell you about this part of my life. But all indicators are pointing to it as the source of the threat."

"Okay, so?"

"There's only been one major change in my life over the past four months. All the guys you met are lovers I've seen for four plus years."

"Dave and Capasso for eleven years, right?"

"Yeah."

He looked at her like her head had split open and Dame Edna had popped out. *"Don't tell me you're seeing yet another man?"*

Her face heated. "Yes."

"Why am I surprised? Is that why you haven't seen your boyfriends in a while? All of them mentioned they missed you. So you're seeing this guy exclusively? Why didn't you tell me?"

Shame coursing through her, she buried her face in her hands. "Because I didn't know I was seeing only him. Not until Jase and Dave and Mike brought it up today. I had no idea."

"How could you not know?" Incredulous.

She pulled her hands away from her face so she could gesture wildly. "Because this whole thing has been so sneaky! I've clearly been deep in denial."

"Why won't you tell me who he is?"

She grimaced. "I'm ashamed, okay? That's the truth." Her entire head blazed to the point where her ears felt like they were on fire.

Matt gaped. "Are you *blushing*?"

"Yes. Stop looking so shocked."

"Sorry. I had no idea you were capable of—"

"Shame?" She laughed. "Well, I am. Very ashamed." She stared at her tea, covered her hand with her mouth, and then finally took a sideways glance at Matt.

He looked utterly taken aback. Then he focused all his attention on her and examined her like a scientist peering at a bug under a microscope.

She cracked up. "I knew I would surprise you at some point." Then contrition gripped her, and her mood soured. She loved sex with BC, but not thinking about him. Or reflecting on her behavior. She picked at the Band-Aid on her left index finger.

"You're not ashamed of the Mafia don, but you're ashamed of this guy?" he asked, his voice pitched high with disbelief.

"Who said I wasn't ashamed of Capasso?" She shook her head and looked away. "I know you don't think I have any morals, but I believe in the sanctity of marriage. I hate what happened with Capasso, and I hate this thing with this guy. At least I didn't know Capasso was married for the first two months of our affair, but I knew about this guy. He was a complete Fuck Accident. Makes me feel dirty. But I don't know what it is about this jerk," she said, exasperated. "I keep trying to break up with him, and I can't seem to follow through."

"Who is he?"

"A rotten, soulless bastard with virtually no redeeming qualities outside of his amazing prowess in bed," she said in a disgusted tone.

"A name?"

She finally made eye contact. "Satan." She mashed her face into her hands. "I hate thinking about him. I broke all my cardinal rules." She slowly let her hands drop.

Leaning in, he raised his brows. "You have cardinal rules?"

"Yes." She held herself taller and her chin higher. "I don't screw married men, I don't screw clients, and I don't screw rich people." She gave a sad shake of her head, and her gaze dropped to the table top. "This guy has been my trifecta of self-betrayal. Which is why now I'm clearly paying the price."

Matt looked like he was nearly salivating. "You gonna give me a name?"

She massaged the tight muscles of her forehead. Her face still nearly radioactive with heat, Hell wished she could shrink inside her clothes and disappear. "Let me start at the beginning."

CHAPTER 4

WEDNESDAY, NOVEMBER 10, 2010, 10:28 A.M.

F ire roasting her insides, Hell fidgeted on a large leather couch in billionaire venture capitalist Brad Collins' plush waiting room. She tapped her foot violently and looked at the skulls ticking by on her watch. Twenty-eight minutes. Unreal. Every part of her wanted to run screaming out the door. She glared at the chic blonde model/secretary sitting behind a polished black desk. But the young Barbie doll wouldn't look up from her laptop.

A chunk of rubber was loose on Hell's left high-top. She ripped it off and checked the secretary—who still wouldn't look at her—then stuffed the tattered piece of shoe in between the cushions of the million-dollar leather sofa. The movement caused her black leather jacket to bunch in the back, causing yet another wave of irritation to prickle her skin. She leaned forward and yanked her worn, old security blanket down to her butt.

She shouldn't have come. Brad Collins was exactly the kind of rich, powerful bastard she hated. She wanted to spit on his expensive carpeting. Probably cost more to decorate his office than she'd spent in rent in the past twenty years.

Her secretary Betsy's parting words chimed in her head. "All you need is a few cash cows that'll feed your coffers so you can help that never-ending parade of deadbeats and losers you love so well."

Hell took a deep breath and looked at her watch. She'd give this guy until ten thirty on the dot, and then she was gone.

A skull ticked onto the six.

She stood, her legs thrilled she'd finally obeyed them. "I'm outta here. Tell your boss that I don't work for the rude."

The young secretary went ashen, and her large blue eyes bugged out. "You can't leave! I mean, Mr. Collins is on a very important call. I'm sure he won't be long."

"I don't care. I'm done," Hell replied, reaching the door.

The woman made a frightened yip, jumped up, and raced over to her. "You can't! People don't walk out on Mr. Collins."

Hell gave a short, barking laugh. "Watch me."

"Don't you know who he is?"

"Yeah, he's a rude bastard and—"

Her pupils went to the size of vinyl records. She gasped and clutched Hell's sleeve. "Shhhhhh. Don't let him hear you say that."

"Hear her say what, Tiffany?" came a deep, smoky voice from behind them.

Hell turned, and there stood Collins, looking remarkably like his pictures. Young-looking for his early fifties, shaved head, with sharp, even features. Deep-set, intense, and intelligent gray eyes. A heavy, dark brow with a large but straight nose balanced by an equally prominent chin. Nice angular jaw. Athletic build. Tall. Kinda hot.

But by the way he stood there like a lord surveying his land, Hell was certain this had been a stupid idea. He was about to come to the same conclusion.

"That you were a rude bastard to keep me waiting for"—she checked her watch— "thirty goddamned minutes," she growled. "I don't care who the hell you are, nobody keeps me waiting thirty minutes."

The man stared at her. Not one muscle of his face moved. Finally he blinked fast, then volcanic fury shot from his gaze. His formidable jaw clamped. His nostrils flared.

Dude was clearly not used to having people call him on his shit.

As if she needed more of a reason to stop this doomed alliance before it started.

"I'm outta here." She turned and put her hand on the doorknob.

"Miss Trent," he bit out. "One more minute of your time."

She made an exasperated noise and turned to face him with her patented Posture of Disapproval: one hip cocked, arms crossed, head slightly tilted, eyes narrowed.

He stood his ground in front of his office door, a good twenty feet away. He wanted her to come to him. More alpha male games. Could he push her out the door faster?

He said, "I want to make this clear, I—"

"Look, I understand you were probably on some bazillion-dollar call with some other important rich person, but you didn't even check with your secretary out here," Hell snapped, pointing toward the girl's desk. "You just expected me to wait. Because everybody waits for the great Brad Collins. Well, I don't. I don't give a rat's ass about your money, power, or status. My time is as valuable as yours, and you just wasted an hour of my life that I will never get back. So find some other private investigator who will wait around and kiss your billion-aire ass. I'm not your woman."

"Miss Trent?" He spoke in a very controlled voice, but from the heat in his eyes and the way his jaw worked, he was clearly holding back a tidal wave of anger.

"Later." Hell turned away, and the secretary stood there, up against the wall near the door—eyes huge, mouth open—looking like she'd just witnessed someone's execution. "And you, honey? You need a new job."

The secretary stared in horror between the two, shaking, and tried to disappear into the wood paneling.

Hell swung back to Collins, who was crossing the room toward her with a very determined and annoyed expression on his face.

She ignored his intensity. "You terrify this girl, did you know that? What kinda boss instills that kinda fear in their people? Like I would work for someone like that? No. I hate rich people. I hate entitled people. And I hate people who terrify their staff. People like you," she said with a sneer.

Collins stopped just in front of Hell, his face hard as granite, his eyes flashing. "Miss Trent, you surprise me. From what I heard about you, I knew you were unconventional, but I had no idea how rude, prejudiced, and narrow-minded you were. In spite of that very enlightening character assassination, I apologize for keeping you waiting. When the fate of twenty thousand people's lives is in my hands, I have a tendency to prioritize the needs of the many over the needs of the one."

She snorted, sent him a bored look, and rolled her eyes.

Fireworks went off behind his gray eyes, and his jaw clenched tighter, accentuating the strong lines of his face.

Her Mating Receptors beeped, and a rush went through her sex. There was a mighty power at the core of the man. Very hot.

Fighting a smile, she crossed her arms, suddenly enjoying herself.

"When was the last time you had the fate of thousands of people in your hands?" he fired at her. "When, if you came to a hasty decision, it could mean thousands of people lost their jobs? From what I understand, you've never even held a full-time job. You don't even own a house. Or employ anyone. Your last secretary left a month ago. But if you want to judge me based upon your Bohemian, live-by-the-seat-of-your-pants, anarchistic, adolescent viewpoint, go ahead." The hair stood up on her arms. Righteous indignation poured from him, creating a field of high-wattage energy that she could palpably feel.

Dude could power a city. She loved him! She wanted to giggle, but she didn't want to stop him. He was wonderful. Great adversary. So rare to find a man strong enough to stand up to her. Especially when what he was saying had seeds of truth.

She briefly checked his package. Dressed to the right, looked good.

"Just think of the friends of yours who have real jobs and mortgages and children," he continued, fire radiating from his body and eyes. "And next time you judge someone like me, ask yourself, who employs all your friends and family members? Like your niece? Who provides hundreds of thousands of jobs? And then look in the mirror, and ask yourself what you've contributed lately."

She finally couldn't help herself and burst into loud guffaws.

Veins popped out on his forehead, his eyes dilated until they were nearly all black, and his shoulders went hard and big. He looked like he wanted to kill her.

She ignored his reaction and had a good laugh. Her animosity toward him vanished. "Damn, I like you, man. And I certainly didn't think I would. You're good. I scare the shit outta most guys. But you got balls."

His brow furrowed hard, and he searched her face, his mouth slightly open. Like he could not get his bearings. He'd clearly expected her to attack. To deny what he'd said.

His reaction cracked her up even more. "You're cute as hell. Take care, Collins." She held out her hand, palm facing downward, ready to take control of the handshake as usual, but at the last second, she flipped her hand up. She'd give the guy the dominant position. His little speech deserved it.

His expression softened a bit, then he looked at her like she had seven eyeballs. Finally, he broke into a smile, took her hand, and shook it.

His smile lit up his whole face and changed his features, making him look younger and more vital. Nice firm grip, warm, smooth skin. Big hands. Long, strong, supple fingers. She caught his cologne. A wave of awareness rippled over her, dusting her skin with electricity, giving her goosebumps. Her sex roared to life.

They met gazes. A spark of primal energy zapped from his eyes and went straight to her center.

Her entire body came alive.

His expression went predatory. He looked at her lips, then sent her a penetrating stare, his mouth hungry.

She almost grabbed him and kissed him. She forced herself to let go of his hand.

"Miss Trent, I—"

"No hard feelings. Try Lance Parsons. He's good. Or Bill

Thompson would be better. Shows up in suits. He, uh, fits," she said, gesturing toward his office, "in all this professionalism shit you got goin' on here."

She turned away and opened the door, inwardly thanking the guy for giving her such a nice treat. She cherished these moments with hot men. A look across a café. A dance at a club. A nice handshake and a quick mental fantasy. As she'd found time and time again, her fantasies were nearly always better than the reality.

"Miss Trent, wait."

One foot out the door, Hell looked over her shoulder. "Yeah?"

"I still want to hire you."

She broke out laughing. "You gotta be kiddin' me."

"No. You're up-front. I'll know what you're thinking. Refreshing. But if you could withhold the character assassinations, I'd appreciate it."

She let go of the door and stepped back into the office, inadvertently blocking the escape of the secretary once more. "No prob. But I don't think I'm cut out for working for the rich and powerful. You're right, I'm super prejudiced and narrow-minded when it comes to rich people. I just hate y'all. Look, you seem like a nice guy, and I don't want to attack you, but I don't know how I'll be able to hold back. I am physically incapable of keeping my mouth shut. You're used to people catering to you. I can't do that. I can't wait for people. Makes me crazy. Well, crazier than normal."

He smiled. "We should only have two meetings. This one and when you give me your report. Surely you can handle a couple hours in my presence."

God, she loved his voice! Deep, resonant, smoky, *hot*.

But working for him? She took a deep breath and examined him. Her sex strongly suggested that she take the job. He was pretty. Full of fire. Her favorites.

Her checkbook made its plea. He was also very rich, and she needed the cash.

But she couldn't lie to herself about the real reason she was considering the job. The man was electric. She had no delusions about them actually getting along, but she could always use fantasy material. This guy looked like a sex machine.

"Maybe. But I still think the healthy choice for both of us is for me to walk out of here."

He laughed, the deep sound rumbling through his chest. "Come on." He gestured toward his office.

She stayed put. "One more chance, Collins. Run now and run fast. This is your last warning."

He grinned, his eyes twinkling. "Thanks, but I think I can handle you." He gave a split-second glance at her breasts, then motioned she should go ahead.

A little energy pulsed through her. This guy was fun. "I'll hear you out, how's that? If I don't think I can help you, I'm gonna be up-front about that."

"Perfect." He gestured toward his office. "Shall we?"

The secretary hadn't lost her frozen expression of disbelief. She stood trapped there, watching the drama unfold, clearly wishing she were anywhere else.

Hell touched her arm. "Don't worry, I won't kill him. But he might kill me. Keep an ear open, okay?"

The secretary's eyes widened in fear. She stole a glance at Collins, her face white.

"Don't worry, Tiffany, you're not in trouble. You clearly did your best trying to control Miss Trent, but you were outgunned and outmanned." He sent Hell a teasing smile.

If her pussy had had arms, it would have waved him inside with semaphores.

"Would you like anything to drink? Water? Coffee? Soft drink?" he asked cordially.

"Got any tequila?" she said with a perfectly straight face.

His brows came together quickly, and his head jerked back a bit.

Hell burst into a big smile. "Kidding. No, I'm good."

Collins snorted and turned to his secretary. "No calls." He shifted his attention back to Hell. "Would hate to see what happened if another phone call interrupted our meeting." The playfulness to his half smile made her smirk.

"You're a brat."

"I think you have the corner on that market, Miss Trent. Please." He gestured to his office, throwing off the timing of her comeback. He was *good*.

She walked past Collins and caught his scent again: a subtle piney cologne mixed with his own unique maleness. Another wave of lust powered through her. Wow.

His opulent office was gigantic and had floor-to-ceiling windows offering views of the rolling hills of Woodside: stands of oak trees mixed with lush, green grasses from the recent rains. A mahogany desk the size of her dining room table stood in a corner with three leather chairs in front. A long, dark leather couch lined one wall. She had half a thought to throwing Rich Boy on top and having her way with him.

His walls were covered in all the obligatory important rich person trophies: photos with other important rich people and awards. Collins with Obama. Collins with both Bushes. Collins with the Clintons. So was he Democrat or Republican? Probably swung both ways, depending on whom he had to bribe at the time. Humanitarian Awards for UNICEF, Habitat for Humanity, and World Wildlife Fund. Read: gave money and no time. The usual. Hell wasn't impressed by any of it.

Collins closed the door.

The thick, cream pile carpeting was so plush she felt like she was wading through it. "Holy crap, Collins. Beats the hell out of my view of the anemic tree and Dumpster. Of course, I had a better view from my jail cell."

"Maybe after this job, you'll be able to afford an upgrade."

"I may have to move, anyway. Rumor has it that they're tearing down the building and putting in condos and offices I won't be able to afford."

"You're thinking too small." He sat behind his desk.

She wandered over and ran her hand over the leather back of one of the chairs. "Probably."

"May I call you Helen?"

"No."

His brow flattened.

She sent him a lopsided grin. "Call me Hell."

He shook his head and gave a reluctant smile.

She slouched in one of the chairs, hanging a leg over one arm while leaning on the other. Normally she showed more respect with clients, but this guy would have to earn it.

He clearly didn't miss her signals and laughed. "You are a character, aren't you?"

"And I'm a Boho non-contributor," she said with a large smile.

He gave a slight shrug. "You pissed me off. You're a well-vetted professional, or I wouldn't have called you."

"You were right. I can't even keep one employee. Maybe I should have learned how to scare them like you can. How do you do that?" She thumbed toward his office door. "I let them walk all over me."

"You just answered your own question."

"Yeah, I hate being a boss. Hate telling people what to do."

He raised a brow, his gray eyes twinkling. "Seems like you'd be good at it."

She chuckled. Damn, she liked this guy. "Well, I have no issues standing up for myself, but I hate responsibility. Betsy rocked. She really kept me together."

"How did you manage to lose her?"

Hell rubbed the back of her head. "Betsy deserved the world, and I couldn't give it to her. A friend of mine who runs a law firm was looking for an office manager, and they're expanding, really goin' places. So I kinda forced Betsy to take the job. But you didn't call me here to talk about me." The middle finger on her right hand stung, and she inspected it. A tiny, irritating cut. She'd forgotten to put back on a Band-Aid.

"If you realize the problem with your business, why don't you fix it?"

"Don't know. Therapist and I are workin' on it. Not making much progress." She laughed, fished out a Band-Aid from her pocket, and tore it open.

His brows came together for a second. "You are a puzzle."

"So what's the case?" She glanced at the wall clock. "No wonder I'm bitchy. I haven't had a toke or food in two hours. Oh, sorry, that was supposed to stay in my head. I'm listening." She took the backing off the Band-Aid and wrapped the bandage around her middle finger. "Got a garbage can?"

He stared at her again like she'd just been released from the mental ward. "Over here." He pointed at a red leather trash can to the left of his desk.

Aiming, she threw the bandage wrapper directly into the can, then pumped her fist. "Score!"

Collins frowned and gestured toward her. "What did you do to your hands?"

She inspected her fingers, which were all bandaged except for one. "I don't know. Always doing something to 'em. Look, my left pinky is fine." She held it up and crooked it, then checked out the various bandages. "Damn, this does seem worse than normal. Oh, yeah, cooking," she said, holding up her index finger. "Chopping vegetables." She waved her middle finger, careful not to flip him off. "Slammed this one in the door of my Malibu. Burned the crap out of these two when I lit a bong in the wind—" She smacked herself on the forehead and made a large gesture. "Why are we talking about this? What's the case, dude?"

He laughed, then collected himself and turned grave. "I am being blackmailed."

"Whoa. Okay, that's a lot more serious than I'd imagined. Thought you might want me to tail your wife or something." She reached into an inner jacket pocket and withdrew a fresh notebook. Lowering her leg to the floor, she sat upright. "Go for it. How did the blackmailer contact you, when did they, what do they want, what are they blackmailing you about, and who do you think it is?"

His expression became troubled. "This is a confidential case. And very serious. I'll need your word that you won't—"

She held up her hand. "Dude, no worries. Comes with the job. But before we start, I have a very important question."

"Which is?"

"Why aren't you going to the police?"

He stared at her intently.

Because he didn't want his secrets uncovered by the cops. "That's what I thought."

"The reason I want to hire you is because I've heard that you've never spilled a secret or betrayed anyone's confidence."

"Not capable. While I clearly can't shut up about how I feel at times, I don't ever share information on clients."

"Is it true you spent three months in jail because you were protecting a client?"

"True. However, I only served three weeks to protect Billie— who was a friend not a client—I served the rest of the time for having a stupid attack in the courtroom and taking on the judge and singing *My Country,'Tis of the Thee* until she sentenced me to contempt. The bitch. Learned a big lesson about shutting up that day."

Collins chuckled. "Wish I'd been there."

"I put on quite a show," she said with a tired eye roll. "At least I was able to clear Billie. Little hard to solve the case on the run from the cops, and then from jail, but no way I was telling the police where she was."

He gave a small, satisfied nod.

"So, answers?"

"A packet got delivered by messenger to my club. No one remembered what the courier looked like."

"What do they have on you?"

"I'm not proud of it, but I had an affair with a woman."

She held back a snort. Pure bullshit. By the solid way he held his head and shoulders, it was clear he was totally proud of it. Bragging even. "She's blackmailing you?"

"No, I don't know who is. I've spoken with her. She has just as much to lose as I do."

"She's married, too?"

"Yes. To a colleague."

"Ooo. Hate that. I've fallen into bed with—Sorry. Go for it. And?"

"If I don't pay four million dollars in unmarked one-hundred-dollar bills by Saturday night, the person or persons will expose the affair, and the deal I'm working on with this colleague will surely fall through, and many people will lose their jobs. And my wife will find out, and that would end my marriage."

"And that would all be very bad. Where's the packet?"

He opened his drawer, withdrew an envelope, and slid it midway across the desk.

Forcing her to get up to retrieve it. She didn't miss the power play, but at this point, she didn't care. Let him think he was more important. She'd bill him extra for Asshole Hazard pay.

Hell sat back down and examined the envelope. "Came in this?"

"No. I threw out the outside envelope."

She looked at him like he was the dumbest idiot on the planet.

He shrugged. "I had no idea what it was. By the time I figured it out, I'd thrown the envelope in the club fireplace."

Sighing, she opened the packet. Ransom note and a stack of eight-by-tens were each individually encased in plastic page protectors.

"I put them in plastic to preserve whatever fingerprints are on them."

"Cool."

She meant to read the ransom note first, but once she caught a glimpse of Collins' naked flesh, she skipped right to the photos. Dude was even prettier naked. Nice ass. Nice musculature. He looked like he was really giving it good to the girl. Looked like fun. She loved the expression on his face. Feral, intense, animal. Nice.

Only problem? No pictures of his cock. Bummer.

"Could she be in on this?" she asked, indicating his lover.

"I don't know."

"Does the colleague want this deal? Is he looking for a way out?"

"Possibly. I stand to gain much more than he."

"What does he get if the deal falls through?"

"A potential sale to a higher bidder."

"Hell of a motive. So, how well do your girlfriend and her husband get along?"

"Not sure."

"Do you guys even talk?"

He gave a small hand shrug. "Normally, we're too busy."

She laughed. "I like you even more."

He grinned, but his smile turned to worry.

"Okay, I'll take the case. But I'll need access to the woman."

"I'll arrange it."

"I may need to poke around here. Sit in on a meeting or two as a fake consultant."

He gestured toward her with an up-and-down motion. "My colleagues will become suspicious if someone dressed like—"

"I won't look like this. I've got a wardrobe of disguises. I'm a chameleon, baby."

He arched a brow. "So, this is what you picked to impress a client on your first meeting?"

Hell chuckled. "Do I look like I'm trying to impress you? When I'm not on a job, I dress for me. You either hire me or you don't. I get so many calls now, if someone doesn't like me or my style, I move on."

He examined her carefully and didn't miss one detail. His gaze lingered on her legs and breasts. "Rather youthful."

"Suits me."

"I went through a punk phase."

"Clearly mine stuck. Okay, you need to give me everything you have on your inner circle. Hot deals and the players. My standard contract has a confidentiality agreement, but I don't need or want any details about the technology of the companies, just the overview and the other people involved. And I need the names of all your enemies. Everyone who might have cause to mess with you. All your girl-friends. What about your wife? Could she be behind this?"

"Sherry?" He sent her an incredulous stare.

"She probably knows about your affairs, dude. This could be to manipulate you into coming home more."

"No. Aside from the fact that she isn't very interested in me, Sherry's naïve as hell. Does not have the mind for subterfuge unless it deals with country club politics. And she has no idea I've had affairs. I've gone to great lengths to make sure she was protected. Thankfully, she believes anything I tell her. Besides, she's involved with so many charities and country club events and opera bullshit, she has no time for me anymore. Now that the kids are grown up and out of the house, we barely have anything to do with each other."

Collins was clearly hurt by his wife's coldness. But if he was cheating on her, what did he expect? Why did he stay married when he had nothing going on with the woman?

"She could still know, and be jealous."

"If Sherry had found out that I'd cheated on her, she'd have left me by now. She made that clear in the beginning."

"Okay, I'll take your word for it. Just write out the names and relationships for me."

"I anticipated that. Here." He slid a stack of papers over to her, but still not far enough for her to reach without getting up.

Jesus.

Hell took the papers, sat back down, and perused the packet. "Cool. I'll start with your girlfriend in question, and work my way out from there. I will involve the least amount of people that I can. Haven't alerted a blackmailer yet." Only once, but it worked out okay, anyway.

He brightened and gave a nod. "Done. Since Saturday is the deadline, you'll have to work fast."

"No worries. But normally the payoff is where we nab the guys. And this idiot blackmailer wants you to drop it at the entrance to Pearson-Arastradero Preserve at ten at night? Must be a total rookie. So easy to stake that out. I have access to some pretty sophisticated GPS devices and satellite intelligence, and that place is wide open. We'll be able to follow the guy anywhere from there."

Collins stared at her in seeming disbelief. "How?"

Ain't tellin' you about Death, honey. "Trade secret. Last two jobs, I
followed the blackmailer back to his or her place, then alerted the
police. Since you don't want the police involved, I'd say let's track the
bastards and then send in your security team to bust them. Once we
know who they are, we'll have them by the balls. I can find out
anything about anybody. Stuff no one else could."

"How?" Then he gave a tiny eye roll and nodded. "I know, trade
secret."

"Yeah. I like to search the homes of the blackmailers thoroughly.
Sometimes they hold out and keep copies of the original docs. Plus
the fact that you might not be the only one he's blackmailing. Bunch
of your buddies could be in danger, too."

"Excellent points. Still, I'd prefer that you solve the case before
Saturday."

"Me, too."

"Job pays ten grand if you can resolve the situation by Saturday
morning. Twenty if you solve it in forty-eight hours."

She stared at him. "I thought you just offered me ten grand."

"I did."

"For three days of work?"

"Yes. Double for two."

A surge of joy went through her. Maybe Betsy had been right. A
couple easy jobs a month would not only fund her business, she
might be able to go to Hawaii once in a while. "I think I like you even
more now." She sent him a beaming grin, withdrew the standard
contract from her pocket, and filled in her fee. Then she handed it to
him. "Sign on the dotted line, and we're in business." She settled back
in her seat.

He perused the short document, nodded, and signed it. He tossed
it on his desk, just out of her reach.

She rolled her eyes, shook her head, and gave a big sigh of disapproval. "Dude, you and your power games. You never stop playing, do
you?"

"What?"

"Don't fuck with me. I'll work for you, but I'd appreciate it if you stopped playing Lord of the Manor. This is gonna be the third time I've gotten out of this goddamned chair for you, and I'm tired of the game." She finally heaved herself to her feet and grabbed the piece of paper.

He sent her a knowing grin. "You're quite something, aren't you?"

"That's what all the boys say." She backed toward the door.

His expression went a bit feral, and he glanced at her tits. "I had you investigated."

"Kinda gathered that."

"So is it true? Do you really have a stable of young studs?" His gaze turned playful. Sexual. His dark eyebrows twitched provocatively, and his mouth went hungry. He didn't seem to be judging her. He seemed aroused.

A torpedo of hormones bombed her sex. Her body ordered her to grab him and throw him on his couch.

Oh, little boy. You'd better not awaken the Beast. Dude was so close to being jumped, he had no idea. She looked at his lips. Super kissable. She smiled widely. "A stable? Sounds like Thompson."

"So? Is it true?" he said in full flirt mode.

"Don't believe everything you hear." She reached the door. "But *that* part of the dossier? All true." With a wink, she left.

His deep laughter rang out behind her.

Wow. Holy God, the man was a sexual King Kong. She needed a cold shower.

Dee-lightful.

On her way out, she took the contract she'd signed with Collins and handed it to his secretary. "Could you do me a huge favor and make me a copy of this?" Needed to eliminate the office copier as the source of the ransom note.

The young woman quickly took the paper, walked to a corner of the office, and ran off a copy. She handed both papers to Hell.

"Thanks, honey. Good luck with your boss. He's a handful."

The young woman said under her breath, "You have no idea."

Hell left and headed to the parking lot. As the hormonal response wore off, her belly felt funny. Something was not right about this. At all.

People in his position didn't hire people like her to solve cases as serious as blackmail. Despite her fame. His defensive tirade had revealed what he truly thought about her.

Thompson was much more professional. Had a huge staff. Collins had already hired him to investigate her, why not have him track the blackmailer?

Collins also employed a security team. She'd already met one of them when she'd first entered the building. A big, hulking dude in a black suit. He'd watched her carefully as she'd interacted with the office building's receptionist. When the receptionist had called Collins' secretary, the Man in Black had called on his cell, and she'd overheard her name. Collins probably had his own SWAT team.

If someone sent him a threatening letter like that, he would have called in his big guns, not a single operator he'd never met before.

Why the hell would he call her to his office to discuss not only blackmail but his affairs? Handing her a big stack of personal information right there? Situations this sensitive were dealt with in the back of a car, far away from home turf. No way would he store the blackmail packet at work. It would be in his briefcase, not in his desk drawer for his secretary to find.

Nor would he risk alerting the blackmailer. The culprit could be anyone near him. He wasn't stupid. Why would he risk having a well-known private detective meet him at his office?

Because Collins wasn't worried about this threat. Maybe because he already knew the identity of the blackmailer. Maybe he thought that Hell was a screw-up and wanted her to expose the blackmailer and blow the whole scheme wide open.

But what could he gain by that? What was his motivation?

Get his wife to leave him?

Come to think of it, he hadn't appeared worried at all. She'd been through three blackmail schemes, and the victim's family members were always freaked out. Sweated profusely, were completely jittery, and had no color in their faces. They certainly weren't thinking about sex. A man who had his life on the line would not be flirting that much. Or playing with her.

Collins had actively tried to distract her. Flirted with her massively. Played on her reputation. Gone for her "weak point." Every single thing he'd said and done had been a calculated move.

Leaving only one possible conclusion: Collins had written the note himself. The blackmail scheme was a scam. He was trying to get rid of his girlfriend, and he was rich enough to hire Hell to scare her away for him. The dick.

She turned around and stalked toward his office. Bastard thought he'd send her on a wild goose chase, did he? She wasn't playing.

Mid-stride, she stopped. Wait a minute. Wouldn't it be amusing to have him pay her to dig around in his personal life? Twenty grand for interrogating his girlfriend and maybe wife? Find the proof that he'd conned her? That would be so satisfying. Walk into his office and slap him with the evidence that he was a total lying jerkwad.

She'd warned him not to fuck with her. The idiot had no idea what he'd just done to himself.

Once inside her Malibu, she held up the ransom note next to the copy of her contract. No little glitchy toner bits at the top. Not the same copier.

Collins must have used his home copier. She'd drop by his place to check. Which would net delicious details about his life.

She burst out in joyous, evil laughter. That dickhead was in for a rude awakening. He may have a lot of money, but he didn't have a lot of brains if he thought he could pull one over on Hell Trent.

CHAPTER 5

WEDNESDAY, NOVEMBER 10, 2010, 12:15 P.M.

Wearing her Boring Businesswoman costume—a gray dress suit with a skirt and a gray wig styled into a tight bun—her heart slamming her breastbone, Hell strode into the lobby of the Embassy Suites in Burlingame. She hoped to God no sweat showed on her forehead. No matter how often she pulled cons on people, it always felt like she was about to walk out on stage in front of an audience of four hundred.

With her posture ramrod straight and her fake, out-of-fashion glasses, she looked like a nightmare Catholic schoolteacher. A woman who must be obeyed.

Hopefully.

She had three hours before she met Collins' concubine at Starbucks in San Mateo. Plenty of time to investigate the scene of the crime and where the pictures had been taken.

Normally, she just asked for help from the front desk when on investigations, but the month before, this same hotel staff had shut her down. All she'd wanted was confirmation on a reservation, but no way. A badge, bribe, nothing had worked. She'd finally had Death hack their system. A last resort when performing her normal work; she saved his formidable skills for high-level tasks.

Hell charged up to the hotel desk, flashed her fake ID at the young female clerk, and demanded to see the supervisor. The young African-American girl nodded and disappeared into a back office.

A few moments later, the clerk returned, followed by a middle-aged Asian lady.

Her heart rate shot higher. Mrs. Andrada, the same manager who'd shut her down just four weeks before, and who'd totally gotten off on the power trip. Beee-yotch.

Please God don't let her recognize me.

Mrs. Andrada wore a tight blue suit and nearly the same pinched expression that Hell wore. "Yes? May I help you?"

Hell's gut clenched. She held herself taller and assumed an imperious affect. "Yes, my name is Gladys Slaughter, and I'm with the Embassy Suites Corporate Enforcement Bureau," she pronounced in a higher tone, with a different pitch than her normal voice. "I'm here on an investigation of a serious complaint of a health hazard in one of your rooms. Room 547. I need to see it now."

Mrs. Andrada frowned. "But—"

"Now. Before anyone has time to cover their tracks," Hell clipped out. "I need to speak with the employees who cleaned the room and who were on duty during the hours of one in the afternoon and seven in the evening of the twenty-eighth of October."

The manager eyed her and crossed her arms. "I've never heard of the Corporate Enforcement Bureau. This seems highly irregular."

She stood even taller. Curving her mouth downward in disapproval, she pulled a file folder from her briefcase, and a pen. She opened the folder and started writing. "Mrs. Andrada has no respect for the corporation, and it is my recommendation that she be transferred to a position that holds less responsibility. Or be terminated." She stopped writing and allowed her heated gaze to burn through the woman. "Is that what you want on my report?" she snapped.

The woman's pupils dilated, and she shrank inside her suit. "I'll get the keys." Turning, she scurried for the back office.

Boo-yah!

Hell fought hard to keep from pumping her fist and hooting.

Mrs. Andrada reappeared a split second later, holding the key. "Please follow me." She hustled by Hell and headed for the elevators.

Hell kept pace alongside Andrada, her chin high. "I need the staff to meet me in their break room. I'll talk to them, one at a time."

"Yes, ma'am. Right this way, ma'am." Andrada gestured to the open elevator, her arm shaking.

She escorted Hell to Brad's suite, smiling with her mouth but not her eyes. By the way Mrs. Andrada kept checking out her outfit and briefcase, she could tell that the woman still had her suspicions. Damn it. She had to convince her beyond a shadow of a doubt.

When they reached the door to Suite 547, Hell turned to the manager and dropped her voice into a near growl. "If you question my authority in front of your staff again and embarrass me like that, I'll personally ensure that you get busted down to manager of the laundry room. Do I make myself clear?"

Andrada went ashen, and she nodded emphatically. All signs of doubt vanished from her expression. Inwardly, Hell relaxed. Some people took more convincing than others.

The manager quickly opened the door and gestured that Hell should go inside.

Hell walked through and blocked the woman from following. "I know where your office is located."

"Yes, certainly," she replied nervously.

"See that the staff is assembled in one half hour," Hell snapped in a snooty tone.

"Yes, ma'am."

Hell closed the door in the manager's face. And then let out a huge sigh of relief. God, conning people was tiring. Especially smart people. Especially smart people she'd met before. But damn, it had felt pretty good to get that obstruction under her thumb.

She turned and headed straight to the bedroom of the two-room suite.

A king-sized bed flanked by two nightstands stood on one side of the room, and opposite, an armoire, vanity, and sink.

Withdrawing the photo, she tried to locate where the camera

must have been. The perspective in the shot led her to the vanity. The middle of the mirror? No. Next to it, and below. On the counter next to the sink, about six inches up.

But how? She carefully inspected the whole area. No signs of removed equipment. She studied the picture again. The photo must have been taken by a camera hidden in one of their belongings. Inside his briefcase or her purse or a small piece of luggage.

Collins or his girlfriend took the shots. Her money was on Collins. He must think Hell was a real idiot.

Still, she needed to rule out any outside interference. On the .0001 percent chance she was wrong. She also needed to eliminate the girlfriend. Somehow she had to find out what they'd brought with them.

Next stop was the employee break room. Hell interviewed four maids and one maintenance man. As expected, nothing unusual had happened with the room. No other inspectors or outside air conditioning people had stopped by that day. Nothing out of the ordinary.

Two of the maids remembered Collins and his lady coming in, and when they'd left, but not what they'd carried.

Hell then ordered Mrs. Andrada to show her the security tapes from that day. Only problem was that there were no cameras in the hallways, only in the elevators. So Hell watched until Collins and his girl stepped on the elevator. Brad carried a briefcase, and his blonde lover, a gym bag. Hell stopped the tape and checked out as much of Collins' briefcase as possible.

The case was large and complete overkill for carrying a laptop. Guys in his position didn't carry large briefcases. The thinner the case, the more power the person projected. Absolutely probable he had a camera hidden inside.

Collins' woman's gym bag was too floppy to sit on a vanity. Still, she might have hidden a camera inside. But what was her motivation in a fake blackmail scheme? Did she want to get rid of Brad?

Her next interview would answer that question.

Hell asked Mrs. Andrada about the suite's guests on the night previous to Collins' tryst. The harried manager reported that the room had been empty the night before.

Which meant either Brad or his girlfriend was the blackmailer. Again, Mr. Snakey seemed the likely culprit.

Hell thanked the shaking and sweating manager, complimented her on a job well done, and assured her she'd look good in her report. The woman almost broke down into tears.

Stifling laughter, Hell left the hotel.

She popped by her house to change back into her normal Hell-wear—a vintage Sex Pistols T-shirt, skinny black jeans, black Converse high-tops, and her black leather jacket—and still had time to walk to her favorite Starbucks, just five blocks away on the corner of El Camino Real and Seventeenth Avenue.

Wednesday, November 10, 2010, 2:03 p.m.

HELL FOUND BRAD'S LATE-FORTIES, CURLY-HAIRED BLONDE IN THE corner of the coffee shop wearing huge sunglasses, a tight, black workout outfit, and a white-and-red baseball cap. Lindsay had a gym-toned yoga body so thin it bordered on emaciation. Strong breeze would blow her into traffic.

Hell approached her. "Lindsay Banning?"

The woman frowned. "Who are you?"

"Helen Trent."

She gave her an up-and-down exam. "Really?"

"Didn't Brad warn you what I looked like?"

"Prove it."

Hell whipped out her identification.

Lindsay examined her offering. "Gladys Slaughter? Embassy Suites?"

Hell laughed. "Ooops." She went through the stack of IDs and fished out the right one. "Here, try this one."

Lindsay gave her a wary glance, checked out her true ID, and finally indicated the chair across from her.

Hell sat. "Now that I've made myself completely trustworthy, tell me all about your life, please." She chuckled, her face warming. "Sorry. Little tired." *And that new weed is stronger than I'd anticipated.*

The woman's face relaxed, but her body was still wound tight. She removed her sunglasses, revealing puffy blue eyes. She'd been crying. Hmmm, fake tears for Hell's benefit? Or real tears? If they were real, Brad was the guilty party.

Aside from the puffiness, Lindsay was a beautiful lady. She had an oval face, high cheekbones, a perfectly straight nose, and full lips. Though she was youthful, her hands gave away her age. Hell guessed she'd had some plastic surgery; her face was a bit too tight. But the woman was extremely pretty. Brad had excellent taste.

Lindsay looked at her lap, then met Hell's gaze. Her pupils got huge, and her lower lip trembled.

Terrified? Of what? Being found out as the blackmailer, or losing Brad?

"Brad told me I should come here to help you, but if someone's following us around and taking pictures of us, don't you think this is dangerous talking to you in a public place?"

Hell motioned downward with her hands. "Honey, no worries. I'm sure you're not being followed. Just calm down."

"How long will it take you to solve this?" Lindsay moved forward into the path of an overhead light. Sweat glistened on her forehead, making her makeup blotchy. The whites of her blue eyes showed. Even more terrified than Hell had originally thought.

"Cases like these are usually solved very quickly. You'll be fine." Total lie. Divorced in two months. Hell withdrew her notebook from her interior coat pocket and got settled. She examined every single facet of the woman.

Lindsay's manicured hands shook. Her brow would have been furrowed if it hadn't been pumped full of Botox. Clutching her keys, she had a leg and foot facing the door, like she was ready to jump up and run. Her back looked tight as a spring. Hell was tempted to yell *Boo!* just to see her hit the ceiling.

Hell faced the woman and assumed her professional pose, body positioning open, sympathy oozing from her pores. "I need to ask you some pretty personal questions, and I'm sorry, I hate invading your privacy, it's the toughest part of my job." She paused for effect and allowed pain to cross her features. People always let their guard down on that line. Giggling inwardly, she salivated for the juicy details of this little tryst. "Whatever you tell me, stays with me," she said, wishing it weren't true. She'd love to tell her cousin Joanne some of her stories. Some were really wild.

But Collins was probably boring in bed. Probably laid back and expected to be adored. She could see him with a smug expression, stretched out on an expansive bed, gesturing toward his cock. *You may suck me off now, serf.*

Lindsay didn't move her defensive posture.

Hell lowered her voice and said in her most heartfelt tone, "I understand how awful this must be for you, and I'm sorry." *Not in the least, you adulterer. You deserve everything you get.*

The woman's shoulders finally dropped a bit, and the big move, she set her keys on the table.

Yippee! Now for the dirt. Hell removed a new notebook from her jacket pocket, and a pen.

Crossing her thin legs, Lindsay fingered her blonde curls. "Okay. What do you want to know?" she mumbled, her face drawn down. She appeared older. Fatigued. Beaten.

"How often do you see each other?"

"Every Tuesday at two. He's my private tennis lesson, and I'm his personal trainer."

"Good covers. Is there anyone in your life who wants to hurt you? Anyone you may have had an argument with recently?"

"No, no one. I've been racking my brain. I haven't hurt anyone... until..." She sighed and fiddled with a fingernail. "Brad and I fell into bed. I mean, we've been flirting for thirty years. The four of us have been friends—Brad and Sherry, and Dan and I—since college. Then, about six months ago, he and I were alone in his backyard. Sherry and Dan were inside having port, and Brad came outside to join me. He looks at me and says, 'Does he know how beautiful you are? I wish I had a day with you, away from here. I'd show you how a man should appreciate you.' Out of the blue."

The way Lindsay's blue eyes shone told the story: she was madly in love with Brad. Which meant Mr. Collins was behind the blackmail scam. Jerk.

Hell maintained her neutral face. "Wow, so what did you say?"

"I laughed it off. But I'd never been more turned on."

"Then what happened?"

"He kissed me."

"And that was it."

"I met him the next afternoon."

"He is hot."

"More than you could know. But..." She worked her mouth and stared at her nails, the line between her eyes deep.

"What?"

Her gaze shot to Hell's. Intense pain emanated from behind her eyes. Her forehead tried to wrinkle but couldn't fight the poison. She dropped her voice to a whisper. "I don't think I'm the only one that he's sleeping with. I mean, aside from Sherry. I think he has a Thursday mistress."

Hell made sure not a muscle of her face moved. What a shocker, Brad having multiple lovers. Not. "I don't know anything about that. All I know is that he cares for you." Clearly she'd be paid more for lying than investigating on this job.

Lindsay wasn't convinced. She looked away and twisted her mouth to one side. "Well...I sort of followed him."

All her senses tingling, Hell leaned in. "Sort of followed him?"

"Well, I didn't really intend to, you know—oh, God, don't tell him!" Lindsay held out her hands in a "stop" motion, her eyes wide, her face white.

Hell made a dismissive gesture. "Honey, no worries. I'm only here to uncover the blackmailer. I won't tell him anything you don't want me to." The lie was so blatant she was surprised her tongue hadn't split in half.

Lindsay clutched her chest and fanned herself with a hand. "He can't find out. He hates clingy women. He told me that in the beginning. And I'm not clingy. I just wanted to know what he was doing, so I followed him to the Fairmont in the City where he met another woman. Some CFO named Gwen. Looks like a bird. Like Big Bird. I don't know what he sees in her."

"Are you sure they were having sex?"

"They kissed, and I followed them upstairs and watched them go into a room. Then I listened at the door and..."

Hell's radar went on alert. This woman was starting to smell crazy. Really crazy. She looked through Lindsay's eyes to deep within them. There was a wild, freaky energy at her core. Her mind was going in fifty different directions at once. Her inner frequency was way too high.

Probably the reason for Brad's scam. "Okay." Hell jotted down the information, trying to look casual. "Did Brad and Gwen see you? Did you wear a disguise?"

"They looked at me but didn't recognize me. I wore a jogging outfit and sunglasses and a purely white baseball cap instead of a white-and-crimson baseball cap. I always wear crimson-and-white because of my alma mater, Harvard. I don't jog, I play tennis and do yoga. Brad knows that. He'd never suspect me in a tracksuit."

The blonde couldn't be this stupid. But clearly Brad was. Unless he'd spotted Lindsay and that's what had prompted him to hire Hell. "Good cover. But that couldn't have made you feel too good."

"No, made me feel so cheap. I mean, I knew he was a womanizer. I'd heard the stories from Sherry."

Sherry knew about his affairs! Of course! Brad was such an idiot.

"But Brad made me think I was the only one he was seeing. I think he does love me. A lot. I think he got scared by his feelings. I think he's using the other woman to distance himself from his true feelings for me."

Hell pretended to buy the delusion. "That's probably it."

Lindsay lit up like a star going nova, and bounced in place. "You think so?"

You poor, whacked-out sap. "I do. So is Brad seeing anyone else besides you and Gwen?"

"No. I followed him daily for a month. Only us two." She said it so matter-of-factly it was clear she'd been pretending to be embarrassed about tailing him but saw nothing wrong with what she was doing. Almost like it was her right to stalk him. Scary. "I know he used to have more girlfriends because he mentioned two other women's names one time when I got him drunk and pumped him for information."

Even scarier. Pre-meditated scariness.

Let's see how scary. "I'll bet you wanted to bust in and kick some ass that night you followed him to the Fairmont."

Her face screwed up into a malevolent sneer. "You have no idea the scenarios that went through my head. A friend of mine has a bunker under his house in Atherton, complete with an arsenal, for self-defense. He has hand grenades, flame-throwers, and every kind of gun you can imagine. All I wanted to do was raid his storeroom, kick that hotel door down, and blast the hell out of the two of them with bombs, then shoot their remains." Her mouth went even uglier.

A chill went through Hell, but she nodded and smiled like the woman had just told her something completely normal. "Yeah, that'd be cool."

Okay, Lindsay was almost to the Boiled Bunny Stage of scary obsessiveness.

Crazy stalker chick alert!

Lindsay nodded, her eyes narrowed, and she got a smug, sinister look on her face. "I swear, if I wasn't civilized, I'd have shot Big Bird by now," she said, full of raw vengeance. "I'm a top marksman. I've won awards. I could take her out with one shot. Brad's fooling himself. He doesn't like her. He's just using her. He belongs with me. That's why you *have* to find the blackmailer. We can't see each other until they're caught." She sent Hell a super-intense, half-pleading-half-warning, psycho look. Like if Hell didn't find the culprit, Lindsay would kill her.

Please don't hurt me, you crazy fuck. "I'm on it."

Lindsay's intensity diminished slightly, and her attention turned inward. She laced her fingers together and worked her hands. "I mean, I'd never hurt him. I couldn't hurt him. I love him so much I can't stand it. I haven't seen him in a whole week. God…" She shook her head. "Don't tell him this." Her gaze darted away, and she covered her mouth.

Talk to me! "Your secret is safe with me." Hardly.

"I love him so much I feel…" She searched for the words, her face full of anguish.

"Like an alien took over your brain and filled you with warm and fuzzy juice?"

"Yes!" she said loudly, pointing. Her eyes widened, and she clamped her hand back over her mouth. "I mean, yes. How did you know?"

Hell shrugged. "Happened to me once or twice."

"Did you ever fall for a man you were having an affair with?"

Never knowingly slept with a married man. "Yeah…oh, it was so bad," Hell said, getting animated. "I was so worried my husband would find out. I had so much to lose. I don't want to think about it." She shuddered dramatically.

Lindsay reached over and grabbed Hell's arm a little too tightly. Woman was so hyped up she was trembling. "That's exactly where I am. I can't afford to be caught. Dan and I are dependent on each other financially, plus there are the kids. Brad has kids, too, and is married to my supposed best friend."

Hell's head jerked back before she could stop herself. "You're *best friends* with Sherry?"

Lindsay frowned, let go, sat back, and crossed her arms again. "Supposedly. But she's weird. I've never really trusted her. You never know what she's thinking. And she hates Brad. Always has. Treats him like shit. He deserves the love I can give him."

"Huh." Hell fought for her bearings. Lindsay said she and Sherry had been friends since college, but she'd assumed they weren't that close. Amazing how people could screw up their lives. But sleeping with *your best friend's husband*?

Sherry was untrustworthy? And hated Brad? Still, maybe Lindsay was projecting negativity on Sherry so she'd feel less guilt.

Lindsay focused on her coffee cup. "But even without the blackmail, I'm not sure how Brad feels about me. He's either really into me or..."

"What?"

She worked her mouth and wrapped her skinny arms around her torso. "It has crossed my mind that he's sleeping with me to get even with my husband. Apparently, Dan hasn't been that nice to Brad. Did some deal that really screwed him over." She stroked the blonde curly locks at her shoulder. "Brad was really upset about it. But that was before we got together. I'm sure he didn't hold it against me. I shouldn't have mentioned it. Brad loves me for me only."

Love wasn't just blind for this woman, it was deaf and dumb, too. Collins wasn't screwing her, he was screwing her husband *through* her.

Talk about Karma. Brad got way more than he'd bargained for when he'd seduced Lindsay. He'd known her for thirty years. He should have picked up that she was a bucket of whacko. Dickhead got what he deserved.

"Brad does make cracks about Dan. He wants to know that he's better in bed than Dan. That I love him more. And I do. God, he's so good. Dan's sweet, but..."

"Not the bad boy that sends you to the stratosphere."

"Exactly! I mean, it's not like Brad doesn't treat me well. He's super nice to me. He always brings me little things to eat, little treats..."

Good doggy. Here's your biscuit, now sit up and beg.

Her willy for the man was wilting fast.

Lindsay got a beatific look on her face, and her eyes went slightly unfocussed. "But I've never experienced anything like him in bed. The things he can do with that..." She gasped, held in her breath, closed her eyes, then slowly let out her lungful. Like she'd ingested a wonderful memory of him like a fine wine and was savoring the taste. She opened her eyes and fidgeted in her seat. "My God."

Hell got aroused. Collins probably did pack a punch in the sack. One sport fuck just to see.

Bad, Hell. Bad girl. "So, have you guys talked about leaving your spouses?"

"Oh, yeah. Well, I have. Lately. Right before this blackmail thing. I finally confronted Brad about our relationship and told him I wanted to take it to the next level. That we should be together. He was all for it. At least, he said he was. I mean, he wasn't happy about hurting Sherry, and he said we needed to take it slow so we didn't burn any bridges. But this blackmail scheme has blown all my hopes out of the water. He said until the case is solved, we have to stay apart. And he's right."

How stupid was this woman? Brad had bought airtime and broadcast a special TV Movie-of-the-Week for her called: *I Am Dumping You By Using a Phony Blackmail Scheme.* She was glued to the set and didn't see the message.

The jerk had so much money he could afford to hire Hell to add a nice layer of authenticity to the scam.

Fucker. Now she just needed concrete evidence to throw in his face.

"He's very smart," Hell said with a definitive nod. *And you're not.* "Let me try to figure out what happened that day the pictures got taken."

"They must have broken into the hotel and hidden cameras in the walls."

"Exactly." *Wrong.* "So when you meet, do you guys bring any luggage with you? Anything regular?"

"Well, sometimes he brings his briefcase, like when he brings me treats or a new sex toy or handcuffs or whatever he wants to play with. That was TMI, huh?"

"No." *TMM: Tell Me More!* "Besides, nothing could shock me." *Please tell me something that will really shock me. Please.*

"He's very inventive. He wants to try all this stuff I never in a million years thought I'd enjoy, but he makes everything so fun."

Details! Where are the details?

"Plus all his focus is on my pleasure. Never had a man who cared so much about getting me off. He gets off on getting me off. He's unreal in the sack. Mind-blowing."

Damn. Now Hell was certain of two things. Number one, the dude was a class A-1, duplicitous, dickhead douchebag. Number two, she really wanted to boff him. Just once. Just to see what he had in him.

But she didn't sleep with the clients. Number one rule. And she'd never broken it. Nor did she sleep with married men.

Up until now.

Mental slap.

Hell referred to her notes. "On Tuesday the twenty-eighth, did he bring his briefcase with him?"

"Uh...yeah. Why?"

"Where did he store it while you guys did it?"

"Why?"

"Do you know where he put it?"

"Yeah, where he always does. By the extra sink in the bedroom, right across from the bed."

"Okay." Proof he took the pictures. *Now I need to throw you off to protect the bastard.* "What do you bring?"

"My workout bag. Has extra underwear and that kind of stuff."

"Where do you put that?"

"In the armoire."

"Good. How long do you guys usually...?" Hell gestured vaguely.

"Two to four hours."

"Four hours?" Hell leaned in. "Really?"

Lindsay brought her voice down. "Yeah, really. I mean, that was in the beginning. The first few times. Then it got shorter because he was worried about spending so much time away from Sherry. The last time he could only stay an hour."

"So four hours... Did you talk and eat or..." *Elucidate!*

Lindsay looked around the room nervously, then leaned in. "No talking in the beginning. We talked more as things progressed because I wanted to know everything about him. But still, we don't talk much. We're too busy."

Hell laughed. "High five, girlfriend!" She held up her hand.

The woman giggled and slapped her palm.

"You rock. Four hours. Yeah. Damn, no wonder you love him. Find some of that, you don't want to let go."

Lindsay shifted in her seat. "All I do is think about him. His hands on me. The way he kisses me and the way he barks out orders. He's so dominant—okay, I can't think about that." She blushed and fanned her face.

Hell was about to come herself.

Lindsay seemed to hear what she'd said and sat straighter. "But it's not just the sex. I love the whole man. He's so smart and well read. He knows everything, practically. I love talking to him, laughing with him. I've never been more in love in my life. Brad is all I think about. All I want. Kind of man you'd kill for, just to have one more afternoon with him. I've never wanted to kill anyone before, but I really did want to kill that Gwen bitch. I told Brad it was okay we took a break, but I made sure he wasn't seeing Gwen Lake."

"You followed him recently?"

"Yeah. He hasn't seen Big Bird in a week. Probably because she's gone. She flies all over the globe as part of her job."

"What does Gwen do?"

"CFO of Bi-Global Com."

"Wow."

Lindsay made a face. "She's an idiot. I taught at Stanford for twenty years. I've got two PhDs."

"Wow. Super impressed." There was her problem: too smart. Couldn't see her nose job in front of her face.

Lindsay smiled, tilted her chin, and sat straighter in her seat. "Brad likes smart women. Sherry's smart but not passionate. About anything. She's always been a cold lizard of a person. Just like her mom and her rotten little daughter, Victoria. I swear, those women don't feel emotion. They're Vulcans."

Hell laughed. "Brad isn't seeing any women right now?"

"Not this week."

"Wonder how a guy like that can go without sex for a minute. Does he like whores?"

Lindsay's mouth opened slightly, and then she scowled. "He's not that sort of man."

"I'm sorry, I meant no offense. I'm trying to do a profile on him."

"Oh."

"In order to help you guys get back together, I have to know everything about him. And he isn't going to tell me that."

Lindsay relaxed. "No, Brad doesn't like prostitutes, nor, thankfully, young women. Lowest he goes is Gwen, and she's thirty-nine. I'm fifty-one, same age as Brad."

"And me. Guess we'll all be hitting fifty-two this year."

"Really?" Lindsay gave her a close, head-to-toe examination, and her nose wrinkled slightly. "Some of us do age better than others, don't we?"

Don't punch her. "Yeah, some of us can *afford* to look better than others."

"And some people don't care how they look."

Hell cleared her throat instead of spilling coffee on the crazy loon. "So you followed him around this past week?"

"No, I don't have time. I have a book coming out soon, and my deadline is approaching."

"So how did—you put a GPS unit on his car?"

Lindsay finally realized that she'd admitted to way more than she'd intended. "Uh." Her attention darted to the floor, and she covered her mouth, rubbing her upper lip with her forefinger. "No. I wouldn't do that. That's crazy."

"So, how do you know?"

Her eyes darkened, she leaned in, pointed, and leveled a Freddy Krueger-like, crazy-ass look at Hell. "You'd better not say anything."

Hell's stomach tightened, and she mentally laid out a quick escape from the coffee shop. "Please don't threaten me. I'm only trying to get you two back together," she said in her best therapist voice.

Lindsay blinked fast and sat back in her seat, clutching her fists to her chest. "I'm sorry. I... Uh." Tears welled in her eyes. "I'm really upset about Brad. I love him so much," she said, her voice cracking. "I don't want him to think I'm stalking him. Or doing anything wrong."

Holy hell, Brad had to get rid of this chick, now. No wonder he came up with the blackmail scheme. But he probably had no idea Lindsay was following him.

"All I want to do is find the blackmailer," Hell assured the freak.

She pulled her fingers downward through her curls rapidly, like she was trying to comfort herself, but her actions came off as manic. "Good. You have to. And fast. I'm losing my mind."

Losing? Lost. "I'll do what I can."

Hell told Lindsay she'd be in touch and left the coffee shop.

One more stop for her proof and then it was time to see her new nemesis. She couldn't wait to throw his duplicity in his evil hand-some face. Seemed like the guy was itching for Karma from every woman he met.

She wished she didn't want to screw him. Sleeping with rich, evil, and married men went against all her rules. But, man, it would be fun to tell him what an asshole he was, jump his bones, and then never see him again.

For sure, the therapist would tell her it related to her deep-seated desire for self-destruction. She agreed.

But sometimes her self-destruction was such a blast she couldn't resist.

CHAPTER 6

H er heart beating fast, her stomach in a tight knot, Hell pulled up to Brad's gated home in Atherton. This shouldn't be easy. Never had to con her way into a billionaire's private residence before. She had no idea if this gag would work.

But in order to prove that Brad was a big fat liar, she had to get to his copier.

The magnetic signs on her Malibu touted her fake business name, *Pro Office Equipment Repair,* along with the phone number to her special answering machine line. She changed the outgoing message depending on whom she was impersonating. Under the phone number, she also had the web address to the fake website. Death had created several dummy websites—complete with positive Yelp reviews—to cover her surveillance activities.

She took a moment, silenced her mind, and slipped into character. Her body partially relaxed. She adjusted her light blue work shirt bearing the fake company logo and brushed a bit of lint off her khakis. Clearing her throat, she pressed the intercom button.

No answer.

Hell's pulse went higher, and sweat trickled down her neck. She reached out to press the buzzer again.

"Yes?" came an accented Latina's voice.

"Pro Office Equipment Repair," she said in a commanding voice.

"What?"

"Pro, as in professional, Office Equipment Repair. I got a call from the secretary of an, um, Collins? First name starts with a B? She said her boss had a problem with his home copier."

"No one tol' me."

Crap. Time to up the ante. "Fine. But apparently your boss was upset and ordered his secretary to pay me double to come out here today."

There was a pause. "I don' know. Mr. Collins don't tell me nothing."

Urgency burned through her. Hell let her anger and frustration leak into her voice. "Fine. Then when he calls me to complain that he didn't get his home copier fixed today, I'm gonna blame you. I'm not taking the responsibility. Collins got the last person at my company who came out here fired for being ten minutes late. Now let me in, or I'm gonna make sure you're the one who's fired, not me."

"Wait. I'm sorry."

The gate buzzed and slid open.

A powerful wave of victory surged through her.

Bingo.

She took a deep breath. Step One complete.

But that had been the easy part. Getting past the guards at the house would be the bitch. There had to be at least one on duty. While Death had furnished her with authentic credentials, Brad's security should be top-of-the-line. She shouldn't be able to penetrate his home defenses. But as she'd found time and time again, even the best rent-a-cops could be fooled. Hopefully.

Her heart revved up, and her jitters heightened, but she stayed focused and in character. She was a copier repair person; she did this all the time. Visited people's houses and fixed their machines. No problem. Easy peasy.

She drove up a long driveway, and the front of the house came into view. Jesus Christ, the building had to be twenty thousand square feet. Mediterranean, terracotta tiled roof, three stories, impressive façade. She pulled past the house and parked next to a black Honda in a row of five parking spaces overlooking a tennis court. Honda must be the maid's car. Also in the line of cars was a silver Camry, clearly another domestic's car. The other car was a shiny, new red Maserati. Probably Brad's.

Her muscles tight with apprehension, she scanned the area but saw no guards anywhere. Plenty of cameras, but no one patrolling.

Huh.

Hell grabbed her toolbox and climbed out of the car.

One side of the tall, arched, front double doors opened as she walked up the stairs. A short Latina in blue jeans and a white polo shirt stood there and motioned toward herself.

Please let this work.

"Hi, I'm Jeanne Simari with Pro Office Equipment Repair," Hell said brightly.

"Come in. I'm Esmeralda." The forty-something plump woman backed up to let her inside.

A buzz started in her belly. Really? Was it going to be this easy?

No. Couldn't be. Wasn't this guy a bazillionaire? Why wasn't Esmeralda asking for identification? Talk about a security breach. Hell could be anyone. What was wrong with these people?

She walked through the doors into a three-story-tall entry hall with an open beam ceiling and an intricately designed marble floor. Directly ahead was a dramatic, curved, mahogany staircase with an elaborately carved railing that led to a second floor. Works of art hung on the creamy yellow stucco walls. Astoundingly gorgeous. Probably originally built in the twenties or thirties, but modernized.

Hell still couldn't believe she hadn't been grilled by a security team. That she'd just walked in the front door. This was crazy. But so awesome!

The short housekeeper held herself with an authoritarian posture. "You have to work fast because I got an important appointment I gotta go on. Here's the rules: you don't touch nothing but what you fix. You don't ask to use the bathroom. You don't do nothing but what you paid for. Collins don't like strangers in their house. They don't like repair people messing nothing up. And I gotta cover up whatever you screw up. So don't screw up, and don't mess nothing up."

While thrilled she'd made it through the house's defenses, she couldn't help but be disgusted with this King Brad and Queen Sherry routine. Hell shrugged. "Whatever."

Esmeralda took a step closer, narrowed her dark eyes, and pointed up at Hell. "No, not 'whatever.' These people are important, and you're not. So you don't mess nothing up."

Hell's stomach tightened. Oops. *Watch it, Hell! Stay in character!* "I apologize. Of course, I'll obey all your rules."

Esmeralda took on an imperious look of satisfaction and crossed her arms over her chest, clearly loving lording her power over Hell. "You better."

"Esmeralda? Who is that?"

A tall blonde lady in her late forties, early fifties, walked into the entryway through an arched doorway on Hell's left.

Sherry Collins. Hell recognized the woman from a picture on Brad's desk.

Hell's stomach flipped and flopped, but she kept her professional affect. This wasn't good. Fooling Esmeralda had been easy. Sherry had to be fifty million times smarter.

His wife was beautiful. And looked remarkably like Lindsay only with straight hair. Collins clearly had a type. Sherry had even features, a long yet symmetrical face with flawless skin. Blonde hair that went to her shoulders and flipped up a bit. Sparkling blue eyes. She wore a cream-colored sweater, pearls, and black slacks that hugged her thin, toned body. With queenly, perfect posture, she glided across the floor.

Why the hell was Brad cheating on this elegant lady?

"Name is Jeanne Simari. I'm with Pro Office Equipment Repair. The secretary of a Bradley Collins called and said something was wrong with a copier in his home office? Gave this address? Put a rush order on it. He paid some big bucks to have me show up here last minute."

Sherry frowned slightly. "He didn't tell me." She gave a tiny roll of her eyes. "Typical. He must mean the copier in his office. Esmeralda, show this person to Mr. Collins' office, will you?"

"But, ma'am, you wanted me to go get that *thing* for you? From my *cousin*?" the short Latino lady said with a weird, exaggerated stare.

Get what "thing" from her cousin? What wouldn't they want to discuss in front of a stranger? Was Sherry on drugs?

Sherry's eyes widened, and she sent Hell a quick glance, almost guilty. Like Hell had caught her doing something she shouldn't.

What were they talking about?

Hell examined Sherry closely. Calm, controlled, but with a slight unsteadiness on her feet. Eyes not as sharp as they should be. Huh. Was Brad's wife a druggie?

Sherry cleared her throat. "Y-yes. The errand. Well, where's Higgins?"

"Off today, ma'am."

"What about Imelda?"

"At the store."

"Oh, fiddle. Josefina is scrubbing the marble floor of the ball-room, and I've just sent Rose to Sak's for me. Fine, Esmeralda, you go. I'll take this, uh, *person* upstairs," she said with a slight nose wrinkle like she found Hell as respectable as a homeless drunk.

Watch out, lady, you might get some middle class on you. Find yourself accidentally buying Two-Buck-Chuck instead of Cristal.

"Thank you," Sherry said to Esmeralda with another guilty glance at Hell. "For picking up those, uh, *tamales*, for the, um, garden club luncheon. Your cousin makes the best."

Completely unnecessary information, and an absolute fabrication. Had to be drugs. But Sherry wasn't too screwed up. Yet. It was only four in the afternoon.

Esmeralda sent Sherry another badly acted "sneaky" acknowledgment, glared at Hell, then scurried off.

These people were pathetic at subterfuge. Like, why the hell would a repairperson care if Sherry were buying drugs?

Damn this whole thing. Hell just wanted to check on the copier and get the eff out of there. Sherry could pick up on her con if she wasn't careful. She did not need to go to jail today. Freakin' two strikes. "Just point me in the direction and I'll—"

Sherry's blue gaze went cold, and her mouth tightened. "My husband doesn't like strangers in his office unless an employee is present. Come, I'll show you," she said with a small hand gesture. She sounded glum, resigned, and wholly inconvenienced. Clearly pissed at Brad. He probably pulled this kind of crap on her a lot.

Hell caught the unmistakable odor of wine coming from her direction. Three glasses so far, she'd guess. "Sorry, ma'am."

"Not your fault." She gave Hell a curt smile, gestured toward the staircase, and walked ahead. "Follow me, please."

The woman clearly loathed repair people. Hell wasn't sure if Sherry even considered her staff human.

Sherry stopped at the base of the staircase, and turned to Hell but didn't face her. "Please watch your step on the staircase, and keep hold of the railing. We've had some unfortunate accidents. We'd love to modify the stairs to be safer, but this came out of a seventeenth-century mansion in England, and we're legally bound to keep it in its original condition if we want to retain its historical significance."

"I understand," Hell said, and grabbed the railing. She took a few steps and saw what Sherry was talking about. The stairs were steep, cut at a weird angle, and were shorter than they should be. Beautiful, but not very practical.

Since there was no way out of dealing with Sherry, maybe Hell could wangle some interesting details out of her about Brad the Dickhead. Keeping her face free of emotion, she worked at breakneck speed to figure out an angle to get Sherry to talk without drawing unnecessary attention to herself. Tricky. She had to come up with a good story. A really good story.

As Sherry climbed the stairs, it became obvious that she'd attended a finishing school. While her balance was a bit off from the alcohol consumption, every movement of her hands and arms and every step she took was carefully controlled, planned, and executed.

She'd clearly had years of practice watching every gesture and containing her body language. Amazing control.

Which meant getting her to open up would be nearly impossible. A human clam. But Hell had pried open many human clams. There was only one way to do it. She had to make Sherry think she was just like her. Sherry would only confide in people of her own class. But how the hell was she supposed convince Sherry that she was a rich bitch while wearing a workman's uniform?

Her heart rate increased and then—*ding*! The perfect story materialized in her brain.

Let the bullshit begin.

"You have a beautiful home, Mrs. Collins."

"Yes, isn't it?" Sherry drawled in a tone that said, *how the hell would you know?*

"Reminds me of my old house."

Sherry stopped mid-step and spun on her. Then clearly decided that Hell was joking. "Oh, yes." She gave one brief titter and continued on.

"Hard to believe, huh? But I had a twenty-five-thousand-square-foot Mediterranean back in Virginia. Built by a senator in the twenties. God, I miss it."

"You can't be serious," Sherry said in a bored, haughty tone. What a bitch!

Hell forged ahead, completely committed to her character. "Wish I wasn't. Magnificent home, really. Five-thousand-square-foot ballroom, Olympic pool, forty acres of lawn. Perfect for entertaining. Last party I had there, we had three hundred people. Governor, some celebrities. Oh, well," she said, letting pain seep into her tone.

Sherry frowned. "How did..."

"Husband left me for his secretary and screwed me out of every penny I had. I was so stupid. I thought if I did what he wanted, he'd come back to me. And now look at me." Hell gestured toward herself with hopefully just the right amount of disgust on her face.

Sherry reached the top of the stairs, turned to her, and gave her a close, head-to-toe examination. "Are you serious?"

Shit. *Come up with an excuse why you don't look like her!*

"Unfortunately," Hell said, stepping up to Sherry's level. She tried to look ashamed. "I know it's hard to tell given my awful appearance. I mean, khakis, ugh. And this dreadful work shirt." She shuddered. "This fabric feels so creepy on my skin, I can't tell you. What I would give for my personal stylist, manicurist, trainer, and masseuse. My hair hasn't been the same since I left home, and my skin was clearly not meant for manual labor." She held up her bandaged fingers. "My poor hands. I can't even look at them. I'm so embarrassed you're meeting me like this."

Sherry seemed properly appalled.

About ten closed rooms and three hallways led off the ginormous second floor landing.

"Doesn't your family have money?" she asked.

Hell looked down at the polished wood floor and worked on an expression that balanced depression with pride. Defeat with resiliency. "He got all that, too. I inherited—oh, not much, maybe four hundred million from my parents—and he *invested* it for me," she said, doing air quotes. "For five years, one bit at a time, he sent it to various secret overseas bank accounts where I couldn't get at it, and testified in court that I'd spent it all. God, I can't go there." She rubbed her forehead and cast her eyes downward but kept her peripheral vision sharp on the woman.

Sherry barely reacted. But the look in her eye belied her true emotion. The story had affected her.

Killer.

"I wouldn't have left the house," she finally said.

Hell was ready. "As it turned out, I thought I'd signed onto the deed, but apparently those papers never got recorded. Tom made sure I wasn't on the title for any of our thirty properties but had lied to me all along and told me I was. He'd had me sign fake documents."

Sherry's eyes widened, and she gasped. "No!"

A charge went through Hell as she pictured the woman with a fishhook in her lip. "Yeah. And his best friend is a prominent psychiatrist, and Tom said if I didn't leave, he'd get his buddy to testify that I was insane and commit me to an institution. Or kill me and make sure my body was never found. He scared me enough so I left."

"Of course you did. Horrible man. You couldn't prove any of this?"

She made sure to underplay her reaction. "His family is much more powerful than mine. They all turned on me. It was awful. At least I got away. I thought the PhD from Vassar would be worth something, but because I didn't work after I graduated, it doesn't mean squat. So I bought this embarrassing office equipment repair business. Only reason I'm here today is because one of my employees is out sick, and your husband's secretary was so emphatic."

"You *own* the business?" Sherry asked, seeming intrigued. Her reaction almost bordered on admiration. Almost. With a hefty dose of pity.

"Yeah, I have three offices, working on more. Just scored a giant contract with Google. I'm rebuilding and making my money back. Well, hopefully. Can you believe it? Just five years ago, I was married, wearing Dior, driving a Lamborghini, box seats at the opera, secretary of the country club, and now look at me. Men." She made a disgusted noise. "They will ruin you. I hope you got yourself a good one, ma'am."

"Yes..." Sherry's attention darted around the area, and she rubbed her chin.

"Don't tell me. He's rotten, too?"

Sherry glanced at her, and a shield went up. Her face hardening, she almost sobered. Hell expected her to change the subject and lead her to the copier. But Sherry stayed put. "Not rotten, exactly, but certainly worthless. Thankfully, he couldn't do to me what your husband did to you. Before we were married, I bound him in an inescapable legal trap that even the best Harvard-trained lawyers couldn't breach. Houdini couldn't even figure out a way out of the legal morass in which I ensconced my dear husband. Mother always said never to trust men. She ensured I kept my family money separate and that our pre-nup was iron-clad."

"Wish my mother would have warned me." Lindsay had told Hell that Sherry knew about Brad's cheating. But how much did she know? "And about the cheating. Not that I'm implying your husband is cheating on you. But I had no idea the sacrifices I was expected to make for the good of his family. Especially turning a blind eye to his affairs." Hell looked through Collins' eyes for her reaction.

Sherry sighed, and the temperature around her dropped to the point where it felt like the air-conditioning came on in the place. "Thankfully, Mother explained that to me as well. If you want family lines to stay strong, you look the other way."

Hell wanted to hoot with elation that she'd made the ice queen open up, but she kept her expression serious and sympathetic. "You, too?"

Sherry gave a slight roll of her eyes.

"I'm sorry," Hell said, and actually meant it. Cheating in a marriage was never okay. Never.

Sherry lifted one shoulder briefly. "At this point, I could care less," she drawled in a bored tone. "Besides, let someone else do the dirty work. I certainly never enjoyed it." She pulled herself up into a self-important posture, but lost her balance and stepped back to catch herself.

Hell stared at her. "He's not even good in the sack?"

"Brad?" she said in a disgusted tone with her upper lip curled. She shuddered and crossed her arms. "Ugh."

She didn't just dislike him, she hated him. Loathed and despised him.

Such the polar opposite sex report from Lindsay's. Brad now had two grades in lovemaking: an A with a million plusses and an F with a million minuses. Did that mean he was really a C student?

"But you're so beautiful, how could he ever cheat on you? Why would he ever need anyone else? I can't believe he's not down on his hands and knees thanking his lucky stars to be married to someone as refined and sophisticated as you," Hell said with just the perfect amount of sincerity.

Sherry beamed and held her head proudly. "I agree."

"You poor girl. I hope you have boyfriends," Hell said.

She pursed her lips in a blink-and-you'd-miss-it move. "I indulged in a few minor distractions and dalliances, but honestly, I grew bored with it all. Unfortunately, there's only been one man for me, and he married another woman." She sighed heavily, filling the air with chardonnay fumes.

Brad had clearly disappointed his wife. He'd let her down early on, and she'd never forgiven him for it. Hell wondered if Sherry had ever given him a chance.

"Sounds exactly like what happened to me," Hell replied. "My fiancé before my husband. He broke off our engagement to marry some gold-digging bikini model. I still love him. I'm not sure I ever loved my husband, Tom. Did you ever love yours?"

Sherry made a face like she smelled something foul. "Hm. Perhaps for a brief period of time when the children were small, but he was such a fool with them—fawning all over them and actually getting on the floor and playing with them—I had to send them away to spare myself the revolting displays. He always loved them far more than me."

Holy shit. Jealous of her own kids. Plus she spoke of her children like they were disposable burdens, like they weren't even human. Like they were possessions.

Sherry prattled on, her face filled with righteous disdain. "For Heaven's sake, I'm the one who carried the little ingrates to term and sacrificed my body so that the great Bradley Collins would have heirs. The least he could have done was put me and my needs first, but no, the ungrateful wretch betrayed me with my own children."

Brad had loved being a father? Sounded like all Sherry liked to do was punish people, especially her kids and husband. No wonder Brad was off in other women's beds. The worship he got from Lindsay probably felt pretty good at first.

Sherry continued with her remote affect. "I don't think he's ever cared about me, to be quite frank. He cheated on me just a month after our honeymoon."

Gee, what a shocker. She probably had the sexual response of a mummy. "What a jerk. So, you two mainly married for the sake of your families?"

"Yes. His father and my father were both heirs to an oil conglomerate and started the Jackson hotel chain. Then they bought a few other global companies. My father passed away just three months ago and—"

"Oh, honey, I'm so sorry for your loss."

The line between her eyes deepened, and she actually seemed sort of sad. Were those real feelings or a display intended to mask her sociopathy?

"Daddy was a great man, revered by all who knew him, even his enemies. Not only did he quadruple our family's fortunes, his leadership in the Republican Party helped end many of those wasted programs for the poor."

Hell's blood boiled. She wanted to throttle the rich bitch. Cutting programs for the poor was something to be proud of? What a-holes! "You must be so proud," she said with as much reverence as she could manage.

Sherry gave a haughty smile. "I am. I was his special princess. He was the only one who valued me the way I deserved. I don't know how I'll ever be able to recover from the loss."

"So difficult." *Great work, Dad. You created a monster.*

"I dearly wish that Jack Collins had been the first partner to die, but the only way that man will die is if someone pours holy water on him."

Hell laughed.

Sherry's eyes gleamed, then her expression turned cold and cruel. "Jack Collins is a totalitarian dictator. Similar to Genghis Khan, only with anger issues. Daddy always taught me to stand up for myself, but Jack takes great delight and sport in crushing and controlling Brad. Of course, if Brad were a real man, he'd cut the strings and stop letting his father control him like a puppet. I never could respect a man who didn't stand up for himself."

"Me, neither," Hell said with disgust. Aah, the son living in the shadow of the father, interesting. Such a typical pattern.

Sherry's shoulders relaxed, and her manner grew a tad more familiar. "I'm sure Brad imagines himself the master of his independence with this ridiculous little venture capital nonsense, but his father is behind all of his successes. Brad deludes himself into thinking he chose the businesses with his own brilliance, but he'll never be able to face the truth that he was spoon-fed the contacts by his father. Unfortunately, he's far too weak, lazy, and stupid to develop his own ideas or cultivate his own working relationships. Brad was a second-rate tennis player in college, a mediocre student, and has never gained the ability to tie his own shoes without the proper instructions and permission from his father. Jack Collins will always have him by his...well, you know."

Sherry would never have revealed any of this without the wine, Hell was sure of it. "What a wimp."

Sherry nodded with a knowing look. "Absolutely. Jack and I loathe each other but are polite for the sake of the family. He loved my father because he was the only man strong enough to stand up to him. So unlike his son."

"Were you both open about this being an arranged marriage?"

Sherry's nose wrinkled. "No. I mean, I always viewed it that way, but Brad adored me. He worshipped me at first," she said in a regal, supercilious way. Like it was all so obvious the world should be falling at her feet. "Until I put my foot down about his advances. I mean, how many times per month is one supposed to put up with all that pawing?"

Um, about thirty would be nice. Hell made a disgusted face. "Men are beasts."

"Revolting."

"So, where's the copier?"

"The what? Oh, in through here." Sherry indicated a doorway to her right.

Sherry liked this conversation. *Good one, Hell. Good going.* As slimy as it was, conning people was her favorite part of the job. She was really scoring some hot gossip today.

Hell walked into the high-ceilinged, wood-paneled office slash library. Tall, glassed-in bookcases lined the cavernous room. Large windows around the top of the space illuminated the area nicely and afforded views of the tops of trees outside with the blue sky beyond. Gorgeous. Masculine. Full of worn leather furniture and expensive leather-bound books. Smelled like him. His huge carved desk was nearly the same size as the one in his office at work. Awards and pictures of him with other rich and famous people filled one entire bookcase. She spotted the copier standing in the corner behind the desk.

"Damn, this looks just like my husband's office. He had this same desk. Okay, getting déjà vu. There's the copier." Thankfully, she knew a lot about most models, having gone through several hand-me-downs from friends in past years.

She walked over to the copier. Above it, along the back wall, was a large shelf stuffed full of tennis trophies. Most were from the seventies and eighties. Looked like he'd done very well. Many first places.

"I can't imagine what I'd do if Brad turned on me like that," Sherry said, her brow furrowed as much as it could be. Her facial muscles didn't look like they'd gotten much of a workout over the years.

"Honey, I shouldn't have told you this. This could never happen to you. He'll never leave you, right?"

All empathy vanished from her face. Her eyes went hard, and her mouth turned mean. "I'd kill him if he tried. After all the behaviors and demands and drama I've had to endure at the hands of that man for all these years, he owes me this marriage and more," she spat.

Holy moly, her hatred of Brad ran deep. "Put up with. He's been mean to you?"

Sherry's eyes widened, and she blinked fast. "Dear God, no." She lifted her chin and sent out a wave of chilling energy. "He wouldn't dare even raise his voice to me. He's just extremely annoying. When he walks in the door, he expects me to drop everything and greet him like he's a monarch returning to his kingdom after a great battle. Expects me to actually sit down with him, have a cocktail, and talk about our day," she said, seeming incredulous. "As if I cared what he does or whom he's spoken with or in which new ludicrous venture he's considering investing his father's money." Her mouth curved with revulsion.

Can you imagine? Your husband actually expecting to *talk* to you? Such abuse. Hell couldn't believe it, but Sherry was starting to make Brad look good.

Sherry continued, looking extremely disappointed. "I've never been able to put my finger on it. He appears devoted and attends all the functions I require. He does everything I want him to do, really. He has good social skills, people like him, and he's a decent bridge player. But...he..."

"Never lit your fire."

"No. He's a pest, really, and he's been home and underfoot far too much lately. I wish he'd just stay at his club."

"So you must be happy that he's cheating on you." Hell poked at the copier but kept most of her attention on Sherry.

"No. The news hurt me tremendously when I first found out. I mean, how does that make me look? However, over time, I've adjusted to the idea and it's even given me some relief. I do believe it's a wife's duty to endure her husband's attentions, but when Brad allowed himself to go bald, I found I could no longer withstand his touch. Ugh. Just the sight of him turns my stomach."

Wait. She kicked Mr. Hottie out of her bed because he *allowed himself* to go bald? Like he purposely chose baldness just to piss her off? What a bitch! "Good for you, honey. I would have done the exact same thing. Who'd want to sleep with a bald guy?" *Me! Me! Pick me!* Hell gave a large shudder.

Sherry nodded, and a cruel smile marred her perfect face. "Like sleeping with the Elephant Man. Even with my eyes closed, I could still see that bald, shiny mess above me. So sickening. Honestly, the man gives me hives."

A jolt of anger made her jaw clench and her hands fist. Nasty rotten witch! How mean to pick on your husband because of his genetics. Woman was nuts.

Besides, bald guys were hot. Especially Brad.

Sherry continued on, clear disdain on her regal face. "Thankfully, he respects me enough not to flaunt his relationships. He never shows up late, he always comes home at night, and never has lipstick on his collar or smells like another woman. He's very discreet. I wouldn't have known if I hadn't had him followed."

Hell's alarms went off. Holy Christ. Brad was so naïve! And Sherry was much more devious than she'd first imagined. "You had him investigated? Good for you! Wish I'd done that."

Damn, how many people were following Brad? Sounded like a parade.

Sherry held her head with a smug tilt. "You always must know what they're doing, even if you don't like it. Knowledge is power. Not only must you find out what they do, you must also document their wrongdoings. I have a file a mile thick on my dear husband. You never know when you'll wind up in court."

"You are my hero," Hell said instead of telling her how scary she found her. Damn, Brad was surrounded by vipers. Sherry was ruthless.

She finally smiled. "One has to look out for oneself. But I don't believe he's serious with any of his whores, even though he doesn't see them in quite the numbers as he has in past years. He used to have half a dozen he rotated through; recently he's down to two tramps. I think it must be his age. He doesn't have the same stamina or something."

Which meant she knew about Gwen, too. Brad was so *dumb*.

"So what happened to the man you really loved?"

She paled, and her face fell. "He married my friend—well, enemy now—let's say ex-friend of mine."

"That's horrible!" Dude was the luckiest man in the world.

"Agreed. And unfortunately, we're in the same close social circle so I see him and her all the time."

"Incredibly unfair." Who was it? How could Hell get her to spill the name?

"Agreed. I thought I'd grow to love Brad, but after a month of marriage, it became clear that wasn't going to happen."

Hell worked on the copier and continued her mind probe. "So what if the gentleman you loved wanted to leave his wife for you?"

"I'd leave Brad like that." She snapped her fingers.

"Even with the hit to your social standing?"

"It would be well worth it. Besides, he's got just as much social power as Brad. I've tried to let him know over the years that I'm still interested, but he hasn't picked up on my hints. Unfortunately, he seems to adore his low-class cow of a wife, Lindsay."

Hell's heart started racing, and she stifled a gasp. Holy God, Sherry was in love with Dan! Wow! She turned away so Sherry wouldn't notice her dropped jaw.

Which meant she also knew about Lindsay and Brad. Her *ex*-friend? Low-class cow? Her enemy? Damn, Brad was an idiot. So was Lindsay.

"I wish I could leave Brad now, but it would stain me in my social crowd without Dan in place. The only way I could keep my position in the club without an important man would be if Brad died. He is fifty-two, that could happen, but, unfortunately, I can't count on him dying anytime soon. It's a shame he's in such excellent health. I've always hoped that his heart murmur would end the whole mess, but he's amazingly robust."

Hell started to chuckle until she realized that Sherry wasn't joking. By her affect it was clear she was revealing her inner truth. Her real thoughts. A cold chill went through her. Holy crap, this woman was a total sociopath.

"I can't tell you how many nights I lay awake praying for my husband's death," Hell said like she was talking about her husband's golf scores.

Sherry nodded and continued on emotionlessly. "I honestly wish I wasn't so concerned about being discovered, or I'd do away with him myself. I've spent many hours fantasizing about how I could manage it, but as of yet, I haven't developed a solid enough plan. Killing him would be easy. Avoiding being caught is where I'm stuck."

Hell's inner Mother Bear came online. All her instincts made her want to run to Brad and protect him from this creepy freak.

Brad needed to dump both his crazy bitches before one killed him.

"I came up with several ways to kill my husband," Hell said offhandedly, hoping she wasn't going too far. "But you're right, they always look at the spouse."

"Exactly. I'm not going to jail for that imbecile," Sherry continued. "Even though killing him would be a public service."

Hell's interior dropped a few more degrees, but she laughed appreciatively. "I'd get the Nobel Peace Prize if I killed my ex."

Sherry snickered. "I wish I could avoid putting myself in danger and leave him now, but a divorce would be disastrous for me," she said with a self-important air. "I'd never make country club president. I'm on the ballot this spring. The elections are coming right up," she said with a tight little smile.

Hell tried for an admiring look. "Good for you. That's not an easy position to come by."

Sherry held herself taller. "No, it isn't. I've been engineering this for years. I'm sure my time has finally arrived." Finally, some light came into her eyes on a subject other than Brad's death.

"Good work. I'm sure you'll be president soon." She turned back to the copier so she could hide her reactions, and to speed the process along. This was getting harder by the moment. Sherry was a tanker truckload of evil, and Hell wanted away from her. She hit the button on the copy machine.

Hell checked the copy. Same glitchy toner bits at the top.

A wave of joy swept through her. Boo-yah! Proof that Brad was a big fat liar! Proof that he'd made up the whole blackmail scheme to have Hell scare away Lindsay for him. What a devious son of a bitch. But it sounded like he needed to be. "I don't know what your husband thought was wrong with this. It seems fine."

"The machine probably ran out of paper. The man is loath to do anything for himself."

"Men are useless." For anything other than sex.

Hell made an additional copy for proof, opened the copier again, gave it a quick visual check, and then closed it. "No, all looks good." She put the copies in her toolbox and headed out.

Sherry walked her to the door. "It was nice meeting you, Jeanne."

"Mrs. Collins—"

"Sherry."

Wow. *Huge.* Hell almost felt like she deserved a prolonged curtain call for her performance. "Sherry, take care of yourself. And good luck."

"I shall. You, too, my dear. I hope you restore your fortunes soon, are able to hire a good stylist again, and get out of that horrendous uniform." Sherry sent her a genuine smile. Hell got the feeling it was her first.

She tried not to run for her car. She slid behind the wheel, let out a huge sigh, and the tension eased from her body. Fatigue set in. The post-performance come-down. All she wanted was a nice, fat joint and an ice-cold beer. She started the car and left the Collins' estate. Time to go home, eat dinner, and then track down Brad.

Jesus, the dude was surrounded by enemies. His father, his scary wife, his freaky girlfriend. Hell wondered if Gwen abused him, too.

Poor guy.

Hell slapped her forehead. What the hell was wrong with her? Had her hormones overridden her logic? Collins was a jerk. Screwing his friend's wife to get even with him?

But his biggest blunder of all?

Mistaking Hell for an idiot.

CHAPTER 7

WEDNESDAY, NOVEMBER 10, 2010, 7:01 P.M.

Brad's beefy dark-haired bodyguard let her into the building, and she sauntered down the hallway to Collins' office.

Pushing through the large mahogany door, she walked into his empty outer room. "Collins?"

"In here," he called out from his office. Damn, she loved his deep, smoky voice. Smoldering hot, like the man.

As soon as she walked through his door, his gorgeous face stunned her to a standstill. A thrill went through her. He looked even better. With his carved, even features, sparkling gray eyes, closely shaved head, and that killer jaw, the boy was beautiful. No coat, he wore a light blue, expensive, button-down shirt with the top unbuttoned, showing a bit of dark chest hair. His sleeves were rolled up revealing sinewy forearms; his right was a bit bigger than his left. Clearly still played tennis. She wanted his lovely, nice, thick hands all over her.

But his eyes were what truly captivated her. Fire in steel. Supreme power emanated from within him. The set to his shoulders, the way he held himself, the man thought he was the shit. And he was.

"Mr. Collins." She swaggered up to one of the chairs in front of his desk.

His eyes twinkled playfully. Such a flirt. "Miss Trent. So, you've solved the case." The smug way he held his mouth said that he didn't believe her.

Smirking, she pulled out the ransom note and the copy from his home office copier from her inner jacket pocket and sent him a look that said she'd seen through his little charade. She set the two pieces of paper on his desk in front of him, sat, and waited for him to confess.

He didn't catch on. Yet. He sent her a questioning look. "Yes. The ransom note and a blank piece of paper? So?"

"If you will note at the top of each page is a glitchy little toner spot from the printer. Both copies came from the same printer." She let the words hang in the air.

His brow wrinkled, and his gaze darted away, just for a millisecond.

She laughed. "You are one evil son of a bitch, Mr. Blackmailer. You should change your name to Bradabus Collins."

"Bradabus?"

"*Barnabus* Collins? The vampire from the sixties TV show *Dark Shadows?* Could be the title of a book about your life."

He lost the color in his face and sat straight up. "*You went to my house?*"

A surge of enjoyment powered through her. Now he was getting the picture. She grinned widely. "Yeah. Had a nice long talk with Sherry."

"You *what?*" His shoulders tightened, his eyes dilated, and his face flushed red. His brows angled hard toward his nose. "You didn't give—"

"Are you nuts? Besides, I didn't have to. She knows all about your affairs."

"*What?*" He leapt from his seat, his face even harder. "Did she tell you that?"

Hell had to hold back an outburst of evil laughter. This was awesome! Mr. High and Mighty beaten at his own game. "Yeah. Told me all kinds of stuff."

His eyes narrowed, and his mouth went ugly. "Sherry never opens up and would never talk to someone like you." Scowling, he walked around his desk, stood too close, and towered above her. "How the hell did you find that out? Did you tell her who you were?"

Her stomach tightened despite her efforts to stop it. She refused to be afraid of this asshole. Dude better back down or she'd turn him into a soprano. She waved a hand dismissively. "No. Calm down, dude. She doesn't suspect anything. She thinks I'm an office equipment repair person."

His eyes went cold, and his lip curled. "Sherry would never talk to a repair person or tell them anything. She considers servants and people in the trades to be inferior. Did you break into my house? How the hell did you get past the staff?"

Clamping her jaw, she pressed her toes hard into her skull-printed Vans. This guy thought he had way more power over her than he did. "No and back the fuck down. I told you. I walked in the front door. Not my fault your home security sucks. I spoke with Sherry because all your staff were deployed elsewhere. She talked to me because I conned her."

"Highly doubtful." His brow went into a deep V, and he frowned, an air of menace about him. "You crossed the line with me," he said in a low tone, his body posture threatening.

Intimidating guy. If she were the kind of person to be intimidated. Hell resisted the urge to pull back and allowed him to crowd her. No way would she even flinch.

Besides, Brad's rabid dog act couldn't compare to Dadzilla's typhoon of emotional violence or Marco Capasso's ruthlessness. Collins needed to take lessons from real experts on intimidation.

But he was starting to piss her off. If he pushed her any harder, he might need his bodyguard.

Eyes narrowed, his mouth twisted, he said, "You should have asked my permission before you went to my house." He edged closer.

A tiny flare of fear made her gut scrunch, igniting her fuse. Her body hot and hard, she squared her shoulders and stood, forcing him to step back. "Hey," she said in a deep, loud growl. She jabbed her bandaged forefinger into his hard chest. "Don't you try to bully me,

Collins. This is on your head, not mine. If you hadn't lied to me and sent me on a wild goose chase, I wouldn't have had to go to your house. You hired me to find out who was blackmailing you, and that's what I did. Your mistake was assuming I was too stupid to catch on to you. If anyone needs to apologize here, it's you. You disrespected me, lied to me, and used me. You fucked up. Not me." She challenged him with the set to her mouth and leveled her gaze straight into his, summoning all her inner power. This bastard had better back down.

He held himself taller, his chin higher, and glowered down at her.

The hair stood up on the back of her neck and arms, but she didn't look away.

"I am still your employer. No one goes to my home and interrogates my wife without my express permission," he said in a loud, sharp voice. "Do you understand me?"

Hell didn't blink and didn't budge. She matched his posture—just short of standing on her tiptoes—stared into his fiery gray eyes, and found herself torn between hitting him and kissing him, which disturbed her even more. "Apparently you didn't read my contract," she replied in the same biting tone he'd used only louder. "Section two states that if a client willfully withholds information or provides false information during an investigation, the contract is nullified, and full payment must be remitted immediately. So back down, Collins, *now*. You don't scare me, and I don't take orders from liars. Besides, I didn't interrogate her, and I didn't blow it. I'm way better than that. Call her and ask her if you don't believe me."

He held her gaze for a long moment, his anger lines deep. "I think I will." With a defiant and heated look, he finally took another step back and pulled out his cell. He only took his burning glare from Hell to punch in the number. "Sherry? Sorry to bother you. I wondered, did a copier repairman come out today to the house?"

Sherry's voice boomed out of the receiver. "Why in God's name didn't you warn me?" she said, her words slightly slurred. She'd clearly had a lot more wine after Hell had left.

He winced, held the phone away from his ear, and broke eye contact with Hell. His expression went from angry to contrite, his shoulders rounded, and he looked five feet shorter. "I'm sorry, I meant to call you…"

Hell held back laughter. Mr. Big Bully turns into Simpering Apologetic Husband in a half second.

He turned away. "Well, Esmeralda could have handled… Oh. Well, I hope they didn't inconvenience you too badly. You did?" He swung his attention back to Hell. "Interesting conversation? *You actually enjoyed a conversation with a worker?*" He looked away again, his body relaxing. "Well, I'm glad you weren't too put out. Did she fix it? Good. Okay, I'll be home in a few hours. I've got to talk to some contacts in China. Okay, bye."

He hung up the phone and studied Hell's face, his mind clicking, most of his anger gone. Curiosity took hold. "You made quite an impression on her. She liked you. Sherry doesn't like people."

Hell stood her ground and held her posture firm. "I'm good."

He gave a slight shrug and walked behind his desk. "Well, she believed you."

"They always do. You owe me an apology."

He stared at her for a long moment. Man was clearly not used to admitting wrongdoing. She held his gaze and tried not to blink.

This would test the dude's mettle. If he didn't say he was sorry, he would be deemed unfuckable, unaccountable, and weak. If he apologized, it would show he had some strength of character.

Finally, he gave a brief nod. "I apologize. I needed to get out from underneath Lindsay and couldn't figure out any other way."

Hell relaxed and was inwardly pleased but kept her face hard. "You should have clued me in. I would have scared her off for you."

"I realize that now. I meant no disrespect. However, I clearly underestimated you, and for that I also apologize. You came highly recommended. Just by your appearance and manner…" He gestured toward her.

"Apology accepted. I get it. Happens all the time. It's partly my fault. I just don't like conforming."

He gave an amused snort.

"After meeting Lindsay, I understand why you did this. She's a bucket of crazy. But you are one lucky son of a bitch I decided to continue on this case," she said, pointing at him. "I found out vital information that will save your sorry ass in the future."

He nodded again, his anger diminishing. He sat down, and his attention darted around his desk. Frowning, he looked at her. "Sherry told you she knows about my affairs?"

Hell sighed and plopped down on the plush leather chair. "Yeah. She knows about Lindsay and Gwen. She's known everything all along."

"Damn." He sat straighter, rubbing his mouth with his hand. "She's never let on."

"I wouldn't say anything if I were you."

He raised his brows in a quick move. "Hadn't planned on it."

"I'd just keep on like you're doing, and don't let her know you know. Or then she'd have to do something about it."

"Yes, she would."

"And don't let Lindsay know. God. She'd probably go straight to Sherry and try to talk her into letting you out of the marriage. Lindsay is bonkers."

He leaned back again, his focus on the ceiling. "This blows me away. I thought Sherry was naïve."

"No. She's known everything about you since the first time you cheated, shortly after your honeymoon—you tacky bastard—and apparently has it all in a nice, neat file somewhere, ready to deploy if you mess up. So I'd watch yourself."

He sat forward, his mouth dropped open, and his eyes bugged out. "She *what*?"

Hell's belly bubbled with elation. Telling this bazillionaire about his life rocked! Mr. All-Powerful who didn't know shit about his own marriage. So satisfying!

She told him everything Sherry had said. Except about him being lousy in bed, that she found him ugly, that she wished he were dead, and her love for Dan. She'd only pull out those nuggets if Collins attacked her again.

Eyes wide, Brad slumped in his chair, his hands on his now very pale face. "My God. I'm such an idiot."

She tried not to gloat. "Right after the honeymoon?"

He made a dismissive noise, and his expression darkened. He looked away, rubbed the back of his neck, then met her gaze. "Had to find someone who would respond to me. Sherry loathes me and always has. I was lucky I talked her into having kids, or we never would have done it at all. I think she's a lesbian."

She allowed herself a brief eyebrow raise. "Perhaps. Certainly, she's a very controlled person." Give him points for noticing Sherry's reaction in bed. Meant he'd paid some attention.

He also corroborated Sherry's story. Hell gave him a pass on the cheating. But what a weird world they lived in.

"I can't believe the information you got out of her. How long were you there?"

"I don't know. Ten or fifteen minutes."

The look in his eyes changed. Admiration shone strong. He saw her as a worthy opponent. Respect, just like that. "Amazing."

Victory pumping through her veins, her body pulsed with excitement. "You bet I am." She decided to leave out the part about Sherry's drinking. Made her look smarter.

He finally relaxed and examined her again. Like he was seeing her for the first time. Stroked his chin. He finally nodded and sent her a grin.

Hell quirked her mouth to one side. "My only question is this: why didn't you just hire an actor to impersonate a private detective to bamboozle Lindsay? Much cheaper."

He shrugged, and his gaze sparkled with play. "Did you mention any of your suspicions to her?"

"Course not. I snowed her for you. She's a freak. Did you know she's tracking your every move? She's got a goddamned GPS unit on your car and has been following you around for the last two months."

Brad gasped, and his pupils dilated. "What?"

Score another point for Hell! Yee-hah! "Yeah, you sure can pick 'em. You knew she was a psychopath, right?"

All the color left his face again and his expression went haunted. "She was always high-strung. It's why she left teaching. After she hit menopause, she couldn't handle the pressures of academia and quit to write books."

"She's lost her bloody mind. And you aren't very observant, dude. She followed you to the Fairmont and watched you go into a room with Gwen."

Brad gaped. "She what?"

Hell told him everything Lindsay had said, trying hard to stay in a conversational tone and not let the unbridled glee invade her voice.

By the end of the report, Brad looked like he'd just had lunch with Jeffrey Dahmer: hands on his head, his forehead beaded with sweat, his gaze hollow. "Fuckin' hell."

This was probably the most satisfying job she'd had in months. "If you have a pet rabbit, I'd give it away."

"What? Oh, Christ. How do I get rid of her?"

"Find the GPS unit, catch her in the act. She'll be mortified. You have more power over her because she loves you, and you clearly don't love her back. Thankfully, she's afraid of you. She wants to follow all your rules. You need to come off as an angry parent. Say that you're worried about her. Insist she get counseling. You can stop her. While she talked about killing Gwen, I don't think she has it in her. I think she was all talk."

"Shit. I knew she was getting obsessive but not this obsessive."

"Kind of Karmic, though, dude. Getting even with Dan by screwing his wife? Tacky shit. And if you don't like her, what are you thinking, screwin' her for four hours?"

He chuckled, and the color returned to his face. "You found out all kinds of dirt, didn't you?"

More than I feel comfortable sharing. "Yeah, so pay me the twenty grand, and I'll be on my way. If Lindsay contacts me, I'll tell her I didn't solve the case, I'm still working on it, and she should keep low. That should take care of her. But as for your security team, you need to kick those guys in the ass because they aren't doing their jobs. One, both Sherry's detectives and Lindsay were following you, and they didn't notice. Two, they allowed a GPS unit to be put on your car. And three, I walked into your house without being asked for identification, holding a toolbox that could have contained weapons or a bomb."

"Jesus Christ. Should have hired you a while ago, just to test my defenses. Believe me, those guys will be hearing from me about this. Damn it. This is totally unacceptable."

"You definitely need better security at home."

"I haven't needed it. The staff serves as guards during the day. But I'll look into it. Can't believe they didn't ask for your ID."

"In their defense, if they had, they would have been shown solid credentials. I have all that covered. Still, if a top security guy had questioned me, he'd have been able to make me."

He grinned. "I don't know. I think you're pretty good."

"That's what all the boys say," she couldn't help but quip.

He laughed and shook his head.

"What I don't get is why you're screwing that lunatic when you could easily get a dame who wouldn't go all *Fatal Attraction* on you."

Shrugging, he said, "She's changed since we started going out. She went off her meds because she's got some new health guru. Gotten more and more unstable. I hope she keeps her mouth shut."

"She probably will. She has a lot to lose. She said she and Dan were financially dependent on one another."

"Her behavior isn't reflecting that fear."

"I think you can turn her around. She may be book smart, but she's dumb as a meatloaf. I couldn't believe the crap she was telling me and didn't connect. 'Oh, Dan screwed over Brad, but that was before we started seeing each other. I'm glad Brad didn't hold it against me,'" Hell said, doing a high-pitched imitation of Lindsay. "Duh! And how she'd pressed you to leave your wife, and then, suddenly, there's a blackmail scheme that's preventing you from seeing her. I mean, come on." Hell pointed upwards. "Astronauts on the space shuttle could see that one."

His gray eyes flashed, and a smile played on his lips. "When did you begin to suspect me?" He clearly loved this game.

She couldn't help but return his smile. Nice he appreciated her smarts, and nice he'd given her the win. "Moment I left this office. Blackmail victims do not flirt as massively as you did. You'd clearly sussed out my *weak spot*," she said, using air quotes, "and tried to exploit it and get my mind off your subterfuge. Which worked well while I was in the room with you, but not when I stepped outside the door and the hormones wore off."

"Why didn't you confront me?"

"Because I'd warned you not to fuck with me, and you did. When people fuck with me, no matter how rich or powerful they are, I fuck back."

His eyes sharpened, but his mouth showed no anger, just a hint of amusement. "Which could net you a whole load of trouble." His words of warning did not match the look behind his eyes. He was still playing.

Hell sat straighter in her chair. "Unlike you, I got nothin' to lose. So when a bastard like you decided to play ball with me—I was like, hey, *game on*." She sighed, shook her head, and her shoulders relaxed. "But then your crazy-ass women started spewing all this shit about you, and I started liking you. And after they were done with their psycho tirades, I found myself wanting to protect you. Insane, huh?"

He grinned ear to ear. "No. Charming."

"Yeah, screw charming. I want my money, and then I'm leaving. You know, I kinda figured from the beginning that something was wrong with you and this whole job. Men like you don't hire single operators like me. Especially when you have Thompson on retainer and a whole security team at your disposal. You have, like, what? Navy SEALs protecting you? Like you wouldn't have hit them up to solve a blackmailing case? Come on."

"I disagree. Thompson has limits. He's not as good as everyone thinks he is. He has a great reputation, but he isn't good at subtleties. I needed a woman to handle Lindsay. And I don't want my security team knowing everything about me. But that wasn't the entire reason I hired you. I also wanted to test you. That wasn't the only case I want you to work for me."

She let out a loud laugh. He was saving face and making it up on the fly. "Sure you were."

"You don't believe me?"

"No. But I don't care what games you're playing, I'm not gonna work for you. You're as trustworthy as the PR director of your dad's oil company. I don't work for liars. I may admire your evilness, but I can't allow myself to be around it. Write me the check, and I'll be on my merry way."

His eyes shined, but his mouth went a bit harder. "Pays a hundred grand."

Her body stiffened like he'd thrown her in an ice-cold lake. She realized she'd stopped breathing, gasped for air, and held her chest to calm the wild heartbeats. "Sorry. Wait. A hundred grand." She coughed.

Hello? He almost got you!

She narrowed her eyes. "No, Mr. Black-hearted Satan Boy, I'm not making a bargain with the Devil."

"Hundred grand for a week's worth of work," Mephistopheles said with a wicked grin.

"No way. You're evil. You take revenge on those who cross you. I'm bound to piss you off at some point, and then you'll want revenge on me, and then you'll have three women wanting to kill your ass."

He looked at her with pity. "Do you really think you're that important?"

The cold blast of rich-boy truth made her gut cave in and her mouth drop open. "Whoa, you're an asshole."

He looked away, probably reviewing what he'd said to her, then glanced at her, unsure, and made a quick read of her. His brow twitched, and he touched his chin in an evaluation gesture.

She said *fuck you* with her eyes, allowed the hurt to turn into hate, and channeled it at him. Dickhead.

His eyes widened almost imperceptibly. He didn't know how to play her, and he'd taken a serious misstep.

Hell sensed his weakness and went for the kill. "Thanks for letting me see a window into your snobby, rotten interior. If you were smarter, you'd have played your cards closer to your vest, and you might have just reeled me in to play your twisted game. But I don't work for arrogant assholes who think I'm inferior. I may be flawed, but I have pride. I only work for people who respect me. You clearly don't respect me."

He closed off his expression. "You misunderstood me."

"No, I didn't. I'm done playing with you." She stood and turned to leave.

"My intent was not to insult you."

"Yes, it was. You've been playing mental chess with me ever since I walked in here this morning. You were just trying to gain control and power over me by belittling me and my importance to you."

"No, I didn't. I simply meant that I didn't think our working relationship would result in any further drama."

"Bullshit."

"I think you're afraid of me and are using any excuse to run."

She faced him, her shoulders squared. "No. I'm afraid of what I'd do to you," she said and meant it. "I've met and matched a hundred guys just like you. They all regretted taking me on." All but one. Marco Capasso had more power than God.

His composure came back with a vengeance. Power emanated from his core. He laughed, his eyes fiery with challenge. "You've never gone up against someone like me."

What a superiority complex! "I've gone against men who had much more power than you," she replied quietly.

He snickered. "Highly doubtful."

By the look in his eye, the man had no intention of stopping his games. He liked playing with her, and he was used to getting his way. While, for some reason, she still liked this guy, she hoped he didn't push it.

"Lots of information doesn't show up on reports, Collins. This is your last warning. You can fuck me," she said, breaking into a quick smile. She allowed her expression to go dead and icy. "But don't fuck *with* me." She sent him her fiercest nonverbal warning from deep within her—a super-charged blast of energy. She'd found visualizing super powers brought her the closest she'd ever come to possessing them.

This guy was clearly used to dealing with strong players. He held her gaze easily, his gray eyes amused and bright. "I like you, Miss Trent."

Dude could charm a lesbian out of her panties. She wanted to stay mad at him, but the spark in his eye and the super-charged energy field that radiated around him, combined with his undeniable charm were messing with her resolve. "Despite the fact that you're an immoral, depraved asshole, I like you, too, dude." *In another universe, I'd have already screwed you by now.* "But I'm not gonna work for you." She turned and walked toward the door.

"Two hundred grand."

She froze to the expensive plush carpet. Shiny new cars paraded through her mind. An iPad did the conga. She pictured her credit cards bills combusting into flames. Out of debt. Just like that.

Glancing back at him, she did a double take. Collins had a dark, predatory, and victorious look in his eye. A hungry smile on his face. Almost licking his lips at the triumph.

He didn't just want to play with her, he wanted to *own* her.

Despite her best efforts to stop her reaction, moisture welled between her legs, and her nipples went hard. Stupid hormonal response! While his deviousness was an absolute turn-on, Hell Trent wasn't for sale. Besides, just because her body wasn't done with players didn't mean her brain wanted anything to do with them.

She sent him a look that told him she was on to his game. "I was right. You sleep in a coffin with dirt from Fort Knox sprinkled on top."

He laughed, which lit up his whole face and made him twenty times more attractive. Easiest way to get Hell Trent into bed was to laugh at her jokes.

Her brain ordered her legs to back away while her body demanded she run over and jump on his big fat one. "Send the check for twenty grand to my office," she heard herself say as she backed toward the door. "Nice meetin' you, Collins." Thank God, her autopilot finally possessed some logic!

She stopped at the doorway, needing one last moment to memorize his face for her fantasy bin. Personality-challenged or not, Brad was the most prime cut of man meat her age she'd met in years. From his riveting gray eyes to his kissable lips and angular jaw, there wasn't one part of his exterior she didn't like. She gave a wistful sigh. "Kinda wish you weren't a rich, evil mofo and I'd met you somewhere else. Would have loved workin' you out, boy. Later."

She left and breezed through the outer office, congratulating herself on walking away from his bait. For once, she saw trouble in man form and turned around and went the other way. Huge step.

She grabbed the doorknob and pulled. A rustling sound came from behind her. She felt heat and smelled his cologne just as Brad reached around her and pressed the door closed.

She took in a quick breath, her heart leapt, and her body ordered her to drop and spread 'em.

A blast of awareness slapped her back to reality. *You do not want to screw Brad Collins! A) he's married and B) he's a son of a bitch.*

Forcing a withering look on her face, she rolled her eyes and sent him an exasperated glare. "Collins, I am so not..."

His handsome face inches away, his gaze captured hers. Dark, roiling, sexually charged energy swirled in his gray depths. Powerful. Heady.

His smoldering intensity plowed through her defenses and sent a wallop straight to her sex. Her clit throbbed. She got wetter.

"...fucking you," she finished in a weak, hypnotized voice.

His steel eyes heavy-lidded, he pulled her to him, his attention dropped to her mouth, and he kissed her.

A blast of hormones rocked her body in a ten-point sex-quake: her nipples turned to rock, her skin electrified, a burst of energy to her girl parts almost made her come. He tasted of bourbon, piney cologne, and his unique earthy flavor as he explored her mouth expertly—dominating, teasing, then conquering. His inner power enveloped her, knocking her off-center, making her soar. She starved for him, his touch, and his dick inside her.

He deepened the kiss, commanding her muscles to surrender.

Her knees and limbs turned to jelly. She was half-aware of clinging to him while making greedy animal noises in the back of her throat. She had to have him. Right then. If he refused to screw her, she'd kill him with her bare hands.

Warning! Sex Accident imminent! Cardinal Rules breach! Stop! You are about to bone a very rich, very married, and very depraved client! Disengage immediately!

Fuck that, roared her sex drive. Just once. One taste.

A hormonally foggy few seconds later, they were both naked, he wore a condom, and he was screwing the hell out of her on the leather couch in his office.

Nothing had ever felt so good or so right.

CHAPTER 8

After a spectacular sex fest, Hell collapsed onto her back on Brad's leather couch, her skin slippery against the smooth surface, her mind a near blank. Warm and fuzzy energy pulsed through her overly happy body. What a ride! Woo-hoo!

She'd known he'd be good but not *that* good. Wow.

Collins got up and walked over to his desk to remove and throw away the condom, giving her an awesome view of his perfectly rounded taut buns, long legs, and V-shaped back.

Her body shook with aftershocks and pulsed with joy. Her sex organs hadn't been this happy in years.

The dude was magic. The best lay since Josh. While she came with her other boyfriends, she didn't come like this. Not these atomic orgasms.

She couldn't speak for a long time. "Holy God," she finally managed to croak. She cleared her throat. "That was outrageous. I haven't come like that in forever. I thought the other guy was a fluke and I was doomed. Damn, that was insane. Thank God there's another one! Hope springs eternal!"

He shot her a hungry grin and tossed the tissue-wrapped condom into his garbage can. "You've only had good sex with two men? I have a hard time believing that."

"I don't lie, and I don't flatter people. I forgot my body could do that. I mean, don't get me wrong, I come with my other guys, but not like *that*. Thanks for reminding me, and ruining me. Shit."

He laughed and returned to her. Sitting on the couch, he ran his long fingers through her hair, then down the side of her face in an affectionate gesture, surprising her. "I thought you had a whole stable of good lovers."

A bit taken aback by his intimate contact, but not unhappy, she nodded. "I thought so, too. But tonight I discovered that I have a whole stable of *mediocre* lovers." Another blast of joy echoed through her nether regions. "Damn, these delicious aftershocks are so fun! You made me come *hard*."

He flashed her a white-toothed grin.

"I love the way you tuned in on me. You read me perfectly and gave me exactly what I needed, when I needed it. Like it was instinctual with you. That's a rare quality. Most dudes, no matter how sweet they are, normally get caught up in the act and focus on their own pleasure. It's the rare man who concentrates so much energy on his partner."

"I don't think I could stand another compliment."

"Don't let it go to your heads. I'm not actually complimenting you. This is an unbiased assessment of your sexual abilities. This venture capital thing is a complete waste of your time. You need to hire yourself out as a sex machine. You owe it to the women of Earth," she said earnestly, then grinned.

He laughed, his face shining, his eyes sparkling.

Another joy aftershock rocked her womb, and she grabbed herself, fully enjoying the rush. "God, this feels so good. Boo-yah!" She flashed him the rock-and-roll sign.

Rarely had she seen a happier expression on a man. Some part of her warned that she might have just created a monster. *Right.* This was the first and last time they'd see each other. Now that he'd had his little conquest, he'd get bored quick. Probably treated the global female population as his own personal sex catalog.

"Hey, Collins, that a bathroom through there?" She pointed to a dark wood-paneled door behind his desk.

"Yes."

"Excellent." Hell quickly dashed to the bathroom to pee and ensure her makeup hadn't turned her face into a Picasso painting.

When she returned, she'd expected him to be dressed, but he was still naked and sitting on the couch. He lit up when he saw her and patted the cushions next to him.

As soon as she sat, he took her in his arms and kissed her. Then he pushed her back on the wide couch and laid next to her, giving her a full body hug, his gaze covetous and appreciative. "You think I'm good, honey, you're on fire."

He touched her breast, then moved down and closed his mouth over the other.

Her hormones sang, and she ground her hips against him. Sinful what he could do with just his tongue and lips.

He pulled away and sent her an amused look. "Exactly what words are tattooed on your ass?"

"It's the Mattel logo."

He burst out in a quick laugh.

She turned so he could see it. He rubbed his hand over her bun, and she kissed his sinewy neck, relishing his scent, warmth, and taste. Dude was serious man candy.

"Why exactly did you feel compelled to get this tat?"

"Barbie and I were born in the same year. Your year, too, actually. Her logo on my ass was the closest I was ever going to get to looking like her."

He hugged her. "You are so funny. I love the skull and crossbones here," he said, touching the small tat by her sex. She thought about shifting over fast so he'd touch her where she really wanted. "What about the skull on your upper arm here with the ribbon above it that says 'Best Before' and some Roman numerals?"

"That's my expiration date."

Frowning, he cocked his head to one side. "Expiration date?"

"I always wanted to know when I was going to die, and I checked, but I don't have an expiration date, so I thought I'd give myself one."

He gave a little snort of laughter. "So when will you die?"

"Sometime after I'm a hundred and four. Note how this says: Best Before," she said, pointing to the lettering. "Originally I was going to say 'Expires On,' but realized that sounded too final and fatal. This way, I can live longer than a hundred and four, I'll just be a little stale."

His gray eyes danced, his smile lines deep. "This all proves it."

"What?"

"I've never met anyone like you before in my life, and I'm very glad that I finally have." He gave her a quick kiss, then said, "Now I need to take a tour of your body with my mouth." His smile turned predatory.

Her clit zinged, and an intense wave of lust rushed through her sex. Dear God, this man was a sexual Svengali who'd taken complete control over her body. Wowza.

He lightly bit her ear, then homed in on the most sensitive part of her neck and sucked and nibbled until she squealed and pushed him away.

He laughed, seeming delighted with her.

She couldn't help but enjoy his attention. Most guys jumped out of bed afterwards, wanting a drink or a snack. In fact, all her guys, with the exception of Roman—and Capasso, but he didn't count— abandoned her about a minute or two after they came. This guy was so fun, and so hot.

But she had to admit—as much as it embarrassed her—his most attractive feature was the mirror of her in his eyes. He seemed to be really into her. The last man to look at her like this was Josh.

Hell's early emotional warning system buzzed her brain, making her muscles harden. One too many Josh similarities for comfort and far too much fun for a Sex Accident with a married man. Time to end this lost morality challenge before she found herself caring about the jerk. "Hey, I should get going pretty soon."

His body stiffened, and the look in his eyes sharpened. "Have a date?"

Was that jealousy behind his eyes? Nah, she must be seeing things. "No, actually. Kind of a dry week until you came along. Just my night for paperwork, laundry, and crap. All the exciting middle-class bullshit."

He relaxed. "So you'd rather do paperwork and laundry than…" He sent her a devilish smile and stroked her thighs.

Her body juiced up and revved into Full Sex Mode, her mind filled with images of his hard dick pummeling her. "Ooooh. Uh, maybe not."

Hell Trent! Time to leave! Once, fine, but twice? You are implying that you care!

He sent her a deadly cool, sensual stare. "Why don't you stay?" His husky, smoky voice went straight to her center, and she resisted the urge to touch herself.

Look, you already fucked him, what does it matter? reasoned her libido.

Good argument. She'd already broken her rules. Might as well fail spectacularly.

She worked hard to maintain an amused yet neutral expression. "I'm up for an encore. Are you?"

He grabbed her hand and put it on his rock-hard cock.

"I'll take that as a yes," she said. Then she pushed him down and rode him.

Off the scale.

AFTERWARDS, AS THEY LAY IN EACH OTHER'S ARMS, SHE CAUGHT THE time on a wall clock in the shape of a gold Krugerrand. "Freakin' nine-thirty? We've shagged for *an hour and a half*? No wonder I'm sore."

"Wuss," he said with a teasing grin.

"You're a drug."

"Are you addicted?"

"If I were, I'd head straight to detox. You're dangerous." Her brow ached, and she rubbed it. "Ow. My face is killing me from my orgasm expression."

He cracked up.

"I'm serious. My face hurts from coming." She massaged her burning muscles. "After seeing those pics and talking to Lindsay, I knew I had to have you. Well, before I part ways with you forever. But God, you are effin' *fun.*"

He ran his hand over her knee and caressed her upper thigh. "I'd like to see you again."

She made a face at him. "Why do guys always feel compelled to say that even when they have no intention of seeing the chick again? Honestly, no games here, dude. I'm beyond them. But this was a really good time."

"I mean it. Don't you feel the connection?"

"Yeah." *Connection, my ass.* Men always said stupid crap like that after sex. Especially good sex.

His expression remained open. There was a pause as she studied him. Then it hit her. He wasn't just saying a platitude, he'd meant what he said. "Oh." She tensed, and her brow furrowed hard. "*Wait, you actually want to see me again?*"

He ran his hand down the side of her face, sending shivers through her. "Yeah. I do."

Ignoring her body's response to him, she made an exasperated noise and looked at him like he was crazy. "Are you nuts?"

He smiled, clearly taking her question as acquiescence. "No."

She gave a short laugh. "*Right.* No way."

His smile vanished, and his attention on her intensified. Then he frowned, seeming confused. Clearly this man rarely heard the word no. "Why not?"

Endless reasons. "Let's be happy with this. Leave me with a good memory of you."

"I could leave you with lots of good memories."

She let out a long, heavy sigh. "Dude, your dick is heroin, and you're immoral. Besides, how could I have become this 'important' to you?" She sent him a don't-bullshit-me look.

He winced, looked away, and the pain lines around his eyes went deep. Not the reaction she'd expected. She'd thought he'd throw the words back in her face. "I apologize. I was leveraging for control—very cleverly I thought—and then said that stupid thing. Sorry."

"Truthfully?" She studied his expression.

He made eye contact with no duplicity on his face. "Yeah. Felt bad as soon as I said it. Came out wrong."

"What were you trying to say?"

"Anything that would make you stay involved with me."

"You wanted me *personally*?"

"Yeah. I wanted this, I wanted you." He kissed her, pulled away, and sent her a sexy smile.

A thrill went through her, and she couldn't believe she was horny again. This guy kept shocking and surprising her. While flattering, it was weird that he liked her this much. Didn't fit his profile. He shouldn't be able to stand her, let alone be sexually attracted to her.

"What are you doing next Saturday?" he asked. He chewed on her neck, sending a cascade of pleasure through her, giving her goose bumps all down her spine.

She pushed him back. "No. Brad, look, I like you, but this is it. Cardinal rule: I don't commit adultery. You're the first Sex Accident I've had since I made my rules, and you'll be my last foray into the Dark Side of the Marital Force."

He seemed undaunted. "We both don't want commitment. We both want good sex. Why not? Afraid you'll fall for me?" He challenged her, his eyes dark.

She laughed at his audacity. She really liked this prick. "No. I haven't fallen in love, uh, ever. I don't do love."

"Really? I thought you were married."

"Look who's talking about love in a marriage."

He gave her a sharp look, then rolled his eyes. "Point taken."

"However, I've never cheated on a spouse, yet I certainly understand why you're cheating on Sherry. I just don't know why you'd stay married to someone who treats you so badly."

"That's because you don't understand my world. And she doesn't treat me badly. I wouldn't let her."

"Bullshit. She treats you like shit. She hopes your heart murmur will get rid of you. The only reason she hasn't killed you herself is because she can't figure out how to get away with it." Her stomach tightened. Oops. Had she meant to say that? Damn stupid sex hormones! Loosened her lips! Both sets!

"What?"

Hell winced. She hated her blabbermouth gene. But what if Sherry wasn't kidding? Brad's lovemaking skills would be a loss to the world.

He squeezed her arm. "Hell? What did she say? She really wants me dead? She actually said that?"

Hell propped up on an elbow and met his gaze. "Unfortunately." She filled in Brad on Sherry's diatribe about him.

He shook his head, then lay back against the couch, grabbed a cushion, and put it under his neck. After making sure Hell was comfortably nestled beside him, he twisted his mouth. "Every time I try to talk to her, she leaves the room. I thought it was menopause or something. Figures she's not over Dan. No wonder they're always at the house. I couldn't figure out why she kept inviting them over. She's continually trashing Lindsay. You think she's serious about killing me?"

"Probably all hot air. But if I were you, I'd keep my eyes open for a while. Just to make sure. Alert your bodyguards that she made some threats. All those other murdered rich husbands didn't think their wives were capable."

His jaw went tight, his eyes fiery. "Bitch. Cutting me off emotion-ally and physically wasn't enough for her, she wants me dead and that asshole Dan Banning living in my house. Wish I could divorce her."

"Why can't you?"

Shrugging, he pursed his lips. "Her father just died, and there are complications with the partnership."

"Jesus. You know, you always have this image of rich people having it all. But not one of you— you, Lindsay, or Sherry—has anything of true value in your life—meaningful relationships—and all three of you are in pain."

Brad chuckled and examined her face. "You think I'm in pain?"

"Yeah. I just don't think you're in touch with it. I think it's a low-level program running deep in your subconscious. I think you're used to being around people who don't like you. You certainly aren't getting the emotional wealth you deserve. Your father's mean to you, your wife's is a total bitch, and you've got a whacko stalker girlfriend. Is Gwen nice to you?"

He clearly didn't see what she was talking about. "Everyone's nice to me. Even Sherry. At least on the surface."

"Your definition of nice and mine are worlds apart. Here you are a bazillionaire, and all I can see is a poor, deprived man living in an emotional desert. Can't believe I'm freakin' feeling sorry for you."

The edges of his mouth quirked.

"Clearly, I'm sick."

He smiled and hugged her tight to his chest. "I think it's charming. What about you? Are you happy?" He pulled away and seemed genuinely interested in the answer.

"Trying. No. I don't know." She lifted one shoulder. "I just get a sense that you and I have some emotional crap in common. In the past, I've also let everyone close to me be mean to me. I see myself in you. Funny, huh? We couldn't be more different people."

He ran his hand through her hair. "I don't know. There's something about you that's very familiar."

"Me?"

"You," he said and kissed her. After a long and thorough exploration of her mouth—making her entire body come alive—he sent her a sweet smile.

A rush of joy went through her, centering on her heart. Loud alarms sounded again. "Well, this has been fun. But I must leave."

He locked his arms around her. "Just a while longer. You know something? I think you're actually a softie, Miss Trent. You come off as this tough punker chick, but deep down you really care about people and are quite sweet. You're not at all who you seem to be."

"And I *seemed* to be a screw-up, which is why you hired me."

He sent her a penetrating look. "No."

"No?"

"No. I hired you because I thought you were cute," he said, the corners of his gray eyes crinkling.

Hell's breath hitched, and she cocked her head to one side. The admission seemed to come out of nowhere. And implied that he'd seen her before. But they'd met only that morning. "What?"

"Yeah. Saw you on TV, and there was a spark in your eyes. You said something sassy to the news reporter and made everyone laugh."

She relaxed against him. TV. Right. "I did?" He wasn't the first man to pursue her based upon her TV interviews. Which she found positively weird.

"Yes. Then, about six months ago, we met." He pushed her back a bit and searched her expression, his own unreadable.

She gave him a double take. Was he kidding? He didn't seem to be joking. She scoured her mind for the memory. Nothing. "No, we didn't. I would have remembered you. You're hot."

"You were pretty drunk at the time."

Her stomach tightened. She swallowed hard and grimaced. "Oh, dear. Where? When?"

"At a club in the City. You were out with two other girls—women —and were sitting at a table next to us. And honey, you were on a roll." He raised his brows and laughed.

Heat crept into her face. *Uh-oh.* "Where?" She could have said anything. A part of her began to look for convenient places in the room to hide.

"At the new place, uh, what's the name? Martini bar in SOMA."

"Belladonna's?"

He sent her a knowing smile. "That was it."

Her stomach balled, and she groaned. Worst fear realized. The Night of Five Cosmos. She crossed her arms as best she could while in his embrace. She only remembered tiny flashes of that evening. Mostly burned in on her mind was the Hangover From Hades the next morning. "Holy crap. But you were there? Where?" A table of fifty and sixty-something bald men appeared in her mind. "Wait. Were you in the group of guys sitting behind me?"

"Yeah."

She gave a little gasp of recognition. "Oh, my God, you were in the Dick Cheney Boy Band!"

He leaned in and squinted. "The *what*?"

Hell tried to stop, but burst out laughing. "Sorry. That's what we called you. Were the rest of your friends bald?"

"I... Maybe so."

"I remember." She nodded. "The Viagra Boys' Choir." She let out some loud guffaws.

"*What?*" The look in his eye was a bit heated, but he still wasn't as mad at her as he should be. Good ol' sex hormones. Natural Prozac.

"Sorry," she said, snickering. "Best lines of the evening. That I can remember, anyway. So funny."

"To you. Viagra Boys' Choir. Dick Cheney Boy Band," he muttered, looking a bit perturbed, but also like he was fighting a smile. "Christ."

"My friends were not impressed with you guys. I'm sorry, but I only have vague memories of that night. How much did we talk?"

"Not much. Your friends wouldn't let you. They didn't exactly hide their contempt for us. But you were quite friendly."

"Jesus, I hardly remember anything. I hate to ask what I said. I remember laughing a lot. Frieda brings out the worst in my conversations. How bad did I get?"

"You were talking about wanting to have sex with Gavin Newsom."

She winced, groaned, and smacked her forehead. But she wasn't surprised. The ex-mayor of San Francisco, and current Lieutenant Governor of California, was a *hunk*.

"That you'd planned to drive around San Francisco with your

head hanging out of the car and your mouth open, just in case his cock happened to be there."

She gasped and covered her mouth. "*I said that?*"

His smile widened. "Yes. 'You never know where Gavin Newsom's cock is gonna be, and you gotta be ready,'" he said, slurring his words and acting out her gestures, doing a rather good imitation of a very drunk Hell.

"Oh, God," she said, mashing her brow into her hand. "In public and everything. I can't take myself anywhere."

"Then you went on a long, involved description of sitting on some guy's bathroom floor, trying to put in a diaphragm, but it slipped out of your grip and launched across the room, stuck to the wall, and oozed down. Not only was the story detailed, the accompanying pantomime was equally informative." His eyes twinkled. He loved telling her this.

Seemed like she was getting some Karma from her earlier revelations about his life.

She rolled her eyes, her cheeks and ears burning hot. "I told that story? Christ. Clearly on Cosmo overload."

"Are you...? No." He tucked his finger under her chin and turned her face toward his. "Are you *blushing*?"

Her face flushed more intensely. She looked away. "No."

"You are!" He laughed and hugged her. "Delightful. I would not have said you were capable. Miss Helen Trent, famous private detective and rabble-rouser, blushing. If I hadn't seen it with my own eyes, I would have never believed it."

"Christ. How embarrassing."

"Blushing or telling the diaphragm story?"

"Both."

"I think you're charming."

"I'm never getting that tanked again."

"You'd had plenty. We went there to discuss a deal, but once you got started, we stopped talking altogether and bought you a round to keep you going."

Her cheeks felt like they were sunburned. "No wonder I'd had five. Four is my maximum and all I planned on drinking. I was wondering where the other one came from. I'm sorry, Brad, but I really don't remem—" Suddenly, his face came into her mind, but he was wearing a goatee. She pointed at him. "You had a beard."

"Yes. Just shaved it off a month ago."

"I remember you! I thought you were cute, but my girls thought you guys were all creeps."

"*Fortune 500* creeps. Not one man there was worth less than a few billion. After you gave me your card, your friends whisked you away. I thought they were going to beat me up."

"They get protective over me when I drink. But they're gonna freak out when I tell them we dissed a group of billionaires."

"Your card is how I found out who you were. I didn't recognize you out of the black leather jacket, like I'd seen you wear on TV and in the pictures on your website. You wore some smokin'-hot tight leopard pants and a sexy black tank that night at Belladonna's. Wait." He pointed to the trail of clothing near his office door. "I think that's the shirt over there on the floor. But the pants were different."

"Yeah, I was wearing my regular leopard-printed pants that night, instead of the red ones I wore tonight."

He laid back, his vision drifted, and a dreamy smile came over his chiseled face. "But the way you danced with your girls, wow. I couldn't stop watching you." His dark gray gaze met hers. "I'd thought I'd wanted you before, but after that night, I couldn't get you out of my mind. I thought about calling you, but I had a feeling you wouldn't remember. I had to figure out another way to meet you."

Warmth spread through her. "Really. So you hired me to scare away Lindsay, and because you wanted to bonk me."

He grinned. "The scaring-away-Lindsay part was an afterthought. All I really wanted was to engineer some time with you."

The warmth within her turned blazing. She could feel her head inflate. So flattering! "So you musta been pretty pissed when I attacked you first thing."

His eyebrows shot high, and he sent her a look like he'd survived a typhoon. "Uh, that's putting it mildly."

"You probably had a whole different scenario in mind. I'd walk into your office, recognize you, and then bone you on your sofa here."

He laughed, but she could tell she wasn't far off.

She narrowed her eyes. "Wait a minute. You thought you'd seduce me by lying to me and making an ass out of me?"

He winced and looked away. "No. I, uh— Okay, my plan was clearly flawed. At first, I was going to have you work a real case for me, but then Lindsay freaked out on me. I decided to kill two birds with one stone. Sorry—"

"You really thought I was that stupid?"

He finally looked at her, no pretense on his face. "No, I thought I was that smart."

She laughed, and he joined her, his expression sheepish, his cheeks a bit pink.

"Jesus, Brad. Some plan, dude."

He shrugged. "I wanted you. Then I found out that you don't sleep with married men."

Surprising. "Thompson found that out?" Impressive. Her rival was getting better at his PI game.

"Yeah."

She chuckled, then sighed. "Lost my mind apparently here. I have that rule in place for a reason."

"Let's forget about it."

"I can't just throw—"

He silenced her with a hard kiss, then pushed away and looked her dead in the eye. "You're hotter than any woman I've ever been with, and I want to see you again." He cupped her face, and his lips closed on hers before she could respond.

Hell's brain went off-line with lust.

CHAPTER 9

Pumped full of righteous indignation, her heart beating hard—yet with a tight and nervous stomach—Hell knocked on the door of the Presidential Suite of the Four Seasons Hotel in Palo Alto. Brad Collins had driven her to madness, and he would pay the price. How was she supposed to move on and pretend she didn't want him anymore when he wouldn't stop pestering her?

A second later, he opened the door, and she had to hold back a gasp. His brilliant smile derailed her for a moment, then she revved up into The Wrath of Hell mode. "What *the fuck* is wrong with you?"

"Well, hello to you, too," he said, radiating extreme pleasure. The jerk.

She blasted by him and into a luxurious suite overlooking the lower San Francisco Bay. Spinning, she faced him. Much better-looking than she remembered. His deep-set gray eyes appeared brighter and more expressive, the carved planes of his face crisper, and his angled jaw more cut. His heavy dark brow set off his prominent straight nose, which was matched by his impressive chin. With his sleek shaved head—along with his chic well-tailored suit that highlighted his broad shoulders and trim waist—this dude was one horrible temptation.

Blocking the memories of the other parts of him and the magic they worked, she forced herself to stay on point. She was there to stop this man from harassing her and nothing else. She thought of the million texts, the flowers, and the unending phone calls this bastard had tormented her with for the entire previous week. "What are you thinking? You can't have me, okay? What the hell is it going to take to get through to that pinhead of yours? How many times do I have to tell you no before you leave me the hell alone?"

It was as if she'd complimented him on his suit. His expression remained happy and bright, his mouth curved with amusement. She wanted to hit him.

"Why are you looking so goddamned happy and amused?" she demanded.

"Because I am happy and amused. Would you like an ice-cold Heineken?"

She'd expected a retort. It took her a second to realize what he'd said. "What?"

"A Heineken?" He gestured toward the other side of the room.

A wet bar lined the opposite wall. Bottles of wine and various types of booze sat arranged on top of the long black bar, along with an array of gleaming glassware.

It was then she spotted her Holy Grail. She took in a short breath. Several chilling Heinekens sat in a shiny silver ice bucket next to the wine collection. A little chime rang in her pleasure center, music swelled in the Pavlovian Response System of her brain, and she salivated. By the sweat on the bottles, she could tell the beer was the perfect temperature. Her beer alarm had been going off for the last two hours, and she'd had to ignore it because she'd had to drive. Damn it, she'd had a crappy day, and the beer looked so good.

What the *hell* was she thinking? She slapped herself mentally. "No, I don't want a goddamned Heineken. I'm not staying, I'm leaving." She pointed her bandaged forefinger at him, trying to appear commanding and all-powerful. "Now listen, Collins, you may be able to get your way with—"

He walked over to the bar.

Her muscles hardened with anger and frustration. "Hey, I'm talking to you."

He turned to her. "I'm listening. Go ahead." He grabbed a bottle of wine and a glass. "I just want a glass of wine to help me digest your points."

His manner was self-assured, confident, and relaxed. Like she wasn't yelling at him. Like they were on a date, and he was listening to her talk about her day. Insufferable!

"Fine. Look, dude, I'm flattered that you want me. I can't deny we had some hellacious righteous sex. You're on a very short list of the best fucks of my life to date. But that doesn't matter." A loud voice from her libido begged to differ. "What matters here are my morals and my rules. I start breaking them, and I'm no better than those skeevy jerks I follow around and catch having affairs. I need to have a code of ethics, or I don't respect myself."

He finished pouring himself a glass of red and joined her. She tried to ignore her hormones dancing at the sight of him, his intoxicating piney-earthy scent, and the power he exuded. He indicated the couch.

She crossed her arms. "No. I'm not sitting, and I'm not staying."

"Do you mind if I sit?"

"No. What the hell do I care what you do? I'm leaving after I get done with my big speech."

"Okay." He sat down.

She glanced down at the coffee table in front of the couch, and her eyes popped. An astounding array of hors d'oeuvres was laid out on the glass-topped, dark wood table. A platter of sushi and sashimi, smoked salmon on baguette, tea sandwiches, a cheese and meat plate with too many varieties of each to count, and bowls of various chopped salads. Plus a plate of fresh-cut fruit, a platter with chocolate-dipped strawberries, and wineglasses full of chocolate mousse. A feast. Including many of her favorites.

Her radar went up. Too many of her favorites. He'd investigated her likes and dislikes. She turned on him with narrowed eyes. "You just happened to have my favorite foods and beer here? What is this? Some kinda Hell Trent Sex Trap?"

He didn't react. "Uh, actually, I was hungry and just ordered some stuff."

She homed in on the look behind his eyes. A gleam lay deep within. He was playing her. Jerk. "Like I believe that."

"Honey, you can believe whatever you want, but I am hungry. Do you mind if I eat?"

"Why would I? Do what you want."

"Great, I'm starved. Just flew in late last night from New York, didn't sleep well, and then today I had meetings all day. Finally got in a nap, but I haven't eaten much." He took a big bite of what looked to be amazing sushi.

Hell's stomach growled. Crap. She'd made plans to meet with friends in an hour, specifically so she wouldn't be tempted to stay. She'd been so focused on what she was going to tell Brad—and she'd been so nervous about seeing him again—she'd forgotten to eat.

"Look, I can't stay," she told her hunger as much as him.

"Okay," he said. "So? Your big speech?"

"Well, yeah. Look, I like you, okay? You're freakin' hot. But at the end of the day, all that matters are my morals and integrity. Marriage is a big deal to me."

He swallowed, wiped his mouth with a napkin, and faced her. "You were married to someone who respected you, loved you, supported you, enjoyed sex with you, and wanted to spend every moment of his life with you."

"He did."

"You had a real marriage. I've never had that. I'm married in name only for the sake of the family business. It's a business arrangement."

She gestured toward him. "But you had kids together and—"

"Sherry wants me dead. Sherry loves Dan. She's never loved me, she doesn't respect me, and she hates me," he said flatly. "You heard her say all those things. I ask you, is that a real marriage? Is that the person I should stay faithful to?"

Hell sighed. "Look, I won't argue that Sherry and you don't have a good marriage, or anything I would even consider a marriage. But I still believe in the sanctity of the union. I believe you two should divorce if you're going to be seeing other women."

"Agreed. But until my father dies, I have to stay with her or my son and daughter will inherit a crumbling empire, and I won't do that to them. A group of investors is following my every move. If they even get a hint I might divorce Sherry, they'll move in for the kill." He turned back to the food and perused the tea sandwiches.

"Why don't you separate?"

"Because Sherry would love nothing more than to destroy what our grandfathers and fathers built just to spite me." He chose an egg salad on wheat triangle. "She'd hurt the children just to get at me."

"How can you stay in the same house with that woman?" Hell demanded.

"I don't. Well, I do. But ever since you told me, I've been avoiding her. I actually haven't seen her in four days." He ate a bite of sandwich.

Hell glanced at the Heineken bucket and then turned back to Collins.

After taking a sip of wine, he said, "That first day after I saw you, I began paying closer attention to what she said and how she acted toward me. I was shocked. I think I've had my head up my ass for the last twenty-six years or in the clouds—"

Hell fought a smile. "I'd prefer the clouds."

He chuckled, then became serious. "Because it was all so plain. The truth was all over her face." He finished his egg salad and began examining the sushi plate again. "I honestly didn't see what was really going on until you pointed it out. That line about feeling sorry for me for living in an emotional desert really shook me."

She'd actually gotten through to him? Or was he putting on an act to trap her?

"You shut down because you had to," she ventured, playing along with him. "But you kinda had to marry her, didn't you? For the sake of the family fortunes?"

He nodded. "Yes. But there were four other girls from prominent families I liked who would have worked just as well in my estimation. True, my father wanted the marriage with Sherry and pressed me. But I didn't mind because I loved her. Probably because she's just like my mother: cold, ruthless, and remote." He chose a California roll and put the whole thing in his mouth.

He managed to eat the entire piece without opening his lips or losing any rice. No way could Hell do that. Rich people must have to practice that kind of stuff so they never embarrassed themselves in front of other rich people.

"I can't believe you heard me. But it makes me really happy to hear you say all that. You deserve better, dude."

"What about you? Are you getting what you deserve?"

She was so tuned into him it took her a second to focus back on herself. And lately, she hadn't really wanted to think much about her life. Because it sucked.

"I've shocked you."

Sighing heavily, she said, "No, I'm, uh...I don't know what the hell I'm doing, truthfully." She toed the maroon carpet.

"Why not?"

She shrugged. "Guess I'm in transition. Yeah, that's a good word for it. From chaos to order, hopefully."

"How long have you been in chaos?"

"Since Josh died—how the hell did you just get me to stay here and talk about my life?" she asked, flinging her arms outward. "Christ, you are good at getting me off point. I have to go. I like you, but I'm not doing this." She took a step toward the door.

"Am I to understand the sole reason for your decision is because I'm married? You have no other objections?"

She stopped and turned back to him. "Well, I'd prefer it if you were poorer. I'm not sure you can relate to me."

"I think we relate pretty well," he said with a knowing grin.

"Certainly, we are sexually compatible." She raised her brows and nodded. "More like sexually combustible."

"Exactly."

"That's not the point." She took a step backwards. "I can't do this." The Heineken called to her, but she ignored its siren song.

"So because I'm rich and temporarily married—"

"Temporarily?"

"Do you honestly think I'm going to stay married to a woman who wants me dead?"

No duplicity on his face, but he was contradicting his earlier statements. "Your kids' inheritance."

"For the last week, ever since I saw you, I've had my lawyers working twenty-four-seven on a way for me to get out of my travesty of a marriage. I will not be married to that woman for longer than is absolutely necessary."

Wow. She really had gotten through to him. Cool. "Good for you."

"What about when I divorce Sherry? Would you see me then? Or are your real objections about my wealth?"

"Uh." This stopped her. What if he did leave Sherry? Would she sleep with him again?

Well, duh, of course.

But something was wrong here. Her stomach was uneasy. A voice screamed at her from the back of her mind, but she couldn't make out the words.

The beer begged her to drink it.

"Why don't you just have one?"

She snapped her attention to him. "What?"

One side of his perfect mouth turned up, and his eyes sparkled. "Why don't you just have a beer? You've been staring at that bucket longingly for the last few minutes."

"Son of a bitch! You are such a pain in the ass. I shouldn't have come. I should have just shined you on." She stared at the beer again. How could one tiny Heineken hurt her? It was just sitting there. He clearly wasn't going to drink it. Would probably throw it out after she left. The maid would get it. In two steps she was at the bar, grabbing a beer. "Christ. I'm so weak! I feel so stupid."

"Why? Because you're drinking a beer?"

"No, because I came here, and I promised myself I wouldn't. And yes, because I can't resist the sight of these effing beers." She popped the top off the bottle and took a nice long draw. The super-cold liquid bubbled deliciously across her tongue and slid down her throat. Her brain did a happy dance, and her entire body flooded with joy. Heaven. She couldn't help herself and took another drink. "Wow, this is the perfect temperature. God, this tastes good."

Collins busied himself with the meat and cheese platter.

Hell finally sat across from him to finish her beer. She'd slam this sucker and then take off. No matter how hungry she was, she wasn't staying.

Damn, he was such a beautiful man. So masculine. Perfectly shaped shaved head. Gorgeous gray eyes that shone brightly with blue and green specks. His beckoning mouth, those magic hands. His hard cock.

The realization slammed her right between the eyes. The truth about why she'd come. She'd been lying to herself all along. Her muscles tightened, and her jaw locked. "Goddamn it! I am such an idiot! I'm so humiliated. Why do I do this to myself?" She threw her head in her hands.

"I hate to ask."

Her face burned hot. She gestured wildly, her body pumping with conflicting emotions. "I'm so ashamed. I can't even stick to my own goddamned rules. If I'd really wanted to get rid of you, you'd be gone. But clearly the only reason I showed up here was not to yell at you but to bonk you. You knew it the moment I showed up, didn't you? That amused and happy look you haven't been able to wipe off your face because you've known ever since I got here that you won."

His eyes shined. He twitched his shoulders. "I'd hoped. You're very unpredictable. But I knew if I managed to get you here, it would up my odds."

She held her head to stop it from exploding. He'd played her! And she'd helped him! Because she liked him so much! Intolerable! "I hate myself!"

"Why? Because we have fun together?"

She finally couldn't stand it any longer and jumped to her feet. She gestured with her whole body and let out her pent-up frustration. "No, because you're married and rich and powerful and horrible and you lied to me when I first met you, and I don't want to be associated with people who do all this mind-fucking and have all this power and craziness and wives and bodyguards and this big ol' honkin' mansion in Atherton and a freakin' zillion-dollar rare car collection," she said all in one breath. She gasped for air and continued with the same fervor. "I've had relationships with powerful men, and they always screw me over. You could destroy me if I pissed you off enough. I don't want to be destroyed."

As the words left her mouth, a halogen bulb went off in her mind, and she froze in place mid-gesture.

Brad was hitting all her Marco Capasso buttons. The power, the prestige, the fancy clothes, the arrogance, the self-assuredness, the bad-boy vibe, the trappings, the money. Everything.

Her heart raced, and sweat broke out all over. "Oh, shit," she said in a quiet voice. Brad was just a nicer, cuter, sexier version of Capasso. No wonder her alarms had been sounding.

"Hell? Why are you looking at me like that? Are you okay?"

She eyed the door. "I can't do this. I'm not goin' here again."

Brad got up and came over to her, but she slipped away, making sure there was a chair between them.

"Why? What did I do?"

Twitchy, she looked between the door and him. "Nothing. It's what you could do to me." Hell took a step toward the exit. If she had walked away from Capasso at this stage of their relationship, she would have gotten away. She'd be free now.

"Hell, please, will you tell me what's going on? You're looking at me completely differently, and your face has gone white. Who destroyed you?"

"No one. I have to go." If she took three huge steps, she could make it outside before he caught her.

Brad approached her, adrenaline jolted her, and she recoiled. He immediately stopped and held up his hands to show her he was no threat. "Please wait. You're reacting to someone else, aren't you? Someone powerful hurt you, and you think I'm going to do the same thing."

Her heart beating out of her chest, sweat trickled between her shoulder blades. She edged toward the door. "You could. You have the power to ruin my life and me. You could kill me, get rid of the body, and make it seem as if I never existed in the first place. You could wipe me off the face of the Earth with one payoff."

Brad didn't make a move toward her, but his face relaxed, and his expression became sympathetic. "Hell, you've investigated my life. How many people have I killed?" he asked in a gentle tone.

He had a point, but her body was certain she was still in grave danger. "Uh, well, none."

"How many people have I wiped off the face of the Earth?"

"None, but look—"

"How many people have I destroyed?"

"Okay, a few business rivals."

"Right. Any women? Have I hurt any women other than a normal breakup? Have I ever hit one or ruined one or destroyed one or killed one?"

This stopped her. Shit. The PTSD was so strong, maybe she was overreacting. She checked his eyes. Much more kindness than Capasso. While Brad had a roguish side to him, he didn't have the darkness at his core that Capasso did. At first that darkness turned her on because she didn't understand it. But once she saw him in action, she knew. That darkness was evil. A narcissism so great he could kill her and believe it had been all her fault. He'd convinced himself that he'd saved her life with that beating.

"Hell? Have I?"

"No."

"You pride yourself on reading people. You've studied me. You know nearly everything about me. Am I capable of doing to you what he did? You probably ignored the signs he gave off in the beginning, didn't you?"

How could he read her mind? "Yeah." She took a deep breath and rubbed her eyes. "Give me a second here." Only when the cool liquid hit her tongue did she realize she'd walked right past Brad and grabbed another beer.

Reeling, her body at battle stations, her mind splintered into memories of defending herself from Capasso and fantasies of how she'd defend herself from Brad. She tried to ground herself in reality, but her mind was out of control.

Glancing over at him, she forced herself to be in the moment. Would Brad Collins hurt her?

She couldn't really picture him beating her. Or stalking her. Even though she got a hint that he wanted control over her. Maybe that was what had triggered her reaction. There was a possessive look in the back of his eyes. But had he hurt anyone like Marco had? No. Had he killed people? No.

"Am I anything like the other guy?" he asked.

"I'm sorting that out now." As far as she knew, Brad was an amazing lover who had lavished more attention on her than any of her previous dates save Josh. No danger except for his initial lies.

His gaze seemed to look through her to deep within. "He didn't just hurt you emotionally. You crossed him somehow, and he physically hurt you. Didn't he?"

Hell turned away, but she didn't want to leave. She wanted to screw Brad and forget all about Marco goddamned Capasso. She drank half the beer before realizing that she hadn't answered him. Shit.

Brad approached her, gently took hold of her arm, and turned her toward him. She was surprised that his touch didn't propel her across the room, he actually calmed her. His energy was so constant, strong, and positive. The look in his eye spoke of nothing but kindness and tenderness. "I've never hit a woman in my life outside of consensual sex games. I only want to have a good time with you, okay? I can guarantee you no woman has ever been afraid of me."

Her focus went to her beer bottle, and she shrugged.

"No one fears me but my competitors. And hopefully some tennis partners once in a while." He ran his hand down her upper arm. "You want me as much as I want you, don't you?"

"Hell yes."

"I'm not the other guy, right?"

"No, you're not."

"So don't let this opportunity for fun pass you by because of your fears. See me for who I am."

Rubbing her forehead, she heaved a sigh. "Sorry, I don't mean to freak out. You don't really remind me of him or I wouldn't be here. It's just the money and your persistence and the trappings are the same."

"I'm sorry he hurt you."

"Me, too."

A layer of fear melted away, and she began to come back to herself. Wow. That was some heavy-duty Capasso PTSD. Great. In front of a witness and everything. Normally, her Capasso attacks happened in the privacy of her own home when she was preparing for her dates with him. She let out a long breath and rolled her shoulders to loosen them.

"Why don't you relax," he said, indicating the couch. "Let's have some drinks and talk."

Finally making eye contact—which wasn't easy—her face warmed and she said, "This reaction really took me by surprise. It's never happened before with someone other than him. I haven't dated anyone as powerful as you, either, except for him. I apologize."

"Nothing to apologize for." He handed her another beer.

She sat down next to him on the couch and turned to him. His gray eyes sympathetic, there was a sweetness about him. He looked at her like he really cared for her, and like she was special and valuable. It had been a while since anyone made her feel this good about herself. The way he handled her freak out said a lot about his character. Damn. He was nothing like Capasso. "Shit. I'm sorry, I didn't mean to get my crazy on you."

"Hell, stop apologizing. You had an involuntary reaction. It's normal when someone hurts you. I'm just pissed he hurt you."

"Me, too."

"But I am having difficulty picturing you taking that kind of shit from someone."

Hell gave a hand shrug. "I didn't see it coming, or I would have gotten out of there sooner. While I knew he'd hurt other people, it pertained to his job. I honestly didn't think he was capable of hurting me. I'd never experienced physical violence before."

Brad's brows knitted together. "His job? What does he do for a living?"

She looked away. "I thought he was a lawyer, but it turned out he was a criminal."

"There's a difference?"

She laughed, the tension easing from her body. "Not much."

He gave her a warm smile and gripped her knee. "I'm sorry, Hell. You didn't deserve it. You do know that, don't you?"

"Yeah. That was pretty clear to me."

Collins asked Hell about a movie he'd seen recently, and she'd seen it, too. They discussed the pros and cons of the plot, and she finally fully got her brain back.

Brad's previous performance in bed began playing through her mind.

"Yeah, I liked that actor but—oh, screw this conversation, I want to jump you," she announced mid-discussion.

He laughed, leaned in, and kissed her.

A bolt of energy struck her clit, juicing her sex. She gripped his shoulders and had to hold back her libido like a team of wild horses. This guy had some awesome voodoo over her hormones.

She pushed him away, breathless. "First you have to promise me something."

"What?"

"You can't call me all the time and text the hell out of me, okay?"

"Agree to see me, and I'll leave you alone until you're in my company."

"Are you blackmailing me?"

"No."

She laughed. "Yes, you are."

"No, I just want you. More than I've wanted any other woman."

"I don't believe that for a minute."

"Let me show you."

He kissed her, and they didn't speak intelligible words for the following six hours.

CHAPTER 10

SATURDAY, NOVEMBER 27, 2010, 7:10 P.M.

Her back crying out in pain, Hell forced herself to smile at Marco and crossed her legs to ease the tension. This ridiculously tight little black dress was so confining and so nastily short she had to sit with her back straight and keep her legs crossed—or her knees glued together—or everyone in the Fairmont Hotel dining room would see her red thong.

Marco didn't seem to realize that she was about twenty-five years past the butt-floss age. So embarrassing!

"Have I told you how beautiful you look tonight, baby?" Marco said, his dark eyes shining. He was in a good mood tonight. Thank God.

"You're lookin' pretty damned hot yourself." *For someone who's starting to look like they belong in a wax museum.*

At fifty-nine, Marco was doing his best to fight aging to the point where he was starting to look preserved. On the verge of embalmed. He'd had a lot more work done since she'd seen him last: his wide-set eyes popped too much, there was an unusual absence of lines on his olive skin, and something about the plastic surgery had feminized his very masculine face. Still, with his sharply angled wide cheekbones, thin nose, and cut jawbone, he was handsome, but the look deep within his dark brown eyes showed his age. Along with some pronounced weariness and wear from his criminal activities and penchant for whiskey and wine.

"How do you like your fish, honey?" he asked.

"Amazing. You want a bite?"

"No, this lobster tail and steak are kickin' my ass. Going to need to unbutton my top button if I'm not careful here." He shot her a blinding grin. His too-white teeth almost glowed. Hell considered putting on her sunglasses to avoid the retina burn.

The oddest phenomenon about Marco was his near complete physical transformation over the past eleven years from a chic, high-priced lawyer into a textbook Mafia don. He'd given up his contemporary hairstyle and now swept back his dyed, dark brown hair in a traditional goombah do, his suits cost triple what they used to, and many gold rings now appeared on his thick fingers. His cologne was heavier, his fake tan darker, and his Don Corleone mannerisms more pronounced. He'd almost become a parody of himself.

Thankfully, he was still hot enough with a thick chest and thinner waist —and the spark in his eyes for her strong enough—to screw him. But it was still going to be a chore.

Mostly because of that jerk Brad Collins. She could almost see him, smell him, and feel his practiced hands on her. Only twenty-four hours before, she'd been in his arms. The comedown to Capasso was profound. Not only did Brad far surpass Marco in bed—along with every other man—Brad looked at her like he adored her. Marco treated her like a favorite car. Last year when she'd seen the Mafia don, she'd almost sort of enjoyed herself. But this year it was pure, unadulterated work.

"Love that dress on you, baby. You should wear dresses all the time."

She grinned warmly to cover her disgust. Dresses made her feel like she was in drag. He used to like her punky style but a few years back began emailing her links to outfits he wanted her to wear so she'd be "more classy and less trashy."

Marco went on a long, involved description of the renovations he was having done to his house on Nob Hill. Riveting as an accounting lecture in junior college. Hell wanted to record his monologue for her bouts of insomnia.

"Your parents are doing well in that retirement home, aren't they? They look good, anyway."

Her heart stopped, and her blood ran cold. *"You saw my parents?"*

"My uncle just moved into the same place. Ran into them just last week. They didn't tell you?"

Her world went dark, and her mind swirled with images of her chained to Capasso forever. She clung to the table and pasted a happy smile on her face. Worst. News. Ever. "Haven't talked to them in a few weeks, no," she said, her voice shaky. She cleared her throat and fought for a neutral expression while the fish did a pukey dance in her stomach.

Thankfully, Marco had been concentrating on removing lobster meat from its shell and had missed her reaction. He looked up from his plate and flashed her a broad smile. "Love your Dad. Quite a talker, isn't he?"

"Yeah. He's, uh, got the gift of gab, all right." More like unchecked verbal diarrhea. Hell still couldn't grasp the enormity of all this new closeness. Now any time she had to see her parents, she might run into Capasso. Which would remind him of her existence, which would more than likely result in him demanding to see her more often.

Fuck! It had taken her *how* long to wean him down to once a year?

No way could she keep doing this. Somehow, someway, she had to get rid of this guy.

"Your niece has grown up into quite a young lady. Beautiful girl," Capasso said with a wistful sigh.

Her stomach dropped. She shivered and rubbed her arms. Where the hell had he seen her? Retirement home was unlikely because Jasmine went to Berkeley and didn't drive.

His thick brows furrowed, and he leaned in. "You cold, honey?"

"No, I'm fine. Just drank too much water too fast." Hopefully, he wouldn't notice that she hadn't had any water. "Where did you see my niece?"

"You know I keep up with your family," he said with a smile and a dark glint in his eye.

A noose of fear tightened on her neck, and Hell had to remind herself to breathe and keep smiling. He didn't answer, which meant he'd probably obtained the information through surveillance.

Son of a bitch. Capasso had some extra sensory perception. As soon as she began to plot to escape him, he'd sniff it out and drop some comment about her family. Every goddamned time.

He continued on, very animated. In fact, the most animated he'd been all evening. "What a knockout Jasmine turned out to be. Probably twistin' some guy up in knots, isn't she? Flashing that smile, that pretty face, those long legs. Makes me wish I was thirty years younger." Completely oblivious to how much he was creeping her out.

Hell had to stop herself from stabbing him with her butter knife. Suddenly, all she could see was his ugliness. For the first time in their relationship, she was completely out of denial. She wasn't there to see an old boyfriend, she was only there to protect herself and her family.

Even when she'd liked him, this motherfucker had never treated her right. He'd never committed to her, and the highest she'd reached was his Number Four. She wasn't good enough to keep and not bad enough to discard.

Marco gave her knee a caress under the table, and she almost yanked her leg away but caught herself at the last minute. Great. Now she was totally repulsed by him. At least the jerk couldn't last long in bed. Funny, what she used to lament she would now celebrate.

He shot her a grin that reminded her of when they were first together. Her heart beat faster, and a bit of her frost thawed. His grin quickly faded into a scowl as he inspected a bite of lobster. Her belly went tight, and she worked her toes against the bottoms of her shoes. Hopefully, he wouldn't explode. When Marco threw a tantrum in a restaurant, he took no prisoners.

His anger turned into resignation, and he shrugged and ate the seafood.

Temporary disaster averted, Hell's mood plunged even further.

She couldn't believe she actually had to have sex with this asshole tonight. How the hell could she make herself do it? Drugging herself into oblivion was tempting, but he only let her have two beers or glasses of wine maximum, and while he always gave her weed, he wouldn't allow her to smoke it around him.

Marco turned to her, gesturing with his fork. "Baby, you're deep in thought tonight. Something bugging you?"

Startled, she sent him a quick smile. "Sorry. A case. Involving a kid," she lied, hoping the kid line would tug at his heartstrings.

"You'll forget about it, right? Don't want to ruin my birthday, right?" He smiled, but there was an edge to his gravelly voice.

Got it. No heartstrings to tug. "Not at all, and I apologize." She pumped more energy into her façade.

"Oh, don't worry about it," he said very magnanimously. "I've just been looking forward to this. You're always the best birthday present I give myself."

Her muscles froze with anger. Her skin prickled, her face heated, and her body pulsed with revulsion and anger. But she didn't so much as blink. She sent him a radiant smile. "I've missed you so much, all I want to do is think about you. Thanks for reminding me." *What an asshole you are. Like you own me, you stuffy dick.* Should have brought laxatives or sleeping pills and dosed his wine.

Hey, now there was an idea. Damn it, why hadn't she thought of it before now?

He held up his wineglass. "To Hell Trent, you've always been a good time, haven't you, baby?" He grinned, flashing his straight neon-white teeth.

She mirrored his smile, torn between driving her fork through his forehead and barfing. Why had her shield of denial given out? How the hell was she supposed to bonk him when all she wanted to do was strangle him?

His attention dropped to her necklace. "Love those jewels on you. Haven't gotten you any in a while, have I? Need to take care of that. Take care of my girl right."

Her alarms went off. Christ, she already felt like the biggest whore on the planet. Any more payoffs for sex and she'd explode. "Marco, you've been so generous with me, these gifts will last me a lifetime. I couldn't be any more grateful than I am." She fingered her opulent sapphire and diamond necklace that had such large gems it bordered on gaudy. Waving the gigantic cocktail ring on her right hand—a forty-carat sapphire flanked by two five-carat diamonds set in platinum—she jiggled her left hand, making the heavy matching bracelet sparkle and clink. "Look at me. Is there any room left for brilliant and amazing jewels?"

He examined her and sent her a salacious grin. "I'd bet I could find some room on that beautiful body of yours. I have to say, Hell, you take good care of yourself. You look great for not having surgery."

Her jaw tightened, and her face flushed with fury. *Stop making it so hard on me to screw you, you idiot!*

"I could hook you up with my doctor," he continued like he was talking about fixing her car. "I'd help you out if you wanted, you know, get a little tune-up on the lines and jowls."

Gut punch. "I have jowls?" she said before she could stop herself.

Marco wasn't the least bit concerned about his comment. "A little. They aren't bad. But if you wanted them gone, I could take care of it for you."

She smiled warmly and grasped his hand in an affectionate gesture like he'd actually said something nice her. In her mind, she threw her wine in his face and drove the spike heel of her shoe into his balls. "You are too good to me." No way could she afford to deny his offer. She'd just let it drop. "How soon can we bug out of here so I can ravish you?" Like getting a tooth pulled, she wanted this travesty of an evening over with. She'd definitely prefer the dentist to this nasty little soiree.

His smile grew bigger. "Always appreciated your enthusiasm, Hell. None of my other ladies are so, uh, eager." He waggled his eyebrows.

Hell fought the urge to barf again and sent Marco a happy grin while scanning the immediate area to make sure no one was witness to her humiliation. The other rich people in the fancy dining room seemed engrossed in their own hoity-toityness. Good.

Thankfully, she'd never run into anyone she'd known when out with Marco. She wanted to keep it that way. Hopefully he'd die soon, and she'd never have to see him again. Pray for his early death!

Their desserts came, and Marco dug into his tiramisu. Hell picked at her chocolate mousse.

"So how's the Lexus running, baby?" he asked between bites.

"Great," Hell said with a giant pasted fake smile. She hated that car more than any of her other crap from Marco. Had twelve-thousand miles on it and it was a 2001. She only drove it to dates with him, and once in a while to do surveillance in snooty areas.

"It's pretty old. I should get you a new one. How about one of those new Teslas? I know you're all into that green movement."

Stop trying to buy me, you asshole! "I love the Lexus, honey. It's still awesome. I keep it garaged, and I only take it out on special occasions. But thanks for thinking of me. You're the best."

He shot her a huge grin. "You never know, I may just surprise you." He winked at her, and she knew better than to argue or protest any further. She smiled at him like she adored him while wishing Dr. Who and the Tardis would show up and take her out of there.

Finally, Marco was done with his dessert, and they left the dining room for their suite. Her limbs heavy with dread, Hell forced herself to slip into happy companion woman.

It wouldn't be that bad. Fuck him, cry for an hour, and take fifty showers. Easy.

Her feet pinched and burning from the super-high torture pumps —another Marco requirement—Hell clicked along next to the Mafia don with her hand on his arm, wondering if she could be any more uncomfortable.

They walked up to the elevator doors, and Marco pressed the button.

"Marco Capasso?" came a freakily familiar, deep, smoky voice from behind her.

All her skin turned to goose bumps, and her stomach dropped to the floor.

Hell turned around and found herself face-to-face with Brad Collins.

Her mouth fell open, and the room grayed out. She gripped Marco's arm for support, took a deep breath, and straightened her spine. *Slip into character, Hell! You're not supposed to know him!*

Shit! Did she conjure him by thinking about him too much?

Her face flushed so hot it felt like her skin was on fire. Having a witness to her humiliation made the whole situation fifty bazillion times worse. She wanted to *die*.

"Brad Collins, how are you?" Marco said, his face lighting up with recognition.

Hell stared between the two in absolute shock. Wait a minute. How in the name of God did Brad and Marco know each other?

The two men shook hands while Hell wondered why the Earth hadn't opened below their feet and swallowed them all whole. This convergence had to be against the laws of nature.

Brad took in her jewels, the dress, and her high heels in a split second. Then he shot her a penetrating look that went right through her.

Nearly wilting with shame, she felt like she had a neon sign over her head flashing the words "Marco's Whore."

Shit. Now he knew who she'd been reacting to on their second date. Why she'd freaked out. Why she'd been afraid of him. For his safety and hers, she'd have to convince Brad that someone else had hit her. That she was willingly seeing Marco.

"Jeanne Simari?" Sherry said with an actual smile on her tight face. "I didn't recognize you with that new hairstyle."

Hell tried not to lose her dinner. But her expression had to be pure mortification. After far too long of a pause, she forced herself to do a quick recall and slipped into her rich bitch character. "Mrs. Collins, I mean, Sherry. What a crazy coincidence meeting you here. Darling," she said, turning to Marco. His dark eyes bright with amusement, he'd clearly caught on to the situation. "I had no idea you knew the Collinses. I was just at their house fixing their copier because Robert ditched out on me, and I was forced to go on the call myself."

Capasso nodded with a knowing expression. "That's unusual. You hardly ever leave the office."

God bless the guy! In that moment, she was actually thankful to have him along. "Yes, because I hate being seen in those horrible khakis. Ugh. However, I had the good fortune to meet Sherry here. But it was so embarrassing that she caught me in my Pro Office Equipment Repair uniform. I'm so glad you got a chance to see the real me," Hell said, gesturing toward herself and flashing what she hoped was a winning smile at Sherry.

Brad coughed, and there was no way she was making eye contact with him.

Capasso greatly enjoyed the scene, his eyes crinkling, his smile huge.

"I'm happy as well," Sherry said cordially. "Your outfit does suit you so much better. Are those Harold Harrington's design? Your sapphire necklace, ring, and bracelet?"

"Uh..." Hell turned to her date. Who?

Marco puffed up his chest, totally full of himself. He reveled in people recognizing the value and brands of his expensive trinkets. Good, at least he was getting some good payoff for this little charade. Make him more pliable later.

"Yes, they are. You certainly know your jewels," Marco said, oozing charm from every pore. He could really turn it on when he wanted to.

Sherry beamed back at him, gave him a head-to-toe evaluation, and her blue eyes lit with lust. She stood straighter, her cheeks flushed, and she pushed a strand of blonde hair behind her ear, in full flirt mode.

Could this exchange get any weirder?

Brad said, "I'm sorry. Sherry, this is Marco Capasso. We met at a fundraiser for the museum. We were on a committee for the night. He's a Harvard man, too. Graduated just a few years ahead of us."

"Pleased to meet you, Mr. Capasso," Sherry said effusively, right on the verge of batting her eyes.

Marco ate up the attention. "The pleasure is all mine. You have excellent taste in women, Brad. Your wife is beautiful."

Sherry lit up like a Fourth of July fireworks display. Even when she'd talked about Brad's death she hadn't been this giddy.

"Please, I'd be honored if you'd call me Marco," he said directly to Sherry. Then he gave her his best *I'd-love-to-fuck-you* stare.

Sherry giggled, her smile so wide Hell was surprised her face didn't rip. Amazing that her facial muscles could stretch that far.

Marco continued, super smoothly. "You've already met my companion, er, Jeanne."

"I have," Sherry said, nodding. She gave a glance at Hell and then zipped right back to gaze longingly at Marco.

"I haven't had the pleasure," Brad said formally. The sharp look in his eyes belied his polished act.

Capasso said, "Brad, this is Jeanne."

Her entire body tight, her heart racing, Hell shook hands with Brad as a mini-movie of their lovemaking played through her mind. The look he sent her cut to the core. He was horrified, he wanted all the information about this, and he wanted it *now*.

Too bad. Besides, in about a minute, he'd decide that he didn't want her anymore. Her mood sank even further, and she was careful to maintain her character. Now that Brad knew she'd been befouled by a Mafia don, he wouldn't call again.

Which was actually fine because after this, she'd never be able to look him in the eye. So humiliating!

The elevator opened, and all four stepped on. The doors closed and it was only the two couples. Hell wondered why she was still alive, why she hadn't expired on the spot. She'd have been more comfortable swimming through an alligator-infested swamp in a bacon suit.

Brad's laser-like stare burned into her.

Hell turned away and tried to smile at Sherry, but she was staring hungrily at Capasso.

Capasso asked Brad about a car, the tension broke, and the two began chatting.

Looked like it took all her strength, but Sherry finally tore her gaze from Capasso, and her focus went to Hell's jewels. "Marco has excellent taste, doesn't he?"

"The best."

Sherry lowered her tone. "You're doing even better for yourself than I thought. Marco is quite handsome, isn't he?"

"He's a very nice man, too," Hell lied perfectly.

Sherry sent a cold look toward Brad and turned back to her. "I envy you. You'll be having fun tonight, won't you?"

Hell sent her a knowing grin. *Jesus, lady, if you only knew.*

Sherry winked at her. "Between his good looks and those sapphires, you must be feeling like your old self."

"I am."

After what seemed like twenty hours, the elevator doors finally opened up.

"Nice seeing you, Brad. You'll be at the museum on the fourth for the preview, right?" Capasso said.

"Yes. I'll be there."

"Excellent, look forward to it. Enchanted to meet you, Sherry," Marco said with a little bow.

Sherry's eyes sparkled, and her cheeks flushed. "Thank you, Marco. Lovely meeting you as well," she said, her voice heavy with lust. Damn, Sherry was practically dry humping Marco's leg. She glanced at Hell. "And oh, uh, nice to see you again, Jeanne."

Hell had to stop herself from laughing.

"Nice seeing you again, Sherry. And nice meeting you, Brad," she said cordially.

"My pleasure," Brad said, shooting her another look that made her want to cringe.

Christ.

The elevator doors closed behind them, and Marco began laughing.

She clutched his arm. "Oh, God, that was so awful! What the heck are the odds of running into Sherry Collins here?"

Marco shook his head, and they walked a short distance before he stopped at a set of double doors. "I thought you were going to faint."

"I almost did."

He slid the card key through the lock, opened the door for Hell, and she walked past him into the suite.

After the door closed behind him, he took off his coat and turned to her with an amused look on his face. "So how long you been knockin' boots with Collins?"

She got dizzy with shock and had to put a hand on the back of a chair for support.

He laughed. "Jeanne Simari? What? You did a job for him lookin' into his wife or something, and then slept with him?"

"Dude, are you having me followed?"

He gave a hearty laugh. "No, but it was so obvious."

"Think Sherry caught on?"

"No. She was too busy staring at your necklace. And me."

Hell finally allowed herself a laugh. "You worked her good, didn't you?"

Marco's smile widened. "It was too easy, and too hard to resist. She sure doesn't like him, does she?"

"Nope."

"Funny, she couldn't take her eyes off of me, and he couldn't take his eyes off of you." His smile was still there, but she didn't like the look in his eye.

Her stomach went hard, and she turned away, focusing on removing her necklace. "He doesn't care about me."

"You've seen each other for a while."

She faced him so he'd believe her. "No. Very new. Couple times. I think we're pretty done with each other," she tossed off like she didn't care.

The look in Marco's eyes remained firm and sharp. "He's not. He wanted to fillet me alive. It was all over his face. He thinks he owns you."

Hell waved her hand dismissively. "No, he doesn't. Believe me, we're nothing to each other." Especially after tonight. She sent him a dazzling smile. "Thanks for covering, by the way. You were brilliant."

He grinned and removed his Rolex. "You sure get yourself into some jams, don't you?"

"Apparently," she said with raised brows.

Marco's smile turned dark, and he nodded. "So you screwed the great Brad Collins."

She suppressed a flinch. *Please don't make this a problem.* She concentrated on the clasp on her bracelet and gave a tiny shrug. "It was an accident. You aren't mad, are you?"

He snorted. "No, why would I be? Kinda gives me a rush, actually. Guy thinks he's king of the world, that he owns you, and I come along to prove him wrong. Screw you right in front of him." He gave a coarse laugh. "Burning that asshole's balls tonight."

Doubtful, but Marco liked the idea, so wonderful. She didn't have to clue him in that she was one of a thousand of Brad's lovers.

"Then I give his uptight Popsicle of a wife one look, and she practically comes right in front of him. Great icing on the cake that Sherry loved your jewels and knew the designer. That was perfect. I just rubbed that society bastard's nose in it. Mr. High and Mighty found out tonight that I could own both his women if I wanted. Actually, your little drama couldn't have worked out any better for me."

Her blood burned hot in her veins, and she had to use every ounce of her strength to stop herself from punching him. "I'm glad." Fuckwad dirtbag shithead. *His woman.* What a *dick*.

His expression turned a bit more concerned. "You know he's a dangerous man, don't you, baby?"

"Yes." *Mostly to my personal resolve.*

"It's better that you're done with him. Outside, he's all cordial and rich, but at the soul of that man isn't a soul at all, it's an offshore bank account."

Ha, look who was talking about souls! "I know. Like I said, he was a quick indulgence, and after tonight, I'm through with him."

Marco shook his head and began removing his tie. "He's not through with you. Not by a long shot. I may need to talk to him for you. Let him know what's what. Who you really belong to." He pulled off his tie and held it taut in a position like he was about to strangle Brad with it.

Her stomach twisted so hard she almost lost the mousse but played it cool. "Marco, why bother? I'm done with him, I told you. Besides, he has hundreds of girlfriends. I talked to a million of them on that case."

He dropped his tie onto the bed and turned to her, his expression serious. "Well, the only one he wants is you. I don't like the way he looked at you. I don't want to intervene, but I will."

Her entire body went to battle stations, and her need to protect Brad overwhelmed her. But she was careful to keep her exterior free of reaction, her patter calm. "Marco, I don't want him, I want you," she said with what she hoped was the perfect amount of earnestness.

His face relaxed, and he smiled. "Good. I know stuff about that bald fuck that would make your hair stand on end."

"My hair is already standing on end."

He laughed, and the tension in Hell's shoulders eased.

Marco kicked off his shoes. "Too funny. I'm here with you, and Collins is stuck with that stiff bitch. No way to make her happy. No wonder he's got tail on the side."

"She's horrible and wants him dead," Hell said, pulling off her pumps. Her toes cried out in pain as she flattened them into the thick carpet.

"She told you that?"

"Yeah, fuckin' bitch," Hell bit out and wiggled her toes.

Marco stopped undressing, and his gaze sharpened on her, his mouth tight.

She cringed, and her heart thumped hard. Holy crap, she'd used profanity! "Oh, sorry."

He sighed and shook his head, his face drawn with disappointment. "Honey, how many times have I told you I don't like my women cussing?" The look in his eyes changed. "Here, I got an idea to shut you up and put that mouth of yours to some good use," he said with a rough grin. He unzipped his pants and beckoned her over.

What would he do if she just killed herself right there in front of him? If not now, later, because there was no way after tonight she was ever doing this again.

Her face growing hot, she swallowed the lump in her throat, and suddenly, it was like she walked straight into a solid steel wall.

What was she doing? No way was she putting that asshole's cock in her mouth. No way was she screwing him. No more. Not again.

"Hell?"

"Uh." She had no idea how she'd do it, but somehow she had to figure a way out.

"What's wrong?" He frowned and put his hands on his hips, his pants at his knees. "Why are you just standing there?"

Adrenaline swamped her, and her heart beat leapt high. Images of him beating her flashed through her mind, and she fought the urge to curl into a ball.

Brad's kind face intruded on her dark fantasies. That's how Marco should be treating her. With tenderness and caring.

A strength filled her center, grounding her, making her feel more detached.

Yes, she was afraid, but mostly that was PTSD from nine years ago. PTSD was not the truth. She wasn't the same woman she was back then. If that fucker tried to hit her now, she'd kill him.

"Hell? Are you okay?"

Oh, shit, she hadn't said anything. *Quick! Excuse Factory! Come online!*

"Uh..." Nauseous, confused, and still very scared, she froze.

"Why do you look so weird?"

Nausea! Sickness! Yes!

"I..." She fluttered her eyes and dropped to her knees.

"What's the matter?"

Clapping her hand to her mouth, she crawled, then lurched to her feet and raced for the bathroom. Slamming the door behind her, she headed for the toilet and pretended to puke.

Excitement and fear filled her and her pretend barfing became real barfing.

She'd never been so happy to throw up in her entire life. Going with it, Hell thought of as many disgusting combinations of food as she could and kept hurling.

While she was absolutely sick, a giddiness took over. She didn't have to screw Marco! She'd gotten out of it! A voice in her head burst out in hysterical laughter. Hell Trent rocked! She was a warrior! No one was going to use her again!

Jowls, my ass. Fucking taxidermied Mafia jerkwad.

A knocking came on the door. "Hell? You okay, honey? You need an ambulance?"

"No," she croaked. "Stomach flu." She made retching sounds because she was too happy to make herself barf again.

"Jeez. You really think so?"

"Sister was just coming down with it two days ago. I thought I didn't get it." She made more sick noises.

· "Jesus Christ. Well, that does it, doesn't it?" he said.

"I'm so sorry, Marco. I ruined our evening." She faked sobbing and pretended to puke.

"Oh, now, honey, I know you'll miss my loving, but I'll make it up to you. We can do it another time, okay? I know you didn't want this to happen."

Hahahahahahahaa!!!

"Look, baby, if you do have the flu, I can't afford to be sick right now. Are you going to be upset if I go?"

A surge of joy nearly blew her body apart. Talk about exceeding her wildest dreams! Hell faked some hurl sounds. "No, I'd feel better if you didn't get this. I'm just brokenhearted I ruined your birthday."

"It's okay, Hell. I just want you to be okay. But I'm gonna go now. Stay as long as you need to; the bill and room service is on me. Stay for a few days until you get better if you want."

"Thanks, honey, I love you."

"I love you, too, baby. I'll call you, okay?"

"Okay."

"Take care, girl."

"I wuh—" She made more barfing sounds.

Hell continued her act until she heard the door close. Paranoid, she stayed in the bathroom for a full half hour, staring at the back of the door.

Finally, heart pounding, her legs shaky, she got up quietly, snuck to the bathroom door, and peeked out. No one was in the room.

Was he really gone?

Still cautious—ready to dash back to the bathroom at any second—she tiptoed to the suite's double doors and checked through the peephole. Nothing. After taking a deep breath, she opened the door and poked her head out. No one.

Shutting the door, she let out a whoop, bounded across the room, and broke into the theme song from *Rocky*. Holding her hands up in victory, she sang the song and danced all over the suite.

Hell Trent *rocked*! Yes!

No more sex with evil criminal bastards! Ever again!

Hallelujah, she'd won!

Mid-dance step, she stopped, and her body went cold.

Marco wouldn't fall for this routine twice. In fact, she was surprised he'd fallen for it once.

How would she get out of it next time? What would she do when he called? She couldn't keep turning him down.

Defeated, she let out a huge sigh and swallowed a lump.

Crap. Right back to square one. Simply figure out how to avoid a high-level criminal you've been trying to avoid for nine years who threatens your family every time you pull away.

She collapsed on the bed in a puddle of depression. Why did his uncle have to move into the same retirement complex as her parents? How could she avoid Capasso now? Screwing him had been her best protection against him. Without that, how was she supposed to keep him under control?

Tears welled in her eyes, and she didn't fight them. Other than dying, she had no clue how to escape his grasp.

Maybe she'd get run over by a car tomorrow.

Better yet, maybe Marco would get run over by a car tomorrow.

CHAPTER 11

WEDNESDAY, DECEMBER 1, 2010, 5:44 P.M.

Hell stood at the door to Brad's suite at the Four Seasons Hotel in Palo Alto. How would she get through this date? She had to convince him that Marco had not been the one to hit her, and that she'd loved being in that horrible little dress and jewels. *Right.*

The door opened, startling her. She gasped and clutched her chest.

Brad stood there with a sardonic smile. "Forgot how to knock?"

"You scared the crap out of me." She laughed to cover her embarrassment but couldn't think of a fast excuse why she hadn't knocked sooner. "Hi, Brad."

His amusement faded into affection. He pulled her inside and kissed her. He tasted amazing, and his easy, masterful dominance made her want to instantly surrender. Clutching his taut buns, she pressed herself against him, loving the feel of his rock-hard dick against her. She breathed in his scent and got even higher off him. She had to have him inside her right then, or she'd explode from want.

He pushed away with a tortured expression. "God, I want to make love to you so badly, but I'll pass out if I don't eat first. I've been running all day, and I was almost late here."

Her body cried out from the let-down, aching for him. She

pushed him back and caught her breath. "Damn, you are so hot. I almost came from that kiss."

He beamed, gave her a quick peck on the cheek, then wrapped his arm around her and guided her over to the food display. The usual bounty was spread out on the coffee table.

Hell took a deep breath and sent an order to her body to calm down. She checked for the Heineken bucket. The gleaming, sweaty bottles of pure delight called to her. "Squeee! Heineken!" She hustled over to the ice bucket filled with her precious beverage.

He chuckled. "Squee? Is 'squee' a word?"

"Yes. Telegraphs extreme excitement."

"I gathered the meaning."

After they ate, he sat back on the couch opposite her and eyed her.

All delusions of easy sex popped like a balloon. Her back went tight, and she heated with frustration. She pointed at him. "We're not talking about that."

His expression turned indignant. "The hell we aren't. You blew my mind."

Anger flared through her, and she held up her hand. "Stop. Rule Number Two: We do not talk about our other lovers."

"Fuck that. You're seeing *Marco Capasso*?" he demanded, his face flushing.

"We're not talking about it." Her heart rate increasing, she grabbed her beer and briefly checked the label before taking a sip.

His attention on her sharpened. "He's the one you're afraid of. He's the one who hit you."

She forcefully stopped all outward reactions and made sure she looked him right in the eye. "No. Goddamn it, I knew you were going to think that. It was another rich, powerful guy who hopefully you don't know."

He leaned in, his intensity on maximum. "He's a fucking Mafia boss, Hell. A Mafia don. Head of his family's business. He's one of the most powerful underworld CEOs on the West Coast. Pioneered much of the Internet crime and is still at the forefront. You can't believe his reach."

She stretched to appear indifferent, her mind racing for the Happy-About-Capasso character she had to assume when she was around those who knew about their affair. "I know. He's an old boyfriend," she tossed off, leaning back in the overstuffed chair. She took a deep breath and made a half-hearted, dismissive gesture as if the subject didn't bother her in the least. "We've been going out for eleven years."

Brad leveled his potent gaze straight into hers. "He's the reason you were afraid of me."

"No," she said with what she hoped was just the right amount of emotion to sound truthful.

Brad wasn't buying her act. "Hell, it's not like I'm going to go discuss it with him. Even I'm not that stupid. Why did he hurt you? Does he hurt you all the time?"

Her stomach knotted, but she squared her shoulders and went into her tough-girl mode. "Brad, you are high. It was another man, and he only hurt me once. I'm not stupid. I wouldn't put up with that shit."

"Sure you would if it was Marco Capasso. He could do whatever he wants to you and get away with it. He thinks he owns you, doesn't he?"

She snorted. "No. God, you are reading all kinds of garbage into an old friendship. We hardly see each other any more."

"How did you meet him?"

She shifted into a more casual posture with her legs crossed. "At a club when I was on the rebound from another guy. I'd just been dumped by Dave, Josh's friend."

"I thought you weren't serious about any relationships after Josh."

Hell continued with her remote affect. "When you are in love with your soul mate and he dies, you believe that there's someone else out there for you. So you go out with an open heart and get it skewered until you realize that a soul mate only comes once in a lifetime."

He tilted his head a bit to one side and squinted. "You want a long-term relationship?" he asked like he hadn't heard her correctly.

Her heart gave a big thump. Crap! How did the truth leak out when she was being so careful? "No. I had my chance at love. He died. Now I live in reality."

He sat back, rubbed his chin, and studied her. "I spotted you, no, Sherry spotted you in the dining room."

"Look, we've talked about this. Let's move on." She turned her attention to the desserts again even though her appetite had vanished.

"I was thinking about you, too. Wishing I was there with you instead of Medusa."

A little rush of joy danced through her. The Truth Voice in her head smashed the hope to paste. *An adulterer will say anything to keep getting free sex.* "You were not." She chose a sugar cookie and took a bite.

"I was, and then Sherry points you out. I didn't recognize you at first. Took me a sec. Couldn't believe that outfit and those jewels."

Her face heated, and she wouldn't look at him.

"Especially after your whole spirited monologue the night before about dresses and high heels and jewelry being enslavement devices. Then I saw who you were with. Holy shit."

Hell's heart rate increased, and sweat trickled between her shoulder blades, but she continued perusing the food offerings and acted as if they were talking about the weather.

He leaned in closer. "Really, all bullshit aside, Hell, you have to get away from that guy. Just being anywhere near his orbit puts you in extreme danger."

Stop the presses! *Really?* "Funny, he said the exact same thing about you."

"Me?"

Hell swallowed and gestured with the rest of the cookie. "You do realize that he knew instantly that we were seeing each other."

Brad's jaw dropped, and he paled. "No." Then an idea hit him. He looked away and said, "Oh." His eyes narrowed, and he nodded.

Hell had no idea what he was reacting to, but she didn't care. "Yes. He warned me against seeing you. What did he say? 'I know things about that billionaire fuck that would make your hair stand on end,'" she said, doing an imitation of Capasso's rough voice.

He sat straight up in his chair, his eyes on fire. "Me? That bastard, I'm nothing like him! I don't kill people! I don't run Internet scams! I don't have people beaten, I'm not in racketeering or prostitution or—"

Hell waved a hand to stop him. "All he does is the white-collar stuff. His brother runs the other part of the family business. Marco doesn't like getting his hands dirty." *Unless it's to beat the shit out of me.*

Brad looked at her like she was an idiot. "Get your head out of the sand, lady. Who the hell do you think runs his brother? Marco's the head of the family now."

"Since Marco's father died, his uncle runs the family." Hell said like it was old news.

"His uncle is in that retirement home now and has stepped down. Six months ago."

Her brain stopped like she'd run into a steel door. Her stomach went cold, and she wrapped her arms around herself. "Yeah..." How did she miss that fucking connection? How blind was she? Her denial went deeper than the Earth's mantle. Marco's uncle went into her own parents' *retirement* home, for God's sake. Message couldn't have been louder or plainer. Who else would be running the Capasso Family?

No wonder Marco looked like a textbook Mafia don; he *was* a textbook Mafia don.

The room darkened around her. How the hell would she get away from him now?

"You didn't know that, did you?"

Hell noticed her trembling hands and gripped her knees. She straightened, and tried to look nonchalant, even though she wanted to have a giant freak out and run screaming down the hallways of the hotel. "I make it a point not to involve myself in his business. None of that has anything to do with me."

Brad's gaze burned into her. "It has everything to do with you. You're on the Feds list. You're a known associate of his."

A wave of nausea went through her, and she burped. Clearly she needed Death to look into all this. Mostly she tried not to think about Marco. "So?" she tossed off. "I've been on the Feds' list forever."

"But now he's the head of his family. And because he's such an amazing player, he took charge of four other families. He controls the entire West Coast now. He's fifty times more dangerous."

Marco's prison walls grew taller around her, and she fought back tears. Then she realized that she'd let Brad get to her. He had a huge objective here, too. Get her away from Marco and score huge points. Just like Marco had done. Both men were trying to show up the other one by bedding her. Screwing each other through her. Very nice.

Time to fight back with a nice club of logic. "You associate with him."

Not one muscle of his face moved. "That's different. We see each other because of the museum. Ours is on an acquaintance basis. I don't have him at my house. I know this is not my place to say anything, but you have to get away from him."

Tell me something I don't know, Captain Obvious. Hell wondered why she was still there and hadn't already left. Duh. Because she really liked Brad and their connection in bed. She just hoped he'd shut up and not totally kill her sex drive.

"He said the same thing about you." She turned back to the dessert plate even though she hadn't finished her cookie.

"Did he order you to stop seeing me?"

Hell paused slightly but kept her attention on the sweets. "He suggested it."

"Yet you're here."

"He doesn't have that kind of control over me." For now.

Brad's intensity heightened. "The hell he doesn't. It was beyond clear that you didn't want to be there with him. When he went to the bathroom, I saw the look on your face. You pinched the bridge of your nose, looked down, and your expression was pained. Like you were ashamed to be there, wished you were anywhere else."

Her stomach wrenched, but she pursed her lips and made an exasperated noise at the back of her throat, trying hard to appear unemotional. "Brad, I swear you missed your calling. You should write fiction."

Brad's intense stare didn't waver. "Both Sherry and I studied you. After a proper display of horror at the table, she became intrigued, borderline obsessed with you two. Even she noticed how miserable you looked, and she can't read people. She figured you were his unhappy kept mistress."

"I'm not," she barked. Her face flushed, and she slammed her beer down on the table, a bit too hard, and some liquid splashed onto the polished surface of the coffee table. "For your information, I was thinking about a case I was working. My life does not revolve around my sex partners," she said in a strong voice, but at the last second looked away from him. *Fuck!*

His dark gaze remained steady and sure. "You aren't the best liar."

She waved her hand and tried to get her power back. "Look, Brad, I told you in the beginning, our affair is between us. Same thing with me and Marco. I'm not going to discuss the personal details of our relationship with you. But you did shock me by calling me. I figured we were done once you realized I was seeing Marco." *Shit!* How did her Number One Worry spill out?

"Why?"

Leaping from her chair, she stormed to the middle of the room, completely exasperated, frustrated, and upset. She didn't want to like this guy. She didn't want to care what he thought. She spun on him, waving her arms. "Because it's crazy, right? It taints me, right? You think less of me now, don't you?"

Brad's head jerked back with surprise. "No, Hell. Jesus Christ, no. I think you got involved with him before you understood who he was, like you said the other night. Now you're in over your head and handling the situation the best way you know how to keep protecting yourself."

Her foundation shifted, pain wrenched her gut, and she found herself even more frustrated. His understanding made her feel more, and she didn't want to feel. "Brad, I don't know how I can get through to you on this. Marco is not the one who hit me," she said, smacking the back of her hand on the upturned palm of her other hand for emphasis.

Brad's stare drilled right through her. "Bullshit. That cowed, submissive woman I saw at the Fairmont isn't you. It was like he'd molded you into who he wanted you to be. Like a Stepford Helen Trent."

Fury boiled in her gut, and she sent him a deadly glare. No one called her weak for surviving. "That's it." She turned and marched to the door.

"Hell, wait."

"Fuck that, and fuck you," she said, her hand on the knob.

"Hell, I'm sorry. Please don't go. I wasn't trying to insult you. I'm trying to help you. You can't tell me you wanted to be there with him."

Perfect opportunity. All she had to do was convince Brad that he'd misunderstood the situation. She turned back to him, assumed her power pose, and deepened her voice. "When have I ever gone anywhere I didn't want to? Who are you talking to? This is Hell Trent here, buddy. Who do you take me for?"

"That bravado is mere window dressing on a terrified woman."

Her gut hurt like he ran her through with a lance. He made her feel skinless. He was far too insightful and knew her far too well, far too fast. Clearly, none of her bullshit would work on him.

Out of defenses and offenses, Hell's mood plummeted. No way could she continue to see Brad. Too dangerous for the both of them. She turned, put her hand on the doorknob, and opened the door.

Brad was next to her in a flash. Reaching past her, he shut the door.

Fear gripped her, her body hardened, and she prepared to defend herself. His expression stopped her and brought her back to Earth. This was Brad, not Marco. He wasn't attacking. He was trying to communicate with her. She had no reason to be afraid.

Pure upset and worry creased his features. "Don't go. I'll stop. I'm sorry. But I can't stand to see you hurt, and he was hurting you. It killed me to watch you bend to that bastard's will. I want to get you out of that. I want to help you."

His need touched her heart, and her shields dropped some. Damn this man, anyway. The idiot did care about her. Maybe it wasn't all a pissing contest with Marco. She wanted to walk out the door, but no man had been this nice to her since Josh.

She leaned against the door. Running her hand through her hair, she shook her head. She had to get him to back off without dumping him. Taking a deep breath, she let it out slowly. "If you want to have sex with me, you'll stop talking about him now. I mean it, not another word or I'm gone."

His face drew down with pain. He walked back and sat at his place on the couch. Grabbing his glass of wine, he drank a long while.

An earlier conversation with Death popped into her mind, and her irritation returned. She straightened her posture and took a few steps toward him. "One more thing, while we're on subjects that make us not want to have sex, could you please stay out of my bank records? Like, what? You wanted to find out how dismal my finances are?"

He gave her a double take, and the heat in his eyes grew fast, scorching her. "What about you? You accessed sealed records. How did you do that? That was you, wasn't it?"

A surge of power raced through her. Thank God for Death. He'd leveled their playing field nicely. "Okay, so we're even." An idea occurred to her to kill the whole Marco argument once and for all. "Wait. You launched your investigation after you ran into me with Capasso, didn't you? You looked into my relationship with Marco, didn't you? And you found out absolutely nothing besides what I already told you, right?" she asked, full of confidence.

The look Brad sent her made the hair stand up on the back of her neck. Her body went cold, and she froze in place. She felt like she'd just stepped into a bear trap.

"No, on the contrary, I found out a lot. A ton you haven't shared," he said with a victorious look in his eye.

A burst of adrenaline made her heart beat so fast it took her breath away. "What?" She found herself standing in front of him with no memory of moving there.

Brad sat back like he held all the cards in their little poker game. "About nine years ago, you inadvertently screwed over Capasso's brother, and Capasso beat you to within an inch of your life for it."

She reeled like he'd smacked her across the face with an iron bar, and had to force herself to start breathing. She used all her powers of acting to keep her face free of reaction. Corroborating his story was as good as committing suicide. She forced a relaxed posture, with her hip cocked. She gave a laugh. "What a bunch of hooey. Who was your source? JD Robb?"

By the way his gaze gleamed, he clearly wasn't buying her story. She knew her performance was off. "According to my source, you tried to get away from him at that point, but Marco wouldn't leave you alone. He stalked you and harassed you until you agreed to see him again. He forces you to continue seeing him."

To have BC openly discussing her biggest secret freaked her out, but she only allowed disdain to cross her features. She snorted. "Who the hell said all this crap? For God's sake, next you'll have heard we ran away and joined the circus together."

"Then how did you end up in the hospital for three days nine years ago with extensive injuries the doctors determined could only be from an assault? Coincidentally, right about the time you got into the fight with his brother."

Hell's vision blurred, and her knees weakened. She took a deep breath and then shook her mind clear, but sat down on a chair to avoid falling down. "If you'd read the police report, you'd know that I don't know who hurt me," she managed to say in a strong voice. She set her face into her most emotionless expression. "I was attacked outside a club in the City. Last thing I remembered was getting in my car to go out that night. I woke up in the hospital."

"Then why did Capasso pay the bill?"

Wow, this guy knew a lot. While absolutely alarmed, Hell relaxed back in her chair to appear truthful. "Because we were going out then, and my insurance sucked."

"The police report stated that you were withholding information to protect Capasso."

Now that was a lie. She'd seen the police reports. She made a noise of disbelief. "That was not in the police report."

The look in his eye remained hard and fixed. "It was in the cops' notes. Thompson asked the cop who'd interviewed you."

Fists clenched, she gritted her teeth, fire scorching her interior. "Son of a bitch! How far did you dig into my life?"

Collins didn't bat an eye. "You dug all the way into mine. Tit for tat, lady. The cop said that Capasso had beaten you up because you helped one of his brother's prostitutes escape. That you knew the girl, were her drama teacher, and grew up with her parents back in San Jose. That her parents asked you to save her. But that you didn't know she was a witness to a murder, nor that she belonged to Capasso's brother when you snuck her out of the City."

Her heart thumped hard, and her stomach fell to the floorboards, but she tried to keep her patter even. "I remember that idiot cop. That drunk creep would say anything for a bottle of booze." She reached for her beer on the coffee table.

"I want to help you get out from underneath Capasso."

She laughed and took a sip of her beer. "I haven't been underneath him in years. He only likes it doggy style."

Brad's face flushed red. "Goddamn it, Hell, I'm not joking. I have the power to get you out of that relationship. You can't take him on alone. That's why he's had control over you for so long, because you've never had anyone powerful on your side."

She ignored his offer and eyed him. "I want to know how you OD'd on coke and gave yourself a heart murmur."

His body jerked, and he lost some color in his face. She'd derailed him. Hopefully, effectively.

Eyes narrowed, he tightened his mouth. "How you accessed sealed medical records is what I want to know."

Mission accomplished. *Now let's talk about you, Brad old boy, and see how you like it.* "I don't know how. I farm all that out."

"You got into the sealed police records in Connecticut, too?"

"Yep. Found out all about your drug bust that Daddy paid to cover up."

A muscle in his face twitched, and the fire in his eyes grew hotter. "That upset me," he said through partially gritted teeth.

"Oh, and I'm thrilled you dug into my relationship with Capasso. For a smart man, you are pretty stupid. You don't think Capasso will find out you looked into him?"

"He's looking into me. Actually, he launched a full-scale hack attack on one of my newly acquired businesses the day after I ran into you. Now I know why."

Her fists tightened, and she resisted curling into a ball. "How do you know it's coming from him?"

"Let's just say I know he's the one behind the attack."

Marco's psychic shackles tightened on her wrists and neck. Her mood fell even further. "Great." She rubbed her forehead. "He probably knows I'm here with you now."

"More than likely."

There was a pause. Hell looked at the door. Should she stay, or should she go?

"You're leaving," Brad said.

As much as a small part of her told her to jet, the rest of her wanted nothing more than to stay. While she was pissed Brad had investigated her life so thoroughly, she'd done the same thing to him. Nor could she argue with his logic about Capasso. But none of that was really the point. The point was Brad's outstanding lovemaking skills, and the way he looked at her. "No. Although, I'd love to kick your ass for delving so deeply into my life."

"You did the same thing to me."

"That's different. I have to protect myself from you because of your wealth and power."

"No, you don't. I'm no Marco Capasso."

Couldn't argue there. "I never took you for a druggie."

"That's a mistake I don't like talking about," he said tersely.

"Well, I don't like talking about Capasso."

He glared, drank some more wine, and then sighed. "I was getting even with my father and almost killed myself in the process. Apparently, I have a sensitivity to coke."

She gestured toward him with her beer. "Why were you dealing in the first place? Like you needed the money?"

"Because my father made me account for every penny I spent. I could have whatever I wanted as long as I justified the expense. I hated his control, so when the coke thing came up, seemed like it was an easy way to make money because I never liked the drug. Worked until I sold to a narc."

"So then your Dad got pissed—"

"See this?" He pointed to a canine tooth. "Implant. Only time he ever hit me. He yelled, 'Collinses make laws, they don't break them! Do you know how that made me look?' Wham! Never seen him so pissed."

"Then you OD'd?"

Shame crossed his features, and he glanced downward before meeting her gaze. "A mistake. I had a few grams stashed that the cops didn't find. I didn't snort that much, but enough to make my heart stop. Thank God my roommate was pre-med, or I wouldn't be here."

She took in a sharp breath. She hadn't realized he'd been that close to death. "Jeez."

His lips tight, he regarded her. "Okay, now that we've dissected my past, what are you going to do about Capasso?"

"Nothing, and none of your business." She looked him dead in the eye. "Brad, honestly, you have to stay out of my life, or I can't have anything to do with you. I only want to have sex with you. I don't need or want your protection." Another total lie, but she'd never accept it from him. She'd only be trading one powerful man's control for another.

He snorted. "The hell you don't."

"Please don't push me out that door."

"I'm not. I'm giving you a way out," he said, his voice full of exasperation. "Take it."

"Do you know any other languages? Because you clearly aren't understanding English." She stood and went to the door. "Look, I like you, but this has become complicated. I'm not getting in the middle of a pissing contest between you and Capasso."

Brad got up and came over to her. "I'm here for you only. I don't care about him; I only want to protect you. Please don't throw me in the same boat as Capasso. I'm nothing like him."

She was about to argue but stopped. He was right. But she was still done with the conversation. She looked toward the door.

His brow went hard over his eyes. "Please don't leave."

"Then shut up about Capasso."

He held her gaze for a long time, then finally nodded. "I just want to fix it for you," he said in a quiet, resigned voice that tugged hard at her heart.

She forced her emotions to shut down. "Nothing to fix. Can we be done now?"

His eyes troubled, he nodded. "Yeah."

She walked past him to the beer bucket. "Good. I need more beer. And food."

"I could use a few glasses of wine myself." He returned to his place on the couch and poured himself a full glass of red.

Hell sighed and downed a half a bottle of beer. Contradicting voices argued in her head. She finally forced them to stop. She was there because she liked Brad and it was just that simple.

Besides, once they started screwing, she'd forget all about Capasso.

At this point, that was all she really wanted.

CHAPTER 12

"So you see Collins pretty often now?" Matt asked and ate his last fry.

Her face still warm from her Brad Collins non-relationship download, Hell shifted in her seat. "Some." She still couldn't face how often she saw him. Too much.

The waitress walked by with two steaming platters: one held a burger combo, the other a triple-decker club sandwich and fries. If Hell hadn't been so stuffed on her BLT and mountain of fruit salad, she'd have tripped the young woman and grabbed the food for herself.

While she'd told him the majority of the salient points of the Collins story, she'd left out many important details to protect herself and Capasso. But mainly herself. No way did she want Matt knowing that much about her. Only enough to figure out who was trying to kill her. "I'm good as long as Brad doesn't send me any more flowers or try to buy me anything. Jerk. Sent me a giant bouquet after our first night. Made me feel so used."

Matt laughed. "Flowers made you feel used?"

She straightened her shoulders and affected her tough-girl attitude. "He was just tryin' to work me. Push my buttons. Control me. I told him if he sent me flowers again, I'd personally shove them up his ass," she said in a growl.

What she'd never tell anyone was that not only had she kept the flowers until they were stinky dead weeds, she'd put his handwritten card in her special keepsakes box. Along with the corks from every bottle of wine he'd drunk over the previous four months, each inscribed with the date. *Pathetic!*

"Did it stop him?"

"Temporarily. But he's determined to get to me accept his stupid gifts. I won't." Her face heated, and her stomach went into knots. "Jerk. I don't even want to see him."

"Sounds like a pretty intense connection."

"I have no idea why. He should repulse me." Her nerves on fire, she rubbed her arms vigorously. She hated reflecting on the affair. How had she allowed herself to become the other woman? Hadn't the affair with Capasso taught her anything?

"Do you love him?"

Alarm bells rang in her head, nearly deafening her, and she had to fight from going into the fetal position. Not *possible!* "No, I'm not capable, I told you."

"You just haven't found the right man yet."

"I found the right man. Josh. But he's dead, so now I screw immoral jerks."

"Does Collins know about the death threat? Does he know someone shot at you two days ago?"

Her heart jumped into a fast rhythm, and she wanted to dive under the table. She didn't want BC knowing anything about her personal life. He couldn't find out that she had feelings. No way could she afford to be vulnerable in front of the guy.

"Hell? Did you tell him?"

"No. I...uh... No."

Matt looked at her with alarm. "He doesn't know?" he demanded. "Have you seen him?"

"No. We had a date last night, and I cancelled and said I was sick."

"Hell, you need to tell him. His life could be in danger," he said like he was shocked she hadn't thought of it.

Like a two-by-four upside the head, the idea hit her hard. She'd been so paranoid about keeping details about her life from BC she hadn't even considered that her attack might put him in harm's way. "But he already has bodyguards," she offered weakly.

"Hell, he needs to know." His tone left no room for argument.

He was right. Her mood turned funereal. The BLT staged a revolt. "This is all getting too serious. I don't want feelings. I don't want serious. But I don't want to die, either. And I don't want him to die. Shit. I should have told him, huh?"

"Let's both see him."

The idea sounded like as much fun as a colonoscopy without anesthesia. "I'd better tell him first." She took out her phone. "Let me send him an email and see if he'll cancel his Tuesday mistress," she said in the same tone she'd used when she'd scheduled her last root canal.

A hard punch to the gut surprised her. *Tuesday mistress.* An image of BC kissing a supermodel turned her interior to fire. Her fists itched to punch him.

Dear, God, no. *Please don't tell me that I actually like him.*

"So you've stopped seeing others, but he hasn't?" Matt said.

A wave of nausea came over her. She erected a steel box around her heart and pushed the idea of his other lovers out of her mind. No way could she deal with her unwanted and unwelcome feelings, not when she was so freaked out. Her coping skills were already at maximum. "I don't know. We don't talk about it. Not my business."

"I feel sorry for you, Hell. I wish you could give yourself better."

Shrugging off the toxic emotions, she squared her shoulders and forced herself to center. "Don't feel sorry for me. I'm actually happy when people aren't shooting at me." Partial truth. She took out her iPhone. "I'm sure he's busy tonight. Even though he has been making more time for me lately. But he might be in India or China or something. May take a week before his schedule is clear enough."

She typed up a text to him. *Tonight?* "That should do it," she said, hitting send. "He probably won't get back to me for a while so we should move on to other—"

Her phone buzzed with a message. *BC: 8 @ the condo.*

"Wow, that was fast. Okay, guess I am seeing him tonight. Damn, Tuesdays and Thursdays used to be Gwen, and she's hot. He's an idiot. And I'll tell him so," she said in a cavalier tone. Very important to keep the hard-hearted Hell story going. Especially now. She typed back: *CU then!*

"You're insane. I just have to say that."

"Well aware of that, bucko."

A text appeared on her phone. *BC: CU naked.* Plus a winking smiley face.

A surge of joy made her pulse race. Damn it.

Well, she shouldn't worry about it. Once he found out that someone was trying to kill her, he'd be running the other way fast.

The realization slammed her like someone had kicked her in the heart with steel-toed boots. Why hadn't this occurred to her earlier? Of course he'd dump her once he heard the news. An easy fling had just become complicated. Powerful married billionaires didn't like complications.

Battling tears, she swallowed a huge lump and hoped she wouldn't lose the BLT. Her future looked even bleaker than before. Brad had reminded her how much fun a man could be. All her other men paled in comparison. Beyond paled—BC made them all suddenly unattractive.

Great. So when Brad was gone, all she'd have left was Secret Teddy and her vibrator. Joy.

Look on the bright side, Hell, the assassin may not miss the next time.

"Hell? You okay?"

Hell jerked out of her mental torture chamber. Matt's weathered and rugged face was etched with concern, and his blue eyes seemed to look through her.

Her mood dropped even further, but she put on a cheery face. Being emotionally naked in front of this guy sucked.

"I'm fine, Matt," she said as sincerely as she could. She grabbed her cell phone and got up.

By the sharp look in his eye, Matt clearly didn't buy her act, but he nodded.

Her heart and gut twisting in agony, Hell headed for the exit, kicking herself with every step for getting involved with Brad in the first place.

Tuesday, March 8, 2011, 8:05 p.m.

HER PULSE POUNDING, HER PALMS SWEATY, HELL STOOD ON THE PORCH of Brad's luxury condominium in Menlo Park and tried to make herself knock on the door.

She did not want to do this. If she couldn't have him, she never wanted to see him again. Beyond that, she wished she'd never met the bastard. She wanted Brad Amnesia.

This two-thousand-square-foot condo had become her personal paradise. Some of the best times of her life had been spent here. Amazing sex, constant attention, and some of the liveliest after-sex conversations she'd had since Josh. Add to that a buffet of unending treats and any alcoholic beverage imaginable, the dates had been unsurpassed. Brad's continued efforts to provide a quality time put every other boyfriend to shame.

But like Josh and everyone and everything else good in her life, of course this affair had to end.

How come every time she tried to have fun, it always turned out to be another emotionally wrenching trap of suffering?

Her throat closed, and tears welled in her eyes. An emotional Vesuvius threatened to blow her apart. She grabbed her feelings with both hands and wrestled them into the vault in her heart. With a spin of the dial, she locked them away, and Strong Hell took charge. She felt taller, harder, and centered.

It's better this way, Hell. Cleaner. After tonight, you'll no longer be an adulterer.

Cold fucking comfort.

She knocked on the door. A split second later it opened, and Brad stood there wearing a dark blue bathrobe, a sexy smile, and nothing else. A field of high-wattage energy surrounded him.

Her knees went weak, and her train of thought derailed.

He sent her a heavy-lidded, predatory stare. "Get in here, beautiful."

You are not here to have sex, woman! You are here to tell him about the murder attempt so he can dump you! "Brad, I'm not beautiful, and we have to—"

He grabbed her and kissed her. A second later, they were both naked and doing it.

Afterwards, she lay in his arms, trying to catch her breath and berating herself for screwing him. Dude was a human drug addiction. Even though, in this case, her drug habit was about to kick her.

She took a moment to shut down and find center again. "We have to talk," she managed to get out in a firm voice. Good. Almost back on track.

"Sounds serious." He brushed a wisp of hair off her brow. "Going to break up with me again?"

"No, we're not together. We're two separate human beings screwing our brains out. You can't split up if you never get together." Denial was wonderful. She loved denial.

He stroked between her legs and grinned. "We're together now."

She curled her toes and fought the urge to jump on him again. "Yes. We are."

"I'll just keep bugging you."

"Dude, I'm not calling this off." *Because you'll do that for me.*

"Good." He kissed her.

She groaned with lust and frustration but finally managed to push him away. Hardening her heart, she tried to feel nothing. "Stop. Let me get this out."

His worry lines deepened. "I'm not sure I want to hear it."

"I'm not sure, either." Her stomach tightened, and her heart beat faster.

"Uh-oh. Is this about canceling last night?" He examined her face. "You don't seem to sick to me. Recovered awfully fast."

"Okay, I lied about last night."

He narrowed his eyes. "What was his name?"

"Not for another man."

His thick brows shot high. "A woman? We could do a threesome." Sending her a salacious grin, he groped her.

She pushed his hands away and couldn't help but chuckle. "Will you please let me get this out?"

"Okay, what's so important that you gave up sex last night? And want to stop having sex right now?"

She took a deep breath and worked hard to keep her emotions locked away. "Someone tried to kill me Sunday morning."

His spine stiffened, and he checked her expression carefully. "Where's the smile? Has to be a joke, right? You're kidding, right?" His face falling, his gaze turned to fire. "Someone tried to kill you on Sunday, and I'm only finding out *now*?" He pushed her back to glare at her full force.

Her stomach convulsed, and shame heated her face. *Prepare for dumpage!* Fumbling for an explanation, she dropped her attention to his chest. "I'm sorry. I didn't think you were in danger, or I would have told you. I just thought your bodyguards would take care—"

"For fuck's sake, I'm not worried about me, I'm worried about *you!*"

She stared at him and tried to make sense of his statement. "Why are you worried about me? I'm fine. Bullets clearly missed me."

His eyes dilating, his mouth dropped open. "Bullets! Someone *shot* at you? When did this happen? Where were you? Were you on a job?"

Pit of her stomach went wonky. On a scale of one to ten, his emotions had gone to fifty. But if he wasn't mad at her for putting him in danger, why was he upset? "Uh, happened on Sunday at around eleven in the morning a few blocks from my house. No, I wasn't working. A guy in a ski mask shot at me with a .38 right after I came out of

Starbucks. Right there on the corner of Seventeenth and El Camino, across from Safeway."

"I saw that on the news. *That was you?* They didn't mention your name."

"I left before the press arrived. I was at the police station for most of the day."

His face reddened, and his brows flattened. "Jesus Christ, Hell. Why didn't you call me on Sunday? Why in good goddamned hell didn't you tell me last night when you called to cancel?"

"Why would I?"

His head jerked backwards. "*Why would you?* Because I care about you, you idiot!"

Anger flared through her. How dare he pull the caring card! While she was okay with being used—she was using him, too—using had nothing to do with caring. "Bullshit you care about me. I have no idea why you're getting all upset."

His hot gaze flaring even more, his mouth hardened. "Don't tell me how I feel, woman. Jesus Christ, you're a piece of work. After all this outrageous sex and all this time together, you don't expect me to be upset when you tell me in this stupidly casual tone that you got shot at two fucking days ago?"

There was her answer. Dude was freaking out at the thought of getting cut off from his sex fix. Of course.

But that made no sense, either. She was one of a thousand lovers. She was nothing to this guy. Something else must be going on with him.

She waved a hand dismissively. "Well, yeah, but I thought you'd be mad that I put you in danger."

"No, I'm upset that *you're* in danger, you moron!"

Right. She looked away and bit her lip. At this point her plate was so full she had no mindshare to try to figure out why he was overreacting. Best to ignore him. Except that if he was freaking out now, she couldn't imagine what he was going to do when she dropped the next bomb. "Somehow I don't think what I have to tell you now is going to help stop all this weird, misplaced emotion of yours," she said more to herself.

"What?"

She finally met his flaming gaze. Her instinct was to hide behind something. "I think the attempt on my life has something to do with you."

His eyes widened, and he took in a deep breath. "*What?* How?"

She tried to maintain her detached, emotionless affect. "The threatening note referred to my sex life. We interviewed my other boyfriends, and they all have solid alibis. We have a few more people we need to find pertaining to them—potentially jealous girlfriends— but today when we were investigating the case—"

"Alibi? You think I tried to kill you?"

"No."

"Wait, what note?"

"Oh, this threatening note that someone taped to my door," she tossed off with a hand shrug.

His face twisted with anger. "Hell! When?"

She lifted one shoulder. "I don't know. Few weeks ago."

"A few weeks! What did it say?"

"Uh...*stop fucking him or I'll kill you, bitch.*"

"Him? Him who?"

"Got me. But now I think they meant you."

"Why you didn't tell me?" His forehead beaded with sweat, and his complexion turned an even deeper red. She hadn't seen him this riled since their first meeting. "Misplaced emotion, my ass, what the hell is wrong with you?"

"Me? What the hell is wrong with you? Why are you yelling?"

"Why am I yelling? Woman, you're fucking crazy! You get a threatening letter, someone shoots at you, and you don't expect me to react?"

"I didn't expect this level of emotion."

"What? You think I'm some cold fish?" He gestured violently toward himself. "That I don't feel? That I'm too *rich* to feel *real* emotions for *real* people? Especially people I spend this much time with? *Why didn't you call me?*"

Hell blinked and searched for words. "Because we're only fuck buddies, and you're married."

"What bullshit. You know Sherry and I are only married in name."

"But you're still married. I hate this whole adultery thing. That's why I keep trying to end this."

He looked away for a moment, his face pained. "I've got every lawyer I know working on the divorce, but apparently the pre-nup we signed years ago has titanium walls fifty feet thick, and none of us expected the changes to our holdings. There's some wording that is totally screwing us, so we're trying to get a judge to give us a pass on the interpretation."

Her stomach scrunched a bit, but she dismissed the reaction and beefed up her emotional armor. How many men had she investigated who gave similar stories to their mistresses? How many stories had Marco fed her in the beginning? She'd already been through the waiting-for-the-married-guy-to-leave-his-wife scenario. She knew how it ended. He stayed married, and Hell stayed single. Yippee.

Besides, no matter what her unruly heart was telling her, she did not want a relationship with a spoiled, rich, serial cheater. Bad boys were for sex, not marriage. "I don't want you to. I have no emotional investment here. This is just recreational sex to me," she said with a hard edge. "Which is why I didn't call you. If you were my real boyfriend, you would have been the first person I called after the police. But you're not."

His face and shoulders drooped, his pain lines deepened, and he actually looked wounded. "I don't know how you do it, but you always make me feel cheap. And used, and low. Maybe I'm not your boyfriend, but I don't even rate high enough as a friend for you to tell me that someone tried to kill you? You don't even consider me a friend, do you?"

Maybe he was going through Male Menopause. Was on his Man Period. "Of course I do. Look, I'm sorry, I didn't tell anyone. Don't take it personally. Besides, I'm totally flipped out about it. How am I supposed to tell someone that?"

"I don't know. How about, 'Brad, I got shot at, and I'm freaked out and that's why I'm breaking our date.' How hard was that?" he fired at her.

She flashed back to the street corner. Sweat broke out all over, her heart went into double time, and she breathed harder. The black metal in the assailant's hands, the flash, her ears ringing, the terror. The abject horror of realizing that someone was trying to kill her. Fear ravaged her thoughts, and she fought for mental clarity. All she wanted was to be back at home in bed holding Secret Teddy.

A voice questioned if she'd been hiding from her true fear by becoming obsessed with Brad dumping her. Hiding in the familiar pain of rejection. Because there wasn't one part of her that knew how to deal with the death threat.

"Hell? How hard was that?" His voice pierced her mental fog.

"Hard. I don't..." Tears burned the backs of her eyes, and she fought to keep from curling into a ball. She'd kept the fear at bay ever since the attack, but all this weird, unnecessary, and unexpected emotion with Brad was pushing her over the edge. She couldn't afford to break now. Not in front of him.

"What?" he asked, giving her a little shake.

"I don't want to deal with it. I'm..." She tried to think of anything else.

But all she saw was the gunman pointing that fucking weapon at her.

Her lower lip trembled, her throat closed up, and a few tears escaped.

The hard lines of his face softened. "Jesus, Hell. I'm sorry. I didn't mean to yell at you. Come here," he said in a tender tone, his arms outstretched.

Her insides hurt like he'd ground them in a meat tenderizer. She tried to detach from her reaction. "I'm fine," she said, her voice quavering.

"Bullshit." He slid closer and took her in his arms. Hugging her tight to his chest, he kissed her on the forehead. "It's okay to be scared. I'm scared, too. I can't believe you almost got killed."

She wanted to push away, jump out of that bed, and run for the door. Or sob her guts out, and neither could happen or he'd know what she felt. With Herculean effort, she wrestled her emotions back into their cages. She couldn't figure out which was more painful, this nonsense with Brad or the attempt on her life.

"I'm cool." She tried to pull away, but he wouldn't let her.

"Just let me hold you, you idiot. For fuck's sake, it isn't weakness. I'd need to be held if someone shot at me."

She finally allowed him to hold her but visualized being at home alone. This was a kajillion times worse than being dumped. She scrambled for a way out. She ignored his strong, warm arms and his piney cologne mixed with his own earthy scent. The feel of his skin against hers. His heart beating. His steady, sure breathing.

Until she realized that BC was all she could think about. How much she craved him. How badly she wished she could trust him. Wished they were in a real relationship.

Her body went to battle stations, and her stomach tightened hard as a fist. Her heart's warning system blared. *Mission abort! Emotional shields have been breached! A long-term-relationship-with-BC thought bomb has penetrated our defenses!*

Good holy God. She'd fallen in love with Brad. Like, actual, real love. She didn't love the dates or the condo or the booze or the food— it was him. The man himself.

Her heart was in such agony she was surprised it didn't spontaneously eject from her chest.

This was the dumbest thing she'd ever done on record. Dumber than her affair with Marco, dumber than moving next door to her parents, dumber than talking back to that judge. The pinnacle of dumbness. The epoch of dumb. She had to get out of there!

"I still wish you would have called me Sunday night," he said softly.

His words cut through her like he'd taken a chainsaw to her guts.

"BC, of course I didn't. We had no plans to see each other," she said, trying to sound cold.

He pushed away and pursed his lips. "You know what I mean. I see you upwards of three times a week, woman. I care for you. A lot. But you shut the door in my face every time the conversation turns toward us."

Tears were a breath away. She looked away to shield herself from his intense stare. "There is no us."

"I spend more time with you than I do with anyone else."

Ditto, but she wasn't going to tell him that. "So what?" she bit out. Pushing away from him, she got out of the bed and headed to the ice bucket in the corner of the bedroom to retrieve a beer and put some distance between them. She had half a mind to grab her clothes, run out the door, and keep running.

She opened a beer and drank a long swig, wishing the cold liquid would take away all her pain and need. The idiot had to be lying about spending more time with her than anyone else. Dude was incapable of going without sex for even a few hours. He had to have a whole team that serviced him. An entire platoon of hot models at his beck and call.

He homed in on her face. "You care just as much about me, don't you?" Clearly fishing. The asshole.

She took an even bigger drink of the beer, then wiped her mouth with the back of her hand. "I don't sleep with people I don't care about."

"You clearly care more about me than you want to."

A sharp, stabbing pain pierced her and she put a hand to her chest. What the *hell* was wrong with this bastard? Why was he trying to get her to admit she liked him when they were in a dead-end relationship? Did he need the ego boost? Or did he just like hurting her?

"We're not talking about this. We need to go back to the real subject here. Which is that one or both of our lives is in danger. From your enemies. Or girlfriends. Or wife. I really don't think it's coming from me."

"Why do you think it's coming from me again?"

She let out a sigh, relieved to get him back on the subject of her attempted murder. "Today I was on the case, and everyone we interviewed had seen this weird old lady following them around. A librarian-looking woman in brown, dowdy clothes with coke-bottle-thick glasses, support hose, and a helmet of gray hair."

He pointed at her. "Wait. I was at Madera at the Rosewood Hotel one afternoon about a month ago, and a strange woman sat at the bar drinking milk and staring at me. Sounds just like that."

"Unsurprising. She followed all my boyfriends around. I still don't know who she is. But watch out for her if you see her. She's dangerous. Today we ran into her and were chasing her, and she pulled a gun on us and—"

His face screwed up with horror. "Hell! What the fuck? Another gun?"

"Yeah, so don't approach her if you see her."

"I won't. But Hell, you need protection, you need—"

"Wait, okay? I'm telling you why we think this is related to you."

"Okay, okay," he said, frustrated.

She sat on the edge of the bed, careful to stay out of his reach. "So after the librarian—that's what we're calling her—pointed that gun at us, we followed her and lost her, but her car license led us to the hotel where she'd been staying. The greasy, fat, nasty manager there said he saw her with a tall blonde lady wearing a yoga outfit who had obviously hired her. He described Lindsay, Sherry, and Gwen."

He made a dismissive gesture and gave a quick shake of his head. "That's crazy. None of those ladies is capable."

"Lindsay's a bucket of whacko, and Sherry's a lot smarter than you give her credit for. And remember she said that she'd kill you if you tried to leave her." Hell took a drink of the beer. "But only if you left her for another woman, which you won't ever do. While you're fucking a herd of us, she couldn't be bothered. As long as you appear to be faithful, that's all she cares about. So there should be no danger from her. But I'll look into her alibi and make sure. I've been wrong about people before."

"Can you do it without contacting her?"

Hell nodded. "I have to. She thinks I'm Jeanne Simari, owner of an office equipment repair business."

He snorted. "Right."

"I'll talk to your maid, Esmeralda. She knows everything, I'll bet. I also need to eliminate Gwen—"

"Not capable. Too level-headed."

"I still need to meet her and eliminate her."

"I can arrange that."

She downed nearly the rest of the bottle. "Lindsay's still high on the suspect list, even though my gut said she didn't do it. But she's got a hell of a motive. I have to talk to her, convince her I'm on her side, and get her to open up to me. I know!" She pointed at him. "I'll tell her that you dumped me. I'll pretend to be totally heartbroken and talk about hating you so she'll drop her guard. We can bond on destroying you. If she's the one, not only will that take me off her hit list, hopefully she'll reveal something so I can nail her for my attack."

He frowned. "Bond on destroying me? Don't go too overboard."

"Lots of material." She grinned, now happier that she'd overcome the earlier emotional strafing run. Then she realized that she had to ask for the list of all his new lovers. Her mood hit the floorboards again. She mentally removed her heart and threw it into the trunk of her car. After a deep breath and the rest of her beer, she gestured toward him. "Since you broke it off with Lindsay, Gwen can't be the only other woman you're seeing. Unfortunately, I need the list of your entire herd." *So I can make up my Hit List and strangle them all.*

His gray eyes troubled, he pursed his lips. "I'm not sleeping with a herd."

Amazing how well the man could lie. "Sure you are."

"Maybe you are, but I'm not. You and Gwen are it. The whole list."

Right. Her pulse quickened, and her irritation built. "Dude, if you're not honest with me, I can't protect myself."

"I am being honest with you. Look to your own *herd*," he said, saying herd like he was saying a bad word.

Her body went hot and hard, and she gripped her bottle tighter.

Glaring, she snapped, "I don't care if you're sleeping with the entire Dallas Cowboy cheerleading squad, I just need the truth."

His jaw tightened, and his gaze fired hot into hers. "I'm telling you the truth. Don't judge me based upon your ability to juggle a team."

She had to stop herself from hitting him. "I'm not juggling a team!" She forcibly made herself calm. "Sorry. I don't want to yell at you. I just don't want to die."

The look in his eye turned steely. "I don't want you to die, either. That's why I think you ought to take a hard look at your other men. I don't think the threat is coming from me."

Unable to keep eye contact, she concentrated on her empty beer bottle. He'd better never find out that he was the only one she was seeing. She'd never live down the humiliation. Well, it didn't matter because she was breaking up with him. All this emotional crap had to stop.

"Hell?"

"What?"

"You *are* still sleeping with a herd, aren't you?"

Her heart rate jumped high. Her body language had given her away! She forced all expression from her face. "That's my business. I don't want you knowing about my other boyfriends." All none of them.

His expression went stony, and his mouth curved downward. "What about Marco Capasso? Seems like he'd be a top suspect."

Her stomach knotted, and she forced it to ease. "Not him." Probably.

BC continued to stare at her.

"It's not. At least that's what he says. Nor is the threat coming from the Bay Area underworld, or my job. He thinks the threat is coming from someone close to me in my personal life. Like, from you."

Brad's face flushed, and his eyes darkened. "Me? That asshole is still trying to separate us, isn't he?"

"We're not talking about him."

"You're still seeing him, aren't you?"

Fury and frustration jettisoned her from the bed, and she stormed back to the beer bucket. "Brad! Do I have to leave?"

"No." He looked away, then turned back. "I just worry about you. People shooting at you, Mafia bosses lurking around."

"He's not lurking. I wish you'd never found out about him." And vice versa. She threw away her empty, fished another Heineken out of the ice, and popped off the top.

"You sure he had nothing to do with it? Trying to scare you away from me?"

"He doesn't care that much."

"The cyber war he launched on me proves otherwise."

Her stomach knotted, and she snapped her attention to him. "He's still after you?"

"He's backed off because we were able to shut him down, but with what's happening with you, I'm sure he'll start up again."

She relaxed. Okay, Brad's paranoia, not reality. Thank God, because she had no real adequate way to protect herself from Capasso.

Brad gestured toward her. "Maybe because I'm armed with big guns, he's shifted to intimidating you. You know he's capable."

Her jaw popped, and she had to force it to loosen. She'd give her liver to go back in time and ensure that neither man had found out about the other. "Don't you think he was the first one I thought of? But I believe him." Not really.

"No, you don't. I see that look in your eye."

Turning away, she shook her head. "You are making up shit to fit your twisted view of reality."

"You're seeing me against his wishes. You even admitted that."

She clenched her teeth and fists and pointed vehemently toward the exit. "Unless you want me to walk right out that door—and so help me God, I will this time—that discussion is closed."

With a brief brow raise, he leaned back and eyed her. "Always throwing up your walls."

She ignored his volley but let out a long sigh. "Except for the fact that I have to know who you're sleeping with right now. Under any other circumstances, I would not want the information. So tomorrow, I'll contact Gwen and Lindsay. Or maybe I'll have Matt talk to them."

"Who's Matt? Is he the 'we' you keep referring to about today's investigation? You hired someone to help you?"

"Yeah." She sat down on the bed again.

He brightened. "Excellent. Now that's a step in the right direction."

"Yeah, well, uh, about that... you're gonna think I'm crazy..." She straightened the covers.

His attention on her intensified. "Who did you hire? Matt who?"

"Matt Sinclair."

BC sat straight up, his gaze blazing. "You *what*? That asshole who put you in jail? Have you lost your mind? You have lost your mind. First you don't tell me you got shot at and you've been getting threatening notes, then you hook up with fucking Matt Sinclair."

"He's good, and I think he can save my life."

"Thompson could, too."

"I can't afford Thompson. Matt's the best value for the money."

"I'll pay for it."

"No."

"Hell, don't let your goddamned pride stand in the way of your life."

"I'm not. He's good. We have a truce right now. So will you talk to him?"

Worry lines deep, he nodded. "Yeah, but I still can't believe this. What happened? Tell me the whole story and everything the police said."

She sighed, chugged half of the beer, and then embarked on the tale. Partway through, he grabbed her and dragged her into his embrace. She barely had time to put the beer on the nightstand. He practically cut off her breathing he held her so tightly. After she finished, he kissed her with urgency.

Dude was blowing her mind. He couldn't really care about her, could he?

A tiny microscopic flame of hope ignited deep within her. What if

BC really liked her? Would he leave his wife for her? A split second later, she took out her mental fire hose and doused the thoughts.

Are you crazy? A billionaire? With feelings for a middle-class tomboy detective his age? Ha!

Besides, this was BC they were talking about. Just because he thought he had feelings didn't mean he had real feelings. He was a human penis who had to be sleeping with a bevy of thirty-somethings. She was nothing more to him than a stand-in for when his young girlfriends were busy working late at Facebook and Google.

She tried to pull away, but he wouldn't let go of her. "Jesus, Hell."

Finally, she managed to push back from him. But when she made eye contact, the pain in his gray eyes shocked her.

Unable to stand his intensity, she looked down at her fingers intertwined in his. "So while this is all going on, we should probably keep our distance." She angled a glance at him.

He paled like he'd just been informed of a family member's death. "Fuck. That."

BC's odd reactions were starting to freak her out. Maybe he was having a mental breakdown. "It's sensible."

"Bullshit. I won't stop seeing you, Hell," he said, his voice laced with need. He pulled her closer to him. "I'll hire more bodyguards."

She pretended to be elsewhere and ignored his bizarre emotions. "You might need them."

"Not for me, for you." He gave her a little push.

"No, I'm fine," she said with confidence she didn't feel. "I've got Matt. Besides, the threat could be over. So I'll have Matt call you, okay?"

"Whatever we need to do to keep you safe." He molded his body to hers, then gave her an emotionally raw look—his gaze both haunted and adoring—and kissed her.

His kiss went way beyond sexual; it was a purely emotional release on his part. He'd never kissed her so tenderly or lovingly before. Like he'd declared his feelings for her in a large Broadway production.

Hell tried to distance herself but got lost in the heady feelings.

She'd forgotten how it felt to be needed. The passion. The intense connection.

A white-hot ball of energy lit up her chest. The intensity spread throughout her body, and she buzzed with a fiery charge like she and Brad together created a perfect electrical circuit. An overwhelming feeling of oneness overcame her.

All at once, she shut down and imagined a thick concrete barrier around herself. Pushing back the tears, she mentally transported back home.

What the hell was she thinking? Getting lost in a liar who slept with legions of hot young women?

Was she this stupid?

CHAPTER 13

A cloud of gloom over her head, Hell sat at her desk and threw a dart at Keith Richards.

Welcome to Misery World. Her heart hurt like she'd sent it through an industrial wringer, her eyes were puffy and sore, while the coffee ate a hole through her stomach. She hadn't been in this much emotional pain since Capasso beat the crap out of her. Since Josh died. Rarely had her life sucked more.

With almost no sleep, her brain was a minefield of horrible images of potential futures. Sitting alone and crippled from an attack in a wheelchair in her apartment in front of a dying Christmas tree. Her funeral with no one in attendance but her cousin. BC smiling in a lounge chair next to a sparkling pool, surrounded by a crowd of gorgeous, bikini-clad supermodels.

Swallowing hard, she threw another dart. Why hadn't she noticed that she was falling for him? How had she let it get this far? How the hell was she supposed to avoid him when the threat against her was coming from his world?

She blew out a stream of air between her lips, fished out a Kleenex from the box, and blew her nose. After dabbing her eyes with a wet washcloth, she forced herself to snap out of it and get back to the case. The sooner it was solved, the sooner she never had to see him again.

All she wanted to do was talk to Gwen Lake and Lindsay and get the interviews over with, but Matt had made her promise to wait for him. Second problem, neither Big Bird nor Looney Lindsay were interested in talking. Brad had given her the women's phone numbers and email addresses, and she'd tried both several times, but neither had responded. Which made the women twice as suspicious and rocketed them to the top of the suspect list.

Matt and she planned to hook up at one. He'd had to take his wife to the dentist for a root canal.

Hell aimed for Keith's crotch and hit his left nut. "Only two and a half more hours and then I can— I am so lying to myself!" She stood. "There is no freakin' way I can wait. Sorry, Matt, but I ain't just sitting here, I'll lose my mind. Besides, with Mr. Sinclair, I think the best way to handle him is to ask forgiveness rather than permission. Gwen Lake probably won't go all *Exorcist* on me like Lindsay might, not if I catch Big Bird at work. Unless she's as insane as Lindsay." She paused a moment to evaluate the potential danger, but her legs urged her to leave. She shrugged. "Only one way to find out."

After reapplying her makeup, Hell drove to Gwen Lake's corporate offices in Redwood Shores, but could not get past the security in the lobby. Gwen was there but was "in meetings."

BC clearly didn't have the influence over her that he'd thought.

No matter. Permission or no, Gwen was going to talk to her.

Hell asked to use the bathroom and, on the way, ran into a maintenance worker. She "accidentally" smashed into the poor Latina and relieved her of her ID badge. After apologizing profusely in Spanish, she left the building and returned to her car. The contents of her trunk had exactly what she needed.

A few minutes later, wearing a janitor's uniform with the stolen badge, a wig, and dark makeup—carrying a bucket with cleaning supplies—Hell became invisible.

With her heart rate high and her stomach twisted, she breezed into the building like she lived there. Security only glanced at her.

Relieved, she hopped on the service elevator and went to Gwen's floor. A minute later, she'd located her office.

Pre-performance adrenaline surged through her body. Hell took a second to clear her mind, push her fears away, and concentrate on her objectives. After a deep breath, she walked inside Gwen's spacious and modern outer office.

Gwen Lake stood in front of a large glass and chrome desk, giving orders to her secretary, a young Asian woman. Hell recognized Lake from her corporate photos.

Tall and willowy, her rival had bright blue eyes, puffy, blonde, neck-length hair, and a fairly large nose. Lindsay had been right, Gwen did look a little like Big Bird, but she was also strikingly beautiful. Like a blonde Grecian goddess. She wore a smart, dark business suit with a pencil skirt, and looked like she'd just gotten her hair done. She looked perfect.

An image of BC screwing the hell out of Gwen flashed through her mind. Her teeth clenched, and jealousy burned hot through her veins. Gwen was tons younger and much better-looking than her. All her instincts told her to punch the woman flat. Rip her apart. Destroy the competition.

Unhelpful!

Blocking the unwelcome porn from her mind, she forced her attention to the job at hand.

"Yes? Can I help you?" her secretary asked.

"Ten minutes with Miss Lake."

Gwen swung her gaze onto Hell. "You're not a maintenance worker. Call security."

The Asian girl's eyes went big. She reached for her phone.

Hell took a small step forward, hands up. "No need. I won't hurt you. My name is Helen Trent, and I need to find out if you tried to kill me."

Gwen's mouth dropped open, and her pupils dilated. "Call them now."

Hell's gut reaction was that Gwen was not behind the shooting. Too shocked, too taken aback, none of her emotions had been masked. No eye movement darting left, she stared into Hell's eyes with fear.

Hell pointed at the secretary. "If you call security, you're going to lose your job, girl. Because this woman will be fired after news gets out to the stockholders that she's being investigated for an attempted murder."

The secretary's pallor whitened, and she put the phone back on the hook.

"Don't listen to her," Gwen said to her secretary. Eyes narrowed, she turned to Hell. "Don't threaten me, or you'll—"

Hell talked over her. "Once the cops find out who you are, they're going to want to have a nice, long chat with you. They, like me, will want a solid alibi for your whereabouts on Sunday morning. If you talk to me now, you won't have to talk to them. I only want ten minutes to ask you a few questions."

"Leave now or be arrested. Call security," she ordered. Scared, not angry. No jealousy, no intent other than to get away from Hell.

Hell had saved her best weapon for last. "Bet the Silicon Valley gossip websites will love this one, won't they?" she drawled. "Isn't your company going public soon? Wouldn't your boss love a huge exposé on your affair with a married billionaire splashed all over the news?"

Big Bird twisted her mouth and put her hands on her hips. "Bitch."

"Look, I don't want to be here any more than you want me here, but someone tried to kill me, and I'm gonna find out who. Your answers satisfy me, and the cops won't even have to know about you."

Her secretary picked up the phone again. "I'll call security."

Gwen stopped the Asian girl with a hand on her arm. "I'll talk to her." She glared at Hell and gestured to her office.

A rush of victory flowed through her. Good. Except now she had to spend more time with the little slag. "Thank you," she said like *fuck you.*

As Hell walked past Gwen, the blonde seared her with her blue gaze. Very pretty woman and not a whiff of danger about her. Hell relaxed. Almost completely convinced she had nothing to do with the shooting. Which was excellent. Now she could focus solely on her hatred of the girl.

Gwen shut the door behind her. "Ten minutes. Get started."

Hell sat in a leather and chrome chair in front of Gwen's large, immaculate, glass-topped desk. The entire room projected power, from the floor-to-ceiling windows overlooking the San Francisco Bay to the chic furnishings.

Hell's face flushed uncomfortably, and she shifted in her chair. What an awful mirror. She was a ragamuffin, homeless gutter dweller compared to this powerful CFO. Why had BC started seeing Hell when he had this sophisticated hottie at his beck and call?

Gwen took her seat and folded her hands on top of her desk, gazing at Hell with the same hatred Hell felt for her.

Hell cleared her throat and imagined being as powerful as the blonde. "Where were you Sunday morning at eleven?"

"A restaurant in downtown San Mateo," she bit out tersely. "Viognier's, over Draeger's grocery store. At a private function. My boyfriend will corroborate that."

The hair on the back of her neck stood up. Far too close to the action. Placed Big Bird ten blocks from the scene of the crime.

But if she had shot at Hell, wouldn't she have come up with a better alibi? From the astounding amount of degrees and certificates displayed on the wood-paneled wall behind her, Gwen was no dummy. Hell's doubts about her involvement grew. "Wait. Did you say your boyfriend? I thought Brad—"

"Brad was a mistake."

Hell must have misunderstood her. "Was?"

"Was."

"You're not seeing him any longer?"

"No."

Why would the girl lie to her? "He told me just last night that he was still seeing you."

"News to me."

Hell stared at her, her mind a near blank with confusion. "You're not lying, are you?"

"Why would I? I hate that bastard."

Her belly bubbling with joy, Hell fought to keep a lid on her elation. She gripped the arms of the chair to stop herself from performing a spontaneous victory dance all over the office. Gwen and Brad were over! Woo-hoo!

Like walking into a wall, Hell's brain and reactions stopped abruptly. Brad had sworn he was seeing Gwen. "Why would he lie to me?" she asked herself aloud. "I've known about you all along. I don't care. I have other lovers, too."

"He's a snake. If he's lying to you, it's only for his benefit."

"Absolutely. So wait, you hate him?"

Gwen snorted. "I barely cared about him at all. He was a convenience and came at a time when I needed someone."

Curiosity surpassed her thrill, and Hell examined Gwen closely. The pain behind her eyes didn't match her neutral expression. "How long did you two see each other?"

Gwen's jaw tensed. "Is this part of the investigation?"

"Look, I don't care about the guy. I have seven other boyfriends," Hell bragged in a rough tone.

Her thin, light eyebrows rose high. "Seven? Why don't you look there?"

"I am. How long?"

"Seven? Really?" Gwen's forehead wrinkled, and the line between her eyes deepened. "How does someone like you get seven boyfriends? You must not be choosy."

Hell ignored the jab. "Very choosy. But it's not hard to collect a group of young, single men when all you want is clean sex with no attachments."

Her angry expression turned intrigued. "Young? How young?"

"Roman, he's a mercenary, is the youngest at thirty-seven. And the hottest. Holy. Moly."

Gwen leaned in. "So you don't see them all at once."

"No. Average about one a week. Some I see monthly, some yearly. They all add up to about a half a boyfriend."

"Interesting. I never could do that. I kept falling in love."

"Not into that myself." *Big fat liar.* "Besides, none of them are worth loving. Especially Brad. What a douche." She inwardly winced. She thought a lot of things about Brad, but never that he was a douche.

"If you don't like him, why are you sleeping with him?"

Hell smiled. "You know why."

"Yeah…" She looked away and pursed her lips.

"So how long did you guys go out?"

"Oh, I don't know," Gwen said with a shrug, feigning indifference, but her pain lines told the truth.

Hell waited.

"About a year or two, I don't know."

"A year or *two*?"

Gwen finally looked her in the eye. "Okay, two and a half years."

"And you never cared about him?"

Gwen sighed, and her attention drifted to her desk. She straightened out a pen to make it align with her laptop. "I did."

"Not worth it, huh?"

The blonde looked up at Hell, her eyes full of fiery rage. "You know him. He's a self-centered prick. It's all about him. A dead end. Initially, I thought he might leave his wife, but he'll never leave that battle-axe. I think he likes the torture. I was too nice *to* him and too nice *for* him."

Probably the truth. "So you broke it off with him?"

Her expression turned even more hurt, and she looked at her lap. "No." Then she frowned, her cheeks flushed pink, and she held her chin high. "I mean, I was just about to. You know, leave him. He just beat me to it."

Hell gasped, absolutely floored. "Wait a minute. *He* broke it off? How could he possibly turn down sex with you?" Didn't sound like BC at all.

Gwen seemed equally perplexed. "I don't know. Came out of nowhere."

"He's insane. You're young and beautiful and super accomplished. What was he thinking?"

She brightened a bit. "That's what I thought. Jerk. I go see him like usual, and I walk into the hotel room, and he's dressed."

"Dressed? Brad?" Hell could not get her bearings.

Big Bird's manner became more confidential, and she lowered her voice and leaned in farther, elbows on the desk. "I know, right? So I ask him what's up, and as soon as he said we should sit on the sofa and talk, I knew he was breaking it off. I just couldn't believe it. I mean, two and a half years, and then he suddenly ends it with no warning?"

"Did he tell you why?"

"He just said he thought it was time to end things. That he didn't think we had a future. He knows I want to get married, and he said he wanted to let me go to find a husband."

Hell's mind hurt. This behavior did not fit the profile of the playboy billionaire she knew. "This makes no sense. Way too altruistic for that guy."

"That's what I thought."

Hell finally made sense of something Gwen had said earlier. "Wait? Hotel? Didn't he get that condo for you?"

"What condo?"

Her stomach felt weird, and her extremities began to tingle. None of this was making sense. "He didn't take you to a condo?"

"No. You meet him at a condo?"

Hell sat back and rubbed her forehead to ease the pain of wrinkling. "Yeah. Okay, this is all too weird. I must be next on the chopping block."

"Obviously."

A bomb of anger went off in her gut, but she held her expression steady. Couldn't let the little bitch get any points. "Like I care. Unlike you, I'm indifferent here. I just want to save my life. So if he dumped you, and

I'm next, the dude must have gathered a whole flock of women by now. He must have rented that condo to save money. Cheaper than renting a hotel room every day. Safer so no one notices his parade of concubines."

Gwen gave a nod. "Makes sense."

Hell finally shrugged. "Still makes zero sense that he'd end it with you. But it sounds like you're doing well. Gettin' a boyfriend this fast? Like, in a couple weeks, right? Good work."

"I met Daniel two months ago, in mid January."

Her train of thought hit a bump. "Wait, when did Brad break it off? I thought this must have happened recently."

"No. Early December."

Hell's stomach dropped to the floor, and she stopped breathing. *Early goddamned December? BC dumped Gwen in December?* Why would he swear he was still seeing her? What a big fat liar! He had to be seeing a whole lot of other women. Had to be. Because the alternative was too disturbing. And weird. And about as likely as an honest Wall Street banker.

Hell finally realized that Gwen had been talking, and she'd missed almost all of it.

"...but it all turned out well for me," Gwen said. "I met Daniel right afterwards, and now I actually have a real relationship that I don't have to hide. What I don't understand is why Brad's still seeing you."

"I don't know. Why?"

She snorted. "Have you looked at yourself lately?"

Hell glanced down at her uniform. "Yeah, I'm in a maid's costume and makeup and a wig."

"I saw you on the news. Don't you normally look like some aging, old, punker freak in a black leather jacket?" she said with a curled lip and a mean smile. She lifted her chin. "And you're a *private detective?*" Her big nose wrinkled, and she took on an imperious expression. "Brad's never dated outside his class. Something has to be wrong. Maybe he's having a midlife crisis. Why else would he suddenly be slumming?"

Her stomach tightened, and her heart stung. *Don't give her any points!* Spitting out the hook, she sat on her reaction. "Only reason you'd take a potshot at me is if you still liked him."

"Or if I loathed you." The hurt in her eyes was clear. She'd loved Brad and was taking out her anger on Hell.

Hell relaxed and let the comments slide. "You liked him a lot more than you're letting on," she said with a chuckle.

"Not enough to kill over. Believe me, he may be good in the sack, but that's it. Daniel is ten times the man."

"You loved Brad."

"No."

Hell made a dismissive noise.

"Okay. I did. Until I found out about *Lindsay*." She said Lindsay like she was saying a dirty word.

"Did he tell you that you were his only lover?"

"Yes. He's a total liar. I ran into him at a hotel we frequented, and he was going into a room with Lindsay."

Hell winced. "Ooo." She pictured catching Brad walking into a hotel room with another woman, and a flash of anger tightened her muscles. She'd want to beat them both bloody. "Well, that sucks."

It also proved beyond a shadow of a doubt that he had lied to her the night before about his other lovers. Dude was a liar. Liars lied. Hopefully, he'd be honest with Matt so they could investigate the rest of his herd.

Gwen looked away and twisted her mouth. Lines of upset wrinkled her perfect alabaster skin. "I thought he'd realize how great I was if he spent time with that lunatic."

"He should have. She's a freak."

Finally, Gwen sent her a look that wasn't filled with hatred. "You got that right. Is he still seeing her?"

"No. After I found out that she put a GPS unit on his car and was stalking him, he got scared."

Her blue eyes widened. "Holy shit."

"I'd warned him when he hired me back in November that she was a bucket of crazy. He was an idiot for sleeping with her."

"What about her? Is she after you?"

"Possible. I don't know why. How could I be a threat? He means nothing to me," she bit out with a cruel edge. *Ha.* "I don't want anything from him but clean sex once in a while." *And a ring.* "Besides, I'm just about to move on. Roman's coming back into town, and he's way more fun than Brad." *Hardly.* "I'm just pissed that some meaningless sex has almost cost me my life." *Meaningless to him.*

"Yet you're still seeing him."

"I'm clearly self-destructive." Really, really self-destructive.

Gwen laughed and seemed shocked that she had. "You must be."

"Have you had any death threats or noticed anyone following you around?"

"No." She shook her head, then her brows shot upward. "Well, there was this strange, squat, little lady in brown I saw everywhere for a few weeks."

The librarian strikes again. Yet another reason Gwen was off the suspect list. "Yes. She followed all of my lovers and all of Brad's. I'm trying to find out more about her."

"Who is she?"

"I don't know. But if you see her, let me know. And don't engage with her. She pulled a gun on me last time I ran into her."

"Isn't she the one who shot at you?"

"I don't know. I have to follow up on all the leads. I'll need your boyfriend's phone number to corroborate your alibi."

"I don't want him involved."

"He won't be."

"I don't want you calling him."

"Either me or the police."

Her eyes went cold, and her mouth tightened. "Bitch."

"I'm only trying to save my life and your humiliation."

Gwen had no comeback for that one.

Her mind reeling, Hell left Gwen's office and drove home to change, but mentally missed most of the ride there. If BC wasn't screwing Gwen, then who else was he dating? Why hadn't he spilled their names the night before? They'd both gone into the affair with the knowledge that the other person had multiple lovers, and she'd never given him any indication that she cared much about him. Why would he withhold the information?

Maybe the number was so high even BC was ashamed. But he'd been pretty open with her about his immorality. Why would he suddenly go mute now?

Maybe his other lovers were so high profile he couldn't afford to get them involved. Knowing him, he could be sleeping with the First Lady or something. That would account for his lies. Damn, he probably wouldn't even tell Matt.

Death would help her out. He could find out anything.

A weird thought occurred to her. BC couldn't just be seeing her, could he?

No way. It was physically impossible for him to be with one woman. And if he were to choose one woman, she would most certainly be blonde, accomplished, thin as a rail, and rich. Not a broke, pink-haired, pot-smoking private investigator with a bit of extra meat on her bones.

A part of her opened a forbidden door, the door to her secret desires, and she peeked inside. How amazingly wonderful and spectacular would it be if BC had fallen for her? Being with him forever? Waking up in his arms? Laughing at his jokes and growing old together? An image of the two of them standing at the altar of the Church of the Redwoods in Portola Valley saying their vows flashed through her mind, and her heart burst with need.

A split second later she took out an imaginary machine gun and shredded the happy picture with a spray of bullets.

When would she learn? Hell's dreams never came true. Only her nightmares.

CHAPTER 14

WEDNESDAY, MARCH 9, 2011, 1:07 P.M.

Hell waved the smoke away from her face, hoping that Matt wouldn't be too pissed at walking into a giant cloud of marijuana. He was due any minute.

She carefully placed the hot tip of the joint into the open mouth of the skull ashtray on top of her desk and applied enough pressure to douse the fire, but not enough to mash the half joint. Weed was so potent these days she only needed a few hits to keep her buzz. If she forgot and allowed herself to get caught up in the enjoyment of smoking, her frontal lobes would solidify, and it would be an hour before her brain could function properly. Dosage was still a tricky issue with marijuana. Each strain provided different effects. She liked buzzy sativa strains like Jack Herer and Sour Diesel for daytime that quelled the abusive voices screaming at her constantly but didn't take away her reasoning. Indica "in da couch" marijuana strains made her incredibly sleepy, so she used them at nighttime.

The joint stopped smoking, and Hell turned back to her computer. A quick Internet search on Gwen's boyfriend revealed little except that he loved golf, polo, and was on the board of a million corporations, and had once been a state senator.

Earlier, on her way to the office, Hell had swung by the restaurant in downtown San Mateo to interview the manager and confirm

Gwen's alibi. She'd shown photos of Gwen and her boyfriend to the tall Middle Eastern man, who had confirmed that the two had been there for brunch with a professional group. They'd arrived at ten thirty and stayed until one.

Didn't mean Gwen couldn't have left the restaurant, driven the five minutes to Seventeenth and El Camino Real, shot at Hell, popped onto Highway 92, taken the next exit at Alameda de las Pulgas or Borel, and zipped back to the restaurant in time for dessert.

Hell grabbed her iPhone and called Gwen's boyfriend. He answered right away and corroborated Gwen's alibi. Big Bird had apparently given him a heads-up. He was actually very gracious.

Hell sat back and turned in her chair to see a junco flit in and land on the young anemic maple outside her dirty office window. Leaves were trying to make a comeback on the skinny broomstick of a tree, but she wasn't sure about its fate. Being the only vegetation in a microscopic patch of asphalt that housed the Dumpster for the building didn't make for a positive future. She watered it weekly, more out of pity than necessity.

Swinging back around, she caught sight of the dying dieffenbachia shriveling in the corner, flanked by the dried, brown philodendron and the desiccated spider plant. Guilt pangs hit her. Why did she water the tree and keep forgetting her plants? Next time someone gave her a houseplant, she'd pass it along. No more vegetation guilt!

Hell opened the notebook on her desk and turned to Gwen's page. Her gut said that Big Bird wasn't capable of shooting her. While Gwen had been hurt by BC, she'd moved on. She liked her new boyfriend too much, and he seemed like a real solid guy. Plus Gwen's job was super demanding. As it stood, she worked upwards of sixty to seventy hours a week. Not a whole lot of time left for stalking and shooting at love rivals.

But until Death cleared her, Gwen Lake stayed on the list.

She leaned back in her chair. Propping her feet up on the desk, she knocked some files to the floor. She reached for the papers, but they were too far away. Shrugging, she settled back, fished out a special one-use Death cell phone from a drawer, and punched the preset number to her favorite tech guru. "Deathy honey? You there?"

His nerdy, too-much-caffeine voice came through loud and clear. "Hell, I was just about to contact you to give you my report. How is my favorite private detective doing today?"

Death's voice sounded extra geeky today, kind of like a radio announcer gnome on steroids. Come to think of it, he kind of looked like a radio announcer gnome on steroids. All he needed was the red pointy hat and the beard. His thick black nerd glasses took away from the image, however.

"Oh, I'm peachy. Anything?"

"I've exhausted my resources, and there is a complete absence of information regarding a contract murder-for-hire on you."

Her heart sank. She grimaced. The little Fear Factory in her gut produced more acid and tension. She grabbed a dart and threw it, missing Keith entirely. Who the hell was after her?

Death cleared his throat. "This is personal, or I would have uncovered a trail by now. The librarian's alias led to that one reference at the hotel. She must be paying in cash because there's no paper trail. All the investigations into you in the past week have been initiated by the local police, who turned up little, William Thompson at the behest of Brad Collins—who was able to penetrate slightly deeper into your information—the Battery Cyber Squad at the behest of Marco Capasso—who got into your computer network fairly far— plus a couple of requests from public computers in libraries in Sacramento and Stockton that were denied."

Hell moved her feet off the desk and sat up. "Wait. When did Brad investigate me? I know he did in early December of last year. Is this a new investigation?"

"Yes. Earlier today, Thompson Detective Agency launched an onslaught. Well, for them. More like a mosquito hovering around."

Her stomach went even wonkier. "Why is Brad investigating me?"

"Why don't you ask him?"

The top of her head felt like a vise was clamping down on it, and she rubbed it. Unable to account for BC's bizarre behavior, she stopped trying. Nothing and no one made sense anymore. "I will. I figured Capasso would be looking into me again. So what about Stockton and Sacramento?" She rummaged through the foot-high pile of debris on her desk for a pen.

"Public computer would suggest that the person does not want to be traced. They actually got around the initial layer of encryption, which isn't hard but proves they know something about computers. I'd say it's a high-level amateur."

"That's the librarian. And in libraries, no less. How appropriate." The tip of a pen poked out from beneath a little toy coffin holding a bendy skeleton. Hell grabbed the pen and knocked into a tall pile of receipts, scattering them everywhere. Rolling her eyes, she said, "Sacramento and Stockton? Kinda far apart, isn't it, for doing investigations?"

"She may live between both areas."

Hell flipped her notebook to the librarian page and wrote down the two cities beneath the growing list of clues about the mysterious lady in brown. "Can you give me the names and locations of the libraries?"

"Already sent."

"Cool." Hell threw her pen on top of the notebook and leaned back in her chair again. "Here's what I need. I found out that Brad lied to me last night and—"

"Shocking."

Hell chuckled and ran her hand through her hair. "Yeah, I know. He told me that he and Gwen were still seeing each other, and it turns out they're not."

"Interesting. With his profile, you'd think he'd lie to cover up an affair, not lie to cover up the absence of one."

"Maybe he's sleeping with someone high level."

"If he is, he's not using his computer or cell phone to communicate with her."

Hell sat up fast, feet flat on the floor. "You hacked his cell phone and computer?"

"I've been inside them since you asked me to back in December."

A rush of tingly energy welled up inside her. She'd forgotten all about that! Her face heated, and she winced. BC would kill her if he knew. Oh, well, too bad. This was about her life. "Awesome." Death's news finally made sense to her, and her Hope Machine jump-started. "So wait. *He's not seeing anyone but me?*"

"I didn't say that, I *said* that he's not communicating with anyone else regarding his sexual activities on any of his known computers or cell phones. But since he became aware that his computers and phone were compromised back in December, he's probably developed work-arounds by now."

A mental image of her and Brad sitting side by side in bathtubs went up in flames, and she slumped in her seat. Shit. Why couldn't she get through to herself? Brad and she would never be exclusive, nor a couple, nor married. Sometimes she hated her delusional optimism.

"However, I have no direct evidence that he has other lovers," Death continued. "When I check his cell and match up his calendar and emails together with the GPS locations, he has no unaccounted-for periods of time."

The chorus of happy voices rose again in her brain, and Hell forcibly shut them down. They were wrong. She and Brad were merely sex partners. No matter how weird he'd acted the night before. "What if he was seeing, like, the First Lady, or someone high level?"

"The trail would be visible from the Space Station."

"Why would he lie to me and say he was still seeing Gwen?"

"Because he's hiding something that I haven't found."

"But if his GPS shows that he was somewhere—"

"He could leave his phone anywhere he chooses. Especially if he is aware of the tracking software—which due to his extensive breadth of knowledge of technology would lead me to believe that he is. He could place his phone so the GPS coordinates match with his calendar."

Her mood reverted to Doom and Gloom, and she looked at the joint in the ashtray, then shook her head. Pot couldn't touch the pain ravaging her heart and gut.

But it was a start. She grabbed the joint and relit it. "Yeah...that's gotta be it," she said in her holding-in-pot-smoke voice. She blew out a cloud and coughed a bit. "Especially after I alerted him to Lindsay's surveillance. How do I find out who he's sleeping with so I can find out if she's the one who's trying to kill me?"

"I would attach another GPS unit to something he carries with him always."

"That stupid phone is the only thing. Wait, his Rolex!" she said with a large flinging gesture of her right hand. The joint slipped out of her fingers, but she caught it at the last second before it landed in a pile of papers. Wouldn't be the first time she'd lit her desk on fire.

"That would work," Death said. "I'll supply you with the perfect equipment."

She relaxed back in her seat and took another tiny hit off the now third-of-a-joint but didn't hold it in because she was getting too high. "Good, okay. Christ, this is all so complicated. Like I would care who the idiot was sleeping with," she said, carefully extinguishing the joint once again.

"Does he know that he's the only one you're currently seeing?"

Sitting straight up, she gripped the phone tighter. "How do you— Oh. Of course you know," she said, slouching again. "No. And he's not going to."

"He will."

She smacked her forehead with her palm. "Oh, crap, Thompson. Like I need anything else to worry about."

"I did warn you about interacting with powerful billionaires."

Hell made a face. "I know. I warned me, too."

"Still, perhaps he could assist you with the Capasso problem."

Her gut caved in, and she involuntarily shuddered. "No, because I'm getting rid of Brad ASAP. And hopefully, Capasso— Oh, crap. Now I got him all interested in me again with this stupid shooting. Damn it." She thumped the top of her desk with a fist and searched for another dart to throw at Keith.

"I do find it fascinating how amazingly talented you are at finding trouble regarding your male companionship."

No darts visible, Hell gave up and let out a long sigh. "Tell me about it. I wish Josh hadn't died."

"I miss him, too."

"I'd give anything to go back in time and cancel that fucking carpet cleaning."

"You must not blame yourself."

"I know." *Right.* Josh had wanted to work from home that morning, but she'd pushed him out the door because she'd been so bent on her spring-cleaning binge. Five minutes after he'd left, a semi-truck had taken him out on the freeway. She doubted she'd ever forgive herself. "Okay, keep an eye on Lindsay's computers and cell. And on Sherry's. They're both at the top of the list. What did you think about Gwen Lake?"

"Not likely your assassin. She didn't communicate with Brad or attempt to for the three months previous to your attack. Unlike Lindsay, who sends him approximately ten emails per day. Mostly questionable humor or links to sites she thinks he'd enjoy."

She'd known Brad still had contact with Lindsay! He'd lied! "Does he write back?"

"No."

Relief washed through her followed by a wave of irritation. She'd give anything to be able to reach into her heart, flip a switch, and stop loving him. "Okay, that confirms it. Lindsay's off the rails and is super obsessed with him. I need to talk to her. But I'm not sure she'll open up to me if Matt is with me. I'm thinking two of us will overwhelm her. But no way is Matt gonna let me go over there alone."

"Are you really giving him that kind of power over you and your actions?"

"Well, no. Apparently. Shit. Well, he's protecting me," she said defensively. "Wow, that was almost a whine."

Death laughed. "I love your cycles of denial. Just keep me on the line when you interview her, and we won't have any issues like the Willow Glen incident with Detective Mallory."

Hell winced. She'd been surprised by a client's husband inside their house, had covered her presence with a theft, barely escaped, then was stopped in a roadblock due to an unrelated police action just a half a mile from the scene of the crime. Even though Mallory knew she'd done it, he couldn't prove it.

"That was bad. Yes, let's not repeat that."

"Sherry Collins' lack of emails is also quite suspicious. She acts as if her computer has been compromised."

Alarms rang in her mind, and she flipped her notebook to the Sherry Collins page. "Really? How?"

"Due to the hook-ups in the Atherton house and the amount of sophisticated equipment present, Collins' household should have constant action. Sherry has almost nil. Maybe five emails a day and a few texts on her cell strictly regarding country club business. No personal email, no shopping, no searching, nothing. From the context of the emails, I know she's using another computer to do research, but I can't locate it."

"Okay, that's weird." Hell jotted down some notes.

"Which does not indicate that she's the killer. It indicates that she's living a double life. She could be involved in illegal activity, could be—"

"The drugs!" Hell exclaimed with a large gesture of her free arm, thankful it didn't hold a lit joint. "I think she's a drug addict. Probably coke or heroin. From my first interview, the exchange between the maid Esmeralda and Sherry alluded to it. I know Sherry likes getting effed up. Did you get any information on Esmeralda?" Hell wrote: *Drugs!!*

"None. I don't believe Esmeralda is her real name. My hypothesis is that she's an illegal immigrant living here under a false identity. No bank accounts, no paper trail. She cashes all her checks and pays her bills in cash. Please get me her fingerprints and a DNA sample."

"How the hell am I supposed to—? Okay, Okay." Hell knew better than to argue. "I'll figure it out." She flipped to the front of her notebook. Under her to-do list, she wrote: Fingerprints and DNA —Esmeralda.

"We will also need a GPS installed on her person."

Another simple task—ha! "Good. Well, not good, but okay. I'll put that on the list," she said, writing down the note. She looked at the astounding amount of tasks on the list and shook her head. "Christ. Why isn't this easier?"

"I apologize that I have not yet been able to determine the source of the threat. I'm utilizing all my capabilities to the task. The world would be a very desolate place without you."

"I know you're doing everything in your power, Deathy. Love you, too."

After some gossip about mutual old friends, they hung up. Hell opened the SIM card slot on the phone and withdrew the card and battery. She went into the bathroom off the main office and flushed the tiny card. After returning to her office, she put a rubber band around the cell phone and threw it, along with the batteries, into the bag of Death phones.

Hell put PN for Probably Not next to Gwen's name on the suspect list on the big dry-erase board set up in the corner of her office. She kicked some files out of the way and stepped back to examine the other names. Sherry/Esmeralda, Lindsay, Tanner, Capasso, the librarian and X. X because there was still a strong possibility none of the people on her board were the culprit. She really couldn't picture anyone on the list shooting her except the librarian.

Must be a lover of BC's he hadn't told her about. Maybe he was sleeping with a friend of hers.

Happy thought.

"Okay, so how do I convince Matt to let me go see Lindsay alone? Have to come up with a good excuse. Also need to cover up my interview of Gwen. Should be easy fooling a highly skilled detective. Piece of cake." She laughed.

Her phone played Van Halen's "Eruption." She stepped through a pile of magazines and catalogs, slipped on a *Rolling Stone*, caught herself, and finally grabbed her phone from the desk.

Matt. Speak of the devil.

Her stomach clenched. Dude still scared her on some level. Such an authoritarian.

Since he was already twenty minutes late, maybe this call was about him arriving even later. That would be cool. Give her enough time to come up with a great lie for why she'd seen Gwen without him, and maybe allow her to sneak off and question Lindsay alone.

She carefully made her way through the paper obstacle course, reached the clear spot behind her desk, and sat down. "Yeah, Matt?"

"Hey, Hell, sorry, but Patty's had a slight complication."

"She okay?"

"Yeah. Just had a bad reaction to the anesthesia and got pretty sick. Better now, but I want to make sure she's absolutely okay."

"Of course, no worries, man." Whew!

"Sorry about this. We can see Gwen and Lindsay tomorrow, okay?"

Perfect! "Good."

"I'm still on for talking to BC tonight. My son is coming to stay with Patty," Matt said. "Do you mind waiting to see the ladies?"

"Not at all."

"Great." There was a pause. "You already went and saw them."

She gasped. *How could he know?* She hesitated just that extra second. "Uh, no, I didn't, I—"

"Damn you, Hell. If this is gonna work, we have to stay on the same page."

"I didn't see them both. I swear on an ounce of marijuana that I did not—"

"Marijuana? What happened to Bibles?"

"I am far more reverent about marijuana than I am about the Bible. I swear that I did not go see them both."

"Which one did you see?"

Hell growled. Damn it. Saw right through that one.

"Hell?"

"Do you want to know what I found out, or do you want to berate me?"

"Both."

She laughed. "I hate that you can see through my lies."

"Starting to get to know you, Hell."

"Great. No, I apologize. I just couldn't sit here any longer." Her attention went to the joint again. No, she needed her brain no matter how much Matt intimidated her.

"We'll talk about this later. What'd you find out?"

Hell told him the short version of the visit.

"Damn, I wish we had more resources," he said.

"I wish I did, too. I can afford you for a month tops, and that's it."

"Don't you have any friends who can help you out?"

"I can't put my friends and family in danger, Matt."

"What about the low-level stuff? Making some phone calls? Following up on peripheral information?"

Hell's mood went even darker, and she rubbed the tension from her forehead. She hated explaining her life to people who were in happy family situations surrounded by people they could count on. "I put out feelers, but no one has stepped up. Look, my life is not like yours. I'm kinda low on loyal people at the moment. Apparently I've been doing the right thing for the wrong people for a long time. People who can't or won't reciprocate. That's why I hired you."

"Sorry, Hell."

"Yeah, me, too. You talk to BC tonight." In a split second, she realized how to slip her plan to interview Lindsay by Matt without him noticing. She just had to pretend that what she was doing was the best approach. She had to take the power. "I'm thinking of hitting up Lindsay later on today," she tossed off. "I want to try something alone before you and I go see her again. Got an angle that should make her open up."

"No. Seeing her alone at her house is too dangerous."

Hell snorted. "Well, she ain't gonna shoot me in front of her servants in broad daylight."

"No. Not without me."

Please don't piss me off. "I'm afraid if we tag team Lindsay right now, we'll spook her. She's too high-strung. Both of us together will overwhelm her. I'll have Death on the line, and I'll record the whole thing."

"I said no."

Like he had that kind of power over her. "Matt, she won't open up if you're standing there."

"Then I'll be nearby."

"I'll wear my Kevlar, just in case."

"You have a bulletproof vest? I thought you didn't like guns."

"I don't like bullets, either."

"Hell, you wait for me," he said, louder and more insistent.

She tried to think of a better argument than her impatience.

"Hell?"

"Give me a second, I'm coming up with a fantastic excuse."

"Listen to me, you hired me to protect you, and I'm telling you this is too dangerous. I hate that you went to see Gwen without me. Hate it. As in, we haven't even begun to discuss it," he barked.

"Okay, okay, I'm sorry. I'll wait." She crossed her fingers.

"Goddamn you, I know you're going over there."

"I won't, Matt," she tried to say with conviction, but her tone was off. Shit! Why couldn't she lie effectively to this guy?

"Damn you, woman." He muttered under his breath. "Give me five minutes."

"What? Why?"

"Give me five minutes before you leave."

"*Five whole minutes?*"

"Hell!"

Chuckling, Hell said, "Okay, okay."

Click.

"Matt?" She hung up the phone and sighed. "What is wrong with this guy?"

The real question: why did she like him so much? She never let anyone boss her around. Well, with the exception of her father. But he didn't so much boss her as bully her.

Hell wrote down what she'd need to pull the scam on Lindsay. Taser, bulletproof vest, big jacket to cover the vest, and more weed for afterwards.

Her cell rang, startling her. Matt. "Yeah?"

"I'll be there in ten minutes."

Damn it, she didn't want his interference. "No, you—"

"Clint's free and is on his way. Patty says she'll be fine. She looks better."

"I don't want you to have to—"

"Hell, fucking wait for me, or I quit!" he blasted through the phone, hurting her ear. He groaned. "I'm sorry, honey," he said, clearly to Patty. "Now you've got me swearing in front of my sick wife," he growled, then hung up.

Hell tried to feel bad but couldn't manage it. All that she could muster was a bit of sympathy for him loving his wife so much. His authoritarian shit could go.

Although he might have a point or two. If by some otherworldly chance Lindsay was the killer, she could murder Hell in her yard and say it was self-defense. But if she were Hell's assailant, she'd already gone through great lengths to conceal her identity. She wouldn't risk calling that much attention to herself. She wouldn't want her home turned into a murder scene.

Matt stormed into her office fifteen minutes later, red-faced, blue eyes flashing. His anger lines were deep on his wide and weathered face, and his head appeared more square or rigid due to his mood. His curly, sandy, and gray mop of hair stuck up like he'd been running his hands through it. "Could you please stop putting yourself in unnecessary danger? It would really help me to save your sorry ass if you stopped questioning potential murderers alone."

Hell wondered why she wasn't more fazed by his temper. Maybe she was actually getting used to him. "Sorry."

"You're not."

"No, I'm not. Is Patty okay?"

"Fine. She just had some health issues last year and I'm para-noid." He looked around for a chair. Spotting one sitting off to the side, he kicked aside some papers, retrieved the chair, and then sat down a little heavily, like life was weighing him down. "She reminded me that when I was on the force full-time she had far more problems. Like with her pregnancies. And I wasn't there."

"Which is why you want to be there now."

"I just worry about her. She tells me I shouldn't. Anyway, I'm here. So how do you want to approach Lindsay?"

Hell quickly came up with a way to frame the plan so he wouldn't suspect she was going to try something that, from the outside, might appear to be insanely stupid. "Okay, the plan is that I go in and see Lindsay alone while you're in your car not far away, listening to and watching the whole thing on the computer. I'll have a microphone in my ear so you can talk to me. You'll be in contact with me the whole time."

His thick eyebrows rose high. "You have the equipment?"

"Trunk of my car. Didn't I show you all that crap?"

"No."

"Meant to. I record my interviews so I can go back later and examine how people reacted to my questions. Catch all kinds of stuff I didn't see the first time." She stopped and stared into space. "Shit, I should have done that with Gwen. Son of a bitch, this case is making my brain scattered. Why didn't I record that?" Shaking her head, she massaged the back of her neck.

"Huh. I didn't think you used much in the way of technology."

"I use whatever I can. Yes, my verbal bullshit skills work the best, but technology has saved my ass since I've incorporated it into my work." She showed him the sole of her right skull-printed sneaker. "Got a tiny GPS I always have in my shoe so Death can track me if I disappear." She set her foot back on the floor.

"Really?"

"Yeah, he tracks me all the time and checks in with me regularly through my cell phone. Makes sure I'm alive and active and haven't been kidnapped. Never know what's gonna happen."

Matt shifted in his chair, sliding a magazine over with his foot. "How does he know if you're on a date or on the job?"

"I send him a text."

"I didn't think you took on dangerous cases, just teen runaways and cheating husbands. You're not really in any danger from kidnapping or anything, are you?"

A little kick to the gut. That memory was burned in on her mind forever. "Unfortunately."

His eyes widened. "You were *kidnapped*?"

Hell gave a sharp nod. "The tracking software helped me find my kidnappers about an hour after they dropped me off."

"That wasn't in any of the police reports."

"I didn't report it to the police."

Matt sat straight up. "You got kidnapped, they let you go, then you tracked them down? Did you confront them? Who were they? Why did they kidnap you? Wasn't that dangerous?"

Hell chuckled, then let out a long sigh. "I tracked them down and confronted them once I found out who they were. Rampart Security mistook me for a real spy. Black-bagged me and interrogated me. Jerks. But I got even with them."

Matt's face twisted with alarm. "Rampart? The mercenaries?" His brow furrowed. "Wait, aren't you dating one of them? Is that how you met?"

"Yeah, kinda. Except Roman wasn't on that job."

"But all those guys are renegade ex-Navy SEALs and Green Berets. Really—"

"Scary-ass mofos," Hell finished for him. "I still have PTSD from that goddamned night. And a few subsequent nights with them."

"Wait, you got even? With Green Berets and SEALs? How?"

"Mainly by sleeping with most of them." She waved her hand dismissively. "But that's a whole long story—"

Matt burst out laughing. "Holy shit, Hell."

"Stop looking at me like that."

"You keep surprising me. And shocking me. What did they do when you confronted them?"

Hell shifted in her chair. "Well, first I had Death arm me with all their confidential information. Then I followed them to a bar, sat down with them, and proceeded to relate each of their life stories. They tried to get all tough, but I knew they were good guys deep down, and I wasn't afraid of them. I told them I wasn't going to stop following them and harassing them until they gave me twenty cases of Heineken, a pound of really good weed, and a hundred grand as an apology. That's when they recruited me to help them on the case, since I had a direct lead to the spy they were after."

"You worked with those guys?"

"Only once." Hell shuddered and blocked the horrifying images from her mind. "That was enough. It's not something I like talking about or thinking about. Those guys operate in a world I don't want to know exists. That's the Big Boys' Club. I prefer to bring down cheating husbands, not armed terrorists dealing in bombs and unstable Middle Eastern countries."

"Hell!" His face contorted into shocked terror.

Talking too much! Hell stood and stretched, then yawned. Someday she was going to need to get some sleep. "We'll need both cars. You follow me."

His eyes wide, he just stared at her. "Jesus Christ. I can't believe your life."

"Wasn't this way before Josh died, I'll tell you that."

He shook himself as if to get rid of her story. "So what's your plan for right now?"

With a quick smile, she walked past him, narrowly avoiding a giant pile of files. "I'll tell you on the way out. Super simple." And hopefully not super stupid. But it would more than likely net exactly the results she needed.

"How ya doin' today, anyway?"

She reached the main door to the office, stopped, and turned back to him, surprised by his question. "Me? Fine, why?"

"Because you got shot at a couple days ago, and the librarian pulled a gun on you?"

"Oh. Um. I'm good. Thanks for asking." She turned away and walked out the door and down the hallway, feeling totally awkward. Was Matt actually starting to care about her?

No, there had to be something weird in the air. Something that was affecting both Matt and BC.

Because neither of these guys cared about her.

Impossible.

CHAPTER 15

H er pulse quick, her body amped for the performance, Hell stared up at Lindsay's immense Colonial house. Six huge, white columns rose thirty feet from the grand porch of the white manse. No one had answered the bell, but she knew people were home.

Hell tried to calm the fear at her core. Beyond her performance concerns, she was just plain afraid of Lindsay. A text she'd received from BC in the car on her way—plus the discovery upon arrival of a black 2003 Honda parked with Lindsay's staff's vehicles—had shot Lindsay to the top of the suspect list. Death had verified that the Honda belonged to Lindsay's gardener. Super easy for Lindsay to borrow.

In order to pick a plan, she'd needed to know if Lindsay knew about her affair with Brad. If she did, then Brad was supposed to lie to her and say that they were through. BC's text had read: *She knew about us, all right. Told her you and I were over. She still went nuts on me. Take care, I think she's off her meds. BC.* Which meant Hell had to go with Plan B. A slightly crazier plan than Plan A, but so be it.

Hell rang the bell again, her hand shaking slightly. "She's not answering," she whispered.

"Maybe she's out," Matt answered in her ear. He was parked out of view down the street watching the scene from the camera hidden in Hell's baseball cap. Her shirt had a microphone disguised as a button.

Matt had used all his powers of persuasion to try to allow him to accompany her. Epic. Failure.

Death's gnome-y voice cut in. "According to my information, I believe she is in the residence. Try again, Hell."

"Okay. Let me perform my one-woman show and see if I can lure her outside."

"First sign of danger, you leave. Right?" Matt said in a tight voice.

Death said, "I also recommend staying outside. Do not go inside the house."

"Agreed to both," Hell replied. "Okay, boys, I'd turn down your volume. This is going to get loud."

"What are you going to do?" Matt asked.

"You'll see."

"Why don't I think I'm going to like this?"

Because you won't.

"Hell has interviewed much more dangerous people in much more violent and unpredictable environments," Death said. "She'll be fine."

"Why am I not reassured?" Matt muttered.

She rang the doorbell again, then lurched away from the door, broke down into tears, and collapsed on the curb in front of her car. Howling in pain.

"Why did he leave me? Why? Wasn't I good enough?" she wailed.

The door clicked behind her, her heart rate kicked higher, but she pretended not to hear and sobbed louder. Sweat ran down the side of her neck, her body overheated from the bulky protection of the Kevlar vest. She'd felt stupid putting it on, but better safe than sorry. She'd been wrong before.

"What are you doing here?" came Lindsay's shrill voice. "You've got your nerve showing up here!"

Hell caught Lindsay's reflection on the side of her Malibu and watched her carefully. "My life is over. Over!" Rocking back and forth, she sobbed violently and threw her head onto her knees—keeping all her focus on Lindsay out of the corner of her eye, looking for tells in her body language.

With her open posture, the loon wasn't telegraphing anything dangerous.

"He left me! He dumped me! I'm alone! All alone!" Hell cried.

Lindsay took a couple steps closer. "I know. He told me. I just talked to him on the phone. He warned me you might be coming by. I'm so unhappy that he was right. There you were grilling me about our relationship when the whole time you were preparing to steal him from me."

Hell finally turned to her and hoped her makeup had reached its Alice Cooper stage. "That's a lie! I liked you and thought you were cool! I went to see him to try to get you two back together again! You made me want to fight for you! Then he twisted the whole thing around and seduced me, but it wasn't my fault. I didn't betray you, he did!"

Lindsay frowned and tried to wrinkle her brow. Wearing tight black yoga pants, a white tee, and blue V-necked sweater, she looked perfect, from her shoulder-length curly blonde hair to her gym-toned body. But she also looked like she'd lost more weight. Her face was beginning to look gaunt.

She narrowed her eyes. "I seriously doubt you went to see Brad on my behalf since he told me he knew about the GPS unit I put on his car."

Shit. *Think fast!* Hell leapt to her feet. "He twisted that around! He conned the information out of me! I fought for you!"

Her lips tightened. "Highly doubtful."

Hell wiped the tears from her eyes with a sweep of her arm. "Fine, don't believe me. But I'm telling you the truth. I'm not your enemy, Brad is."

She shushed Hell. "Keep your voice down. I don't want the gardener to hear." She scanned the immediate vicinity, then motioned toward herself with skinny but ropy arms. "Someone's bound to hear us out here. Come inside."

No way! "Why? So you can hurt me in there? No. I came here to ask you to stop trying to kill me because you don't have any reason anymore. I know it was you who shot at me!" She tuned in completely to Lindsay's facial and body reactions.

Pursing her lips, the blonde rolled her eyes and put her hands on her hips. "Oh, for pity's sake. If I had shot at you, you'd be dead. I'm a top marksman. I've won awards. I wouldn't have missed."

No startled reaction, no attempts at covering her emotions, Lindsay's manner was straightforward and earnest. Hell inwardly relaxed a bit. Maybe Lindsay wasn't the one.

Lindsay motioned toward the front door. "Now come inside. I can't risk anyone overhearing us."

Hell shook her head and took a step toward her car. "If you're not the one who's trying to kill me, then I have to go find out who is."

"Wait. I need to know some things, but I can't talk out here. I think I might know who's trying to kill you."

Hell's heart gave a thump, and she focused all her attention on Lindsay's eyes. Was that true?

"Don't go in the house, Hell," Matt warned.

Even though she was no longer worried about her safety, Matt was right. Lindsay could still want revenge. She could make up some crazy story about Hell breaking into her house and attacking her, and Hell had no time for jail.

"Why can't you just tell me out here?"

Lindsay gestured vehemently at the door. "Could you please keep your voice down and come inside?"

"I don't trust you. You could lure me in there and kill me," Hell said, this time being absolutely truthful.

Lindsay made a disgusted noise and shook her head. "If I were going to kill you, I surely wouldn't do it in my own home. Do you want to know who I think shot at you or not?"

"Don't go in there," Matt repeated.

Lindsay seemed irritated, but not at the level of craziness she was the last time. No whites of her eyes showing, no signs of immediate danger. Maybe BC was wrong, and she was back on her meds.

"Come in already!" Lindsay urged.

Matt and Death would kill her if she went into the house.

But Hell saw no other way. Lindsay clearly wasn't going to open up within earshot of her servants. The risk was worth the information.

Pulse jumping higher, Hell stuck her hand into her pocket, closing it on her Taser, just in case. She gave a quick check with her gut. Not too tense. She'd probably be fine.

Hell followed Lindsay into the house.

"Hell! Shit!" came Matt's expected response.

"You are putting yourself in unnecessary danger," Death added. "She could be lying about knowing about your assailant."

Yeah, yeah, yeah, shut the eff up, boys.

The blonde indicated she should go into a room to the left of the entry hall. All her radar on Lindsay, Hell slipped past her and into a large wood-paneled room.

"Keep your eyes on her," Matt ordered. "Christ, Hell, she could shoot you and say it was self-defense. Except that we have this all on tape. Still, I wish you would get the hell out of there."

"I concur," said Death.

Trying to ignore the crazy people worrying in her ears, Hell scanned what looked like a library. For Matt's and Death's sake, she quickly planned three escape routes: out the French doors that led to the back gardens, through the open side of a large picture window facing the front yard, or out another door that probably led to the kitchen or a hallway.

Hell turned back to Lindsay.

The blonde's posture and energy had changed.

The hairs rose on the back of Hell's neck, and her stomach and feet felt funny.

Lindsay looked taller and bigger. She clearly felt more powerful and in control here in her home. Hell didn't like the look in her eye. Her vibe was intense, vacillating between fiery hatred and cool curiosity.

Shit. What if Lindsay was the one? Hell had just walked into her trap.

She slowly edged toward the French doors that led outside.

"I don't like how she looks, Hell. Do you see the change in her?" Matt demanded.

No duh. Hell wished she could turn off the volume, but he was right. Damn, this might have actually turned out to be stupid. At least there would be a record of her death.

Hell came to a stop right in front of the French doors. Her limbs urged her to run. Normally, she listened to her body's reactions, but what if Lindsay turned out to be her assailant? The case would be solved, and Hell could sleep again.

Besides, Matt was just down the street. He'd get there eventually.

"Good, hang out there. Christ, this is killing me to watch," Matt said.

"I can have police there in three minutes," Death said. "Tap the microphone if you want me to call."

Hell kept her hands away from her shirt and tuned into Lindsay. "So who do you think it is and why?"

"I want to know about you and Brad," Lindsay said.

Hell's insides tensed with frustration. Lindsay knew nothing. She just wanted the details of her relationship with Brad. She allowed her irritation to show. "You don't know anything about who's trying to kill me, do you?"

"I do," she said with confidence. "But I want some information in return. Things he won't tell me. When did he leave you?"

Hell held the crazy woman's gaze, showed no emotion, and allowed her energy to grow cold. "You first. What do you know?"

"When did Brad leave you? I know as of two days ago you two were seeing each other at the condo near Sand Hill," she said, her focus on Hell intense.

Hell's heart stopped, and it felt like the bottom dropped out of the room. "How the hell would you know that? And how do you know about the condo? Did he take you there?"

Lindsay barely blinked. "No, but I hope that you don't think just because he got that condo for you and you two have spent three days a week there together since January that it really meant anything to him. He never loved you. He loves me."

The pit of Hell's stomach went cold, and she glanced at the French door, instinctually running through her escape plan. Lindsay clearly had had Brad followed. But how? His security team had been alerted, his car swept daily for GPS devices. How the hell had Lindsay managed it?

Had she hired the librarian? Or had she gotten better at the job? If she'd been following them personally, then she might be Hell's assailant.

Lindsay continued on with an elitist affect heavily tinged with anger and vengeance. "I hope you didn't think he ever cared about you. You were his stop-gap whore until he settled the business merger issues with Dan and could come back to me where he belongs."

"Uh...yeah."

Lindsay brought herself up to her full height, oozing self-importance. "In all that time you two spent together, did Brad happen to mention that his greatest dream is to be the father of my children? I froze my eggs when I was thirty-two, and I still have several left. We're going to do in vitro fertilization. Of course, while we'll be creating our children in a lab, we'll be making love daily, and for longer than the measly six or eight hours you two screw."

Hell froze to the floor, the willies overtaking her, and she gave a quick shudder even though she tried to stop it. Lindsay was clearly off the rails. Hell knew for a fact that BC didn't want any more kids. They'd had a long discussion about parenthood just the week before. Hell glanced at the handles to the French doors. She could be out of that room in a couple seconds. "Uh, no, he didn't. But clearly Brad loves you more." Before she ran, she needed the truth. "How do you know about the condo? You kept following him? I know you didn't put a GPS on his car because his team sweeps for them."

Lindsay took on a self-satisfied expression, her gaze full of righteous vengeance. "But you don't. You were easy to follow. I followed you back to your creepy apartment that day you interviewed me at the coffee shop, and you didn't notice me at all, did you?"

Goose bumps rose all over her body.

"Hell? Leave now."

"I concur," said Death.

Her mind also screamed at her to fly, but she needed the whole story. "Why did you follow me initially?"

Lindsay sent her a condescending stare and stood taller. "Because I was wondering if Brad had found himself another whore. You really weren't that special. I've followed every woman he's ever met. I was actually surprised at how few he was screwing. From Sherry's stories, I thought he had more. But following you really paid off. You went to Sherry's that day, then back to your apartment, then you went to Brad's office. God, the noises you make. He's good, but he isn't *that* good. Did you make up that sexual animal act to entrap him? Didn't work, did it?"

Hell's body heated with rage and fear, and she fisted her hands. Part of her wanted to escape, part of her wanted to beat the bitch's face bloody. "You tried to kill me, didn't you?"

"Maybe, maybe not," she said with a smirk.

"Hell, leave now," Matt ordered in a no-nonsense tone.

"Please," Death added.

But Lindsay's act wasn't convincing. She might just be embellishing her story to scare off Hell. She could have hired the librarian to follow Brad, and that's how she knew so much. "I don't think you're my assailant at all. I think you're just making up this shit to scare me. I think you hired someone to follow me."

Lindsay's face hardened, and her eyes glittered with anger. "I did so follow you. I was actually pretty disappointed at times that you didn't notice me. Especially the night at the Fairmont back in November. Actually, that was just a happy accident. I'd gone there to follow Brad and Sherry, and lo and behold, there you were, dressed up in sapphires and diamonds, sitting with a sophisticated man in a suit," she revealed with a gleam in her eye.

Hell's heart rate jumped, and she grabbed the handle of one of the French doors.

"At first I thought you were in actuality a high-priced whore, but I couldn't figure out why anyone that obviously rich would buy an old bag like you, so I dug further. You really do have some interesting men in your life, don't you? But a Mafia don? Really?"

"Hell, now." Matt's tone left no room for argument.

Hell agreed but first needed to warn this idiot blonde. "People who dig around in Marco's life have a tendency to disappear."

Lindsay snorted with laughter. "Like I'm afraid of some throw-back Mafia idiot. Doesn't he know that the Mafia is totally outdated? They have little power any longer. The Mexicans and the Asians have all the power now. Everyone knows that."

The woman was half-sane, half-delusional, and super smart. Hell couldn't figure out if she was homicidal or insane or both.

Hell squared her shoulders and deepened her voice. "You are playing a very dangerous game, lady. Especially if you shot at me. Marco doesn't like his friends getting hurt."

Her eyes narrowed, and her mouth turned ugly. "If I decide to kill you, I'll get away with it. No Mafia idiot will scare me off. Besides, all I have to do is tell people that you threatened to kill Brad, that you came here to try to enlist my help for your revenge plot, and I can kill you legally. I'll look like a hero to him and our future children and the world. So listen to me carefully, you crazy pink-haired freak, you stay away from Brad and me. Or I won't miss the next time."

Hell's heart rate shot higher.

"Now, Hell, or I'm coming in to get you."

Was Lindsay confessing? Or just making a hyped-up threat to get rid of the competition?

Hell set aside her fears and tried to read the crazy woman. "You leave me alone, or you'll regret it."

Lindsay sneered. "You don't scare me. I have enough money to make you disappear without a trace. Or maybe I'll just cripple you and make you so ugly no man will want you again, not even your Mafia boss. You'll die all alone in that pathetic flea trap in San Mateo. Now get out of my house before I shoot you here." Brutal energy emanated from within her. Her shoulders got bigger, her eyes crazier.

Hell practically ran to the front door.

Lindsay laughed but made no move to follow.

As soon as she hit the front porch, she raced for her car. Once inside, she locked the doors, started the engine, and took off.

"I'm very relieved that's over, Hell," Death said.

"An understatement," Matt said.

As soon as Hell cleared the gates, she shuddered violently and broke into a cold sweat. "I wish I could say I'd just eliminated her."

"No shit we didn't eliminate her. Wow," Matt replied.

"She is more dangerous than your original estimation," Death said.

"Yes, but to what degree? Is she copping to the attack to scare me off, or is she the real culprit?"

"Unclear," Death said. "I'm not convinced of her innocence or guilt."

Hell drove down the block, pulled up next to Matt's car, and rolled down her window.

"I couldn't tell, either," Matt replied.

Death heaved a sigh. "I will hack into her home computer and report back."

"Thanks, Death."

"Be seeing you, Hell." He clicked off the line.

Hell removed the tiny earbud and put it in her pocket.

"Damn, Hell, no more of this," Matt bit out. She couldn't see his eyes behind his shades, but his anger lines were deep. He pointed at her. "No more questioning potential suspects without me there, period. You got that?"

"She wouldn't have said any of that with you there."

"You're right, but at least you wouldn't have been in danger. No more or I'm off the case."

"Matt."

"I need to have some power here. You clear everything with me first, or I walk. I mean it."

Tears threatened. Unexpected and alarming. Of course Matt would abandon her when she needed him the most. Hadn't everyone? She gave herself an inward shake and swallowed hard. No showing weakness. "Come on, Matt."

"No. You won't charm me. Let me do my fucking job."

"Okay, okay. Jeez." The old Matt finally reared his ugly head. Figured.

Her capitulation didn't appease him. The lines on his weathered face stayed set and angry. "I'm not playing this game with you."

"I'm not playing a game."

"The fuck you aren't," he spat. "You've been playing a game with me ever since you hired me. You don't give me the full details, you hide information, you go off half-cocked, provoking the very people who could be trying to kill you, and you don't let me protect you. This has to stop. Now." He jabbed at the ground in a sharp stab.

He had a point. Several of them. Shit. Tears welled in her eyes. She let out a long sigh and broke eye contact. Running her index finger over the sore spot between her eyes—careful not to wipe her tears— she shrugged and turned back to him. "Okay. Look, I'm not used to having anyone help me other than Death."

His hard expression didn't waver. "I know, you told me. Get over it. Stop hamstringing me and expecting me to take your shit. I won't."

"Okay. I got it." With one giant internal shove, she made her tears go away and hardened her emotions. "I agree. I'll do my best not to go behind your back. I'll run everything by you." A feeling of claustro-phobia came over her, like Matt had just wrapped her in a straight-jacket. She twitched her shoulders to relieve the psychic pressure, and her attention went to her steering wheel. Her jaw burned from being clenched too tight, and she stretched it until it popped. "Sorry, you're hitting my authoritarian buttons."

"You're not a teenager, and I'm not your father. Grow up, and let me help you."

She squirmed, her body antsy with frustration. She didn't want to fight him. She'd hired him. "You're a hundred percent right." Top of her head hurt from being so tight, and she pressed her fingers into the muscles. "I couldn't read Lindsay, and I can always read people. I'm flying blind. Normally, within a few minutes, I know what's going on. But not now, I'm effing powerless. Which scared me and freaked me out even more."

"You're too close to it. You'll be okay. Just let me in."

"Sorry, Matt. Wasn't my intention to hire you and not let you help me. I just hate needing people."

"We all need people, Hell."

"I don't," she said quickly.

"Bullshit."

"Okay, let me put it this way, I can't need people because ever since Josh died, I've had no one but Death, and he never leaves his bunker. Well, and Joanne, but she's got a kid in college and no mate, and is barely keeping her head above water. When no one is there for you but an old friend on a computer, you have to figure it out on your own."

The hard lines of Matt's face softened. "Sorry, Hell."

Her heart ached, her throat closed, and more tears escaped. Why was sympathy so hard to take? It was like her pain wasn't real until she saw it reflected in someone else's face. "Don't be," she said in a surprisingly nice, strong voice. "I'm fine. Look, you're gonna see BC later, right?"

"Yeah. Where will you be around nine thirty, ten tonight? I see BC at eight in San Carlos."

Nausea roiled her gut, and she shifted in her seat. The horror! BC and Matt discussing the affair. Could any idea make her sicker? "Home. Call me on the landline. I talked to Death, and all of BC's whereabouts coordinate perfectly with his calendar. So if he is sleeping with someone else, he's purposely leaving his cell phone behind and sneaking around to see her and not communicating with her on any known phone or computer."

"Jesus, Death is good," Matt said, looking uncomfortable. "Here's your equipment." He passed her a computer and a little bag of accessories.

She took the stuff and set it on the seat next to her. "Brad's not going to want to open up to you, more than likely, but you can handle that."

"I can. You going home now?" he asked.

"Yeah, after I do some grocery shopping."

"Get some rest, will ya?"

"Do I look that bad?"

"No. I just know you're not sleeping well. Need to take care of yourself, that's all."

Hell stared at him, perplexed. The dude's caring act was starting to smell real. And maybe not motivated by money. She tried not to squirm. Why didn't she like him being nice to her?

He squinted at her. "What?"

"Nothin'. You're right. I'm tired. Make some food and watch a movie. Charge my cell. Turn in early."

"Good, okay. I'll call you tonight."

"Killer. Later." Hell started her car, and with a wave, drove off.

Matt didn't care about her, he just wanted control. Manipulating her by appearing to have real emotion for her so he could soothe his ego and take charge of the situation.

Too bad, buddy. This is my life.

Although he did make a good point about putting herself in needless danger. Damn it.

What she couldn't figure out was what BC had seen in Lindsay and Gwen outside of their beautiful exteriors. Did he like cold, crazy bitches? Did he think that Hell was a cold, crazy bitch?

She had been pretty cold to him. Pretty easy to see why he could interpret her behavior as crazy. Great. Attracted to her defensive act, not her true self.

Still, their continued alliance made no sense. If BC hadn't left his wife for Gwen or Lindsay—two women in his class—he sure as shit wouldn't leave Sherry for Hell. She was a passing trifle in BC's life, and she'd better wake up and get that through her head.

Her mood plummeted as she headed toward the freeway.

Her stomach balled, and she finally allowed her tears to run free.

Good job falling for an unattainable, Lothario billionaire, Hell.

If she were as talented at making money as she was at getting herself into amazingly painful situations, she'd be as rich as BC by now.

Wednesday, March 9, 2011, 7:25 p.m.

WEARING HER BLACK LEATHER JACKET, HELL LOUNGED ON THE OUTDOOR chaise in her patio and smoked a joint, a Heineken in her other hand, still shaky from recording her video journal entry. She wished she hadn't had to relive recent events, but it was the only way to process the mess that was her mind. She used to keep a written journal but found it took too long. Now she could just record herself on her computer and get her thoughts out quickly. Death had helped her set up precautions so no one could ever see the videos but her. Not only would she lose the majority of her friends and family if the footage was released, the things she'd admitted to would get her sent to prison for the rest of her life.

She coughed, looked down at the half joint, and put it out. Her lungs really couldn't take this much weed. Normally, she only smoked a few hits during the day, but the attempted murder and her PTSD had turned her life into a 420 festival.

Her ten-percent-charged cell phone appeared in her mind.

"Holy crap. How many times am I going to forget to charge that stupid thing?" She heaved herself to her feet and went inside, careful to close the sliding glass door behind her to keep out the night chill.

She set her beer on the coffee table and headed for her bedroom.

Walking inside the messy tragedy, she noticed all the skull paintings were skewed, and she still had eight boxes of books stacked high against one wall that she'd intended to give away months before. She kicked aside a pile of magazines and books and spotted her cell lying partially under the bed next to her computer. She'd shoved her laptop under there earlier to get it out of the way while she'd changed.

The end of the charger cord poked out from beneath her bedside table on the floor between a Maglite flashlight and her vibrator.

She dropped to her knees and reached for the cord.

A thunderous explosion rocked the room, a shelf full of books fell on top of her, and she was plunged into darkness. Her whole head rang.

Fight-or-flight juices dumped into her system. *What the hell?*

Her left leg and part of her ass cheek burned. Dust filled the air, and Hell coughed. Pushing the shelf up and off her, she crawled out from underneath the piles of books.

Sharp impact to her forehead. Pain cracked through her skull. "Ow!"

A gas leak! A pipeline had blown up her neighborhood just like in San Bruno! Her heart beat faster. Power crews had been working on the line down the middle of the block.

She had to evacuate. But first she had to see.

She frantically felt around on the floor near her bedside table until she came upon her Maglite. The flashlight lit up a beam of thick dust. She grabbed a T-shirt and tied it around her nose and mouth. Her eyes filled with particulate matter. She blinked it away and squinted.

Something wet ran down her face. Water from a leaking pipe? She wiped away the liquid and checked her palm. Bright red. Her heart rate ramped even higher. "Fuck!"

She stood and searing, spiking pain came from her leg and butt. She shined the flashlight on her thigh and gasped. Her jeans were pock-marked with red spots. More blood!

Hell aimed the beam through her door to the living room. She couldn't make out anything through the heavy dust. Should she break out her bedroom window?

Wallet, cell, and computer!

Computer case was next to her computer. She fell to her knees and shoved the laptop inside the black leather case, along with her cell phone and charger cord. She patted her jacket pockets and found her wallet. Good!

Hell heaved herself to her feet on shaky legs. Computer under her arm, flashlight in hand, she approached the bedroom doorway.

She wanted to go out through her living room, but that way might be blocked. But she had to get out fast. The apartment above her might come crashing through her ceiling at any second.

"Hell? Where are you?" came a loud, gruff shout from beyond her living room.

She wasn't alone! Lars, her next-door neighbor. Thank God he was okay!

"I'm here!" Hell yelled.

If he had gotten there that quickly, his daughter and grandkids had to be okay. They lived in the same duplex. Maybe the whole neighborhood hadn't been destroyed.

"Hell? Can you walk?" he shouted.

"Yeah! I'm coming!" She shined the flashlight on the debris-filled floor and made her way toward Lars' voice.

Parts of her pinball machine lay entwined with pieces of Sheetrock, all piled on top of her pitted and destroyed furniture. She crunched over shards of glass from the sliding glass door, unable to believe the scene. Total apocalypse.

Lars appeared out of the dense cloud in front of her, his mouth and nose covered with his shirt. "Are you okay? You're bleeding."

"I can walk, no broken bones."

"Let's get you out of here." The big man put his arm around her and guided her out of the wreckage.

Hell stepped over boards and piles of crap, suddenly realizing she was outside on her patio. The sliding glass door and part of her exterior wall had been blown away.

"Watch out for the hole!" Lars warned.

A three-foot-wide black and smoking crater lay in the center of her patio. Her fence was blown outward, lumber strewn all over the building's main walkway.

She stopped and stared in confusion. "Wait, wasn't this a gas explosion?" she asked Lars.

"No, Hell. Come on, let's keep going."

"No? What was it?"

Lars didn't answer and kept moving her toward the street. Hell saw no signs of other damage anywhere.

Melissa, Lars' wife, ran up to them as they approached the sidewalk. "Hell!"

"I'm okay."

A huge crowd of neighbors milled on the street. Dogs barked, and sirens wailed in the background, but it all sounded weird through the ringing in her ears.

Hell couldn't get her head around the scene. "What else exploded?"

Lars' face was granite. Why didn't he want to tell her?

"Lars? What else got blown up?"

He gave a short shake of his head. "Nothing, Hell. Just your place."

"I don't get..." Adrenaline poured into her system, and her heart went into near cardiac arrest. "Someone just tried to kill me with a bomb?"

"Hand grenade or pipe bomb."

Her knees weakened, and her mind grayed.

Lars caught her and held her up. "You're okay, kid."

Melissa took Hell's other arm and guided her next door to their home. "Come on, hon. I have to check you out."

Hell barely registered the fire trucks and police cars arriving on scene. She couldn't think.

Tears of fright blinded her.

Good. Holy. God.

CHAPTER 16

Matt sat across from Brad Collins at the swanky wine bar in downtown San Carlos. From its burgundy leather seats to low lighting and warm wood interiors, the place was as far from a Matt hangout as possible. No big-screen TVs showing sports, everyone wearing suits, no one talking loudly, no one drinking beer but him.

Everything about Collins was sharp. Angles to his face, his nose, his jaw, but mainly the look in his eye. Smart, sophisticated, and from his guarded expression, a player. Adorned with all the trappings of his class. From the Rolex to the thick diamond and gold wedding band to his expensive, tailored suit and spotless, leather dress shoes, his whole vibe screamed money, privilege, and power.

Matt tried not to hate him, but why should this prick get all the breaks? Mostly he was born into the right family. That was his whole contribution to society, born into a rich dynasty. What the hell did Hell see in this douchebag?

After some awkward introductions, Matt began his questioning. "So aside from Hell, how many other mistresses are you seeing?"

Brad pulled at his collar, and his attention darted to his pressed dark slacks. He blinked fast, then leveled his intense focus at Matt. "I don't want Hell to know this."

"Kind of difficult seeing as how I work for her."

Collins' gaze went hot, his jaw clenched, and the line between his eyes deepened. "I don't want her to know because I don't want her to leave me."

Perplexing. And intriguing. Hell knew he had other lovers. Why would she care? "Okay…"

"I stopped seeing all of them but her. The last one, over three months ago. They were like water compared to the best wine the Napa Valley has to offer," Collins said with a near beatific mistiness in his eyes.

Matt had to stop himself from going into a coughing fit. Hell? A fine wine? More like cheap whiskey. But Brad wasn't acting like he was slumming. He was acting like he was in love with his equal.

Was it possible? Was the billionaire only seeing Hell? Matt would go along with his little story and see where it went. "There's some strong motive for your exes to hurt Hell."

"No, they're both professional career women."

"Gwen and Lindsay. That's it?"

"Yes, just the two for the last two years. Well, Lindsay I'd only seen for six months. Before her, Gwen was it."

Matt studied his face and didn't pick up any duplicity, but the man was a practiced liar. "Look, Collins, I won't judge you, and I promise I won't tell Hell. At this point, I just want to save her life. I can conduct the interviews without her knowledge. But I need to know the entire list of suspects. If you care about her, please tell me."

Collins' face flushed, and anger flared in his gray eyes. "I'm telling the truth."

Matt waited.

"I am," Brad said tightly, his face a deeper red.

"Someone high level that you're hiding for security reasons?"

He snorted. "When the hell would I have time?" He threw up his hands. "I see her upwards of twenty hours a week. I play tennis three times a week, and work forty-five to fifty hours a week. Besides, I'm fifty-two years old. How much sex do I really need at this age? Twenty hours a week is enough, believe me."

Matt's mind exploded. "*Twenty hours of sex a week?*" he said way too loudly. His face went hot, and he checked the vicinity to see if anyone heard him.

Two guys at the next table stared at them with their mouths open.

One said, "I want twenty hours of sex a week." They both raised their glasses.

His face frying, he turned to Collins. "Sorry."

Collins waved his hand, his smile lines deep. Matt had to give him credit, he rolled with it.

Laughing, the billionaire leaned in. "Didn't want to burst their bubble, and thanks for the thought, but we don't screw the whole time. Like I said, I'm fifty-two." He sat back with a satisfied, smug grin. "But we have way more sex than I've had in years. Rest of the time, we make out, eat and drink, and laugh. She's the funniest woman I've known."

Twenty hours of naked fun time and sex. Per week. Shit. He and Patty were lucky to get twenty minutes. Overcome with jealousy, Matt had to mentally slap himself back to the interview. "Makes sense to me, but Hell's pretty convinced you must have other lovers."

All shred of humor vanished from Brad's face. "She judges me based on her own situation, but she's wrong. She wouldn't believe me last night when I told her. Of course, I had to lie to her about Gwen, so please don't tell her."

Matt almost believed him. "She already knows."

Collins' eyes popped, and he leaned forward. "How?"

"She talked to Gwen today."

Collins slumped. "Great." He sighed and looked like he'd lost all his money in the stock market. "So this is all a moot point because she's going to leave me now, right?"

Why would the guy put on such a big act for Matt? Did he really care what a private investigator thought? He was a power player, used to telling people what he wanted and getting it instantly. Would he really put out all this effort for subterfuge? From where Matt was seated, the guy's emotions came off as true. "I don't think so, but I don't know, and I don't want to be involved in your relationship."

Collins shot him a quick grin. "Take your head off, wouldn't she?"

He chuckled. "Uh, yeah." He was beginning to believe Hell was the only woman Brad was seeing. For twenty goddamned hours a week. Twenty! He cleared his throat. "Okay. Did either of the ladies take it badly? Gwen or Lindsay?"

"Yes, both. Gwen handled it the best. She knew we'd break up eventually. But Lindsay...she's another matter. She even showed up at my office late this afternoon, ranting about Hell planning to kill me, of all things."

Guilt pangs hit his gut. What the hell was wrong with him, letting her go alone into that idiot's house? He could have stopped her if he'd tried hard enough. He had to get control over her.

Collins shook his head. "Almost took dynamite to pry her out of the office. Christ, she can't take no for an answer."

"Hell had an angle she wanted to play. I'll admit, she got Lindsay going. She seems a little high-strung."

"High-strung? She was a raving maniac this afternoon. Spouting all this nonsense about saving me and implanting her frozen eggs. I'm still trying to figure out how she convinced herself that I want her kids. I don't even want my kids half the time. Kidding. Truth be told, she freaked me out."

"Do you get the sense she was the one who tried to hurt Hell?" Matt asked.

"Like I said, I can't see her doing it, but..." He shrugged.

"What did you tell her when she told you about Hell?"

"That I'd hired extra bodyguards. I let her believe I'd broken it off with Hell. Lindsay thinks I'll be calling her soon."

"Did you allude to that?"

"I barely got a word in edgewise. As usual."

Matt wrote down some notes, then took a sip of his Anchor Steam. He'd felt like an idiot ordering a beer, but he'd never developed a taste for wine. "We'll keep her at the top of the list. What about your wife?"

Brad's eyes went cold. "What about her?"

"Does she know about your affairs?"

"Yes. According to Hell. But her mother told her to expect me to cheat and to look the other way, so she does."

"You lost all interest in her?"

"Yes." He looked down at the floor, then back at Matt. "We were wrong for each other."

"Why stay together?"

"The family business. But I've been working hard to engineer things so it won't come apart when we do divorce. Ever since Hell told me my wife wanted me dead, I've been divorced in my mind." He leaned closer. "I don't want Hell to know that I'm legally ready to start proceedings. She knows I intend to divorce Sherry, but she doesn't know how close I am. She'll take it the wrong way. Too much pressure, and she'll bolt."

"You seem awfully worried about what both of you describe as an ongoing one-night stand."

Collins raised a brow and moved back in his chair. "She describes it that way."

"You want more?"

There was a pause as Collins worked his mouth, then he finally gave a slight nod. Clearly uncomfortable parting with the information. "Yes, but she's a difficult person to corral."

Matt snorted. "You can say that again."

A look of intense frustration creased the billionaire's face. "Defensive. I never get the feeling I'm actually talking to her. Closed off. Yet the most mind-blowing lover I've ever had. In bed she acts like I'm the most powerful, most attractive man she's ever met. She acts like she worships me when we make love. Never experienced anything like it. But afterwards, if I try to talk her about us or her personal life —subjects other than her work or anything about me or current events or movies—she shuts down and is gone before I know it. Slips right through my fingers."

"Sounds like Hell."

Collins shook his head and let out a long sigh. "My other girl-friends were so different. I don't think they cared much for what I did for them in bed. They were solely focused on themselves. Talked about their emotions ad nauseam. And my money. How we would spend it, what we would buy, where we could go. What they wanted me to buy them. Hell has forbidden me to buy her anything. Beyond that, she loses her mind if I try to give her gifts. Threw a wrapped package at my head one night; took me a full hour to calm her down. I finally had to rent a condo so she couldn't pay for the hotel room. The idiot doesn't have a couple grand for a goddamned hotel room. What the hell's wrong with her?"

Matt inwardly snickered. Hell wouldn't let anyone control her, not even a powerful billionaire.

Collins continued in a heated tone. "All my other girls tried to get me to leave my wife and marry them. Not only won't Hell acknowledge that we're in a relationship, she won't talk about her feelings for me. Ever. She's gotten me to open up about almost everything. What I didn't tell her, she found out on her own. Apparently she had some hacker genius probe deeply into my life as soon as we became involved, and she uncovered things about me that no one else knows."

Death strikes again. "Like?"

Collin's mouth tightened. "I'd rather not discuss it. Suffice to say, her friend has prodigious powers in computer hacking. Accessed sealed medical and court records."

"Jesus." The more he found out about Death's capabilities, the more he wanted to know who the guy was. Sounded like he could topple governments if he wanted to.

"Scared me, frankly. But when I saw that she'd only gathered the information to protect herself and that she wasn't capable of betraying me, I got over the invasion."

By the hard edge to the look in his eyes, Matt guessed his dick had gotten over the invasion, but Brad not so much. "You're a billionaire. Lot of power. Probably scared her."

"And she's curious as hell." Brad sipped his wine.

Matt chuckled. "Hallmark of a good detective."

Collins set down his glass, and his body language opened: legs a little farther apart, his shoulders more relaxed, his shields lower.

"Still, I've never met any woman—or man, for that matter—who didn't talk about themselves. Most of what I know about her I got from Bill Thompson's report and our first night together. Because she didn't think our encounter would be anything but a one-night stand, she revealed more about herself that evening than during any of our subsequent dates. She only shares crumbs of her life."

Matt was surprised at this guy's passion for Hell. A little too much passion. Maybe he'd arranged the gunfire to scare her into quitting her other men. "So you want more than just an affair and want her to leave her other men for you."

"Yes, but if you tell her I said that, I'll deny it."

"Pretty jealous, huh?"

Brad's jaw hardened. He leaned back and narrowed his eyes. "Not enough to pay someone to shoot at her. I was playing tennis when it happened. You can corroborate that with my club and my tennis partner that day. I'll give you his number. As far as proving that I didn't hire someone to shoot at her, well, I don't think there's a way for me to do that. But I'm not capable of hurting her. I want more from her, but I want it to happen naturally. I don't want to force her."

Matt didn't pick up any signs of duplicity.

Brad eyed him, and not in a friendly way. "What about you? You're the one who hates her. You're the one who put her in jail. I have no idea why she hired you because I would still love to kick your ass."

Interesting. Guy wasn't just there for the piece of tail. He actually seemed to care. Give him a couple points for that. Matt couldn't help but smile. "I only put her in jail for three weeks. Hell is responsible for the ninety days extra. Pulled a hell of a stunt in that courtroom."

"She said you really grilled her in the interrogation room." The look behind his eyes darkened.

Matt was careful not to show any remorse. "I won't apologize for that. She aided and abetted the prime suspect in a murder. More than that, she protected the perp and hid him—or her—from us."

"She's loyal."

"She's a pain in the ass."

BC broke his disapproving expression, humor lightening his features. "I can only imagine the trouble she gave you."

"Never met anyone like her. I didn't hold back, either. Even though she was a woman and I normally interrogate them differently, I went after her with everything I had, and she didn't crack a hair's breadth. But I just met a whole new person in the past few days. I'd misread her. I had no idea who she was."

Brad nodded, his thick black brows high. "She's got a hell of a shield around her."

"A foot thick. But a very good person," Matt said, a bit surprised he was admitting aloud what he'd just barely realized.

Collins gave a quick smile. "That's big, coming from you."

"She hasn't had a fair shake in life."

"No. I think her father is abusive," Collins said, fishing.

Matt twitched his shoulders. "She doesn't talk about her family."

"She doesn't talk about anything. I want to help in any way I can with the case. Any preliminary ideas?"

Matt's suspicions about Collins had faded. He seemed too straight, too in control of himself and his emotions, and too rational. And he clearly loved her. "I think it's either one of your girlfriends or one of her boyfriends. Or your wife."

"Sherry..." Brad chuckled. "No way." He frowned, and his focus on Matt intensified. "Wait, I thought you ruled out her other boyfriends."

"Mostly. Still have a couple questions I need answered about one, and the girlfriends of another. But since Hell hasn't seen anyone but you since early December, my gut is saying the threat is coming from someone connected to you. While her ex-boyfriends are bummed she ended things, they don't have a cross word to say about her. I didn't pick up any signs of danger from them except for one. But he's a civil attorney with no criminal history and a solid alibi."

Brad stared at him, blinked, then moved closer, eager. "Hell stopped seeing her other men? In early *December*? Are you sure? She told you this?"

Matt cringed, and his face heated. "Shit. Hell's gonna kill me. You have to keep that between us," he said, pointing. "I'll never solve the case if she finds out I blabbed her most precious secret."

Brad's mouth slowly turned into a smile. Then he beamed like he'd just made a killing in the market. "None of them in three months? Only a few weeks after we started seeing each other?"

"Damn this subterfuge between you two. Really hard to keep straight what I'm not supposed to tell you and what I can. All I want is information so I can help her."

Brad laughed a joyful, relieved laugh. "So it's not just me. She's in love, too." Man looked like he'd won the America's Cup.

"She'd never admit it in a thousand years. Not even to herself. Wait, you're actually admitting that you love her?"

"Yes. Very much. This is excellent news," Collins said, his chest puffing up. He took a manly swig of his drink. Sat like his cock grew a foot in length. His gaze gleamed, and his smile went sly. "She's an amazing actress." He gave a victorious laugh. "Here we've been exclusive for over three months, and I didn't even know it. And neither does she."

Matt couldn't help but be pissed off at the guy. Hell deserved better than this prick.

Brad examined him. "You think I'm hurting her, don't you?"

"Yeah. I do, actually. So if you don't mind me asking, you say you love her, but what are your intentions? Just going to use her like your other mistresses until you get tired of her?"

Brad burst out laughing. "You are rich. Two days and you've become her adopted father."

Not true. But he couldn't deny she brought out the protector in him. He couldn't help but want to care for her. Maybe because no one else had. "So?"

Collins continued chuckling. "I love it. My intentions. Well, I've been in love with her since our first night. She's never far from my thoughts. I go to bed with her in my mind and wake up wishing she were next to me. I've never felt anything like this. Might be the only time I've ever truly loved a woman. Taken me completely by surprise."

He seemed to be telling the truth.

"While she's sworn she has no feelings for me, clearly she's been lying to protect herself." He sent Matt a searching stare.

Matt said, "She'll never admit it."

"That's why you don't have to worry about me broaching the subject of her dumping her other men. I know it would send her screaming out the door."

"You're probably right. I have as little control over her as you do, and I'm going to have to work on that to protect her right. I chewed her ass this afternoon about that Lindsay stunt. She barely accepts my help. I think she fired her secretary because she hated asking her to do anything."

"Does she need more protection? She won't have to know it's there. I'll provide you with whatever you need."

"I wanted Hell to hire more people, but she said she can't. Doesn't have the cash. She can afford me for one month and that's it."

"Order more protection," Collins said with a decisive nod. "Just don't let her know about it, nor that I'm paying for it. Twenty-four hours. You coordinate it all, right?"

Matt hesitated. Hell would kill him. But if she were dead, all of this would be a moot point. She'd hired him to protect her. He'd never made any promises about *how* he would help her. Worst thing she could do was fire him, but he couldn't see her doing it. "Excellent. Only thing she said she'd let me do was install a surveillance system in her apartment so I can check on her during the night, but I told her all I'll be able to do is watch her get killed. We're putting that in tomorrow. I want to do more, but she's refused. Won't do anything for herself. I don't know how she makes it. Dead plants and paperwork strewn all over."

"Tell me about it," Brad said with an upward toss of his hand. "Woman worries me half to death. Lives in a place she calls Casa de Vortexa or The Vortex, filled with pedophiles, drunks, drug dealers, and computer hackers. Even though she says it's an anomaly in an otherwise great neighborhood—and my sources in law enforcement corroborated that—I want her the hell out of there, but I don't dare broach the subject."

"I wouldn't."

"She won't listen to me at all," Collins said, gesturing sharply with both hands, getting very animated. "Smokes pot constantly, drinks a lot, puts herself in dangerous situations. Jesus Christ, she comes late to a date just a month ago, bleeding, her clothes torn from fleeing from a homeowner after getting caught *breaking into his house!*" he said emphatically, waving his arms.

Matt pursed his lips. Why Hell didn't have a mile-long rap sheet he'd never know.

Sweat beaded on Collins' forehead, and his gaze hollowed. "She had to steal an iPad to cover her tracks, jump fences, and run through yards, got chased by the police, and barely missed getting caught. Crazy!"

"Did she say why?"

Brad relaxed a bit. "Yeah, she had the keys. A divorce case. Wife assured her that the husband never got home before five, but he came home sick and surprised Hell. She ran out the back door, and he saw her jumping over his fence." His face flushed a deeper red. "It was on the goddamned news that night! Thankfully, they mistook her for a young Hispanic kid who'd been burglarizing houses in the area, but, Jesus, she was so cavalier about it all. Laughing like it was all so funny. I was *horrified.*"

Matt had to hold back laughter. Of course, if he were in love with her, he'd have duct-taped her to a wall by now just to keep her out of trouble.

"Out of control," Collins said with another wild wave of his hand. "I know she's in therapy, but it's clearly not helping. Now people are trying to kill her. I was up all last night with nightmares that she was getting shot, and I couldn't save her." He rubbed his forehead. "Fucking crazy woman." He turned his intensity onto Matt. "Please, Sinclair, do what you can for her."

"I will."

Despite his earlier misgivings, he was starting to like this rich asshole.

Brad leaned back in his chair, the lines on his face deepening. "Meanwhile, I have to accelerate the divorce proceedings. I'll call my lawyers tonight and file tomorrow. Of course, I have no idea how to go about the conversation of a future with Hell without her running."

"If you divorced Sherry, Hell would probably come around."

"You think?" Collins said, his face brightening.

"She had eight boyfriends until you. Now she has one. Do the math."

Collins laughed, and then his face took on a shine. He looked like he lost a few years in age.

While over the moon for her, the man still better do the right thing by her. Jury wasn't out on this guy, but he'd taken himself off the unsub list.

Brad took a long sip of his wine. "Who do you want to hire?"

"Thompson."

"Done. I'll make the call. Set up whatever plan you think will work the best. I'll tell him you're in charge."

"Good." Plus that would put him in touch with another very successful local PI. He could use the contact.

Collins leaned in, opened his mouth, then shut it. Shook his head and moved back in his seat.

"What?"

His lips tightened, and the line between his eyes deepened. "Hell would kill me if she found out I said something about..."

"About what?"

"Oh, fuck it. There is one person in her life that I think might be behind the shooting."

"Who?"

"I know I shouldn't say this, Hell has forbidden me to talk about him, but did she tell you about her association with the Mafia don?"

How did he know about Capasso? Did he have her followed?

"Capasso?"

"Yeah." The icy look behind Collins' eyes said it all. He hated the man.

"How did you find out? You said she never opened up to you."

"Ran into Hell and the don at the Fairmont one night shortly after we started seeing each other."

Matt sat up, hungry for the information. His curiosity had been piqued earlier when Lindsay had mentioned running into Hell with Capasso up at the Fairmont. He'd wanted to probe further into the interaction but knew Hell wouldn't willingly reveal anything about the Mafia don. "Really?"

"Yeah. Very surprising and very strange. Hell didn't look or act like herself."

Collins relayed the story, giving Matt a disturbing picture of Hell's date with Capasso. Hell in a tight black dress, covered in jewels, acting submissive and cowed? *Hell Trent?* A flaming fire ignited in his gut, and his hands fisted. An overwhelming urge to strangle Capasso overcame him. No way would she dress or act like that unless her life depended on it.

"She seemed mortified when she ran into Sherry and me," Collins said. "Ashamed. I know he's threatening her into seeing him. I know it."

After they solved the case, Matt had to convince her to let him help her get out from underneath the criminal's control. No one should live like that. Poor kid.

He gave his head an inward shake. What was he thinking? He was running as soon as the job was over. He couldn't allow himself to get caught up in the drama of Hell's life. He had other priorities: like the mortgage on his house and his kids' college expenses.

Besides, she hated him. She'd never in a million years let him help her.

"Did Hell say anything about him?" Collins asked.

Matt shook his head. "No. But when she was talking to him on the phone, she looked afraid. White-knuckled the phone, sweat on her forehead, pale and jittery."

Collins' back stiffened, and his eyes heated. "He called her? When?"

"Yesterday."

"Okay, she told me that," he said, easing back down in his seat. "She hasn't seen him since November, right? Since I ran into them."

"Yeah, probably. She said she only saw him once a year, on his birthday. So that fits," Matt said.

Collins gave a slow nod. "That's what she told me. Still, I'd still take a look at him. There's something wrong there. He may be trying to separate us."

"Agreed. And I think you're right, that he forces her to see him. I just don't know why she hasn't gotten away from him sooner. Why he has such a hold on her. Did your detectives uncover anything about their history?" Matt asked.

"Only hints of a fight Hell had with Capasso's brother about ten years ago. Over an underage prostitute. According to the rumor, Hell saved the girl without realizing she was Capasso's brother's possession, nor did she know that the girl had just witnessed a mob hit."

Matt's stomach went hard. "Christ."

"Hell denied the whole thing when I confronted her, but her eyes dilated. Also right around the time she had the fight with Capasso's brother, Hell ended up beaten to shit in the hospital."

The image of a battered Hell lying in a hospital bed shocked his system. Fury raged within him, overheating his body, making him break out in a sweat. His instinct to protect her became overwhelming. Here were the real answers. "You sure?" He gripped his beer tighter.

His expression even graver, Collins nodded sharply. "Yeah. Fractured ribs, fractured jaw, internal bleeding. The list of injuries was extensive. She was in ICU for twenty-four hours, then spent two more days in the hospital before she was released."

A wave of intense nausea hit Matt, and he flashed on a minimovie of all the beaten women he'd seen in his career. Horrible shit. To find out that Hell had suffered the same fate as the countless victims he'd interviewed made him sick to his core. "Damn. How did you find that out?"

"Hell has talented hackers and so do I. Of course, when I told Hell I knew about the beating, she told me the same lie she told the cops: she was attacked by a stranger and didn't remember the attack. A cop who was on the case that Thompson talked to, a McConnell, confirmed that Capasso had beaten her because of a problem with his family business. That afterwards Hell tried to end it with Marco, but he wouldn't let her go. That he threatened her into seeing him, using her family's safety as leverage."

His mood darker, Matt shook his head, his jaw so tight it hurt. All rang true. Poor Hell. "No wonder. Christ."

She had to let him help her. After they were done with the case, he'd insist. Yes, they were still enemies, but there was no way he could allow her continue to suffer under that mob boss monster's control.

"Good luck trying to get her to talk about it."

Matt would find out what happened. "I'll keep digging. But she really doesn't think the threat is coming from him. And if what you're saying to me is true, it makes no sense that Capasso would sneak around and threaten Hell. If he has absolute control over her, he'd just come straight out and order her to do what he wanted."

"Unless he was trying to manipulate her. He has to know who she is. He's been seeing her for eleven years. I can't imagine he beats her all the time. I can't see her taking that. He's getting older. Maybe he's trying a subtler approach now."

"I'll get her to tell me." Matt's phone rang. Hell. "Speak of the devil. Yeah, Hell?"

"Matt?" Her voice cracked. Beeping noises in the background.

The pit of his stomach went cold, and his body hardened. Something happened to her. "Yeah, Hell? What's going on? Where are you?"

"I need you to come over here." Her voice shook.

His heart rate shot up, and he gripped the phone tighter. Urgency possessed him. He had to get to her and yesterday. "Where? Hell, what happened?"

Sobbing.

Adrenaline flooded him. Matt sat straight up in his chair. "Hell, talk to me. What happened? Where are you?"

"Mills-Peninsula Hospital in Burlingame."

Matt leapt out of his seat. *"The hospital?"*

Brad stood, looking like he was going to attack him and rip the phone out of his hands. Matt made an executive decision and hit the button for the speakerphone but held his finger to his lips. Collins responded with a terse nod.

"Yeah," she said, teary. "Could you come over here? I'm in the ICU for observation, but I'm trying to get them to release me because I can't afford this."

Brad's jaw dropped.

Hell said, "The cops are driving me nuts with questions, and they all want to talk to you."

Matt's heart beat hard against his breastbone. "Cops? What happened?"

Loud sobs came out of the speaker.

Brad's expression turned even more alarmed.

Matt had to loosen his grip on the phone so he wouldn't crush it. "Hell, honey, calm down, and tell me what happened."

"They bombed my back patio and blew up my apartment! They almost killed me!" More violent crying.

Matt took in a huge breath, and sweat dripped down his back. How had she survived?

Brad gasped and put a hand to his chest, his eyes wide.

Matt said, "Holy shit. Are you all right?"

"Y-y-yeah. I was lucky. I got hit with shrapnel all along the left side of my leg and butt—but not too deep, I think. But I'm hurtin', man. I'm alone here, and scared, and the cops really freaked me out, and I called my cousin and sister, and they're coming but won't get here for a while, and I need to work on the case, but I'm so terrified right now I can't stop shaking."

Her tone wrenched his heart. He'd kill whoever did this to her. "You hold tight. I'm coming now."

"O-okay." She sounded about five years old. "See ya." She hung up.

Matt headed out of the restaurant, Collins hustling alongside.

The billionaire looked frantic. "I'm coming with you."

"Could be a lot of press around this."

"I don't care."

"Follow me in your car. I don't know how long I'll be there."

"Okay."

His system jacked with adrenaline, his body battle-ready, Matt ran stoplights and broke nearly every traffic law as he drove to the hospital. That attack was all his fault. Goddamn it! He punched the steering wheel. She shouldn't have been left alone. It was clear from the first moment he'd taken the case that she'd needed constant protection. He should have stood up to her. He shouldn't have let his emotions for her fuck with his job. His first real job as a civilian, and he was blowing it. All because of his anger for a woman who was clearly not the depraved slut he'd thought. She was a nice, kind, giving, sweet person trapped in the body of a crazy woman. With very few people in her corner.

Time to put his prejudice for her aside. Time to put his hatred and their past behind him. Solve this case and save her life.

He might piss her off, he might overstep his boundaries with her, but no way was she dying on his watch. It was time to take control and protect her.

No matter how much she fought him.

CHAPTER 17

E ars ringing, head throbbing, Hell lay in the uncomfortable hospital bed wishing she were anywhere else. The left side of her leg, thigh, and hip burned and stung, all pockmarked with shrapnel wounds. The skin on her hip bone had been sheared off and was her biggest injury, about two-and-a-half inches in diameter and gross. Another big gash on the side of her knee, about two inches long and a half inch wide, hurt like a son of a bitch. Five stitches in her forehead from the bookshelf completed her new Frankenstein look.

But her appearance was the least of her problems. The bomb hadn't just destroyed her apartment, it had destabilized her mental foundation. Fragmented thoughts warred with each other. Relief at surviving the bombing battled the terror of future attacks fought the horror of isolation. She'd never felt more alone in her life. All she had were eight lovers who didn't give a crap about her and a family who had abandoned her years before. The only person she could count on was her cousin Joanne, and thank God she was on her way. But having a team of only one person —who already had a full life and a daughter—left a giant, gaping chasm in Hell's life. Times like these put a spotlight on the emptiness.

She wanted nothing more than to crawl into bed with Secret

Teddy, but he was gone, and her safe place was in shreds. Somehow she had to keep it together, but she was right on the edge of completely losing her mind.

To make her situation even more intolerable, she was stuck in the goddamned hospital. Even though her private ICU room was spacious and modern, the gnarly disinfectant/cleaner smell assaulted her, the monitor next to her wouldn't stop beeping, and the automatic blood pressure cuff kept puffing up so tightly she swore it was about to sever her arm. To add to her joy, her high-deductible health plan meant even more debt.

One more thing and she'd need a padded cell.

Matt walked through the door, looking much more worried than she would have expected. What had changed?

Even though she didn't trust him, the sight of him calmed her. Thank God she'd hired this guy. He'd help her. He was solid. An amazing cop. One smart thing she'd done.

Too bad she hadn't had the money to follow his advice and hire bodyguards after the shooting. Might have helped.

BC appeared at the door. Completely out of context. Took her a long second to understand he was really there.

The world tilted, then twisted and turned, making her already-convoluted sense of reality even more surreal. *What the hell was BC doing there?*

Oh, shit, Matt had been interviewing him! Son of a bitch!

The degree of caring in the men's expressions was almost shocking. She put her hands to her chest, dragging the IV tubes with her. She didn't want them to see her this vulnerable. She hated that she'd started crying on the phone.

BC pushed past Matt, his face full of emotion. She wanted to run.

Fighting tears, she forced a smile. "Hey, BC."

"Hell, Jesus." He wiped his eyes.

Overwhelmed, she burst into sobs.

BC put his arms around her and brought her close. "It's okay, baby, I'm here."

Torn in half, one part of her reveled in his comfort while the other part wanted to strangle him. All she'd longed for since Josh died was this kind of comfort and attention. To have it coming from a married man, a man she could never have, plus the all-encompassing love she felt for him made her agony nearly unbearable.

The bomb was looking like the easy part of the ordeal.

He kissed the top of her head. "I'm going to make damn sure nothing like this ever happens to you again."

Hell fought to ground herself and stood on her feelings. The tears stopped, but they were a breath away.

She pushed him away, but he brought her back close. "You can't be here, Brad. The cops will question you. Everyone will find out."

"I don't care."

She ran the back of her hand across her eyes. "I hate having you see me like this."

"What? Human?" BC asked.

She chuckled. "Yeah. Human."

"Jesus, Hell, someone nearly killed you." He squeezed her. "It's okay to be scared."

"But I don't want to."

He kissed her cheek and shot her a reassuring grin that gutted her. Pulling away so he could stand, he stayed close to the bed and kept hold of her hand.

Matt came up on her other side and patted her forearm. "Are you all right?"

A different Matt stood before her. Gentle, kind, caring. Confusing! "No. Goddamned bomb destroyed my *Tales From The Crypt* pinball machine, my TV, my kitchen, destroyed my apartment. I got pinball shards in me, too. Tons of crap embedded in my skin. Apparently, with shrapnel wounds, they don't remove the bits of metal and wood and books and whatever else blasted into my body. All of it will 'work its way out' eventually. I can't imagine the joy."

BC tightened his hold on her hand.

"What happened right before?" Matt asked.

Hell calmed a bit and thought. She shook her head. "Nothing, man. Not a thing. I was out there smoking a joint, walked inside, and kablooey! Missed being blown up by like thirty seconds."

Matt's forehead wrinkled deep. "Damn, Hell."

BC nearly crushed her hand, then eased off. "Jesus."

Hell scratched the edge of a bandage on her forehead. "One cop who'd been in combat in Iraq said that if the bomb hadn't exploded exactly where it did, and I hadn't been in that precise position in the back bedroom behind the boxes of books and bookshelves, I wouldn't have made it. The force of the blast missed my little area, and I got hit with a minor amount of the shrapnel. It hasn't been confirmed yet, but from the wreckage, the vet guessed it was a hand grenade."

"Damn," Matt and Brad said at the same time.

"My whole head hurts and is still buzzing. But we know who it has to be. Lindsay must have done it. You have to go to her house and question her, Matt. I didn't tell the cops because I didn't want you involved, BC, but here you are. They're gonna question you, and the affair is bound to come out," she said, her voice pitched high with upset.

Brad's expression didn't change. "I don't care. All I care about is you." He wiped her cheeks. She wished he'd just stop. He was making her feel, the last thing she needed.

Matt said, "Until we have all the evidence, we shouldn't jump to conclusions, even though your reasoning is sound. You got Lindsay all riled up this afternoon. This is quite a coincidence if she didn't do it."

"Exactly," Hell said.

"So were you knocked out?" Matt withdrew a small notebook and a pen from his inner jacket pocket.

"No, and thank God for my neighbors. They came and got me out of there. But the place is..." Tears stung her eyes, and her throat closed. "Destroyed."

BC rubbed her shoulder.

"So the police arrived shortly after that?" Matt jotted down some notes.

"Yeah. Melissa had checked me out initially—she's a nurse—but there was so much blood everywhere, it was hard to tell. Most of the blood came from the wound on my forehead. She said I was gonna be fine. And I am. Except for this side of my leg and ass here are almost hamburger." She gestured toward her left thigh.

"Christ," BC said.

"The bomb blew out a bunch of windows in the condo complex next door, and the surrounding apartments all sustained damage. Thankfully, I'm the only one who got hurt. But I was and still am totally overwhelmed and—"

"Of course you are." BC ran his hand down her shoulder.

Her body responded to him like a starving dog being fed a steak. How soon could she send him away? Where was that nurse with more drugs?

"So nothing unusual?" Matt asked.

"Bomb was pretty unusual."

Matt snorted. "Smart ass."

Hell smiled, which felt good. "Nothing out of the ordinary, no. Cops followed me here to the hospital and insisted on questioning me while I was getting stitches. Not sure I helped them much, because I was trying to not involve BC, and I'm so screwed up."

Matt indicated the door with his head. "Joe's out in the corridor. Cops are putting a twenty-four-hour guard on you."

"Jesus. Yeah, I saw him earlier."

BC said, "I'm calling some outside help, too, Hell."

"BC, no. I—"

His face turned to granite, and he jabbed a finger in her face. "You shut the hell up, woman."

She leaned back and glared. "I'll argue with you later."

He raised his chin. "The hell you will."

Hell rolled her eyes.

In the doorway behind BC, the lead detective—a lantern-jawed, dark-haired mountain named Serra—poked his head in the door and stared between Matt and BC, then disappeared.

Her gut tightened, and a wave of shame coursed through her. BC had been made. Now the whole world would know about their affair. *Shit.* "Dude, you blew it by coming here. Lead detective, Serra, just stuck his head in and saw you. I'm trying not to get you involved."

"Well, I am involved, and I want to stay involved." Brad's intensity heightened.

She guessed it wasn't every day he had girlfriends getting blown up with bombs. Why else would he be there and look so freaked out? "Well, be prepared for a grilling. Great, now this is gonna be in the news, and I'm gonna look like this giant home-wrecking whore." Her mood spiraled downward even further.

"Hell, stop," BC said. "No one is going to call you a whore. I'm the philandering Silicon Valley venture capitalist."

"And I'm the one clearly gunning for your money. I thought I couldn't hate this situation any more, but apparently, I was wrong."

"Hell, stop. Everything will work out, you'll see," BC said.

"Sure." Hell made a face at him.

He shook his head and grinned.

Her sister, Irene, walked into the room and gasped when she saw her.

Hell's body tensed further, and the machine beeped faster. Shit. First time in years that a family member had met one of her boyfriends and he was married. Could this situation get any more fun?

In one of her usual gray, boring, skirted business suits accented by a white shirt with a dated ruffled collar—along with her shoulder-length curly gray granny hairdo—Irene looked like a nun. Her tight, prune-y mouth and the deep wrinkles grooved around and between her brown eyes told of all her years of disappointment with the world. A free and loving person in her twenties, over the years, Irene had become a blend of their conservative, narcissistic, spoiled-brat parents. Became all that she once loathed. Sad.

But Hell's main issue now was Irene's big-ass mouth. She was a direct pipeline to their parents, and Mom and Dad did not need to know about Brad. Shit!

Hell put on a fake smile. "Hey, sis."

Hopefully, Irene was not up on local venture capitalists. With any luck, she wouldn't recognize BC.

"Irene, this is Matt Sinclair, a guy who's helping me solve my case and—" *Don't say his last name!* "Uh..."

BC extended his hand. "Brad."

Irene shook hands with him and thankfully didn't seem to notice Hell's awkwardness. Matt offered his hand, and Irene took it.

Matt moved back and allowed Irene access to her bedside. But BC wouldn't let go of her hand. Which was an odd move for him. Why was he staking his claim on her in front of her sister?

Irene hugged her as best she could, then pulled away with her worry lines etched deep. "Elly, for God's sake, are you okay, sweetie? A bomb? Why didn't you tell me on the phone? You said you'd been in an accident."

"I didn't want to worry you. How'd you find out?"

"You're all over the news."

The beeping of the monitor grew even faster. "Oh, crap. Tell me Mom and Dad don't know. Tell me."

"They saw it on TV. You have to talk to them. They're freaking out."

Hell tried hard to maintain her sanity. "No, I don't. Not now. No way do I want to talk to that big asshole."

Irene's lips tightened. "Elly, they're old, and they can't take the stress. They have to hear your voice or Dad will have a heart attack, and Mom will have a stroke."

The problem with that? "I'll call them later. I can't take Dad's shit right now."

Irene looked at her phone. "Too late. Here." She stuck her cell in Hell's face, forcing her to let go of BC's hand.

Her body went hot and hard, and she clamped her jaw. "Irene! I told you I don't—*Are you trying to make me feel worse?*"

Irene shrugged and sent her a nasty smirk, a flare of victory in her eyes. Ever since Hell had moved away from living next door to her parents, the whole family had turned against her, pissed they actually had to step up to help care for the old farts. Even before then Irene had treated her like shit, ever since she'd married her conservative butthole of a husband, Martin. Why had Hell called her? Stupid moment of weakness.

Dad's voice boomed from the phone. "Irene? You there? What's going on with Elly?" A part of her wanted to go into the fetal position while her old battle-worn side emerged to protect her. This brutal motherfucker had terrorized her since birth.

With a glare at Irene, who remained resolute, she finally put the cell to her ear. "Dad, how ya doin'? This is Elly," she said in a cheerful tone. She slipped into Placate-The-Crazy-People Mode. Only way to survive Parent Attacks was to say whatever they needed to hear. One false move and it was Parent-ageddon.

By the sharp look in BC's eyes, he didn't seem too happy with Irene, either.

Dad's normal growling and clearing-throat noises blasted through the receiver followed by, "Elly? That you? Jesus Christ, you're all over the news! What the hell happened? You gave your mother a heart attack!"

Hell shut down further and kept her affect clean of emotion. "Dad, calm down. I'm fine."

"Don't give me that bullshit. If you were fine, you wouldn't be in the hospital. Someone blew up your apartment with a bomb? Tell me what happened."

Hell sighed. If she were prone to spontaneous combustion, this would be the time. "Like the news said. Someone threw a bomb, maybe a hand grenade, on my patio and—"

"Jesus Christ! No, shut up, Marilyn, she's fine. I'm finding out! Here I'll put you on speakerphone."

Panic hit her. Not the speakerphone! Not her mother! "No!"

Her mother owned her soul and only let her borrow it occasionally. Mom's voice was like a firing squad to her heart.

"Elly?" Her mother sounded weepy.

Hell's heart shredded, and tears filled her eyes. "Hey, Mom."

"You have to stop all this, Elly. You have to stop."

Of course it was all her fault. "Mom, I didn't do anything. I was attacked." Hell wiped her eyes with the thin hospital blanket.

"We're too old for this, Elly. I just can't take it."

She gripped the phone harder, and her back tensed so hard it ached. "Mom, I didn't get bombed to hurt you. I try not to get blown up, mostly. Really, my primary goal in life is not to be blown up."

Out of the corner of her eye, BC stared at her with a frown, clearly upset by her side of the conversation.

"Still, you're doing something to cause all this, and it just can't go on," her mother pressed.

Hell let out a long breath. Every time she'd ever been injured or fallen off her bike or gotten sick or was upset, her mother acted like Hell had purposely done it to hurt her. She forced her voice to be even more calm and controlled. "Mom, don't worry. I'm fine. Honestly. Got a little bit of shrapnel, but my books saved me. Not a big deal."

"Goddamn it, Helen!" Dad thundered.

Hell jumped a bit, hurting her leg, and held the phone away from her ear. "Ow." Amazing how Dad's yelling hardly fazed her anymore, but Mom's teary self-pity always ripped her guts apart.

"It's a goddamned big deal when someone throws a fucking bomb at you," Dad stated indignantly. "Now what kind of bomb was it?"

Here we go. Dad barely had a high school education but was an expert on everything. He believed that global warming couldn't possibly raise sea level because he'd been on a cruise ship once and had seen "all that water."

"Elly? What kind of bomb?"

"I don't know, Dad," she replied in a tired voice. "Kind that blows up your apartment."

"You said it could it have been a grenade? Now I know all about grenades. Why, during the war, I saw a guy with his arm in shreds, I mean *shreds*, skin hanging off the bone like chicken skin, veins flapping like red spaghetti, blood everywhere—"

She almost barfed, and the beeping of the machine grew more

rapid. She swallowed hard. "Dad! No gross-out stories, or I'll hang up!" Next he'd work his bowels into the conversation.

"John! Shut up!" Mom ordered.

"Stop yelling at me, the both of you. I know what I'm talking about. Now when I was in World War Two, I threw a couple hand grenades. This was in Paris..." Dad proceeded to launch into a long, involved, barely related story.

Relieved yet furious and resigned and frustrated and repulsed and disgusted and hurt and a million other emotions that her parents always elicited, Hell covered the receiver, rolled her eyes, and lay back. "Christ almighty, he won't shut up."

"He means well," Irene said in a patronizing tone.

The vise around her stomach tightened a notch. "Hardly."

Irene pursed her lips.

What was even nicer in the Trent Family was that when someone beat you up, there was always another person there to tell you it was all your fault. Hell seriously needed a family-ectomy.

A few minutes later, her father wrapped up his soliloquy. "So tell that doctor that that's how we used to handle grenade wounds, you know, back in the war. I don't expect those fancy Hillsborough doctors know anything about that. Let me talk to the doctor. He there?"

"No, Dad. Look, I gotta go."

"Elly? You're on TV again," Mom said. "It looks like they caught the man. He doesn't look nice at all."

Adrenaline jolted her. "Who? A man? Someone turn on the news. Mom says that they caught my attacker."

"Got it," Matt said, and turned on the flat screen hanging on the wall next to the whiteboard.

Breaking News! the screen flashed. *San Mateo Bombing!* Tanner came on screen, yelling his innocence while two cops hustled him into a police car.

Hell's jaw dropped, and a sense of urgency overwhelmed her. "Tanner? He couldn't have done it! Why didn't they talk to me before they arrested him? Matt, go get the cops, and bring them in here. This is crap! Damn it, I have to get out of here and go clear him." She sat up.

"The hell you do!" Matt and BC barked in unison.

BC pushed her gently back into the bed.

Hell glared. "I'm fine."

"You're not fine," Matt, BC, and her father said at the same time.

"You're staying here," Matt said firmly. He stood with his back and shoulders straight, the picture of power and control. "You can't do anything in your current condition. Besides, that's why you hired me. Let me do my job, okay?"

"He's right." BC wore a similar no-argument face.

Hell didn't know how she'd suddenly gotten surrounded by immovable men, but when she got her brain back, she was going to do something about it. "Whatever. Clearly this isn't the time to argue. You don't think Tanner did it, do you, Matt? Has to be Lindsay. How can it be Tanner?"

"We don't know the evidence yet, Hell. Here." Matt grabbed the cell from her hand. "Mr. Trent? Mrs. Trent? This is Matt Sinclair, and I'm a private investigator working for your daughter. The police have just come into the room to talk to Helen. I'm going to hand you off to Irene, all right? Great." He handed the cell to her sister.

Everyone checked the door. No police.

In that moment, she fell in love with Matt Sinclair. Not romantically but intensely. "You're a rock star, Matt."

He gave a little nod, the look behind his eyes strong and sure.

BC smiled widely. "I should have done that."

Irene held the phone with a shocked expression, then narrowed her eyes and put the cell to her ear. "Mom? Dad? I'll call you right back."

Her sister hung up, lifted her chin and a half, and her wrinkled, thin lips flattened. "That wasn't very nice, Elly," she said to Matt. She glared at BC, then Hell. "They love you."

Hell twisted her mouth. "Doubtful. They get all their frequent flier miles from the guilt trips they lay on me."

"Oh, Elly, if you'd go see them more often, they'd be nicer to you."

Hell tried to think of a response other than *fuck you*. She kicked herself for calling her sister. How soon could she get the moron to leave?

Her cousin Joanne came rushing into the room, her dark eyes wide. "Are you okay?"

Her entire body eased. Just the understanding in her cousin's face centered Hell and made her feel safer. The only one in the family she could trust. The only non-narcissistic-freak-of-nature in the bunch.

Hell tried to give her a bright smile. "Fine, cuz."

Joanne made a face and swept dark hair out of her deep brown eyes. "Fine, she says when a bomb destroys her apartment." Her make up was a bit runny, like she'd been crying. While Hell was sorry she'd worried her cousin, at least someone in the family cared about her.

Joanne always dressed chic but simple and looked thirty years younger than Irene even though their difference was a mere six years. Today she wore a berry cardigan over a black scoop-necked T-shirt paired with white close-fitting slacks, which highlighted her thin, fit body. Her contemporary shoulder-length hairstyle suited her youthful, symmetrical features.

Hell smirked. "Yeah, when a pizza place says their pizza is the bomb? Don't order it."

Everyone laughed but Irene.

Brad backed up, and Joanne took his place, taking Hell's hand. "I'm just so glad you're okay."

Hell returned her cousin's grip. "Me, too, kid. Told you I'd never leave ya."

Joanne sent her a loving smile, warming her to the core. No way could she have survived the family without her help. She was the only other person who understood the cesspool of abuse that was the Trent Family.

"You're on again, Hell," Matt said, pointing to the TV in the corner.

Her blown-out apartment appeared on one side of a split screen; on the other, a news interview she'd done the year before.

Hell gasped and clutched her chest. "Shit."

Joanne stepped sideways to the foot of Hell's bed, allowing Brad to return to her side.

"Take it easy, Hell," BC said. "You came through it fine. That was all just stuff. Stuff can be replaced. You can't."

"Listen to him," Joanne said, checking out every square inch of Brad.

Irene's x-ray vision seared into him.

How did this happen? How did her worlds collide?

Understanding came over Joanne's face. "You're BC." She'd heard the Brad stories ad nauseam.

"BC?" Irene asked, looking between her and Brad.

Hell's throat went tight. "BC is his nickname. Brad, this is my cousin, Joanne."

"Pleased to meet you," Brad said cordially, shaking Joanne's hand.

Irene's gaze sparkled. "So how long have you two been going out? Why haven't we heard about him, Elly?"

She gritted her teeth. "Because we're not at that stage yet, Irene," she bit out.

Irene checked out Brad, then her attention went to his hand in Hell's. "Seems as if you are to me." She gave her a sinister smile.

Hell's stomach lurched, and a little wave of panic made the machine next to her beep faster. Not only had she lost her apartment, she'd lost her privacy. Within minutes, Hell and BC's relationship would be broadcast all over the Trent Family News Network. She couldn't wait for when they found out he was married, which they surely would. Which would just add to her humiliation and pain when she dumped Brad because he wouldn't divorce Sherry. Or when Brad dumped her because he was Brad.

At least her billionaire lover presented well in his zillion-dollar suit. Irene had freaked when she'd met Dave and gotten a gander at his blue Mohawk, facial piercings, and tattoos.

Joanne sent her a silent little sly smile of approval topped by a quick eyebrow raise.

While pleased by her cousin's reaction to Brad, this was the worst disaster that had ever befallen her. She needed to get rid of the group and fast.

Matt stepped forward on her left.

Hell shook her head. "I'm sorry, Matt. Joanne, this is Matt. He's helping me solve the case."

Joanne was too far away and settled for waving at Matt. Hell purposely avoided mentioning his last name. Joanne would kill him if she knew who he really was.

Irene stared a hole through BC. Hell had to get her to leave. How was she supposed to heal when she was enduring an emotional blanket bombing?

Joanne patted her unhurt leg. "So, Hell, what's the prognosis? They're releasing you soon, right?"

"Yeah. I'll be fine. All superficial injuries. I was really lucky."

"Thank God," she said, and her shoulders dropped a bit.

"No worries, cuz. We're gonna find this bastard and nail 'em. Well, after I sleep for a week." Hell yawned dramatically.

"We should let her rest," Brad announced.

While she didn't like him throwing his weight around, he'd gotten Irene to nod. At this point, anything that got rid of her sister was good for her. She'd deal with Brad's weird, misplaced, protective boyfriend behavior later.

"I have to call Kendra," Joanne said, referring to her daughter in college. "I was talking to her when you called. She's totally worried. I'll be right back. My extra bedroom is all set up, so as soon as you're released, we can go home, okay?"

Guilt made her face heat. "I can stay at a hotel."

Joanne rolled her eyes. "For God's sake, no way. I'm taking care of you. I took tomorrow off. You're staying with me, and don't argue."

Like Joanne needed this huge disruption in her life. "I hate to bother you when you're so busy."

"Yeah, it's such a bother when my favorite cousin's apartment gets bombed. I mean, it happens so often. Like, what? Five times this month already?"

"I know, I just—"

"Hell, relax, that's what I'm here for. Do you remember my shoulder surgery? Or the other hundred things you did for me? Jeez, you are the hardest person to help. Just tell me what you need."

Hell's throat closed, and she pushed back the tears. "Thanks, cuz."

Irene sent a guilty glance between her and Joanne. "I'd love to help, but I have to get ready for the fundraiser for Martin's reelection campaign." She assumed a regal posture. "My husband is United States Congressman Martin White. I don't know if Elly told you that," she said, directing her proud announcement to Matt and BC.

Both men nodded respectfully, but they clearly weren't impressed.

Joanne and Hell exchanged their usual silent mutual looks of contempt for Irene. Which made Hell feel a bazillion times better.

Irene prattled on. "He's a real rising star in the Tea Party now with the introduction of his new bill to immediately deport all the illegal immigrants and make sure they don't receive any type of aid. We're thinking of a presidential run in four years."

Like anyone cares about your racist bullshit, Irene. Shut the fuck up. "Irene, don't worry about it. Joanne lives closer. You're an hour away and clearly busy." Also a total asshole.

Her sister's face relaxed. Never could count on her. Why couldn't she remember that?

Irene gestured toward her. "Look at the bright side, you get to go shopping to replace all your, uh, furnishings. Maybe you should take this as a new beginning and create a normal adult environment for yourself," she said in a perky tone. "A place you could be proud of."

Hell's stomach hurt, and her face flushed. "Good plan. Besides, that giant playpen is gonna be hard to replace, along with the huge high chair and crib. At least the rubber nipples for my beer bottles are easy to source."

Her sister's face screwed up tight, and her frown went to her boobs.

BC coughed into his hand, and Joanne outright laughed. Matt's jaw twitched, but he kept his hard expression.

"First Hell needs to heal," Joanne stated protectively. "At least they caught the guy. I'll be right back." She left.

Irene stood taller. "I've got to go, Elly. Now make sure you go see Mom and Dad," she said, using her Patronizing Princess voice. "After this little fiasco, you really owe them a visit."

Hell's blood turned to fire and she balled her fists. "Little fiasco? Someone *bombed* my apartment, Irene, and almost killed me. No way am I taking Dad's crap."

"It takes two to have an argument," she stated like a hall monitor reciting the rules. "You never take responsibility for your side of things."

"Oh, right, it's all me, I forgot. Ever since I was two, I launched my evil war on him, right? Isn't that when he started comin' after me? That's when Mom said she had to start protecting me from him," Hell bit out with a caustic edge.

"You don't have to get sarcastic. We all know Dad had some minor anger issues at one time, but—"

Rage heated her body hot, and she glared at her sister. "Minor? One time? He's never stopped attacking me, Irene."

Her sister sneered. "That's your interpretation, but you've always been overly sensitive. You can't blame all your problems on Dad. This bombing is a perfect example. I mean, with a crazy job and a life like yours, are you really surprised it led to this disaster?"

"Uh, yeah, actually, I—"

Her sister continued without missing a beat. "We told you your sordid life would end like this, but did you listen to us? No. And far be it for you to think about your impact on the family. Did you even think about what this might do to Martin's reelection campaign? He really can't afford this type of publicity."

Irene was so lucky there wasn't a baseball bat handy. "Are you for real? Like I fucking planned to get bombed just to ruin your fat dickhead of a husband's career? You don't even care that I almost *died*, do you?"

Irene's eyes darkened; she took a step forward and pointed at Hell vehemently. "Don't you take out your anger on me, Missy. Can't you see how you're the problem here? You're the one with the depraved life and ridiculous hair and marijuana addiction. Have you thought that this might be God's will? That God sent the attacker to bomb you, to wake you up, and set you on the right path? That's the first thing I thought, that this attack might have been the best thing that's ever happened to you."

Her vision blurred, her jaw went to her chest, and it took all her strength not to leap out of bed and punch her stupid asshole sister.

BC stepped forward, his hand raised, his face hard, his eyes flashing. "That's enough, Irene. Hell's had enough for one night. You said you had to leave. Why don't you?" He stood tall, his shoulders big, and jerked his head toward the door.

Irene turned all her hatred and anger onto BC. She curled her lip. "Who are you again? You don't look like one of her usual low-class, criminal, punk-rock boyfriends. You almost look sort of normal, and strangely enough, her age. I thought she only dated young boys."

Hell's body flamed hot. She sat up and opened her mouth to yell, but Brad cut her off.

"I'm her friend. And I say she's had enough of your *sisterly love*," he snapped, his jaw tight. "Leave. Please. Now." He pointed toward the door.

"Hmmm." She gave him an up-and-down examination, and a look of revulsion came over her pouchy lined face, making her jowls even more pronounced. "Ever since her husband died, she's used her grief as an excuse to sleep with an endless parade of losers. Looks like she's found herself another low-life gigolo scumbag to inhabit her bed."

The beeping grew super fast. "How dare you call him that!" Hell pointed at the door. "Get out! Of this room and my life! Forever!"

"You heard the lady," BC said, his voice low, his eyes dark.

Irene sneered. "When you get your head out of your ass, go see our parents before they die. But I'd leave the overdressed creep with the fake Rolex behind if I were you. Mom and Dad don't need reminders of your sordid sex life." She turned and stormed out.

"*Bitch!*" Hell yelled at her sister's back.

Hell's head was so hot her forehead burned, and she was covered in sweat. She made a violent gesture. "Why did I call her?"

BC rubbed her shoulder. "I'm sorry, Hell."

"Wow," Matt said.

"No, I'm sorry, BC. She was way out of line, even for her."

"Don't apologize. You didn't do anything wrong," BC said. "You just reached out for support and got beaten down instead."

Hell tried to cool her flaming cheeks with her hands. "Story of my family life. Sorry, guys, you didn't need to see that little embarrassing display."

Matt waved his hand dismissively. "Nothing to apologize for, Hell. You sure didn't do anything wrong."

BC snorted. "I'm the one who's sorry. I almost slapped her."

"I almost killed her. Thanks for coming to my defense, BC. And you earlier, Matt."

Matt smiled at her warmly. Brad grinned, making her heart swell. Pain followed, deflating her hope. She had to get rid of him.

BC looked at the door, then back to Hell. "Funny thing is, I've met her before on several occasions. I can't believe she didn't recognize me."

"You met my sister?" Hell asked, incredulous.

"Fundraisers and functions for her idiot husband."

Hell frowned. "I didn't think you belonged to the Caucasians for White People Caucus."

He snorted, then laughed and gave his head a quick shake. "You aren't too far off. Irene acted nothing like this woman I just met. Figures anyone who's with that asshole blowhard would be personality-challenged. Her husband's going to have a heart attack when he finds out what she said to me. My father owns that stuffed shirt." He got a slow, evil smile on his face. "I can't wait to remind her of our conversation. 'Hi, Irene, remember me? I'm the overdressed, gigolo, low-life scumbag with the fake Rolex you met in the hospital.'"

Hell giggled. "Please bring a video camera. I'll want to see all the lovely shades of green she'll turn. But damn, if Martin ever finds out about us, he'll freak. He thinks I'm the Antichrist."

"You are," BC said with complete sincerity and without skipping a beat.

Hell and Matt laughed.

"Glad you're okay, Hell." Matt put his hands on the bedrail. "I'll start on the case and report back in the morning, okay?"

"Yeah. Clear Tanner if you can, okay?"

"Police must have solid evidence."

"I don't believe it. Canvass my neighborhood and—"

"Hell, you don't think I'm gonna go home and knock back a beer, do you?"

She loved this guy. "You rock. Thank you. I..."

"Hell, stop. I got this. I'll find out everything I can. You're right, I don't think Tanner is capable. But Lindsay sure is. I'm going to her place first."

"She's gotta be the one trying to pin this on Tanner."

Matt gripped her forearm. "You don't worry about that right now. Let me follow up on a few things, and we'll connect tomorrow. Your only job is to heal up and get better. Let me handle this for you, okay?"

She relaxed back in the bed. "Okay. But damn, I hate being lame and not being able to help."

Matt pursed his lips and shook his head. "You're not lame, you just got blown up by a damned bomb, you dork. Besides, you're paying me good money to help you and watch you get tortured by your family. Of course, that was just a bonus." He winked.

She laughed at not only his joke but his sudden familiarity and lack of animosity. What had changed?

"You take care. I'll see you in the morning." Matt sent her a genuine grin that warmed her. With a small salute and a wave at BC, he left.

Leaving her with Mr. Emotional Godzilla, who was just about to destroy her Tokyo. She was already a walking exposed wound—literally and figuratively—last thing she needed was feelings for an unavailable lover. Tortures of the Damned.

BC took her hand again and kissed it tenderly.

A tsunami of emotions flattened her shields. With every single bit of her reserves, she slammed the gates shut and battled the tears. She was seriously beginning to hate this bastard.

"You're going to your cousin's?" he asked.

"Yeah." She looked down at her bandaged arm and then at the IV. Anything to escape his powerful gray gaze.

He ran his hand down her upper arm. "Why don't you stay with me at the condo? Let me hold you all night?"

Her heart crushed to the size of a walnut. What was he trying to do? Kill her? "No, BC."

"Why not? I think you need it. I know I do."

"This isn't right, dude. You're married. We're just having an affair, okay? You're not my boyfriend."

"The hell I'm not. Get out of denial."

She wanted to cry again. He was right. The dude was her goddamned boyfriend. In fact, her only boyfriend. "Crap. I don't want to do emotions. Emotions are bad."

"Hell, will you listen to yourself?" He leaned in with an urgent expression but then pulled back and relaxed. He shook his head. "No. This is not the time or place to have this discussion. We need to talk about our relationship, but not now. The only thing that matters right now is that you get better."

"Why don't you let me call you in a week or so after I've healed and—"

His brows came down hard. "Are you insane? I'll see you tomorrow."

"I'll probably just want to sleep."

"I still have to see you." His expression turned vulnerable and raw. "You almost died, Hell. I can't stand it. I don't know how I'd live without you."

Hell's hope soared, making her gut burn. She got instantly annoyed. What was wrong with him? "BC, you'd be fine. With your wife and zillion other mistresses."

"I'm not seeing anyone but you."

She blinked, the gears in her head careening out of alignment. He made no sense. Finally, she managed a frown. "What? Oh, bullshit."

He shot her a sweet smile. "It's true. After having Cristal, you don't want Coors."

The floor shook. The world tilted on its axis. All the pieces of the puzzle settled into place. How he hadn't seen Gwen or Lindsay in months. Gwen not knowing about the condo. His over-the-top emotions of the night before. All his weird behavior.

Red alert! Battle stations! Please report to the bridge!

She wanted to run out of the room.

He took her hand once more. "No one compares to you, Hell. Besides, when do you think I'd have time to date anyone else? We see each other every other day, almost twenty hours a week."

She pulled her hand away. "I thought I was getting sloppy thirds."

He chuckled. "No. I broke up with all the others, Hell. You're the only woman I've slept with since early December."

She gasped, her heart beating harder. "What? Jesus, isn't that like a million dog years to you? How many fuck years is that?"

"Hundreds."

She laughed for one second, and then her world crashed around her shoulders. This was the dumbest thing she'd ever done in her life. He'd slice her heart to bits and serve it back to her on a bejeweled, solid-gold platter.

"Don't look so terrified, Hell. I won't hurt you. I couldn't hurt you. All I want to do is be with you. Now and forever."

Blackness consumed her, and she fought for clarity. Shit. He felt it, too. Damn it. She thought she'd been the only one. "Will you stop? You're totally freaking me out."

"That's obvious by the look of sheer terror on your face."

"I'm a little beyond acting right now."

"You're still doing a good job. And I know why. Because you haven't seen any other men besides me since early December, either."

Her brain froze instantly, like he'd injected liquid nitrogen directly into her skull.

Matt.

She clenched her teeth. "I'll kill him."

"He didn't mean to let it slip. He wasn't happy with himself."

"I'm not happy with him, either. I wasn't gonna tell you."

"Which is stupid."

"No, it isn't. It's called: you're married, and I'm protecting myself. Son of a bitch. There's no way you'd leave Sherry."

"I just talked to my lawyers. They're filing for my divorce in the morning."

All the breath left her lungs. Her brain collapsed in on itself. She held her head and forced herself to start breathing. "Please stop. We are tabling this stupid discussion right now, or my head will explode."

He smiled at her with exasperated affection. "God, I love you, Hell."

Her jaw dropped, and she froze in terror. She held up her hands in a defensive pose. "Aaaugh!! The L word! Stop! Stop right there. No, you don't."

BC grinned, leaned in, and kissed her.

Vaporizing her thoughts.

When he pulled away, she reached for him, pulled him back, and kissed him hard. All without wanting to.

Then she realized what she'd done and ended the kiss.

He sent her a knowing smile. "It's okay to be in love with me, Hell. I haven't ever felt this way about a woman before. This is real, honey. I'm madly in love with you."

"Don't mind-fuck me right now. Just let me call you. Okay?"

"No. I need to see you. And you need to see me. Let's just stop the bullshit. Especially considering how close I was to losing you. I know you love me just as much."

"So what? That means we've both lost our minds, that's all."

His eyes grew brighter, he smiled widely, and he kissed her again.

Sirens blared in her brain. How did he get her to admit that she loved him? Thick steel doors closed off her heart. How the *fuck* did this whole horrible thing happen?

When he pulled away, his eyes were goofy with love.

She hoped he could not hear her inner scream.

He grinned. "I can't wait to be free to marry you."

Her mind went blank for a moment. The information was so huge it just bounced off her brain. Then deafening sirens blasted throughout her head. *Mission abort!*

"I shouldn't overload you. I'm sorry. I just love you so much, and I've been wanting to tell you, but I didn't know how you felt because you've been so good at hiding your feelings."

Hell wished she were on a rocket ship to the moon.

He kissed her once more, which was a relief because if she tried to talk, all she'd do is bellow in fear.

He pulled away and sent her a look that made her shiver. Her body was certainly on board with his plan but not her brain. Not by a long shot.

"I'll call you in the morning. You need anything, call me."

Snap out of it! End this stupid relationship now before your heart implodes and dies! "BC..."

"Get some rest. Good night. And I love you." He kissed her on the cheek, winked, and walked out with a giant smile on his face and a bounce in his step.

Leaving behind a huge vacuum in his wake.

This was terrible. Like, the most terrible thing ever to happen to her in her entire life.

Josh.

Well, outside of Josh dying. This was the Number Two Horrible Event. Even worse than marrying Donny. Or getting the shit kicked out of her by Capasso.

How come she wasn't just expiring on the spot? Didn't people die from this much stress?

Besides, BC didn't know the real her, he only knew the small part of herself that she shared with him in the condo. He'd fallen in love with someone who existed only in his imagination.

Even if there was a remote chance that he'd actually fallen in love, how long would it last? Until some supermodel sashayed up to him. He'd lied to Sherry, he'd lied to Hell on several occasions, which meant he'd lie to get his way. Only reason he would mention all this love and divorce business was because he wanted Hell exclusively but still wanted his chickies on the side. Just like Capasso.

Great. She'd found another Marco Capasso. Brad might love her, but he was still a demon. There was no bloody way she was getting into a relationship with another demon.

Hell punched her palm. "Shit!"

In that moment, she desperately wished she'd been smoking that joint on the patio when the bomb had gone off. No more pain. She'd be with Josh, and everything would finally be peachy. She'd been seconds away from freedom.

Why had God spared her?

CHAPTER 18

Matt drove down El Camino toward Hell's place, more upset than he'd been since he'd been fired. A bomb to take out Hell? Overkill or what?

Hell was right. Tanner wouldn't do that. Matt saw the tender way he was with her. The kid didn't have it in him. Someone had set him up.

Lindsay was at the top of the list. He'd driven straight there and had knocked on the door. A maid had answered and said that Lindsay wasn't home yet, and Mr. Banning was out of town on business. The gardener's black Honda was gone, too. He'd waited until the backup arrived from Thompson. As soon as Lindsay came home, she wouldn't be able to go anywhere without them knowing it.

Matt drove around the streets surrounding Hell's neighborhood, scanning for a black Honda or any sign of Lindsay. He'd located a couple Hondas of the right year, but none of the hoods were warm. Finding nothing, he headed to Hell's place.

The police had cordoned off Hell's entire street. Matt parked a block away and made his way past the crowds of neighbors to the cops at the front lines of the barricades. TV crews questioned whomever would talk to them.

Matt spotted Joe Piccolo in the law enforcement throng.

His old partner motioned him over. "He's okay, guys. Let him through."

Two uniforms moved out of the way, and Matt joined Joe.

Joe's tight curly hair was now gray and starting to thin, but he still kept his tall, lean body in top shape; his pecs, shoulders, and arms were hard and big, and his waist was as narrow as a twenty-year-old's. However, the youthful olive skin of his face was finally starting to show his age. His hooked nose seemed more pronounced, and the lines were now deep around his close-set brown eyes.

"Matty, how ya doin'?" They shook hands. "Figured you'd show up."

Matt could feel the eyes of his old coworkers on him, and his face warmed with shame, but he pretended not to notice their attention. "What d'ya got?"

Joe turned away from his colleagues, probably so they wouldn't overhear the conversation. "We picked up that Tanner whack job right down the block. Crazy motherfucker. Lost his mind when my guys approached him. Threw two uniforms into someone's yard before seven guys tackled him. They had to Tase him, like, three times. Barely did anything to him. Screaming about how he was innocent and protecting Hell and how much he loved her. How we were gonna get her killed because they had the wrong guy. Blah, blah, blah. Nuts."

Joe's report confirmed Matt's suspicions. But he didn't want to voice his opinion yet. "Sounds like it. Any direct evidence?"

Joe snorted, seeming amused. "Do we. Fuckin' hand grenade in the trunk of his car—bomb guy's first impression was that it was a grenade. Then we found the pin in the bushes in the walkway near Hell's. Plus we found a .38—a different one because we confiscated another .38 the first time we arrested him. We're gonna run ballistics to see if this gun is the one he used to shoot at Hell over at Starbucks. Plus they found a copy of the threatening letter taped to Hell's door. Plans of her apartment. Freakin' receipt for the bullets. We got him in the bag."

More overkill. Hard to believe the cops hadn't questioned the insane amount of incriminating evidence. "Awfully neat and tied up."

Joe did a double take and frowned. "What? You don't think he did it?"

"I don't know. I met the kid. I don't think he's capable. I think someone might be setting him up for it."

Joe's face went pained, and he waved a hand. "Aww, Matty, don't go makin' this more complicated. If you'd seen him an hour ago, you wouldn't have any doubts." He motioned around himself. "People saw him around here this afternoon, walkin' up and down the block in front of Hell's place."

Matt stepped closer. "Really? Who told you that?"

"Neighbors next door, and the guy who lives above her. Plus a bunch of other people."

"Damn." Either someone did a number on the kid, or the vet really had snapped.

"If it weren't for all the evidence against Tanner, I'd be looking at her neighbors here in the complex," Joe said, jerking his thumb behind him. "Everyone who lives here is pissed off at Hell. Course, two of 'em are in jail right now."

"For what?"

Joe shook his head and gave a rough chuckle. "When we made our safety check, we found a pound of meth in one couple's place. Then this other neighbor of hers, a computer gamer freak, went nuts and attacked my guys when they went to his door. Dude had been up for a week playing some online war game—all these water bottles full of pee on the ground around him—he thought the game had come to life, and we were there to kill him. He thought the grenade had been meant for him."

"Jesus."

Joe grimaced, his eyebrows high. "Nut wagon had its work cut out for it tonight."

Matt wrote down the notes on a small pad of paper. "Damn. Anyone else spotted around here at the time of the attack?"

Joe gave an indifferent shrug. "Neighbors saw a woman jogger run away from the scene."

"Which neighbors?"

"Those people over there." Joe pointed to a couple huddled in front of the duplex next door to Hell's place. "They were the first ones on scene. Friends of Hell. Nice people."

"I'll go talk to 'em in a minute. Anything else?"

"Couple residents heard someone running out of the place but didn't see anyone. But since we already got Tanner on the scene, this is all sewn up, Matty."

Clearly they were satisfied they had their man. "Keep me in the loop, okay?"

"You got it. Just don't let the other guys know I'm helpin' ya, okay? They're still pretty dicey about you."

Matt glanced over at Smith and Garcia, two San Mateo detectives who'd been glaring at him. "I think it's pretty obvious."

"I know. Just be careful. They know you're in a new job and tryin' to help Hell, but they don't like it. I already told 'em to back off you."

Matt nodded. "Thanks. We still on for poker on the twentieth?"

Joe lit up with a wide smile. "Yeah. Usual suspects, my place, seven. Can you have Patty make that awesome ceviche again?"

Matt pursed his lips, then smiled. "Yeah." Patty's ceviche was a top request.

"Oh, before I forget…" Joe grabbed a dark backpack near his feet and handed it to him. "Here. Hell's stuff."

Matt took the skull-printed pack.

"Her, uh, well." Joe looked over at the group of cops, then lowered his voice. "There's, uh, junk she'll want in there."

Matt frowned, then shrugged. "Thanks."

Joe glanced around, moved closer to him, and lowered his voice. "I put most of her dope in there. She'll need it. Good thing she kept it in the freezer."

"I'm sure she'll appreciate that," Matt said with a chuckle.

"And, uh, there's also something else important to her in there,"

Joe said, the line between his eyes deep. He jabbed a finger in Matt's face. "But don't laugh at her."

"Why would I laugh?"

Joe whispered, "I got her teddy bear in there."

Matt's eyes must have bugged out past his nose. *Hell has a teddy bear?* For the life of him, he couldn't picture that leather-clad rabble-rouser holding a damned stuffed animal.

Joe nodded sharply, his expression serious. "Don't laugh at her, and don't give her a bad time. I made that mistake and made her cry."

"What?" Matt had no reference for this new information. Crying over a teddy bear? Hell Trent?

Joe nodded, his face drawn with regret. "I was at her house when we were seeing each other, and saw this bear and teased her, and she burst out crying, and I felt like the biggest asshole in the world. Her parents neglected her as a kid, and all she had was that stupid bear. She got drunk and told me all kinds of stuff. Made me real mad. So go easy on her, will ya?"

More of the Hell jigsaw puzzle fit into place, and his sympathy for her grew. All fit with her sister's ugly diatribe. "I had no intention to do anything else."

Joe's expression softened. "You like her, don't you?"

Matt snorted, then smiled. "How could I not?"

A grin split Joe's face. "I knew it. I told you she was good people," he said, lightly punching him on the arm. "You two just hit it off wrong."

"We sure did."

Joe's attention went over Matt's shoulder. "Okay, Matty, I'm gettin' eyeballed. You'd better move on."

"Okay, and thanks." They shook hands once more.

With a small salute, he left Joe and walked over to Hell's neighbors, ignoring the stares of his former colleagues.

"Hi, I'm Matt Sinclair, and I work for Helen Trent. Could I ask you two a couple questions?"

The man was tall and stocky with thick salt-and-pepper hair, a gray goatee, piercing brown eyes, and a distrustful expression. Late forties, early fifties. The woman was around the same age, thin and pretty with dark eyes and shoulder-length light brown hair.

"Already talked to the cops," the male bit out. "I don't recognize you. Are you sure you work for Hell?" His attention went to Hell's backpack.

"Yeah. Just left her at the hospital. Her friend, that cop over there, just handed me her backpack to take to her."

Guy remained unconvinced. "Can I see some ID?"

The woman elbowed her husband. "Lars, I'm sure he's okay."

"Melissa, how do we know he's not the press and lying to us about the pack?" he asked out of the side of his mouth, his hard stare on Matt.

She nodded. "Oh. Good point."

Matt took out his PI license and badge and showed them to the couple.

"What a pretty little badge you got there, Matty old boy," came a nasty voice from behind him. "Did you get that at the Dollar Store?"

"No, I heard he got it at Toys "R" Us," replied an equally sarcastic voice in a lower register.

Matt turned to face Smith, a balding, white jerk with a broken nose, and Garcia, a wide-faced Mexican with thick lips and a full head of graying dark hair. Both wore rotten leers.

His body went hard, and his gut twisted. "Tom, Don, how are you guys?" All he wanted to do was punch them bloody, but he wasn't rising to their bait.

"We're fine, *Mr. Sinclair,*" Tom Smith said. "Now why don't you run along and let us real detectives do our jobs." He made a shooing motion.

Matt's inner core turned to lava, but he wouldn't allow himself an outward reaction. He made sure to keep his tone even. "I'm not bothering anyone. Hell hired me to help her."

The married couple began staring at him with extremely unfriendly expressions.

Took all of Matt's strength to keep his poise.

"Smith! Garcia! Over here!" Rafael Jersey, their immediate superior. He met gazes with Matt and turned away.

Matt's gut caved in; he almost felt the physical punch. His face flushed. He hadn't believed it when Rafael had turned on him. They'd gone through the academy together.

"See ya later, Sherlock," Smith sneered.

Matt's jaw clenched tighter.

Don Garcia nearly busted a gut. "Where's your Mystery Van, Fred? Or are you playin' Shaggy now? Where's Scooby-Doo?"

Smith laughed heartily and clapped his asshole partner on the back. "Yeah, don't forget your Scooby Snacks!"

The two dirtbags broke into the theme song from Scooby-Doo and walked away, singing and flipping off Matt behind their backs.

Matt closed his eyes for a second, took a deep breath, and shook off the fury. He turned back to the couple. "Can you tell me what you saw and heard before and after the attack?"

"They sure love you." Lars nodded toward the two retreating douches.

"We have some history, yes." Matt lifted his chin higher and made sure no shame showed on his face.

After a long few seconds, Lars finally nodded. "We didn't see much. Some lady runnin' by I've never seen before. A jogger. But she looked like she could be from around here. Black yoga pants, black sweatshirt."

"She wore a white-and-red baseball cap with the ponytail pulled through the back," Melissa added.

Matt wrote down the details. "What color was her hair?"

"Blonde," Lars answered.

Melissa said, "What I thought was weird was that she was wearing sunglasses at night. We were standing right out here with the dogs when she ran by. I said to Lars, 'Honey, I think that lady's gonna run into a pole.'"

Lars' eyes went wide. "Then the explosion."

"Scared us half to death. Dogs went crazy." Melissa nodded emphatically. "Lars had a heck of a time getting them in the house.

Then we ran over to see what happened and found Hell..." Her face fell, and she shook her head. "Poor thing."

"She was pretty bad," Lars said, his expression haunted. "I can't believe she survived the bombing. Did you see it in there?"

"Not yet."

"Terrible." Lars' jaw clamped, and the look behind his eyes darkened. "I hate to see her hurt like this; she's good people. I think it was that Tanner guy. He was here, you know. Earlier tonight. I told him to get lost. He was hangin' around outside my house. He's been around here a lot the past four months. Well, except while he was in jail."

"Did he leave before the explosion?" Matt asked.

"Yeah. But that doesn't mean he didn't come back."

"Huh. Hell doesn't think it was him."

Melissa elbowed her husband. "Lars, what about the cop?"

"What cop?" Matt asked.

Lars pushed his hands downward, shushing his wife. "He's this guy's friend, Melissa." The barrel-chested man jerked his head toward Matt.

Matt's stomach flipped, and the hair stood up on the back of his neck. "Joe? Joe was here earlier?"

Lars and Melissa exchanged glances.

Matt checked to see where Joe was, then turned back and lowered his voice. "Look, I know I was talking to him just a few minutes ago, and he gave me this backpack of Hell's stuff to give to her, but I'm working for Hell. Was he here earlier?"

Melissa looked to Lars, who finally nodded. She turned to Matt. "Yeah, about an hour before the explosion."

Matt's skin prickled. "Joe," he whispered.

"Musical instrument," Lars finished. "Piccolo or something? He was sitting across the street in his car, looking at Hell's place."

"Jesus Christ." Matt heaved a sigh.

Lars narrowed his eyes at Matt. "He's a friend of yours, isn't he?"

Matt gave a short nod. "He was my partner for ten years, but I don't trust anyone." He looked Lars dead in the eye. "Hell is my only priority," he said in a strong tone.

Lars' shoulders relaxed. "Okay." He turned to his wife. "We didn't see anyone else, right?"

"No more than the usual suspects in the neighborhood."

Matt flipped back to his notes about the jogger. "I want to know more about the woman runner since you saw her right before the grenade went off."

"She was about my height, don't you think, Lars? Five six?" Melissa asked.

Her husband nodded. "Yeah, about."

"How did you notice the color of her baseball cap?" Matt asked. "Red and white, right? Wasn't it dark?"

"She triggered our security lights," Melissa said, pointing up toward her driveway. "I was worried about her because she was dressed in all black, and I thought the cap didn't reflect enough."

"What about her body type?"

"Gym-toned, skinny," her husband said. "Like lots of the ladies up in Baywood and Aragon." He gestured up and behind him. "This part of town has got lots of rich ladies like that. I mean, not here on this block, but over a couple."

"I grew up here. I know the area," Matt said.

Lars gave him a nod. "Really? What high school?"

"Hillsdale, class of '79."

Melissa broke into a wide smile. "I went to Aragon. Class of 1981."

Matt grinned. "I have a lot of friends who went to Aragon around that time. What group did you hang out with?"

"I was in band."

"So was my buddy. John Gilford?"

She brightened, clapped her hands, and bounced in place. "Oh, Johnny! All the girls had crushes on him. Played the trumpet. What happened to him?"

Matt chuckled. "Sorry to disappoint you, but he's married to a guy named Bill, and they're both in San Francisco working for the city."

Melissa laughed delightedly. "I knew it! He was so pretty and so nice. We loved him."

Matt went over names of friends with Melissa. They had many

connections in common. By the couple's now open body language, it was clear they were much more trustful of him. Nice turnaround considering the earlier smear campaign.

Matt noticed the time on his watch, almost midnight. "Sorry, I gotta get back to the case. It's getting late. So the woman you saw was thin and about five six?" He wrote down the details.

"Yeah."

"Straight or curly hair?"

"Curly," Melissa said.

Lindsay.

"So you think the jogger had something to do with it?" Lars asked. "Don't you think it was Tanner?"

Matt shrugged. "I don't know. Maybe. But sunglasses at night isn't very normal, is it?"

Lars shook his head. "No. So you saw Hell. How is she?"

"Shaken, but physically, she's doing well. Really lucky."

"Poor girl," Melissa said. "We love her. She's so nice."

"If I were you?" Lars said. "I'd check out the other residents of her place. You know we call that place Casa De Vortexa—"

"Or the Vortex," Melissa chimed in.

"—because of all the freaks living there. We've had problems with most of them. Buncha drunks and drug users."

Matt glanced over at Hell's building. "Yeah, two have been arrested just tonight."

Lars smiled widely. "That was great. I'd still check them all out. Never know about some of those nutjobs."

"Anyone else in the neighborhood got a grudge against her?" Matt asked.

"Not that I know of," Lars said.

"Everyone loves Hell," Melissa said. "We've lived here twenty-five years, and she moved in only eight or so years ago, and she knows people we've never met before. Every time I see her on her walks, she's stopped and is talking or laughing with someone."

Lars crossed his thick arms. "The only problems she's had are with her ex-boyfriends and her neighbors in the Vortex."

"Good thing she's getting out of there," Melissa said. "She put a deposit on the duplex over on the other side of us, right there." She pointed up the block. "She's moving there in a couple months."

"If it's okay with you, I may want to talk to you again," Matt said.

"Okay," Lars replied.

"Thanks, you two have been very helpful."

Matt canvassed the area, and four more neighbors had spotted the mystery jogger running from the scene. On the next block, behind Hell's house, a retired firefighter in a wheelchair had watched the jogger scramble into a late-model dark sedan that could have been a black Honda. She'd peeled out and headed for El Camino Real. The firefighter had thought it was strange that she'd been wearing sunglasses at night and seemed to be in a panic. Car hadn't turned over the first time, and she'd pounded the steering wheel in frustration. Matt noted every detail.

Matt wandered back to Hell's apartment, but no one would let him near the scene. Smith and Garcia took great delight in denying his request and sang the Scooby-Doo song at him until he left. He'd have to return with Hell in the morning.

He got in his car, called his wife to tell her he'd be home even later, and headed to Tanner's place in the City. He'd see if anyone was awake and would talk to him. See if that mystery jogger had been anywhere near his building that evening.

While still mad at himself for the attack—and humiliated by his run-in with his old coworkers—Matt had a fire in him he hadn't felt in recent memory. Even toward the end of his career, he hadn't felt this focused or alive. He was going to solve this case and save Hell's life.

Make those bastards back at his old station house look like amateurs.

Friday, March 11, 2011, 11:08 a.m.

MATT HEARD HELL YELLING FROM HALFWAY DOWN HER BLOCK.

Hell stood in front of her building, waving her arms and screaming at some newspeople. "Get your fucking camera out of my face, bitch! I just lost my home and almost died! How the *fuck* do you think I feel?"

His muscles hard, he ran for her.

A gaggle of news vultures had circled her. Her cousin Joanne was doing her best to protect her, but Hell had gone rabid.

"*What?* Fuck you, I'm not a fucking slut! Come over here and ask me that question again, you little piece of shit!"

He shoved people out of his way, wedged his body between the cameras and Hell, and gently took her by the shoulders. Her appearance made his heart wrench. The crazed, feral look in her dark eyes screamed asylum escapee. She wore a black, skull-printed hoodie and matching sweats and looked like she hadn't slept. Ten years older with huge circles under her eyes. The bruising and wound on her forehead made her fair skin look pasty.

The newspeople shouted questions at him. Several remembered him from his public disgrace. He hardened his shell and pushed his feelings down. No way would they get anything from him. Not even a reaction. Fuckers.

"Can we go into Lars and Melissa's garage without their permission?" he shouted at Hell over the cries of the news creeps.

Hell jerked her head in the direction of the driveway. "Lars is right there, waving us in and trying to control his dogs."

"Let's get you inside." He put his arm around her, brought her close, and moved forward with his other arm out, pushing news people aside.

Joanne rushed to flank Hell on the other side, following Matt's lead.

Once Hell was safe down Lars and Melissa's narrow driveway, Matt turned back to the cameras and blocked them from following. "This is private property. Back up *now*."

"What is your relationship with Miss Trent? Are you one of her lovers?" a young Asian woman yelled at him.

A tall, balding man in glasses called out, "Did you start sleeping with her when you were kicked off the force for corruption? Are you jealous of her other lovers?"

"Did you know about her other lovers?" a twenty-something black guy asked loudly. "Did you know the suspect?"

Without one muscle of his face moving, he turned and walked away. They began to follow. He stopped, swung back on them, and deployed his patented "Kill" expression that cowered even hardened felons.

The newspeople stepped back onto the sidewalk, but continued to shout questions.

Matt joined Hell and her neighbors inside their open garage, out of view of the cameras.

Lars and Melissa greeted him, very friendly and familiar. Nice to have some positive energy in the sea of negativity. Lars handed Hell her computer bag.

She looked inside and said, "This computer is it. All I have left in the world except for my black leather jacket, a six-pack of beer I had in the trunk of my car, and some weed." She gave them all a bright smile. "Least I have all the essentials, right?"

The group laughed.

The pressure on his gut eased. The old Hell shining through was a welcome sight.

Joanne asked, "Don't you have a full storage unit somewhere?"

Hell raised her brows. "Yes, the Tomb of Josh and Hell. I think I'd just rather set fire to that storage unit. Talk about more emotional torture."

Lars and Melissa seemed as curious as Matt about the "tomb."

Hell noticed their expressions. "Twelve years ago, a month after my husband was killed on the freeway, I packed up my entire three-bedroom house in a fit of grieving. Haven't touched it or looked at it since."

Lars said, "Harry and I can help you load it up and move it next door in a couple months."

Hell broke into a wide grin. "Thanks, honey."

Matt stepped forward. "Hell, can we talk later?"

"Yeah, Matt. Wait. What have you found out?"

He nodded toward the street. "I don't want to talk here."

"Can you follow me to Joanne's?" She faced her attractive, dark-haired cousin. "Is that cool, cuz?"

Joanne nodded, flashing a nice smile. "Sure."

Matt's heart skipped a beat, and he forced himself to look at Hell.

Hell said, "We're gonna stop by In-N-Out on the way down to her place."

"Why don't you give me Joanne's address?" Matt asked. "I want to do some digging around here for a while."

Hell homed in on his face. "You found something, didn't you?"

"Nothing concrete."

"Tanner's been set up, huh?"

"Inconclusive."

She snapped her fingers. "I knew it! It's Lindsay, isn't it?"

"Don't know. I want to talk to Lindsay and Brad's wife first."

She frowned. "That might not be easy. They must both know about BC and me by now. Did you see the papers? One of those jackals out there tied BC to me. Took a picture of him coming out of my hospital room. Plus one of my old boyfriends must have blabbed. My sexual exploits are all over the paper. The only thing saving me is the damned tsunami and Japan's earthquake. Which is so over-the-top awful I can't cope with it right now. I have a bunch of Japanese friends, and a good buddy is teaching over there right now."

Matt rubbed the tired muscles of his forehead. "Terrible, isn't it?"

Hell pointed toward the hills on her right. "A freakin' tsunami is hitting Half Moon Bay and the coast as we speak. I have some guys I went to high school with who are fishermen." She made a waving motion. "But I can't deal with all that on top of this."

"You need to sleep," he said.

She patted the front pocket of her leather jacket. "And not answer my phone. It's off right now, Matt. Just come down there, okay? Give us an hour."

"I may need a bit more time than that."

"Take all you want. I may be asleep. Just wake me up."

"I may not let him, Hell," Joanne said. "You need to rest."

Matt grinned. Hell's cousin's caring made her even more attractive. "You got a great cousin here, Hell." And in another universe, a woman he'd be greatly interested in getting to know better. With her pretty features, sweet curves, and sparkling deep brown eyes, Hell's cousin was a looker.

Joanne blushed a bit, and her smile widened, showing off her straight white teeth. A jolt went through his dick, and he loosened his collar. Wow! Been a long time since he'd had his heads turned. Felt good. While his body belonged to Patty, his mind was his own.

"The best in the universe," Hell said emphatically.

Joanne pursed her lips but kept smiling. "You are too, Hell."

"I don't know about that." Hell looked down the end of the driveway, and her face hardened. "God, now the gauntlet."

Matt briefly put his hand on her shoulder. "I'll protect you from them." He walked ahead.

Hell caught him by the arm, her face full of emotion. "This goes deep, Matt."

He fought his instincts to sweep her into his arms and hold her. "We'll solve this thing," he said gruffly with a nod.

Hell sighed, her worry lines deep. "I'm glad I let BC hire some guards for me. They're out there. I told them to stay in the car. Don't want 'em all hovering."

Matt raised a brow. "They could have helped you with those newspeople."

"I thought I could handle the onslaught. Apparently not." She rolled her eyes.

Matt walked out ahead of her and shielded her as best he could, but the reporters swarmed them like flies on a cadaver.

"Is it true you're sleeping with Brad Collins?"

"Is it true you're sleeping with Collins and six other men?"

"Do you sleep with them all at once?"

Hell's face turned deep red, and her body trembled hard. About to combust.

He blocked the cameras. "Keep moving, Hell."

The guards stepped out of the car as they approached, and Matt motioned for them to hurry.

Thompson's muscle—a tall Latino man and a fireplug of a white guy—rushed over and helped shield Hell until she got into Joanne's car. Matt and the two guards exchanged cards.

Matt watched Hell leave and returned to her building, followed by the news crews.

He stopped in front of the Vortex and held up his hands. "No comment. If you try to follow me, I'll have you arrested." He deployed his scowl, and they backed off.

He pretended to have permission, stepped around the barriers, and walked down the cement pathway to her place. Or where her place used to be.

His heart sank, and a wave of nausea went through him. Looked like a war zone.

Joe had texted him and confirmed the bomb squad's initial determination: a standard M67 military-issue fragmentation grenade had been used in the attack.

A jagged, gaping hole big enough to drive a car through was where Hell's sliding glass door and part of her wall had been. At the base of the remains of the wall was a three-foot crater in the cement patio with a twenty-foot radius of destruction where the grenade must have landed. Her living room was now piles of metal, wood, Sheetrock, and furniture that had been partially eaten away by shrapnel.

Something about the scene was so desolate. So empty. So lifeless.

This woman who had no one and nothing now had even less. Why did the horrible things always seem to happen to the same people? While he'd certainly had his share of rotten luck, he was a rich king compared to Hell Trent.

A narrow path had been made through the debris, but not much had been cleaned up yet. Broken boards had been haphazardly stacked in a pile just beyond her apartment. Twisted shards of what used to be lawn furniture and a barbecue lay next to the wood.

The assailant had to walk down the walkway at least twenty-five yards before throwing the grenade, with only four seconds to run away. Hard to believe no one got a good look at the perp. He stood in the place where the unsub must have launched the weapon. Matt carefully checked all around him. To his right beyond a wall of bushes—and pitted trees from the blast—was a condo complex with several blown-out windows. Four upper-floor balconies had views of the walkway. Cops must have talked to the residents.

Time to find out if people were too scared to talk or if they really hadn't seen anything. Matt gave the area another long look, then headed next door.

He'd crack this case and save the crazy woman's life.

Then maybe she wouldn't be so crazy anymore.

Friday, March 11, 2011, 1:25 p.m.

MATT WALKED UP THE STEPS OF LINDSAY'S COLONIAL MANSION. Thompson's guys had told him she was home. He'd decided to try a surprise visit. See if he could catch her unprepared.

Hopefully, he'd have more luck here. Earlier, he'd talked to six of Hell's neighbors who'd had a view of her patio and walkway, and no one had seen anything. Almost everyone had been watching *Jeopardy*.

He rang the doorbell, and chimes sounded from inside.

A minute later, one side of the tall, white double doors opened.

A thin, toned, and pale woman his age with blonde curly hair stood there wearing a scowl and a red-and-white baseball cap. Just like the one the jogger had worn.

Lindsay herself.

In a tight, white tank and black, calf-length yoga pants, if she turned sideways, she'd disappear. Her chest bones protruded, and veins popped out on her too-thin, wiry arms. While she was technically pretty with even features, her obvious many plastic surgeries and overly worked-out body gave her a hardened, harsh, manufactured edge. Like a nightmare Barbie doll come to life.

Yoga outfit? Check. Skinny blonde woman? Check. Motive? Check.

But the red-and-white baseball cap was the money.

Glaring at him, she pointed down the driveway. "Didn't you see the 'No Solicitation' sign? How did you get through the gate?"

"Gate was open. I'm not selling anything, ma'am, and I'm sorry to bother you."

"Who are you?"

He took out his badge and showed her. "Matt Sinclair." Now for the magic words that should get her to open up. "I'm working for Brad Collins."

Her blue eyes sparkled, and she took in a short breath. "Brad? Well, finally. Why didn't he call me? Why is he contacting me through you?"

A little more blood pumped through his veins. Felt like his old self. "He wanted discretion. That's why I didn't call. I was hoping to catch you when your husband wasn't around. I also didn't want your maids to overhear."

She narrowed her eyes. "Well, then why were you talking to those people out there? The ones in the surveillance van? Didn't think I noticed, did you?"

His gut twisted. Damn it. Thompson had been made.

She pulled herself up to her full height and affected a condescending expression. "Didn't think I was smart?" She stopped and frowned. "Wait a minute." Leaning closer, her eyes lit with recognition, and she pointed at him. "I've seen you somewhere recently. I never forget a face. I have an eidetic memory. Even though I've been having issues lately. My doctor says it's because I refuse to take my meds, but she's wrong. So why were you talking to my enemies out there? You'd better give me a good answer, or I'll make a citizen's arrest and send you straight to jail."

Matt made sure not to react. He kept his posture professional, his face neutral. "Those people are not your enemies, and neither am I. On the contrary, Brad hired me and those people to watch and protect you. He's concerned that all his girlfriends are in danger," he said with perfect sincerity. Thank God his bullshitting skills hadn't left him.

"Brad hired them?" she practically shouted. Then she clamped her hand over her mouth and checked over her shoulder to inside the house. After a second, she breathed a sigh of relief and turned back to Matt. "So he loves me, doesn't he? He sent you here to tell me that he loves me, and he's sorry about standing me up last night, right?"

Matt's mind stopped, then clicked into high gear. Why did she think she'd see Brad last night? Was the billionaire lying to him and Hell? "Uh..."

Lindsay nodded, and her face relaxed with understanding. "That's what I thought. Okay, come in, and tell me everything Brad said." She scanned her yard and driveway, then stepped back into the house and motioned that he should come inside.

No way. She felt far too powerful and in control in her own home. He'd seen her change with Hell. He wanted to keep her off-balance.

He gestured toward a side of her vast front porch. "Ma'am, if we could talk out here, it would be better."

Her forehead wrinkled as much as it could. "But why?"

"Brad was concerned that your house might be, uh, compromised."

"Compromised?" She gasped loudly and clutched her chest. "My house might be bugged? Oh, God!" Her face went whiter, and she gripped the doorjamb for support.

"We're not sure."

Composing herself, she took a deep breath. She glanced down the hallway over her shoulder and then walked outside, shutting the door behind her. "No, I don't believe I am. Or I'd already be divorced, or in jail, or worse—" She sent Matt a worried glance. "Never mind." Lifting her brows, she cleared her throat and crossed her arms. "Where was Brad last night?"

Wait, *jail*?

She leaned forward. "If he sent you to give me some lame excuse why he stood me up, I'd like to hear it."

She'd either prepared for this and was cementing her alibi for the night before or she genuinely thought that she'd had a date with Brad.

Matt chose a plan on instinct, hoping he'd get the right answers out of her. "He didn't tell me why he missed you."

Her frown reached her chin. "Well, I know where he was, at the hospital, because it was all over the news. What I don't understand is why he went to that whore's side just because her apartment got bombed. That should have sent him into my arms, not to her stupid hospital bed. I was waiting for him. Why didn't he just come see me?"

One point for her guilt. "I don't know that, ma'am."

Her demeanor became even more heated. "I told him that she was dangerous and he should break it off with her. Especially because I only have a few more years to use my eggs, and if we don't jump on the in vitro fertilization procedure quick, we won't live long enough to enjoy our grandchildren."

Matt's skin prickled, and his stomach went cold. Wow, she was just as crazy as he remembered. And there was her clear motive for attacking Hell.

Lindsay went on like he wasn't even there, the pace of her delivery growing faster and more frantic. "I knew he was going to be late, his letter said he would, but why didn't he show up? You know what? This is all Karma. This is what he gets for leaving me in that hotel room. This should teach him to cheat on me with that whore."

She certainly sounded like she'd had a date with Brad and had waited for him at a hotel. Either that or she'd imagined the entire evening. But part of her rantings sounded rooted in truth.

She gestured violently, waving her arms. "He doesn't even love her! He loves me! He wants my children, not hers! I have the prime frozen eggs, and she's a barren, menopausal wasteland. We were supposed to talk last night about our future and our children. All we need is his semen, and we can move forward with the process."

One point for Lindsay being totally insane. "Uh..."

"Did Brad tell you that we're going to Tahiti and make babies? Well, we can't make babies; we have to get them implanted. But we can pretend we got pregnant in Tahiti and tell our children that's where the magic all happened. But Brad knows all this. Why did he send you?"

Two points for Lindsay's complete insanity, and, finally, a pause. "Since your husband doesn't know me, he thought it was the safest way to communicate with you. Brad's worried that your husband is suspicious."

She nodded and made a very quick dismissive gesture. "Oh, yes, yes, of course. I just don't understand why he went to the hospital. I mean, if your low-class whore of a girlfriend got bombed and splashed all over the news, wouldn't you want to distance yourself from her? Wouldn't you want to break it off just to make sure you weren't associated with her?"

Huh. More points for her guilt.

He maintained his professional affect. "I only work for Mr. Collins; I'm not privy to his decision-making rationale."

She stepped closer, and he got a whiff of her perfume. Strong and nauseating. He was glad Patty didn't care about scenting herself. In his mind, women already smelled pretty enough.

"Why didn't he message me or have the hotel staff alert me?" the crazy blonde demanded. "Why did he use all that cloak-and-dagger stuff with me—like the secret letter last night and sending you today —and then risk everything by showing up at the hospital, knowing he was walking smack dab into a crowd of reporters? He makes no sense."

Brad wasn't the only one not making sense. "I'm sorry. He didn't mention the letter. You got a secret letter from Mr. Collins?"

Her brow furrowed, then relaxed. "Yes. I'd been waiting for word from him. I knew he'd contact me. Prove to me that he still loved me and wanted my babies."

More points for scrambled brains. "He didn't mention the letter. He doesn't tell me everything, ma'am. But if you could fill me in on exactly what happened last night, I could help the two of you much better." *Let's see if you're making up this crap or telling the truth.* "Now he sent you a letter by mail?"

She made a face and chuckled. "No, silly. Then it wouldn't have been secret. I found it on my dresser. He must have paid one of his maids to sneak it over."

Was she hallucinating? "Did you see the person who delivered the message?"

"No. But his housekeeper, Esmeralda, and my gardener are cousins. I figured that's how the note got there."

Her body language was open. The look in her eyes showed no duplicity. But she could just be fully committed to her delusion. Or be an exceptionally good actress. He'd been fooled before.

Matt nodded definitively. "Makes sense. So, in the letter, he invited you to..." He gestured toward her.

"The hotel. With all the instructions. I followed them all. Tell him that."

She was certainly acting truthful.

"I will. The instructions said...?" He tried to appear detached and not very curious. Like he was writing down details about what color paint she wanted on the exterior of her home.

Her posture relaxed, and she rubbed her chin. "Well, inside the envelope, along with the key to the hotel room, was a letter with explicit instructions on how to meet so we didn't get caught because Sherry has surveillance on him. That's who I thought those people were outside in the van." She made a shooing motion with one hand toward Thompson's people.

"And you knew it was Brad's letter from his handwriting?"

"No, the note was written on a computer. He doesn't have time to write personal notes. He's a very busy man. I knew it was from him because he signed it."

Ever heard of forgery? "Okay, and what did the instructions say?"

"To wear the yoga disguise, and make sure I wasn't noticed going into the hotel. He was so paranoid I'd be seen, he told me to park on a side street and walk a quarter mile to the hotel. I went in a side door near the restaurant, snuck up the back stairs, and waited for him in the room, but he never showed."

Wow, this story had become elaborate. A little too elaborate. Either someone smart was manipulating this woman or she was totally crazy. He pretended to study his notes. "What hotel was that again? The..."

"Embassy Suites."

He nodded. "Right, the one on..."

"By the airport, in Millbrae."

"Of course." He wrote down the name. If she were telling the truth, it would be easy to verify who made the reservation and who picked up the key and when. "So did you notice anything unusual at the hotel? Did anyone see you? Was there anyone out of place? Anyone you noticed?"

She shook her head and ran her hand through her blonde curls. "No. Since I didn't see anyone, I didn't see anything unusual. Just got in and out without anyone seeing me."

He smiled. "Good work."

Lindsay could have easily come up with this script beforehand. Anticipated the questions and written some lines to prove her innocence. Come up with perfect excuses why she had no proof of her alibi.

She returned his smile. "Tell Brad I also burned the instructions and the letter after I read them, just like he told me to," she said like a proud eighth-grader reporting to a teacher. There was something off in the age she projected. One minute she gave off the vibe of a professional adult; the next she sounded and acted like a good little seven-year-old princess. But mostly, she sounded like a full-blown whackjob.

"You'll tell him I followed all his instructions, right?" Lindsay's expression needy, she moved closer to him, invading his space.

He fought his inclination to step back and held up his notebook in front of him as a shield. Concerned he looked too defensive, he relaxed his posture, shifting his weight to one leg. "You bet. Good, you burned all the evidence. I'm sure he'll be pleased. Where did you burn the letter?"

She stayed too close to him. Like she'd transferred her need for Brad onto him. The combination of her perfume and myriad beauty products nearly choked him. But he couldn't move and risk losing her temporary trust in him.

"In the fireplace in my bedroom," she said, using her little girl voice. "Then I got rid of the ashes in the toilet, just like the letter said, so there was zero evidence left." She gave a proud smile.

"Good work." He needed proof she'd actually gone to the hotel and that she'd received a letter. He'd be talking to her staff shortly. "So you went to the hotel around when, and you stayed there for how long?"

"I arrived at six and stayed until I saw Brad on the ten o'clock news. Then I cried and finally cleaned up enough to leave." The raw, emotional hunger in her eyes intensified, and she gripped his arm. Her tight, tiny hand reminded him of the jaws of a Chihuahua. "Tell him I wasn't seen. Tell him that."

He fought the urge to shrug her off. "I will," he said in a confident, deep tone.

She heaved a sigh, let go of him, and, thankfully, took a step back. "Then I went to his and Sherry's house, hoping to catch him before he went inside the gate. I staked Collinswood out for an hour, until I saw him in the window and realized he'd beat me there. Then I screamed for a while and drove home around eleven forty-five."

She sounded lucid and crazy at the same time. However, she did confirm Thompson's report about her arriving home just about midnight.

"Okay. Do you still have the hotel key?" Matt asked absently, looking at his notebook with his peripheral vision tight on Lindsay.

"No, I threw it out on 280 on the way home like he asked me to. He wanted to make sure there wasn't any evidence left of my trip to the hotel so Sherry wouldn't catch him. That's why he didn't call me and why he asked me not to call him. So there would be no evidence linking us together."

He glanced at her. There was something off about the look behind her eyes, besides her obvious craziness. Like she was hiding something. Another point for her guilt.

He'd be calling Brad directly to confirm her story. He hoped the guy wasn't lying to him and Hell.

"Good, perfect. I'm sure you following all his rules will make him happy."

Her shoulders drooped with relief, her face relaxed, and she let out a long sigh. Like she was very happy he'd believed her story.

Either she'd fabricated the tale to cover her guilt or she was totally off her rocker.

Or a third possibility: the mysterious murderer had turned this woman into his or her personal marionette. There could be a master puppeteer behind the scenes, playing the whole group. Sending Lindsay secret letters and ensuring she had no alibi while simultaneously setting up Tanner for the fall. Maybe the assailant had framed them both, and depending on how the bombing went down, they'd have their choice of victims to blame. Maybe Lindsay had been the bomber's backup plan.

Of course, how many murderers plotted and executed these types of elaborate machinations? Nearly zero. Most murders were simple crime-of-passion affairs and spawned from jealousy. Plenty of that floating around in this case.

He needed to know the depth of Lindsay's hatred of Hell, and if she had access to hand grenades and guns. "Brad asked me to find out how you were doing."

Her mouth dropped open, and her face flushed. "How I'm doing? How the hell does he think I'm doing? He went to that skanky bitch's side last night instead of coming to see me!" She pointed vehemently off in the distance. "So what if she almost died? I have babies to make! I'll bet she bombed her own apartment just to keep Brad and his semen away from me. That's *my* semen! I need that semen! Trent doesn't want me to have his babies! I know that's what this is about!"

The hair stood up on the back of his neck, and he had to suppress a bad case of the willies. "Uh..."

She made a stabbing motion with her forefinger directly into his face. "You know she threatened to kill Brad? She came right here into my home and told me she wanted my help to kill him. She wanted to torture him, kill him, then dump his body in the desert. Does he know that? Does he know she wants him dead?"

Matt realized that she'd stopped talking and was looking to him for confirmation.

"I don't know about that, only that Brad wanted me to find out if you were all right."

"Well, I'm fine. Wait a minute. This makes no sense. Why is Brad worried about protecting me? They caught the man who bombed the pink-haired troll. It was some Iraq vet, some mentally ill lover of hers. The case has been solved."

Perfect opportunity to hit her and hit her hard. "We believe the vet may have been framed for the crime. We think there is another perpetrator."

All the color left her face, her mouth dropped open, and she clutched her chest. "But the evidence was overwhelming! He was seen on her block that day. He had the evidence in his trunk and in his apartment! Wait! Does this mean Brad won't be seeing me because he thinks the bomber is still at large? He thinks she's still in danger? Shit! This isn't fair! The vet clearly did it!"

An *I'm Guilty* sign flashed over her head in giant neon letters. How the hell did she find out all these details that hadn't been released to the public yet? He only knew about Tanner's apartment because he'd been there and had seen it. Hardly anyone knew the facts of the case. Except for the bomber.

He forced a hard yet unemotional look on his face. "I have no idea what Mr. Collins' plans are, ma'am."

Did Lindsay have some police friends who'd leaked the information to her? But why would she care so much about who had hurt Hell if she weren't the killer? If she loved Brad this much, she would have only cared about where Brad was and what he was doing.

Lindsay did a double take, moved closer, and examined him closely, then a look of recognition came over her face, and she pointed. "Now I know where I saw you. I was staking out the pink-haired troll's office the other day, and I saw you and Trent come out of the building." Her expression turned threatening and ugly.

He stopped breathing. Holy crap, this woman was creepy. Exactly the type who killed for jealousy. He couldn't believe she'd admitted to the stalking—of both Hell and Brad.

She stepped closer and sneered. "You're working for her, aren't you? Trying to pin this bombing on me so she can steal Brad from me."

He didn't flinch. "No, I'm working for Brad," he replied easily. "He wanted me to investigate her. That's why I was there."

She wasn't buying it. "I overheard you say you were working for her."

He kept his expression sincere. "I was trying to convince her to hire me so I could work undercover in her business. Brad was concerned about their relationship."

She tilted her head, and the whites of her eyes showed. "Wait. There's something not right here. I don't believe you. I think you're here for another reason. You're trying to get information from me." Her eyes widened, and she took a step back. "Brad doesn't think that I had anything to do with her bombing, does he?"

"Ma'am, he—"

She moved closer and stood taller. "If Brad doesn't believe that the vet bombed Trent, he sent you here to interrogate me, didn't he? Because you just interrogated me, didn't you?" She poked him in the chest. "Hey, you tell him just because I have access to grenades, and would love to see her dead, doesn't mean I did anything. Besides, if I wanted to kill her, I'm smart enough not to get caught."

His heart beat faster. Wowza! Was that a confession? "Uh, I'm sure you are."

She chuckled in a superior way. "I have an IQ of 165. I would have made damned sure to create a better alibi than waiting for Brad in some hotel close to Trent's apartment."

"Sure you would have." She might be smart, but her IQ had certainly not done her any favors. Problem with gifted people was that they always underestimated people who didn't share their intelligence level. He'd brought down a couple of genius murderers who didn't think they had any chance of getting caught by a bunch of dumb flatfoots. "May I ask something?"

"Certainly."

"How do you have access to grenades?"

She did a double take. "I didn't say that. Did I? Oh, I did. Yes, yes, anyone can get them if they really want," she said with a dismissive motion. "They aren't hard to come by. As for me, I have connections through my shooting club. A friend of mine has a practical arsenal. You know, for when all the poor people stage their uprising and launch their war on the rich." She spoke as if this were a well-known fact and a total inevitability. "He has a bunker. He's prepared."

The hair rose on his arms, and his stomach hollowed. "Good for him. So you belong to a shooting club?"

"Yes, which also proves that I'm innocent," she said like it was all so obvious. "If I wanted her dead, she'd be dead. I wouldn't have missed." She laughed. "I wouldn't have missed the first time at Starbucks. I'm an experienced marksman. I've won awards. And I wouldn't use a measly .38 pistol. I'd just blast that bitch between the eyes with my .44 Magnum." She pantomimed shooting a gun. "Blam! And that would be the end of it. But I would never do that because I can't raise Brad's children from jail, now can I?"

How did she know that a .38 pistol was used in the shooting at Starbucks? That detail had not been leaked to the media. If she wasn't the killer, how did she get that information?

But talk about incriminating herself. Motive? Check. Means? Check. Opportunity? Check.

Matt forced a neutral look on his face. "I don't think you attacked Miss Trent. I'm only here to protect you."

As soon as he left there, he'd contact Joe and find out if anyone had ever pressed charges against the blonde crazy. Maybe Death could do that job more easily; he had access to sealed records. Hell's Internet man could probably also determine how Lindsay had obtained the information about the .38 pistol and Tanner's apartment.

Lindsay's expression contorted into a mask of angry contempt, and her vibe turned hostile. "I'm beginning to think this has nothing to do with Brad. I think you're lying to me. I don't think those men were hired by Brad. I think they were hired by *you*." Her eyes blazing, she stepped toward him, daring him.

He stood his ground. Even though she was creeping him out, he couldn't show any fear. "No, ma'am, they were not."

"Bullshit," she spat, her face flushed. Her ever-vacillating expressions reminded him of all the meth-heads and mentally ill people he'd busted. Hands on hips, she hardened her face, and the look in her dilated eyes turned weird, verging on maniacal. She pointed at him, narrowly missing his face. "I think you're a big liar, Mr. Fake Detective. I *will* be calling Brad to find out if you're a liar. If you *are* working for that witch, I'll have you and those surveillance people out there arrested. I have your car licenses memorized, and your fake badge and your faces. I have an eidetic memory. I won't forget you," she seethed in a rapid-fire assault. "I'll take you down like I take down all my enemies. No one is coming between me and my future children! Not you and not that pink-haired troll!"

With a crazed expression, she disappeared inside the house, slamming the door behind her.

Matt stared at the tall arched double doors, brows at his hairline. He shuddered. What a freak.

Was she the killer? How could she not be the killer?

Because she was a total whackadoodle. Unfortunately, her mental problems could explain her entire performance and story.

But if Lindsay was telling the truth about the secret letter, then the enemy they were fighting was even more sophisticated and devious than he'd first imagined. He had to talk to Brad's wife and see if she was capable of the Machiavellian scheme.

But first he had to make sure that Brad hadn't sent Lindsay a letter.

Matt went straight to his car and called Brad.

Collins answered immediately, sounding frantic. "Sinclair? What have you got? How's Hell? Why won't she answer my calls?"

"Uh, she's fine. I mean, not great, but okay. She probably hasn't called you because she's asleep. She didn't get much rest last night."

"Right, right. God, I'm so worried about her. I know she's at her cousin's. My guards are watching her. I want to go see her, but I don't want to upset her. I know she's overwhelmed and tired. Let me know how she is when you see her. I wish I could move her into the condo with me, but I don't want to move too fast with her and freak her out. Shit. You called me for a reason, didn't you?"

Matt thumbed through his notebook. "I'm at Lindsay's and just talked to her."

"That must have been fun," he bit out, his tone cold.

"I need you to be honest with me."

There was a pause. "Okay..."

"Did you have a date with Lindsay last night?"

"*What?* Are you crazy?" Collins sounded floored. Matt didn't pick up that he was faking his reaction. "That whacko? God, I never want to see her again. Wish I'd never met her. Christ. Fucking freak. She sends me twenty emails a day no matter how much I try to stop her. Wait. Why are you asking me this? Did Lindsay say we had a date?"

Matt was surprised at how relieved he was by Brad's reaction. "Yes, that you sent her a letter with a hotel key and explicit instructions regarding arriving at the hotel unseen. She swore you had a maid deliver the letter to her room. Claims she found it on her dresser."

He was quiet for a moment. "Wow."

"She says she was waiting for you at the hotel and was upset you'd gone to the hospital to see Hell."

"What? How did she know I was— Oh, shit, it was on the news. Or is she still stalking me?"

"She could be. Lindsay mentioned that she'd been watching Hell the day she hired me and saw us coming out of Hell's office building together. She recognized me. So, apparently, she's still up to her old tricks."

"Damn it."

"She was out last night when Thompson's guys got on her about ten, and she came home at midnight wearing a yoga outfit. When I just talked to her, she was wearing a red-and-white baseball cap."

"Like the woman who was seen at Hell's last night." Brad's voice was laced with hatred and anger.

"Yeah."

"Shit. It's her, isn't it?"

"Not enough evidence yet, but she's at the top of the list." Matt circled Lindsay's name in his notebook. "Have you ever used a secret letter to communicate with her?"

Collins made a dismissive noise. "No. I always called her. She probably had a delusion I sent her the letter, and that's why she went after Hell. Did she say where she waited?"

"Embassy Suites."

"Out by SFO. Right. Christ. We used to meet there. She must have hallucinated the whole thing. Probably had another breakdown. Look, clearly she's nuts, but do you really think she's capable of bombing Hell?"

"Not sure. Is she prone to making up elaborate stories like that? She had precise details about what the instructions said. Throwing the hotel key out into traffic to get rid of it, wearing a disguise to the hotel. Has she done this sort of thing before?"

"I don't know. She tells stories, that's for sure. And, yeah, she always provides so many details it's amazing she can fit them all in that whacky brain of hers."

"So it's possible she made up the letter?"

"Probable, even. I've never sent her a letter, never given her instructions like that."

"Who has access to her house other than her and Dan and the staff?"

"I don't know. Wait, you think that someone was setting up Lindsay for Hell's attack?"

"If they did, they went to great pains to ensure she had no alibi."

"Who would do that? Capasso. Capasso is that smart."

"Capasso wouldn't have bombed Hell's apartment."

"Are you sure? This would have been an easy job for him. So

many suspects he could have lured them all to Hell's block. The vet and Lindsay."

"We don't know anything for sure yet."

"Right. And it's entirely probable that Lindsay's just completely lost it and tried to bomb Hell herself. I'll alert my bodyguards to be on the watch for her."

Matt shifted in the driver's seat of his car, realizing that he'd been sitting on a pen. He grabbed it and put it back in its holder on his dash. "I think Lindsay loves you too much to hurt you. But she is obsessed with you. And crazy. It's possible she went after Hell."

"Ever since she got this new health guru, she stopped taking her meds and lost her mind. Damn it, if that bitch hurt Hell, I'll strangle her myself," Collins said through gritted teeth. He sighed heavily. "Are you going to see Hell now?"

"Yeah. Well, after I get some lunch."

"Tell her I want to see her, okay?" Brad said with a whiff of desperation in his voice. "Tell her to call me."

"I will." Poor bastard really had it bad for Hell.

Matt hung up, sighed, and shook his head. Problem with unbalanced suspects like Lindsay was that it was difficult to determine if they were demonstrating their mental illness or guilt.

Matt coordinated with Thompson's men, letting them know they'd been made. Thompson was sending a better-concealed surveillance vehicle: a van from a local utility company.

Hopefully, if Lindsay was the guilty party, she'd try something soon. Hell needed this ordeal over.

CHAPTER 19

H ell tried to get comfortable in Joanne's cushy leather chair, but her leg was killing her. Painkillers and pot helped a little but not enough. Not only did the grenade wounds hurt, her whole body was sore from having all those books and crap fall on her.

Matt had just arrived and sat opposite her on a leather settee.

Joanne lived on the bottom floor of a lovely house in the Los Altos hills—a super-pricey, exclusive South Bay town comprised of large parcels—which she rented from the widow owner. Decorated simply but tastefully with a sophisticated edge, her two-bedroom apartment was furnished in leather and wood with watercolor paintings of flowers on the walls and a few art glass vases and colorful paper-weights placed about. The view out the floor-to-ceiling windows was spectacular, showing off the rolling hills and woods sprinkled with zillion-dollar estates.

"So what about Lindsay?" Hell took a sip of iced tea Joanne had brought her earlier.

"No solid evidence linking her to the crime." His eyes shined. "Yet."

"Yet? I knew it was her!" Hell bounced in place, making her wounds sting.

Matt held up a hand. "Wait. Before you get ahead of yourself, listen." He filled her in on Lindsay's crazy tirade about the letter, expecting Brad at the hotel, and her access to guns and grenades. He also relayed the information about the bomb squad's findings.

Hell clapped her hands. "She soooo did it, Matt!"

Matt sent her an amused smirk. "No direct evidence yet, Hell. Craziness, lack of an alibi, and wearing a yoga outfit and a red-and-white baseball cap is not guilt. We don't know where she went because we just got on her late last night. We only know when she came home. However, I do know that there was a reservation at the Embassy Suites under the name Lindsay Banning."

Hell's head snapped back. "Really?"

"Yeah. And I talked to the reservations clerk, and a woman fitting Lindsay's description had rented the room earlier in the day."

"Oh. So that means she's crazy, or guilty?"

"Don't know that yet."

"Did you talk to her maids to see if they delivered a letter?"

"I didn't feel good staying around. I'm going back. But if Lindsay made up the hotel reservation part, and if there was a letter, she probably wrote it herself."

Hell let out a long breath. "Was she driving the Honda?"

"No. She was in a Bentley. Honda didn't show up until this morning, along with the gardener."

Hell furrowed her brow, which burned. She had to forcibly relax her forehead. "Ow, I can't even react normally without my face hurting. So is she using another black Honda? Are there two?"

"Must be, if it was her. But we don't know for sure. All we know is that she went somewhere, came home driving her Bentley at midnight, and Brad hadn't made a date with her."

"You talked to him?"

He nodded. "Yeah. It was clear he hadn't had a date with her."

Hell wished she weren't so relieved. "Damn, Embassy Suites is far too close to my apartment. She could have bombed me."

"Can you have Death delve into her past and see if there have been any charges filed against her? Any police records? Any lawsuits for personal injury that have been settled? We need to know if she has a history of violence."

"I had him do a cursory background check. I'll have him probe deeper. I want to call him before you leave."

"Good."

Joanne walked into the room and handed Matt a tall glass of iced tea.

He lit up and sent her a bright smile. "Thanks, Joanne."

"You're welcome." Her cousin checked Hell's glass. "You need more?"

"In a minute. I'm good."

"Just let me know." Joanne turned her attention to the small dining table near Matt and grabbed a magazine off the top.

"You're spoiling me."

"Not possible." Joanne grinned and left.

Matt watched her leave the room, his gaze lingering. He clearly liked what he saw. How cute! Matt had a crush on Joanne! Hell decided not to mention it. She didn't want to make either of them uncomfortable.

Matt's focus returned to Hell. "Lindsay's either totally crazy and innocent, totally crazy and guilty, or someone smart is setting her up. We'll find out. Lindsay won't do anything from now on without us knowing it."

"How? You're here, and the only person I hired— Oh, cool, you used the GPS tracking thingies that Death sent to my office?"

Matt looked away and rubbed the back of his neck. "Uh, no." He put on his hard-cop face and looked directly into her eyes. "At the risk of being fired, I accepted help from BC to tail Lindsay. I put one of Thompson's guys on her last night."

Hell wondered why she wasn't angry. She actually felt sort of relieved. While also being annoyed. She didn't like owing BC. "I'm happy and unhappy at the same time."

"I knew you wouldn't like it." Matt's authoritarian edge didn't fade. "But you hired me to help you and solve this case. I never promised not to accept outside help to do the job."

Hell pursed her lips and sent him an eye roll. "That's why I let BC hire the bodyguards. A) I can't afford them and B) if the threat is coming from him, I might as well let him pony up some cash to protect me. But I don't like his interference. He's...he's another one of my problems that I need to solve. But for the moment, you're right, it's about my life."

Matt's shoulders relaxed. He'd expected a fight.

"I'm not mad, Matt, don't worry. I trust you. Do what you need to help me, and don't second-guess yourself. My head is so messed up I'm unable to make great decisions. Just take care of it."

He smiled. "I think that grenade actually knocked some sense into you."

"Or completely blew all the reason from my brain. I know it's Lindsay. I know it is. I got her too riled up. Shit."

"You can't blame yourself for the actions of others, Hell. Especially unbalanced rich women." Matt pulled off his dark blue jacket, revealing a short-sleeved, lighter blue shirt, which highlighted his thick shoulders and hard back. His right forearm was big and ropy from playing tennis, but he had a stocky body suited more for rugby or football. Darling man, really. With his intelligent sky-blue eyes, wavy, sandy-brown graying hair and wide, squarish face, dude was a man's man. Not her type, but hot. He draped his jacket over the arm of the settee and relaxed back.

"What did the cops say when you told them about Lindsay? You must have told Joe."

He shrugged. "They think they have their man."

"You couldn't clear Tanner?"

He looked at his iced tea glass. "Uh, no."

Her belly tight, Hell sat up. "What?"

Matt frowned and shook his head.

"He was spotted in my hood?" Hell prayed his answer was no.

He gave a grim nod. "By six people, hanging out in front of your house yesterday afternoon."

Her mood blackened, and she slumped in her seat, trying to ignore the twinge in her back and the jab of pain in her hip. "Shit.

After he got out of jail, he calmed down and texted me, worried about me. Said he wanted to protect me. I told him I had it handled. Damn him, anyway. But how could the evidence support the guilt? Placing him at the scene isn't enough."

His mouth curved with disgust. "Whoever set him up is good. Joe gave me the lowdown." He relayed all the evidence that was found on Tanner and his car. "...And a copy of the note taped to your door."

Hell's skin flushed with shame, and the weight on her shoulders grew heavier. The setup was so complete. Such totality. "Dear God."

"Yeah. There's more. I talked my way into Tanner's place last night. Unfortunately, your pictures are splashed all over his apartment."

A cold chill came over her, releasing a bit of guilt. "Creepy. I didn't know that. Was that part of the assailant's setup?"

"No, you getting shot and his arrest sent Tanner further into his manias and his obsession with you."

"Son of a bitch." Hell rubbed her arms and held herself.

"His last journal entry was about how God was giving him a second chance. He couldn't save his team back in Iraq, and he couldn't save his mother from her drug overdose, but he could save you. He transferred all kinds of stuff onto you. According to my buddy, between the time he was arrested last time for the shooting at Starbucks and now, he's added even more photos."

Hell shuddered. "Great. How come no one told me about the pics in his apartment before this?"

"Joe didn't want to scare you any more than you already were. I told him withholding information from you had put you in more danger."

"Sure did. Now I'm really glad I had you with me when I saw him in jail."

"Yeah. Plus Tanner's computer revealed all the emails he's been sending you."

Hell's lower back complained, and she shifted her weight. "Damn it, making him look like the attacker was like shooting fish in a barrel. He'll never get out."

"We'll solve it. He won't be in there forever."

All her thoughts tunneled to one: The Fear Channel. "Meanwhile, the true assailant will kill me."

Matt pointed at her. "No, they won't, Hell. Not while I'm here." Strength and conviction radiated from him.

The edge came off her fear, and she let out a heavy sigh. She'd never had such a good man in her corner before. Not since Josh. But even he hadn't been this centered and together. "What about Sherry and the librarian? Are the cops just ignoring all the questions we had about them?"

Matt's gaze darkened, and he twisted his lips. "Yeah. Past ignoring it, they think the ideas are ludicrous. Joe had a good laugh about it. Thinks we're reaching. Unless we come up with some concrete evidence, like blood, DNA, grenades, guns, or camera footage of Lindsay or Sherry actually committing an act, there's no way in hell the cops will go near them. Both women are too powerful, too rich, too connected. Lindsay and Sherry run in the social circle of the president of the United States, for God's sake."

Hell rubbed her forehead, hit her wound, and hissed. "Son of a bitch. I hate rich and powerful people. This sucks." She picked up the backpack Matt had brought her and unzipped it. All she saw were bags of weed. The pungent odor of green bud filled her nostrils. She laughed. "Joe didn't just grab one bag of pot from my freezer; he put my whole stash in here."

"He was worried about you."

"Apparently. Almost freakin' two ounces. Christ, I'd better put this in more plastic, or Joanne's house is gonna smell like a dispensary. Joe must have smuggled it out past his friends." Her favorite stuffed animal peeked at her from beneath the bags of dope, and her heart leapt. "Secret Teddy!" She withdrew the bear and hugged him tight. "Thank God." A comforting warmth overtook her, and she felt safer.

Matt smiled. "Joe said you'd need him."

Hell's face heated. She hadn't meant to have a big emotional display at the sight of a stupid teddy bear in front of someone.

"Hell, don't be embarrassed." He looked at her with what appeared to be fondness. Unexpected.

She glanced down at her bear and still felt like she'd been caught sucking her thumb in a crib. "Please don't tell anyone, okay?"

"I wouldn't." Fatherly energy emanated from his kind blue eyes and confident posture.

The tension eased from her spine, then lurid visions of her being bombed popped into her head, and her adrenaline spiked. She did her best to hide her reactions, but if Secret Teddy had been a real bear, he'd be dead from asphyxiation. She'd woken up screaming for five years after Capasso had attacked her. Couldn't imagine the devastation the grenade had done to her subconscious.

A warm spring breeze scented with fruit blossoms, wet earth, and new plant growth wafted through the screen of the open sliding glass door, blowing away the pot smell. Surreal how beautiful and serene the day was compared to the war going on inside her mind and body. Hell zipped up the backpack to stem the weed odor.

Matt worked his mouth and looked at his notebook, then at her. "Let's talk for a minute about Sherry." His eyes lit.

Excitement filled her, and Hell sat straighter in her chair. "What? Tell! Tell!"

He smiled, his blue eyes crinkling. "I talked with their gardener because Sherry has apparently retreated to her mother's in Marin to hide from the news and tabloids. Ever since the story broke about you and BC, there's been an encampment in front of their house."

Hell grimaced, and her face flushed. She couldn't believe everyone knew about her sex life now. Horrible. "Jesus."

"Anyway, the gardener, Lloyd Meeker, had some interesting tidbits to share." Matt checked his notes. "Disgruntled guy, clearly. Hates the Collinses. He said that Sherry had made a big deal out of getting a headache and going to bed early last night. She'd told the entire staff that she was ill. He couldn't figure out why she'd told him because he's not even the lead gardener. Then he said as he was leaving that night around five thirty, he saw Esmeralda driving by and called out to her because he'd wanted to coordinate with her about renovations to the driveway, but she wouldn't stop. Which she's never done before. She wouldn't even look at him."

Hell leaned toward Matt. "You think Esmeralda helped sneak Sherry out so she could throw that grenade at me?"

"I don't know. I wanted to talk to both women—Sherry and Esmeralda—but neither was around. Only person I found was Meeker. I'm going to track down the entire staff and see what I can get out of them. See if anyone saw her get into the car with Esmeralda, anything else unusual. But Brad's butler has been in England for the last week, and their mechanic is on vacation, so I just have to track down the cook, the head gardener, the maintenance man, and the housecleaner. Then I'll target Esmeralda and Sherry. If their stories don't corroborate with the staff's, I'll put a tail on both." He winced. "Even though I hate asking Brad to pay to follow his wife."

Hell snapped her fingers, then pointed at him. "Death sent me those small GPS trackers. They're at my office. We can put them on Esmeralda and her car. Sherry's too. That'll save BC some cash."

Matt's weathered face drew down, and he clamped his lips tight for a moment. "Hell, I'm uncomfortable with the illegal stuff."

"I know, but I don't want to die."

"You have the bodyguards; you'll be fine," he said decisively. "Besides, I don't think Brad's about to run out of money anytime soon."

"True."

"But I really want a face-to-face with Sherry if I can get it, as soon as possible," Matt said. "Get her confidence and see if I can eliminate her. Then I won't have to put a tail on her."

"Okay, good. So you canvassed my hood. Anything else we need to know about the case?"

Matt pinched the bridge of his nose and met her gaze. His face clouded.

"What?"

He lifted his chin, his eyes dark. "Joe was seen last night before the bombing."

Her stomach hollowed, and she broke out in a cold sweat. "Holy shit, is he stalking me again?"

Matt's brows came together hard. *"He stalked you?"*

She bit her lip. "Yeah." She sighed. "I thought he was done with all that. Damn it. But Joe wouldn't try to kill me. His heart isn't bad like that. Still, it creeps me out."

"How long did he stalk you? And when?"

"I don't know how for long, but it happened toward the end of our affair. Maybe for six months or so, I'd catch him in weird places. Took me a long time to catch on, actually. Once I really figured it out, I told him he was scaring me, and freaked out on him. That seemed to shake him up, and he stopped. Or so I thought. Maybe he just got sneakier."

Matt rubbed his mouth and sat back in his seat, shaking his head. "No wonder he knew so much about your exploits—I mean, lovers. You did your best to hide your sex life from everyone. Damn, he displayed all the signs of a stalker, and I just thought..."

Hell twisted her mouth. "I was a slut."

His face flushed, and he shrugged. "Sorry. That's how he made it sound."

"Do you think he did it?"

"No. But I'm making sure of it," Matt said. "I'm meeting him later to get a face-to-face and confront him over this shit. See how he reacts. I'll know."

"I'd rather have it be Tanner at this point. Joe..."

He made a stop motion. "Let's not jump to any conclusions. I can't imagine Joe would bomb you. He's a cop, he loves you, and he's worried about you. It makes sense he'd be keeping an eye on your place."

Hell let out a long sigh. "Right. And Joe's a sweetheart. A bit creepy around the edges, but okay. He's gone to bat for me a lot. I'd hate to find out he was the one behind it."

Matt nodded firmly. "He's the only one in the department who stood by me. But we have to eliminate him."

"Right. So what about Gwen?"

"Gwen's in Europe for the week." He glanced at his notepad. "Was there three days ago."

"Thank God, one person off the list. Didn't think she'd done it. Okay, I just have to go here, what about Tanner? What do you really think?"

Matt crossed his ankle over his knee and draped his arm along the back of the settee. "I think there's too much evidence against him. Even though he's crazy, he's smarter than that. If he really wanted to hurt you, I think you'd be dead by now. He certainly wouldn't be hanging out at your house all day on the day he committed the crime."

"Damn it, it has to be one of BC's women. It just has to."

Joanne snorted loudly from the other room. "Like he has this collection."

Hell said, "He did have a collection. We both did."

Joanne walked into the room. "You're monogamous for the first time since Josh, right?"

Hell's belly tightened. "Repulsive, but yes."

"You guys must really like each other."

"Apparently. He even dropped the bloody L word last night." Hell's heart began beating faster, and she broke out in a sweat. Talking about her attempted murder was much easier than this conversation. A voice in her head suggested moving to Europe.

Joanne gaped. "How did you possibly manage to keep that to yourself last night?"

Hell chuckled and shrugged. "I was still in shock. Am still in shock. Besides, it doesn't mean anything. He's married and a big fat liar living a lie. I had a stupid attack, which I will recover from shortly and return to my own herd, where I belong. But yes, apparently we have actual feelings for each other, and I couldn't be more disgusted with myself or him."

"Hell, it's natural," Joanne said. "What did you say when he said he loved you? Did you tell him you loved him back?"

"Not exactly, but I didn't deny it very well." She smoothed the edge of a bandage on her forearm.

"Do you love him?" Joanne asked.

Hell snorted. "I hope not."

"You do, don't you?"

She made a face. "I'm trying to stay in denial."

Joanne walked all the way into the room, stopping by the dining table near Matt, and rested a knee on a chair. "Makes sense, Hell. You see him pretty regularly, right?"

Hell traced the leather piping on Joanne's chair with a forefinger. "Um, I guess lately we've sort of seen each other almost every other day. Not that I noticed."

Joanne made a little yip. "Every other *day*? How did you not notice? I knew you saw him occasionally, not *every other day*. How much time do you spend with him?"

"Twenty hours of naked fun time a week," Matt bit out with a dark look.

Hell snapped her attention to him. "How do you— Oh. Brad admitted it?"

"More than admitted, bragged." Matt's dismal expression grew even darker.

"Bragged? Brad? Why— Wow, you don't look happy."

Matt pursed his lips. "I've been married thirty years. How much naked fun time per week do you think I get?"

"'Bout ten minutes," Hell responded without missing a beat.

He shook his head, and Joanne laughed.

Chuckling, Hell said, "If BC and I had been married for thirty years, we'd be the same. Josh and I certainly didn't do this toward the end."

"Well, no wonder you aren't seeing the other guys. You don't have any time," Joanne said, still with a giant grin.

"I can't believe I didn't notice," Hell said with revulsion.

Joanne glanced at the kitchen, then turned to Hell. "I need to finish the salad dressing. Let me know if you need anything." She smiled and turned to leave. "Twenty hours a week, and she doesn't notice. You are so funny."

"When I go into denial, I go all the way."

"Take your painkillers," Joanne said from the next room.

"Yes, Mom."

Matt referred to his notepad. "Since I haven't talked to Sherry, I want your take on her. Truly, your gut instinct, what do you think?"

Hell relaxed back in her seat, thrilled for the subject change. "While she said she'd kill Brad if he was only seeing one woman, and that seems to be the case now, I can't really see Sherry getting her hands dirty. She's a princess and hates Brad. Now Lindsay is Boiled Bunny crazy about him. She said she'd kill just for another afternoon with him."

"Jesus, what is it about that guy?" Joanne asked from the kitchen.

"Got me. I mean, I apparently love him, but I have poor taste in men."

Joanne snorted. "Except for Josh."

"Except for Josh." Hell sipped her tea. "As for Lindsay and Sherry, I truthfully can't picture either of them lobbing a flippin' hand grenade onto my patio." A wave of dizziness came over her, and she slouched deeper into her seat to rest her head on the back of the chair. The exhaustion was catching up.

"We'll find out," Matt said and stood.

"Before you go, let me check in with Death and get him on Lindsay." Hell grabbed her cell from the coffee table and lay back in her chair. She punched in the one-use emergency number on her phone because she didn't have any of his special phones with her. "Deathy?"

"Hell, glad to hear your voice. How are you?" His gnome-y geek voice was deeper and more gravelly than normal. He'd either just woken up or he'd been awake for a few days.

"Not great but alive. What did you find out?"

"Esmeralda is definitely into drug dealing."

Hell perked up, her heart beating faster. "Really? Hey, I know you hate this, but I need Matt to hear this, and I'm too exhausted to remember what you said and repeat it to him. Can I put you on speakerphone?"

"If you must."

"Thanks, honey." Hell hit the speakerphone button.

Matt's eyebrows went high, and he sat down.

"Yes. Her name isn't Esmeralda, it's Maria Ruiz," Death reported. "She has a rap sheet a mile long and several outstanding warrants: two here, four from Mexico."

"Wow." She and Matt exchanged looks.

"Her brother is a high-ranking member of a Mexican drug cartel."

"Shit. So she's the one who shot at me?"

"Unsure, but I doubt she'd put herself in danger like that," Death said. "She accepted the job with the Collinses three years ago to lie low while the authorities searched for her—and more than likely to set up the Collinses for blackmail or to steal from them. The warrants are still active. Sherry pays her under the table."

Matt pursed his lips and shook his head.

Reality slap. Rich people believed the rules didn't apply to them. Another reason it would never work out between her and BC. "You'd think Brad would be better at vetting people," Hell said.

"Sherry runs the household and does all the hiring and firing," Death said. "Many wealthy individuals hire illegals to save money but don't realize that a frequent con of local cartels is to entrap them. Professional criminal organizations infiltrate a rich person's life by placing a domestic who gathers financial and, if present, incriminating evidence against them and then bleeds them dry through blackmail or embezzlement. Or they force the wealthy to use their private jets for transporting drugs."

Matt gave a slight nod. Clearly he'd had experience with the same kind of people and scams.

"Ooo, icky, creepy, and fascinating all at once," Hell said.

"Yes, so that may be the type of arrangement that Esmeralda or Maria has successfully achieved, or perhaps she is merely hiding."

Hell nodded sharply. "I have to plant that GPS on her. I was just about to do that when I got blown up."

Matt's face tightened. Hell would more than likely have to do the job herself.

"Okay, Deathy honey," Hell continued, "I need you to figure out if

Marco Capasso was the one behind the bombing. I don't think he'd go that far to control me, but I need to eliminate him."

"I can check his networks and periphery, but it could take some time. I can enlist the assistance of the General."

"Awesome. How's he doin'?"

"Quite well. We drank an entire bottle of Scotch last night and watched the last season of *Dr. Who*. I have no memory of the finale."

Hell laughed. "How long do you think it will take you?"

"Unsure. But it will be a top priority. However, in my informal analysis of the situation, Capasso's motivation is the weakest. He already believes he has control over you. I haven't noticed any new probes other than the slight extra attention directly following your shooting. I would assume this new attack will concern him and he will be doing his own investigation."

"And if your theory is correct, and he launches his own investigation, that will clear him."

"Yes."

Hell heaved a huge sigh. "I hope we get some people off the suspect list soon. Hey, can you do a little more digging into Lindsay's background and see if she has any history of violence? Even way far back?"

"Absolutely. Since I've already made a preliminary check of Lindsay's background and found no criminal history, if she has committed crimes, then the cases are sealed or the charges were dropped and the cases settled out of court. I will find out. Honestly, Hell, how are you doing? Do you require any personal assistance? The General has expressed much concern. Do you wish us to hide you?" Death's tone was tender and sweet.

Her heart warmed at her old buddy's affection and caring. "Not right now, honey, but thanks. But you never know. However, I will be needing extra help from you in the next couple weeks."

"Of course. You are my priority."

"I love you, Deathy."

"I love you, too, Hell. I am so very sorry that this happened to you."

"Me, too. Lost a really good pinball machine."

He laughed. "Don't worry, Hell. We'll find the perpetrator and destroy them."

Hell thanked him, and they said their good-byes.

"Not very smart of Sherry to hire an illegal," Matt said. "Especially when she has no idea who she's hired."

Hell put her cell on the table next to her tea. "To our knowledge. Maybe Sherry knows who Esmeralda or Maria is and hired her for a reason. Sherry's on drugs. Maybe she wanted an easy, untraceable source."

"Brad should know. He needs to protect himself."

Her stomach scrunched. "Yeah..." No way did she want to talk to him.

"Do you want me to handle it?"

She sighed with relief. Thank God she had Matt working for her! "Yeah. I'm just worried if we upset the balance of the household, we won't catch my assailant."

"I'm sure Brad will take that into account."

"Look, she's been there for three years. A few days won't matter."

Matt's expression remained firm. "He needs to know now. Besides, he's paying for this surveillance."

Hell's skin prickled. "This why I didn't want him paying for it, because it's splitting our loyalties here."

Matt held her gaze and blinked, thinking. "We can come back to this after you've rested. I have to agree with Death about Capasso. His motivation is the weakest."

"Good. I agree, too. Why, after eleven years, would you start attacking me? And like he'd hide it? He'd just come out and tell me what he was doing."

Matt got to his feet. "Still, it's wise to have Death confirm it, just to make sure. You never know what a jealous man might do. If he knows that you and BC are exclusive, he could be rattling your cage to get you to return to him."

"That grenade was a bit above a rattle. But better safe than sorry."

Matt took a step toward the door. "I'll find out what's going on with Sherry and keep an eye on Lindsay. You take care, and I'll call you later. Bye, Joanne, and thanks."

Joanne stepped outside the kitchen, whisking something in a bowl. "Bye, Matt."

He sent her an extra-bright smile and left.

Joanne walked up to her, stirring what smelled like balsamic vinegar, basil, fresh garlic, and olive oil. "Wow. Hell. Your life's really...um..."

"Exploded?"

Her cousin snorted, then nodded. "Yeah. I mean, for twelve years you've avoided serious relationships and just played with The Stud Stable, and now you're spending twenty hours a week with a billionaire. Matt, an old enemy, is now an ally. It's weird. Something's happening, girl. You haven't been in love since Josh."

Hell made a disgusted face. "Yeah, thanks, heart, for picking a cheating billionaire Lothario. Loving him will get me exactly nowhere."

Joanne smiled. "You don't know that yet. He loves you a lot more than he's even told you. I saw the look in his eye. He was freaked out at the thought of losing you. I think he's going to leave his wife for you."

"God, I hope not."

Her cousin shook her head and chuckled. "Come on, Hell. You love him, he loves you. You spend all your free time together. You honestly, deep down, don't want a future with him?"

"No," Hell said with much conviction.

Her brows came together for a moment. "Is this because you're afraid of getting hurt or because you don't think it will work?"

Hell let out a long breath. "Reasons are endless. Hormone flu will wear off in a year and a half, and that's how long it will last. Really, bottom line? He isn't worth it. I would not have picked this guy for a mate. He's absolutely without morals. He's an adulterer, he crushes his competition using smear campaigns and backdoor dealings, he rigs elections, he slept with Lindsay to get even with her husband,

and that's only the tip of the iceberg of the bad things he's done. He's treated me great, but he's not a good person."

"Whoa, that's not good," Joanne said with a frown. "He seemed so nice and caring."

She shrugged. "He *is* nice and caring. And he's a demon. I wish it were more black and white. I wish he were a better man. To me, he's a sweetheart. Better to me than any man ever has been with the exception of Josh. He's the first man to look at me the way Josh did. I know his love for me is real. I just don't trust him. I think he'll get bored once he gets his conquest, and he'll move on, right about the time I open up to him."

"He is in his mid-fifties, right? Guys do mellow out."

She blew out some air between her teeth. "Okay, aside from my lack of trust in him and his deep-seated immorality, he's too rich, too entitled, and far too used to getting his way. Everyone caters to this guy. He's a bulldozer. He gets what he wants because he doesn't stop until he gets it. No matter what. You know me, I'm a codependent. He'll have me trained like a dog. I'm not going there again."

"But you have awareness now."

Hell twisted her lips. "Great, so I'll be a self-aware dog."

Joanne laughed. "I don't think you'll let him do that to you. I think you've underestimated your psychological change since Josh."

"I still don't trust him."

"Only someone who really loves you would risk his marriage to be there for you with all those cameras around."

"I'm telling you, he was only upset because his fuck-hole got damaged."

Joanne gave an exasperated laugh. "You are hopeless." She returned to the kitchen. "If he leaves his wife, I'd give him a chance," she called out. "But you're right, until he's single, you can't trust him."

"Thank you. Which is why I'm dumping him."

"Has he phoned?"

"Probably."

"You aren't going to talk to him?"

"No, I'm going to sleep."

"Good idea. When you wake up, the soup and salad should be ready."

"Thanks, cuz, for everything."

"You don't have to thank me, but you're welcome. Now go take a nap."

Hell heaved herself to her feet, limped down the hallway to the guest room, lay down, and fell asleep about thirty seconds after her head hit the pillow.

Saturday, March 12, 2011, 7:35 a.m.

HELL AWOKE IN A COLD SWEAT, HER HEART POUNDING, LEG BURNING, relieved to see it was finally morning. All night she'd been trapped in a twisted reality of horrifying nightmares and half-awake terrors. Every forty-five minutes to an hour, she'd jerk awake in a blind panic, frightened to the core of her soul.

No matter what she did, she could not feel safe. She tried to meditate, but every time she cleared her mind and started to relax, her alarm system would sound. *Incoming! Man the battle stations! Arm the weapons! Prepare for war! Don't let your guard down or we'll die!*

When she did manage to sleep, she was tormented with frightening fantasies of various death scenes. Her body torn apart. Being eaten alive by wild animals.

For someone with a bad case of PTSD, having her apartment blown apart had not helped her disorder. Nor had all this unnecessary emotion for BC. Her head felt like it was on the verge of combusting.

Disoriented, she wanted her own bed. Which was now in shreds. Even Secret Teddy wasn't providing much comfort.

Most importantly, while BC's bodyguards should make her feel protected, they were making her feel trapped. Like BC had ensnared her permanently in his billion-dollar web and hired guards to keep her there. She *had* to escape.

In between nightmares, she'd tried to think of places she might feel safe. A resort at Shasta Lake seemed the best option. A lovely lakeside getaway with rustic cabins, where she'd stayed regularly over the previous twenty years.

But was it safe there?

Was it safe anywhere?

Whatever she did, she had to do it quickly. She had to find a way to sleep.

After a challenging shower—she lost count at forty individual wounds ranging from tiny to half-dollar-sized, all concentrated along her left side—she carefully applied antibiotic cream to the polka-dotted mess of her leg and butt, then checked her cell phone. A hundred voice messages and fifty texts. Mostly from BC.

Shit. She did not have the strength to face him. She felt like she'd die without him. Which meant she had to stay away. She couldn't fall back into her old patterns. Her sickness had convinced her that she loved him. She just loved the torture. Life wasn't good unless it was bad.

Shasta Lake.

Hell pretended to be a lot saner than she was when she approached Joanne with her plan. She didn't mention that she was in the middle of a panic attack. She acted together and lucid, and it only took a few minutes to pull one over on her dear cousin.

Joanne's bargain was that she'd sneak Hell out only if she promised to call once a day. No problem. She could easily be sane for a few minutes a day.

Using the old hiding-under-a-blanket-in-the-backseat trick, Hell and Joanne easily drove past the two guards.

Freedom.

CHAPTER 20

SATURDAY, MARCH 12, 2011, 10:01 A.M.

M att drove through the tony suburb of Atherton, bristling at all the money on display. It wasn't right. People like him who'd worked hard their whole lives in civil service deserved better. These bastards who were born into money and never did an honest day's work in their lives—or the high-tech, IPO, twenty-something brats—got to live surrounded by unbelievable luxury while everyone else suffered. America had become a rich person's world. All the politicians were bought. Everything was corrupt. An honest man like him was an anachronism in today's cutthroat world of short-term profits. Everything he held dear was in jeopardy because the lawbreakers had taken over.

His priest kept telling him there was hope, but Matt didn't see any. The good were persecuted, and the bad were celebrated. Period. Look what had happened to him. He'd given everything to that force. Everything to his profession. Fought temptation, never took anything he didn't earn, and criminals disguised as cops had taken him down. Disgusting. A bad taste filled his mouth, and he spat out the window.

He turned the corner. Three news vans were parked in front of Collins' high-walled estate. He drove past them to the ornate black iron gate and pushed the intercom button.

"How do you know the Collinses?" came a voice from right beside him. "Will you talk to us? Can I have your name? Why are you here? Are you a relative?"

"Fuck off," he barked with such vehemence the reporter paled and backed away. He inwardly smiled. God, that felt good.

"Hello?" came the reply in a heavy Spanish accent from the intercom speaker.

"This is Matt Sinclair. Brad Collins sent me to interview the staff."

"He don't tell me nothing. Oh, yeah. You were coming tomorrow."

"Can you let me in?"

"Okay." A loud buzzing, and Brad's sculpted, fancy iron gate opened.

He drove up the themed concrete drive, past mature trees and flowering foliage, past the towering Mediterranean fortress, and parked overlooking a tennis court.

He checked the list of employees in his small notebook. Esmeralda the housekeeper/manager. Cook Imelda Garcia and her husband, Mario, the maintenance man. Housecleaner Josefina Martinez. Head gardener, Jill Johnson. Car mechanic, Patrick Granger. Brad's butler, Archibald Higgins. But the mechanic and butler had been gone during the attacks and were apparently still on vacation.

Only person Matt had managed to talk to was the head gardener's assistant, Lloyd Meeker.

As he approached the house, one side of the tall, arched, dark wood double doors opened. A short, stout Latina wearing blue jeans and a yellow polo shirt stood there.

Matt greeted her in Spanish, and she brightened.

"Your Spanish is good, señor." She stepped outside and closed the door behind her.

Odd move. Why wasn't she inviting him inside? "My wife is from Jalisco."

Her smile widened. "Very good. I have cousins who live there."

"I'm Matt Sinclair, and you are?"

"Esmeralda Santos."

The plant from the drug cartel. The illegal. Matt's attention intensified on the felon.

"What can I do for you?" she asked. She stood between him and the door like a human iron gate.

He pointed behind her. "Can we speak inside the house?"

"No. Sorry, we redoing floors."

Which was a lie. The look in her eyes was off, and he didn't like the tight line of her mouth. Like she was afraid the truth might spill out. Guilty body language. No varnish smell. No work trucks anywhere in sight. Why didn't she want him inside?

From what he knew, she was playing the part of a housekeeper and didn't want any unnecessary attention focused on her. Whatever she was hiding was worth the risk.

He needed to alert Brad. Hell might not want him to, but Brad needed to know.

He checked his notepad and looked back at her. "You've probably heard about the commotion regarding Mr. Collins."

"Oh, yes. Mrs. Collins very, very upset. She pack and leave to her mother's house in Marin yesterday. We all worried for her."

"Who else is here today?"

Her brows knitted together. "You mean the staff?"

"Yes."

She looked behind her at the house, then turned back to Matt. "Uh, mostly everybody gone because we redoing floors. Mr. Higgins, he gone home to England for last two weeks. Patrick, the car guy, he gone on vacation. Imelda and Mario shopping at Costco."

Matt checked his book. "Is Josefina here?"

"She no work today."

"What about Jill, the head gardener?"

"Jill and Lloyd, her helper, off today."

"So you're the only one home."

She looked him in the eyes and didn't blink. "Yes." She didn't want him talking to the rest of the staff.

Matt held her gaze for a long moment. Her shoulders hunched, and her worry lines deepened. He shifted his weight to one leg and referred to his notes. She let out a small sigh. Wow, was she on edge.

He glanced up and pretended to focus more on his notebook than her but kept his peripheral vision locked on her. "All right. So Mrs. Collins is gone to Marin, and she left yesterday. When did she find out about Mr. Collins and his...uh..." He gestured vaguely.

"*Puta*? I mean, uh, woman?"

Matt inwardly flinched. *Puta* meant *whore* in Spanish. Guess whose side the housekeeper was on. "Yes."

"Don't know," she said with a shrug. "She no talk to us about things. I hear her yell, that's how I know she find out about Mr. Collins."

"What day was that?"

"Yesterday." Her eyes narrowed, and she began to retreat within herself. "Don't they catch the man who blown up *la puta's* apartment? Why Mr. Collins want you to talk to me about this?"

This woman was taking a big risk with this choice to confront him. If she'd helped Sherry attack Hell, why would she want any unnecessary attention on her so soon afterwards? Maybe the scam she'd been setting up was about to happen. Maybe she was expecting a delivery from the cartel. Even better, maybe she'd just received a drug delivery from the cartel.

"Mr. Collins wanted to make sure none of this came back on him," he replied casually, as if his questions were routine and of no consequence. "He needs to keep his privacy and was concerned about the *police* interviewing his staff that—"

Esmeralda's eyes went huge, and her back stiffened. "The *policia*? They come here? Now? When?"

Gotcha. A little surge of power went through him. Damn, he'd missed this part of his job. He kept his face free of emotion. "He wants to make sure they won't come here."

Her rigid posture eased. "Oh. Good." Then she did a double take. "I mean, I don't got no problem with police. I talk to them if they come."

She was so obviously rattled Matt half expected her to burst into a confession. She was certainly guilty of something.

He hid a smile and glanced at his notes. "So you live on the property?" He indicated the area with a small movement.

Her brow furrowed, her eyes full of suspicion. "Yeah," she said hesitantly.

He pretended not to notice her terrible acting. "Do you get along well with the Collinses? They good bosses?"

She frowned. "Yeah, why you ask? Of course, I like the Collins. They pay me good, I do good job. They never complain. Why Mr. Collins want me to talk to you?" She put her hands on her hips and glared. "What's this about really? You sure Mr. Collins sent you?"

He didn't react. "Yes. He told you I'd be talking to you. You don't remember?"

"He said someone. I don't know who he said. Show me you ID." Mean, dark energy emanated from her eyes.

Convicted. Either she was setting up the Collinses for a scam or using them in a drug operation or hiding. Or all three.

Matt held up his badge. She took great care in examining it carefully. She pulled back, crossed her arms, and closed off her expression.

"So you like working for the Collins."

"I already say that," she bit out, now openly hostile.

Matt looked at his pad, then watched her face carefully. "Did you deliver a letter to Lindsay Banning's house on Thursday afternoon, the tenth of March?"

Her head snapped back, then her face hardened. "What? Do I look like postman? No, I housekeeper. I don't deliver nothing to no one."

Her defensiveness certainly wasn't helping her. Time to push her a bit more. "The gardener, Lloyd, said you left at five thirty in the afternoon of March ten and wouldn't stop when he flagged you down. Where were you going?"

Her eyes widened, and she took a step toward the house. "I don't know. I was off work." Then she made an obvious attempt to look like she didn't care. She tapped her finger against her mouth, squinted, and appeared to pretend to think. "I went shopping."

"Where?"

She scowled and shrugged. "What does it matter where? I go shopping."

"I'm just asking some simple questions. What are you hiding?"

Gasping, she threw up her hands. "Who said I hiding anything? Do I need a lawyer?"

"Why would you need a lawyer?"

"You asking me all these stupid questions." She gestured sharply, her tone pitched high, her face reddening. "How do I know what I do two days ago? I busy here, you know. I have job. What do I know where I go all the time? I ask you what you do two days ago, you probably don't know, either."

Matt didn't react physically and didn't allow any emotion to seep into his voice. "You seem awfully upset over a couple routine questions."

"Not upset. Tired," she said, waving her hands. "Well, of course, I upset. Mrs. Collins upset and leave. I don't know if I have job if they divorce. Everyone upset here. And now you questioning me like I'm criminal. How should I not supposed to get upset?" she demanded, fully riled.

"I'm not treating you like a criminal," he replied calmly. "I just asked where you went after work Thursday night, that's all."

She took a deep breath, fought for words, then blurted, "I told you, shopping at the store," she said with a sharp gesture.

"What store?"

"I don't know! I no have time for this. I have work to do." She took a step backwards.

He followed. "Mr. Collins wants you to talk to me."

Her face twisted with fear and anger, and she jabbed a finger in his chest. "I call Mrs. Collins. I bet *she* no want me talking to you. Mr. Collins divorce her, you want to take all her money for Mr. Collins, don't you?"

He tried not to smile. She might be a criminal, but she sure as hell wasn't very good at it. "No."

"I no believe you. I go now. I have work." She put her hand on the doorknob.

"Mr. Collins won't like it," he said.

Her mouth dropped. She spun and pointed at him wildly. "You upsetting me! I don't want to be upset! Everyone upset! Now everything bad!"

Matt made a downward motion with his hands. "Please calm down. You're not in trouble. I just want to know where you went the other night. Lloyd, the gardener, said it was unusual that you didn't stop, and you drove right by him."

"He know nothing." She flung her hand toward the tennis court. "Lloyd always lying. He a drunk. You listening to a drunk now? I bet Mr. Collins no want you to harass me. You harassing me," she said, screwing up her face and stabbing at him with her forefinger.

Time for some misdirection. He allowed his body language to turn casual and checked his notes again. "So you went shopping, okay," he said like she hadn't just been yelling at him. "And Mrs. Collins was sick that night."

She stopped moving and stared at him. "What?"

"Mrs. Collins was sick that night, two nights ago. She told the gardener and another staff member that she was sick and was turning in early. Do you take care of her when she's sick?"

Her shoulders relaxed, and she crossed her arms. "If she ask, yes."

"So you left early two nights ago while Mrs. Collins was sick?"

She gasped, and her pupils dilated. Then she snapped into an indifferent expression and shrugged. "She sent me to the store to get her painkillers for her headache," she tossed off like she'd just thought of it.

This housekeeper was clearly vying for Worst Liar of the Year. "Okay, so you went to the store for Mrs. Collins." Matt flipped the pages of his notebook, put his finger on a line of text, and stood taller. "But you said earlier that you were off work."

She wasn't fazed. "Yeah, I just remember. I was off work. I do favor for her."

"Do you do favors for her like delivering things to friends? Do you know Lindsay Banning?"

Her eyes went large, then she resumed her fake, uncaring expression. "I don't deliver nothing to no one. And yes, I know her, she friends with Collins."

"Has Mrs. Banning been here recently?"

"No, because Mr. and Mrs. Collins having big fight over his *puta*," she said like he was totally stupid. "I work now. I don't talk to you no more." She turned, walked into the house, and slammed the door.

She could have very well snuck Sherry out that night. She could have delivered the letter to Lindsay. She could have taken part in the bombing.

But if she was part of a drug cartel that was setting up the Collinses, there would be myriad reasons she wouldn't want to divulge where she'd been.

Whatever reason she was lying, it was clear he needed to tell Brad his suspicions, despite Hell's objections. Collins needed to do a complete investigation into his household and its finances.

Matt walked around the estate but didn't find anyone else. There were a couple cars in the employee parking area behind the eight-car garage, which meant someone else besides Esmeralda was inside. The housekeeper was probably preventing him from talking to the staff, worried they might have witnessed something that night. Might have seen Sherry sneaking out to the car. Or the other staff might be involved in the plot against Collins, if there was one. He'd have to come back.

He slid behind the wheel of his car and called Brad.

"Sinclair, have you seen Hell?" The billionaire's deep, gravelly voice was taut with tension and higher than normal.

"Yeah. Earlier."

"Why won't she answer my calls?" Yet another vocal pitch upwards.

"I don't know. You'll have to ask her."

"She's running on me, isn't she? She's freaked out about everything, and she's blaming me, isn't she?"

Matt sighed. "She is not blaming you. Look, I'm uncomfortable being in the middle of your relationship. I told her the same thing. I won't be held responsible for exchanging information between you. I'm only in this to save her life."

"Okay, okay. You're right. I'm just going out of my mind. I can't get a hold of her, we're all over the news, Sherry's got the kids screaming at me— Shit, sorry. I haven't slept, and I'm punchy." He took a large breath. "What did you call about?"

"I need to warn you about an employee of yours."

"Who?"

"Esmeralda Santos. Her real name is Maria Ruiz, and she's a criminal with several arrest warrants: two here, four from various states of Mexico. Her brother is a high-level member of a Mexican drug cartel."

"Holy shit. I'll fire her."

"Wait. Before you do, you need to know what she's been up to and what she knows about you and Mrs. Collins. If there are any legal issues, she may have evidence that will incriminate you. She may be setting you up for blackmail."

"Holy crap. Sherry hired that idiot. I never liked her. Something was off, and I couldn't put my finger on it. I'll call my financial and security guys."

"Utmost discretion is required here. Make sure your people don't alert her. I got her rattled enough. We need her calm and unaware so we can find out what she's been up to. She could still be involved in the attack on Hell. She and Sherry could be behind the bombing."

"Sherry? No way. I think." Brad went quiet. "Shit."

"If there's even a remote possibility, we don't want Esmeralda destroying evidence or going to Sherry."

"This is insane."

"Nothing is proven. We need more information."

"I'll get right on it." He made an exasperated noise. "Jesus Christ. You know, if I hadn't met Hell, I wouldn't have known any of this. My entire household has been against me. I had no idea how much Sherry hated me. I wonder if my wife knows about Esmeralda, or Maria, or whatever her name is."

"No idea."

"And you can't ask Sherry directly because it may tip off Esmeralda," Brad snapped with disgust. "That and Sherry isn't speaking to me now. Look, Sinclair, as much as I hate my wife, I don't think she's involved. She may have hired Esmeralda, but I can't see her plotting an elaborate scheme like this. Last night I couldn't sleep, and I kinda poked around in her room. Actually did more than poke. I went through everything and found nothing."

"If she's smart enough to set up Tanner for the grenade attack, she's smart enough to cover her tracks."

"God, I hope not. The kids couldn't handle it." His voice was laced with pain. "They already hate me and blame me for everything. If their mother turns out to be a true psychopath, it would crush them."

"Let's not worry about that right now."

"Right, right. Goddamn, this is just too much. So what do you know about Lindsay? Any new information since Thompson's been on her?"

"No, but we have Hell's computer guy looking into her background. Let's see what he turns up." Matt's cell buzzed, letting him know he had a text. "One second, Collins. I'm getting a text, and it could relate to you."

"Go ahead."

Patty: *Hell was just here. Said she's leaving the Bay Area.*

Matt's heart rate went crazy. "Holy shit! Collins?"

"Yeah?"

"I have to call my wife. You'll be at this number?"

"Yeah. Hope everything is okay."

Matt had better warn him. "My wife just texted me. Hell's left the Bay Area. She didn't tell me anything. We were supposed to meet in two hours. I have to call and find out what Hell said."

"Son of a bitch! I'm calling my guards! Call me back!" Click.

His hands shaking from the adrenaline rush, Matt punched in his home number.

"Hi, honey," Patty said. "Helen was just here. She didn't look good, and she said she was leaving to find somewhere safe. She kept repeating that she didn't feel safe."

"What was she doing at the house?"

"Dropping off a five-thousand-dollar check."

Two weeks! "Jesus Christ! Did she say where she was going?" He wiped the sweat from his forehead.

"No. When I asked her, she started crying."

Matt's mind went dark. How was he supposed to protect a woman who'd disappeared into some PTSD nightmare? "She gave you no hint where she was headed?"

"No."

"I'll find her. I love you, and I'll talk to you later."

"Love you, too."

His phone rang just as he was dialing Collins. Thankfully, it was Brad.

"She escaped my guards! Those idiots just let her drive right by them!"

Matt pursed his lips and shook his head. "They weren't expecting her to sneak out."

"Where did she go?" Collins sounded like he was one step from the funny farm.

"I don't know, but I'll find out. She doesn't have that much of a head start. I'm going to her office now to search for clues. I'll find her."

"God, this woman will be the death of me! Please call me as soon as you have anything! Anything!"

"Will do." Matt hung up, dropped his detached-for-the-client act, and punched the steering wheel. "Goddamned woman!"

As he drove out of Brad's estate, he felt almost as crazy as the owner. He'd known this case would be a pain in the ass, but it wasn't in the ways he'd expected. Not in his wildest imagination would he have predicted his affection for Hell would be driving him harder than his professional needs.

What was it about this girl? Shouldn't he be happy with the money and not seeing her for two weeks?

But he knew he wouldn't breathe again until he found her. Their connection wasn't sexual, but it was certainly familial.

He made a loud, dismissive noise.

Great. Just what he needed. More crazy family members.

CHAPTER 21

Clutching Secret Teddy—a half-empty beer in front of her—Hell huddled in a chair on the back porch of her rustic, cedar cabin overlooking Shasta Lake as the light faded from the blue-purple sky. Nestled in a stand of oaks that served as home to a group of acorn woodpeckers, the resort—a group of fifteen cabins of varying sizes with a large dock—served the summer boat crowd. Hell and a couple in their thirties who'd come to fish were the only ones currently checked in.

The crisp, March mountain air bit into the exposed flesh on her hands and face but filled her senses with the comforting smell of lake water, pine, and oak. Her down jacket and microfleece pants helped some against the cold, but she knew she'd have to go back inside shortly.

She'd made herself come outside, finally, just to keep her head together. Hiding in the cabin all day hadn't done anything to diminish the fear. The walls had begun to close in on her.

Because she'd had a relatively normal trip up to Lakehead the day before—stopping at the outlets in Vacaville to pick up a few bags of clothing, underwear, and shoes—she'd thought her escape had cured her PTSD and gotten her brain working right.

She couldn't have been more wrong.

Nothing she'd done since she'd arrived had made her feel safe. No amount of beer or weed the night before could touch the terror. No matter what she did, she couldn't get centered.

She'd barely slept. Every time she closed her eyes, she saw a shadowy figure coming to kill her. She'd thought this little cabin and the memories of her fun summers there would provide her with a sense of safety. But not this time.

When she wasn't having nightmares, she was reliving past traumatic events. Her living room exploding. Marco Capasso beating her. Dad screaming at her. Her brother-in-law spewing his disgust at her. Her ex-husband Donny emotionally destroying her. Matt in that interrogation room, berating her, breaking her down. Black-bagged and terrorized by the Patriots. Caught in the middle of the raging gun battle between Rampart and their enemies: the deafening noise, the smell of gunpowder, the bullets flying.

When she wasn't shaking, she was crying. When she wasn't crying, she was puking. When she wasn't puking, she was smoking pot to control the nausea and trying to get liquids and food inside her. So far she'd managed to keep down a few soda crackers and a bit of chicken soup.

The night before, she'd barricaded the front and back doors and had lain awake listening to every sound outside—the rustling of the branches against the old cabin walls, the train across the lake, and an occasional car on the road below the cabin. The cars were her true fear. Bringing killers to her doorstep.

No way could she make sense of reality. She'd been on panic attack benders before, but none like this one. Normally, a couple days spent under the covers of her bed did the trick. But now she had no home. No safe bed. No safe place at all.

Fucking PTSD. Right back to three years old: lost in a terrifying world with no one there to hold her and reassure her. No one there to comfort her. Only this horrible blanket of terror smothering her, engulfing her, with no way out.

Tears filled her eyes. She blinked them away and reached for her beer with a shaking hand.

A rapping came from far away.

Hadn't the woodpeckers returned to their nests already?

The rapping got louder.

It was coming from her front door.

Adrenaline slammed her, and she almost dove off the back porch. If it hadn't been ten feet off the ground, she would have. Someone was there to kill her!

Trembling, she held herself, racing for an escape plan. Why hadn't she grabbed the gun out of her office safe?

"Hell?" came a loud man's voice.

She jumped a foot off her chair and clamped her hand over her mouth to stop the scream.

Wait. The voice was familiar. Too familiar.

Matt.

It couldn't be him.

"Hell? I know you're in there!"

Yes. Matt.

She slumped into her seat with relief, then her body hardened with anger. Her jaw set. How dare he?

A half second later, an avalanche of fear buried her. Paralyzed and trembling, she hugged herself hard. She wanted to run, but if she moved, he'd find her for sure. She couldn't face him. Not now! Not when she was so far gone. She couldn't handle him. She couldn't protect herself. She was absolutely emotionally naked, and he'd destroy her.

"Hell? Come on, open up. I'm not leaving."

No way. She held herself even tighter and closed her eyes. She could make him go away if she just thought it hard enough.

"Hell? Damn it! Open the goddamned door!"

How could she get rid of him?

"Hell? I'll get the key from the manager. You know I'll do it."

"Fuck!" She covered her face with her hands.

The sound of leaves crunching under footfalls became louder and louder.

"Hell?" Matt's voice from directly below her.

She kept her face buried in her palms like she had as a child. If she didn't see him, he couldn't see her.

"Hell, are you okay?" Very worried tone. Completely unexpected.

The tenderness in his voice tipped her over the edge, and she began sobbing.

"Jesus, Hell. Let me in, okay?"

"I can't handle it, Matt. You have to go away. I can't take it."

"Hell, jeez, I'm not going. I certainly wouldn't leave you like this."

Without wanting to, she yelled, "Why? You fucking hate me! All of you hate me! Go away, just go away!"

"Wow," he said in a soft voice.

Making her feel about sixteen hundred times crazier. This is why she avoided people when she was this far gone. She couldn't handle the mirror of her instability. She was almost okay being lost in her terror, she was used to it, but when she saw her illness reflected in the eyes of others, it overwhelmed her.

"Hell, let me help you."

She closed her eyes tighter, but the tears wouldn't stop.

The porch creaked, and a loud thump made her look up.

Matt had climbed up the side of the porch and was now facing her, his face lined with concern.

Every cell in her body screamed at her to hide. Her legs twitchy, she wanted to sprint to the next town. "You have to go, Matt. Honestly, I'm on the edge here and I can't..."

He approached her slowly like she was a wild cornered animal, pulled out the bench from the picnic table next to her, and sat down a few feet away. "Talk to me, Hell."

"No." She wiped her eyes with a sleeve, her arm trembling. "Matt, you have to go. I don't feel safe. I can't get safe. I can't handle you. I can't handle anything." A tsunami of emotions whirled up inside her, threatening to blow her mind apart. She held her head between both hands. "I can't take any more hurt. Just go away."

"I'm not going to hurt you."

"Bullshit! Everyone hurts me, especially you! You're mean, you hate me, you've broken me down, I'm not safe with you. I'm not safe, period, and I can't protect myself right now. You have to go."

"Hell, I don't hate you. At all. I like you. A lot," he said in a gentle tone. "I was wrong about you."

"No, you weren't," she spat. "If there wasn't something wrong with me, people wouldn't be so mean to me. I'm sure everyone's just upset that goddamned grenade didn't blow me up. That would have taken care of the Hell problem once and for all, right?"

"Jesus, Hell. No. Do you know how many phone calls you're getting? How many people are worried about you?"

Adrenaline pumping, her heart rate went higher. Those calls meant nothing. Matt couldn't possibly understand her world. "They're all users. They don't care about me, they only care about what I do for them."

"Hell..."

"Doesn't matter, anyway. I don't trust any of them. I don't trust anyone. I'm freakin' lost, Matt. I've never been this terrified. Never been this far out there before. Literally, I have no place that's safe for me anymore. Nowhere I can go."

"Joanne loves you."

"I'm not bringing my level of danger to her right now. You and I both know that Tanner didn't blow up my place. The librarian was not hired by Tanner. Whoever hired her ordered that hit on me. It's gotta be either Lindsay or Sherry, and they have unlimited bank accounts and numerous ways to rid me from the face of the Earth."

"I have to agree with you."

"Right. So I have no home, no refuge, I've lost my mind, and people are trying to kill me. I'm totally ashamed that you're seeing me weak like this. The goddamned PTSD makes me fall into this pit of fear sometimes, especially if something scary happens to me. Normally, it takes me about two or three days to crawl out, but I've never been hit this hard."

Matt sent her an understanding nod. "I know about PTSD. I know what being in mortal danger is like, and I know what it did to my head. I was shot during a really tense standoff with a murderer—not bad, a flesh wound, but it was terrifying. I've never been that scared in my life. Really shook me. For months afterwards. I wasn't good with Fourth of July for a while there."

She could relate. That battle with the Patriots had had the same effect on her. She'd recently gotten to the point where she loved fireworks again. Guess it would be a long time before she'd enjoy them again. Her shoulders relaxed a bit. Matt's understanding made her feel better.

"Do you know what causes your attacks?" he asked.

Hell glanced at her beer bottle. "Really terrifying childhood." She did not want to elaborate.

Matt paused a second, then asked, "Your parents were abusive?"

Hell nodded, wishing she could forget all about her past.

"Were the authorities called in?" he asked gently.

Heaving a huge sigh, she said, "No. We looked like a great, healthy family from the outside. But we couldn't be further from that." She tried to hold back, but the words spilled from her. "Dad's a rage-aholic beast, and Mom was cold and angry. But since I've had PTSD my whole life, I'm normally okay with it. But when over-the-top crap happens to me like when Capasso beat the shit out of me, or I when I was caught in the middle of an urban war zone with Rampart, or some creep shoots at me personally and then blows up my place with a hand grenade, and my affairs are splashed all over the goddamned news—and I know I'm about to get emotionally beaten up by my father and brother-in-law—I just can't take it. I crack."

"I can see why."

"Yeah, and on top of all this crap, now BC falls for me, and I fall for him. Making me even more vulnerable and emotionally wrecked. And then I hire you, a mortal enemy, to help me. What the hell was I thinking?"

For some reason, he barely reacted. His face stayed calm, his eyes clear, his manner strong and weirdly comforting. She felt like she was talking to a priest.

"I'm not your enemy, Hell, I'm your friend. You'll be fine. You just need some sleep."

She sighed and rubbed her arms. "I don't know, man. It's like all the nightmares of my childhood have come true. Someone really is trying to kill me. Someone really is trying to destroy me."

Matt's pain lines appeared briefly. "I'm here to help you, if you'll let me."

Maybe he got the PTSD thing, but he'd never understand what it was like coming from a family like hers. "I can't, Matt."

"Why? Everyone needs help once in a while."

"I don't." She looked down at her lap, ashamed of her past, ashamed of her need.

"Bullshit."

She didn't meet his gaze. "Can't afford to need what I can't ever have."

"You've just been around the wrong people, Hell. There are plenty of people in this world you can trust."

"Ha."

"There are. You just haven't met many yet. And there clearly aren't any in your family. So, when you were a kid, did they beat you, or..."

Hell kept her attention on her hands and wished she could change the subject, but something about Matt was drawing her truth from her. "No. They beat the others."

"Not you?"

She took a long draw off her beer but didn't make eye contact. "No, I sold my soul to make sure they didn't. But there was always a constant threat of violence. Dad was crazy, screaming all the time."

"Do you know why?"

"Yeah. He was being oppressed and undermined by his parents at the family business, so he'd come home and drink and take it out on us."

He winced. "What about your mom? Didn't she try to protect you?"

She heaved a huge sigh. "No and yes. Sometimes. Even though she held that against us, too. She screamed at me once in a huge argument when I was nineteen, 'I've been protecting you from your father since you were two years old!' Like I somehow owed her for that."

He shook his head.

The memories of her past flooded her, and the soul-sucking helplessness she felt as a kid raged back. She fought the darkness that threatened to consume her. Closing her eyes, she hid her face in her hands. Had she ever felt competent to care for herself? Had she ever felt safe?

She fell into silence, wishing her past would just disappear and go away.

"I think it will help you to talk about it, Hell," he said gently. "It will help me help you definitely. But if you can't, that's cool. I don't want to push."

Hell was so sick of the weakness and fear. So tired of the overwhelming exhaustion from fighting on her own for so long. So done with the feeling like all her lifeblood was draining from her.

She glanced at him, and something about his wide, sympathetic face and soulful blue eyes stopped her. The look on his face reflected back the truth she knew deep in her heart. She hadn't deserved the treatment she'd received as a child. Or as an adult for that matter. Beyond that, this man was on her side and wanted to help her.

"You're fine. I'm the mess." Her attention went to her beer.

"Was your father abusive all the time?"

"No. That was, and is, part of the problem. He's also funny and charming. Generous and caring. But then he'll get a bug up his ass and destroy me out of nowhere. Never know when he's gonna erupt. Started in on me when I was a toddler. I used to go to sleep curled into a ball, holding my teddy bear and shaking like hell." She glanced down at the stuffed bear in her lap, and met his gaze. Raising one eyebrow, she said, "Clearly, I've come a long way since then."

His angry expression lightened and he smiled. Then he became serious again. "Did he abuse your mom?"

"No. Just us."

This seemed to surprise him. "Huh. So what was your mom like?"

A moth flitted into her face, and she batted it away. "Basically a princess who thought she'd married the hot rich kid who would provide her with maids and cars and riches beyond her wildest imagination. But instead of being fabulous and having servants and lying around a swimming pool, she found herself a mother of three with a fat, downtrodden, depressed, alcoholic husband. She hated everyone and everything."

The line between his eyes went deep. "Damn, Hell."

She hugged Secret Teddy. "Plus Mom wasn't exactly cuddly. Didn't like touching us or holding us. Left me alone in my room for hours in a playpen or crib. Mom told me once, 'You couldn't let the baby see you when you walked by the door, or they'd want you.' She said it like what she was saying was completely acceptable and not totally psychotic."

Matt paled. "Christ."

Hell withdrew some tissues from her pocket and blew her nose, feeling more centered. "I learned early on that if I wanted love or attention, I had to take care of myself. Or be extra cute and earn her attention. Ergo the theater degree and my pathological need to entertain and please people. Only way I had any value was to be whatever Mom needed me to be. The more I anticipated her needs and met them, the more I got from her. The less I asked for or expected from her, the more I got."

He twisted his lips. "You wonder why some people have children."

Hell uncrossed her legs and recrossed them with her other leg over her knee. A sting of pain came from her wounds, and she hissed. "I know, right? I asked her why she had kids when she hated being a mother so much. She said, 'We didn't think back then, we just did things.'"

He snorted.

"At least my sister was there for me when I was little. She took care of me so much I called her 'Mom.'"

"That's good."

"Thank God, or I'd be a total basket case. I know, weird, she's such a horrid bitch now, but she saved my ass when I was a baby. Then turned on me when she married Congressman Dickhead. Lost her when I was thirteen." Her heart stung, and she increased her hold on the bear.

"I'm sorry."

"Me, too. I really loved her. Really looked up to her. I couldn't believe it when I lost her. I still have a hard time getting my head around it. Ergo the call I made to her when I was in the hospital." Hell took a sip of her beer. "But even Irene couldn't make up for Mom's neglect. Mom is responsible for my whole inability-to-bond-with-or-trust-others shit. It's just like feral animals, if they don't bond properly with a human as a baby, they aren't able to bond with people later. And I didn't bond properly with my mother because she didn't hold me enough. Like my therapist said, 'You can't bond with someone who isn't there.'"

His eyes widened. "Jesus."

She looked down and realized that she had Secret Teddy in a death grip. Big surprise. "In her defense, Mom's mother treated her the same, and so did her mother. I come from a long line of people who don't know how to love each other and whose love receptors were never fully developed. All of us, my mother included, have the hunger for closeness with others with no way to satisfy it. We're all permanently love-starved. Drives us all crazy."

"That's sad."

Her throat was a bit parched from talking and crying. She took a drink of beer, and the cold liquid soothed her. She realized something else was soothing her. Matt listening to her and giving her ground for her pain. "My biggest problem is the gaslighting within the family," she said, gesturing with her beer. "Everyone inside and outside the family has always told me how lucky I am to have such a supportive, amazing family, when the truth is that we're all being ripped to shreds. Plus we all want to believe the happy family myth so badly we perpetuate it. Total 1984 shit. Love is hate, hate is love."

Matt shifted on the bench, stretching out his back. "Still, you moved out of your parents' house a long time ago, Hell. Hasn't your therapist helped you to let go of some of this?"

Hell rolled her eyes and shook her head. "I was so love-starved, and so convinced that I'd hurt my Mom with my birth—and forcing her into this horrid nightmare of caring for me—I was determined to make it up to her, prove my worth, and get her to love me. Prove I was worth loving. So I bought my grandmother's house from the family and moved next door to my parents when I was in my late twenties and became her and Dad's personal slave to redeem myself and earn their love."

His eyes widening, his mouth fell open. *"You lived next door to them?"*

Hell laughed, and then her smile faded. "For thirteen long, arduous, horrible years," she said with revulsion. "Me and Josh. Dumbest thing I've ever done. I thought if I worked hard and made all these sacrifices, they'd all finally love me. But all the move did was reinforce my worthlessness and turn me into my parents' possession. I endured more abuse from my siblings and father than is nearly humanly possible. My therapist said most of her patients who were in situations like mine are all dead. Weed and my need to help my clients has kept me alive." Beer was freezing her hand. She set the bottle on the picnic table next to her.

Matt shook his head. "Damn. But you did wake up and move eventually."

"Yeah. At the time of Josh's death, we were planning on moving because Mom and Dad's incessant demands were killing us. Then Josh died, and Mom and Dad were actually great and supportive for the first month. I thought maybe Josh's death had changed them, and they were finally on my side. But a month after he died, Dad announced I was done grieving, accused me of being selfish and self-indulgent, and demanded I get back to serving his fat ass."

Matt made a loud dismissive noise. "A *month?*"

Hell chuckled. "Yeah, how did he put it? 'Everyone knows any longer than a month of grieving and you're just wallowing in self-pity. If you really cared about anyone other than yourself, you'd just move on.'"

"What?"

She took a sip of her beer. "When that didn't work, he accused me of disgracing Josh's memory. He even said the words, 'Josh would be ashamed of all your moping and mooning.' That finally uncorked me. I screamed at him for a good, long while, then I walked next door, put my house up for rent, and was out in two weeks."

He nodded sharply. "Good for you."

"And as it turned out, it was good for my parents, too. They found out that they couldn't live on their own without my help. Half the reason they were forcing me to care for them was so they could stay in denial and pretend they were still in their forties instead of their eighties. I mean, initially, the whole family freaked out and beat me up for *abandoning Mom and Dad*, quote unquote," she said, doing air quotes. "But Mom and Dad ended up moving into a retirement home with a bunch of their friends, and now they're living the high life with their buddies, drinking and laughing every day."

"Well, that *is* good."

Heaving a sigh, she relaxed back in her chair. "Yeah. But you know something else? A neighbor of mine, Allyn Cook, said the other day when I was bitching about all this crap, 'They may be terrible, but you turned out okay, didn't you?' And he was right. I *am* okay. I like myself. And now that I'm starting to figure out why I'm so terrified all the time and feel so bad when I need something from someone, I know at some point I'll be able to fix myself."

Matt smiled. "Sounds like you're on track. And now that your parents are being cared for, you can keep some distance, right?"

"I wish."

He did a double take. "What?"

Hell shrugged. "They're too old, Matt. I can't do it to them. I just figured out the family dynamics—and how they've affected me and my psyche—in the past six months. They only have a few more years left, and I can't stress them out now by leaving them. They couldn't take it. They depend on me too much. Even if they're horrible, I'm not. No matter what they did to me, I have to answer to my own conscience. I'm not abandoning my elderly parents."

He shook his head and waved his hand. "They're getting plenty of care in that home."

Hell's stomach knotted tighter. "Yeah, but Mom needs me. She's too frail, and too emotionally dependent on me. Dad's this hurricane, and she relies on me to keep her sane. It's a sick relationship, but at this point it's too late to change. I just have to ride it out until they die. So I go and play my role and lie to her and tell her how great it is to see her, and I entertain her. Bring her treats. While Dad and Martin destroy me. Real fun."

"Christ. Sorry, Hell," he said. "At least you're figuring out what's going on in your head and life."

"Thank the Lord. My intellect has always been my saving grace and my way out. But with my shaky foundation, these attacks are far beyond my ability to cope."

He leaned in, shoulders squared. "You need to let me help you."

She stroked her brow, hiding behind her hand. "I don't know how, Matt. I'm so far gone right now I'm having trouble making rational decisions. I'm having difficulty making sense of reality."

He leaned back, but his posture stayed confident. "One step at a time. I know you wanted to jump off the deck here and run when I arrived, but you stayed right here and talked to me no matter how much you wanted to hide. That's a step. You're not crazy, Hell. You've just been through too much. Look, we can take as much time as you need here to stabilize mentally, and you will stabilize. Just don't shut me out, okay? You hired me to help you and protect you. Let me do my job."

Her vision cleared for a moment, and she studied him. He wasn't a monster police detective attacking her. Not a judge in robes sitting high atop his bench peering down at her viciously. Just a nice, open, sweet man offering her his help.

A man she'd just given five grand.

She started laughing.

Matt's face screwed up with confusion.

Hell shook her head, still chuckling. "I'm just so messed up, it's funny. Can't even ask a guy I hired to help me for help. Pathetic."

His expression softened. "Not pathetic—like you said earlier, learned behavior. You did what you had to to survive childhood. And your tools worked, didn't they? You survived a pretty bad situation, didn't you?"

"Yeah."

"So your methods worked, right? Don't beat yourself up for them. You have the awareness. Just allow yourself to ease into a new way of doing things. No one can get through life alone. There are people you can trust in the world. I'm one of them. I don't quit a job once I start. I'm here, and I'm not going anywhere."

Dude was a freaking beacon of light in the storm that was her mind and life. She'd been so lost in Crazy Land she'd forgotten what it was like to be rational. "Okay, now I don't feel stupid for hiring you."

He smiled.

"Sorry, man. It's hell being Hell." A piney-scented breeze blew through the back porch area, chilling her. She held herself tighter.

"You'll be fine. You're a lot more together than you give yourself credit for."

"Ha."

"You are." He leaned back and crossed his leg, resting his ankle on his knee. "I just went through your whole office. I thought you lived in total chaos. Your financial books are immaculate."

"I haven't balanced the checkbook in a month."

He made a mock-shocked face. "Wow."

"No, I know. I keep the tax stuff together. I've always kept my financials in order. Always had a head for numbers."

"Your client files are detailed and organized. All the paperwork that's vital to your work is in order. Your reports to your clients are exemplary. It's your billing system that sucks and your information files that are scattered all over the place."

"I like to do a good job for my clients," she said because she was running out of excuses for screwing herself.

His fatherly/priestly/therapist-y vibe was turned on high. "You have a stack of invoices to get out to clients that total over twenty-five grand."

Her heart gave a hard thump. "Really? That much?" She tried to sound casual and hide her alarm. Twenty-five *grand*? No wonder her checkbook balance was so anemic.

"Yeah."

She sighed heavily and turned her attention to her beer bottle, running her finger around the mouth. "Yeah, most of my clients don't have a lot, and have kids to care for. I hate asking them for money."

Out of her peripheral vision, Matt's intense gaze burned into her. "Do you hate paying your dentist?"

"No. Oh, I know. But these are people who really needed the help."

"Like you do when you go to the dentist," he replied pointedly.

Out of responses, she finally looked at him and made a face and a waving motion with her hand. "Now don't be throwin' all this logic at me."

He smiled. "It's okay to care for yourself, Hell, and it's okay to ask for help. You need to learn how to do both. And right now, it's vital you trust me and let me help you," he said in a firm voice.

She took a big breath, feeling trapped and safer at the same time. "Okay."

"We need to go back to the Bay Area. Now what about BC's bodyguards?"

She shifted in her seat. "I don't know. It was part of the reason I ran. I want out of that whole mess. I love him, but I can't be with a married man."

"He told me he was divorcing his wife. I think he's already filed the paperwork."

Her heart leapt, and she punched her hopes back down to nothing. "Right." Same lies he told her.

"I believed him."

Hell turned to him and looked him directly in the eye. "Let's be real for a minute here. The man is an adulterer. How long do you honestly think he'd be faithful to me? A year? Two, maybe?"

Matt shrugged. "If he's getting all his needs met with you..."

A good man like Matt couldn't understand a how a player like Brad thought. "He might have told you he'd filed the paperwork, but that doesn't mean he did. He's a liar, Matt. Liars lie. I heard the same song and dance from Capasso. Married men string you along forever.

I don't have forever, Matt. I'm in my early goddamned fifties, soon to be in my mid-fifties. I'm not waiting for Brad."

Matt finally nodded with understanding. "Still, overall, I think this thing with Brad was good for you. It means you're getting through your grief over Josh. You're opening up again. That's good."

"Not sure about that." Hell massaged the painful line between her eyes with a forefinger.

He reached over and gripped her forearm. "You'll be okay, Hell." He let go. "And I have to apologize to you. For everything I said to you in that damned interrogation room."

She flipped her hand dismissively. "Matt, you were just doing your job."

"No. I crossed a line with you, and you and I both know it. And I apologize." No animosity on his face, no hardness, and yet his brow and eyes showed slight worry and contrition. He clearly meant what he said.

"Aren't you always that way in interrogations?"

"No, I had it in for you. I'm ashamed to admit it, but it's the truth." He rubbed his forehead and shrugged. "Joe was my partner, and you'd hurt him." Frowning, he gave his head a quick shake. "But it went beyond that. The night before, I'd had an argument with my eldest son. You reminded me of him. The defiance, the anger. He even wore a leather jacket like yours. He'd gotten into this Goth thing and wanted to drop out of school, and I lost it and... Shit. The guys told me you were okay. Even Joe was mad at me for what I did to you. It was clear after the first five minutes you weren't going to give up Billie."

"I had to protect her."

"I know. So I took the anger I had at my son out on you." His mouth curved with disgust.

"You didn't really get to me that bad, I was just tired. And you sounded and acted a little too much like my father."

The pain lines around his eyes deepened. "I'm sorry, Hell. It's not right. What I said to you, or what your father did to you."

She made a dismissive gesture. "Matt, it's all water under the

bridge. But thanks for telling me about your son. Makes sense why
you were so emotional. As usual, people aren't mad at me. It's not
about me at all. My dad is the same way. He's mad at his mother. He
destroys me the way he wishes he could have destroyed her. My sibs
beat me up the way they were beat up. Like we were saying, all
modeled and learned behavior. I just wish I would have woken up
sooner to the nasty patterns and gotten away before Mom got so
dependent on me. I have no idea how to be a good person and
abandon my mother." Her stomach tightened, and her mood took a
dive again. "They are totally going to rake me over the coals for this
stupid sex scandal. Dad's gonna destroy me. Mom will be ashamed of
me. Tons of fun."

"Sorry, Hell. I have no idea how I'd have made it the last few years
without my dad, my wife, my mom, and my sons holding me up."

She snorted. "You're a lot more functional than I am. I'm a basket
case."

"No, you're not. I'd be dead if I were you. I don't have whatever
you have, Hell," he said, gesturing toward her. "That grit. That will to
live. I lost my job and took it like it was the end of the world. When I
see your life and what you've never had and what you've endured and
what you're enduring, it just doesn't compare to what happened
to me."

"You can't compare lives, Matt."

"Yeah, I can. Watching you has been a real wake-up call for me. I
had no idea what I had. Here I've been taking my family for granted,
my wife, my kids, just lost in my own suffering. I needed to stop and
realize how lucky I am. And how lucky I was that you called me."

Straight-faced, she pointed at him. "Now you're going too far."

He chuckled. "You helped me make my mortgage payment this
month, Hell. No one else was calling me. I've got a stink on me that
no one else wants to touch. You know if our situations were
reversed, I would have been overjoyed to deny you the job, and that
makes me sick. You were gracious enough to get past your hate
of me."

She gave a hand shrug. "You were cheap, and I was desperate."

"Maybe initially, but within an hour, you'd lost your anger and were very sweet to me. And you've been nothing but kind ever since."

She lifted one shoulder. "You're a good guy."

"Not to you. Not until now. As much as I pride myself on being an upstanding member of society, I wasn't with you. I haven't been fair to you at all. And you didn't deserve it." The look in his eye was clear, his voice strong.

"It's okay, Matt."

"No, it isn't." He blinked and rested his arm on the picnic table. "You're just such a completely different person than I thought you were. I don't know why I was so blind. You're a really good person, Hell." He sounded like he still found it somewhat surprising.

"Thanks. I try." A feeling of pride welled up inside her. Rare but nice.

"I really admire the way you are with people. They shine when they're around you. Not just your friends but grocery clerks, waitresses, people you don't know, you always joke or laugh or compliment them, and pretty soon you're talking like old friends. Joe can do that, too. I always admired that in him. But you really see the best in people, bring out the best. I...don't really know how to do that."

Hell smiled. "I learned early on to be free with your compliments and stingy with your criticisms."

"I try, but I can see where people could do better. I try not to criticize—and sometimes what I say comes out sounding like it—but I'm really just trying to help people."

No wonder the guys at the station house called him Mr. Persnickety. "I try to manipulate people so they are happy when I'm criticizing them and might actually listen to what I'm saying."

He grinned. "Maybe I should learn how to do that. But I don't know how, so I want to say one more thing here."

"Uh-oh."

His smile widened. "No, it's good. I wanted to say that I think you have genuine talent as a detective, and I'd like to see you build up your career—*and actually bill people*—make some money, and make that business really work for you. Get some people in there to help you."

Hell sighed. "I do have people who help me occasionally, but nothing regular in a while. I just can't deal with it." She took the last long drink of her beer, finishing it.

"We all need help, Hell," he said with an open gesture of his large hands. "It's why we live in tribes and communities. It's why I dedicated most of my life to law enforcement. To help people. Because people need help. It's not a flaw, it's reality. We all need to eat and breathe air. That doesn't make us bad people, it makes us human. You were made to feel ashamed for your basic human needs, which makes no sense. See the illogic of the situation here, Hell. We all need help, we are all interdependent on each other, and there's nothing wrong with that. You aren't weak or wrong or bad because you need help."

It was like Matt opened a whole new previously undiscovered door in her mind. The idea was so radical, so counter to everything she'd learned, she couldn't get her head around it. Asking for help made her a total loser. Asking for help made her a greedy, abusive, self-centered, spoiled-brat user.

He gestured toward her. "You do realize your pathology is completely ironic. What do you do for a living? You help mainly wives of deadbeat dads. Without you, they and their children wouldn't be okay now. You don't look down on them for needing help, do you? You don't think they're flawed because they hired you, do you?"

"Uh..." Unable to make an intelligent comment back because her brain couldn't make the leap yet to accepting his point, she moved on. "Well, I also don't let people close to me because I don't want to get my fucked-upped-ness on them."

"People can take care of themselves, Hell."

Another parry of logic that derailed her. Another totally new concept that made no sense. "Huh. Maybe so. I don't know. I'm still not convinced you're the guy to help me."

"I am. I misjudged you, and you've misjudged me."

She finally made eye contact. "Come on, Matt. Be honest."

"I am," he said simply with very little emotion. "I see it's really our differences of style that has rubbed me the wrong way. I've changed my mind about your morals, your lovers, all that stuff I used to judge so harshly. I didn't see what was really going on. I saw a crazy woman assuaging her pain in the beds of lots of men."

"There's some truth there."

He gave his head a firm shake. "No. You had much more control than I gave you credit for. All your men are nice, responsible men. I saw the relationships were honest. Everything mutual, and no one was committing adultery. Well, except for you and BC. That's an anomaly for you. I can see you don't feel good about it. All the things you do, and have done, for others show your true character. All the rest is bullshit. What I'm trying to say is that I not only admire you, Hell, I respect you." The look in his eyes was steady and true.

Hell had no idea how to respond to this epic turnaround. "Wow."

He raised his brows briefly. "Yeah. And that's something I never thought would happen."

"Me, neither."

"Yeah, because I'm such a stubborn lunkhead at times. And I'm sorry..." He reddened, looked away, and rubbed the back of his neck. Shaking his head, he turned to her. "I have to say this: I take full blame for your apartment getting blown up. I should have been there to protect you. I should have taken control of the situation and done what I thought was right. I knew you needed more protection, but I didn't say anything because my prejudice against you blinded me."

"No, Matt, that was my problem. Not yours."

His serious expression didn't waver. "No, it's mine. I'm ashamed to admit it, but I have to if we're to move forward. I didn't do the job to the best of my ability, and I want to make up for that now. I want to protect you, help you, and get this asshole."

The strength in his gaze made her feel protected and like she wasn't alone. But he shouldn't be taking responsibility for the damned grenade attack.

"Jeez, Matt. I appreciate what you're trying to say here, but it wasn't your fault. Besides, you might have pissed me off if you crowded me too much." He still wasn't convinced. Best to continue on, or they'd be arguing all night. "Look, let's not worry about the past, and deal with the present. A part of me just wants to run."

"Hell, if someone wants you dead, they will succeed eventually if you don't stop them. We have to solve this to protect you."

He was right. Unfortunately. "Okay. I think."

"Trust me, Hell. I won't let you down."

No way did she trust him, but he had tracked her down. He seemed to care. What if he was a caring person? She hadn't met many of them before. How would she recognize one? But she had just spilled her guts to the guy, and all it did was make him open up more to her.

"I mean it, Hell."

She held up her hand. "Give me a minute here." She closed her eyes and concentrated on her breathing. And calming. *Should I accept Matt's help?* she asked the team of voices in her mind.

Yes! several voices practically thundered back.

She chuckled and opened her eyes. "Well, that was pretty clear. Felt that one all the way to my bones."

"What?"

She sent him a half smile. "My gut is telling me to accept your help."

His shoulders and face relaxed. Open, shiny energy emanated from him. Like his steel walls had fallen down, and she saw inside, and there was a very sweet, good, Catholic boy there.

Matt was honorable. He'd managed a successful career, a thirty-year marriage, and he'd raised three accomplished sons. Not exactly a usual friend of hers.

Maybe the Universe had answered her prayers.

Either that or Satan was playing more tricks on her.

"So it's really late, and I'm in no shape to drive back to the Bay Area," she announced.

"I rented the cabin next door."

She pursed her lips. "Awfully sure of yourself, weren't you?"

"Lack of self-confidence has never been one of my problems."

Snorting, she thumbed behind her. "You want some food?"

"You have food?" Incredulous.

She laughed. "I *am* trying to take care of myself. I have chicken soup I made today, macaroni salad from Granzella's, and a bunch of veggies in microwave bags from Trader Joe's. Plus enough beer to survive the Apocalypse."

He grinned. "I'd love a bowl of chicken soup, and a beer."

"So would I."

They stood. Her hip and leg burned, and she winced and groaned.

"You okay?" he asked.

"Fun with healing. I'll be fine."

Matt nodded and allowed Hell to walk ahead of him. She started to move past him but stopped and gave him a quick hug, then clapped him on the shoulder. "Thanks, man."

He gave her a smile that warmed her to the core. "You're welcome."

Hell walked into the cabin and a weird feeling overtook her. Was it...? No. It couldn't be. She couldn't be feeling hopeful and safe, not under the circumstances. Must be the beer.

A voice in her head begged to differ. She slapped the voice away. No matter what Matt had said, she couldn't depend on him or open up to him any further. People were untrustworthy. Period. Especially straight, upright Catholic boys. He was merely a temporary Band-Aid on a giant gaping wound.

But as she took the soup out of the fridge—and Matt made a joke about the pile of candy and cookies on the table—she couldn't help but admit the human Band-Aid was giving her some mighty relief.

CHAPTER 22

SUNDAY, MARCH 13, 2011, 8:12 A.M.

Hell sat opposite Matt in a booth at Shari's Restaurant in Red Bluff, drinking coffee while they waited for their food. The decaf was fresh and tasted great.

Matt gestured with his cup. "Meant to tell you last night, I talked to Joe."

Hell's heart did a little kick. "Yeah?"

"Really don't think he did it."

Hell relaxed. She trusted Matt's judgment. Even if she didn't trust him.

Matt continued, "He admitted he'd been watching your place lately. Worried about you. And he copped to what he did to you a few years back."

Hell's eyebrows went high, and she leaned in. "You confronted him about it?"

"Yeah."

"How did that go?"

Matt gave a hand shrug, and the relaxed look on his face reassured her. "He was embarrassed. You really got under his skin. He admitted he'd gone a little nuts for a while there. He said you were very discreet, and there were only a couple guys you were seeing. He'd made up a lot of the story to get my sympathy."

Her body tensed from the memories of her frustration and fear. Not a fun chapter of her life with a goddamned cop stalking her. Police could get away with anything. Especially against someone with a prison record.

Hell made an exasperated noise at the back of her throat. "I told him up front that I wasn't into monogamy. I made it plain. I told him I had other lovers."

"He didn't believe you. Not until he saw it with his own eyes, and then he was pissed."

"What an idiot."

"He has issues with interpersonal relationships. We had our problems. He doesn't listen well. Good man, good heart, great cop. But he sometimes only hears what he wants to." Matt's phone rang, and he looked at the number, then at her. "Collins. You want to talk to him?"

"No." She'd already ignored five calls and ten texts of his so far that morning.

"Okay." He put his phone away. "So what's the plan, Hell? Where are you going once we get back? My offer still stands."

"Dude, you're sweet, but I have to smoke pot, and I'm not doing that at your house."

"So where will you go? I mean, I know you don't want to, but you may want to accept BC's offer of protection."

"Nope. I want nothing to do with him. I can take out some money from my retirement account and pay for a few months of a bodyguard. I may do that if I really can't get any sleep. But first, I'm going to try staying at various hotels. Live out of my car and decide last minute on accommodations. If I don't know where I'm staying, they won't know where I'm staying."

"Unless they follow you."

"I'm pretty good at losing tails. And I'll rotate my plates, the junk in my back window, and the bumper stickers." She sipped her coffee. "Plus Death will alert me if I show up on any networks."

He chuckled and shook his head. "Whatever makes you feel safe. And as long as I know where you are."

"You bet. Under this one condition: you don't tell BC or anyone."

"Okay." His gaze settled on her. "So what are you going to do about him?"

She massaged the sore muscles of her forehead. "Avoid him for right now. I'm barely together. I couldn't handle that scene."

Her phone rang. Dad. Her gut clenched, and she winced and instinctively recoiled, hunching her shoulders. "Speaking of not being able to handle scenes."

"BC?"

"No. My asshole father. No way am I gonna answer it. Good, it's going to voice mail." She breathed a sigh of relief.

"Is it possible he might have information about the case?"

"No. This has to be about the slut story that's making the rounds."

"Earthquake in Japan and the nuclear threat kind of wiped you out of the news. Maybe they didn't hear."

Hell made an exasperated noise. "Are you kidding? I have a huge family. Someone probably told them, most likely Martin. Anything to get my father yelling at me is good for him." She looked at her phone. "But you do have a point about the case. And I didn't tell them that I was leaving the Bay Area." She went to her Messages box, sifted through the hefty list, and discovered ten earlier voice mails from Dad. Her heart rate jumped. *Mom was hurt!* "Damn, I missed a whole bunch of his calls. Crap, I hope Mom's okay. Her heart isn't good. I should have checked this sooner." She chose his latest message. "I'll let you hear it in case it pertains to the case."

Her dad's voice came booming out of her phone. "Goddamn you! You call me back! This is your father, and this is the tenth fucking call I've made, and you'd better call me right back! I'm furious with you!"

Her muscles went to battle stations, and she fought the inclination to dive under the table. Or throw the phone into her water glass.

Well, at least Mom was okay.

Matt's eyebrows went high.

Instead of shutting off her cell, she decided to let Matt hear the whole message. Most people didn't truly believe her about her father until they heard one of his tirades. "All the papers and TV stations are calling us, asking about your goddamned sex life! How many goddamned gigolos did you sleep with? Sounds like you were fucking a goddamned football team! I didn't raise you to be some round-heeled tramp! Some two-bit whore! Call me back!" Click.

Each word knifed her gut no matter how hard she tried to protect herself. In nearly every interaction with him, Dad managed to hurt her. But Dad in Full Asshole Mode was the hardest. She hoped her appetite would return before she received her food.

Matt's mouth dropped open, and his eyes went wide. Then his ears went back, his lip curled, and his shoulders hardened. "You almost die, and this is all he cares about? Doesn't he understand someone is trying to kill you?"

"Welcome to my world." Hell couldn't believe how awesome Matt made her feel. To see the true mirror of Dad's abuse was so healing. Instead of everyone taking Dad's side, instead of people blaming her for Dad being mean to her, finally, someone saw the truth. Dad was the one at fault.

Matt was fired up. "Here you are up in some cabin *alone*—shaking and terrified— and he can only think of hurting you more? Like you had control over the media and someone bombing you? He didn't even talk to you first to find out the truth? Just tried and convicted you based upon the garbage in the news?"

Hell smiled, basking in all this lovely truth. "Dad's not really into reality."

"I can't believe he called his own daughter a tramp and a whore," he seethed. "I hope you aren't listening to that bullshit."

She shrugged, realizing that Matt was more upset than she was. She was so used to the abuse, nothing that came out of her dad's mouth surprised her anymore. "I committed a cardinal sin. I made him look bad in public. Dickhead. Like I'm gonna call him back. Right away, Dad. Can't wait to get more of that love and support." She continued scrolling through her message list. "Looks like my brother-in-law left a message just twenty minutes ago. I can't wait to hear his precious character assassination."

"That's Irene's husband, the congressman? Is he as bad as she is?"

"Worse. Check this out. You think my dad is bad, here's a little window into my dear brother-in-law's love for me."

He held up his palm, his brow furrowed. "You don't have to, Hell."

"Oh, no, I'm loving this. You have no idea how much you're helping me right now." Hell hit the Play Message button and retreated far within herself. A part of her clutched an imaginary Secret Teddy.

"Elly? This is Martin. I'm sorry for what happened to you with the bombing and all, but you have to admit you brought the situation all on yourself. I mean, what do you expect when you're fucking all these scumbags?"

"Holy shit," Matt said.

"Isn't he a sweetie pie?" Hell bit out with a smirk.

"The papers are full of your sexual exploits! There was only one decent man in the whole bunch, and congratulations, you've permanently stained him. You've ruined Brad Collins. Jesus Christ, what you've done to me, you stupid bitch. His father, Jack Collins, practically put me in office!"

"That's right, he did." Hell giggled. A silver lining!

"And you repay me and him by seducing his married son and ruining his life? This could cost me a future election! Did you forget that I am being groomed for the presidency? Without Collins' money and support, I can't win! You could have just cost me my entire political career, you thoughtless slut!"

Her gut twisted, and the pain built. "Okay, that was a little below the belt."

"You can turn it off," Matt said, his forehead a mass of wrinkles, his jaw set hard.

"No, let's listen to the whole thing." She needed to associate the horror and alarm on Matt's face with her brother-in-law's tirade. That was the proper reaction. Not acquiescence. Not shame. Not laughter. Horror.

"Your nymphomania is infecting the whole family like an AIDS epidemic, and I'm going to put a stop to it! You are not to come near my family again! You don't contact my kids, you don't drive by my house, you are dead to us!"

"Good," Hell said and meant it.

"God forgive me for saying this, but it would have been the best thing for me and this family if that bomb had killed you."

A hard punch to her heart and gut took all the breath from her lungs. Hell clutched her chest. "Whoa."

Matt gasped, his expression blank from incredulity.

She couldn't believe her brother-in-law had actually spoken the words. He'd actually told her he wished she were dead. Wow. Now there's some truth for ya. Hideous truth.

"Your nieces are ashamed of you. We're all ashamed of you," he continued, sounding like he was foaming at the mouth. "And I'm sure Josh is, too, wherever he is. I'm just glad he's not alive to see the depths you've sunk to." Beep.

Hell felt smaller, expendable, worthless. Like her world had turned desolate. Like she was standing alone on an empty battlefield with nothing but burned-out shells of buildings and piles of ashes surrounding her. She fought the tears and rubbed her stomach to try to ease the agony. She honestly had no one and nothing. No family, no husband, no support. Only enemies who wanted to hurt her or wished she were dead. "That asshole. That horrible wretched asshole."

THE PAIN ON HELL'S FACE SAID IT ALL. MATT COULDN'T GET HIS HEAD around the comments. His heart hurt for her. All he wanted to do was hold her. Reassure her. "Jesus Christ, what a bottom-feeder. You don't listen to that, Hell," he said, pointing at her forcefully. "You erase that message and forget everything he said. You don't need that poison in your mind."

His words had little effect on her. She looked like a beaten, abandoned, four-year-old waif. "I have to keep it, Matt, so I don't forget.

Because I will forget. I'll go to Christmas, and that bastard will get me again. I have to get better at distancing myself from the abuse. Not let it get to me. Give up hope that these people will ever be nice, give up hope of ever being loved by them, and go in there with my shields up and my armor intact. I've been trying, but I keep failing."

"You aren't failing anything. They are failing you. You have to get away from them, Hell."

"I can't. Not while Mom's still alive." Tears ran down her cheeks.

"Doesn't she know how much your father and brother-in-law hurt you?"

"No. She's too focused on herself. No one in the family understands how much I hurt because I make sure they don't. If I try to protect myself from the abuse or react to it, I get blamed. The majority of my family are mean to me, and the minority that isn't pretends the abuse isn't happening. So I end up getting beaten up by everyone."

His gut burned, and he longed to take away her pain. How would you make it without your family? Not only did she lack her family's support, they actively attacked her. Tried to hurt her as much as they could. How would you survive that? "Forget about them, Hell, and start your life over. You have great friends and Joanne. You can rebuild your life."

She sighed heavily. "As soon as Mom and Dad are gone, I will. Yeah, thank God for Joanne. She's the only one who gets it. But I'll be fine, Matt. I've made it this far. I won't let those bastards win." The look in her eye was that of a wounded warrior, but one who hadn't given up the battle. She might be down, but there was still that strong part of her that would never say die.

His admiration for her grew. When she got away from her family, she would heal. Maybe this whole experience would be the catalyst that finally pushed her into her corner and got her out of the situation sooner.

But my God. Leaving your whole family. He couldn't even face thinking about it. He'd be absolutely lost. No Christmases? No

Thanksgivings surrounded by all the people who loved you and supported you and were so happy to see you coming through the door? How the hell would you survive? He'd almost lost his mind along with his job and reputation, and his brother and father, plus Patty and the boys, had kept him together. Kept him strong. So did his faith. How would you find the strength to survive if all you had to rely on was yourself?

Hell took a sip of her coffee with a trembling hand. "God clearly put me here to test me. But She/He/It has severely overestimated my capabilities. Sometimes I think the load is too much for me to bear."

She wiped her eyes, and his instinct to protect her became overwhelming. He'd only heard tirades like that on the job in broken homes. Not from supposedly upstanding congressmen. What a horrible man. Of course, Hell's father was in the same class: lower than dirt.

Matt thought of his father when he'd broken the news to him about his felony charges. Dad had said he believed in him and reassured him that God wouldn't have chosen him for the challenge if he couldn't handle it. That there was a reason for the betrayal, and eventually it would reveal itself. In the meantime, he'd rise above the muck and make a success of his new path.

If it weren't for Dad, he wouldn't be the man he was. If it weren't for Dad's guidance, he had no idea where he'd be.

Hell listened to a few more messages, the look behind her eyes haunted and hollow, and then hung up. "I was right. I have nobody but Joanne and Frieda. And I can't let them near me right now for their protection. God, who'd figure that the worst part of this grenade attack was not that I almost got killed and my apartment got destroyed but that I lost all my privacy. Now I'm Queen Slut. Mother of All Whores. As if things couldn't get any worse, now everyone either wants to beat me up for my sex life or wishes I was dead."

Matt reached over and gripped her forearm. "He was just trying to hurt you," he said with a squeeze. He let go and sat back. "This will all blow over, Hell. If your parents are as old as mine, they'll forget as soon as the papers do."

"I hope you're right. Let's move on," she said, putting away her phone. "I need to focus."

He was so glad he wasn't her. Once he got his career back on track, he'd be dialed. Everything would be perfect again. The machine would be back online.

He couldn't imagine her world. The chaos. The loneliness. Even though he could relate to a bit of it. Being the only truly moral person in the department had isolated him. When he was being set up, he hadn't seen it coming. No one had warned him.

Trusting the wrong people had been his downfall. But at least he knew how to trust.

Hell didn't. Because she didn't have anyone she could trust.

Sunday, March 13, 2011, 4:20 p.m.

HELL WAS DROOLING EXHAUSTED BY THE TIME SHE CHECKED INTO THE Doubletree in Burlingame. A hotel she'd picked mainly because of the fresh-baked warm cookie they give you upon check-in.

As she settled into her room, her phone rang. Matt. She put the phone to her ear and resumed loading her plug-in cooler with Heinekens. "Miss me already? I'm touched."

He snorted. "Yeah."

"Sherry wasn't home?" She stood, and a muscle in her back twinged. Rubbing the sore spot, she limped over to a chair and carefully sat down. The wounds on her leg stung, and she winced. Clearly time for more painkillers.

"Nope. Gone to her mother's in Marin. We're watching Lindsay, and she's still at the top of the list. But we still have to consider all the options, like your boyfriends. I know you don't think any of them did it, but I still want to clear them, okay? Plus they might have information we could use."

Hell stretched to one side and shifted her weight, trying to find a comfortable position on the big overstuffed chair. "You're right, they do. I just got off the phone with Mike and Dave. Both saw the blonde yoga woman who'd hired the librarian. Blonde ponytail, black yoga outfit, white-and-red cap, skinny, toned frame. She'd totally stuck out and had been completely incongruent with her surroundings. Went to one of Dave's performances at a nightclub and hung around Mike's tattoo shop, looking at his portfolio, but never scheduled an appointment. Both saw her again in subsequent days at fast-food joints, staring at them and not eating the food. They'd both gotten pretty creeped out. Mike said he'd tried to approach her, but she'd disappeared before he could confront her."

"So again, she wanted to be seen. Which both implicates and puts doubt on Lindsay. While she confessed on several occasions that she stalked you and BC, she didn't want to be seen in either of those two instances. Unless this is part of an intimidation plan to get you to break up with BC or vice versa."

Hell delicately scratched a super-itchy spot on her leg where some shrapnel was working its way to the surface. "Possible."

Out the window next to her, a plane flew low over the Bay on its descent into San Francisco Airport. Hell wished she could just hop a flight and escape her entire life.

Matt cleared his throat. "What about your other guys?"

Hell shrugged. "Jase has been out of town for the last two weeks on a case in San Diego and hasn't seen or heard anything. Roman is out of the country, and has been during the whole deal. My other three guys—Hans, William, and Frederick—haven't been in the San Francisco Bay Area in four months: two live in Europe, and one lives in New York. So that takes care of that."

"What about Capasso? Did Death clear him?"

Her body tightened, and she gripped the phone harder. She wished she never had to see Marco or talk to him again. "Not yet, but like we discussed at my cousin's house, he has the least motive. I wish I could send you to interview him, but you're not supposed to know about us."

"Yeah, I don't think he'd be very open to talking to me seeing as how I jailed several of his men. I know you don't want to, but you need to talk to him yourself and make sure he's not involved."

Her stomach balled. "Yeah, I know."

"Sorry."

"Don't be. We have to eliminate him."

"Why don't you get some rest today and talk to him later," Matt said. "I'll come by there around ten tomorrow morning, and we can make our next plan of attack."

"Perfect. See you then."

"Hydrate and get plenty of sleep, right?"

"Yep. Thanks, hon." She clicked off with a slight warm feeling welling up inside her. Matt was a rock. She wished she could hire him full time.

Hell felt guilty about not returning the thirty phone calls, million emails, texts, and Facebook messages from her clients and friends, so she made a quick fake Facebook post. "Thanks for all the well wishes and inquiries about my health. I'm doing fine. I should be back to work soon." Total. Lie.

One last call to her cousin to make lunch plans the next day, and Hell was done. Yay! Time to rest.

As she moved her thumb to turn off her phone, it buzzed in her hand. Roman Jagger's smiling picture greeted her. His wide blue eyes, carved face, and ripped chest made her heart skip a beat as usual, but her body's reaction didn't last. Damn that billionaire!

Roman was her nicest boyfriend. Super hottie and a total sweetheart. A little young—thirty-seven—but mature beyond his years. She wished she loved him as much as she loved that idiot Brad.

"Roman, baby, how are you?" she said cheerfully, assuming her upbeat companion persona. "I haven't heard from you or seen you in six months."

"How am I? How are you?" His rough, low voice was fraught with worry. Surprising yet heartwarming. "Burke just called me and told me what happened." Burke Cherlenko, his coworker at Rampart Security.

She made a dismissive puffing noise. "Oh, I'm fine."

"Bullshit. I want to come out there, but I'm stuck here for another few months."

"Where's here?"

"Can't say. Burke wanted me to pass along a message from him and Rampart: you need anything, give him a call. Captain, Rollin, and he are in the Bay Area. I'm sending you Burke's new number."

She'd had the most overly dramatic affair with Burke ten years before, soon after Rampart had kidnapped her. Charming bastard. A hugely decorated veteran, he'd been fun but totally crazy with PTSD from serving in Afghanistan. Rarely slept and had turned into a controlling dickhead. "Somehow I don't think I need a crazy mofo to help protect me from another crazy mofo."

Roman laughed. "Burke's changed. Really mellowed out."

"Ha."

"He just got married."

Hell burst out in belly laughs. "Good one."

"No, really."

Hell gasped, floored. "That mercurial Lothario player? Burke got *married*? This is *Burke Cherlenko* we're talkin' about, right?"

"Yeah. He married Sam Murdock."

"What? Sam?" Hell pictured the fiery redhead giving Burke hell. "Oh, my God, that might actually work. She's a wild woman. Partied with her on many occasions. She's my neighbor Emma's best friend. She'll kick his ass."

Roman gave a short laugh. "He needs it kicked. Give him a call, okay? They were all worried when they heard. Even Captain."

Carter Blackstone, AKA Captain America, the CEO and fearless leader of Rampart. Hell had tangled with him on countless occasions. "Right. Dude thinks I'm an immoral blight on law enforcement."

"Down deep he really likes you, Hell. He's just not used to people questioning his authority."

"He needs it questioned. Look, tell them I'm fine. Really, I am."

"Let me guess, you're alone in a hotel room, clutching your teddy bear, smoking pot, and shaking."

Spooky how well he knew her. "Nope."

"Liar. Could you do me a favor and stay alive for another few months until I come home? And will you please call Burke?"

"I'm fine. But if I need Rampart, I'll call 'em. Right now, I have it all handled. Do your job. Save the world. I'll be here when you get back."

"You are the hardest person to help. Damn, I miss you, Hell."

"I will. And I miss you, too." Ish. Damn it, she used to really love this kid. Stupid Brad the Brain Poisoner!

She hung up and collapsed back onto the bed. Exhausting. Such a brilliant idea to date a mercenary whose sole purpose in life was to rescue damsels in distress. Thank God Roman was stuck in some foreign country. That's all she'd need.

While she was touched that Burke was still fond enough of her to care about her, no way would she allow Rampart Security to help her. They had bigger things to worry about than one demented private detective.

No more phone calls! She let out a long breath and flicked on the iPhone's screen to finally turn it off.

The phone buzzed in her hand. Marco Capasso's name appeared on screen. Her gut crunched tight, and she shuddered. Was he behind her attack? He'd called the day before, but she hadn't responded because she was too afraid. But she had to know. Besides, she'd promised Matt.

She tried to get her thoughts straight and held herself tight. "Hey, M."

"What the fuck is going on, Hell? A fuckin' hand grenade? Are you okay? You need me to come get you?"

Adrenaline dumped into her system, and she almost threw up. Holy crap. Was this part of his plan? Blow up her apartment, then come and rescue her?

"Hell? You there?"

"Yeah, sorry. No, I'm cool." She rocked back and forth, trying hard to maintain her composure. Even if he wasn't behind the bombing, she couldn't let him know how far gone she was, or he'd show up and send her right over the cliff.

"How are you?"

She couldn't completely lie, or he wouldn't believe her. "Not good."

"Poor girl. Let me help you."

Turn this around! "I'm crawling with cops. I can't put you in that kind of danger."

"Fuck the cops, I can provide better protection."

"You do not need them around you. I won't do that to you."

He chuckled. "Her place gets blown up, and all she can think about is protecting me. One of a kind, Hell. Love you, girl."

"Love you, too."

Wait. How did he know she still needed protection? Tanner's arrest was all over the news. Only reason he'd know is because he was behind the attack. A chill came over her.

"So why don't you think it's this army vet kid, Tanner?" he asked.

"How do you know I don't think that?"

"Because you're deep in hiding, and you sound totally freaked out." Like it was all so obvious. "Besides, how much evidence was found on that kid? Just from the news, you can tell he's being set up."

Amazing how Marco could sound innocent and guilty at the same time. "Yeah. I think he's been framed. But don't worry about me, I'll figure it out. I'm hiding pretty good."

"Is that *billionaire* helping you?"

"No."

"You told me you were done with him."

"I am."

"I mean before. Were you just blowing smoke up my ass?"

She tucked into the fetal position, her heart pounding. She forced her voice to be strong. "No. He tracked me down a couple times, and I saw him because I want his contacts so I can work less and charge more to rich clients."

He laughed.

She relaxed a bit, stretching out on the bed. "But now I think the threat may be coming from him."

"I can look into it."

"Don't worry. I have people."

"Yeah, fucking Sinclair the ex-cop douchebag. I've been meaning to call you and chew your ass for that. What the hell happened to your brain, girl?" he demanded.

She steadied her voice and accessed her practiced excuse. "I know he messed you over. It's part of the reason I hired him," she said in a surprisingly cavalier tone. Good. "To get even with him for you and me. It's been a total blast subjugating him and torturing him. I mean, how could I resist shoving his failures in his face? He came crawling to me for the job. Made me feel awesome. Total Karma, man. Plus he's super cheap, and he's got a little talent. I think he can help me."

Marco gave a good, long, hearty laugh.

Hell sighed with relief.

"Okay, now I see your angle," he said. "Why did I doubt you, Hell? You're rich, girl. Fuckin' rich. Give that bastard hell."

"I am."

"Too funny. Still, I'd like to help you out. If you came and lived with me, no one would bother you."

Hell gasped as if the idea was so awesome she couldn't stand it while trying to withhold a long bellow of terror.

Dance and dance fast, Trent!

"I am not putting you in danger," she said in her no-bullshit tone. "You have too many people dependent on you to get mixed up in my drama. Think of your kids and your other ladies. And your business. You have enough to worry about."

There was a long silence, and Hell almost passed out from fright. If he insisted, there would be nothing she could do but go along with him.

"You're right, baby. I hate it, but you're right. I've already got the Feebies up my ass. I can't afford to attract any more attention than I already am. Besides, they'd frame me if I got close to you, just to bring me down. Then whoever that bastard is who's after you would get ya. Can't stand that thought. Look, I'll do what I can from my end. Someone knows something."

"Please don't get involved with this. Honestly, I'd never forgive myself if something happened to you."

"Love you, girl. Always loyal to me, aren't you?"

"Always." *You psycho fuck.*

"You'll call me if you need something. Say the word and I'm there. And when it's all done, come by. I miss you. Like I said before, I want to see you more often. Like we used to."

She choked back puke. "That'd be awesome."

"Love you, baby. Ciao."

"Love you, too. Bye, M."

Hell hung up, turned off the phone, and broke out in sobs. Her life was way too much to handle. Was that all an act, or was Capasso behind her attack?

In her twisted state of mind, she just couldn't tell. All she knew was that she was sick of everything. Goddamned Mafia dons and billionaires trying to control her, everyone slut-shaming her and blaming her for the bombing, while some asshole was still trying to kill her. If she didn't have such a strong sense of self-preservation, she'd end the whole mess. A bullet to the brain, and she'd have total peace. Tempting.

After calming down, she curled up with some room service and tried to watch a movie. BC kept intruding on her thoughts. She knew at some point she'd actually have to have a conversation with him, but not while she was teetering on the precipice of sanity. The night before, she'd gotten the first few hours of real sleep since her apartment had blown up, and only because Matt was sleeping next door.

She tried to eat some roasted chicken and Caesar salad, but her mouth and stomach weren't cooperating.

Time for an appetite enhancer. Hell stood on the toilet and smoked her one-hitter pipe, carefully and slowly blowing the smoke into the fan in the ceiling. Which was annoying, but she couldn't afford to get kicked out of the hotel for weed, even if she was smoking it legally.

A knock came on her door.

Her heart leaping into her throat, she jumped down from the

toilet and stared in horror at the back of the bathroom door. *Mayday! Mayday!* She wanted to dive under the sink. *Who was it? Who had found her?*

Her whole body trembled, and sweat broke out all over. They were going to kill her. They'd found her, and they were going to murder her. She could jump out the window. No, tenth floor, too far up. She had to call 911.

Flinging open the bathroom door, she ran to her bedside table, dropped her paraphernalia, grabbed her phone, and turned it on. She started to punch in 911 when she stopped herself.

Wait. Hold on. Was this an appropriate reaction? Were her fears out of control?

What if it was one of the hotel staff? No, she had the *Do Not Disturb* sign out.

Her pulse whooshed in her ears. The food threatened to make a comeback. Assassins!

Another knock came on the door, this time more insistent.

Shaking, she huddled by the bed, frozen with fear.

Who knew she was there?

Capasso! She was dead!

Wait. Capasso wouldn't dare, not with the threat of the cops.

Maybe Roman had found out her location and had sent Burke. Damn, she didn't want to deal with this!

What about Matt? Could be him. Her shoulders relaxed, and a bit of her brain seated. At least Burke or Matt wouldn't kill her.

A super-strong knock. Whoever it was sounded impatient. Maybe Matt had found out something.

She hesitantly snuck up to the door and checked through the peephole.

BC.

Gasping and clutching her chest, she reeled back away from the door. "Shit!" Her vision blurred with tears, and she stumbled against the bed and sat, wrapping her arms around herself in a death grip. "No way," she whispered. *How did he find her?*

He knocked again. "Hell, I know you're in there. Answer the door."

She curled up in a ball and shut her eyes tight. She couldn't take another powerful man hurting her. Marco, now Collins? A surge of nausea sent the food up her throat. She swallowed hard.

"Hell, I mean it. Open the door. We have to talk."

She rocked on the bed, her body shaking harder. Nowhere safe to hide. Nowhere safe to go. She began hyperventilating.

"Hell, open the fucking door! I'll keep yelling until security gets here."

Tears ran down her cheeks. Terror overwhelmed her. She opened her eyes and frantically scanned the area for a hiding place but found none. The room darkened and became ominous. The walls began to undulate and move in on her.

"Hell? Answer me!"

All at once, she was off the bed and at the open door. Her vision was so blurry she couldn't see. All she knew was that she had to protect herself. She had to attack and get rid of the predator.

"You have to stay away from me!" she screamed at full volume. "You're killing me!"

From what she could tell, BC looked blown away. Eyes big, face white, mouth open. "Hell, what happened to you?"

"Truth happened to me! Get away from me, and stay away! I never want to see you again!"

"Jesus Christ, you've lost it," he said to himself. "Hell, listen to me, I love you and—"

"You don't love me, you love *fucking* me! I'm not your whore! I'm a respectable person who deserves respect! Not some back-alley, double-dealing, sneaking-around bullshit!"

BC pulled at his collar and looked around the hallway. "Hell, could we please talk inside?"

"No. There's no talking going on here. There's only you leaving."

"Hell, I don't know what happened between now and the last time I saw you, but you're not okay, and you need help. When was the last time you ate? Have you slept?"

Her body heated so hot she broke out in a sweat. "Don't you pull that caring crap on me, you asshole!"

Despite his blurred image, she could tell that his expression was pure worry. "But, Hell, I do care about you. I love you. You're my future."

Fury poured from her center, and she had to stop herself from pounding his face in. "Stop lying to me! Stop hurting me! You used my love against me just so you didn't lose your fuck-hole! Because that's all I am to you is a fuck-hole!"

Hell's rage cleared her vision. She'd never seen this kind of pain on his face before. Like his whole family had died in front of him.

Her gut seared in agony, and she blacked out for a split second, completely emotionally overwhelmed. The one thing in the world she couldn't stand was hurting someone. Especially someone she loved.

Nausea slammed her. She spun and raced for the toilet. She lost the meager amount of food she'd been able to down earlier. Images of being old and alone in a derelict apartment filled her mind. BC next to a hot young blonde. A collar around her neck with Marco holding the leash. She couldn't stop barfing.

Finally, the puking melted into sobbing, and she sunk down next to the toilet and wailed.

All she wanted to do was love people, but all she'd done was hurt them. She'd never find peace. She'd never find love. Doomed to this cycle of agony for eternity. Why wouldn't God just let her die?

Something touched her leg. Terror filled her. She screamed, reared back, and smashed her head against the tiled wall. Pain cracked through her skull, and she cried harder.

BC was crouched down near her, his face drawn down, his eyes full of worry. "Hell, Jesus."

She hid her face in the crook of her arm. "Go away, just go away," she sobbed.

"I'm not leaving you like this. Holy shit, your leg is bleeding. I gotta call for help."

Her fury returned with a vengeance, and her tears vanished. She pulled her arm away and faced him. "You do and I call the cops on you and get a restraining order!"

"I—"

"Can't you see you're tearing me apart? Can't you see I'm not safe? I finally find this place and feel a teeny bit safe, and you come here to destroy me. I can't take the pain! I love you, and I can't have you!"

"Yes, you can have me, I'm right here."

"No, I can't. You're already committed to another woman, a woman you have no intention of leaving! I don't want a married man unless he's married to me. And that is never going to happen with you, so get the hell out. Now! I mean it!"

She stood, grabbed him, and shoved him out the bathroom door. He tried to fight her, but she pushed him through her entryway, out the door, and into the hallway. She pointed toward the elevators. "You get out, and you stay out. Of my life forever!"

With a pained, exasperated look on his handsome face, he cried, "I'm leaving Sherry! I want to marry you! I filed for the proceedings, but Sherry's lawyers countered with a totally unexpected move! I can win, I only need a little more time!"

A bomb of fury exploded inside her, nearly blowing her head off. It took all her strength not to wrap her hands around his neck and strangle him. "Liar!"

She slammed the door, but he stuck his foot in at the last second and pushed it open. "Hell, don't! You're sick, and you need me!"

"You wanna see me again, then show me the divorce papers!" she snarled. "But we both know you don't have the balls to leave Sherry, so *fuck off!*"

He tried to say something, but she pushed hard on his chest, sending him reeling backwards, and closed the door in his face.

She locked the door, fell against it, and slid to the floor in a heap.

BC pounded and yelled, but the noise barely registered.

Wrapping her arms around her knees, she plunged down a very, dark, deep hole.

While she'd never have the guts to kill herself, she desperately wished that she'd fall asleep that night and never wake up.

Monday, March 14, 2011, 10:05 a.m.

AFTER A LONG, HORRIBLE NIGHT OF TRYING TO KEEP FOOD AND LIQUIDS
inside her, Hell awoke to Matt knocking on her door. She cracked the
door and told him she was too sick to work or talk, and to come back
the next day. He looked incredibly worried about her, but she shut
the door in his face and staggered back to bed.

She cancelled her noon lunch date with her cousin with a short
text and ordered breakfast from room service. She managed to get
down an egg and some toast. Housekeeping made a welfare check
shortly after the food arrived, and she pretended to be fine. But by the
alarmed expression of the housekeeper, she knew the older Filipino
lady didn't buy her story. But the woman did leave her alone.

She'd rarely felt this sick. Heart sick, fear sick, or physically sick.
A part of her was concerned about the two big wounds on her leg and
hip, but she didn't have it together enough to clean them out. Since
she hadn't been able to consistently eat, she hadn't been able to keep
down the pain meds or the antibiotics. She hoped she'd get some rest
that morning, a bit more food, then later on she'd take care of the
shrapnel wounds and find a new hotel. But at the moment, the best
she could do was sip on some orange juice to restore her electrolytes.

After draining the OJ glass, Hell fell into fitful sleep.

She was hot. Really hot. Her ears rang, and her head pounded. So
overheated. Sweat pooled between her breasts as she lay on top of the
covers. Her tank top and pajama bottoms stuck to her skin. No air in
the room. She breathed more deeply, and faster, but still couldn't get
enough oxygen. Stifling.

Why couldn't she focus? Everything looked pixilated and wavy.
Curtains were moving like they were in the wind, but the windows
didn't open, and there was no breeze in the room.

Did someone dose her with LSD?

The bed wrenched violently, and she fell headlong into an inky, black nothingness.

CHAPTER 23

MONDAY, MARCH 14, 2011, 10:41 A.M.

M att rubbed the back of his aching neck, his stomach gnarled, as he drove to Collins' estate in Atherton, his mind filled with Hell.

She'd looked worse than terrible, like she was at death's door. Damn it, why wouldn't she let him help her? She'd practically slammed the door in his face.

But what had happened between yesterday and just now? How could she have gotten worse?

He'd left a message for her cousin, asking her to check on Hell. Maybe Joanne could get through to her.

Next best thing he could do for her short of kidnapping her and taking her to the hospital or home to care for her was continue on the case. The quicker it was solved, the faster things would calm down and the sooner she could heal.

Damn, he'd never met anyone stubborner. Except for maybe himself.

At least it looked like he'd be getting direct access to Sherry. He hadn't believed it when he'd called the Collins residence and Sherry had actually gotten on the phone and had agreed to talk to him, face-to-face. He'd thought he'd have to pull out the big guns and allude to finding incriminating evidence that might be linked to her, but she'd readily agreed to see him.

The gates opened as he pulled up. Was she watching him from the windows? Seemed a bit too inviting. Like she actually welcomed him there. Why the hell would she want a private investigator in her home asking such personal questions?

Whole thing felt wrong.

Matt parked in his now usual place overlooking the tennis courts.

When he approached the arched wood double doors, one side opened. A tall, strikingly beautiful, blonde woman around his age stood there. She wore a sleeveless blue top and tight-fitting white slacks showing off her toned body.

Only rich women could afford to spend so much time on themselves. Matt tried to withhold his judgment.

"Mr. Sinclair?" Sherry asked.

"Yes, ma'am. Matt Sinclair. You can call me Matt."

"My pleasure," she said, seeming surprised by his appearance. "Won't you come in?"

"Thank you."

Sherry backed up and allowed him inside.

Matt removed his sunglasses and stepped into a three-story-tall entry hall the size and grandeur of his church. A large, carved mahogany staircase rose to the upper floor. Three arched doorways and several closed doors led off the ornate marble-floored entry hall.

Ostentatious as hell. Could feed an entire city on the entry hall itself. He had a childhood buddy who installed artsy marble floors for rich people. Insane cost.

"Beautiful house, Mrs. Collins," he said in an upbeat tone.

Her blue eyes sparked brighter, and her mouth curved into an even wider smile. From what Hell had said, Sherry wasn't acting her normal self.

The truth hit him so sharply he almost felt the physical slap across the face. She was attracted to him.

Holy smokes. His stomach knotted. "Mrs. Collins, I—"

"Call me Sherry," she practically purred.

Hell would not believe this one. Matt swallowed hard. "Sherry."

She gazed at his shoulders, then did a quick inventory of all his main features and returned to his face. Her smile widened even farther, and she looked at him like he was on her dinner menu.

Matt tried not to squirm, but she made him feel naked. While in his younger days he'd received a good amount of attention from the ladies, it had been awhile since a woman looked at him like this, and never this hot this fast. Maid upstairs and everyone in the house had probably gotten Sherry's signals. Shifting his weight, he cleared his throat.

She gestured to the room on their right. "Shall we talk in the living room?"

"Certainly. After you," he said, slipping into his chivalrous mode. She liked him; he could use it.

Very handy that he wasn't attracted to snobby white women, because this lady, even in her early fifties, was gorgeous. What the hell was wrong with Collins, anyway? While Hell was an attractive girl, she wasn't an elegant, upper-class woman with perfect features.

Sending him a radiant smile, Sherry glided ahead with a walk that seemed put on. Like it wasn't her natural gait but one she'd adopted to make herself appear more refined. Phony as hell. He'd expected her to be a bit more down-to-earth since her family's wealth dated back to the Mayflower—and most old-money people he'd met were more normal—but not this woman. Look in the dictionary under Rich Bitch and there was a picture of Sherry Collins.

The living room was just as grand as the entry hall. Furniture was so hoity-toity and delicate he didn't want to sit on it. Front window displayed a giant water bill of lush, green tropical plants and flowers so perfect they looked fake. He thought of his yellowing camellias and anemic azaleas that had barely bloomed this year. Both he and Patty had been too busy to do yard work and too broke to hire a gardener.

He checked the floors. While shiny clean, they didn't look like they'd just been redone. No varnish smell. "These floors are amazing. Do you refinish them often?"

She smiled. "Not in a few years, but we do pride ourselves on keeping them clean and polished."

Thank you for confirming Esmeralda's lie.

Sherry indicated a spindly-legged chair near a long couch. Victorian, that was the style. Probably. Matt went over and stood near the high-backed upholstered chair, waiting for her to take her seat.

She sat on the sofa a bit too near his chair.

He sat and had to hold his leg at an unnatural position to avoid touching hers. As he reached into his jacket pocket to retrieve his notebook and pen, the heat of her gaze burned into him. He rolled his shoulders, turned to her, and assumed a sympathetic affect. "I appreciate this, Mrs. Collins—Sherry. I know how difficult this must be for you, and I'm sorry."

She looked down for a split second, and an instant of pain crossed her regal face. Then her intense blue gaze met his. "Yes, it's been all quite awful. Are you married, Matt?"

"Yes, ma'am. For twenty-eight years."

"Good for you. Happy?"

"Very much."

"You're lucky. Brad and I were never happy. I suppose all this was inevitable," she said with a small, controlled gesture of her left hand.

"I'm sorry." He needed to make her think he was on her side. "I want you to know that just because I'm working for Miss Trent doesn't mean I approve of her choices or lifestyle." He allowed his expression to grow troubled. "Quite frankly, this has all been very distasteful for me."

Sherry's eyes took on a little glow. Perfect. "Yes, I'm sure it has. For a moral man such as yourself. I did a little checking on you, I must confess."

Alarm bells sounded loudly in his mind. Investigating the investigator? What did she have to hide? "So you knew I was married," he tried to say in a casual tone. He kept on his game face. Couldn't give away any tells.

Sherry held herself with perfect posture like she'd practiced sitting as well as walking. "Yes, but I wasn't sure in what type of marriage you were. You see, I did some research to find out what frame of reference you possess. A moral man will see my issues differently than, say, a man who commits adultery."

"Good thinking, Sherry." *Listen to what she says, old man.* Perps always revealed more than they meant to, especially if they were trying to manipulate the investigator. This woman had clearly wanted to stack the deck in their little exchange. Intriguing.

She gave a slight smile that could be construed as approval, but it was clear her smile muscles hadn't been used much. "Your wife has a lot to admire in you with your impressive resume and solid background."

She must know about his disgrace. Why was she trying to butter him up? Because she wanted him to buy whatever story she was going to feed him. Strike one.

"So unlike Brad." Her mouth slightly curved downward, and she did an eye roll.

"I'm trying not to judge, I'm only trying to solve this case," Matt said.

She regarded him, and her brow wrinkled almost microscopically. "Curious how you thought you needed to talk to me. I thought the culprit had been caught and put in jail. The evidence was overwhelming. I thought the case was closed."

Look on her face was unreadable. This woman had spent years masking her emotions, but there was a dark energy behind her eyes, deep within her. A hidden maliciousness. After years of talking to perps and being around the bad guys, he'd learned the signals, the scent, the vibe of criminals. Didn't mean she was the assailant, but it did mean that he needed to be wary of her.

Let's see how she reacts to the first bomb. "Your confusion is understandable. We have reason to believe the suspect in jail might have been framed." Her eyes dilated slightly. She was either behind the attacks or genuinely shocked. "We're just tying up all the loose ends to make sure the right man is in jail, and that Helen is safe. I hate to ask these questions, but I have to cover everything. The slightest bit of information could be the key."

She moved back almost imperceptibly. "How could I know anything? Does Miss Trent really believe that I would go so far as to toss a hand grenade onto her patio?"

"No," he said like he found the idea ridiculous. Wait. How did she know the grenade was thrown onto the patio? Was that detail in the newspapers?

"I mean, could you picture someone like me doing something like that?"

"No." Truthfully. But she seemed to know far too much about the incident. "While neither Hell nor I believe you had anything to do with it, you might have some information that could help us. You may have seen or know something that you don't realize is related to the crime."

Her shoulders relaxed. Nice tell. "Is it true the grenade destroyed her apartment?"

"Yes."

"How ghastly. And she didn't get hurt?"

"Oh, she got hurt."

"That's terrible." Her lips resisted smiling, but her eyes shined with joy.

Could she be the one? Of course, if some creep slept with Patty, he'd be pretty happy if the man got hurt. Still, this woman had just launched herself to the top of the suspect list.

"I know you were here when the attack happened," he said like he believed it.

"Yes. I was in bed with a migraine. My staff can corroborate that." She looked him dead in the eye and wasn't giving off any signs that she might be lying. But if she were the culprit, she would have practiced for this moment. "It really is embarrassing nasty business when your husband cheats on you, and it gets all over the news."

"I can't imagine. This shouldn't take long." He referred to his notebook and list of questions.

"While I'm incredibly unhappy about the affair, this isn't the first time Brad has cheated on me," Sherry eagerly volunteered.

"It's not right."

"It surely isn't. A man like you would never consider it, would you?"

"No, ma'am. I believe in commitments, and I believe in marriage."

"Of course you do, because you're honorable. Which, pardon me for saying so, makes no sense why you'd work for someone as low as Miss Trent."

He inwardly flinched, and he squelched a rise of anger. Amazing how oddly protective he'd become over Hell. "Surprised me, too."

Her features drew down with pity. "I'm so sorry about that awful business with your police job."

His stomach tightened. Of course she'd found that out. She was either their assailant or she was trying to distract him from something else she didn't want him to find out. Maybe about her drug addiction?

"Clearly you were framed," she added. He couldn't tell if she believed it.

"I was."

"Because of your honesty and forthrightness."

"Yes."

"Because you caught your coworkers committing illegal acts and rightfully reported the activity."

"Yes." His whole body got the heebie-jeebies, but he resisted the urge to shake them off. He couldn't let her know how much she'd gotten to him. Why the hell had she found the need to not only investigate him but to let him know that she had? To warn him, threaten him, or throw him off?

Sherry continued with a superior affect. "It's terrible how they let that travesty take place. It's getting so all the honest people are being driven out. I mean, what does it pay to be a good person these days when all we get rewarded with is betrayal? Our situations are very similar. I gave Brad everything I had to give a man, and clearly it wasn't enough. Now his dalliances are affecting me socially. My children have, at least, taken my side. But, of course, why wouldn't they when I haven't done anything wrong?"

Only guilty people professed their innocence like this. But Sherry throwing a hand grenade at Hell? Maybe she figured it was such an outlandish idea for a society lady to bomb a rival, the mere strangeness of the act would eliminate her from the suspect list.

"I'm glad you have the support of your kids," he said.

"You have three boys, yes?" she asked pointedly, but also like this information was readily available everywhere.

His heart rate shot up. Wow. "Yes, I do."

"Did they stand by you?" By her non-reaction and seeming lack of interest in how her information might be affecting him, she clearly hadn't even considered that Matt might have a problem with her investigation. Was she a sociopath?

"Yes."

"You're lucky." She looked down at her perfectly polished nails. "I hope my children continue to do so. They're all I have left. Well, aside from Mother." She seemed genuinely upset.

"Terrible."

"I'm sorry, I keep babbling on. What were your questions?"

"Well—"

"You must have already questioned Lindsay," she said with a sharp edge to the look behind her eyes.

"Hell did." Here it was. The next part of her plan. Throwing someone else under the bus. Which meant she was either getting even with Lindsay for sleeping with Brad or trying to misdirect Matt away from her own guilt.

"I think you'll get a lot closer to solving the mystery once you speak with her." Her mouth went hard.

"Really? Why?" he asked, playing dumb.

"Isn't it obvious?"

"Nothing's obvious to me right now, Sherry."

"She's obsessed with Brad. She's the one who's been following him around. You must know that."

"Yes, but how did you know that?"

"Brad told me," she said without a moment's hesitation. His gut told him that she had rehearsed this scene backward and forward.

"Oh, of course," he said, acting badly. Purposely rattling her cage. He pretended to jot down a note.

"You can't suspect me of all this nonsense."

"No, I do not," he said with sincerity. *Yes, I do.* But he would continue to send her mixed signals and see how she reacted.

"Even though I have a perfect right to be upset with Miss Trent."

"You certainly do," he said with much conviction.

Her eyes narrowed slightly, and her thin lips tightened. "She probably told you that she conned me several months ago when on a case for Brad, which is apparently how they met."

"She told me the story."

She gave a small snort. "I have no idea why she'd continue to see Brad when she's also dating a Mafia don who's fifty times more handsome, gracious, and cultured than my ugly, old, bald husband. Did she tell you about Marco Capasso? Isn't he the more likely source of the threat?" A little surge of victory appeared in her eyes.

Yes, she'd carefully crafted this entire scene. "Uh. That's right, you ran into Hell with Capasso up at the Fairmont."

"Yes. Of course, I thought she was Jeanne Simari, the office equipment repair business owner." Her gaze filled with seething hatred, and her nostrils flared like she smelled something foul.

Her fury had dislodged her mask a bit, allowing him to see the killer viper underneath that he'd previously only sensed.

Let's encourage the viper to come out and play.

"Yes. I know this means little to you, but she—" He furrowed his brow, affected a pained expression, looked away, and rubbed the back of his head. "I won't even try to defend her. What she did to you was rotten. And she knows it."

"Yes, but only because Brad hired her. I know Brad's the one to blame in all this." But her eyes didn't match her words. She blamed Hell.

But did she hate her enough to kill her?

"He didn't help," Matt agreed.

"So what type of questions do you have for me?"

"I wanted to know if you've seen a short, squat, older lady in brown following you around."

She stared at him blankly for a moment, then blinked fast. "I don't think so... Wait, yes. Yes, I did. She was outside the Circus Club gates the other day. I noticed her because she drove a car similar to my maid's. I thought for some reason Esmeralda had come to find me. But when I drove past, it clearly wasn't my maid. The woman was Caucasian, wore thick glasses, and was unfortunately, uh...well, her features..."

"Ugly?"

"Yes. I don't normally like to throw out judgments such as that. People in the lower classes can't afford the luxury of a good doctor or stylist."

If Matt had had an interest in the woman, it would have died right then.

Sherry continued without seeming to take notice of her insulting language. "Then the woman followed me to my hairdresser and on to the jewelers. But when I came out of the store, she was gone, and I never saw her again. I was about to call the police."

A complete fabrication. Or was it? Sounded plausible, yet her delivery reeked of practice.

"She followed all of Hell's and Brad's associates," Matt said, making sure his expression was neutral.

"Well, isn't she the one you're looking for?"

"One of the ones."

She looked away and stroked her chin with her long, manicured fingers. "I wonder if she knows Lindsay."

"Why?"

Turning back to Matt, she flipped a palm upward. "Well, the car. The black Honda that looks like Esmeralda's. Lindsay's gardener has one, too. Lindsay was forced to borrow it one day. So humiliating for her," she said with a little self-indulgent shoulder crunch and a cat-that-ate-the-canary grin. "I greatly enjoyed it." Her posture went ramrod straight again, and her smile faded into freezing-cold hatred. "That was shortly after I found out about her betrayal."

"Really."

"I know the car that the assailant drove during the first attack on Miss Trent was a black Honda," she tossed off, glancing down at her nails. "At least, that's what I read in the papers." The look at her hands was intentional, the line delivered to make her appear as if she were innocently passing on information.

Alarm bells sounded louder. "I'm impressed with how much you know about the case." Was she privy to some information that Lindsay had given her? Lindsay could still be the culprit, and Sherry could be directing him her way to get revenge.

The look in her eye sharpened, and she smiled a fake smile. "Well, after Brad was caught at the hospital with Miss Trent, I studied all I could online about the attack and Miss Trent. You'd be surprised at how much information is available."

"Wealth of information out there nowadays." Especially if you paid people to uncover it all and spent hours studying it.

"Because I was so distraught about Brad potentially leaving me, I needed to know how close he was to her. And if he was still seeing Lindsay."

"I'm only here to find out who's trying to kill Miss Trent."

"I'd look at Lindsay."

"Because she stalked him?"

"Because she always swore if Dan ever cheated on her, she'd kill whomever he slept with. She said that to me on several occasions. Now that we're not friends any longer, I feel comfortable betraying her trust. Since she could care less about it. Lindsay could have transferred this jealousy onto Miss Trent and followed through on her threats." No tells that she was lying. But the woman seemed quite deft at weaving truth and fiction.

"Interesting." He pretended to take notes. "I can't imagine how that would feel to have your best friend sleep with your spouse," he said, oozing sympathy.

"It hurt deeply," she said, without any sign of duplicity.

"Terrible."

"I'm so glad you understand. Nowadays people seem to expect cheating."

"Not me."

"You're a Catholic, aren't you?"

The pit of his stomach went cold. Did she know his blood type? "Yes. Does it show?"

Her eyes widened for a split second, and then she laughed a slightly uncomfortable laugh. "I apologize. An article I read about your case mentioned that you were Catholic, and since I am, I remembered. The reason I mentioned it was because we were both taught that adultery was a sin. We both come from the same religious frame of reference."

"Yes, we do." Why did he get the feeling she was lying about how she'd obtained the information? And why the *hell* would she want all this information on him unless it was to manipulate him into putting him on Lindsay's trail or to cover up her own guilt?

But Sherry throwing a hand grenade at Hell? He could not see it. She might hire someone to do the job, though. But a *hand grenade*? Why not just shoot her?

"So the way I see it, if the threat to Miss Trent is coming from Brad, Lindsay would be the top suspect. Even though that doesn't make sense." She turned away and rested her mouth on a forefinger. "I can't see her bothering with a hand grenade, and where would she get one?" She brightened, and her eyebrows rose. "That's right. Her friend Marcel Livingstone has that bunker filled with weapons. She spoke about his grenades and arsenal. And there was that time that she told me she'd considered bombing a mutual acquaintance at the club, a woman she disliked, but I believe that was all talk. Lindsay is still much too sophisticated to do something crass like that."

Sherry either thought Matt was really stupid or she genuinely believed that Lindsay was involved. Still, talk about overselling an idea. He was surprised that she hadn't brought out a leash, tied it around his neck, and dragged him over to Lindsay's house.

A migraine at home was Sherry's alibi for the night Hell was attacked. How hard would it have been to leave unnoticed? Esmeralda drove right by Lloyd and didn't stop. Sherry could have easily been in the backseat or trunk.

Sherry continued smoothly. "But from what I understand about Miss Trent, the culprit could be half the state. How many people has she put in jail? How many men have lost their fortunes in the divorce cases she's worked? Wouldn't those people be the more likely sources of the threat?"

"We're still following up leads. You could be right," he assured her.

"I'm sure I am. Or it's Lindsay. What about that Gwen Lake person? Have you questioned her?"

"Yes. Hell did. But she and your husband stopped associating back in December. She's moved on and is in a relationship now."

"Oh, really? Cow. Pardon me," she said, putting a hand to her chest. "This has all been so upsetting."

"I thought Brad cheated on you shortly after the wedding."

"Yes. But the information has never gone public before. That's where the true damage lies. Our social circle—while somewhat flexible with changing circumstances in relationships—still frowns on publicity of that kind. I've gotten a few sympathetic calls, and hopefully I won't be ostracized. I especially hope it won't ruin my chances for country club president. It all depends on whether or not Brad and I decide to stay together. While he's filed for divorce, I believe his lack of preparation belies his true feelings for me. If he'd been serious about leaving me, he wouldn't have left a giant legal loophole in the documents. If we stay in the marriage, everything should be fine. That's my hope, that these dalliances with Miss Trent and Lindsay are just more of his passing fancies, and that all this divorce nonsense will fade like his eventual interest in his concubines."

A presidency in the country club was clearly worth staying in a loveless marriage. Or maybe it was about the money. "I hope so, too, for your sake. I mean, if you split up with Mr. Collins, wouldn't that affect your finances?"

She laughed. "Dear God, no. In fact, I'll be richer. Well, if he died, I'd be the wealthiest yet. While I joked to Miss Trent about wanting his heart murmur to lead to something fatal, now I've come to think it's not such a bad idea," she said with a straight face. Clearly, she was speaking her truth. "Serve him right for splashing me all over the news."

A chill went over him. "Yeah," he tried to say with conviction.

"Of course, if he divorces me, I'll be just as wealthy without him." She looked at her surroundings and pursed her lips. "I would miss this house. This is his family's estate." Poison filled her voice. She clearly hated Brad and his whole family. "I had to actually sign a paper that said if we ever divorced, he'd get the house. When I've spent the last twenty-six years improving it and making it livable. His mother had horrid taste. His father wouldn't know a balustrade from a colonnade. A cornice from a Rock Cornish game hen."

Matt laughed because she seemed to want him to.

She beamed. "I took this godforsaken mansion and turned it into a showplace. Not that Brad ever noticed or cared."

"He seems pretty busy with work."

She sneered and gave a harsh laugh. "Brad's only busy trying to show up his father with that ridiculous venture capital nonsense and by bedding as many women as he can. His father and he are two of a kind. Brad always rages about how much he can't stand his father when he's a cardboard cutout of the man. Jack Collins always has been a skirt-chasing bastard who only thinks of his money."

Her hatred for her husband ran more deeply than Matt had first thought. If the attempts had been on Brad's life, he'd look no further than Sherry. "You deserve better." Most definitely not.

She brightened. "Agreed. I have considered the idea that divorcing Brad might free me to find someone more suitable. Someone with honor and integrity." She looked at him like he was a fancy diamond ring she was considering buying.

Matt's body heated, and he cleared his throat. "Yes."

"Someone like you."

Whoa! His face flushed. "Er, uh, thank you, ma'am." He fought the instinct to get up and run for the door, and forced himself to calm. Whatever Sherry wanted, her main purpose seemed to be to distract him.

She smiled widely. "You still have the humility to blush. You really are quite charming, aren't you? I don't meet many men like you. Real men with real jobs who have worked hard to support their families. Honorable, faithful, church-going men."

"Believe me, ma'am, I try hard, but I'm not perfect by any stretch of the imagination."

"No one is, but you come closer than any of the men in my class. No man I know cares about his wife, children, and his church the way you do." She gave a knowing smile. "You must have really needed Miss Trent's money, didn't you?"

Play along! He affected a bit of shame and looked down for a moment. "Yes."

Sherry laughed. "I thought so. You probably loathe her as much as I do."

"I...well." He shrugged. "I hate being around that depravity, but I have to feed my kids." He tried to look rueful and resigned.

"You should come work for me." Her blue eyes lit with hope.

He couldn't believe it, but working for Hell was like a heavenly paradise compared to this socialite succubus's offer. "Love to, but I signed a contract and accepted payment. I always fulfill my obligations, even to someone like her." He held himself tall and proud.

"Even if saving her life is the wrong thing to do."

A spike of shame roiled his gut. Exactly what he'd thought about Hell at the beginning. Shouldn't have been so hard on her. He should have been able to see through her self-defensive act. "Yes."

"Please consider my offer. I could use a man like you on my team." And clearly in her bed. "I'd love to hire you full-time. I'm sure you'd find your, uh, benefit package, quite substantial." She gave him a covetous look and actually had the audacity to glance at his chest and hands.

His gut caved in, and he had to fight hard not to shudder.

"I'd pay you much more than the measly five hundred a day Hell Trent is paying you."

He almost flinched but caught himself. Jesus Christ, how had the woman found that out? Had she bugged Hell's office? He'd make sure to sweep it later.

Sherry leaned in so close their knees touched, and he had no room to move away. "I could easily triple that for you. Plus give you a month's vacation," she purred. "We've been known to allow our staff on vacation to use our various homes for their pleasure. We offer many perks," she said with what he was sure she thought was a coy grin and then leaned back. Her manner did not come off as flirty, it came off as superior. Ugly.

"Please consider my offer," she said with a sly smile. "Maybe being around a man of honor would help me recognize one in my own class."

He loved the way she kept referring to herself as from being from another class. Like she was a higher being. No wonder Brad had cheated on her. But he shouldn't have bothered. He should have divorced her years ago. Sherry was a vapid, social-climbing waste.

Amazing how someone so beautiful could turn so hideous so fast.

"I'll definitely take it under consideration. And thank you." He sent her one of his most charming smiles.

She flashed him her overly white teeth, clearly thinking she'd won him over.

He stood, his body thrilled he was going to finally escape from this witch. But first, he needed her to believe that she'd convinced him. "I'm sorry for bothering you. I told Hell this was a waste of time and money. An elegant lady like you going after her? Ridiculous."

He carefully checked her expression. While her face didn't move much, there was clear triumph in her eyes. Perfect. Now that she believed she'd accomplished her mission, she should be easier to catch and convict. If she were the culprit. She could just be covering up a drug habit, like Hell suspected.

He needed to know if Esmeralda was helping her with the attempted murders or supplying her with drugs. Brad would help him with that. The Mexican Mafia would be no fun to take on, but then again, it might get him in good with the Feds. That might make it easier to get an investigation into his frame-up and dismissal.

Just as he stepped across the threshold, Sherry slipped him a card with her personal cell number on it. Then winked at him.

Gross. He sent her a smile and forced himself to walk normally to his car.

As soon as he shut his car door, he allowed himself a full-body shudder.

CHAPTER 24

As Hell awakened, her hotel room's bright white ceiling came into focus. She'd had one of those weird dreams that seemed real. She'd woken up in a hospital, freaked out because she couldn't afford it, torn off her hospital gown, redressed in her pajamas, and escaped right past the nurse's desk. After wandering around a scorching-hot parking lot, she'd gotten so tired. Luckily, she'd found a magical shady bus stop for safety and shelter. She'd curled up on the bench and had gone to sleep.

So funny. A magical bus stop. Stupid dreams.

Her vision was blurry and almost tunnel-like. Why did she feel so terrible?

A wave of cold hit her, and she shivered. "I'm cold." Her voice came out a bare whisper.

A middle-aged blonde woman wearing a nurse's uniform appeared above her.

Adrenaline slammed her, and she screamed.

Her blue eyes wide, the woman gasped and reeled back, clutching her chest.

"Where did you come from?" Hell croaked.

"You scared me," the woman said, fanning her face.

"You scared me. Who are you? A nurse? Why is my voice all

scratchy?" Hell tried to move but seemed glued to the bed. Her arms were so heavy, like they weighed a thousand pounds each. Her tongue was dry and tasted like a sock. Reality was so fuzzy. Was she awake or dreaming?

"Doctor?" the nurse said over her shoulder.

Her heart rate shot higher. "Doctor?" Why would she need a doctor? And how did a doctor and a nurse wind up in her hotel room?

A white guy around Hell's age with short gray hair and a trimmed beard came into view. "How are you feeling, Helen?"

"Horrible. And freaked out that there's a doctor and nurse in my room when I fell asleep alone in here." Her vision cleared more. Her room didn't look like her room at all. "Wait. Why does my room look different?" Was her mind playing tricks on her?

Her sight came into sharp focus. She was in a large, beautiful hotel suite twice the size of hers facing a wall of windows that overlooked a balcony and the night sky with an almost-full moon.

More fight-or-flight juices dumped into her, and she gasped and sat straight up in bed. "Where the hell am I?"

The whole room spun and darkened. Her back hit the mattress hard.

The doctor took her by the shoulders. "Easy, Helen, easy. You're fine. Just stay calm. You almost pulled out the IV."

Took her a second to clear her head. The room came back into focus. "What IV?" Then she noticed the tube going into her arm, and a wave of fear made her belly and back tense. "The hell I'm fine. I fell asleep in my hotel room and I wake up— Where the hell am I?"

"You're at the Rosewood Hotel on Sand Hill Road. I'm Dr. William Gregory, but you can call me Bill, and this is Nancy Morgan, your nurse."

Her heart beating fast, Hell gripped the sheets hard. "Rosewood Hotel? I can't afford this! How did I get here? I can't afford my own doctor and nurse. Why the hell would I have a doctor and nurse, anyway? What happened to me?" The urge to run overwhelmed her. "Doesn't matter. I have to get back to my cheap hotel."

"Please calm down, Helen, you're fine. Mister—"

"I am certainly not fine." A digital clock next to her read 8:12 p.m.
Her pulse jumped higher. "I'm missing nine freakin' hours!"

"Please try to remain calm, Miss Trent. You went into shock in
your hotel room. You don't remember the hospital? Or the drive here,
or our previous conversations?"

"Hospital?" Hell tried to sit up, but a wave of dizziness kept her
horizontal. That dream couldn't have been real! "Shock?"

The doctor patted her arm. "You must stay calm, Helen."

"What hospital? How did I go into shock?" she demanded.

"Your electrolytes were off, and apparently, you drank an entire
glass of orange juice and it—"

"I drank the juice *for* the electrolytes— Shit, I forgot the salt. Wait.
How did I end up here? And how come I'm not still in the hospital?
Who transported me here?"

"Brad found you unconscious in your hotel room and called—"

Terror turned to rage, her weakened body hardened, and she
clenched her jaw and fists. "Brad kidnapped me? That son of a bitch!
How dare he? Shock, my ass! That bastard made it all up and
kidnapped me! I told him I wanted him gone out of my life, so he
fucking kidnaps me? I'm calling the police!" she yelled, her anger
centering her.

Dr. Bill's eyes widened and he took a step back, seeming aghast.
"Miss Trent, he didn't kidnap you, he saved your life."

Hell scowled and narrowed her eyes. "Oh, sure, did he pay you to
say that? This is bullshit. I'm half-dead, I can't defend myself, and the
bastard kidnaps me!" She tried to gesture violently, but the IV
stopped her.

Dr. Williams' face reddening, he blinked fast and looked at her
like she was insane. "Listen to me: he didn't kidnap you. He called 911.
You went to the hospital by ambulance, and then when he turned his
back, you escaped from the ER, and he found you at a bus stop on El
Camino, semiconscious."

The pit of her stomach went wonkier. That dream could not have been true. She was probably talking in her sleep, and Brad had used the story to placate the doctor. "Bullshit! You're a liar, and he's a liar!"

The doc heaved a huge sigh. "No, I'm not," he said in a less-than-patient voice. "You went into shock. I can attest to that because when I arrived here, I confirmed the diagnosis."

"Right. He paid you to gaslight me, didn't he? Creep probably drugged me," she bit out. "And you're one of his bought toadies." She narrowed her eyes and sneered. "You're probably not even a doctor. Now get lost, I'm leaving." She sat up, but the room went topsy-turvy, and she had to lie down again.

"You aren't going anywhere, Helen. You stay put," the doctor said forcefully, pointing down at her. Then he pulled himself up taller, appearing incredibly offended. "I've known Brad thirty years, and he's not capable of that. And I'm not capable of that type of behavior."

Hell's frustration built to the exploding stage. "I said, *get lost*," she growled while pointing toward the door with her IV-free hand.

"Is she awake? Is that Hell I hear?" Brad stormed into the room, a super-worried look on his handsome face.

Spearing her heart in half and taking the breath from her lungs. She covered her reaction and let her upset fuel her fury. "Get out! All of you!"

His gray eyes wide, his jaw dropped. "Get out?"

The doctor and nurse stepped back to let Brad close to the bed.

The doctor wore a deep frown. "Brad, Helen is under some fairly significant misconceptions about her situation, and she won't believe me. She's already fired me, ordered me to leave, and threatened me with police action. She thinks we drugged her, kidnapped her, and are holding her here against her will."

Hell's head almost blew off her shoulders. "Thinks? *Thinks!* Fuck you! It's the truth! You all kidnapped me, and I'm calling the cops!" she threatened as viciously as she could.

"*What?*" Brad demanded, staring at her, seeming floored.

"Maybe you'll have better luck convincing her of our good intentions," the doctor said. "We'll be outside. Please make sure she doesn't pull out her IV. She's already tried to leave twice."

"Third time's the charm," Hell interjected loudly. "Once I can stand, I'm out of here!"

Brad's confused expression turned to fire, and he glared down at her. "For crying out loud, will you stop hurting yourself?" He turned to the doctor and nurse. "Bill, Nancy, thanks. I'll handle this."

Handle this? Like she was some ridiculous problem? Asshole! She wanted to sit up and point at him dramatically but was too dizzy, so she settled for scowling. "You will not *handle* me! Get the hell out before I call the cops and have you arrested!"

Behind Brad, the doctor and nurse slipped out of the room.

BC rolled his eyes, his face etched with fury. "Goddamn, you are a pain in the ass. You almost died, you idiot!" He gestured at her sharply. "You went into shock!"

"Yeah, and you took advantage of the situation and kidnapped me and paid those people to lie to me! And I'm still not sure I went into shock. You could have drugged me, for all I know, and then lied to that doctor! Don't tell me you're not capable!"

He looked heavenward for a moment, then blinked a bunch of times and leveled his hot gaze straight into hers. "Listen to me, you fucking idiot, I did not kidnap you. I did not drug you. I saved your life, and you're welcome. However, had I known last night that you were about to go into shock and almost die, you can bet your sweet ass I would've kidnapped you," he seethed through gritted teeth.

Something about his vehemence and fury made her pause. What if he was telling the truth? He couldn't be. Could he?

No way. Even though nothing about his expression read duplicity.

Raging voices screamed conflicting messages at her. *Run! Stay! He's lying! He's telling the truth! You almost died! No, you were fine!*

She lay back, unable to make sense of the situation. All she wanted was to get away from him. If she couldn't have him, she didn't want to see him. Especially when she was so weak and out of it.

Sweat beading on his forehead, his eyes slicing into hers, he gestured at her sharply. "I've been kicking myself for leaving you there. I ordered my lawyers to fix that goddamned legal loophole Sherry's lawyers found in the initial divorce filings, and get me the signed papers as fast as they could, but fuck, you still almost *died* before I could get back there to show you the damned things and ask you to marry me. I had to bluff my way inside with help of a housekeeper. And then, Jesus Christ, I find you lying there looking dead. I thought you'd *died*, Hell. I lost my mind." He jabbed his forefinger into her face, his gaze burning. "No more of this bullshit, you hear me?"

Suddenly, the words *divorce papers* and *marry me* pierced her foggy skull. Her jaw hit her chest, then a wave of emotion flattened her. She closed her eyes and started hyperventilating. This was all too much. Shock? Death? Divorce papers? Was he lying? What was real? Tears worked their way to the surface, and she had no strength left to fight them.

His weight on the bed next to her tipped her toward him, and he gathered her in his arms. His scent and warmth enveloped her. Her body wanted to melt into him, but her brain wanted to bolt.

"Don't cry, Hell. You're okay. It's gonna be okay."

She made a weak attempt at pushing him away. "No, it's not. Why are you lying to me? Why are you hurting me like this? I can't take it."

"Hell, I'm not lying. I'm divorcing Sherry. I want to marry you. I love you. I wouldn't lie about this, I wouldn't manipulate you, and I wouldn't hire actors to play doctors. Nor would I drug you and kidnap you, you moron. I love you, and I'm taking care of you. That's all that's happening here."

Anger flared through her again. She was too sick and tired to play games with rich and powerful men. He had to be lying. "Bullshit! Stop lying to me! You're rich. You can afford any young, blonde, skinny, accomplished wife you want. You'd never pick an old, broke, middle-class tomboy. I'm just your strange stuff."

He looked at her like she was brainless. "You are the stubbornest human being I've ever met. No. You're wrong about me. I love you. And I'm not letting you push me away when you're so sick. I'm taking care of you whether you like it or not. I did leave Sherry for you, and

I've shown you the papers three fucking times already, and you clearly haven't remembered any of it."

Hell stopped trying to think and cried for a while. Waking up to her worst fears and her greatest dream had overloaded her circuits. But she didn't fight his embrace. His strong arms felt too good, too right. As she calmed, he pulled her tighter to him, making her feel safer. But she still couldn't believe any of this was real.

Brad let out a long sigh. "When I got to the hospital, those imbeciles could have cared less about you. Pissed me off the care you were getting, so I stepped out to call my own doctor. When I got back, they were all gone, and so were you. I thought they'd taken you somewhere but no. I freaked out. Assholes just let you walk off when you were so out of it. Then my bodyguard found the blood drops, and we followed them."

She gasped and pushed away to face him. "Blood drops?"

"Yeah, you ripped out your IV."

She tried not to panic. "Shit!" Horrifying.

"We found you barefoot in your SpongeBob pajamas, passed out at a bus stop, blood all over you."

Her body tensed, and the tears returned, only now from fright. Son of a bitch! The dream wasn't a dream at all! She was wandering alone and out of it? With no protection? Anything could have happened to her. What if she'd managed to get on the goddamned bus?

BC nuzzled her. "It's okay. I found you in time."

A sharp pain came from her right foot. She wiggled her toes, and the bottoms of her feet hurt. How far had she walked barefoot? She tried not to panic. "I almost died. What if you hadn't found me?"

"We don't have to think about that," he said in a calm, sure tone. "All that matters is that I did, and I'm taking care of you. Good care. I've got the doctor, the nurse, bodyguards. No one will ever hurt you again. I promise."

She pushed away from him. "Except you when you leave me for the supermodel. BC, I can't do this. I appreciate the fact that you just saved me, but this isn't going to last. You'll be on your way with another chick in about a minute. You've never been faithful in your life."

"The hell I haven't," he replied indignantly. "I never cheated on Rachel Lather, and I was with her from the time I was seventeen to twenty-two, five years, until she left me."

"Really?" she sniffed. Brad handed her a wad of tissues, and she took them and blew her nose. "Thanks."

"You're welcome, troublemaker. I am absolutely capable of fidelity, and I promise to be faithful to you. I know my relationship with Rachel was a long time ago, but she was my only other serious relationship besides Sherry. Only reason I cheated on my wife was because she wouldn't sleep with me or let me touch her, and she hated me. I didn't want to cheat, Hell. I want a real wife who knows how to be faithful and loyal."

He was still missing a giant point: their worlds would never mix. "But I don't have your breeding. All your ladies said the same thing, that you'd never date outside your class, and that you were slumming. You people don't marry people who aren't part of some giant, corporate dynasty."

"And you heard this from whom?" he asked, looking at her like she was totally stupid.

"Your... Well, they have a point."

"Hell, stop. You're scared and making up obstacles because you're afraid of getting hurt. Well, me too, Miss Nine Boyfriends. Hell, look, I love you. You, Helen Elizabeth Trent, you. All of you. The reason I was with those ladies was because I didn't know anyone like you existed. I didn't know I could have this much fun with a woman. How could I ever possibly be interested in one of those girls after meeting you?"

Damn, this man could argue. "I don't know. All I know is that you terrify me, and I don't want to be terrified."

He brought her closer. "You're only scared because you haven't slept or eaten in days, and someone blew up your apartment, and no one has been taking care of you. And the last man you loved died, and you've been too alone ever since. All you need is some food and rest, and a couple days with me to see that this is all real, and you'll be fine."

"Did you really file for divorce from Sherry? I thought she found a legal loophole."

"We closed it. Papers are right there on your nightstand. Open them up."

Hell grabbed the manila envelope, dragging the IV with her. She opened the top and withdrew the papers. A quick inspection revealed that he'd told the truth.

Damn.

She put back the divorce papers and closed her eyes once more. This was not a possibility. She'd screamed all that stuff at him about leaving Sherry, but she'd never expected him to do it. She could not get her head around it. It was a strange dream.

Maybe that was it. Just a weird dream. But she felt so awake.

"Hell?"

In her warped state, there was no way she could process this, so she stopped trying. She made a concerted effort to relax. "I'll just go along here because I don't know how to handle any of this. We were done in my mind with no way back. I never in a million years considered a real relationship with you. This is crazy."

"I know this is a lot to take in. Especially considering how sick you are. Just hold on."

She looked up at him, blown away by the love in his sparkling gray eyes and the sweet expression on his handsome face. "This can't be real," she whispered.

He smiled. "We fell in love months ago, Hell. You're just catching up, that's all. But I'd like to hear it from you. You still haven't said the words."

"What words?"

"The L word. Do you love me?" Vulnerability appeared deep within his gaze.

She closed her eyes and threw her head back onto the pillow. "Oh, God."

"Oh, God, what?" he said, sounding very worried.

She sighed and shook her head. Then looked directly into his intense depths. "'I love you' seems so paltry and meaningless compared to how I feel about you. And now I'm terrified I've opened up, and you're gonna kill my heart."

Beaming, he hugged her tightly. "No way. But I knew it. You've felt a lot for me from the beginning, haven't you?"

She nodded but for some reason had to avert her attention to the covers. "You're absolutely correct," she said quietly. "All the evidence has been there; I just didn't want to look at it. Until I couldn't ignore it. The day I told you about the shooting at Starbucks is when I realized I was in love with you. I should have figured it out sooner. I kept the flowers you'd sent until they were stinky dead weeds, I—"

"What flowers— Oh, the flowers I sent after our first time together?"

"Yeah."

He laughed joyfully. "The ones you swore you'd shoved in a blender?"

"Yeah. Those flowers. I still have the vase at my office," she admitted, her face heating.

"You what?"

"Stop looking at me like that."

"Holy shit," he said with a giant smile. "How did you do all that and not know you loved me?"

"If I'd allowed myself to see it, I wouldn't have been able to continue seeing you. I honestly really thought you had lots of other women."

"When would you think I had time for them? We spend twenty hours a week together. Hell, I'm your age. How much sex do you really think I'm capable of?"

"I don't know, but I hope to find out," she cracked.

He laughed and kissed her temple. "Honestly, Hell, think about it. You know how much I work. You know I play tennis three times a week. Add up the hours and tell me when I had time for anyone else but you."

Holy crap. He was right. "Wow. We've really been faithful to each other, haven't we?"

"Since early December."

"Cool." Happiness rose up inside her, and a split second later, her doubts came out to douse the dreams with ice water. "But you don't really know me, BC. I've put on this act for you. For everyone. I'm not always that person you see."

"We've been spending a lot of time together, Hell. You're not always this live-wire comedian. You get quiet with me from time to time. Enough for me to see that softer side of you."

"We'll see what you think in a couple months."

He blinked fast, examining her. "You have an interesting dichotomy. Some part of you—when you open up emotionally—believes you are unworthy. Yet you're also that woman who nearly killed me in my office that day because you felt you were being disrespected."

"I don't feel unworthy. I'm concerned about how we started this relationship. I've never started off a love relationship as an affair. I handle my affairs very differently than my relationships."

"I think we know each other pretty well. I've been open with you."

"Yeah, but all we've done is have sex. Which, believe me, is the most fun I've ever had, but we haven't socialized with our friends, we haven't met our families, and we haven't gone out in public together."

He didn't even so much as blink. "I think we'll handle all that just fine. I can't stand my family, my kids aren't speaking to me, so that takes care of that, and you're done with your family, right?"

"Pretty much."

"I talked to Joanne for a good half hour, and we got along fine after she realized how much I loved you, how I'd left my wife for you, and how all I cared about was your well being."

Where the hell did he get all this confidence? Maybe rich people had a special catalog where they ordered extra surety. "How did you end up talking to Joanne?"

"I called her to let her know where you were."

"Cool. Thanks." She pictured herself living in his giant, horrible house. Talk about a fish out of water! "I just don't know how to reconcile the difference in our incomes and lifestyles. When I look at the man here, this fun person I've spent all this time with, I have no doubts. Of course, you being clothed is taking some getting used to..."

He laughed.

"But the few times I experienced your world, it made me want to run screaming back to the Vortex. All that money and stuff, it freaks me out."

"Hell, I'm just that guy you spent time with in the condo. That's who I am. All the rest is bullshit." Dude reeked with certitude.

Hell frowned. "I don't fit in at your country club. At all."

He laughed like all her worries were so ridiculous. Not quite on the verge of patronizing her, but close. "Hell, you are so cute." Okay, that was patronizing. Why wasn't she angrier? "You're right, I haven't seen this side of you. No part of you has been insecure."

She lowered her voice and tried to appear as sane as she could. "I'm not insecure, I don't feel unworthy, I hate being bullied. Your world doesn't like old, pink-haired, leather-clad tomboys. I'm not making this up. You don't know what it's like being someone like me. Besides, your world has already tried to kill me twice, and we were hiding our affair. I can't imagine what will happen to me now that it's all out in the open."

Finally, his cocksureness faded a notch, and he became serious. "Hell, this is an isolated incident, I can assure you. No one is going to come after you. I'm going to make sure of it. All your attacks happened when you were alone. You won't be alone now. You'll be surrounded by my people and guards. You're going to be fine. I promise. I love you, and you are safe."

His sincerity touched her deeply. She ran her hand down the side of his face. "Really? We can have that amazing bliss we found in the condo? We can have that all the time?"

"Yeah, Hell. All the time." He kissed her. "Now will you let me take care of you?"

No way was she starting off a relationship with a bunch of need. "I totally appreciate it, but now that I'm relatively lucid, I can take it from here. If you can spare a bodyguard, I'll go back to my hotel room, get some sleep, and then we can hook up tomorrow sometime when I'm feeling better?"

His brow went into a deep V. "Are you out of your fucking mind? There is no way in hell you're leaving my sight, woman."

Great, Trent. Two seconds into being a couple, and he was already yelling at her. "Honey, I don't—"

"You let Josh take care of you when you were sick, didn't you?" he countered, the look in his eyes sharp.

"Well, yeah, but we were living together and—"

"We're in a relationship now, right?"

"So you tell me. I mean, yes, I accept that. My brain is not there yet. Look, I—"

"Fine. Then we'll deal with this in the abstract. What do partners do for each other? They take care of each other, don't they? He wouldn't have let you go alone to some hotel room when you were sick, would he? He'd have kept you close to ensure you received the care you needed. Because he was your *mate.*"

"Yes, so—"

"Let me do my job."

It was like someone threw a switch and changed the channel on her life from single and alone to in a relationship. She was no longer a she, she was a we. With a freakin' billionaire who had more resources than she could imagine. The switch was so extreme she couldn't process it.

"Hell?"

"I'm here." He was going to win this argument. As freaked out as she was, he was probably right. "Logically, I can't help but agree. But you have no idea how hard this transition is for me."

"I know you better than you think I do. Will you just go along with my doctors and me? Will you just trust me?"

"I'll do my best. And sorry for fighting you when you're trying to be nice to me. I'm not exactly sane."

"It's okay, honey, you've been through hell, Hell."

"Not sure my nickname is helping me right around now."

He brought her to him and kissed her.

She got dizzy with heady love and clung to him. Shoving back the sudden tears, she ended the kiss, and stared into his gorgeous gray eyes. So hard to grasp that the deep love radiating from his gaze for was her.

When he pulled back farther, she noticed her stuff neatly stacked in the corner of the room. Her plug-in cooler, suitcases, toiletry bag, plus coats and sweatshirts with Secret Teddy perched on top of the pile. Her stomach went funny, and fear began to grip her. "Wait. You checked me out of my hotel room? So now we're living together? Did we jump a step here?"

He pulled her close once more, a big smile on his face. "Well, since you don't have a home, I thought it would be a good idea to provide you with one."

Uh-oh. She didn't need a provider, she needed a mate. And she still wasn't completely convinced she needed that, either. "I have a home in two months. I put a down payment on a duplex."

"Look, we don't have to deal with this now," he said with a squeeze and a confident expression. "For the next two months, you live with me. Then we'll see if we jumped the gun, okay?"

He seemed supremely sure of all this. Hell's brain was still somewhere back at her apartment before it got bombed.

But the thought of being by his side all the time was the greatest gift anyone had ever given her. More than a dream come true, a dream beyond her wildest imagination. The secret dream she'd been hiding from herself since the beginning with him.

His brow wrinkled. "Unless you don't want to spend the night with me—"

She shook her head. "No. I do. It's all I want, which scares the crap out of me. I'm terrified, BC. And overwhelmed."

He squeezed her. "Again, let's come back to this in two months. You've got enough to deal with right now."

"Okay. And thanks," she forced herself to say instead of giving him the twenty-five thousand reasons living with him this soon was a terrible idea. "Sorry for accusing you of kidnapping me. I wanted this so badly, wanted to be with you so horribly, I just couldn't even face considering that it might be a possibility. I honestly have felt bad about sleeping with you while you're married. I hate adultery."

He smiled and kissed her. "I know. And I love you for that."

"I love you, too, BC. A whole, whole lot."

His gray eyes positive and bright, she'd never seen him look so happy. He really loved her. Actual, real love. For her.

Hot, bubbly energy spread throughout her body, centering on her heart. She hugged him tight and breathed in his scent, unable to comprehend her luck.

He nearly crushed her in a hug.

Was it true? Was he the one?

Could she count on him?

He kissed her on the forehead. "Also, if you're wondering where your car is, it's parked in the parking lot right out front. Your keys are over there on the dresser."

"Great. Cool."

"Now here's my plan," he said. "The doctor comes in and does his thing, then I hold you all night so you can sleep."

Sounded like Heaven. "I've never had any better offer in my life. Even though I'm going to pay you back for all this. I want copies of all the bills."

His face twisted with anger, and his eyes filled with fire. "Hell, Jesus Christ, noooo" —he blinked fast, his whole expression changed, and he smiled—"oookay. Okay. Fine," he said cheerfully. "So you'll let him see you, and you'll do what he wants? Right?"

She frowned and narrowed her eyes. "You're bullshitting me to manipulate me."

His happy expression didn't change. "Would you expect any less of me?"

She laughed.

He sent her a very real, exasperated smile. "Can we please deal with the money issues later and take care of you now? Please? That whole letting-me-do-my-job thing we just discussed?"

Her stomach tightened. This was not going to be easy. Every time she'd given up control in the past, it had cost her dearly.

Except with Josh.

But Brad Collins was no Josh Miller, and she needed to remember that. No man had been like Josh. She couldn't expect that level of commitment out of anyone.

But for the moment, she needed care, and Brad was offering it. She'd have to be suicidal not to accept it. She sent him a weak grin. "Sure."

His face relaxed, and he sighed. "Excellent." He turned serious once more. "Also, Dee McIntyre is stopping by tomorrow. I don't want to cross any boundaries here, Hell, but you need help. You almost died."

Her heart gave a thump, and her insides twisted. Yes, it was boundary-crossing, but mainly she didn't want to face her therapist. Dee was going to kill her for not contacting her sooner. Hell wanted to argue with him so badly. "Okay."

"Now let's let the doctor see you. Bill?"

The doctor appeared in the doorway, wary.

"Sorry," Hell said. "Someone has been very diligent at trying to kill me, and it's made me pretty crazy."

The doctor smiled, and his shoulders relaxed. "How about we take one more person off the list—you—and you follow my care instructions, okay?"

"Okay. I'll do my best to not be annoying. Can I have food now? I'm starving."

The doctor nodded. "Yes. Although, let me order for you. I want to make sure it's easy on your system, and you can keep it down."

"Well, I wasn't going to order hot wings and a pitcher of beer. I was thinking more like chicken soup with a side of sautéed vegetables and about six gallons of water."

More relief came over his face. "Good. Perfect."

"I'll order that from room service, shall I, doctor?" Nancy asked.

"Yes. If that's okay with you, Brad."

"Of course."

The doctor got a serious look on his face. "While we wait for your food, I want to talk to you about your wounds. Two were infected."

Hell gasped, and her spine stiffened. Brad put his arm around her and rubbed her shoulder. "No wonder my hip hurts. Okay, now I'm freaked out even more."

"We caught the infection in time, and you'll be fine. I'll give you something for the pain, and an antibiotic."

Brad kissed the side of her head. "You're not yourself, Hell. All you have to do is listen to Bill, and you'll be fine."

"Okay."

The doctor continued on.

Hell partially listened but mainly beat herself up for allowing her wounds to get that far.

Then something about the doctor and his tone struck her. He was talking to her like was she in kindergarten and didn't understand English very well.

Inwardly, Hell both relaxed and became annoyed. Doctor was clearly overdramatizing the situation because he thought she was such a whack job. She put on her fascinated listening face and tuned out. Whatever. She'd stopped trusting doctors a long time ago. A full eighty-five percent of her experiences with them had been negative. She'd been poisoned, misdiagnosed with cancer, and nearly all the pills she'd ever been prescribed had made her violently ill. She was at one end of the bell curve, and no doctor ever wanted to hear that.

As Dr. Bill went on about taking better care of herself, blah, blah, blah, Hell realized that she'd actually committed to Brad. Her thoughts returned to darkness, and she gave herself a good, solid mental kick in the ass. She had no doubts about her feelings for him, but the dude was a Casanova billionaire and the least trustworthy man in her life. Talk about a bucket of dumb. Why not skip the whole mess, skewer her heart, and slow-roast it over a campfire?

Hell glanced at Brad next to her. His gray fiery gaze caught hers and zapped her right to the core. Like he saw straight into her, past all her defenses, and saw deep inside and loved what he saw. Loved her. All of her.

A wave of white-hot energy ripped through her, making her lighter than air. A shiny energy field lit up around him, almost like a halo.

Alarms sounded, and her heart rate jumped. She squeezed his hand like everything was great, but turned back to the droning doctor and pretended to listen. This was too good to be true. Her dreams always died horrible, miserable, torturous deaths. This was merely the beginning of an even more spectacular failure.

After the doctor finished up his ultra-boring lecture, BC proceeded to grill him on how to handle any and every possible contingent problem that could arise with her. As his interrogation became both exhaustive and inventive, Hell made a mental note not to loan BC any more medical thrillers.

Thankfully, the food arrived while the men discussed her like she wasn't there, and Hell dug into a steaming bowl of tasty chicken and vegetable soup with warm sourdough bread, which breathed life back into her brain cells.

Finally, gratefully, BC shut up and the doctor left. Hell finished her meal and headed directly for the shower. After redressing her wounds and brushing her teeth, she felt slightly more human. She curled up next to BC in bed while he watched a car show, and realized it was the first time they'd been in bed together without having sex. Weird.

Yet something about the normalcy of the situation brought her great comfort. While certain to be temporary, screw it, someone was taking care of her for a minute.

Good.

CHAPTER 25

J osh hugged her. *"I love you, Elmo, bundles and oodles."*

Her face in his big, warm, muscular chest, she breathed in his musky scent and relished his rough, unshaved chin against her temple while his long hair tickled the side of her face. He'd never felt so good. His large, buff arms enveloped her, making her safe and happy.

She stood on her tiptoes and nuzzled his neck. "I've missed you. Where have you been?"

"Around, Elm. But now that I know you're gonna be okay, it's time for me to jet."

Panic struck her, and her heart rate jumped high. "No!" He tried to pull away, but she wouldn't let him go. She hung on, starved for his embrace. "But I want to be with you. I've missed you so much."

"You'll be fine, Elmo. Now I gotta go."

Twelve years of longing ripped her apart. "I love you! Don't leave me!" She couldn't go through it again. She couldn't lose him again. She couldn't face that horrible pain. If she just held on to him hard enough, he couldn't leave her.

He rubbed her back. "It's okay, honey. We'll always have us. No one can take that away." He pushed away to face her, his large blue eyes radiating love.

His sweet face! Tears ran down her cheeks, and her heart filled with him.

His expression turned serious. "But you have to let me go now. Because it's not about us anymore, Elm, it's about you and what you need. Be where you are. Be with him."

She broke into violent sobs. How could he reject her and throw her into a relationship with Brad Collins? "Brad will break my heart! You never would! I want you, not him!"

As the words left her mouth, she realized that she had cheated on him! She cringed, and her face heated with shame. "I'm so sorry I slept with him and fell in love with him! I cheated on you!"

He ran his large hand over her head. "Elmo, calm down. No, you didn't. I died. You were supposed to move on. All I wanted was for you to find someone to love."

Her heart tore like the two men were playing tug-of-war with it. She loved Brad as much as she loved Josh. How had this happened? It was all so confusing! How could she love two men at once?

Josh's expression was confident and peaceful. "Elmo, you and Brad are supposed to be together now. Nana Miller says he's one of the good ones. He got a little lost, but you'll straighten him out."

"Nana Miller?" Josh's paternal grandmother had been very special to her.

"Yeah, she's the one who got you two together. She's here, and sends her love. But the most important thing, and the reason I like Brad, is because he loves you as much as I do. None of the other guys did, but he does. So now, I'm gonna jet."

Her pulse jumped high. "No! Don't leave me! Brad scares me!" She held on to him with everything she had.

If she stayed in his embrace, she could go back in time and be with him. All she wanted was the safety of the past.

Josh's hold on her loosened, and he began to glow like a light bulb. Soon, he radiated such bright energy she had to look away. She reached for him, but her arms found nothing but air.

His voice came from all around her. "Love you, Elm. See you in the Light."

Sobbing, she cried out, "Don't leave me. I'm afraid!"

Josh materialized back in her arms, and she hugged him tight.

"Don't be afraid, I have you," he said. But his voice was deeper and of a completely different timbre. He smelled piney, not musky, and his body shape had changed: smaller, thinner, and wiry. Instead of standing, they were lying down in bed in a dark room.

Hell couldn't make sense of it. WTF? "Josh?"

"No, Hell, it's me, BC. You're okay. You're dreaming."

Josh? BC? Who was holding her? Smelled like BC. Sounded like him.

Oh, shit, she'd been dreaming about Josh and had woken up in BC's arms. Surreal. "BC?"

"Yeah."

"Is this real?"

"Yeah, babe. It's real. You're at the Rosewood Hotel with me, and everything's going to be all right." He turned on the light, and they both blinked against it. His eyes met hers, and he lit up with a smile.

A rush of love went through her. "I had a dream about Josh."

"Yeah?"

"He said good-bye. He told me to be with you. That I wasn't betraying him by loving you. I was in his arms a second ago, and now..." She nearly crushed him in a hug.

"I gotcha, babe." He held her tight and gently rocked her.

"I don't know how to trust you. I want to, but I'm so afraid. I don't want to lose you. I can't go through it again. Losing Josh almost killed me. I can't lose you. I couldn't stand it."

"You won't lose me. Not a chance. You'll see. You'll keep waking up in my arms."

"Jesus Christ, I sure hope so."

"I love you, Hell. Bundles and oodles."

"What did you just say?"

"That I loved you."

"No, after that."

"What? Bundles and oodles?"

"Yeah." Goose bumps rose all over her skin. "You're freakin' me out. Did I say that in my sleep?"

"No. My nanny always said it to me. That she loved me bundles and oodles."

"Really? That's weird. I've only heard it from Josh."

"Josh used to say that?"

"Uh-huh. Just said it in the dream."

"That *is* weird. Nanny Mary was great. One of the people who loved me the most in my life."

"I don't think you've told me about her."

"I'll have to remedy that sometime. But now, I want to know how you're feeling and what you need."

"What time is it?"

He looked over her shoulder, then met her gaze. "Six thirty in the morning."

"Wow. This is the first time I've slept more than two hours in days."

"I'd like to think I'm helping."

"You can take full credit. Man, you are fifty times better, no, a bazillion times better than a teddy bear."

"Rarely have I received such a compliment," he said, kissing her on the forehead. "You want some food? Let me order for you, okay? Eggs and toast and fruit, maybe?"

"I don't want you to go to any trouble. I can call."

He leaned in, his thick, black eyebrows high. "Hello? My job?"

Uncomfortable, but cowed by the steely resolve and need in his eyes, she nodded. "Eggs and toast and fruit, perfect."

He smiled. "Okay."

BC called room service and then took her in his arms again.

She snuggled against him. "Sorry I called you Josh. I..."

"Don't. I'm the first mate you've had since him. Makes sense. Actually makes me feel better. You haven't loved anyone like this since him, have you?"

"No. Not at all. I think I'd been clinging to him without realizing it. Like it was okay if I got my physical needs met with other people but not my emotional needs. I felt like I was cheating on him if I really liked anyone."

"Sounds like you're ready to make peace with that part of your life."

"I am. While the mystical side of me believes I really just saw Josh, clearly a part of my subconscious needed to give myself permission to let go of him and embrace this. Whatever this scary-ass thing is we're doing here."

"It's called love."

"Scares the crap out of me."

"Me, too, Hell, me, too."

"Good. Glad I'm not alone." She sighed and snuggled against him.

He rubbed her back. "Not anymore. I felt like I won Wimbledon when I woke up a few minutes ago and you were next to me. This is the first night you've willingly intentionally spent the night with me." He kissed the side of her face.

She giggled. "Yeah, those couple five in the morning 'Oh, shit!' surprises when I woke up in the condo and thought I was home."

"I loved those times. One night, I think it was in early January, I just held you and watched you sleep."

A warmth came over her heart she hadn't experienced in years, her throat closed, and tears rushed to the surface. She hadn't been loved like this in so long she'd forgotten how it felt.

An earlier exchange they'd had came to mind. "No wonder you freaked out that night when I showed up at the condo kinda messed up."

He pushed back, his mouth open, his eyes wide. "Kinda messed up? You were bleeding, Hell. You'd just run from the cops and had bruises and scrapes all over you. How was I not supposed to react?"

Oops. Oh, yes. Relationships. Crap. Now it was coming back to her. She turned her attention to neatening the covers. "Why did I bring that up?"

"I'm glad you did." He sent her a grave look. "We'll have to have some discussions about your job. It would be very challenging for me to bail you out of jail."

The rusty part of her brain that handled pesky males began to oil and work. She leaned back to face him. "Hey, that's the first time I've had to run from the police in years." *Year. Six months, tops.* "Believe it or not, I avoid drama. Look, when I told you that story, I had no idea of your feelings. I initially lied, if you remember, but then that stupid newscast came on, and I reacted before I could think." *And I would have kept lying had I been able to foresee the future.*

He frowned, his face reddening. "Are you trying to reassure me or worry me more?"

Best way to smooth over an argument was to pretend there was none. "Look, it all worked out fine. We're good. I won't bring the cops to your door. Promise." *At least for the next few months, anyway.*

BC opened his mouth to say something, then shut it.

She knew what he was thinking. "You're about to offer to support me so I can quit my job."

"No. Well, yes." He twisted his mouth. "But I'm getting a hint that you wouldn't go for it, even though it would make me very happy to do so."

She let out a long breath. "I don't want to go into this all right now. I'm too tired and overwhelmed. But I'm willing to discuss any topic." *But I'm not quitting until I'm too old to run away from the cops.* "And I am also acutely aware that I just leapt into an arena that is much more visible to the public and the media. I won't do anything to get you or me in trouble, I promise." *Amazing how well she could lie when she needed to.*

He clearly wanted to say more, but sighed and kissed her.

Time to put BC on the No Information List. Last thing she needed was micromanaging by a man with more resources than God. Thankfully, she had Death monitoring her and her devices. She wouldn't put it past BC to stick GPS units and microphones in all her possessions and clothes. His caring was adorable, but he clearly needed to be contained.

Time to invest in lip glue.

∾

AFTER FOOD AND TEA, THE SUN CAME UP. HELL TOOK A QUICK SHOWER in the suite's large, marble master bathroom, changed the dressings on her wounds, and slipped into comfy, relaxed-fit yoga pants, a Sex Pistols T-shirt, and a black hoodie with a white skull on the front. When she emerged from the bathroom, she found BC waiting for her on the newly made bed. Wearing a black T-shirt and jeans, he'd showered and shaved and looked scrumptious. She eagerly joined him, and he brought her close to cuddle. He felt wonderful. And as much as her brain was still scrambled, she felt more centered than she had since her apartment had been blown up. She almost felt safe.

Something about their five-room suite in the Rosewood Hotel seemed familiar as well. While one of the priciest places around, the hotel's choice of décor was more austere, simple, and chic than ostentatious.

"Hey, I wanted to ask, how did Sherry take the news?" Hell asked.

His body went rigid, and his face fell.

Great, Trent, let's ruin the mood. "I'm sorry. You don't have to tell me. It's okay."

"No, it just... She was pissed. And not because she loved me. She admitted that she'd never loved me, but that I owed her the marriage. First thing out of her mouth was, 'How dare you! Now I'll never make country club president! You did this on purpose to ruin my chances, didn't you?'" he said, doing a high-pitched, screechy imitation of her.

"No."

His gray eyes wide, he nodded. "Yes. I didn't think she could shock me, but she did."

"I'm sorry, honey."

"Don't be. You woke me up. And saved me. God, she's a rotten bitch. She recounted all the horrible things I'd done to her in this litany, this torrent of verbal abuse. Touted all the sacrifices she'd made, like staying with me even though I'd gotten old, ugly, and bald."

Hell gasped. "But you're so hot!"

He kissed her on the cheek. "Thanks for that."

"Even though she didn't love you, you still wounded her pride. Old, ugly, and bald, my ass. She just wanted to hurt you."

"She is malevolent. I had no idea how soulless and unfeeling she really was." His thick dark eyebrows high, he shook his head.

"Probably made you feel better about the divorce."

He snorted. "Ecstatic." His eyes darkened, and his lip curled. "Rotten bitch. Wish I would have left her years ago. Like, the month after we got married."

"She gave you kids," Hell offered.

His miserable expression didn't change. "Yeah, and they like me about as much as she does. I haven't been able to reach my daughter emotionally since she was a little girl, and even then she was pretty standoffish. Now she's as closed off and cold as her mother. And my son resents me. Which is my fault. I should have fought Sherry when she wanted to send them away to boarding school. Neither of the kids ever forgave me for that."

"But Sherry was the one who sent them away."

"Well, she didn't frame it that way, and I didn't do a great job of keeping up with them. I'd just started the venture capital thing when they went away, and I got all caught up in eclipsing my father and forgot everything else in my life. Including the people in it. I've made a lot of mistakes in my life, but my kids are the worst."

"Maybe you can work on making up for that."

He glanced at her, and then his focus went to a loose thread on his jeans. "I've tried reaching out. My son is definitely more open to it. Took an internship last year at my company, and we actually got along well. He finally let out some of his anger, and we talked. That's when I found out that Sherry had told the kids that boarding school was my idea."

"Jesus."

Brad turned to her. "I surprised him, the way I reacted. I don't think he completely bought my side of the story, but I think he might eventually forgive me for letting him down. We share a lot of interests. But Victoria is always going to hate me. Her mother did a great job of poisoning her against me."

"I'm sorry, BC." She took him in her arms and held him tight.

He hugged her. "Don't be. I deserve it all." He released his grip.

Hell scanned the room. "Hey, do you know where my phone is?"

"Charging over on the dresser there." He pointed across the room. "It was nearly dead when Brittney brought it here. She was the one who packed up your room for you. I hope she got everything."

Hell wanted to get up, but her body didn't want to move. "From what I've seen, it's all there. But I need to tell Matt and Joanne where I am. They're probably both freaking by now."

"I've been in contact with both."

"That's right, you told me you picked Joanne's brain. Good. And you talked to Matt, too, that's right." She grinned at him and patted him on the thigh. "Hey, you're acting like a boyfriend and everything."

"I knew they'd both be worried."

He'd accessed her phone. Hell's stomach gnarled. "So did you see who else called?" she said in what she hoped was an innocent tone. Hopefully, Capasso hadn't.

BC didn't seem to notice. Cool. "You received several calls, most names I didn't recognize. I only responded to Matt and Joanne."

"Okay." She let out a long breath.

"You're worried about Capasso, aren't you?"

Her stomach caved in. Shit. She had to balance this carefully. Let Brad into her heart but not her secrets. If she corroborated what he thought Capasso had done to her, he'd want retribution. "Nah. I can handle him," she tossed off.

"Your eyes just dilated."

Her body went on alert. "You stay out of it. That's between him and me."

"What are you going to tell him?"

She rubbed between her eyes. "That it's over."

Brad made a dismissive noise.

She gripped his arm. "Dude, everything will work out fine. I know how to handle him." Then she let go and moved back a bit. Super-unpleasant prospect.

"Don't lie to me, Hell."

"I'm not lying," she lied. "He has a wife and four other mistresses and can only take so much Viagra without killing himself. He may think he cares a little about me, but once I make it clear that I'm with you now, he'll get over it."

"That story was right, wasn't it? He beat you up for saving that young prostitute."

She looked away before she could stop herself. "No. Brad, look, I want our relationship to be clean. Let's let go of the past."

"I would if it didn't involve the present. He still thinks he owns you, and I want him to know that he doesn't."

Her irritation built, and she faced him. "What? That you do?"

"Hell," he said in a warning tone.

"Sorry. I don't like talking about Capasso, okay? Let me handle him. You promise right now, you won't talk to him."

He glanced downward. Her alarms went off. That's all she'd need!

"Brad, I mean it."

He turned to her, his face churning with upset, pain in his eyes. "You haven't been able to handle him for eleven years. Why do you suddenly think you'd be able to now?"

Like a gut punch to the solar plexus, the realization hit her hard. Brad was uncontrollable. Urgency possessed her, and her heart rate increased. Capasso would love nothing more than to kill him. "Brad. Listen to me. Don't do it. I mean it. That's my life, not yours. I have to have clear boundaries here. You have to listen to me. I'm not your property, I'm not his property, I'm my property. And he has been good to me."

His eyes darkened. "By putting you in the hospital?"

She tried to maintain direct eye contact. "He didn't put me in the hospital. That story was wrong."

His lips tightened, and the look in his eyes steeled. "We shouldn't start off a new relationship on a foundation of lies."

She sighed, leaned back against the bed, and put her head in her hands. Marco would kill her and Brad without a thought. Maybe this whole thing wouldn't work after all. Tears came into her eyes. Torn in half with only a few spare brain cells.

"Hell, I'm sorry. Please don't cry. I have to protect you."

She took her hands away from her face. "I'm not in danger," she snapped. Total. Lie. Okay, this sucked. The man was quickly becoming proficient at reading her. She'd never had a dude pay this much attention to her. Hopefully, his intensity and interest in her life would wane soon, and he'd click into Normal Boyfriend/Husband Mode: oblivious, wrapped up in work, only paying attention to her for sex, food, and occasional companionship.

Brad started to say something but stopped.

She wiped her eyes and heaved herself out of bed, which hurt a lot. She groaned.

"What do you need? I'll get it for you."

"Just getting my phone."

Hell's heart rate went higher, and sweat broke out on her forehead. Marco might still be behind the attacks. And if he wasn't before, he might be now. This relationship could push him right over the edge. She had to see him as soon as possible, tell him that it was over between them, and hope he didn't freak out. She retrieved her phone and went to the messages. Then climbed back in bed with Brad even though she wanted to bolt.

But how was she supposed to face Marco? A) She couldn't take care of herself yet, and B) she couldn't leave Brad, not now. Besides, if Marco planned on killing her, there would be nothing she or Brad could do to stop it. She might as well spend her last few days on Earth happy.

"Let me see who called. Brother. Don't care. Crap. What the hell does Martin want? Hasn't he tortured me enough?"

"Uh..." BC frowned and bit his lip.

"What?"

Rubbing the back of his neck, his attention went to the floor.

Muscles tensing, Hell prayed it wasn't something horrible.

"What?"

He took a deep breath and looked her straight in the eye. "I was worried you were dying and wanted to alert your family members. So I searched your phone, saw his name come up in a few messages, and I know him. But since your sister is such a bitch, I thought I ought to get a sense of how the relationship between you and him was, so I..." The look behind his eyes began to heat.

Her face flushed with shame, and worry ate at her stomach. Hopefully, BC hadn't believed any of Martin's poison. "You listened to his messages." She needed to make sure that if she almost died in the future, she destroyed her phone first.

BC's carved face turned to granite; his eyes stormed with fury. "That horrible fucking asshole. I wanted to drive over there and wrap my hands around his neck and squeeze until his eyeballs popped out."

A little thrill went through her, and she relaxed. "Ooo, I like that visual." While sorry he had to hear it, her heart warmed with this newfound ally. She wasn't alone. What affected her, affected someone else. And that someone else had power. More power than any other boyfriend she'd had.

BC gave a flash of a smile, then his face went hard again. "I can't believe the stuff that came out of his mouth."

"He's been worse." Hell propped herself up on her pillows a bit more. Pain lit up her leg, and she hissed and winced.

BC's whole vibe had turned warlike. He held himself taller in bed, his gaze sharp. "No more. You know I'm talking to him about this."

Buzzy energy raced through her at the thought. "Fine. I'd like to burn those bridges. I need a new life. A new tribe. A new family. I'm leaving all those assholes behind. Well, once Mom and Dad are gone."

"Only one who seemed the slightest bit concerned was your brother, Frank."

"He's okay."

"Your sister left you a really nice message," he said in a sarcastic tone. "I'm sorry, Hell. Only my father is mean to me. You have a whole collection of people. But your men are nice. Were nice." His eyes grew troubled, and he worked his mouth, then rubbed his lips. "I'm sorry, I heard a couple of their messages. I couldn't stop myself, and it was low, even for me."

While alarming, he openly confessed to what he'd done, and he wasn't happy with himself. Good. "It's okay, BC. This is all pretty extreme. I know you just want to protect me." BC reminded her that her voice mail could contain more anger bombs, and she honestly couldn't handle any more abuse at the moment. She set her phone on the nightstand.

"I won't do it again, I swear," he assured her. "I don't want you in my phone, either."

Her back stiffened. *Gurk. Sorry, already inside.*

"But I have to say it reassured me," BC continued, thankfully not noticing that she'd tensed up.

Right back atcha. Only when she'd heard and read his messages did she realize how tame and normal he was. He might come off as a big deal to the world at large—and have an edge in bed—but down deep, with his friends, he was just a kind, sweet boy.

BC said, "The only nice people in any of those messages were your guys. Or your ex-guys. Totally different tone. I think they all care about you more than you believe. I think most of them are in love with you." He didn't seem jealous; he seemed relieved.

"Doubtful, but they were nice. None cared as much as you."

He kissed her.

Her brain went fuzzy. She could only think of getting naked with him. "When can we do it?" she asked impatiently.

He laughed. "Later. Matt's going to be here any minute."

"This is the longest period of time we've spent together without having sex. I don't want to start a trend here."

He grinned, and his eyes sparkled.

Brittney, BC's PA, stepped in the room. "I'm sorry to bother you, but there's a Matt Sinclair here to see Miss Trent?"

"Speak of the devil," Hell said. "Send him in. And please call me Hell."

The dark-haired young woman looked to Brad for confirmation, who nodded. She smiled at Hell. "Okay, Hell."

The girl disappeared.

Matt walked in the room, bursting into a big smile upon spotting her. "How's the patient?"

So different than just a week before. He actually liked her now. Go figure.

"Better. Food and rest has been a miracle cure. Helped to have a live teddy bear sleeping next to me, too." Hell held out her hand, and Matt came close to the bed and took it.

BC leaned over, extending his hand, and he and Matt shook.

Relaxing back against the headboard, BC gave her knee a squeeze. "Should I leave you two alone?" he asked, looking like he wanted to stay.

Hell gave it a split second of consideration but saw no reason for him not to be there. Then she wouldn't have to repeat everything later with her Swiss cheese memory. "No need. Besides, this case involves you. Unless you have any objections, Matt?"

"None. So how are you feeling?"

"Great," she tried to say with conviction.

BC pursed his lips and nudged her. "Great she says with shrapnel deep in her side and a Mafia boss calling her and someone trying to kill her."

"I'm fine. Okay, so, Matt, what's the scoop?"

His eyes took on a victorious shine, and he grinned. "I found the librarian."

CHAPTER 26

Hell's heart leapt into her throat, and she sat up straight in bed. Swinging her legs over the edge of the mattress, she put her feet on the floor. A wave of burning pain from the wounds on her hip and thigh prevented her from jumping up to dance. "You found the librarian? Where? When? How?"

Matt gave a conspiratorial grin. "Secret." He settled into a sleek, modern, boxy white leather chair opposite the bed. Wearing a tan jacket, a light blue shirt, and dark slacks, he looked sharp this morning. With his thick, wavy light brown and gray hair, intense blue eyes, and pleasantly weathered square face, the dude was a looker.

BC scooted down the bed and sat next to her.

She made a face and bounced on the bed, hurting her leg and hip. "Ow. Just tell me."

Matt chuckled, his eyes crinkling. "First, I sifted through the photos of every PI in Northern California. Nothing. Then I thought about her. If she was a PI who broke the law, she might have gotten into trouble. So I searched for PIs who'd lost their licenses in the past few years. Finally found a Miss Judith Jones in Sacramento, recently released from jail on assault charges. Picture didn't completely look like the librarian, but the woman was ugly enough to be her. So I drove up, found her now shuttered office but couldn't locate her. But I did find the bar where she hangs out. And this picture of her." He stood, walked over, and handed her his cell.

Hell wondered why he had such an expectant look on his face. She examined the pic on his phone. Two older, leather, S and M/biker lesbians in an embrace. Both had very short gray hair. Neither looked like the librarian.

"One on the left."

Hell zoomed the photo and finally recognized the squat nose and weak chin. But other than that, the woman looked completely different, all dolled up in black leather chaps, a leather jacket, and a leather cap covered in chains. "How did you know this was her?"

Matt gave a satisfied smile. "Bartender was quite forthcoming with information. She apparently hates Judy because she stole her girlfriend. Couldn't wait to tell me everything."

Hell stared at the picture, unable to reconcile her first impression of a dull, boring PI with this tough hellion. "I can't handle this. So is she into sadomasochism, or is she a biker?"

"Both. She's also got a pretty substantial rap sheet and an old murder charge that was dismissed for lack of evidence."

Hell gasped. "Murder? Crap. She wasn't just fooling around with that gun. She would have shot us."

Brad stiffened beside her, and she put her arm around him to reassure him.

Matt nodded. "Judy Jones is one bad apple."

Hell gestured with the phone. "So she *was* wearing a wig."

"Yeah, and a disguise."

"But her face wasn't disguised. Wow, she got hit hard by the ugly stick. Course, if she shaved her face, and wore a more flattering hairstyle and some makeup, she'd clean up okay. Looks like she works hard to accentuate her worst features. I mean, can she smile? She's even scowling in this photo." She held up the pic as evidence. "So what was with the assault charge? Who did she beat up?"

"She intimidated a cheating husband while on a case for the wife and ended up beating the crap out of him. Broke his arm with a tire iron."

Hell's jaw dropped, and she pointed at the photo. "Her?"

Matt nodded, his eyebrows high. "Yeah, she's apparently vicious as hell. Has a bad rep in the S and M scene as a Dom who goes too far. Gets in a lot of bar fights. Is a total badass. Or thinks she's a badass. Bartender said she used to run with a biker gang, then decided to become a PI to try to go legit but ended up basically being a hired thug."

"Librarian, more like the Killer Death Librarian. Terminator Librarian." Hell assumed a straight-shouldered pose and a severe expression. "Your book is late?" she demanded in a bad Austrian accent. "I vill beat you viss a tire iron! Quiet! I say quiet or I shoot!"

The men laughed.

"How old is she?" Hell handed Matt his cell.

He took the iPhone and returned to his chair. "Fifty-eight."

"I knew she wasn't much older than me. So who hired her to track me?"

Matt put his cell in his pocket and crossed his ankle over his thick knee. "Haven't got that yet. But there may be no trace between them. No history. She's known for her discretion with clients and only works for cash."

"There goes Death's help. Shit."

"Still, we'll find her. And when we do, we'll make her talk," Matt said with a confident tilt to his chin.

Dude was the picture of a stalwart cop. Broad-shouldered, clear look in his eye, professional, experienced. Thank God he'd been disgraced, or she'd never have gotten someone this skilled for so cheap. Even though she felt a little bad about paying him so little. She made a mental note to try to scrape together a bonus for him at the end of the job. That was, if she was still alive to give him one.

Hell turned to BC. "Does Sherry have a connection to Sacramento?"

Brad shook his head, his tanned scalp catching the light from the bedside lamp. "Not that I know of. No. Her mother's in Marin. I'm not sure she's ever been to Sacramento, except to drive through."

"What about Lindsay? Any connections to Sacramento?" Matt asked.

BC's eyes widened. "Her mother lives there. She grew up there. Her whole family lives up there. Shit."

A little rush went through Hell, and she pointed at Matt. "Bingo. What's the surveillance on Lindsay revealed?"

Matt didn't seem as excited as she, but then again, his life wasn't on the line. "Nothing concrete so far. Just that same incriminating activity the night of your bombing. Taking off in a yoga outfit and coming back home late."

"Yeah. Last I checked, Death's monitoring Lindsay's phones. But I haven't talked to him since you and I were at Joanne's. We need to find out if Lindsay had assault charges levied against her in the past. But if he found out anything significant, he would have called me."

"She may have a prepaid phone she's using to contact Jones," Matt said.

Hell tsked. "Yeah. Damn it. We need to know who she's calling. We need that connection between her and Judy Jones. I think we'd better plant some bugs in Lindsay's house."

Matt's expression hardened. "Illegal activities could muck up the case."

Hell prickled with annoyance. She always broke the law and never got caught. Well, rarely got caught. "We just use it for our own purposes. Then we direct the cops to do their own investigation once we find something."

Matt held up his hand. "How about we approach the job a bit straighter? Like, we wait and question Jones. She may easily give up Lindsay, and then we don't have to break the law."

Hell considered this. "Huh. Usually, I break the law, then cover it up later." The men's attention sharpened on her. Her heart gave a start. Shit. Her Brain-To-Mouth Disease could really screw her with these guys. Out of the corner of her eye, she caught BC staring at her. Hell purposely kept her focus on Matt. Even though he didn't seem very happy with her suggestion, either.

His lips tight, Matt said, "Hell, if I ever have a chance at clearing my name, I can't risk getting caught in a scandal now."

Yes, and I wish hadn't said that. "You're right. Sorry, since I don't have the authority to use certain surveillance techniques available to law enforcement, I've developed some work-arounds. I don't technically break the law." Backpedal, backpedal, backpedal. Total utter lies. Now to throw someone else under the bus to deflect the blame away from herself. "Death does. He takes all the risks for me. And his work can't be traced back to me."

Both men relaxed a bit. Yay! Her amazing powers of bullshit had returned!

"Ask Death if he'll work for me," BC said.

Hell made a puffing noise. "He won't."

"Why not?"

"He doesn't like you."

"Why not?"

"Because you're a rich, evil bastard who's won my heart."

"Jealous?"

"Yes. And he knows everything about you. Except your heart. And if you didn't know that part, you may judge the other parts of your life rather harshly."

"I see," he said, clearing his throat and looking uncomfortable.

While a scoundrel, the boy was especially attractive this morning. With his nicely shaped, sexy bald head, thick black brows, sparkling gray eyes, square jaw, and kissable mouth, every cell in her body wanted to screw him and never stop. She forced her brain away from thoughts of attacking him and onto the subject at hand.

Hell looked at Matt. "Okay, but what about putting a tracker on the librarian's car? That's legal for us to do." Not really, but if she said it with enough confidence, maybe the men would believe her.

Matt shook his head. "No need. Jones's not going anywhere. She's an only child and the sole caretaker of her mother."

Hell gave a knowing nod. "And her mother's in Sactown?"

"No, Pleasanton in a retirement home," Matt said. "Jones drives down there three times a week. Apparently, it's the only thing she does that isn't self-serving. According to the bartender, she dotes on her mother."

"Huh. Oh, that's why she was on the computers in Pleasanton and Sacramento."

Matt leaned forward. "How did Death know about the librarian's computer activities if—"

Hell gave a wave of her hand. "He didn't. Early on, jeez, only, like, a week ago, still, a long time ago in a galaxy far, far away, Death reported that there were four people trying to access my information. Thompson at the behest of this guy." Hell thumbed toward Brad, who coughed and reddened. She almost named Capasso. *Aaauugggh!* Her stomach tightening, she continued, "And two amateurs using library computers in Sactown and Pleasanton."

"Who was the other one?" Matt asked.

"Uh, Patriots, I mean, Rampart Security. My old buddies were worried about me." No way was she bringing Capasso into this conversation.

BC's contrition faded quickly into stoniness, and he sent her a laser-edged look. "You were in my information, too. And you're still inside my phones and computers, aren't you?" He elbowed her.

Hell's face heated, and she grimaced before she could stop the reaction.

He ripped into her with his dark gaze. "You *are* in there, aren't you?" he bit out in a very unfriendly tone. "One of my guys thought he had a hint of an intrusion, but the evidence vanished as he was watching. I know it wasn't Capasso. His guys are good, but not this good. That's Death's signature, isn't it?"

Hell looked away, glanced back at him, then moved her attention to her hands. "Sorry. Tryin' to save my life. I'll have him stop."

She could almost get a tan from the heat coming out of Brad's eyes. "How the hell— Damn, I really want to hire that guy. Do have any idea the level of sophistication of technology I have access to? I have some of the top guys in the country working for me. And your friend Death just navigates around them like they're preschoolers," he said with a large, sweeping gesture.

"Yeah, he's good, all right."

She could tell by the steely hunter look in Brad's eye that acquiring Death for his team would always be a top goal. Too bad.

"I'll never meet him, will I?" Brad asked.

"You might. But you won't know it."

Brad's attention on her intensified, seeming like he took her statement as a direct challenge to his authority. *Get over it, buddy. You may own my heart, but you'll never have my mind.*

Matt said in a very diplomatic tone, "So after you get some rest, let's go see the librarian, okay?"

"I want to go now," Hell said. "Yesterday."

BC sent her an incredulous stare. "Hell."

Matt nodded toward BC. "Listen to him."

Hell pondered this. Despite the shot of adrenaline regarding the librarian, she was just about to pass out from exhaustion. Her stomach still felt funky, she was dizzy, and her leg and hip hurt like hell. "Damn it. I do feel terrible. I could use another day's rest."

"Another day?" BC asked in a leading tone, looking at her like she was mental. "You need at least until Friday."

"Let's go Friday. But only if you're better," Matt said.

She stared at them both, fairly startled. Both were acting very fatherly. She'd never had anyone be fatherly in a good way toward her with the exception of her late partner. It felt really good, and really wrong. What usually followed any kind of fatherly help was emotional Armageddon. Dad never stopped until you were a little smoking cinder of nothingness.

BC put his arm around her. "Hell, you okay?"

Realizing that her expression had turned fearful, she forced a smile. "Yeah, fine." She made herself snap out of her mini-freak-out. Something told her that her future was paved with mini-freak-outs over people finally being nice to her. "Okay. You're both right," she said in a bright tone. "Let's go Friday, okay?"

"Okay," Matt said with a big smile.

But BC still stared at her. Damn it, he wanted to know everything she thought, and could tell when she was being duplicitous. Not good. She did not need the man in her head. She had to get better at the game. She'd forgotten what a balancing act relationships were. Especially new ones.

Hell had a question, and also desperately wanted to change the subject. "How's Tanner doing in jail?"

Matt's face fell, and he briefly looked at the floor.

Hell's body tightened. "What?"

He let out a long sigh, his upset clear. "He went nuts. They had to sedate him and put him in a prison mental ward. He's restrained and not doing well, unfortunately."

Hell recoiled, guilt wrenching her insides. "But he didn't do it." She wrapped her arms around herself.

"You and I know that, but the cops don't, and Tanner is not helping himself by freaking out."

There wasn't much she could do to help him with that. "Shit."

BC leaned against her. "You guys have completely cleared him?"

"No," Matt cut in. "But it's very clear to me that he's been set up. Way too much evidence. But the local cops have their man and don't want to look any further. Bombings freak out the public. Catching the guy that soon made everyone feel safer."

Hell made a disgusted noise. "No matter what I told them. Or didn't tell them."

Matt sent her a grave look. "Cops know you're holding out on them, Hell. They asked me about Capasso."

Her pulse quickened, and she stopped breathing, then forced herself to start. Her face flushed. Damn it! She didn't even want his name mentioned in front of Brad! "Great. Wait, what did they say they knew? What did you say?" All her attention went to reading Matt's mind. Would he tell her everything?

Matt uncrossed his legs and shifted in his chair, but his focus didn't leave her face. "I told them that Capasso had no motive. That you weren't seeing each other but once a year."

"They want him to be guilty, don't they?"

"They'd love to pin anything on him, yes." Matt nodded, removed a small notepad from his jacket pocket, flipped through it, and stopped on a page. He briefly read it, then looked up. "They interviewed him, but he had an airtight alibi since he was at an art opening, and there was a film crew on scene. Plus he apparently took them to task for even implying he might be involved. My buddy said while she wanted to keep hammering him about your attacks, it was clear to her that he was telling the truth. Not that they cared. If they could have, they would have pinned it on him just to take him down."

Hell let out a breath she hadn't realized she'd been holding so long. But she still couldn't quite believe Marco was innocent. Death would clear him once and for all when he was done with his investigation. "How did you get all this information? Cops wouldn't say anything to me."

"One of the ladies and I go way back," Matt replied, gesturing with his notebook. "I vouched for you. I mean, it's pretty obvious why you wouldn't open up about Capasso, and she knew that. Always lookin' for an angle to play, but she finally gave up. But she really likes Tanner no matter what other evidence I presented. She doesn't think that Jones' involvement is relevant. She thinks she's a lesbian who might have a crush on you or something."

Hell rolled her eyes. "Christ."

Matt snorted and smiled. "This girl—uh—woman and I go way back, but she and some of her co-workers don't like messes and want neat, wrapped-up answers even if they're not the truth. They're going forward with the case against Tanner." He shrugged.

"Shit." Hell looked down, her shoulders slumping. BC put his arm around her and brought her close. Her body relaxed, and a warmth went through her heart. God, she loved this guy.

"Don't worry, Hell," Matt said with a confident expression. "It's got to be Lindsay or Sherry. Now all we have to do is prove it."

Hell said, "Let me talk to Death and see if he's been able to clear Marco. And see what he found out about Lindsay's past." She turned to Brad. "Honey, could you get me my backpack on top of my suitcase over there?" She pointed to her pile of stuff in the corner of the suite.

Brad stood, retrieved her pink skull backpack, handed it to her, and took his place beside her on the edge of the bed. She zipped open the top of her pack and withdrew a Death phone from the plastic bag of cells.

"You have special phones?" Brad asked.

"Yeah, have to. One-use phones. He scrubs them and gives them back to me." She punched a preprogrammed button on the cell. It rang once, and he picked up. "Deathy? You there?"

"So happy to hear your voice, Hell," came his nerdy, radio-announcer-on-steroids reply. "I've been worried about you. Are you all right?"

"Fine."

"Am I correct in assuming you are in the company of Brad Collins at the Rosewood Hotel?"

Death saw all. "Yeah."

"He did file for divorce."

"I know. He gave me a copy of the papers."

"That was unexpected."

Hell snorted and glanced at Brad. "Tell me about it."

"I assume you are now in a public relationship with him?"

"Apparently. My brain hasn't exactly caught up with it."

"I hope you aren't trusting him."

Hell blew out some air between her teeth and gave a couple laughs. "Of course not."

"Good. If the relationship progresses much further, you'll need protection against his father's network, better known as the Cabal. They won't be happy about your alliance. Your association with Rampart has put you on their enemies list. We'll need to compile a dossier of their misdeeds and lock it away to protect you. Inform them that if something happens to you, the evidence against them will be released on the Internet."

The information was so overwhelming, Hell couldn't begin to process it. A chill went over her, and she shuddered. "Christ."

Brad brought her in for a side hug, and she leaned into him, feeling slightly better.

Ironic. He'd both put her in extreme danger and saved her.

"But first things first," Death continued, "we need to keep you alive now."

"Good plan. I mean, they can't kill me later if I die now."

Both men's attention sharpened on her. Death snickered.

Hell pretended she hadn't said anything alarming. "I need to know about Marco." Her belly tightened, but she hid her fear. Brad had to think she was unconcerned about Capasso.

"Yes, certainly. Both the General and I have done extensive investigations into his network, and no attack of any kind was ordered on you."

Her stress level eased a notch. "Okay, good."

"On the contrary, since the grenade attack, he's had his people trying to uncover who is at fault. He has sent out orders that you are to be protected, and if any information surfaces regarding you or your assailants, he is to be informed immediately."

Hell wanted to fully relax but needed to hear it once more. "So, honestly, in your opinion, do you think Capasso was in any way responsible for what's happened to me?"

"No. The General concurs."

Hell melted into a little puddle and almost slid off the bed. "Thank God. I didn't know what I would do if it were him."

Brad rubbed her back.

"However, I'm not certain how long Capasso's interest in your well being will last once he discovers your new relationship with his rival. He's launched several attacks on Brad's network of late."

Hell's stomach balled, and she gripped the bed with her free hand. Great.

Brad apparently heard Death's statement and leaned closer. After a second of consideration, she moved the phone so he could hear, but put a finger to her lips. He nodded. Lucky for BC, Death had amazing diction and a clear, strong, although nasally, voice.

Hell said, "Capasso did the same thing a couple months ago."

"Yes. However, this time, in deference to your new situation, I terminated several attacks on Brad's behalf. But he needs to improve his security."

"Could you let him know about the holes in his net?"

"I'll send my findings to his chief of network security, Gary Holloway. He's a talented man, but narrow-minded. He can't always see the whole picture."

"Brad wants to hire you." Hell glanced at BC next to her, who looked like he was practically salivating at the idea.

Death laughed.

"That's what I told him."

Brad made a face. Sighing, he got up and walked around the bed to behind her.

Matt stretched out his long legs and scrolled through the messages on his iPhone.

"I am always available to you," Death said. "However, aside from the threat his father poses to you, Brad is involved in several illegal operations of which you need to be aware. Using offshore bank accounts and money laundering through several countries, he's able to manipulate the price of the stock in his new companies."

Hell tightened her mouth, and a sting of embarrassment heated her face. Nice reality slap. Yes, Brad loved her, but he was still Satan. "Nice."

"I've created an extensive report for you to review. While most of his practices are the norm for people in his tax bracket, Collins pushes the limits and has made himself vulnerable."

Hell rolled her eyes and made a disgusted noise. "Great."

"While he could presumably buy his way out, he could expose you personally to unwanted attention by the government."

Hell's back and neck tightened, and she stretched her neck. "Peachy." No way would her success rate be as high without her unconventional methodology. How would she conduct her business under the scrutiny of the law? Navigating through Matt's obstacle course of morality had proved challenging enough.

"He's actually quite tame compared to his father," Death said. "His father makes Brad look like a Boy Scout. I'm sending you a full report on his father's misdeeds so you can begin to understand his power and reach. Quite extensive and elaborate machinations manipulating the entire global economy. He's exponentially more dangerous than anyone you've ever faced and makes Capasso look like a dime-store hood. Jack Collins is the current leader of the Cabal, the notorious organization Rampart Security fights. The Cabal created that little war you inadvertently joined when you worked with Rampart five years ago."

The dark clouds over her head opened up and drenched her. "How lovely." News just got better and better. Okay, so Brad wasn't Satan, he was Spawn of Satan.

A cup of coffee in his hand, Brad sat next to her and did a double take at her. Hell probably had on her Hate Stare. She tried to relax her brow and ease the fire in her gaze.

Death let out a long sigh like he was reluctant to tell her something.

Her stomach tightened. "What?"

"Not to be dramatic, but the more I think about it, the more it becomes clear we shouldn't wait on setting up your protection against Brad's father and the Cabal. Even if you and Brad don't last, they may not wait to find out. I'll get right on it. I actually can't overstate the danger. While you were merely having an affair with Brad, you presented no problem. With the advent of your now open relationship with his son, you will quickly become a target for removal. It would not be out of Jack's character to hire an assassin."

A hard virtual kick to the chest took her breath away.

BC and Matt sent her sharp glances.

She forced her expression to go neutral and her breathing to return to normal.

Death continued. "I'll have the dossier containing proof of one of his more heinous transgressions completed and secured tonight."

"Jesus."

Brad's focus on her intensified. Matt frowned. Hell pretended not to notice.

"Soon, you'll need to present the blackmail package to Jack. He must be encouraged to keep you alive. He and the Cabal will be concerned about your long-term prospects of becoming Brad's wife.

Since Brad is expected to one day take his father's place in the evil organization, I can say with certainty they will not want you by his side when he takes that position of power."

A chill went over her, all her muscles tightened, and she shuddered. "Holy Christ," she said instead of screaming. She wanted to run out of the room and keep running. Brad? Not only in the Cabal, but running it? The news was so huge it almost didn't fit into her brain. Sweat broke out all over her, and she had to fight to keep her mind and body from launching into a full-blown panic attack.

Matt put down his phone, looking like he was just about to ask her what was wrong. BC completely tuned into her facial expressions, and body language. She had to cover.

"Have no concerns, we will keep you alive," Death said.

"You bet," she said enthusiastically, trying to appear upbeat and not the least bit concerned. She smiled and chuckled, pretending that Death had just said something funny.

After a moment, Matt returned his attention to his phone, and Brad began picking lint off his trousers.

She let out a long, silent breath of relief, but her heart continued to pound. *Good Holy God.* Brad in the Cabal? Her teeth clenched so hard a molar squeaked. This was insane! This was crazy! This was— wait a minute. Wait just a goddamned minute. What was she thinking? Like she and Brad had a future? Ha! Their relationship had the shelf life of fresh fish. What the hell was she worried about? All her fears dissipated, and the tension in her body eased.

"Are you still there?" Death asked.

"Oh, sorry. Yes. Any reason to suspect that person we were discussing might be involved in what's happening now?" Hell kept her tone perky.

"No. Your relationship just went public. Jack Collins doesn't rush into decisions. Since I help the Patriots—Rampart—keep tabs on the Cabal's operations, I'm aware of most of their activities. I haven't seen your name crop up in four years."

She let out a nice, long sigh.

"But I expect to see you in their communications shortly."

Her stomach tightened, and she gripped the phone harder. *Stop worrying, Hell, you and Brad won't last the week.* She tried to shake off her fears and relax.

"Back to your new boyfriend," Death said. "My conscience is requiring me to warn him directly about a product of one of his current Internet companies. The app has been designed with a carefully constructed vulnerability. While it's designed to hurt Brad's company, it will most certainly hurt his innocent customers."

Hell looked at Brad with alarm.

His thick black brows high, BC leaned in closer.

"Say that again, honey, one of his companies' products is sabotaged?" Hell asked.

"Yes. Looks like the signature of one Stephen Mussen, if I'm not mistaken."

BC's eyes went wide, and his mouth dropped open. Then his face reddened, and he looked like he was about to rip the phone from her hand.

Hell silently gestured at him to listen, and react later. BC's brow a deep V, he gave a sharp nod.

"Mussen designed the system purposefully to have easy backdoor access to the computers in which the program is installed. I believe your new mate—along with many of his customers—could be being set up for thefts and/or blackmail schemes."

"Christ."

BC's eyes went dark, and his face turned to stone.

"I found three other instances of irregularities with various products in which Brad has invested," Death reported. "Along with the issues with his personal computer networks. He needs to be alerted so that you and his customers have zero vulnerability."

"I'll let him know. Could you send me a quick overview of the problems?"

"A courier should be arriving shortly with a thumb drive for Brad. I will be contacting his network manager myself. We knew each other in our past lives."

Brad sighed, and his shoulders relaxed a bit.

"Aren't you dead?" Hell asked.

"Brad's manager knows one of my new online personas. We've shared information recently. He has no idea he actually knows me. Or knew me."

"Okay, cool."

Death continued, "Also regarding Lindsay's past. She apparently assaulted two people, one of her sorority sisters and her son's live-in nanny. In both cases, the charges were dropped, and, I assume, a substantial payoff was made."

Hell's heart beat a bit faster. "What did she do to them?"

"Slammed her sorority sister over the head with some type of trophy, apparently in a jealous rage. According to the report I uncovered, Lindsay believed that she should have won the award," he said.

"Great. What about the nanny?"

"Slapped her across the face and cut her lip. Again, they settled, and the charges were dropped."

Hell nodded. "Okay. So she's prone to violence, which tilts the guilt scale further in her direction."

"Agreed. If you personally require my further assistance, the General and I have determined several safe locations where you may hide and rest."

"I can't thank you enough. I hope I'm okay for right now."

"Brad does have sufficient personal protection for the moment. It's his networks that are somewhat porous."

"I'll tell him."

"And, of course, his father will present some challenges to your future security. But I believe the information I'll gather will effectively convince Jack Collins and the Cabal that keeping you alive is in their best interest."

While Hell was still triggered, she forced herself to set aside her fears. This was a temporary situation. Soon, she wouldn't even be on the radar of the Cabal and Jack Collins because she and Brad would be done. "Good. Thank you, sweetie pie. Love you so much."

"Awww, I love you, too."

Hell hung up and put a rubber band around the phone, indicating it had been used. She opened the card slot and withdrew the SIM card. After pocketing it—she'd flush it down the toilet later— she closed the phone, returned it to the bag of phones, and slipped the plastic bag back into her backpack. Brad didn't miss one of her actions.

Matt asked, "What about Lindsay?"

Hell relayed the information.

Brad nodded. "I remember when the incident with the nanny happened. Lindsay, of course, made it sound like it had been self-defense, like it was this giant mistake. And that the only reason they settled was to keep the story out of the news." He shook his head, looking like he'd lost a dear friend. "But I can't believe Mussen's setting me up. No wonder he proposed those changes recently. I knew there was something wrong with that request. There was a look in his eye I didn't like, and he was sweating like hell."

"Don't do anything until you read the report," Hell said. "Mussen could have a Trojan horse or some self-destruct code embedded in the program, along with his other scams."

Brad's jaw went tight, and he shook his head. "Son of a bitch. But, hey, thank your friend. Sounds like he's saved my ass."

"I will." Hell looked him right in the eye. "Death also revealed a bit about how you run your businesses," she said cheerfully. "Very enlightening." She sent him a big grin and a dark look. She wasn't going to mention anything in front of Matt, but she wanted Brad to know she didn't approve of his misdeeds.

His focus sharpened on her, a slight shadow of shame came over his face, and he looked away. "Huh."

"Yeah. We can discuss all that later," she said in the same faux perky tone.

Brad swallowed hard and checked the time on his Rolex.

Good, at least he had somewhat of a conscience. Christ. Fucking rich people.

Her thoughts veered back to the horrifying information regarding Jack Collins, the Cabal, and Brad's future, and her body hardened once more. But how much of a threat could she honestly present to

Collins and the Cabal? She'd only worked with Rampart once. Death had always been overly paranoid. He could easily be overstating the danger.

She shouldn't worry. Just concentrate on today and not worry about tomorrow. Especially since tomorrow was pretty much guaranteed to be Brad-Free.

Matt asked, "Brad, what did your guys find out about the household? Hell, I told BC about his housekeeper Esmeralda's involvement with the Mexican drug cartel so he could protect himself. With the caveat he didn't alert Mrs. Ruiz."

Hell's heart rate jumped, and she gripped the bedcovers, then forced herself to calm. While working with others hit her control-freak buttons, Matt was one of the best. She had to let go and trust him. "So Esmeralda's still at the house?"

BC nodded. "We're being cool and just watching her."

Hell relaxed even more. "Okay, good."

"She has no access to the finances," BC said. "I had no idea this was going on, but my butler, Higgins, has been handling the budget and finances for the house for the last fifteen years. Sherry delegated the responsibility and never told me. I've got the security guys keeping an eye on Ruiz. We've bugged her quarters and will be monitoring her."

"Where's Sherry?" Hell asked.

Brad's face hardened. "After she had her giant tantrum, she packed her bags and headed straight back to Marin to her mother's. I'm sure they're having a great time dissecting me."

Brittney walked into the room. "Mr. Collins, I'm sorry to bother you, but your father is on the phone for you. He sounds impatient."

Hell's body went cold, and she suppressed a shudder. Probably going to order Brad to dump her. Guess it was as good of a time as any to discover what kind of control Jack had over his son.

"Why didn't he call me on my phone?" Brad asked, pulling out the smartphone from his pocket. He checked the screen.

"He did, but you didn't answer."

"Oh, right. Forgot to turn it back on. I'll take the call out in the living room, Brittney. Great. He probably found out I left Sherry. This should be fun. If you will both excuse me, I'll try to make this short." His face weary and resigned, he kissed Hell on the cheek, stood, and left the room.

Matt looked at BC until he left, and then leaned in. "I have to tell you what happened with Sherry. Wow."

Her interest was instantly piqued, and excitement filled her. From the look on his face, this information was red hot. "What?"

"I didn't want to say anything in front of BC, but man, what a weird scene. She came on to me, and I mean, *came on to me.*"

Her mouth dropped open, then she bounced in place, starved for the info. "Really? Tell me everything and quick."

Matt relayed the incredible story of his interview with Sherry.

Hell was shocked, amused, and fascinated. This was not the Sherry she'd met. At all. "Let's keep our eye on her. But BC won't believe this stuff about Sherry. Can you deploy his guys to watch her?"

"Uncomfortable with that, Hell, but it probably would be smart. You should talk to BC about it."

"So you really think Sherry's capable of my attacks?"

Matt's expression grave, he gave a quick nod. "Yes. Yet there is still the possibility it's Lindsay, but Sherry is clearly guilty of something. She was working me hard. I don't like how much she knew about me and you. And I'm nearly positive she was lying about her alibi the night you got bombed. She could have been in the car with Esmeralda when she drove by the gardener and wouldn't stop. But her lies and her leaving the house might have nothing to do with the case. But she really wanted me to believe it was Lindsay. Whole thing was about hating you and shifting the blame to Lindsay. She orchestrated the whole interview from start to finish. Where I sat, where she sat—"

"So she could rub knees with you."

He shuddered. "God, she was creepy. Really, something is seriously wrong with that woman. At first, I thought she was pretty good-looking, but toward the end, all I saw was her ugliness."

Hell nodded. "She has an amazing exterior like Lindsay. And

Gwen, BC's other ex. I cannot figure out how the dude ended up wanting me."

"Hell, you're a very attractive woman, and you know it."

"Hey, don't get me wrong, I like how I look. But I'm not cut, pasted, and blonde. His previous three exes look like sisters. And I look like their weird, adopted step-cousin once removed."

"You're still insecure about this whole thing, aren't you?"

"Duh. He has legions of supermodels throwing themselves at his big, fat wallet, and he picks a broke, old, tomboy detective? He's crazy."

"About you," came his deep voice from the doorway.

Hell winced and flinched but rolled with it. It wasn't like her insecurity about the relationship was this huge secret. "And he's an eavesdropper."

"An eavesdropper who'd have to be deaf not to hear you. Your voice carries, honey."

"Yeah, that's a problem." A wave of dizziness overcame her, and she rubbed her eyes. Wow, she was tired.

BC came into the room, sat next to her, put his arm around her, and pulled her close while facing Matt. "She'll get over being insecure once she realizes that I'm not going anywhere."

So either Jack hadn't ordered Brad to dump her or Jack didn't have much control over his son. "True. If you keep being here, I'll start believing it's real. But not when I'm still this effed up. Matt, darling, I want to talk about the case, but I'm about to drop. I just got the two-second warning that I need to sleep."

Matt heaved himself to his feet and stretched. "Then sleep, Hell. We can talk later."

"Good."

Matt nodded and took a few steps toward the door. "Let's try to catch Jones in Pleasanton on Friday. She might be more willing to talk when she's visiting her mother. She'll definitely be more vulnerable when she's not on her home turf."

"Excellent. And the drive is much shorter."

"That's what I was thinking. Take care of yourself." Matt moved to the doorway.

BC stood. "I'll walk you out, Sinclair."

Matt gave a quick nod and left the room.

BC hugged her and kissed her on the temple. "You rest, honey. I'll be out in the living room."

"Okay."

BC left, shutting the door behind him.

Hell lay down and, despite all the warring voices in her head, instantly fell asleep.

MATT WALKED THROUGH THE LIVING AREA OF THE LARGE, EXPENSIVE suite, headed for the door.

Brad caught up to him and stopped him with a hand on his arm. "Can I talk to you for a minute?" he asked in a lowered tone.

"Sure."

The billionaire glanced at the closed door to Hell's room, gestured toward it with the coffee cup in his hand, and then turned back with an intense look in his eye. "I'm worried about Hell. Just yesterday, she almost died. Her wounds were nearly gangrenous. She's not well mentally. I don't think she should go out on Friday, but this is all new, and I don't want to put my foot down. Yet. Still feeling my way here."

Good thing Hell had this guy in her corner. "I agree, but you can't stop her. Don't worry, I'll take care of her. Make sure she eats and stays hydrated. She'll probably sleep the whole way. Passenger seat reclines. Patty always sleeps on long trips. If we solve the case, it will go a long way to healing her."

BC frowned and nodded. "I used to worry about her, but now that I'm finding out what's really gone on in her life, and is going on, I'm terrified for her. I'm having a really hard time not jumping in and taking over. What she's gone through!" he said with a wild gesture of his free hand, almost spilling the coffee in his other. "Casually drops these stories about being black-bagged and kidnapped by mercenaries." .

Matt couldn't help but smile. Hell was going to give this guy a heart attack. "Rampart guys?"

"Yeah. You knew about that?"

"She just told me the story the other day."

Brad rubbed his forehead. "Christ. Never been in a relationship with someone who put themselves in dangerous situations on a regular basis. And never loved any woman like this." The billionaire sighed. "One more thing." His face went hard; he glanced at the door to the bedroom and sharpened his gaze on Matt. "Has Hell spoken to you about how she's going to handle Capasso?"

"No."

Brad stood tall, chest out. "He isn't going to be happy about our engagement. His current Internet attacks on my networks have made his intentions clear—he's already declared war on me. I've decided to meet with him face-to-face to let him know that it's over between them, and she's under my protection now. That his attacks on my companies aren't scaring me."

Matt's stomach tensed. The confrontation between the two titans could send Hell right over the edge. "I wouldn't go behind her back on this one. She's afraid of him. Could backfire on you."

"I want to take the brunt of his anger, not her."

"If you'd read his case files, you wouldn't go over there."

Brad didn't bat an eye. "I did. I know what he's capable of. I also know he hates violence and deploys it infrequently. Makes absolutely no sense to escalate the war, not with someone as well armed as me. Once I look him in the eye, I'll be able to tell where he stands: he'll either fight for her or let her go. I'm going to convince him to do the latter."

"Dangerous."

Not one doubt on his face. "I'll have guards."

Matt snorted. "You're crazier than Hell is."

"You see why we make such an excellent couple."

"She's gonna kill you."

Collins smiled. "She isn't used to having someone on her side yet. Been alone too long. Had too many people come after her and beat her down. She's never had the armament to win before. I think she'll like it once she gets over the initial shock of someone helping her."

"What has she said about it?"

"That she'll handle him." He made a disgusted noise. "Like she's done such a great job for the last eleven years."

Matt sighed and shook his head. "You two are going to kill each other."

"No. She'll get over the invasion once she sees the results. But you're right, I expect yelling and screaming and pouting and threatening. Then she'll calm down, and everything will be fine."

Matt pointed at the mug in Collins' hand. "Did you put LSD in that coffee?"

Brad laughed. "I know she won't be easy to deal with. But she's worth it. I'm going to save that woman whether she likes it or not."

The set to his jaw reminded Matt of himself. This guy might be right for Hell. He might be able to handle her.

Matt said his good-byes and left and headed to Lindsay's to meet with Collins' guards.

He hoped Hell wouldn't kill BC for overstepping his boundaries.

But Brad was probably right, showing a strong front to Capasso might be the only way to get rid of him. Matt just hoped Hell was okay with it. While an odd couple, Hell and Brad actually seemed to fit together.

Could this be God's work? Had He brought the two sinners together to rebuild their lives and walk the better path?

Was that why Matt had come into Hell's life? He and Patty had discussed at length the ramifications of his influence over her, the good he could do for her and was doing for her. Patty believed what he did, that God sent you where you were supposed to go.

Even though he'd still found no meaning in his frame-up and firing in disgrace when he'd worked so hard and had made all the right choices. Patty had told him the same thing that his father had, that God had not turned His back on him, He'd just sent Matt on a different path.

Yeah, some path. Path of Undeserved Shame.

Hell could not be part of that future, could she? What could he learn from her? Nothing that he could see.

But in the short term, she was definitely helping him keep the kids in college, and him and Patty in the house.

He needed to call Mindy and have her clean up Hell's office and answer her phones. Mindy sat alone with nothing to do, while Hell's paperwork piled high and her phone rang continuously. If things didn't work out with Brad, Hell would need a job after the case was solved.

Why did he have such a pull toward the crazy woman? Strange.

But he couldn't deny it. Like the billionaire, he wanted to protect her and take care of her, too.

CHAPTER 27

Holding BC's hand, Hell walked out of the lobby of the Rosewood Hotel, trying to ignore her itchy wounds. She'd started to go stir-crazy in the hotel room and had convinced Brad to take her out for an early lunch. She glanced over at him in the morning sunshine. He wore cool black sunglasses, black jeans, and a long-sleeved, white, button-down shirt with the sleeves rolled up revealing his buff forearms. Yummy. Mostly she'd seen him in suits. She loved his more casual look. Also helped her to not stand out in her black capri yoga pants and vintage Batman T-shirt.

They walked down the cement stairs toward BC's limo waiting at the curb. His guard, Victor, a tall, buff, black, ex-military dude in his early thirties with a supreme ass, walked just ahead of them, scanning the area.

Hell hadn't felt this safe in weeks. BC beside her, his guard there, finally things were calming down. All she had to do was talk to the librarian, and bingo, the case would be solved, hopefully by the next day. Her life was really turning around.

They stopped at the limo. Victor reached forward to grab the door handle.

A loud explosion came from the far right parking lot, and Hell jumped, her heart racing, while simultaneously, Victor jerked his head to the left, and a small spray of blood splattered the car.

Gunfire!

Adrenaline dumped in Hell's system. She grabbed a stunned BC and threw him to the ground behind an adjacent planter, out of the line of fire, and dove on top of him. "Stay down!"

"I'm supposed to be protecting you!" BC moved to change positions.

Her body pumping with fight-or-flight juices, she fought him. "Stay put, dude! Be a man later!"

More explosions rocked the area, and the waist-high cement planter sheltering them cracked. Cement dust filled the air.

Victor, blood dripping from his chin, crouched low to the ground, using the limo for cover. He took out his gun. "You two stay there. I'm going after the shooter!"

Leaping to his feet, Victor ran past the back of the limo, heading for the parking lot.

More gunshots echoed through the area. Chunks of asphalt and cement sprayed everywhere.

The shots stopped, a car door slammed, and tires screeched.

Hell pushed off BC and leapt to her feet.

Victor lay on the ground just beyond the limo, writhing in pain, holding his knee.

A black Honda rocketed toward the exit. She could barely make out the driver: a blonde woman with curly hair wearing a white-and-red baseball cap with her ponytail coming out the back.

Lindsay!

Hell's vision shifted. "That fucking bitch!" Overwhelmed with rage, her body hot and hard, her mind tunneled to one thought: *Get her!*

Thankful she'd grabbed her car keys, she tore off for her car in the parking lot close to the exit while keeping an eye on the fleeing Honda.

"BC! Take care of Victor!" she shouted over her shoulder.

A part of her registered the pain coming from the wounds on her thigh and hip, but she didn't care.

Her mind became super sharp, her hunter instincts activated. That bitch's ass was hers. No one did this to her and BC and got away with it. She would take her down or die trying.

The black Honda jetted out into traffic and hung a right, cutting off a couple cars, which skidded and honked.

Hell would catch her ass and beat the holy shit out of her.

As she leapt into her car, she thought she heard BC yelling for her to stop, but his crazy masculinity issues were his problem. Her problem was putting an end to her nightmare. No one blew up her goddamned apartment and got away with it. No one shot at her and took away her sense of safety and went back to living a life of luxury. That bitch was about to be stopped. And stopped *hard*.

Her heart beating fast, sweat breaking out all over her body, Hell squealed out of the parking lot.

The light was red, but there was no time to stop. She glanced at the traffic coming down the hill. Two cars approached the intersection. This would be close.

Hell gunned the engine and launched out of the parking lot.

Out of the corner of her eye, the grills of two sedans seemed to fill her entire side window.

Bellowing, she kept the pedal to the floorboards, forcing her attention on the road ahead.

Horns blared, and tires screeched.

Hell braced for impact while pushing the Malibu to its limits.

A few seconds later, she realized that no one had hit her. She'd made it! Must have dodged the accident by centimeters. Boo-yah!

She briefly checked her rearview mirror. The drivers were screaming and flipping her off, but everyone seemed unhurt. "Too bad, people, but I've got a murdering bitch to stop!"

The Honda was a good three-quarters of a block ahead of her. Where was Lindsay going? Home? She was headed that direction, but what a stupid place to hide.

Maybe she didn't see Hell behind her.

Wherever she was going, Hell would catch her. Lurid visions of slamming the bitch's head to the cement driveway flashed through her mind. Beating her face in. Kicking her bloody. When Hell got her hands on that skinny little c-word, Botox wouldn't help her.

The Honda drove straight through the light at Alameda de las Pulgas, continuing down Sand Hill.

Hell approached the intersection, praying she'd make the light.

A white Lexus pulled directly in front of her.

She slammed on her brakes to avoid hitting the moron. "Fuck!"

The light went yellow, and the Lexus stopped.

Hell skidded to a stop, narrowly missing the Lexus. She checked to the right to see if she could buzz around the obstruction. A van blocked her. Stuck! Her impatience nearly blew her head off. "Son of a bitch!"

The Honda disappeared from sight.

"Goddamn it!"

She pounded on the steering wheel until the light changed green. She finally blew by and around the other cars and raced through the small roads of Atherton. Tall, ornate fences lined the sidewalk-less streets, protecting the zillion-dollar estates of the tony Peninsula enclave.

Hell skidded around the corner of Lindsay's street. The gate to her estate was open. Didn't mean she was there.

"Lindsay, you better be here, you beeyotch!" Hell yelled, blasting past the gates.

The black Honda was parked on the opposite side of the house in front of the six-car garage.

Victory filled Hell. "Gotcha! Woo-hooo! You are *mine!*"

Her body juiced for the fight, she stopped halfway down the driveway, turning the car sideways with the passenger side toward the house to block Lindsay from leaving. No way would she get away now.

Hell leapt out and stormed around the front of her car, stepping over the river rocks that lined the driveway, then got back onto the intricately arranged pavers.

"You fucking bitch! Get out here, and face me like a woman! You chickenshit asshole! I'm gonna kick your ass for what you've done to me! Blowing up my apartment and trying to shoot me twice! You're dead meat, bitch!"

Hell marched across the driveway and climbed the stairs of the Colonial mansion's wide porch. "You *bitch*! Get out here!"

The front door of the large home opened, and Lindsay emerged. Wearing her trademark red-and-white cap, black yoga pants, and a black turtleneck shirt, the thin blonde approached her, her expression almost emotionless.

Her lack of reaction made Hell even madder. "You fucking bitch! Trying to kill me! I'm gonna—"

"I won't let you kill Brad!" Lindsay shrieked, the whites of her eyes showing. Her face twisted into pure madness. "He's the father of my children! You won't kill my babies!"

Hell stopped, and all the hair stood up on the back of her neck.

Lindsay advanced, her entire body shaking. She pointed at Hell. "All you want to do is kill our love and kill our babies!"

Frozen with fear, Hell forced her legs to back away. She clearly hadn't planned this out well. Hadn't even occurred to her that Lindsay might have completely lost her mind.

"Baby-killing whore!" Lindsay seethed in a weird growl.

Hell grimaced, turned, and ran for her car.

Just as she reached the Malibu, she checked over her shoulder.

Lindsay lifted up her shirt, revealing something large, black, and angular against her pale skin.

A semi-automatic handgun.

Hell's heart rate skyrocketed.

Lindsay withdrew it and pointed it at Hell. "No one's killing my husband and babies!" she shrieked.

Hell dropped to the ground just as the gun went off.

Blam—*pank*! The bullet hit the side of her Malibu, not a foot from her head.

Her heart pounded so intensely she could barely breathe. "Holy shit!"

She scrambled around the front of her car and ditched behind the tire.

Hell scanned the area around her for weapons. River rocks were right in front of her. Grabbing a smooth chunk of granite, she ducked down to look underneath the car for Lindsay's feet. When Lindsay took a break in firing, she'd nail her.

"Murdering whore!" Lindsay yelled.

Bang-*tank*! Another shot hit the side of her car.

Hell flinched, and sweat trickled down her neck. In that moment, her aversion to owning a gun vanished. If she got out of this alive, she was buying some armament. Screw this pacifist shit.

Footfalls on cement. Lindsay's neon green sneakers appeared on the other side of the car.

Zero time.

Her pulse thundering in her ears, Hell stayed low to the ground, ready to spring.

"Baby-killing, pink-haired troll!" Lindsay bellowed. "I'll kill you before you kill my children! My babies are going to Harvard, you hear me? *Harvard!*"

Sirens wailed far off in the distance.

Lindsay moved toward the back of the Malibu.

Now! Hell leapt up and threw the rock.

Lindsay ducked. The rock went over her head, and she righted herself and aimed.

Hell flattened to the driveway.

Blam! A rock lining the garden bed exploded. A spray of debris peppered her, stinging her arms and face. Her heart beat so hard she could barely breathe.

"Murderer!" Lindsay screamed.

Hell wiped the dust from her eyes, grabbed another rock, and darted around the front of her car. She quickly peered through the car windows and ducked back down.

Lindsay stood at the back of the Malibu, a wild look in her eye, holding the gun with both hands. "Whore!"

Blam! The tall blue flowering bush right next to her blew apart. Hell yipped in fright but stayed down.

"Mrs. Banning!" came a loud, gruff voice from the base of the driveway.

Who the hell was that?

Hell popped up quick to check. A stocky white dude about thirty dressed in a suit slowly approached Lindsay, who was now facing him. Man had a gun! Thompson's guy! BC's surveillance was paying off! Yay!

"Put down your weapon!" he ordered.

In a quick movement, Lindsay raised her hand and fired. "Fuck you!"

Dude recoiled and landed flat on his back. He didn't move.

It happened so fast Hell almost couldn't make sense of it. She stared at the lifeless man. Then the blood chilled in her veins, and terror struck her. Good. Holy. God! Lindsay had killed a man!

Do or die, Trent!

Her body shaking, Hell homed in on her target and threw the rock full force.

The blonde's attention and gun still focused on the dead man, the rock hit her on the side of the neck and knocked her sideways. The gun went off in the direction of the man. Lindsay cried out, put her palm to her neck, and fought to keep standing.

Her body pumping with adrenaline, Hell lunged for more rocks. She grabbed another fist-sized chunk of granite and threw it at the crazy woman, nailing her in the jaw.

Lindsay's head snapped to the side, and she screamed. Grabbing her face where she'd been hit, she fell to her knees. Blood ran down her neck.

Hell scooped up another rock and charged her, throwing the rock as hard as she could.

The rock caught Lindsay in the shoulder and bounced off.

Bummer!

Right as she reached her, Lindsay lifted the gun and pointed it at Hell's chest. "Baby-killing witch!"

Hell shoved the end of the barrel out of the way with her left hand—burning her palm— and the gun went off with a wild, skyward shot. Her ears rang, and gunpowder stung her nostrils.

She landed a solid right to Lindsay's cheek, her head jerked to one side, and Hell tackled her to the ground on her back.

The gun flew out of the blonde's hand and clattered to the driveway, just out of reach.

Hell's body pulsing with fury and terror, she straddled the surprisingly strong and wiry stick figure and punched the whacko with a series of the hardest hits she could manage. Lindsay's head snapped back and forth, and she screamed in pain.

All at once, Hell couldn't breathe.

Lindsay's hands were wrapped around Hell's throat! She hadn't even seen her move!

Lindsay squeezed hard. "Die, baby-killer, die!"

Stars obscured Hell's vision. Choking, furious, and freaked out, she grabbed Lindsay's hands, dug her nails into the maniac's knuckles and fingers, and pulled hard.

Lindsay shrieked and loosened her grip.

Hell yanked her attacker's hands away from her throat, gasped for air, then came down hard across Lindsay's nose with her right forearm. "Fucking whack job!" she croaked.

Lindsay's head slammed back against the pavement, and blood spurted from her nose. She bellowed in pain.

Hell took her by the ears and pounded her skull against the cement with all her might. "I'm not trying to kill your babies, you idiot!"

Shrieking, Lindsay grabbed the front of Hell's T-shirt and yanked upwards while bucking with a strong, undulating yoga move, sending Hell flying through the air over her head.

She tucked as quickly as she could but hit the driveway hard with her right shoulder. Pain shot through, but she kept rolling and leapt onto her feet. Spinning to face Lindsay, all she saw was the giant, black barrel of the gun inches from her face.

Hell gasped, her heart leaping into her throat.

Lindsay looked certifiable. One eye was swelling shut, her other eye was wild and crazy, and her curly blonde hair stuck up all over. Blood ran in rivulets from her nose.

Hell knew this was the last face she'd ever see. She said a quick good-bye to BC and Joanne. But she wasn't going out without a fight. She prepared to lunge.

"Stop! Drop your weapon, or I'll shoot!" came a loud voice from behind her.

She yelped and jumped a foot, clutching her chest. Matt! Thank God!

"My babies will *live!*" Lindsay aimed at Matt, her hand shaking.

Matt's wife and kids! He couldn't die!

Hell leapt for the gun. Lindsay jumped backwards and pointed the weapon at her.

"Matt, get down!" Hell latched on to Lindsay's gun hand and pushed down.

Blam! The bullet ricocheted off the pavement. Hopefully, it hadn't hit Matt.

Lindsay screamed, "Murdering bitch!" and kicked Hell.

Pain shot through her shin, and she bellowed and stomped down on her opponent's foot while focusing on controlling the gun to ensure it didn't go off again.

Matt grabbed Lindsay in a bear hug from behind and picked her up, immobilizing her.

Yay, he was okay!

Hollering, Lindsay released the weapon.

Hell grabbed the pistol, ran away a few yards, and unloaded the cartridge, ensuring the semiautomatic was empty.

Lindsay howled as Matt fought to keep her under control.

"Let go of Mrs. Banning!" came a new voice. Lindsay's house manager, Jeremy, a tall, thin older man, ran toward them.

Lindsay turned toward her servant. "Jeremy! Help! They're trying to kill my babies! We have to kill them before they kill us!"

Hell yelled, "No! Don't! She's lost it and pulled the gun on us! She killed a man! Check down the goddamned driveway!" She pointed vehemently at the dead body.

The man rushed forward and pounded Matt on the back. "Mrs. Banning wouldn't hurt anyone! You let go of her!"

Hell ran into the melee. Matt tried to protect himself while holding on to Lindsay.

Jeremy full-on attacked Matt, punching and kicking him. Hell jumped on the old guy's back and locked her arms around his neck.

Impact to her jaw, pain rocked through her head, and Hell saw the sky and then hit the driveway hard, stunned.

"She has my gun! Hell, watch out!" Matt cried.

Hell shook her head to clear it and sat up. The end of a pistol appeared in front of her face, and beyond it, a bloody and crazy Lindsay.

Her heart stopped. This was it. Getting out of this situation once, yes, twice, no.

Matt had Jeremy in a tight hold on the driveway. "Stop fighting me so I can stop your boss from killing another person!"

Lindsay's face swollen and bruised, she didn't react to Matt's shout. She snarled, "Baby-killing whore! Die!"

Hell winced and hid behind her hands.

"Don't shoot her, Lindsay! Then we can't be together!" came a deep shout from near the front gate.

BC!

Lindsay's expression went from insane, demonic rage to peaceful innocence. She glanced over her shoulder while keeping the gun trained on Hell. "Brad? I'm so glad you're here! I was just going to call you! I'm saving our children! She tried to kill your semen and my eggs! I'll be right with you after I stop her!" She began to back away while stealing glances at Brad.

Hell's head still ringing, her insides went cold. She'd never been this close to this much crazy in her life.

"Don't kill her, or we can't be together!" BC yelled. "My plane is ready. I've made reservations at that resort in Tahiti you wanted us to visit. Remember our plans?"

She continued backing down the driveway, still with the gun on Hell. "Yes, I do. Wonderful, Brad. But I need to kill her first, or she'll try to murder our babies!"

"No! I don't want you to shoot off that gun. It could backfire and, uh, hurt your eggs. Just drop the gun. I'll protect you. And our babies. My security team is here and will take care of Trent. Come on, let the professionals do their work, and we'll go to Tahiti."

Her features softened even more, and her shoulders relaxed. A weird, beatific expression came over her beaten-up face, making her appear even more deranged. She stopped, raised her chin high, and sent Hell a smug smile, revealing bloody teeth. "See? He loves me. Not you. We're going to Tahiti and make babies. Beautiful babies who will go to Harvard."

She turned and walked toward Brad. "I'm coming, Brad." Almost like nothing had happened. Spooky as all get out.

"Put the gun down, Lindsay," he called out.

She looked at the gun in her hand, seeming surprised. "Oh, right, gun." She laid it down about ten yards away from Hell and continued on. "I got your text the other night, Brad. I wore the yoga outfit. Why didn't you show up at the hotel?"

Lindsay wasn't just insane, she was hallucinating. Death had complete access to BC's phones and he'd never sent a text to the lunatic. Something about her craziness dulled Hell's anger.

Matt snuck up behind Lindsay and tackled her to the ground. Hell checked on Jeremy to see if he was a threat. The old man stood there looking alarmed but made no move to intervene. Clearly, he'd finally caught on to the situation.

Lindsay screamed. "Get off me! I have to make babies with Brad! Brad! Save me! Save my eggs!"

Brad joined Matt, and they both held Lindsay on the ground.

Hell knew she should get up and grab the gun but was too dizzy from the hard hit to her jaw. A couple more seconds of rest, and then she'd move.

While she desperately wished it hadn't happened, the murder would ensure Lindsay never got out of a mental hospital. Thank God.

Hell checked the dead body. The legs moved.

Yay! He was alive! Thank God.

Wait. This meant that Lindsay could plead out, get a slap on the wrist, and be back out in a week, ready to terrorize Hell all over again.

Hell's attention went to Matt's gun lying in the driveway. Possessed by a sudden urge to grab it and shoot the crazy bitch to put an end to her terror, she had to hold herself back. No more jail. But this was all seriously fucked up. Now her nightmare would never end.

A police car pulled up, sirens blaring. Another squad car arrived just behind the first. Good, they'd take care of Lindsay and the hurt man.

Lindsay wouldn't stop shrieking. "Why are you doing this to me? Arrest her! She tried to kill Brad and my babies! Brad! Tell them I was only protecting our children!"

Four police officers rushed up to Matt and Brad. While Brad held Lindsay, Matt showed them his ID. Lindsay began screaming unintelligible words. Another cop approached the wounded man.

Drama over, Hell rested on the pavers, wondering why she wasn't interested in standing. Suddenly, she just didn't give a fuck. The ending she'd so counted on, a nice and clean ending to her trauma, had become a new morass of torture. Psyche evals, excuses, high-priced doctors and lawyers, and tons of court appearances and bullshit, with the bottom line meaning that Lindsay would get away with everything she'd done to Hell.

Typical. Everyone in her life got away with hurting her. She never got retribution or validation for her pain. The situation always turned to the abuser. Excusing the abuser. Worrying about the abuser. Making sure the abuser got their needs met.

Hell's breathing became rapid. Images of all the people who had hurt her went through her mind like a hellish movie clip show. Dad screaming at her. Mom freezing her out. Capasso beating her. The news media slut-shaming her. Martin unleashing his bile on her.

Her train of thought splintered. More sirens sounded in the background, planes flew overhead, Lindsay screamed, but everything slowed down and quieted. None of it seemed real.

Pain began to radiate through her hands. She looked down and was surprised at her swollen and bloodied knuckles. Warm liquid ran down her face. She wiped her cheek, and her palm came away bright red.

Her vision tunneled. Her breath filled her ears. Something hard hit the side of her body, and she smelled hot cement.

HELL STARTLED AWAKE ON A ROLLING STRETCHER. TREE BRANCHES passed above her with the blue sky beyond. A paramedic was on one side with BC on the other with a seriously panicked look on his face.

"What?" she asked, confused.

"Hell, are you okay?"

The paramedic, a young red-haired man, patted her on the shoulder. "Ma'am, just lie still. You'll be fine."

Adrenaline dumped into her system. "Wait!" Hell cried out. Then she got dizzy. "Stop the stretcher! I don't want to go to the hospital. I'll be fine. Just give me a minute here." Last thing she needed was a ride in an ambulance and trip to the goddamned hospital. That would break her already broken finances. She already owed twelve grand she didn't have from the grenade attack.

The paramedic's expression remained firm. "You may have a concussion. You lost consciousness. You need to be checked out."

"No, I don't. Let me off this goddamned thing."

BC nodded. "Hell, I'll be with you the whole time. You won't—"

Hell sharpened her gaze "No. *I'm* in charge here. Not you people. Now let me up."

Took her a good ten more minutes of arguing before the idiots would listen to her. Only thing she allowed them to do was give her an icepack and clean up her hands. She pretended like she was fine, but was on the verge of fainting the entire time.

Hell walked away from the ambulance, her legs shaky, the horizon tilting occasionally. She prayed she wouldn't pass out and do a face plant into the sidewalk.

BC, his x-ray vision tuned in to her, put a firm arm around her back.

After a few steps, her knees weakened and he increased his hold on her.

He frowned. "I shouldn't have let you talk me into this."

"Just get me to your stupid limo, please?"

He sighed. "I'll have the police come to the hotel and take your statement there. I'm calling Bill on the way."

"Don't make a fuss. I'm just a little overwhelmed. I'll be fine."

BC helped her into the limo and she collapsed on the backseat.

He sat next to her and gently ran his hand over her head. "You are not fine. Stubborn and crazy, maybe, but definitely not fine. I'm going to have Bill meet us at the hotel."

"Don't be dramatic." The interior of the car was moving so much she squinted at him.

"She says, looking like she's about to pass out."

"I'm not," she lied.

"Bullshit. By the way, *what* were you thinking?" he demanded. "If I hadn't shown up when I did, you'd be dead."

Lindsay's crazy face and the gun flashed through her mind. Her stomach knotted hard, and she breathed in and out fast and fought tucking into the fetal position. *Take it easy. It's all over, Hell.*

"Hell?" He ran his hand gently down her arm.

Her equilibrium took a swirl. She closed her eyes and slowed her breathing. *Safe spot. Find your safe spot.* She pictured being back in her old apartment, in bed with Secret Teddy. *You'll be fine, kid. Just relax.* "I'm fine."

"You keep telling me that, but I'm not buying it."

"Honestly." She forced her eyes open and sent a direct order to her body to *calm down.* "I'm cool."

"The hell you're cool." He stared at her, his mind clicking. He looked like he was contemplating calling back the ambulance.

A little spike of adrenaline cleared her head. "Dude, please. I think I'm allowed a few minutes to just lie here after what just happened to me. Without all the drama of the damned hospital and doctors, okay? I know what I need to do to take care of myself."

"I understand that you need a bit of time to regroup, but please do me a favor and don't use extreme illogic to prove your point. You demonstrated beyond all doubt in the previous hour that you have zero idea how to care for yourself."

Her body tensed with anger. "Hey—"

"When there's a crazy woman with a gun trying to kill you, you run *away* from her, you don't go chasing after her to get shot at again. I'm kicking myself for not being able to stop you, but you had too big of a head start. By the time I reached the entrance to the hotel, you were already out in traffic, wreaking havoc," he said with a flinging gesture of his right hand.

While he had some points, Hell had done her job. "I needed to stop her."

"You call the police," he stated firmly. "That's their job. You solve the mysteries; they arrest the crazy killers. Right?"

No way was she giving in on this point. She'd done the right thing. Maybe the wrong way, but she'd done her job, which was to protect and defend herself. "Well, since the person who tried to kill me finally got caught, I'd say this situation won't come up again. Besides, I solved the case, didn't I?"

His jaw tightened. "Please don't waste any more words defending your lunacy."

For some reason, their argument was centering her and grounding her. While also annoying her. Weirdly normal.

Brad opened his mouth to say something but stopped. He sighed, and his brow wrinkled with worry. He massaged her unhurt leg.

With the threat of the hospital over, and because everyone had finally stopped making her move, her vision stabilized. The nausea receded, and she finally felt a tad bit better, despite the pain coming from her hands and head. Hopefully, BC's doctor would bring some painkillers.

Matt appeared outside the limo.

"Matt, you want to meet us back at the hotel?" BC asked.

"Yeah. I'll follow you after I go to the police station and make my report."

"Hell's in no condition to go the police station," BC announced. "I'm going to arrange for them to meet us at the hotel. Matt, could you make sure Hell's okay until I get back?"

All he needed was an orchestra for a music swell. "I'm fine."

"Shut up," they both said.

BC kissed her on the cheek. "I'll be right back." Amazing how he could go from stern dictator to tender lover in a split second.

"Okay."

He shook his head. "Crazy woman." The look in his eyes sharpened. "You do realize we'll be discussing the choices you made today in depth later."

She waved her hand and then fluttered her eyelids and pretended to feel sicker than she did. "Whatever, just go so we can get back to the hotel." Dude had some wake-up calls regarding how much power he had over her. Like, none. He owned her heart and girl parts, nothing else.

His expression softened, then fell. "I really don't like the way your eyes look, honey." Anguish in his gaze made her gut twinge, and a blast of hot shame coursed through her.

She couldn't discern which was the bigger mind-fuck: almost dying and solving the case or realizing that her actions and decisions no longer affected just her. Thank God her emotions were mostly stuck in an ice chest somewhere.

"I'll be right back," BC said and left.

"That was some idiot move you pulled, *Batgirl*," Matt bit out.

Hell was momentarily confused until she realized she still wore the Batman T-shirt. Seemed like she'd put it on twenty years before.

Matt stepped in and sat across from her. "What was your plan? Get Lindsay to shoot you so she'd get arrested?" Heat radiating from his eyes, he was nearly as angry as Brad.

Adding to her brain warp. While she'd been praying for someone to come along and care about her, she'd forgotten the consequence: people in her face. "Yeah. Worked brilliantly, didn't it?"

Matt glared at her and pursed his lips.

"All joking aside, thanks for saving my ass back there, Matt. I almost had her, but damn, what a freakin' whack job. Did you hear that weird crap she was screaming? And she shot that dude without a thought. Scary shit, man."

Matt continued slicing into her with his hot gaze. "Scary was when I pulled up, and I see Lindsay tossing you over her head in some karate move, and then she has that gun in your face. Thompson's man, right there in the driveway, dead. I thought it was over for you, Hell. It almost was," he said, his voice higher, his tone urgent.

Hell ran her hand over her head, hit a sore spot, and winced. "Yeah, that wasn't exactly all planned out the way I would have liked. I'm glad the cops got here quick."

Matt gave a huge sigh, shook his head, and finally relaxed back in his seat. He pointed at her. "Yeah, weird thing was they were responding to a different call. Intruder next door. Neighbor saw a thin guy in a watch cap and dark glasses run through his yard, followed by a short, fat, Hispanic man. Supposedly knocked over a bunch of lawn furniture and kept going. He thought they were in his pool house. Cops didn't find anything."

"That *is* weird."

He blew out some air between his lips, and his mouth twisted with disgust. "Old guy, probably teenagers running through his yard, and he flipped out. People around here call if the wrong leaves drop on their property."

"I know. This is BC's world. I don't fit."

His face relaxed into a fond smile. "You'll do fine, Hell. He really loves you."

"I think you're right. Did you tell the cops about the librarian?" she asked.

"I will."

"I still want to talk to her."

"Authorities probably won't be that interested, depending. Looks pretty open-and-shut at this point."

Hell's side hurt, and she shifted on the seat into a more comfortable position. Thankfully, her balance stayed true. Her head was clearing. Which was great because she had no idea how long she could keep BC from forcing her to go to the hospital. "Why did Lindsay hire the librarian?"

"Intel. To watch you. To make you paranoid. Maybe try to get you to give up Brad because initially she probably didn't want to kill you, just scare you off."

Hell wasn't convinced. "Will you go see the librarian with me? I have to at least ask her a few things. See her face-to-face."

He lifted one shoulder. "If you want to."

"I just want to tie up this loose end. I probably ought to rest for a couple days, but could we go next Monday?"

He grinned. "Sure. Troublemaker."

She relaxed on the bench seat. "Okay, good."

BC stuck his head in the door. "Cops are sending a detective to the hotel."

"Thanks, honey."

He gave a nod, and he and Matt exchanged places.

"I'll see you two at the hotel later," Matt said as he backed away.

Hell waved at him. "Okay, Matt. Thanks so much, dude."

Brad held out his hand. "Thanks, Sinclair. For saving her life."

Matt smiled and shook with BC. "My pleasure." Then he pointed at Hell. "And you, try to stay out of trouble and away from gun-wielding psychopaths for a few hours, okay?"

She smiled. "I'll make a concerted effort."

"I'll help," BC added with an edge to his voice.

With a sharp nod at BC, and a salute at the both of them, Matt disappeared.

"Now there was the smartest thing I've done in a while," Hell said.

BC twisted his lips. "And here I thought you were an idiot. Well, I still think you're an idiot."

"You already said that."

"You're damned right." He moved to her and rubbed her leg. "I'm supposed to protect you, not the other way around. Throw me to the ground and dive on top of me," he grumbled. "'*Be a man later*'? Really?" He glared.

Hell couldn't help but chuckle. "Sorry, but you could have gotten us killed with all your masculinity issues. How's Victor?"

His face reddened, and his eyeballs popped. "Masculinity issues!" He stopped and turned away. "Don't yell at her, Collins," he said to himself and heaved a big sigh. He looked at her, his anger somewhat contained. "Victor'll be fine. Shot in the knee and leg but hopefully not too much damage. Took a chunk of meat off his chin, but no bone. He's at Stanford Hospital now." He moved in beside her and took her in his arms. "Jesus, Hell."

She cuddled against him, adjusting a few times to ease the pressure on various sore areas. Her brain was still all over the place, but her body was very happy for the warmth and love.

He ran his hand down her shoulder. "I can't believe the threat came from me. I really thought it would turn out to be Capasso."

"He doesn't care that much."

He kissed her on the top of the head. "I know you're still worried about him."

Her heart thumped hard, and her stomach tensed. "Let's not think about him right now."

"Sorry." Sighing, BC shook his head. "What am I going to do with you?" he asked softly, more to himself.

"Hold me like you're doing right now."

"I love you, Hell."

"Love you, BC."

A second later, tears surprised her. And then didn't surprise her. He held her tighter.

Thank God, it's over.

CHAPTER 28

Hell blinked awake to BC walking in the room, showered, dressed, and smiling. "How are you feeling, honey?" he asked.

He joined her in bed and wrapped his arms around her. She snuggled against him.

Solving the case, plus three days of rest, had done wonders for her. Her jaw had finally stopped aching, and the wounds from the grenade attack had mostly healed. Skin was tender in spots, but no more itching and no more pain. Her shoulder injury from the bad dive roll at Lindsay's was another matter.

"A bit better, I think. Brain meltdown has subsided."

"Good. Are you sure you're well enough for the trip to Pleasanton?"

She stretched, her shoulder complained bitterly, and she winced, then yawned. "Yeah. Easy. If I need to, I can sleep in the car. Matt's a good driver. Besides, don't you have to prepare for battle with the succubus?"

His eyes went cold, and his face hardened. "Unimaginable fun."

"Sorry, baby."

"Today should be our last meeting. Dad's lawyers reached an agreement with Sherry's family team."

"Wow, dynasties. We poor people only have to divide our debts."

"She's going for blood and getting it. But I could care less. Whatever I have to pay is worth it to get rid of her." He sighed, met her gaze, and his features softened, his eyes sparkling.

Warmth filled her body, centering on her heart.

"You make me feel like the luckiest man in the world." He put his hand to her cheek and kissed her. When he pulled away, he said, "And I'm a little concerned about this trip today."

Hell did a little flip with her hand. "I have to see that librarian, and then I'll be done. Just a couple more questions answered, and I'll be satisfied."

"Speaking of that, I just got off the phone with the lead detective on the case." BC thumbed toward the living room. "They found reams and reams of plans in Lindsay's house. How she'd pinned the shooting on Tanner. Copies of the threatening note taped to your door. Where she'd gotten the hand grenades, the whole shebang—no pun intended. Plus they found more grenades and the gun she used for the Rosewood shooting."

"She used two different guns that day?"

"Apparently. Now they have them both. Plus the rest of her arsenal. Lindsay's got quite a collection."

Hell twisted her lips. "Damn. In retrospect, it seems so obvious. I mean, except for the anomalies."

"What anomalies? The librarian?"

"Did the cops mention her?" she asked.

"No."

"There was no evidence linking Judy Jones to Lindsay found at the house?"

"Not so far."

"I thought for sure by now Lindsay would be trying to throw all the blame on the Terminator Librarian."

He ran his hand over her head. "They aren't exactly listening to what she says, since mostly she rants about saving her babies. They've got her all drugged up, anyway. She's lost in La La Land."

"Christ." She pulled up the covers, readjusted, and nestled close to him.

He frowned. "Lindsay's going for the insanity defense. With her lawyers, she can get it. They've already paid off Thompson's man, the one she shot, so he's not anxious to testify."

Anger flared through her, and her jaw tensed. "Son of a bitch."

His brow furrowed. "And then there's Jeremy, Lindsay's house manager, the guy you fought, who keeps trying to convince anyone who'll listen to him that Lindsay was home with him during the attack at the Rosewood. No one believes him. He's practically her family, been with her since she was a kid. Thankfully, Lindsay's gardener and his wife, one of Lindsay's housekeepers, made sworn statements they'd both seen her sneak out the back door and drive away a half an hour before the attack. With all the gunshot damage to the Honda from Victor's return fire, and Lindsay's DNA all over the inside of the car, the case is open-and-shut."

Her mind darkening, Hell shook her head and let out a long sigh. "Watch, Lindsay will get a goddamned ankle bracelet and will be back at home in a week, plotting to kill me all over again," she spat. She sat up in bed and propped herself against the headboard. BC moved to fit next to her. "People always hurt me and get away with it."

BC took her hand and sent her a reassuring look. "I can't imagine they'll just let her off with probation. The district attorney wants her blood. Apparently, she made him look bad in a recent book of hers on criminal behavior."

"Thompson's guy will be such a great witness, won't he?" Hell said, dripping with contempt. "And what the hell was wrong with him? Didn't he see Lindsay flying in the driveway? What took him so long to come help me?"

"He saw Lindsay, but he was in a fake power company van parked down the block, watching the place from a surveillance camera mounted on top of his vehicle."

Hell snapped her attention to him. "So they got footage of Lindsay coming back? Did they get a good shot of her face?"

"No. But with that curly hair, it was clearly her. She turned toward her passenger seat as she passed by the van, so all they captured on film is the back of her head. But Lindsay's red-and-white baseball cap was clear, along with the black turtleneck."

"That's weird. Like she'd spotted Thompson's guys again and knew they were there?"

"No, she was reaching over to grab something. Then, where she parked, on the far side of the house, the angle was blocked by a tree, so the footage shows just a glimpse of her running into the garage. But the camera clearly caught all the action in the driveway with you, Lindsay, Matt, Jeremy, and Thompson's guy."

Hell picked a piece of lint off BC's T-shirt. "Why didn't Thompson's dude protect me better? He walks up, and she just shot him. I can't believe he survived."

"He almost didn't. He wasn't wearing Kevlar. He's one of Thompson's surveillance nerds and isn't trained in protection. Apparently, she missed his heart by inches, and all the major arteries. Luckiest shot ever. Don't worry, honey, maybe she won't go to jail, but she'll be locked up for a long time in an institution."

"I hope so. God, she was bonkers. Of course, I should have figured that out earlier. I mean, being *that* obsessed with you? Come on. Talk about *crazy*." She glanced at him sideways with an evil little smile.

He narrowed his eyes, pulled her on top of him, and smacked her ass a couple times.

Her shoulder ached, but a lovely zing went through her clit, and she could only think of having him inside her. Despite her injuries and bruises, sex was worth the pain. "Don't start what you can't finish," Hell said in a husky voice.

His eyes dilated, and his wood came to life, pressed against her thigh.

They kissed, and her entire body pulsed.

She slid off and began to unzip his pants, then glanced at the clock. "Oh, shit, it's almost eight!" Her sex drive shut down immediately. She stopped and turned to get out of bed.

BC caught her, pulled her back, and held her fast. "Oh, no, you don't. You don't rev my engine and then stop it cold."

"But Matt will be here in an hour, and I have to shower and eat."

His hungry smile widened. "I'm up for the challenge."

"But BC, don't— Ohhhh. Don't stop."

Monday, March 22, 2011, 9:15 a.m.

WEARING BLACK YOGA PANTS, A PINK SKULL T-SHIRT, AND BLACK
Converse high-tops, Hell dashed into the living room clutching her
skull-printed messenger bag and black leather jacket. Jeans were
more appropriate for the situation, but the skin on her hip was still
too sensitive.

Matt and BC sat opposite each other on the cream-colored,
square, leather living room couches, drinking coffee.

"Sorry I'm late, Matt. I, uh...slept in."

BC let out a short, barking laugh.

Hell sent BC a withering look.

Matt pursed his lips, fighting a smile. "You two make me sick."

Her face heated. "Can we go now?"

Matt snorted, stood, and gestured toward the door.

BC grinned. "What time will you be back?"

"Like, two, probably. Right, Matt?"

"Between that and three, yeah. Depending on the traffic."

Brad got up and came over to her. "I'll be in Burlingame. I should
be back here by four at the latest."

"Okay."

They kissed and pulled away. BC winked at her.

Her body hummed, and a little powerful burst of lust throbbed
through her loins. She beamed back. What this man did to her.
Wowza.

Hell relaxed in the passenger seat of her car as they drove along
580 headed east through the rolling green hills between Silicon
Valley and the Central Valley. Patty had needed his car, so they'd
taken hers. After Matt's initial disgust at the messy interior, he finally
deigned to drive it. BC had offered his Bentley, but they'd declined.
Like driving a large, expensive billboard.

They made small talk, then lapsed into silence. She wondered if she should tell him about the part of his car she'd busted off. Now that they seemed to be almost sort of friends.

"You want to tell me something," Matt said. "What is it?"

Hell broke out of her reverie. Matt had his mind-reading face on. She sighed and looked out the window. "I'm not sure hanging out with a detective is a good idea."

He chuckled. "About the case? Lindsay?"

"No. Okay, fine. When I was in your car a week and a half ago, I sort of accidentally tore off a part of the trim on the—"

His face flushed. "You! I blamed my son. Shit. Of course it was you. You're the only juvenile delinquent who's been in my car recently. Poor kid. Now I have to go crawling to him. Why didn't you just tell me?"

"Because our alliance was super tenuous at that point."

"Where is that piece of trim? Please tell me you didn't throw it out. You know that costs three hundred bucks to replace? Only comes in a set with a whole lot of other pieces."

She couldn't help but giggle. "I stuck it in a seam of the carpet. I'll get it out for you when we get back. Sorry."

"For all that's holy, my poor son. No wonder he was so mad at me." He sighed heavily. "Probably have to get him that new iPhone," he muttered under his breath.

"I'll pay for it."

"I might let you." He twisted his mouth and shook his head, but he wasn't as mad as he should be.

Did he really like her?

Still a good time to thank him. "Thanks for sending Mindy to my office and straightening out all that crap. I shouldn't have let it get that far."

"It's okay, Hell. She wasn't doing anything at my office but surfing the web."

"Well, good. I'm glad it all worked out."

Hell had been thinking about her business and how helpful Matt had been. While it was the most insane idea she'd ever come up with, she was heavily considering a partnership. But she didn't have the first idea of how to start the conversation. He'd laugh her right out of the car.

But they had nothing else to do, and this would be the last period of time they'd spend together. Maybe she'd try a short fishing expedition. "Sooo, Matt."

"What?"

"What are your plans now that we've solved the case? I mean, after today, we're done."

He lifted a shoulder. "Yeah. Just going back to my office, I guess."

Silence. He wasn't picking up on the hint. Time to be plain.

"About that." Hell let out a big sigh. "I know this is weird and terrible and frightening and otherworldly and will probably cause the instant destruction of the universe as the two polarities meet, but—"

He grinned. "That's quite a buildup."

"But..." He was going to say no. Why had she even thought about it? "No. You'd never go for it. And it's crazy. I shouldn't have even brought it up." She turned her attention out the window.

Her stomach hurt a bit. No, it was her heart. Oh, Christ. Why did the thought of his rejection bug her so much? Ridiculous. Such her typical pattern. Find someone who thinks there's something wrong with her and try to get them to like her.

"What?"

She didn't bother looking at him. "Never mind."

"Hell," he said in a warning tone.

She sighed heavily. "Okay, fine. Here's the deal. I am clearly messing up my business. With the publicity of the Candler kidnapping case—and now being in the papers all the time with the bombing—the volume of offers I'm receiving has grown past my ability to handle them. You're a really good detective and—this is crazy and I know you still probably don't actually like me underneath that pleasant exterior of yours, but—"

"My exterior is pleasant?"

"Matt! Okay. I'll just say it. Do you want to form, on a trial basis, a business partnership with me? I know we'll have to settle a million details and agree on stuff that won't be easy, but I think the two of us sort of complement each other. Together I think we could kick some ass. We'll know pretty fast if it won't work. And if we find ourselves trying to kill each other, or if we do kill each other, our zombie bodies can walk away with no hard feelings."

He blinked fast and examined her. "You're serious. *You want to form a partnership with me?*"

"I know it's insane, but yes. On a trial basis. I can talk to a part of society you can't, like young people and degenerates, and you're the straight cop guy who can handle the rich people and professional corporate people that I terrify. I'm good at undercover work, but I need a partner. I have a few actor friends who help me with small jobs, but no one else professional or licensed. I mean, you and I did well at Lindsay's— Oh shit, that's a bad example, and I shouldn't have brought it up." She grimaced.

She couldn't read his expression, but he wasn't laughing, and he wasn't mad at her. He actually seemed sort of intrigued.

"No, I'm glad you brought it up. While I am flattered by your offer, I'd need to have some ground rules, or I *would* kill you."

"I figured we have a lot of details to hammer out. What's the first ground rule that came to mind?"

"Well, quarterbacking the initial Lindsay scam when you went into her goddamned house unarmed and pushed all her buttons while I was stuck on that lame surveillance system out in the street, I would have devised something else. She was clearly too dangerous to play with, and you'd misread her. You were lucky she didn't kill you that day."

Hell shrugged. "Yeah…"

"And this last cowboy move of yours, that cannot happen again." He sent her a sharp glance.

"I apologize. I went nuts. I barely remember the trip to Lindsay's. Or any of that scene. Just images, I was so pissed. That won't happen again."

"It better not. I can't work with someone who isn't on the same page with me. The main point is, you listen to me when I tell you I don't like something, or I think something is too dangerous," he said with a sharp, pointed gesture. "We decide what our plan is together. You don't go off half-cocked and expect me to save you from six blocks away."

"I can do that."

He checked her face and turned back to the traffic. "Really?"

"Sure. Our next case will not be personal. I'll be completely different when I'm not the victim and people aren't trying to kill me. I welcome your advice. I also need structure. I'm too old to live like this any longer. I want to make my business a success instead of the chaos it is now. I want to build it up, get a better office, save up, and buy myself a house in Aragon or Homestead."

His brow furrowed. "But you're in relationship with a billionaire, Hell."

"I know BC could wave his pinky finger and a castle would appear, and then what? How would that make me feel? I wouldn't appreciate it. Only the things I've earned have meant anything to me. I've been dependent on others forever and have hardly taken my life seriously. I want to grow up. You're an excellent example for me. I can learn a lot from you."

"Makes me happy to hear you say all that, Hell. I could certainly use the business and the money. Be great to make my mortgage. Maybe let Patty retire so she can do her tapestries. But there are some deal breakers for me."

"My weed."

"Yes."

"Non-negotiable. Well, Matty, it was a nice dream. I can still fill your calendar. I'll just refer them to you. I'll figure it out. I always do." She turned away and gazed out her window, bummed but not surprised. She knew he wouldn't accept her for her. Why did she ever think he could?

"That's it? You're going to walk away from our partnership because of marijuana?"

"Yep. And for the record, *you're* the one who's walking away because of marijuana, not me." She continued focusing her attention outside. The passing green hills were covered in giant wind turbines, spinning, creating electricity.

"But you don't need it."

"That's not for you to decide," she snapped more harshly than she'd meant. She sent him a hard look. "If one of the conditions of our partnership is that you get to make my medical decisions for me, then I don't want you for a partner."

He concentrated on the traffic, his features drawn down. After a few moments, he turned to her. "Really? You'd turn down something that could be good for you for your drug addiction?"

"You see it as an addiction. I see it as medication."

"You really think it's medication? Not an escape?"

She made a disgusted noise. "Dope is not an escape for me. Do I look like I'm escaping? I'm stoned right now."

He blinked fast, the lines on his weathered face deep. "Well, then why do you do it?"

She heaved a sigh. "I thought we had this conversation."

"That was before I was considering a future with you, and I can't really remember what you said."

"Fine. Weed takes the edge off. It tones down the terror and pain at my core and allows me to be normal and not some high-strung freak. Up until the morning Lindsay shot at me, I was able to keep my emotions under control enough so I didn't have to smoke pot during the day. But for right now, between my PTSD and the recent attack, weed is the only thing keeping my head from exploding. If I'm doing it, it's because I need it. I'm not suffering to demonstrate to you what I'm like when I'm not medicated."

"So you don't want to do it during the day?"

"No," she said like it was obvious. "Hopefully, we'll have the case totally settled, and I won't be terrified soon, and it won't be an issue. But for a while, I'm gonna be doing it as often as I need it. We'll have to find an office with access to a roof or a courtyard or a balcony or something. I won't smoke inside or around you. I clearly didn't care in my old office."

He bit his lower lip and blinked hard. "I don't like it."

"And I don't like it that you don't like it," she countered in a strong tone. "Weed's been demonized for a century, only made illegal during the Depression to put brown people in jail. Humans have been using it for thousands of years. Only thing bad that will happen if weed gets legalized nationally is all the 7-Elevens will run out of Doritos and M-&-Ms."

He snorted. "Must have been hard to go cold turkey in jail."

Hell burst out laughing.

"What?"

"I was more stoned in jail than I've ever been in my life."

Matt's jaw slackened. "What?"

She snickered. "Yeah. Dude, I was dating a local Mafia don. He owns guards in that place. I had more gourmet food and weed than I knew what to do with. Kept that whole cellblock stoned and fed the entire time I was there. Everyone had my back. Actually had some good times in there. Some of those ladies were really wild."

His brow hardened, and his mouth curved downward. "Glad I didn't know that. Jesus Christ." He glanced at her. "How do you do it?"

"How do I do what?"

"Charm everyone to the point where they ignore all your crazy behavior? Or worse, encourage it."

"We'll never know."

He sighed heavily. "Pot really bugs me, Hell. But it hasn't affected our working relationship. Your natural stubbornness and unwillingness to ask for help have been the problems."

She let him think out loud and decided not to volunteer anything. He had to want to be her partner. She wasn't going to convince him.

He slowly shook his head. "But it's stupid to walk away from a partnership because I don't like that you smoke pot. I don't know, Hell. I just can't believe you even suggested this deal. We don't exactly have a great history."

Hell raised her brows. "I'd like to forget our past and concentrate on this last week, when we both met completely different people. I think it'll work. Only thing we have to lose is our minds."

He laughed. "I can't believe I'm even considering it."

"*Odd Couple*, for sure." She nodded.

"I am not Felix."

"You are *so* Felix."

"I guess you are Oscar."

"Unpleasant mirror."

He smiled. "How long of a trial?"

"Six months? A few cases? Until we find ourselves trying to kill each other?"

"We'd get a six-month lease on a place?"

"Yeah. Both of our offices are too small. We need two offices with a waiting room for Mindy."

"Where?"

Hell eased down in her seat. "I like San Mateo. Built up a good rep there, and there is cash in them thar hills. With you we could break into Hillsborough. Ka-ching!"

He ran his hand through his thick, wavy hair. Then he shrugged and took in a deep breath. "Honestly, your choices and opinions bug the shit out of me, Hell. I don't know if I can come to terms with our differences."

"Me, neither, but I'm willing to try. You drive me nuts with your fastidious, anal, OCD bullshit and Puritan, narrow-minded, black-and-white view of the world. And your view of me. But I think you can help me with detective skills, and I can help you. Because if you're gonna make it in this business, you're gonna have to learn how to drop the cop thing at times. Bend the rules a bit here and there."

"I'm going to agree to disagree."

Hell looked out the windshield at the traffic. "Maybe it won't work."

"No, actually, I think it will."

Her heart lifted, and she turned back to him.

He continued, "We just can't have any illusions about our differences. Let's work a few cases and see how it goes. It's worth a shot.

You have things to teach me, too. As much as I hate to admit it. I'd like to see what it's like to work with you when you aren't the intended victim and we're not dissecting your life."

Hell nodded, struck by how happy the thought of working with him made her. "It'll be much different."

He gave her a double take and examined her face closely before turning back to the road. "This isn't part of that threat you made to me in the interrogation room, is it?"

"What?"

"When you said that I would pay for what I'd done to you?"

Hell had forgotten what she'd said until that very moment. "Oh, yeah. No. But it is a great idea." She sent him an excited smile. "A two-for-one. I get even with you—and improve my business—just by working with you," she said cheerfully.

He made a face.

"And, hey, dude, if this all works out well, I want to help you get your badge back."

His head nearly came off it snapped so hard in her direction. "What?"

"Yeah. We both know it was a setup. There have to be clues. Let's figure it out."

His brows high, he seemed shocked. "Really? You'd help me?"

"We'll be partners, won't we? I can get into places you can't. I have access to a lot of those players. We can use Joe."

Matt's face fell, making his lines deepen. "He won't want to help. He's retiring next spring."

"We don't have to let him know we're using him."

"Hell..." he said in a warning tone. Then his stern expression broke. "Actually..."

She patted him on the shoulder. "Don't worry, Matt. We'll figure it out. But for right now, let's meet, say, next week?"

"Okay." Matt chuckled, turned back to traffic, and shook his head to himself. "If you would have told me two weeks ago I'd be entering into a partnership with Hell Trent, I'd have told you you were crazy."

"You're the one who put me in jail, dude."

"I know. You're crazier than I am." He leaned over while keeping his eyes on the road. "But you know what really pissed me off about you?"

"Oh, do tell."

He gave a quick grin. "Not personally. Professionally. You broke that goddamned Candler kidnapping case in a day and rescued Brittney," he bit out. He jabbed a finger her way. "I'd been solid on that sucker for a week, working almost twenty-four hours a day. How the hell did you do that? You made me look like an idiot."

"Oh, God, Matt," she said, her shoulders slumping. "It wasn't talent. The kids trusted me is all."

"Everyone knew you knew the kids."

"No, you don't get it." She examined him. Would he screw her on this? Probably not.

"What?"

"This had better not come back on me. You promise me you won't go after Brittney?"

"Of course not," he said with a wave of his hand. Then he stopped and stared at her. "Wait."

"Yeah. Brittney was never kidnapped."

"What the fuck—I was right!" He swerved a bit but quickly straightened out the car. "That little bitch staged the whole goddamned thing, didn't she?"

"Yeah, but she wasn't a bitch, she was trying to protect her—"

"No wonder!" His face flushed and twisted with anger, he gestured at her with a stabbing motion. "You bald-faced lied for that little bitch?"

She didn't let her emotions rise to meet his. What she'd done was right. "She's not a bitch. She'd been molested for years by her stepfather, Mr. Beloved Decorated Fire Chief, and was trying to protect herself by faking her own kidnapping and running away. She couldn't take it anymore."

Matt gaped, his attention snapping between her and the traffic. "What? Are you kidding?"

"I wish. She was too scared to ask for outside help because of her stepfather's contacts in the police department. And his status in the community. He's a freakin' local hero. Her mother knew about the abuse and wasn't protecting her, and she was desperate."

His anger deflating, he said, "Holy shit. How come I didn't know that?"

"Because it would have blown the whole case wide open, and she wouldn't have been able to keep her scholarship to Yale and become the doctor she's on the road to becoming now. Her mother and five half sibs were dependent on that creep. It was a total mess. I hated that case." The muscles of her scalp were so tight she massaged them to ease the pain.

"Jesus Christ. Larry Candler's a child molester? That makes me sick. We did a fundraiser together. And during the kidnapping case, he had me wrapped around his little finger. That bastard! God, the picture-perfect caring father! We all thought it was so great how he adopted her and treated her like his own child. Ugh. God, that poor kid."

Hell frowned. "He thought he was in love with her. He told her that he married her mother so he could be with her."

He made a disgusted face. "Gross. But how could you force her to go back into that house to—"

"I didn't. He stopped hurting her."

"How do you know?"

"I can't go into that." It had felt so good to kick that bastard in the balls. Candler had snuck into Brittney's room to rape her but instead had gotten a surprise he'd never forget. Hell would love to tell Matt the story, but no one in the Auntie Vigilante Squad spoke about their work. The AV Squad had been formed thirty years before with a group of female friends who helped settle domestic disputes when all other avenues had been exhausted, with fists and batons if necessary. "Suffice it to say, he never molested Brittney again. Now she's in college, anyway, and away from the creep. Still, we're keeping an eye on him and his other kids. He doesn't dare slip."

"You and some people are watching him? Who?"

Talking too much! "Look, the point is I didn't outsmart you and solve the case. I just helped cover for Brittney. Took me forever to convince her to go back home that day. We came up with some fake evidence and a good story, and I have zero idea how all the kids involved managed to stick to it, but they did."

"I knew something was wrong with that!" Matt smacked the steering wheel with the heel of his hand. "Whole damn thing was made up," he said, seeming incredulous. "Man, that tape from outside the abandoned warehouse sold me on the kidnapping. Angle showed part of the van and the men, just enough of them to be convincing. Who were those guys? Some of your old actor buddies from college?"

"No, couldn't put those people at risk of going to jail. The guys, quote unquote, on camera were me and an orphan kid I hire sometimes who can be trusted to keep his mouth shut. Plus he's so young he'd never serve time for helping me. We both played a few roles. We kept changing jackets and masks and coming back into view of the camera. I picked that location specifically because of the security cameras next door. I blocked out the action like a movie shoot."

"Jesus. The deception," he said, his voice a mixture of awe, surprise, and disgust. "Like hell you didn't outsmart me. Most criminals aren't as crafty as you."

Hell shrugged.

"That's why you wouldn't reveal your sources. You almost went to jail again."

"Yeah, it was close. But I am sorry, Matt."

"Apology accepted. You did what you thought was right. And you're right, we would have thrown the book at the girl if she hadn't been willing to give up the fact that she was being molested, even with her connections."

"She still doesn't understand how bad it would have been for her."

"No wonder Candler was all over my ass. He wanted to see Brittney before any of the cops talked to her. He said he had to make sure she was all right, that she would only trust him. And there I was, admiring him because he cared so much about his stepdaughter. Christ, that makes me sick. So obvious in retrospect."

"Don't be so hard on yourself. I knew Brittney, and when she started bawling and telling me what that bastard did to her, I was shocked, too. I'd known Candler for years. I was totally blown away. Dude is so charismatic, so outwardly kind, and so good at running that department. And he did save an entire classroom of school-children from burning to death. He's a monster and a hero."

He was quiet for a moment. "At least you came out looking like a miracle worker."

She snorted. "Yeah, conquering hero," she said in a dismal tone. "I think I single-handedly caused a spike in Costco's alcohol sales after that fun little event. Took a few years of life off my liver."

After a few moments, he turned to her. "You know I admire that you put yourself on the line like that, but you wouldn't be good to anyone in jail, mostly you."

"Yeah, I know." She shrugged. "But I couldn't walk away from that girl. I had to save her. And her whole goddamned family. Same way I couldn't walk away from Billie, the transsexual prostitute. In each situation, I was their only hope. I just think God calls upon you some-times. Besides, as I found out, I can survive jail. Billie would have been gang-raped and killed—"

"They have special wings in the jails for transsexuals."

"Billie's cousin is a cop who wants her dead for shaming the family. Last time Billie went to jail, her cousin made sure she was sent into the general population. She almost died in that attack."

"Oh."

"And by the way both cases started, it was beyond clear to me that God—or the Universe or whatever—had manipulated the situation to bring us together. I'd have to have been deaf, dumb, and blind to miss the signs. I never go to Redwood City but had to get a part for the Malibu. I called seven places, and this automotive place on Veter-an's Boulevard was the only one that had it. So I pull up next to a car in the parking lot for the parts store, I turn, and find myself staring right into Brittney's face. I hadn't been to North Beach in, like, four years, but that day, a client got into a car accident and asked me to go to a strip club to pick up her child support check. I'm pulled over in SOMA under the freeway because I got lost when I took a shortcut, and I'm checking Google maps, when Billie comes screaming by me, covered in blood, totally freaked out. Now tell me, was I or was I not chosen by God in those instances?"

His eyebrows high, he gave a slight nod. "Maybe so, but I also believe God wants you to take care of yourself."

"Yeah..."

"I'm just saying it would be good to learn that it's okay to walk away sometimes. Maybe you had to be there in those two cases, but I've learned over the years that you owe yourself, too."

"Can't argue with that."

He chuckled. "Hell Trent called by God. Not something I'd ever considered."

"God loves pot-smoking, pink-haired tomboys, too."

Matt blew out some air through his teeth and sent her a half-smile.

CHAPTER 29

As they got closer to the librarian's mother's rest home, Hell turned to Matt. "How do you want to approach this? She won't want to talk to us."

"I'll grab her, drag her into the car, and we'll threaten her. We tell her that if she talks to us, we won't turn her in. She gets crazy, I have my gun."

"I have my Taser with me." Hell patted her front jacket pocket.

"Good. We may need both."

They entered the driveway to the nursing facility and parked near the entrance.

"She'll know my car," Hell said.

"She won't be expecting you here. You wait up here with your Taser handy." He indicated the front seat with a downward motion of his hand. He pointed out Hell's window. "I'm going to wait in that alcove by the entrance. I'll grab her as soon as she comes out."

"Okey-dokey."

Hell was dozing off when Matt waved at her and signaled he was ready.

Her heart rate shot up, and she got the Taser ready, but didn't see the librarian anywhere. Only person around was a stout older woman in jeans and a black T-shirt with a short, gray buzz cut, walking toward Hell. Maybe the librarian was still inside, and Matt had seen her through the window.

Matt left his hiding place and walked up behind the woman. But... *Der!*

Damn, the librarian looked different. Thick nerd glasses, a too-tight, short-sleeve, Harley-Davidson T-shirt, and motorcycle boots. As she got closer, her features became more familiar. Still, what a transformation. Much tamer and more normal than the leather-and-chain outfit from the photos Matt had dug up in Sacramento. Zero similarities to her librarian persona.

Matt grabbed her arm and stuck the end of his gun into her back. Judy resisted, but he maintained control. After a few exchanges of words, Judy calmed and went along with him.

Hell had to admit that while Judy's clothes suited her better, they hadn't done much for her appearance. She might as well be wearing the support hose and the helmet of a gray wig for all the good the jeans and T-shirt were doing her.

Matt marched her to their car, opened the door, and shoved her inside.

Hell's heart rate high, all her senses tuned into the librarian's body language, she showed her the Taser. "One move, Judy, and I'll zap you with this thing."

She screwed up her face into a malevolent snarl, her brown eyes huge behind the thick lenses. "You can't do this to me. This is illegal. I'll call the cops as soon as you let me go, and you'll both go to jail."

Hell sent her a sardonic smile. "Anyone's going to jail around here, it's you, my dear. As an accomplice in my attempted murder. Lindsay's in jail. It's only a matter of time before the cops find out about you."

She narrowed her eyes. "You don't scare me."

"We should. We have your future in our hands. However, I really have no interest in calling the cops on you. I just want information," Hell said in a calm, sure tone. "You tell us what we want to know, and maybe we'll forget we found you. But if you piss me off, you can kiss your freedom, and maybe your life, good-bye."

Judy held her chin up, and three long, white hairs caught the sun streaming in the window. "You're not gonna shoot me. And the cops have got nothing on me."

"But Lindsay does," Hell fired back. She took off her sunglasses for effect. "Her maid confided in me that Lindsay recorded all your meetings and has them in a safe deposit box, ready to deploy. Plus an entire dossier on you. Your criminal history, the murder charges that were dropped, all your pathetic financial information, whatever she could get on you."

She sneered. "You're lying. That bitch wasn't wired. I checked."

Hell smiled. "You missed her necklace and earrings. And the whole setup hidden in the trunk of the Honda."

Her brows drew down, and she frowned, her anger lines deepening. "Shit," she spat. "That rich bitch. I knew I shouldn't have gotten involved with Miss High and Mighty."

A surge of victory powered through Hell. Yay! She'd bought the lie!

"When did Lindsay hire you?" Matt asked.

Judy sighed. "About six months ago. To track her boyfriend and all his girlfriends."

"Six months ago?" Hell asked. "But I wasn't seeing him then."

"It was only a couple of blonde bitches before you."

"Another blonde?"

"Yeah, he had two. Then you."

"But Lindsay Banning was one of them," Hell said.

Judy nodded. "And the other two."

Hot anger burned through Hell's veins. "I knew he had another one! Why the hell didn't he tell me when I asked him?"

A nasty smile curved Judy's pouchy face. "Are you really this stupid? He's using you."

Hell almost agreed but caught herself. Bitch was confusing her and knocking her off point. She made a waving motion with her hand. "What was Banning's plan?"

Judy shrugged. "She didn't reveal that to me, but it was pretty clear she wanted to kill you all. And him."

Hell pointed at Matt. "I knew she wanted to kill Brad! I knew she was shooting at him, not just me at the Rosewood."

"Oh, yeah," she said in a superior way. "She wanted to kill his girl-friend and him, and pin it on the other girlfriend."

Matt nudged Judy. "She told you this?"

"No, but I figured it out from what she wanted me to do. She point-blank asked if I knew a contract killer. When I reacted nega-tively, she told me it was all a joke. She swore she just wanted to scare you. The bombs, everything, none of it was meant to hurt you. Bull-shit. She wanted you dead. I saw that look in her eye, and I know that look. She was hungry for your deaths. Really hated Brad Collins for dumping her for you."

Hell gestured with the Taser. "She said all this?"

"You don't have all those guns and sniper gear like she had at the storage locker if you're not serious about killing people. At first, it was that Gwen Lake chick and Barbara Hoffman she wanted to kill."

"Barbara Hoffman?" Matt asked. "That's the name of Brad's second blonde?"

"Yeah," Judy replied. "But I didn't follow Hoffman much. Only when I was following Brad did I come across her. This was six months ago. But like I said, I didn't follow her, only Collins. And Gwen Lake for a while. Then you started seeing him, and Banning modified her plan. Set her sights on killing you and Brad and pinning the murders on Barbara Hoffman."

"What storage locker?" Matt asked.

"One out by the bay," she said like everyone knew about it.

"Where?" Hell asked.

"San Mateo. Out by Seal Point Park. On J. Hart Clinton Drive."

Hell knew the storage facility. She'd spent many wonderful after-noons at the park across the street, taking walks along the Baylands and Coyote Point, enjoying the seabirds and watching the planes land at SFO.

"Why didn't Lindsay mention the storage locker in all those docu-ments she had at home?" Matt asked.

Jones shrugged. "I read about that. Makes no sense. She said she kept no paperwork, no phones, no weapons at home that could be tied to her attacks. And from what I saw, she was pretty meticulous. Banning must have lost her mind because I couldn't believe all the incriminating stuff they found at her house."

"Give us the space number," Matt fired.

Judy looked between the two and did a smug tilt with her head. "Maybe."

"Tell me," Hell ordered. "It's the least you owe me. That bitch tried to kill me, and you helped her."

Judy sat up, defensive. "No, I didn't. I honestly didn't put it all together until recently. I didn't want her to kill you," she stated adamantly. The hard edges to her face softened. "You're too cute." Then she ogled Hell like she was a tasty bit of chocolate.

Hell's stomach lurched. She tried hard to keep her expression neutral.

Matt coughed.

"I had no bullets in the gun that day on 280 when you guys almost caught me," Judy continued, her demeanor much friendlier. "You scared the shit out of me. That bitch Banning hadn't paid me yet, and the rent was due on my mom's rest home here, and I knew I wouldn't get any dough out of that rich bitch if I got caught. I didn't want to hurt you, I just wanted you to leave me alone."

Hell and Matt exchanged glances.

"Oh," Hell said.

Judy gave Hell an up-and-down look. "What I don't get is why you're running away from your sexuality by screwing all those guys."

Hell snorted. "You watched me with all those guys, and you still think I'm gay? I'm fifty-two. You don't think I would have come out by now?"

"You're in denial," she stated with confidence. "All you need is one night with a good woman." She leaned in with a hungry, come-hither smile revealing nicotine-stained teeth. "I could show you a world you never knew existed," she said in low, husky voice, permeating the area with stale cigarette breath.

Hell leaned back and fought the urge to shudder. "Spare me the speech, I've heard it a million times. I'm masculine. I'm butch. And straight as hell."

The librarian turned to Matt. "The more they deny it, the more you know it's the truth," she said in a sing-song voice.

A muscle twitched in Matt's jaw, but he kept his expression firm. "What's the storage space number?"

She sent him a superior grin. "I don't have to tell you anything."

His gaze darkened, and his face hardened to stone. "I still have contacts in the police department."

She laughed. "Oh, please. They all think you're a rotten traitor."

Matt's shoulders went hard and big, and his eyes blazed red-hot. "No, they don't. You don't know anything about me."

Judy greatly enjoyed this. "The hell I don't. A nice Catholic boy like you on the take? I'll bet your priest is proud of you."

Matt's eyes dilated, his face flushed, and he fisted his right hand.

Hell jumped in quickly before Matt killed her. "So why did Lindsay risk everything by shooting at me in her driveway the other day? She could have played it cool."

Judy turned to Hell, her expression relaxed, but by the rigidity of her spine and the way her body was turned toward the door, it was clear she'd received Matt's threat. "Just proves my theory that she lost her mind. I mean, to the point where she even looked different to me on the news the other night. I think she wore a disguise when she hired me."

"But she used her real name?" Hell asked, incredulous.

Judy nodded and didn't give off any tells that she was lying. "Yeah, I thought that was weird. Smart people can be so stupid. Especially rich people who think they know everything. That Lindsay bitch was a real know-it-all. Super uppity. I charged her extra for her attitude."

"Why did you let all my guys see you?" Hell asked.

"Part of Banning's plans. She wanted people to know they were being followed. Wanted to create an atmosphere of paranoia. Especially to set off that Tanner whack job."

A jab of pain nailed her gut. "Poor Tanner."

"Had to admit he was fairly cute for a man, even if he was crazy.

All those young studs you were screwing were hot for men." Her face twisted with incredulity. "Which makes no sense why you'd go for Collins. Old and ugly compared to the others."

Hell pointed the Taser at Judy. "Were you the one who planted the grenades and evidence in Tanner's car?"

"No, Banning did that," she said, assuming more of a tough-girl attitude. "I told her I'd follow people, intimidate people, but I wasn't planting any guns or bombs in anyone's car. Not for less than a couple hundred grand. But, goddamn, that bitch was tight. Would only pay me a grand a day and no more."

Hell said, "She may end up taking you down with her."

"I wonder why she didn't already say something about you," Matt asked and glanced at Hell.

"Because they've got her so drugged up," Judy said. "But I knew I shouldn't have trusted her. She's too crafty."

"What did that Barbara Hoffman woman look like?" Hell asked. "And where did you see her?"

The librarian grinned. "Jealous, huh? I'm telling you, he's gonna break your heart."

Hell rolled her eyes.

"I followed Hoffman to the Circus Club, a yoga place downtown Menlo Park, and a couple chi-chi restaurants. Usual hangouts of Collins' women. Hoffman looked like all his women but you. I think he orders them from a catalog. They all look like they came off an assembly line that produces snobby, rich, skinny, blonde bitches."

Unsurprising and surprising at the same time. "Why didn't he just tell us about her, Matt? I mean, like I would care? I was seeing nine guys."

Judy's mouth fell open. "Nine! That's the total count? I only saw you with five."

"Hadn't seen the other four in a while," Hell couldn't help but brag.

"Where do you find the time? I had two girls once, and they almost killed me."

Hell lifted a shoulder. "Didn't see 'em much."

Judy made a dismissive noise. "You saw five in one week when I was following you."

Of all weeks to follow her. "That was an unusual week." A very crazy and tiring week where she was trying to cleanse herself of her overwhelming desire for BC.

"Then you dumped them all for the old, bald fool." Judy gave a sad shake of her head. "Has to be the money."

"I had another rich boyfriend. Money doesn't make a man."

Judy appraised Matt, then spoke to Hell. "If it's not the money, this one is cuter," she said with a nod his way.

Matt cleared his throat and flushed red.

"That's against the laws of nature," Hell said.

Eyes wide, Matt nodded.

Hell pointed the Taser at Judy. "I want a look at that storage unit. Give us the space number, and we won't volunteer that we found you."

"Will you let me go?"

"Yes," Hell said.

"Space 330. But you can't get in even if you wanted. Door is alarmed, and you need a key or a code to get in the front gate."

"What's the code?" Matt asked.

"I can't remember," she said like he was an idiot to ask. "You also need to disconnect the alarm on the unit or the front office will be alerted. Plus you drive right by that front office."

"I can handle all that," Hell said with confidence.

Matt looked at her like he didn't believe her. He had no idea of Death's reach.

Judy chuckled derisively. "Bullshit. You aren't that good. If you were, you would have figured out Banning's game way before this."

"Try figuring out a case where you're the vic. And you have to interview all your boyfriend's girlfriends while getting shot at and having your home blown to bits."

She raised her brows briefly in acknowledgment. "If I liked the guy as much as you seem to like Collins, I would have taken care of the others at the first sign of danger. Done a preemptive strike."

"I'm not into violence."

"Yeah. You could kill. We all can," she said with a hollow look behind her eyes.

Hell swallowed hard. "Okay, let's go check out the storage locker and call it a day," she said to Matt.

"You're letting me go." Judy's eyes narrowed slightly, she looked between the two. Hell had the feeling she was just about to attack.

They'd gotten what they came for. No use in fighting the crazy sociopath or incensing her further. "Yeah. Right, Matt?"

Matt had changed his posture; he'd clearly read Judy's intent. "I'm good with it."

Jones put her hand on the doorknob and turned to Hell. "Collins dumps you, you know where to find me. I'm tellin' you, I can take you places he can't."

Hell fought the urge to barf. "Thanks."

Judy sent her a weird hungry smile and left.

Matt climbed out of the backseat, slid behind the wheel, and burst out laughing. "Now you know how I felt when Sherry came on to me."

"Ewww, eww, *ewwwww*." Hell vigorously rubbed the gooseflesh on her arms. "That was vile."

"You get hit on a lot by lesbians?"

"Yeah, they think I'm one of them. Funny, people who are so against stereotyping always stereotype me because I hate dresses, high heels, and girly crap. It's all so stupid. Who came up with edict that all women have to wear dresses and high heels? Total female enslavement devices. Make us weak and vulnerable. Have you ever tried to run in a short skirt and heels?"

Matt loved this. "Can't say as I have."

"I've always hated skirts and dresses. Here's my underwear. So yes, I've always gotten hit on by girls, but normally they're much cuter and don't gross me out."

The interest on his face grew. "Do they tempt you?"

"No. But I like the attention. Especially if they're adorable and charming and want to buy me drinks."

Matt chuckled and started the car. "Okay, enough excitement for the day. Let's get you back to the Rosewood."

"Are you crazy? We're going to the storage unit."

"But Hell, I—"

"I don't care if I'm dying, I have to go see that thing. Let's do it!" Hell flashed him the rock-and-roll sign and a giant, excited smile.

Matt laughed but shook his head. "BC made me promise to get you back to the hotel right after the interview."

She pursed her lips. "BC isn't my doctor and doesn't have power of attorney over me. I'm an adult who is completely capable of determining what I need. And I need to see that storage unit. Besides, BC will be busy until at least five. He's meeting with Sherry and their lawyers and hopefully making their final agreement on the divorce."

"But Hell—"

"What he doesn't know won't hurt me. Or you. I know you want to go there as badly as I do. Don't deny it. Come on, Matt, let's go."

Matt stared at her for a moment, then grinned and backed out of the parking space. "The subterfuge between you two starts so early."

Hell let out a laugh from the back of her throat. "With him? The subterfuge hasn't stopped since the moment we met."

"Perfect basis for a long-term relationship."

"With Satan? It's the only way."

CHAPTER 30

As they approached the storage facility, Hell's body buzzed with adrenaline. She forced all the worst case scenarios from her mind. Accessing the storage unit shouldn't be too hard, but they were breaking umpteen laws. Hopefully, it would all go smoothly, and Matt wouldn't decide to end their partnership before it started.

Matt pulled her Malibu into the driveway for the storage business. "Locked gate. I forgot to ask the obvious. How will we get in here?"

"Watch and be amazed." She put her Death phone to her ear. "Deathy? You there?"

"Yes, Hell. I have you on screen," came his gnome-on-steroids voice. "Allow me to open the gate for you."

The gate made a mechanical humming noise and slid open.

The tension in her muscles eased.

Matt's eyes widened, and his jaw slackened. After a moment of hesitation, he drove through the gate.

She grinned. Kinda fun to show the newbie some of her tricks. "Play it cool, Matt. Here's the manager's office."

He relaxed his face. They slowly drove by the small, attached office of the complex.

Inside, a dark-haired woman stood behind a counter.

Hell smiled and waved like she and the lady were old friends. The storage employee beamed and waved back.

They cleared the window, and Hell let out a silent sigh. She didn't want to show Matt anything but supreme confidence. She sat straighter. "Okay, have you hacked into the alarm system?"

"I'm inside, yes," her tech guru replied.

"Disable the alarm for space unit three three zero."

"Done. Be sure to notice where the cameras are, and keep your bolt cutters out of sight," Death advised.

"You betcha. Matt, just keep driving slowly toward the unit." She gestured ahead.

He shot her an alarmed glance.

"Pretend like we're visiting our own locker," Hell said. "Since it has a car in it, it has to be a big one." She pointed at the far end of the storage facility. "See those units at the back? I'll bet it's there. I'll handle the manager if she comes out," she assured him. "Just follow my lead."

His brow wrinkled, and he shot her a sharp glance. "Do you break the law like this all the time?"

"I do if I want to find out what's going on. Once I know the truth, I work on gathering legal evidence."

He pursed his lips. "How many investigations have you blown?"

"Only a couple. This method works for me, Matt. I realize I'll have to compromise my evil ways when I work with you. But it's harder to gain access to the places I need to go without the authority. No one has to talk to a private detective, and I can't get warrants for searches. I have to wing it."

"I guess. Just seems like there must be a better way than putting ourselves at risk for arrest."

"No chance," Hell said, putting on her tough face. She assumed the proper uncaring posture to match her expression.

Matt made a dismissive noise.

They entered the back of the property filled with the bigger storage lockers. Luckily, the section was currently devoid of people or vehicles.

He pointed to a double-wide unit coming up on their right. "That it? Number 330?"

She felt like a racehorse at the starting gate. "Yeah. Pull up in front." This unit could reveal all the final details about her attacker.

Matt looked around the area nervously. "I hope this works." Sweat beaded on his forehead, and his eyes were too wide.

This break-in was nothing compared to some of her stunts. If he wanted to be successful in the PI game, the dude was gonna have to man up and get his halo tarnished.

Hell jumped out, happy to get moving. She popped her trunk, slipped on some nitrile gloves, and put a pair in her pocket for Matt. She grabbed her digital camera, bolt cutters, and a replacement lock. Careful to turn away from the cameras, she cut off the old lock from the storage unit and stashed the heavy thing in a pocket of her jacket. She flipped open the hasp, looped the new lock through the eye, and left the padlock open with the key inside.

She ditched the cutters and old lock back into the trunk and withdrew her phone from an inner pocket. "Okay, we're in, Deathy."

"I see that. Good work. Keep me on the line in case you need me to reroute a police response."

"Okey-dokey. Thanks." She slipped her Death phone into the front chest pocket of her jacket where it would get the least abuse and where he could still hear her voice.

Matt's gaze darted about at all the surveillance cameras. His whole posture screamed "I'm *guilty!*" "Hell, the cops are going to want to know how we got in here."

Hell fought her irritation. He'd better not blow it. She forced herself to reply calmly. "We're going to give them the keys to the lock and say the librarian gave them to us. That we decided to check it out to see if it was worth passing on. To see if she was lying to us."

"She'll tell them otherwise."

"They won't believe her," Hell said decisively. "Here." She shook his hand, slipping him the nitrile gloves. "Put 'em on out of view of the cameras."

He gave a quick check at the security cameras, angled his body to shield his hands, and put on the gloves. Then he rolled up the garage door.

The black Honda was parked on the left side of the unit.

She gasped, her heart thumping hard. While hoping Judy had told the truth, she hadn't quite believed her. "Holy crap. Lindsay's lair."

"Sure looks complete, doesn't it? Wow." He stepped inside and flipped on the florescent lights.

Hell withdrew her digital camera from her pocket. "I'm going to document everything before the cops do. I want to make sure no one ditches any evidence." She took a picture of the car. "But that's weird. Wasn't the Honda at Lindsay's last time I saw it? How did it get here?"

Matt slowly walked farther into the unit, checking it out as he went. "I don't know. Maybe she has a couple of them."

His expertise came through in the way he scanned the area. He didn't miss a thing. Thankfully, his shoulders had relaxed, and his eyes were no longer popping. Slipping into work mode had clearly calmed him. Good.

Along the right wall, opposite the car, was a white plastic folding table strewn with papers. Beyond the table in the far corner stood a tall, gray, metal storage cabinet.

Hell took in the honey pot of incriminating evidence like she was devouring a particularly delicious buffet. No way would Lindsay ever get out of jail now. Thank God. *Vindication!*

She stood back and took a photo of each quadrant of the room while Matt inspected the car.

She approached the table to get closer shots of the contents. Papers and a few small boxes were scattered over the surface. She pulled back the flaps of one of the cardboard boxes.

A hand grenade lay inside, nestled on a bed of paper.

She gave a little shriek, her heart thumping so hard she couldn't breathe for a second. "Matt, grenade."

"Shit." He joined her and examined the gnarly explosive. "We really need to call the cops. And the bomb squad."

"Clearly." Hell's body gave a sharp shudder. "I have to look through these papers, but I'm gonna use a pen to move them. I'll be careful. Never know what the whack job has lying around."

"Okay. I'll check out the metal storage closet." He moved past her to the corner.

She searched the pockets of her leather jacket for a pen and found candy wrappers, a fuzzy peppermint, an old shopping list, and a lighter, but no writing instrument.

Matt opened the tall cabinet and took in a deep breath. "Hell? Check this out."

He stepped aside revealing an impressive array of weaponry. Automatic rifles, pistols, assault weapons, and shotguns lined the walls of the locker.

A wave of cold chilled her. Why was she still alive? "Christ. Talk about overkill. I'm only one unarmed person. How could Lindsay possibly think she'd need all this to kill me? Bitch is crazier than we thought. Thank God she didn't have the assault weapons when I followed her back to her house after the attack at the Rosewood."

"No kidding."

Hell carefully documented each and every weapon in the cabinet, trying not to picture all the damage the arsenal could have caused her.

While Matt examined the contents of the trunk of the car, she returned to the folding table. She still needed a damned pen to move the papers. She tried the last pocket of her jacket and found a pencil. Huzzah! She poked through the stack of papers, snapping pics of each. Most were receipts for guns, the car, and her surveillance equipment, all bought by Lindsay Banning. A veritable treasure trove of incriminating evidence. While very shaken, Hell felt like she'd won the lottery.

She moved aside the last receipt, revealing a small card. Looked like Lindsay's driver's license. The loon must have mistakenly left it behind.

Hell focused her lens and took a close-up of the card.

Something was off about the photo.

Hell took the camera away and examined the license closely.

The woman in the picture was not Lindsay.

It was Sherry Collins in a curly blonde wig.

Hell's heart rate shot high, and she yipped. A nuclear bomb of realization exploded in her mind.

Sherry had impersonated Lindsay.

Sherry had hired the librarian.

Sherry was the killer.

Finally, Hell found her voice. "Matt!" was all she got out as she pointed vehemently down at the license, her finger trembling.

"What? You look like you've seen a ghost." He came close and examined the card. His head snapping back, Matt gasped, his mouth open wide. "Holy shit."

Her body charged like she'd grabbed the third rail on the subway. She jabbed her forefinger at him. "Sherry planted all that evidence at Lindsay's!"

Matt pointed back, his blue eyes bright, equally excited. "The tall, thin intruder in the watch cap next door to Lindsay's the day of the shooting! The two people who ran through the neighbor's yard. Sherry shot at you and BC, then drove to Lindsay's and escaped through the backyard, probably to an awaiting car."

"The tall man and a short Latino?" Hell said with a wild gesture. "Esmeralda. Lindsay's gardener is Esmeralda's cousin. No wonder he swore he'd seen Lindsay leave the house before the shooting at the Rosewood. Esmeralda probably paid him to lie. Jeremy, her house manager, had been telling the truth all along! Sherry must have passed the gun she used at the Rosewood to Lindsay's gardener, who planted it in the house before the cops arrived. Sherry was probably out of her mind with joy when she saw the news reports and realized that Lindsay's breakdown had played right into her hands."

Matt stared at all the papers, then turned back to Hell. "Now we know why the librarian said that it didn't look like Lindsay on TV. Because she'd been dealing with Sherry all along."

Her heart rate neared cardiac arrest range. "Oh, Jesus God, Sherry's meeting with Brad right now! The librarian might have called Sherry to tip her off that we'd talked to her! If Sherry realizes we're on to her, she could hurt Brad! I have to call him to warn him!" She whipped out her cell phone and hit the button to call BC, her hands shaking so hard she almost dropped the phone.

"Empty gun case here, Hell." Matt gestured at a corner of the table. "But I can't picture Sherry shooting up a lawyer's office. And I doubt the librarian called Sherry. What's her motive?"

"To make sure that Sherry didn't kill her for ratting her out. Maybe get more money from her. Sherry could lose it in that meeting."

"You don't go through all this planning and suddenly start shooting up a lawyer's meeting. Sherry's too smart for that. At this point, she thinks she's gotten away with it. Lindsay's in jail, isn't she? I don't think Sherry would risk all that money, not to mention her status. Her big dream is to be in the society pages, not in the headlines for murder."

Hell was not convinced. BC's phone went to voice mail.

Bouncing from foot to foot, Hell wanted to fly there. "Christ! He's not answering! I'll text him." *URGENT! Cancel the meeting! Sherry's the killer. We have proof. CALL ME.*

"Where is he meeting her?"

"Burlingame, like, ten minutes from here."

Matt gave a firm nod, then pointed toward the car. "Better to be safe than sorry. Do you have Brad's bodyguard's number?"

Hell headed for her car, so anxious she wanted to jump out of her skin. "Shit, no! How stupid! Brad fired Thompson after the shooting and hired a new team I haven't met yet."

"We should call the cops about this locker and Sherry on our way." Matt made a sweeping gesture and flipped off the lights.

"Agreed."

Matt stepped out and rolled down the unit's door. Hell snapped the lock shut and withdrew the keys.

They hopped in Hell's car and took off for the entrance.

He frowned as he cleared the gates. "Shit, the police won't believe me. They're going to want solid evidence before busting a rich, connected lady like Sherry Collins." Meaning his reputation had screwed him. He made a left onto Seal Point Parkway, his pain lines deepening.

Matt was so upright and forthright she kept forgetting he had no credibility in his old world. "Yeah, and if we blow it, we could be in jail while Sherry's back there destroying evidence. We have pictures of the stuff but that's it."

"Let's confront her and see what happens," Matt said. "She and I have a rapport. Let's see what she says in a room full of lawyers."

"Crap, I hope BC doesn't tell her before we get there because I just sent him that text. She could shoot him if she thinks she's cornered."

Matt's eyebrows rose. "Let's hope he doesn't."

Her pulse leapt higher. "I'll text him again." She withdrew her phone and typed: *Don't confront Sherry. Pretend you don't know. We're on our way. Ten minutes away. Stall her.* "Still no response." Her stomach twisted, and a weird, cold feeling overtook her extremities. Something was wrong. "He always gets right back to me. I don't like this. I want to call the cops."

Matt took the exit for 101 North. "Hell, he's in a room of lawyers with his ex, trying to save his empire. As much as he loves you, he's a little busy right now."

Despite his logic, Hell's nerves stayed on fire. "I got a bad feeling."

He merged onto the insanely busy Peninsula freeway. "We'll be there shortly. Besides, Brad's one of the best-protected men I know. Both he and his bodyguards know that Sherry has openly spoken about wanting him dead. They'll be on alert."

She thumbed behind herself. "Still, I should have grabbed one of her notebooks."

He gave a firm shake of his head. "Which would have contaminated the scene. Relax."

Hell tried, but she couldn't stop the voices in her mind screaming that something was *terribly wrong*. Probably just her PTSD. "You're right. Crap, I played right into Sherry's hands. I totally caused that whole scene at Lindsay's."

He jabbed a finger at her. "Hell, no, you didn't. She did that. You just went to her house unarmed to talk to her. Don't you dare feel any guilt about that. Lindsay tried to kill you."

"Because I pushed her so hard."

"No, because she's crazy," he stated adamantly.

Whatever. Hell always felt guilt for everything bad that happened in her sphere. Part of her fun psychological pattern. Her mental damage probably also accounted for the sirens blaring in her mind and body.

At that moment, she remembered her Death phone. She pulled out the burned cell from her pocket. "Death? You hear all that?"

"Yes, I did. Quite a surprising development. You wouldn't think a sophisticated society lady would resort to such crude methods to gain her objectives."

"No kidding."

"Also surprising, Sinclair isn't the vindictive, egotistical bastard we thought he was, is he?"

Hell smiled at Matt. "Under certain circumstances, I'd say yes, but in regards to me now, no. Anakin is turning out to be a good ally."

Matt sent her a worried glance.

"I'm relieved you've turned him to the Dark Side," Death said with a chuckle. "Shall I stay on the line?"

Hell shook her head. "I wouldn't worry about it. You heard Matt, and he's right. BC has bodyguards. The librarian more than likely didn't alert Sherry. That would put her in danger. I'm sure everything's fine. Even if my gut is churning like a washing machine."

"Alrighty then. Please keep me apprised of your progress."

"I shall. Love you, Deathy."

"Love you too, Hell."

Hell shut off the phone, withdrew the SIM card, and tossed it out the window onto the 101 freeway.

Matt drove fairly fast but within the law. No matter what she told herself, Hell could not calm her heart or body. Covered in sweat, she trembled like a little nervous Chihuahua. She kept texting BC and calling him, but he wouldn't pick up. Matt was probably right. Sherry was bent on financially ruining Brad and their kids. He and his lawyers were probably performing some pretty amazing legal gymnastics to keep her and her legal team at bay.

Matt parked in front of the law offices. BC's Bentley was parked two cars over.

Hell stepped out of the car.

Loud popping noises came from inside the office. A woman screamed.

Gunfire!

Adrenaline jacked her system, and her heart rate skyrocketed. "Holy shit! Sherry's lost it!" Without another thought, she sprinted for the door.

"Hell! Wait for me!" Matt cried.

Hell was already at the entrance. Pushing open the doors, she ran inside.

A man lay in the carpeted hallway directly in her path. She skidded to a halt.

Freddy, BC's new bodyguard, was on his back, his sightless eyes staring at the ceiling, his torso covered in blood.

Hell gasped and clutched her chest, her mind freezing.

A woman's cries came from behind a desk on her left.

BC's voice boomed out of a room two doors down the hall on the right. "No, Sherry, don't!"

"You bastard! You took everything from me!"

Blam!

BC let out a blood-curdling scream.

Hell's vision tilting, her instincts took over.

Save him!

She leapt over the body and raced toward the room.

"Hell, wait!" Matt's faint cry barely registered.

Her body primed to kill, Hell ran through the open doorway. On the left side of the conference room, Sherry stood pointing a smoking gun at BC, who sat on the floor, leaning against the wall holding his thigh, his hands covered in blood, his face contorted in agony. Sherry moved the gun over and aimed at his crotch.

Sight clouded red, Hell charged the murdering socialite. *"You fucking bitch!"*

Sherry's mouth dropped open, and she swung the weapon toward Hell.

"No!" BC yelled.

"Sherry, stop!" Matt ordered.

Sherry's face twisted into a malevolent snarl, and she fired.

A searing punch of white-hot pain impacted Hell's left shoulder.

Her upper torso recoiled from the shot, but she didn't lose her momentum. Ears ringing, she dove through the air and knocked Sherry onto her back. They landed in a heap with Hell on top.

Hell grabbed hold of the gun, burning her hand, and punched Sherry hard with her other. Sherry's head snapped to the side, but she kept hold of the weapon. Hell yanked on the gun, but her injury had weakened her, and she couldn't wrest the weapon free.

In a quick move, Sherry jerked the pistol out of her grip and smashed Hell's left temple with the solid chunk of metal.

Blinding agony rocked her skull, she saw a flash of light, and then she was on her back, stunned, her head and shoulder splitting with pain.

Get up, Hell!

"Sherry! Hold it!" Matt yelled.

Gunshots blazed. Deafening. Gunpowder stung her eyes and nose.

Save your ASS!

Hell's body pumped hard with fight-or-flight juices, but her limbs were slow to obey her, and her head pounded horribly. She held her upper arm/shoulder to stop the bleeding and tried to find shelter from the gun battle. The room looked like the twisted and out-of-focus reflection of a fun-house mirror. Conference table was a couple feet behind her. She needed to crawl underneath.

She glanced back to check on Sherry. The smoking end of a gun appeared in front of her face with the blurry bitch beyond.

Her heart rate went crazy, and more adrenaline dumped into her system. She held up one hand as best she could in surrender, while keeping pressure on her gunshot wound with her other.

Sherry appeared to be leering, her features reminiscent of Heath Ledger's Joker. "Now, you rotten whore, you will die along with your boyfriend here, and both of you can enjoy the afterworld together." Her voice sounded far away, tinny, and distorted.

Hell's vision focused. Sherry held her left side with one hand, the gun in the other. Blood seeped through her fingers where she held her abdomen.

Matt must have shot her. But where was he? Had she killed him?

"Sherry, put down your weapon," Matt said from somewhere behind Hell and the conference table.

Thank God, he was still alive!

"Matt, didn't I kill you yet? What a disappointment." Sherry kept the gun trained on Hell's face. "If you come any closer, I'll kill Miss Trent."

Sherry was going to kill her, anyway. She saw no way out. But if Hell died today, she was definitely taking this psychopath with her. She had to get past her pain and injuries, clear her head, and figure out how.

BC sat against the wall about fifteen feet away on Hell's left. He hyperventilated and groaned as he moved his blood-covered hands and changed position. "Leave her alone. I'm the one you want to kill."

Great, just what she needed, another dead soul mate. "Shut up, BC!" Hell croaked.

"Shut up! Both of you!" Sherry demanded.

"Put the gun down now, Sherry," Matt ordered.

"Brad, one more word and I kill her. Matt, I'll put it down when I'm done. Now, you loathsome bitch, you crawl for me." Sherry grabbed Hell by the hair with bloody fingers, drilled the gun into her right temple, and dragged her toward BC.

Excruciating pain took Hell's breath away. She screamed in agony and scrambled along on all fours, trying to keep up with Sherry.

"Stop hurting her!" Brad cried out.

Sherry halted near BC, just out of his reach, yanked Hell to her feet, and locked her arm around her neck, the whole time keeping the hot end of the gun jammed into Hell's right temple.

The stench of her own burning hair filled Hell's nostrils, and tears rolled down her cheeks. However she killed the sociopathic creep, she'd make sure to hurt her as much as possible in the process.

"I haven't even begun to torture your little whore yet, you bastard!" Sherry seethed through gritted teeth.

Sherry made a quick outward movement with her left arm, then drove her fist straight into the gunshot wound on Hell's shoulder.

Blinding pain shocked her system. Closing her eyes, Hell howled but couldn't do anything to defend herself with the gun at her head. Her legs shook hard.

BC yelled, "Leave her alone, you fucking bitch!"

Her heart tore at BC's anguish.

Sherry laughed joyously.

Hell breathed hard to control the fire in her shoulder and temple and forced her eyes open to take in the scene. Matt crouched behind the conference table on the left side of the room, his gun trained on Sherry. Out of her peripheral vision, below her on the right, she could just make out the top of BC's head. A man groaned from underneath the table near Matt, probably one of Brad's lawyers.

"Let go of Hell, and drop your weapon," Matt ordered in a calm tone. "So far you've only killed one man, Brad's bodyguard, and just wounded others. If you stop now, with your connections, you'll only get a few years."

"I didn't kill any lawyers? Not Timothy or Jonathan?" Sherry asked, sounding extremely dismayed.

Matt briefly checked the floor to his right. "No, but they'll die if the paramedics don't get here soon."

"Well, then, I'll just have to take my time." She groaned and bent over slightly like she was having difficulty standing upright.

Sherry's abdominal wound was weakening her. She was favoring her right side. Problem with stomach wounds, they didn't always kill fast. Sherry could last for hours before she died, while Brad's wound could kill him soon if he didn't get help. Luckily, by her own limited blood loss, it was clear the bullet in Hell's shoulder had missed the biggest arteries. Hurt like a mofo, but it wasn't bleeding profusely. But BC didn't have long.

"You're shot. Let me call the paramedics," Matt said in a neutral tone.

"No, I want to die. I have no reason to live any longer," Sherry said and grunted.

"What about your kids?" Matt asked.

"The little ingrates. I hate them," she spat. "Junior Brad and Princess Brad are lucky they're not here, or I'd do the world a favor and kill them, too. Wretched creatures."

Hell gave a tiny gasp. Christ, the cold, murdering Gorgon truly had no heart.

"But you have your whole life to live," Matt said. "Surely you can get past this betrayal."

Sherry gave a short laugh followed by a groan. "I have nothing and no one. Judith Jones just alerted me that you'd found the storage unit in San Mateo."

Fucking librarian asshole!

Sherry continued, dripping with hate, "But that wasn't the worst of it. Ten minutes before that, Diana Hollingsworth had called me to inform me that I'd lost my bid for the presidency, and it would be better for the club and the rest of the members if I quit my job as treasurer."

Yeah, getting shunned at the club, much worse than shooting or bombing people. Perfect motive for a mass murder. Her twisted reasoning enhanced the horror.

The socialite tightened her hold. Pain speared Hell's shoulder and she groaned. "Then the icing on the tea cakes," Sherry continued with disgust. "How did Diana put it? That perhaps a year or two abroad might be the appropriate course of action to spare my friends the embarrassment of my current situation. Odious trollop! She practically ordered me out of my own town to hide my head in shame because my husband couldn't keep his cock in his pants. Vile, social-climbing, two-faced cunt."

Matt's aim on Sherry hadn't wavered once. "Being a mass murderer will stain you much more than this little scandal."

Sherry cackled, coughed, then moaned. "I'll no longer care when I'm dead. I just can't figure out upon whom I wish to inflict the most pain. My vile miscreant of a husband or his whore." She punched Hell's gunshot wound.

Hell's mind blanked from the impact, then she let out a scream that shook the windows. She was just about to puke or pass out.

"Leave her alone!" BC cried out in a hoarse tone. Shit, he was fading. If he didn't get medical attention soon, he'd be a goner.

Matt stood and stepped out from behind the table.

"Matt, no!" Hell yelled.

Matt ignored her, his attention fixed on Sherry's face behind her. "Sherry, put the weapon down or I will fire."

"Back off, Matt. I will shoot them and myself, no matter what you do."

"What will that prove?" he asked, taking another small step forward.

Sirens wailed off in the distance.

"The same thing it proves now. That marrying Brad Collins was the single worst mistake of my life," she bit out. "I should have done away with him sooner. I had so many opportunities, just never could follow through." She turned Hell to the right, probably so she could look at Brad. "You do realize you almost didn't survive New Year's two years ago. I'd brought the poison with me to Switzerland and was in the process of adding it your hot toddy when you surprised me with that beautiful Heinz Gassman diamond necklace. I was so taken aback I decided to a give you a reprieve. Besides, we were going to the Bilans' the next day, and it would have ruined that date, and I so wanted to see Tina's new atrium. But now I wish I would have killed you. What a disappointment you are, you worthless piece of trash."

A chill went over Hell. Sherry spoke about killing Brad as if the act had the same emotional weight as getting rid of an old car.

"Me the disappointment?" Brad hurled up at her, his voice strained but strong. "You just admitted you've planned on killing me for years, you rotten bitch! You just shot me, you abomination! What the hell did I do to you but love you, care for you, and marry you? I did everything for you!"

The vigor in his voice gave Hell a tiny bit of relief. Maybe he'd managed to stop the bleeding.

Sherry snorted derisively. Leaning a bit to the right, she kept the gun firmly at Hell's head. "You did everything for me, poppycock! You gave me nothing! You deserve to die for all the disappointment, the repulsive sex." She shivered. "Besides, as I've discovered, killing is quite simple, really. Pleasurable, even. I greatly enjoyed killing Freddy. I can't wait for your lawyers to die. Of course, killing those two should qualify me for a postmortem award."

"You disgusting psycho bitch!" Brad fired at her. "You were the worst wife anyone could have. Fucking you was like fucking a corpse!"

Oh, God, he was trying to save Hell by getting Sherry to shoot him!

"BC, no!" Hell screamed.

Sherry yelled, "Rotten bastard! So it's a corpse you want? Here, allow me to oblige." She lowered the gun from Hell's temple.

Hell reached up as fast as she could, grabbed the weapon with her right hand, and yanked.

Sherry's body jerked, pushing Hell forward hard.

As she fell, the gun ripped from her grip. She landed on the carpet at BC's feet. Pain annihilated her shoulder and arm, and she yelled.

Gunshots blazed above her. She covered her head as best she could with just her right arm, mashing her face into the carpet.

Something super heavy, warm, and soft landed on Hell's legs. She turned and found herself looking right into Sherry's glazed eyes. Blood poured out of a bullet wound in the center of her forehead.

Screaming, Hell scrambled away.

BC, now closer to the door, grabbed her and pulled her into his arms, but his grip was weak. His eyes were going unfocused. Shit, he'd lost too much blood. "Are you okay?" he slurred.

"Brad, stay with me!" Hell took her hand away from her wound and placed it on BC's thigh.

Matt appeared next to her, holding a tie in his hands. "Move, Hell, let me get the tourniquet on him. Put the pressure on your own wound."

Relieved Matt was alive, but terrified for BC, Hell quickly moved back and clamped her hand hard on her shoulder. Matt located BC's gunshot wound and tied the tie around his upper thigh, just above the wound.

"Stay with us, BC," Hell said.

He opened his eyes. "I'm here. That bitch isn't killing me today."

The strength in his voice and gaze reassured her.

Hell glanced at Sherry's body.

Surreal. She knew she should be feeling more relief, but her mind had entered the Barely Able To Think Zone. None of this seemed real. She smelled the gunpowder and blood, saw the carnage and Sherry's dead body, but she couldn't get her head around the scene. It was like she was watching it all on a TV from a different part of town. While the searing pain in her shoulder and head reminded her that it was real, they were the only tells.

"How are my lawyers?" Brad rasped.

Matt checked over his shoulder, then turned back. "They're holding on. I managed to get a tourniquet on one of them. The other just got grazed by a bullet but got knocked out when he fell. He's just coming around now."

"Thanks, Sinclair. For saving them and us," Brad said with a groan.

Hell looked up at this brave man who'd saved her life twice, and gratitude pierced through the hazy mess of her mind. "You rock, Matt," she said, her voice cracking.

He sent her a warm smile, then grimaced. "You're both very welcome." Matt's pain lines were deep. He had a red splotch on the upper arm of his jacket.

"Did you get hit, Matt?" Hell demanded.

He rubbed the area a bit. "A little. Not as bad as you two."

She snorted. "How can you get a little shot?"

"Police! Everybody on the ground or we'll shoot!" came a loud roar from the doorway. A crowd of cops swarmed into the room in full riot gear. "Hands on your head!"

A new blast of fight-or-flight juices flooded her. Her heart rate high, her mind tumbled straight back into the Vortex of Horror.

"We're the victims! We've been shot! Don't hurt us!" Hell cried out.

"Hell, do what they say and do it fast, or they'll shoot you," Matt ordered sharply.

She obeyed as best she could, but her shoulder killed her.

After a long couple minutes of overwhelming terror—and insane pain from far too much jostling and manhandling by the cops—the police finally accurately assessed the situation, and the paramedics rushed into the room.

This time, Hell didn't refuse the ride to the hospital.

CHAPTER 31

T*he light went out of Brad's eyes. He slumped to his side.*
    "No!" Hell cried.

Sherry stood over his dead body holding a smoking gun. She turned and grinned at Hell. "Your turn, you loathsome trollop," she bit out, leveling the gun at Hell's face.

Hell screamed a soul-wrenching bellow.

"Hell! Wake up! You're dreaming!"

Heart pounding, she awoke in Brad's arms.

"You're having a nightmare, honey," he said in a soothing tone.

She cried harder and clung to him as best she could with her right arm, her body trembling, her left arm locked in a night sling with a wedge pillow. "I dreamed she killed you. Then she was gonna kill me." Her stomach was so tight it burned. So hard to believe he was alive. So hard to believe she was okay.

He stroked her hair and rocked her gently. "It was a dream. I'm alive, you're alive, and that sorry bitch is dead. Just relax. Everything will be okay."

Listen to him. You're alive. She's dead.

Hell buried her face in his chest, soaking in his scent, warmth, and love. The scary fog slowly cleared. "Goddamned PTSD. That's how many times I've woken up screaming in the past seven days?"

He kissed the top of her head. "Um, several, you poor thing."

"I just want to sleep without seeing that horrible bitch's face. Or getting shot."

"I'm sorry, honey." He wrapped his arms around her more tightly, careful not to hurt her shoulder.

"How are you doing? What time is it?" she asked. Light came from above the suite's curtains, indicating the sun had come up.

"Around seven. I'm okay. Leg is still killing me, but I took some Vicodin, and it's better. How about you? How's the shoulder?"

She gently moved her arm, and a sharp pain came from her wound. "Hurting. I hate this sling, but at least it keeps my arm from moving. But this adjustable king-sized bed is killer. Best idea you've had in a long time." She patted the comfy mattress he'd had delivered to their Rosewood Hotel suite.

He smiled. "I'm glad you like the bed. But I think *you're* the best idea I've had in a long time." He leaned in and kissed her.

Her body came alive, pulsing in all the fun spots. What this man could do to her sexually, let alone to her heart. Amazing how she could be horny seconds after waking up from a nightmare. He was a maestro.

He withdrew with a loving grin. Wearing only dark blue silk sleep pants, he looked especially delectable this morning. From his tanned, V-shaped upper body with its light dusting of dark chest hair to his long, lean arms to his sparkling gray eyes and strong jaw, BC reeked masculinity. The shape of his shaved head was perfect, his age lines so distinguished, his smile so radiant.

"I still can't believe I get to keep you," she said.

His eyes dilated. "I'm never leaving you. Ever."

She let out a big sigh. "Good."

"Speaking of that..." He shifted his attention to his bedside table. Wincing and groaning, he disentangled from her and moved the back of his bed upwards into an almost sitting position.

Hell rubbed her eyes with her right fist, yawned, and hit the button on her bed controller to match the position on his side. As the mattress rose, her shoulder twinged, but the pressure on her lower spine and hips eased. She peered at his naked muscled back, curious.

He reached into his bedside table drawer. "I've been meaning to give you this."

"What?" Probably talking about her iPad. He'd borrowed it the night before.

He turned toward her holding a small red velvet box.

Her heart leapt into her throat, and she sat straighter, ignoring the complaint from her wound.

He grinned and opened the box.

An emerald-cut white diamond the size of an ice cube was flanked by four large baguette diamonds, two on each side, all set in platinum. From Cartier.

She'd been expecting an engagement ring at some point, but nothing this enormous. The diamonds were so huge the ring almost didn't look real. Bloody thing equaled the entirety of her net worth: house, cars, and retirement.

Her interior heated with shame and embarrassment. Like parking a Maserati in the driveway of a dilapidated old house with a yard full of weeds. Where the hell could she wear this thing? Her friends would never speak to her again. Her family would beat her like a piñata. She'd get murdered for it while doing surveillance. She immediately wanted to reject the ostentatious rock, but when she saw the look in his eyes, all she saw was Brad handing her his heart on a platter. Touched to her soul, Hell choked up.

His eyes wet with emotion, he said, "Hell, I've never loved anyone like this, nor desired any woman this much. I think you're perfect. I'd be honored if you'd accept me as your husband. Hell, will you marry me?"

Her heart burst with a powerful surge of energy, and she threw her arm around him, hurting her shoulder, but she didn't care. "God, yes!"

How she'd longed for this connection. This closeness. This joining. She couldn't believe she'd found true love again.

He laughed and held her tight, then kissed her, thoroughly and

luxuriously, like he was savoring a particularly fine wine. Her girl
parts demanded his attention. Too bad she and Brad were still too
damaged for sex.

When she pulled away, he was grinning ear to ear.

She nuzzled him. "Thank God I found you," she whispered.

"I didn't even know love like this was possible. Do you like the
ring?" He presented the ring again.

She loved him, and the idea of marrying him, but not the ginormous rock. Not only was it completely incongruous with her style, its
mere existence went against her entire ethos. How many people
could this ring feed and house? But she couldn't disappoint Brad. Her
fears and prejudices weren't his problem. To cover her truth, she put
her hand to her chest. "How could I not? Belongs in a museum."

"Why the brow wrinkle? Not the right style? I can take it back."

Shit. This guy could read her far too well. "No, it's gorgeous."

"So?"

"I adore this because you gave it to me. I wouldn't want any
other." Thankfully, this was merely the engagement boulder. She'd
nudge him into a more modest wedding set later. Hopefully, he
wouldn't notice that she'd permanently ditched the glacier. "It's really
perfect, BC." For some spoiled brat rock diva. Some idiot princess.

He relaxed and looked at the bauble. "I know it's probably too
much ring for you, since you haven't adjusted to being with a rich
guy, but I really loved it. And this was a compromise." He met her
gaze and raised his thick, dark brows. "I wanted to get you the sixty-
carat ring, but even I had to admit it was ridiculously huge. So I
settled for the twenty-five carat ring. Well, forty carats with the four
baguettes."

Her stomach went hard, and her face flushed hot. Along with the
voices screaming at her that she was singlehandedly causing the starvation of Earth's children, others screamed at her that she was in
grave danger. Fear gripped her, and she took a deep breath.

"What's wrong, honey? Your eyes just went wide, and you look…"

"Sorry. No, I'm good."

He sent her a patient look.

She put more effort into her performance. "No, really, this ring is just amazing."

"Are you sure you like it?"

She looked him straight in the eye. "Yes. I love you, and I love this ring, and you couldn't make me any happier right now. Well, unless you stuck your cock in me."

He chuckled and groped her. "As soon as we can." He kissed her and pulled the ring out of the box and handed it to her. "Try it on."

Rather than burying the ring in her underwear drawer as she really wanted, she put on the freakishly huge thing and forced a happy smile. Technically, it fit perfectly. But the sparkling Stonehenge did not belong on her hand.

She flashed on Capasso presenting her with jewels, and her stomach twisted.

Logic intervened. Capasso had given her the jewelry equivalent of cement overshoes, drowning the remnants of her self-esteem and ensuring his continued ownership. This crazy giant diamond on her hand was a declaration of BC's love.

She held up the ring. "How did you know my size?"

"Measured it when you were asleep."

She snapped her attention to him. "You did not."

He sent her a cheeky grin. "Did so. Couple months ago. The night you'd done a bunch of shots at a bar with the Roller Derby ex-felons to prove you were one of them instead of a private investigator working for one of their spouses. You staggered into the condo an hour late, absolutely faced."

She winced and cringed. She'd tried all sorts of tricks to dump the booze rather than drink it, but she'd still managed to go about four shots over her limit. She barely remembered the taxi ride to Brad's condo and had vague images of throwing him down on the bed and jumping him. "Sorry about that. I always felt bad. I should have canceled the date."

"No, I loved it. You were a total animal." He chuckled and shook his head. "I was wondering how the hell I was going to con you into putting on the ring sizer. Then you showed up drunk off your ass, attacked me, performed a short, hilarious comedy routine, and passed out. Provided me with a perfect opportunity."

"So let me get this straight. I show up totally blotto, displaying some of the worst behavior I'm capable of, and you still wanted to propose?"

He squeezed her hand. "I was thrilled. One of the only nights I got to hold you all night. First time you let me drive you home the next morning."

"Oh, God, that hangover. Horrible. I was so worried I was going to puke all over the beautiful leather interior of your Bugatti. Wait a minute, you were thinking about proposing to me even way back then?"

He smiled, his gray eyes shining. "I told you that when I find what I want, I go after it. Never fallen in love this fast, this hard before. You were all I could think about."

She nestled in his arms and basked in his warmth and love. So happy he chose her. So happy he wanted her permanently. He made her feel safe. The ring didn't, but he did. Finally, she'd come home.

"I'd better tell Tiffany to get a hold of my publicist so she can announce the engagement."

Hell's heart rate tripled, and her joy ride ended abruptly. "Why don't we wait until the media stops feasting on us? Sherry's body isn't even cold yet. Your announcement will not help us escape our over-publicized *deadly Silicon Valley love triangle*. I'm so sick of that label: love triangle. Actually, in our situation, a love polygon was much more accurate."

He snorted. "I don't care about what people think of us. I'm telling everyone I love you. Screw anyone who doesn't understand. I don't even want to be associated with that sociopathic bitch."

"That will be awhile."

"I know. But I'm going forward with the announcement."

Hell smiled to cover her fear. She could see the headlines now: Deadly Silicon Valley Love Triangle Engagement. Private Investigator Hooks Billionaire Lover. Pictures of the bloody ring would be splashed everywhere, and people would crawl out of the woodwork to destroy her. Humiliate her. Gold-digger! Tramp! They'd be asking BC how he felt marrying a slut.

"In the next couple weeks, we'll need to schedule a meeting with my personal financial manager," BC said. "Sign you on to the mutual checking, get you all set up with debit and credit cards."

Alarms blared, and her body stiffened. More horror! Take his largesse, and she'd have no power with him and no respect for herself. "Thank you, but I don't want to take anything from you. I'm going to earn my own money, buy myself another house, and prove to myself that I can live on my own with just my earnings. I've been relying on other people's money forever. Burned through Josh's life insurance. No more. I only spend what I earn."

He pushed away and stared at her, his face blank. "No. Are you serious?"

"Yes."

"I thought all your refusals to take my money were because we were having an affair."

"No."

His forehead wrinkled briefly. "You took money from Capasso."

Her jaw clamped down hard, and she narrowed her eyes. "Mention his name one more time in an argument, and you'll find this giant ring lodged firmly in your colon."

His expression darkening, he looked away. "Sorry, sorry. I just..."

"For the record, I never took money from him. I was forced into accepting the jewels," she snapped.

"No, I know. That was stupid of me," he said with a dismissive wave. "You just totally shocked me." He blinked and frowned. "Really? *None* of my money?" he asked in a higher register.

Her posture relaxed, but her stomach stayed tight. "No, honey, I don't need it. I can handle all my personal finances fine without your help."

His mouth set, and his focus on her sharpened. "Don't give me that shit. Your cards are maxed out, your checking account has seven hundred bucks in it, your savings is down to four thousand bucks, and all your bills and taxes due now add up to double your cash on hand. You are flat broke. Matt took five hundred grand from me. You'll do the same, and more."

"Jesus Christ, it's disconcerting how much you know about me. But you didn't factor in my accounts receivable. Now that people have stopped trying to kill me, I can get out the invoices."

"You need money now, not in a month."

"I have a twenty-five-thousand-dollar rental insurance policy payout coming next week from my blown-up apartment. That plus my accounts receivable will get me through until I can work again in a couple weeks. Look, I appreciate you trying to take care of me, but I can do it myself."

He pursed his lips. "If I was anyone else in my income bracket, you'd be suing me. And you'd get a ton."

"Brad, give it up. I'm not bending on this. I love you, but I'm not taking your money."

He looked at her like she was totally deluded. "I don't know how you're going to do that and stay in a relationship with me. I'm not compromising what I spend or where I go or what I buy."

"I didn't ask you to. Or expect you to. I have no judgments about what you do with your money."

"It will be *our* money once we're married."

"Let's not deal with that right now. After we're married, we'll settle the financial stuff." She sent him a confident smile, like she expected no problems. All she had to do was put off the wedding until she could come up with a perfect strategy to keep their money separate.

His brow went through a series of movements while he processed this. He finally let out a long breath, and his shoulders twitched. Abdication. Thank *God*. Probably temporary, but she'd take it.

She moved onto her back, flipped up her left hand—careful not to move her arm—and pretended to admire her ring. Hopefully, she wouldn't have to wear it for long.

"So I can't buy you gifts?"

Her stomach tensed hard again. *Great work-around, Brad.* All he'd have to do is say whatever money, expensive car, or tropical island he wanted to give her was "a gift."

Truth was, she loved little presents from her mate, especially chocolates and flowers. But she knew Brad well. This wasn't about giving her gifts because he loved her, this was about controlling her and forcing her to accept his lifestyle. If she opened the door to accepting his gifts just a crack, she'd lose all her power.

Besides, the last thing she wanted was to be seen driving an expensive car, wearing expensive clothes, or showing off expensive jewelry. She'd no longer fit in with her friends.

She sighed. "Can we deal with this later? Like, after tea?"

"Is it because you're trying to prove to people that you aren't with me because I'm rich?"

"No. I don't care about other people. I only care about how I feel."

"So you don't care how I feel? You don't care that I get pleasure from buying you things?"

Her face flushed, her irritation shooting through the roof. "You may get pleasure from buying me gifts, but I don't get pleasure from receiving them. Isn't that your point? To make me happy? All I need or want is your love, compassion, and understanding."

He stared at her like he wanted to crack open her skull and read her thoughts. "You don't like gifts because of Capasso?"

"No, and will you please stop bringing him into this discussion?"

"Sorry. I just... I don't understand. You're the first person I've ever met who didn't like gifts."

Her mood went darker, and she stared down at the ring but hated it as much as the conversation so she focused her attention on Secret Teddy, sitting in a chair in the corner of the room.

Not only was she concerned about maintaining the balance of power in their relationship and losing common ground with her friends, whenever anything good happened to her, someone in her life beat her up or abandoned her for it. She'd been conditioned over the years to hide her good fortune from others, but that strategy was impossible with Brad. How the hell would she protect herself now?

She gave herself a mental slap. So what if she got abused in the future? The only thing that mattered was making Brad happy now.

She sent him as genuine of a smile as she could and kissed him on the cheek. "You know what? I'm being a tweak right now. Of course you can buy me gifts." She took him by the hand. "But, look, would it be cool to limit presents to birthdays and Christmas? Would that be okay?" Since her birthday and Christmas were months away, she'd have tons of time to guide him toward more modest purchases. No cars, no houses, no jewelry. Chocolate, booze, or flowers. Period.

He smiled and gave her hand a squeeze. "Of course." He blinked a bit, his smile faded and his brow wrinkled as he continued to stare at her.

Damn him, he was starting to see through her defenses.

She pretended not to notice his attention on her and put on a cheerful face. "I need a shower." She turned away and planned the least painful way of getting off the bed.

He put a hand on her arm. "Hell, I know you want to make me happy. But I have a feeling you're telling me what you think I want to hear right now to please me. I appreciate the intent, but I need the truth. Unvarnished. You'll be my wife. I need to know what you really think. My money and this ring are upsetting you, and I want to know why."

No. Fucking. Way. People always said they wanted the truth, but if you actually told them, it was usually the last thing they wanted to hear. She relaxed her face. "Honey, I'm really tired right now. I just woke up, and I haven't even had tea. Don't read into my reactions."

His gaze intensified, like he was trying to do a mind meld with her. "The day I hired you, you were very open about your prejudice against rich people. You made it clear you equated wealth with dishonesty, abuse of power, and privilege. Throughout our relation-ship, your views—while not directed at me—have remained strong. I thought when you fell in love with me, you let go of some of that prej-udice, but I'm beginning to see that you haven't. Over the past few weeks, I've watched you resist what's offered you. I see you struggle with the servants. I see you fight my entire world. I've kept attributing it to the shell shock and PTSD, but now I see your resistance goes beyond that. You genuinely seem averse to my world to the point of hostility. Which, you must admit, is problematic going forward."

The arrow of truth struck her right between the eyes. Good points all. Great. Not only would she lose friends and have her old world turn against her, she had to fight her own beliefs and ethics and change the way she thought to truly accept her new husband. So easy! She looked down at her hand in his.

"Please talk to me."

She glanced up, and the vulnerability in his eyes nailed her.

But she couldn't let his need sway her into a useless, upsetting conversation. "Dude, honestly, I'm tired, and I just woke up, and I'm not up for a big discussion this early in the morning."

Concern etched his features, and his gray eyes searched hers.

She patted him on his unhurt leg. "Honey, stop worrying. You're mapping your fears onto my half-dead, zombie-like reactions. Look, my apartment just got blown up, I watched you almost die, I thought I was going to die, we just started a relationship and got engaged, and my entire life is being dissected in the news. I think I have a right to be a little freaked out right now. If I'm giving off weird signals, I think it has more to do with our recent circumstances than our future or how I'm dealing with your servants and world."

"I just want to make you happy," he said, seeming a little lost.

"You are. Stop worrying."

He didn't look convinced.

She let go of his hand and scratched the side of her leg where a piece of shrapnel was working its way to the surface. Time to pretend everything was fine and ignore his emotions. The more she defended or excused her reactions, the more she signaled that she was hiding her true feelings. Time to shut up.

He reached over and gently took hold of her left hand, trapped in the sling, and looked at her ring. "I know you're faking liking this ring," he said, glancing up at her with a penetrating stare. He let go. "How about we do this: wear that until I can get you an engagement ring that suits you better. Even better, why don't we pick out our wedding sets together? Something modest we'll both enjoy wearing."

She let out a long breath, and her back relaxed, but she tried to keep her face neutral. She couldn't show too much emotion or he'd know how much she hated the ring. "You're probably right. I mean, I can't really wear this doing my work."

He snorted. "And I also get the feeling you really don't like that ring."

"How could I not? It's beautiful."

He gave her a look that went right through her. He twisted his mouth to one side. "Please don't feel like you have to have a certain response to please me. What pleases you pleases me. I want your honesty much more than platitudes. That's why I want you to talk to me and tell me how you feel."

"I will." Eventually. Probably. Maybe. "I mean, I am." *Shit!*

He gave a brief chuckle and shook his head. He looked at her and started to say something but stopped himself.

Good.

She nuzzled him, and he kissed her on the forehead.

Weirdly enough, as much as he was annoying her with his attempts to make her happy, he was also making her feel safer. Most guys didn't pay this much attention to their mates. BC really cared about her. So unfamiliar. But still very welcome. While she'd never fully trust him, because she was incapable, she could see where he'd eventually be right up there with Josh on The Most Trustworthy People in her life. She hugged him tight, then pulled away and smiled.

"I'm here for you," he said, moving some hair from her brow. "I want to know what you think, and what will make you happy. But I can't help you with your prejudices. I want you to be open to accepting what's offered to you. Just give my lifestyle a chance. Try to embrace it rather than fight it all the time."

"I will. I promise." *That I will get better at hiding my disgust of your ostentatiously repulsive lifestyle.*

His shoulders and face relaxed, and he smiled. "When do you want to have the wedding?"

Hell's stomach lurched, and she stiffened. For some reason, she'd completely forgotten she had to go through a ceremony to get married. "Uh, I don't know." *Never?* "After I heal would be best."

His eyes took on a shine. "I can't wait. I want a big wedding: big fancy ballroom, lots of food, great band, few hundred people, the works," he said way too enthusiastically.

The idea hit her like a thousand-pound rock being dumped on her head. She'd rather lick all the toilets clean in Central Park than endure another wedding. Especially the kind BC envisioned. The *horror*! A) She hated wearing dresses, B) she loathed being the center of attention, C) she despised all the traditional mandatory rituals: weddings, funerals, graduations, award ceremonies, etc. Intolerable social prisons disguised as parties where everyone pretended to get along even though they all wished they were somewhere else. Imbibed tons of booze just to make the situation bearable. Atrocities.

"Your face went white. Let me guess, you don't want a big wedding."

"Uh. No. I mean, sure," she said brightly. "Whatever you want. Good."

He raised a brow. "And the Bad Acting Award goes to... Try again, only this time with feeling."

She laughed, then made a concerted effort to look happy. "No, really. Sounds great, honey." All she wanted was to forget this conversation, forget the stupid ceremony, and be several years into a marriage with him.

He sighed heavily and sent her a tired look.

Come on, Trent! Act, baby, act!

She leaned into him. "Sorry, honey. Look, I'm just really exhausted. And overwhelmed. Can we deal with one big thing at a time? Let me get my head around the engagement, then we'll deal with the wedding plans, okay?" She looked deep into his gaze and tried to make her eyes sparkle with joy.

He smiled, and his shoulders relaxed. "Of course. I don't mean to overwhelm you. I thought it would make you happy."

"It will," she lied. "I mean, it does. But let's talk about it later." Like, in forty years or so.

"Okay. Oh, one more thing before you shower."

"Yeah?"

"I love the hotel, but I want to go home and sleep in my own bed. With you. I want to move back to Collinswood. I'm having Sherry's things removed and her room cleaned out. The house should be ready in a week, week and a half."

The room darkened and went cold. Her stomach twisted, and she recoiled and gripped the sheets. How many shocks was the bastard going to subject her to before tea? "I really don't want to live where Sherry lived," she blurted before she could stop herself.

His brow turned into a big V. "I know, I know. I hate that she lived there—and there's a big part of me that doesn't want to go back—but I can't let her win. If I don't move back, Collinswood becomes the Sherry Collins Memorial Mausoleum. I can't let her take Collinswood from me, along with the last twenty-six years of my life."

Hell pulled the covers up but really wanted to be holding Secret Teddy. "Would that really be such a bad thing? New start, maybe?"

"No," he said in a tone that left no room for doubt. "That house means the world to me. My grandfather lived there, my father lived there, I grew up in that house. It's my home. My foundation. I have to go back. I thought you'd be okay with it."

She tried to think of a better response other than: *No, no, fuck no.* She couldn't disappoint him, but she couldn't move into Sherry's house, either. He'd been right earlier, she had to communicate with him and make her needs known.

She turned to him. The raw need in his eyes slammed her.

Suddenly, her mouth opened, seemingly all on its own. "I can't imagine a place I'd least rather live, but I certainly understand your need to reclaim Collinswood, so I'll help you."

Shit! Her goddamn need to please was going to kill her someday.

Thankfully, BC seemed more focused on his dreams of Collinswood rather than what must be sheer terror in her eyes.

His gray eyes sparkling, he said with a grand gesture, "I want you to make that house yours. Transform Collinswood into a place where you'll enjoy living. Remodel it, paint, whatever you want to do."

Coat of paint on a shithouse still makes it a shithouse. "Sure. Sounds like fun," she tried to say in a convincing way. She looked at the clock, and her thirst for tea grew stronger. Along with the desire for about six joints.

This little exchange also proved another point: Brad didn't want to know her true feelings, he wanted her to want what he wanted. He'd compromised a bit on the ring, but there was clearly no room for argument about where they were going to live.

A voice in her head warned her that this transition was going to be one of the hardest in her life.

He hugged her tight. "God, I love you, Hell. I never knew it could be like this. That I could have someone who cared so much about me." He pulled away and ran his hand down her face. "To wake up next to you, sleep next to you, it's a dream come true."

Hell grinned, warm energy spreading through her. Right when she began to worry about their future, he reassured her. He was just so solid. So sure of himself. So sure of their relationship. "Right back atcha."

"Hey, I apologize about the proposal. I had so many plans. Really wanted it to be dramatic and spectacular. You know, candles and a special romantic view." His face full of emotion, he said, "But I had to be engaged to you *now*. I had to have you as my fiancée sooner than I could arrange the big deal."

The love in his eyes reached right in and gripped her heart. "Don't apologize for your proposal, honey. It was perfect."

He kissed her, then said, "I'll call for breakfast, okay?"

"Okay."

He ordered their usual, then got up slowly, and, with a large groan, moved onto his crutches. After several adjustments to balance himself, he went into the bathroom, wincing with every step.

Hell lay back on the bed and sighed. It had been twelve years since she'd had to negotiate a marriage, and her skills were rusty. Since Josh died, she'd had total freedom and never had to compromise. She'd forgotten how difficult fairness was to achieve between a couple. How much work it took to make sure both parties were happy.

She frowned. Of course, voicing one's true opinion was the key to achieving that fairness. Which she'd completely blown. She should have fought harder against moving into Collinswood.

Would she have let Josh talk her into this move? No. What was it about Brad that was different? Maybe it was just the whole situation. Being thrust twenty-four-seven into the machine that was BC's life had stripped her of her identity and autonomy. She awoke when he did, ate when he did, did what he did. She had instantly become his other half, with his half dictating her half. She'd never been sucked whole into someone else's reality before. Josh had moved into her home and her world.

Hell hadn't just lost her previous life, she'd been given a full new one.

What she would give for just a few hours alone on her patio at the Vortex. Just being quiet. Just being herself. Then she could straighten out her head.

She stared at the new frightening addition to her finger. The crazy paperweight of a diamond ring didn't seem real. None of her new world seemed real.

Why couldn't he have been poor? Or at least in the middle class?

Another mallet of truth bashed her over the head. Didn't matter if she didn't accept his money—by agreeing to be BC's wife, she'd joined the one percent. She was now part of the Collins' coal and oil empire. Part of the evil that was destroying her world. She had become all that she loathed. Her own mortal enemy.

Her brain began to rattle and shake, her sanity taxed to its limits.

What she needed was a nice dose of denial right about now. Yes, denial, her old friend. She loved denial.

Hell slowly heaved herself out of bed, and her shoulder cried out in agony. Breathing deeply to control the pain, she grabbed her weed and pipe and stepped out onto the verandah. Time to take a break and stop thinking. Besides, thinking had rarely led to anything positive. She loved the man, and she was marrying him, and it was just that simple.

A voice laughed loudly in her head.

Love, yes. Simple, no.

CHAPTER 32

After breakfast and a painful shower, Hell relaxed next to BC on a sofa in the suite's living room. She sipped on a cup of jasmine tea, and he drank his specially-flown-in-from-some-foreign-country-grown-in-a-remote-jungle-harvested-by-wildebeests very exclusive, very expensive coffee. He read the *Wall Street Journal* while she played *Scrabble* on her iPad.

Someone knocked on the door.

"Yes?" Brad called out.

The door opened. "Mr. Collins?" A young Indian woman stepped into the room, one of Brad's many staff members.

"Yes, Zara?"

"Congressman White and his wife are here to see you."

Hell's stomach balled, and she wanted to go into the fetal position. "Great. Did you announce our engagement?"

Brad frowned. "No."

"Fuck. Martin and Irene have some ESP. 'We sense Hell's having a good day. We must go ruin it.' Make them go away."

"No, let them in," Brad said in a loud, decisive voice.

"Yes, sir." Zara left.

The tension in her body at maximum, she almost punched him. "Brad, they're only here to beat me up. Didn't I tell you that every time something nice happens to me, someone comes along and beats me up for it?"

"No, you didn't tell me, but they most certainly will not beat you up. Hand me your phone." He reached for it.

"What?"

"Hand me your phone," he said with such intensity she gave him her cell.

He quickly searched for something and a little evil shine overtook his expression.

While she was curious, her insides fried, her face heating. "We just got engaged. I'd like at least one day to be happy before someone ruins it."

"They won't ruin it, trust me."

She blew out air between her lips. Guess she had to be flayed alive in front of him to make him understand.

Wait, BC had told her a week ago that he'd listened to Martin's message on her phone, and it had pissed him off. So why was he subjecting her to that asshole's abuse now?

BC's father had put Martin in office. Maybe he had to be nice to him. Maybe he was going to try to get Hell and Martin to be friends. Her stomach tightened so hard it hurt. Martin was the consummate politician; for sure he'd bamboozle Brad. Most people missed the subtle barbs and insults Martin threw at her and tried to convince her she'd misinterpreted the situation. She'd been locked in this cycle of invalidation of her abuse her entire life. She couldn't take much more. She looked at the door to the verandah, seriously considering dashing out there to hide.

Phone in one hand, Brad put his other arm around her shoulders in a protective manner and widened his legs, his body in a power position.

Whatever her fiancé was up to, she wanted no part of it. If Martin got too mean, she was out of there.

"Elly!" her sister exclaimed with a giant fake smile, her arms wide as she glided into the room wearing one of her ugly skirted suits.

Hell's first instinct was to slap her.

Irene's asshole dickhead of a husband waddled in behind her. Dressed in a gray suit, Martin appeared exceptionally white, bloated, and pasty today. Amazing how all old Republican men looked the same. Martin was like the love child of Karl Rove and Dick Cheney.

Hell's mind took a quick tour of Martin's previous abuse, and she tried to calm the fear at her core. Emotionally terrorizing her was the congressman's favorite pastime. Just like dear ol' Dad. Together, they made quite a team.

Hell glared at her sister, but made no move to stand. She wanted to scream *fuck off* but was too afraid to really speak her mind. "Irene, why are you here? Did I almost die wrong again? Did I get shot wrong? How did I make you look terrible today by almost getting murdered?" Her stomach tightened, and she prepared for the artillery shelling.

Her sister batted her lashes at Brad and laughed nervously. Her cutesy act was totally incongruent with her gray, curly, granny hairdo, gray suit, and pink, ruffled shirt. Like a flirty nun. Disturbing. And totally unexpected. Why wasn't she attacking?

"Why, Elly, what a thing to say," Irene said in her kiss-ass voice.

Hell had only seen her like this on TV in interviews and around her parents. She must be afraid of Brad.

"You know I love you. Why haven't you returned my calls?" her sister asked in the same fake tone.

Hell's blood boiled, and her jaw clenched. "Only reason you're being nice to me is because Brad's sitting next to me. If I were with the tattooed DJ, you wouldn't have even deigned to call."

"That's not true, Elly. We've always been close. I don't know why you're acting this way." Still with the nervous laughter.

Sick of whatever game her idiot sister was playing, Hell turned to Brad. "I need alcohol. Like, a tanker-truck load. Like, five hundred proof."

Brad wasn't paying attention to her. All his focus was on Martin, and it wasn't friendly. He looked like he wanted to skin him alive.

Martin seemed oblivious to Brad. He was too busy sending hateful energy to Hell. He turned to BC and turned on his false charm. "How are you, Brad? You can't imagine my surprise when I saw the news and realized you were dating my sister-in-law," he said with a strained smile. He couldn't even act he was so clearly pissed, confused, and upset by the relationship.

"*Marrying* your sister-in-law," BC bit out. "I proposed this morning, and Hell agreed to be my wife."

Hell held up her left hand from the sling as best she could and waved her fingers at the hideous couple. Her ice cube flashed like a mirror ball.

Pure envy filled her sister's eyes. Irene's features drew downward to the point where the entire lower half of her face appeared as if it had melted. Her self-esteem came solely from her luxury goods and highfalutin friends and holding her money and connections over other peoples' heads. Hell suddenly being richer than Irene was probably one of the worst things that had ever happened to her.

The color left Martin's face, and he gripped the back of a chair for support. He stammered, coughed, and tried hard to smile but came off looking demented and crazy. "Great. News," he said through gritted teeth with a pasted-on smile. All of a sudden, he snapped into Politician Mode, stood tall, and a warm, fairly genuine grin came over his puffy face. "Great. Couldn't be better. We'll be related now, won't we? Your father will be happy he got *me* in the deal at least, right? Some compensation to sweeten the pot."

The words physically stung. The sick bastard couldn't be nice to Hell even when he was trying his best.

BC's jaw tightened so hard his skin whitened. He looked like he was about to pop. Hell didn't know what he was going to do, but she was pretty sure she was going to like it. His heated gaze lasering into Martin, he held up her phone and pressed the button.

Martin's message played loudly.

Mayday! Mayday! Hell winced, hunched her shoulders, and fought her inclination to run out of the room. Martin and Irene were going to kill her. Any time she'd directly challenged them or her father about their abuse, they'd escalated their attacks. She'd learned long ago to take as much of their shit as possible with a smile on her face, then go hide and cry. Brad's deliberate provocation would not end well.

As Martin's poisonous words echoed through the suite, his face went through all the colors of the American flag: first he turned beet red, then went white, then an odd shade of blue from not breathing. He finally gasped in a large breath, and his expression contorted as he fought to maintain a false smile.

His infamous line blasted out of the cell: "God forgive me for saying this, but it would have been the best thing for me, and this family, if that bomb had killed you."

Hell's interior seared, and she held her belly. No matter how many times she heard that message, it still hurt.

Irene's jaw went to her sagging breasts, then she leveled her Death Scowl at her husband. Martin grimaced, and his shoulders rounded.

Hell couldn't believe it. Irene was actually mad at Martin for saying that crap?

Brad made everyone listen to the entire message, then he punched it off. He pulled her close, kissed her cheek, and withdrew with his pain lines deep. "I'm so sorry for making you listen to that filth again." He turned on Martin, and his mouth went ugly. He pointed up at him. "You, asshole, are on notice," he barked in a deadly tone that came from deep within him, probably somewhere near his balls. "When my old man is gone, so is our money. Like, the second after they declare my father dead, the spigot will be turned off. One negative word about her, or me, and I will turn all my resources against you. You know what I'm capable of."

A chill went through her, followed by a thrill. No one would be mean to her again. Especially Martin and Irene. Not with Brad in her corner. Damn, her fiancé was formidable. More importantly, he'd seen through the couple's bullshit. Yay!

Martin stood taller and affected a concerned expression, which came off as condescending. "Now listen, Brad, that message was taken completely out of context." He gave a couple fake laughs like it was obvious no one should be taking his words seriously. "I don't know what lies Helen has filled your head with—and I'm not one to talk bad about someone—but I came here as a friend to warn you. Stay with her, and she'll be your ruin."

Hell filled with nausea, and her face burned with shame.

Brad stiffened beside her. "Watch it, White. That's my *wife* you're talking about."

Despite Brad's protective words, she wanted to hide with Secret Teddy. Clearly her relationship with BC would give her no protection from her abusers. She also couldn't help but worry Brad would be influenced by Martin's filthy lies. So many people had believed the monster. The old adage, *where there's smoke, there's fire,* had always totally screwed her.

Martin continued on in a cocksure manner. "Thankfully, she's not your wife yet. Hopefully, I arrived here in time to save you from the worst mistake of your life. Mark my words, if you don't break off this ridiculous engagement with this mentally ill nymphomaniac—"

Brad was off the couch and, in two steps, had Martin by his collar, all without his crutches. "*What did you call her?*" he growled.

Hell stared at her fiancé's back, her mind a near blank. Was this really happening?She could count on one finger the times people had stood up for her. Astonishing.

Martin's face even whiter, he looked petrified. "I..." He closed his eyes, then opened them wide in a panic. "You can't marry her! She's a delusional drug addict! She'll bring you down! She'll shame you like she shamed us! She went to jail! Go ahead and beat me up, but you can't change her depravity!"

Unreal. Didn't matter if the dick was in front of a firing squad, he'd still use his last breath to disparage Hell.

Favoring his left leg, Brad shook Martin. "You are so lucky Hell is a lot nicer than me. If she hadn't begged me not to hurt you when I first heard that fucking message, I would be beating you to a pulp right now. I'd get away with it, and you know it." He pushed Martin away hard.

The porker stumbled, but Irene caught him.

BC gestured to Hell. "This woman is a hundred million times

more decent, caring, generous, and giving than you. She lived next to your in-laws for fifteen years and took care of them so you and Irene could be the toast of the town in Sacramento, then Washington. She took care of your brother-in-law when he was in the car accident and nursed him back to health while you were attending parties in DC. The only reason she went to jail was because she was protecting an innocent woman."

"A black, transsexual prostitute, you mean— Don't hit me!" Martin held up his hands defensively, his simpering, wussy, true self on full display.

While Hell greatly appreciated Brad's efforts, he should give it up. Wouldn't matter if the Pope beatified and canonized her, Martin would still say she was the Devil.

Brad took a step toward him, dragging his right foot a bit, the rest of his body poised for attack. "You pathetic parasite! Hell sacrificed everything for your rotten family, and all you did was beat her up for it and persecute her!"

Martin gestured dramatically at Hell. "She abandoned her parents when they needed her the most! When the family needed her the most!"

"After fifteen years? She'd just lost her husband! She had a right to live her own life!"

Hell wanted to say *yeah* but didn't want to throw off Brad's rhythm. Still, she couldn't believe the gloriousness of the situation. Finally, some real truth.

Narrowing his eyes, Martin curled his thick upper lip. "Do you know the sacrifices I made in my career because my wife had to fly to San Jose to pick up the pieces that Helen left behind? She owed us, and she let us all down!"

"Owed you? For what?" Brad demanded.

"I'm a member of Congress!" Righteous indignation radiated from his every pore. "She's a worthless tramp! Only value she's ever had was serving this family, and she couldn't even come through with that! Then she goes and gets us splashed all over the news by saving that sick, black, transsexual degenerate! I had to endure pictures of her everywhere with that freaky pink hair, those disgusting tattoos, and black leather jacket! Then she disrespects *a judge* by desecrating '*My Country, 'Tis of Thee*'—which went viral on the Internet, I might add. To top it all off, *she goes to jail!* Do you know how that made me look? I have a reputation to maintain! But she doesn't care about the importance of my work! She only cares about herself! This latest fiasco proves it! You may be too mesmerized by her sexual powers to see it, but she's the entire reason your sophisticated and well-bred wife tried to kill you!"

Brad's face reddened, and his eyes darkened. "You'd better shut up and right now, fucker."

Martin continued on, sounding like he was making a heated political speech. "Fine! Don't listen to me! Let her destroy your life and reputation! You'll find out what the rest of the world knows when she cheats on you and ruins you! Helen Trent is nothing but a worthless, lazy, self-centered *slut* who's more interested in her drug addiction and football team of lovers than—"

Suddenly, Martin was on the ground, holding his jaw. Hell hadn't even seen Brad's fist move.

Her love for Brad surged, and warm, lovely feelings mixed with the underlying fear of Martin's and the family's retaliation.

Irene screamed and rushed to Martin's side. "You are getting a very skewed version of who we are," she flung up at Brad. "I don't know what she's told you, but she lies."

Brad bared his teeth. "Weren't you the one who called me a low-life, gigolo scumbag the last time I saw you?"

"I didn't know who you were! That's not my fault! She sleeps with criminals! She's a whore!"

Her sister's words pierced her heart, and Hell put a hand to her chest. She could take Martin's vitriol mostly, but not her sister's.

Brad turned to Hell. "Can I hit her now? No, she's not worth it." He glared down at them. "Martin's the only whore here. He's the one who sucks my old man's cock for money so he can keep his day job. Speaking of whores, Irene, if I were you, I'd ask your fat paragon of virtue here about his taste for high-priced, barely legal hookers. Like the ones I bought him when we were in Vegas last August."

Hell gasped. Was this true?

Irene stood, narrowed her eyes, and put her hands on her hips. "Like I believe that. You're lying to throw the blame off my sick sister!"

Brad grinned and held up his iPhone. "Smile, Fat Boy's on *Candid Camera*. Doesn't he look handsome next to his little prostitute?"

Her sister stared at the screen and stopped breathing. Martin's jaw hit the floor. Eyes blazing, Irene turned to her beached whale of a husband, her face in a full sneer. Martin's guilt was written all over his chubby face.

Hell wanted to leap to her feet and dance. Holy shit, proof! In her wildest fantasies, she never thought she'd see Martin deposed from his throne.

BC pointed at Hell. "Hell never cheated on her husbands, but you've cheated on Irene, you big, fat heap of lard. Not only with as many whores as you can screw but with your girlfriend of twenty years, Gloria Della. You probably know her, don't you, Irene? Gloria was Martin's secretary until just last year."

All the color left Irene's face, and she leaned on the dining table. After a moment, her face contorted into pure rage. "I knew it! You weren't comforting her that day I caught you in each other's arms! You were screwing her, you fat piece of shit!"

Hell almost hooted. What a sick burn on that asshole! Story just got better and better! Woo-hooo!

Even though, on some level, Hell couldn't help but feel sorry for her nasty sister. Typical. She still had compassion for the bitch even if her sister had none for her.

Martin tried to stand but couldn't heave himself off the floor. After a ton more effort, he finally stood, puffing loudly, his triple chins wagging. He straightened his spine, and his round face transformed into the picture of innocence. He waved a hand dismissively and gave a couple flippant chuckles. "Now, Irene, you know that's not true. I've never cheated on you. Gloria *was* upset that day. Her dog had just died. I've never had inappropriate relations with that woman. Never! Those pictures weren't of me and prostitutes, they were dancers at a donor event I was forced to attend. You don't think I *enjoyed* that evening, do you?"

Irene pursed her lips and narrowed her eyes. "What about Jane Hopkins? Melinda Jenkins? Shelly Capistrano? You slept with all of them, too, didn't you?"

Martin's blue eyes went wide, then he relaxed and gave her an oily smile. "Now, Irene, your imagination is going wild and—"

Brad cut him off. "I have a file with the entire list, complete with photos and dates, if you'd like to see it," he offered Irene in a pseudo-polite tone. "Maybe you'd like to give the information to your lawyer for your upcoming divorce negotiations."

Martin stared at Brad, his face full of alarm, then turned back to his wife and stammered, but nothing intelligible came out. Finally, with sweat pouring down his red brow, he pointed at his spouse. "Don't listen to his lies, Irene! He's making all that up to hurt us! Your sister's sickness has infected him! He's gone crazy!" He turned to Brad. "You don't scare me, Collins! You've clearly lost your mind!"

Irene glared at Martin, then Brad, her frown reaching her pearls. "Fuck you both." She hustled out of the room.

Eyes narrowed, Martin glared at Hell, then Brad. "You don't want me for an enemy, Collins."

Brad took a step toward him, his posture threatening. "My father doesn't buy politicians like you without leverage. Aside from photos and video footage of you with your whores and girlfriend, we have enough evidence about your financial misdeeds locked away to put you behind bars for the rest of your putrid life."

Martin pointed at him, his pudgy hand shaking. "You're a liar! I've protected myself! I know for a fact no such evidence exists! My reputation is beyond reproach!"

"Consolidated Properties," Brad said in a quiet, low voice.

Martin's face became the color of marshmallows. Then he got enraged. "I'll take you down with me, Collins! I have just as much dirt on you and your father!"

Brad held up his phone. "Dad's going to love hearing that little quote. In your own words. Beautiful."

Martin went silent, his lips tight, his face turning deep crimson. "So much for trying to warn you, Collins. I hope she ruins your life the same way she's ruined ours." Without another word, he turned and left the room.

A couple seconds later, the door slammed in the next room.

Hell laughed joyously. Suddenly, she was crying. Pain engulfed her, and she dissolved into racking sobs. Why had they always been so mean to her?

BC's arms came around her. "It's okay, honey. Take it easy. They're gone and can't hurt you anymore."

"What did I ever do to them but care for their parents and remember their kids' birthdays and host Christmas parties and do all this shit for them? I mean, is it so hard to be nice to me? I'm a good person, goddamn it, and I'm so angry I've let them treat me this way. Did you hear that bastard? I'm so useless I should give up my whole life for the family so he can go off and suck corporate cock and make millions by selling his soul? Could they show me an uglier picture of myself?"

BC rubbed her back and hugged her tight. "No. But Jesus, what an asshole." He gave a harsh chuckle and pulled away to face her but kept her close. "I have the reputation of Mephistopheles. You're the one who went to jail to protect a black transsexual prostitute. This is the first relationship that will redeem me in the public eye, and he says you're hurting me?"

Hell looked down at the ring, and another sting of pain went through her. They made her feel like she wasn't worth the rock. "Yeah."

He squeezed her. "Honey, don't listen to them. I know they've beaten you down, but they spoke pure lies and vitriol. There wasn't one word of truth to any of their statements."

"It's hard when they've been telling me this crap since I was a kid." Hell shook her head, wiped the tears away, and sighed.

"Which says everything about how horrible they are and nothing about you. Martin doesn't treat you badly because of anything you did or said. He and your father treat you badly because you're the youngest and the weakest in their eyes. They hurt you because they can get away with it. So they can feel powerful. They are small, insecure men who feed on the pain they inflict on others to boost their egos. It isn't about you at all. It's all about their tiny, flaccid dicks. Only thing you did was be born into the wrong family."

She shrugged, unconvinced. "I do wear weird clothing, and I don't act like a normal person—"

"So what? Nothing you could wear or say, nothing you could do would upset people who truly loved *you*. True family is about unconditional love. They'd love you *for* your style. *For* what you said. *For* who you are. They wouldn't try to change you. They'd celebrate everything that was you. Like I do."

A surge of love for Brad and a wave of happiness cut through her pain. Her inner foundation felt firmer. These were the words she needed in her head. These were the ideas that needed to become the basis of her psyche. "Thanks, baby. You aren't exactly describing my experience."

"I know. It's a harsh reality, Hell, but you don't have a family. You need to give up on that group and stay away from them."

I wish. Hell sighed heavily. "After Mom dies, I will." She blew her nose.

He frowned. "She let all the abuse happen, Hell."

"I know. But even if she's been cruel to me, I can't do it to her. I'm going to be there for her in her old age despite how she treated me."

His expression remained firm. "I think they brainwashed you and still have complete control over you. I think—"

She quieted him with a hand on his hard unhurt thigh. "Look, I agree that I need to leave the family eventually. But I know how abandoned and alone I felt as a kid and I can't do that to anyone. Especially not someone as frail, old, and partially demented like my mom. She's just too fragile. She wouldn't understand, and it would hurt her health if I wasn't there for her. She won't last forever. I can take the abuse until she dies. Then I'm done. I feel no such obligation to my father. He'd better hope that he dies before Mom or he's going to be one very lonely old bastard."

He regarded her for a moment. Then gave a slight acknowledgment and brought her close. "I love you," he whispered in her ear.

She kissed him on the cheek. "Thanks for standing up for me, honey. I'm a little shell-shocked, but I'll be okay. You were wonderful. You have no idea how much your defense and your words mean to me. You're helping me more than you could know."

He grinned, and his focus went to her mouth.

They kissed and hot energy electrified her whole body. Only other man to do this to her was Josh. But the connection with Brad seemed fifty times more intense because Brad was fifty times more intense.

Not to mention protective. Wow. That part felt super damned good.

In fact, everything about Brad—with the exception of his money and mansion—made her feel good. She could feel his inner strength shoring up hers. She'd never had anyone this powerful in her corner. It was remarkable, unsettling, but so encouraging. She might actually be able to feel safe someday.

What a mighty gift that would be.

Wednesday, April 3, 2011, 5:15 p.m.

HELL STRETCHED OUT ON THE TWO-PERSON TEAK CHAISE ON BC's expansive Hawaiian lanai and gazed at the Pacific Ocean. The sun peeked through the magnificent gray and white rain clouds on the horizon. The intoxicating aroma of the surrounding plumeria trees, along with the ocean breezes, filled her senses. The crystal-blue water beckoned to her but, as she'd quickly discovered, swimming in the ocean with an effed up shoulder was very painful. As disappointing as her limitations were, she was also well aware that this was Brad's Oahu vacation home and neither he nor the house were going anywhere. They'd be back. Often, if she had a say about it.

Hell sipped her mai tai, and tried to accept her new, slightly pock-marked body. The stippling of shrapnel wounds along her left side were still raised and red, along with the gunshot wound to her shoulder. At least she no longer required bandages. She hadn't wanted to wear her black-and-white, skull-and-crossbones-printed bikini, but Brad had insisted. While she didn't look too bad for a fifty-something broad—a small fat pad on her belly seemed to be the only defect aside from her scars—the way her fiancé looked at her made her feel like a twenty-one-year-old supermodel.

BC slid open the screen door and came out on his crutches. "Hey baby, how's the drink?"

She held up her glass, toasting to him. Not only was the balance of fruit juice and rum perfect, he had completed his masterpiece with a tiny purple umbrella and pineapple chunks on a skewer. "Your mai tai making skills are exemplary. This rocks."

He smiled and slowly lowered himself down on his side of the large chaise. He slipped, sat down hard, and let out a loud groan. "Shit, that hurts."

"I'm sorry, honey."

"I'll be fine." Wincing, he carefully adjusted his position on the thick pad.

His long, lean, tanned body, even with the bandage around his right thigh, was a luscious buffet of man candy. Dude totally competed with the horizon and ocean for most beautiful landscape. He wasn't overly buff, but his muscles were beautifully toned. She loved his pecs and the light dusting of dark hair on his V-shaped upper body. He wore dark blue swim trunks that were just the perfect length and size: not too long like a surf rat, not too short like an old guy in denial. Just tight enough to show off his package, but not so close he looked like a gay centerfold. He turned, making his abs tighten, and the sun glinted off his ropy muscles, sending a charge through her.

Even though it had nearly killed them, the night before they'd managed to have the first sex since Sherry shot them. Almost not

worth the pain, as they had both concluded while laughing like hell
—and groaning—at their clumsy and painful session.

He finally relaxed, sighing heavily. He turned to her and gave a
brief eyebrow raise. "I already feel saner here. God, it was nice to get
away from the cameras and press."

"Yeah, and since we took off in your personal plane at night, no
one knows where we are. I have to say, this part of you being rich
rocks." She flashed him the rock-and-roll sign and sent him a big
smile.

He grinned and grabbed her hand. "The contrast between my last
trip here and this one couldn't be more stark. I swear, the ocean
sparkles more, the house seems brighter and friendlier, the food
tastes better, everything is better with you. I love you so much." He
leaned over and kissed her.

Intense love for him overwhelmed her. Suddenly, she was fighting
tears.

He pulled away and furrowed his thick, dark brow. He wiped a
tear from her cheek. "What's wrong, honey?"

"Nothing. I'm just so grateful." She rubbed her eyes and forced
the tears to stop. Last thing she wanted was to ruin her vacation by
being a big, blubbering baby.

Brad pulled her into his arms. "It's okay, sweetie. Everything's
going to be okay from now on."

"I know, that's why I'm crying. You have no idea how bad it's been
for me since Josh died. This change is so extreme. A few months ago
—and for forever it now seems—I was alone in the Vortex. Now here
I am with the man of my dreams, in a fucking bazillion-dollar,
gorgeous, work-of-art home," she said, gesturing around her. She
pointed to the ocean. "Overlooking an amazing private beach with
your own pod of dolphins living in the cove. Unbelievable."

"I paid those dolphins to come here and entertain you, just so you
know." He winked.

She smiled and wiped her eyes. "Whatever you paid them isn't
enough." Emotions overwhelmed her once more, and she swallowed

hard. "It's just so unreal, A) that I found love again, and B) that the relationship brought all this great stuff with it."

"And not-so-great stuff. I still feel bad that I put you in danger."

She made a face. "Like you did it on purpose. Besides, you'd be dead by now if that bitch hadn't come after me."

His expression fell. "I couldn't believe her detailed plans for killing me. All those poisons they found in the storage unit."

Leaning into him, she said, "Poor guy. At least she left a prosecutor's dream of evidence behind. The lead detective was so happy. He said it was the easiest case he'd ever had. No one could possibly misinterpret her intent when she'd handwritten out all her plans in that journal."

His expression grim, he gave a brief nod. "She was certainly thorough. Amazing how much time and effort she put out for her scheme. Setting up Tanner, then Lindsay for her crimes. Buying a car that matched Lindsay's gardener's car. Following around all your men and ensuring they saw her. Taking over Lindsay's identity: the credit cards in her name, the phone number, and computer account. Plus the acquisition of that arsenal. Like she was starting her own war."

"Well, Esmeralda—I mean, Maria Ruiz—really helped with that. She and her drug cartel family buddies and their ready supply of hand grenades and assault weapons."

He shook his head. "Well, Miss Ruiz will be in jail for the next thirty or forty years, then she'll be deported."

"Thank God." She took a sip of her drink.

"Still too good for her," BC bit out.

She gestured with her mai tai. "Yeah, same with Jones. Freakin' measly fifteen years."

He shrugged. "We needed her testimony," he said, and took a long draw off his cocktail.

She snorted. "I still can't believe that horrid little troll convinced me and Matt that she hadn't planted the grenades and evidence on Tanner. Jones was better than I'd thought. I mean, it made sense. I was trying to figure out how Sherry managed to get all that stuff in

Tanner's car without Mr. Paranoid himself noticing, and also while she was busy bombing my apartment."

Pain lines marred his perfect angular features. "Unreal you survived that."

"Seriously. Creeps me out that all these people were lurking around outside my apartment, committing these crazy crimes, and I was oblivious, just sitting there eating dinner and smokin' weed. I'd checked the area that night, too, man. I didn't see any of them. How did I miss Joe *and* Tanner *and* the librarian *and* Sherry? Feel so stupid."

"Don't."

"Easier said than done." She turned to him. "So I overheard you on the phone talking to the lawyer about Looney Lindsay. Please tell me she's stuck in the mental institution and not getting out."

"You heard that, huh? Barry wanted me to know that her lawyers just mounted a solid case for her release."

Her heart rate jumped high. "No!"

He held up his hand. "Don't worry. There's no way. Thankfully—well, not really thankfully—she shot Thompson's guy. And the judge on the case is not in her pocket. Lindsay's back on her meds and has regained some of her sanity. If she's sane, she'll go to jail."

Hope filled her, and she relaxed. "That would be awesome."

"Another thing in our favor: the DA is gunning for her. She made him look bad in a recent book of hers. Even though Lindsay's people paid off Thompson's guy, who is now not eager to prosecute, it's out of his hands. He'll be forced to testify."

"Good." Hell took another sip of her mai tai, and took a second to savor the fruity-rummy taste. She gestured with her glass. "Speaking of mentally imbalanced people, thanks again for having your VA friend hook up Tanner with those services. I think he's got a real chance at recovery now."

BC smiled, and his attention went to the bandage on his thigh. He lifted up an edge, shifted it, and winced. "No problem. Thank God things are finally mostly resolved." He eased back in the lounge, resting his head on the padded cushion. "Calm has been restored at the house. Higgins is taking over as household manager, and the rest of our staff checked out. None were involved with Esmeralda's scheme or Sherry's. They're cleaning out the last of Sherry's stuff. Collinswood will be ready for us shortly."

Her stomach twisted, but she was careful not let her face react. She'd rather be moving into a cardboard box under the freeway. Or her old jail cell. She'd give her left tit to be moving back into her old apartment in the Vortex. All she wanted was the familiarity of her own surroundings.

Hell looked down at her drink and found only ice cubes. Christ, she'd just chugged the whole cocktail without realizing it. She shot BC a nervous glance, then put the glass down on the table on the other side of her. Talk about a giant tell.

They sat for a few moments in silence, watching the ocean.

She turned to him and lifted her chin. "Hey, I have a question."

"Yeah?"

Hell regarded him. "Did you guys have to call it Collinswood? You do realize that in *Dark*—"

His expression turned instantly annoyed, and he sat up. "Yes, yes, in *Dark Shadows*, Barnabus's mansion was called Collinwood," he snapped. "Ours is *Collinswood*," he said, emphasizing his *s*.

She sent him a pitying look. "Dude, that's close enough to be almost insig—"

His face flushing, he made a stop motion with his hand. "Yes, I know. I endured more teasing in school about it than you can imagine. Look, we called the damned thing Collinswood before that stupid show aired, okay?"

She giggled.

"What's so funny?"

"You're awfully upset about all this, Bradabus."

He narrowed his eyes and grabbed her and chewed on her neck. "I'm going to suck your blood!" he proclaimed, doing a bad imitation of Bela Lugosi.

She squealed and pushed him away with her good arm.

"Jonathan Frid didn't do a Hungarian accent."

"No, but he was a lousy vampire. So are all these modern-day vampires. Only vampire worth imitating is Bela Lugosi. He was the man." He brought her close. "Look, all joking aside, I know you don't want to move into my house. And I don't blame you. I can't say as I'm looking forward to it, either. It won't be easy, and I know it, and I'm sorry to ask you to do it. But I need you to do this for me. I really love Collinswood," he said, drawing out the *s*, "and I want to map over the Sherry memories with new memories of you and me and our love. I have good childhood memories of Nanny Mary there. Playing in the gardens when I was a kid. My grandmother was kind to me there. Since my family has been in pieces my whole life, that house is really all I have left."

The need in his eyes moved her. "We'll make it work."

"God, I love you." Her hand caught his attention. "And I love the new Mokume Gane engagement ring. That designer guy Michael Daniel was right, the old, Japanese, gold metal-working process makes the ring appear almost wood-patterned." The diamonds embedded in her tricolored gold ring caught the sun. "Chic, avant-garde, and traditional." He flashed her a bright smile.

Hell gazed down at the unfamiliar ring on her hand, and the warmth in her heart surged. Really was beautiful. Plus she wouldn't get killed for wearing it. "I love it." She almost said that she also loved his matching ring, too, and that she couldn't wait for him to be wearing it, but thankfully stopped herself. She had to endure the wedding first, and she'd still rather be drawn and quartered than face that horrid spectacle. Better to keep silent. So far, she'd managed to evade all conversations about setting a date.

He smiled, brought her to him, and kissed her again. When he pulled away, he looked like the happiest man in the world.

Her heart inflated to near bursting, and her body felt like it was on fire with love.

Millie, the cook and caretaker of the property, spoke through the screen door. "You two ready for pupus? I got some fresh poke all ready for you, and guacamole and tortilla chips."

"Bring it on out, baby!" Hell said.

Millie giggled. "I'll be right back."

Brad sent Hell an admiring grin and thumbed toward Millie's retreating back. "You know I've never heard Millie laugh so much. I didn't even know her. She's a kick. I feel so dumb. Here I had this great person caring for my house and I never even thought of her. You've introduced me to my entire staff. They're all such great people."

Yes, darling, the people who work for you are actual people. Never ceased to amaze her how tuned out BC had been to his entire world. "Millie rocks."

He sent her an easy smile and ran his hand over her head. "I love my life so much more than I ever have. And it's all because of you." He kissed her again.

She lost herself in him, relishing the intense feelings flowing through her. Felt so good to love this fully again.

He pulled away with a big smile, then looked over his shoulder toward the living room. "I hear Black Sabbath."

Hell's gut crunched. The Fear Voice in her head told her that the moment between her and BC had been too perfect and her parents were calling to ruin it. "I'm ignoring my phone today. I'm on vacation. Oh, crap, it might be Joanne. I'm hoping she can come out here on Friday. She was supposed to get back to me." Careful to keep her shoulder immobile, she heaved herself out of the chaise with her good arm.

She stepped inside the cavernous living room with its high ceilings and ginormous open windows that featured the magnificent tropical landscaping of the estate. BC's "small vacation home" had turned out to be a traditional Hawaiian home on steroids. Seven thousand square feet of oceanfront tropical paradise with an Olympic-sized pool and tennis courts. Really amazing. Hell still couldn't get over her fiancé's posh universe. Pure craziness.

She grabbed her phone off a bamboo side table next to a matching leather and bamboo couch and hit the button to check her missed calls, expecting to see Joanne's number.

Her heart stopped beating, and her blood ran cold.

Capasso.

The room darkened around her, and she almost threw up the mai tai. Her body began shaking, and her instinct to hide overwhelmed her.

Fuck.

For some naïve, stupid reason, she'd thought his lack of communication over the previous three weeks had meant that he'd given up on her.

Of course he wasn't done with her.

But that didn't mean she wasn't done with him.

She had to stop herself from throwing the phone on the floor and stomping on it. Shaking off a shudder, she turned off her cell and put it back on the table.

Fuck you, Marco.

Millie appeared with a platter of scrumptious-looking food in her hands. "You ready? You want to eat in here?"

"No. Come on, let's go outside!" Hell said faking her cheer, hoping her fakery would stop the terror and bounce her back to actual happiness. She opened the door for Millie, her hand trembling. Thankfully, the older Filipino lady didn't seem to notice.

Grinning ear to ear, Millie walked outside and presented the appetizers to BC.

"That looks great, Millie," he said with much enthusiasm.

Hell closed the screen door, sent her body an order to calm down, and tried her best to mentally shut the door on all thoughts of Capasso.

This was her time now. For her and only her. All she wanted to think about was Brad and her future with him. Screw her past.

She cleared her mind, took her place on the chaise, and dug into the poke.

As the fresh ahi melted in her mouth and its subtle flavor—combined with the sesame oil, green onions, and soy sauce—delighted her, she caught movement out of the corner of her eye. Her dolphin friends had returned and were breaching the surface of the water.

Brad pointed and exclaimed, "Check 'em out! That's so cool!" Pure joy radiated from his gray eyes.

Gratitude overwhelmed her once more. The contrast between Brad and the Italian dickhead couldn't be more extreme. Brad was a sweet boy who loved her for her. Capasso was her father in an expensive suit.

She let out a long sigh and glanced upward.

Thanks, Universe.

THE END

Hell Trent and Matt Sinclair will return in *Hell House.*

HELL HOUSE

WEDNESDAY, JUNE 10, 2011, 12:05 A.M.

F ocused on her iPhone, Helen "Hell" Trent crossed the second-floor landing of her fiancé Brad Collins' Atherton mansion, headed for the dramatic, curved, mahogany staircase that led to the first floor. *On my way,* she texted to her partner, Matt Sinclair. Hell did a flourish with her index finger and hit *send*—a little too hard. The phone launched out of her hand and tumbled to the plush dark blue carpet a few feet from the top of the stairs.

"Stupid phone."

Hell bent down and grabbed her cell. A glint near the floor caught her eye as she stood. Curious, she knelt down to inspect the source of the light.

Fishing line stretched taut across the top of the staircase about seven inches off the ground.

It took her a long second to grasp the situation.

Her heart began pounding. Sweat beaded on her forehead.

At midnight, she was the only resident of the house on the second floor. BC was in China.

She was the intended target.

Tears rushed to her eyes. She reached into the interior pocket of her black leather jacket with a shaking hand and withdrew her new, snub-nosed Smith and Wesson .22 pistol. Holding the gun with one hand, she called Matt with the other.

"Matt? Get over here now. Someone just tried to kill me."

"Very funny."

"Matt," she said, her voice cracking.

"Holy shit, I'm on my way. How?"

"They strung fishing line across the top of the Death Stairs. Thick enough to trip me good."

"Wait. Death Stairs? That carved, mahogany staircase right there when you first walk into the house?"

"Yes, the same antique stairs that killed BC's grandmother and crippled a maid."

"What? *Killed BC's grandmother?* Why the hell did they keep them after—"

"Apparently, the staircase came out of some famous, seventeenth-century, European mansion. BC says they can't change or improve the thing because of its stupid historical significance. And, of course, recognition in a historical registry far outweighs safety at Collinswood."

"That's why you use the servants' staircase. I thought it was because you parked your car in the back because Brad hates the Malibu so much."

"No. No one uses this staircase. Everyone uses the elevator or the service stairs. But, today, in a *strange twist of fate*, the service stairs are being refinished and the elevator just happened to break down. *Handy* timing, huh?"

"You gotta get out of there. Now."

"Can't risk it. They'll cover their tracks. I knew the staff would try to get rid of me, but not this way."

"Hang tight. I'll be right there."

"O-okay."

Hell called 911 and reported that someone had tried to kill her. Dispatch said she was sending officers to the scene. The lady wanted her to stay on the phone but she didn't want to risk it. She had to have both hands free to defend herself.

She took pictures of the fishing line—probably thirty or forty-pound test—but the images didn't come out well on her phone due to the dark wood background of the stairs and lack of good lighting. She needed more proof. Matt or the cops had better get there before the murderer found her.

Everyone in the house had known she was leaving at midnight. The assailant had to be hanging out waiting for her demise. Whoever showed up first would be the culprit.

She looked down at her gun and winced. If her assassin was armed with an automatic or a shotgun—or if there was more than one attacker—her little Smith and Wesson wouldn't provide much protection.

Lights came on in the marble-floored entry hall below.

Hell's heart rate tripled, and all her focus went downstairs.

Higgins, the butler, stepped out of the arched doorway to the dining room, dressed in a shiny maroon bathrobe and dark slippers.

Adrenaline slammed her system. She aimed the gun at him. "Stay where you are!"

The tall, silver-haired Englishman screamed and threw his hands up, launching a rolled newspaper high into the air. His pale blue eyes huge, he leapt back into the dining room, out of sight. "Dear God, she's gone mad!"

So that was his game: attack her and pretend he hadn't. Sneaky bastard.

"Great acting, Higgins! You won't get rid of me that easily, you asshole! I'll make sure you go to jail for the rest of your miserable life!"

"I'm calling the police! They'll throw you in a padded cell where you belong!" he yelled from just inside the doorway.

Her jaw tensed so hard it popped. Bastard was an uncompromising, judgmental princess. A murdering, dickhead princess.

Voices from the dining room. Someone else was with Higgins. Was the staff all in this together?

Her heart beat so hard she could barely breathe. She moved to her right a bit and bent down behind the carved mahogany railing to get better protection.

Sharp pain speared her shoulder, and she grunted. "Stupid goddamned gunshot wound. Stupid goddamned BC's world trying to kill me all the time." She wiped the tears away, a sliver away from completely losing her mind. She'd already been super disoriented living in BC's ugly, horrible mansion surrounded by his ugly, horrible staff, but this attack sent her right back into the PTSD Horror Zone. "Screw this. If I survive tonight, I'm moving out and never coming back."

Marco Capasso flashed through her mind. Had the Mafia don paid off someone in the household to hurt her?

No. The jealous whack job would kill Brad before he'd kill her.

Hatchet Face, the cook, poked her head out from the dining room doorway. Hell's system revved higher. She was in on it, too! No surprise there. The forty-something Mexican lady with sharp axe-like features and beady dark eyes had hated Hell from the moment they'd met. Just two weeks before, the nasty witch had escalated their feud to all-out war when she slipped laxatives into Hell's food.

"Stay back, or I'll shoot!" Hell bellowed.

Hatchet Face screamed and disappeared.

"I'll get my gun. She no kill us," Mr. Creepy, the maintenance man, said in his thick Mexican accent. Hatchet Face's husband, Mr. Creepy was a fifty-something, square-bodied thug with soulless, dark brown eyes.

"You're trying to kill me, you assholes!" Hell yelled.

"What's going on?" A new, high, feminine voice came from the dining room. The head landscaper, Jill, a young woman in her late twenties. The only staff member who'd been nice to her. Hopefully, she wasn't involved.

"Trent's lost her bloody mind," Higgins exclaimed. "I told you she was a violent, depraved monster! I told you something like this would happen! I'm calling Mr. Collins immediately!" he pronounced in his super-effeminate, melodramatic way.

While Hell could care less about Higgins' sexual orientation, the

Gloria Swanson wannabe was the nastiest queen she'd ever had the misfortune to meet.

"Go ahead, Princess Prissy Pants! I'll tell him you creeps all tried to kill me! Not only will he fire your asses, you'll all be in jail! No one tries to kill Hell Trent!"

Sirens sounded outside.

"Thank God!" Hell and Higgins said at the same time.

Heavy knocking on the door. "Police!"

"Mario, go through the side door, and let in the authorities," Higgins ordered. "We don't dare put ourselves in the line of fire of that madwoman! The homicidal tramp would kill us all without a thought!"

What she would give to punch the prima donna flat.

More loud knocking from the front door. "Open up, it's the police!" came a deep shout.

No one moved.

"She won't shoot with the cops right there." Jill appeared in the entry hall, wary, eyes wide. Wearing a white T-shirt and gray sweat pants, the young, thin blonde held up her hands. "Don't shoot. I'm opening the door."

"I won't shoot you, Jill," Hell bit out. "I'm only trying to protect myself because someone in this house just tried to kill me."

Jill darted to the front door and opened it. "She's got a gun!" she cried and pointed up at Hell.

A crowd of police rushed in, guns drawn, all pointed at Hell. "Drop your weapon!"

Hell's adrenaline shot through the roof, and she tossed her gun a few feet away. "It's dropped." She held her right hand up but couldn't raise her left very high due to the lingering problems with her gun injury. "Don't shoot me. I'm Hell Trent. I live here, and I was protecting myself. I called you guys because someone in this household just tried to kill me."

"On your knees! Hands on your head!" the lead cop yelled.

"For crying out loud! I'm the one who needs protection!"

"On your knees! Get those hands where I can see them!"

Three cops rushed up the staircase, weapons trained on her.

Her head exploding with fury, Hell got down on her knees and lifted her arms. Horrific pain burned her shoulder. "Ow! I'm so telling Captain Mulroney about this. Hey, watch out for the fishing line tied at the top of the stairs! Don't contaminate the crime scene!"

"I don't see any fishing line," the lead cop bit out, a baby-faced, blond kid. "Now get that arm up higher!"

"You idiot! I can't! My shoulder is injured! Don't you know who I am?"

"A crazy woman with a gun?" he sneered.

"Hey, Goodman, that *is* Helen Trent," said the cop behind him, an Asian in his early thirties. "She *is* a friend of the captain's. Didn't you see the video of the shooting on the Internet? She's the private investigator who took a bullet to save her boyfriend, the billionaire Collins guy who owns this house. Our office handled the case."

The young blond cop stopped and narrowed his eyes at her. "I don't care whose friend she is or if she's a big Internet star, she threatened those people with a gun."

"Hell?" Matt yelled from the front door, surrounded by cops. "Officers, I'm a private investigator, Matthew Sinclair. That's my partner up there, Helen Trent. She just called me and said someone tried to kill her."

"Don't listen to him!" Higgins cried from the dining room. "The violent Trent maniac tried to kill me!"

"Shut the fuck up, Higgins!" Hell grunted with pain. Her shoulder felt like someone was drilling a metal rod straight through it.

Goodman kept his gun's aim sharp on her. The other two cops' attention went between Matt and Hell, but they didn't lower their weapons.

A stocky cop in his early fifties with a gray flat-top pushed by Matt. Jake Anderson. Relief flooded her. An old friend and, once upon a time, not a bad lover.

"Jake!" she exclaimed.

"Goodman! Wong! Montague! Drop your weapons! That's Hell Trent!" Jake barked, his gruff voice deep.

The Asian cop behind Goodman lowered his weapon and put it away. "I told you."

The other cop holstered his weapon as well, but Goodman kept his gun trained on her.

Goodman narrowed his eyes at her. "Lieutenant! She has a gun and threatened to kill those people!"

Jake barely reacted to the news and started up the stairs. "I seriously doubt it. But if she did, she probably had good reason."

"She had no good reason other than she's a violent predatory animal!" Higgins shrieked.

Jake sent the butler an irritated glance and kept climbing. "Goodman! Drop it now! That's a direct order!" he commanded.

Reluctantly, the blond kid slowly brought down his weapon.

Hell's Fear Dial dropped a couple notches, and she let out a long breath. Her body trembling, she brought her arms down slowly. Searing pain cut through her shoulder, and she hissed. Rubbing her shoulder gently, she groaned.

She heaved herself to her feet and grunted loudly. "Son of a bitch, that hurts."

"What is wrong with you imbeciles?" Higgins yelled. "I demand that you do your jobs, and arrest that horrible woman! She tried to kill me!"

"Can't imagine why," Jake said under his breath as he walked by Goodman.

Hell's sanity returned in that moment. God Bless Jake and his timing. Collinswood had been like living in a House of Mirrors with all the mirrors reflecting back an insane woman. While she'd known all along the staff was being mean, without validation, it had been like reliving her childhood: emotionally destroyed by people who denied their abuse and blamed her for her reactions.

She pointed at the top of the stairs. "Watch out for the fishing line strung across the top step. Damn gunshot wound's killing me." She carefully rolled her shoulders to loosen them, her left complaining bitterly. "Apparently, Goodman here doesn't have an Internet connection and hasn't paid attention to any of the investigations going on in your department lately."

"New transfer. Little too gung-ho. We're working on it." Jake looked down the stairs and motioned toward himself. "Hey, Matt, come on up. You guys, let him through. Sergeant Escobar?" He pointed toward the dining room. "Don't let any of those people leave. Secure the whole estate." He turned to the young blond cop next to him. "Goodman, downstairs. Help Sergeant Escobar. And try not to shoot anybody, okay?" Without waiting for Goodman's response, he continued upward. "Sorry about all this, honey. Report said shots were fired." He stopped below the top step.

"No. Come to think of it, I'm not even sure my gun is loaded." Hell rarely kept bullets in her pistol, concerned about accidents.

Behind Jake, Goodman glared at Hell like his overreaction was her fault. He clearly still thought she was guilty of something. After a dark look at Jake's back, he finally descended the stairs.

While relieved Jake and Matt were there, her body was still wound tight as a rubber band stretched to its breaking point. Sweat trickled between her shoulder blades, and she couldn't calm her heart.

She tried to act cool and casually pointed at the fishing line. "Someone in this house tried to kill me by tripping me, and I was afraid they'd finish the job before you got here, so I got out my gun," she said like she was a tough girl and not a terrified three-year-old like she felt. She gave Jake a brief history of the staircase.

Jake nodded, checking out the antique woodwork. "Stairs sure are cut at a weird angle. I can barely get a foothold on them they're so short. Yeah, if you fell from there," he said, pointing at the top of the stairs. With his index finger, he followed the route of where she would have fallen. His eyes widened, and he shook his head. "Jesus. Be a miracle if you survived. Even if you did, you'd probably wind up paralyzed."

Hell shuddered. "No one normally uses the damned thing, but today, coincidentally, the back staircase is being refinished, and the elevator is out of order."

"Nothing suspicious there," he joked. He kept climbing until he reached the top and leaned down to check out the line. "That's not very friendly. Damn, girl, you just don't get a break, do you?"

"Has the entire world gone insane?" Higgins yelled. "I demand you arrest that homicidal maniac! She tried to murder me in cold blood!"

Her body flared with heat, and she fisted her hands. "Shut up, you simpering piece of crap," she snapped. "I know you're behind this."

"Vile harridan!" Higgins shrieked. "Officers, you must arrest her! No one will be safe until she's behind bars where she belongs! She's a lunatic! A degenerate drug addict who threatens me with violence and harasses me daily! She's unhinged! A dangerous, gun-wielding miscreant! She belongs in an asylum, not Collinswood!"

Whack job was lucky the cops were there.

Jake rolled his eyes. "Escobar, escort that *gentleman,* and the others, into the living room. We'll set up the interviews in there."

"Why am I being treated like a criminal?" Higgins demanded. "Are you daft? I worked for royalty! My reputation is beyond reproach! I will not stand for this abuse! I demand to see my lawyer!"

Jake shook his head and sent her a look like he found Higgins as crazy as she did. She let out another long breath. So awesome to finally have validation. Yes, Higgins was a crazy asshole. If only Brad could see that.

Of course, it would probably help if she'd actually told Brad what had been going on between her and his butler, but she couldn't bring herself to disappoint her fiancé. Higgins had worked for Brad for over thirty years. BC loved the man.

Jake stepped over the fishing line, scooped up her gun, and joined her.

Hell smiled and gestured toward the house. "Welcome to Kinder-gartens of the Rich and Famous."

The older cop laughed, and they hugged. His rock-hard arms and warmth reassured her. With his thick jaw and chest and thin waist, Jake always reminded her of a human bulldog. Only handsome.

Higgins continued screeching in the background as the cops herded him and the other staff members into the living room.

Jake pulled away and handed her the Smith and Wesson, butt first. "So what? You missed us so much you got these people to try to kill you?"

"Exactly." Hell shot him a grin and slipped the gun into her jacket pocket.

Matt climbed the stairs, inspecting them closely as he went.

She still couldn't believe someone had tried to kill her. Again. So hard to get her head around it.

Jake patted her unhurt shoulder. "We'll secure the scene until the detectives arrive. This the only threat? The line?"

"I don't know. I hope there isn't anything else. But there definitely could be more." She filled him in on the battle with the cook and the laxative episode.

He winced. "Jesus Christ. I thought you were living the high life here, kid."

"No. Tortures of the Damned. I also got into it with Brad's son, Nick. He got up into my face one night and called me a slut. Really intimidated me with his posture and fury. I think he was on drugs, but he was scary."

Jake shook his head.

Hell continued, "Good plan to check out my room and car and my entire route from the bedroom to the gate, just to be sure. Elevator needs to be examined to see if it's been tampered with. Check if it actually broke down or if someone just flipped a switch or undid some wires to make it appear out-of-order. Also, the reason the back staircase is being refinished is because someone spilled a corrosive liquid on it just a few days ago. No one's come forward, of course. Brad thinks it was the maid, who was afraid she'd have to pay for the work. Now it's urgent we find out who. If we can't get a confession, there has to be fingerprints or some physical evidence left behind. The whole scene reeks amateur. Fishing line? Like a murder planned by a seventh grader. Has to be one of the staff. Hopefully, not Brad's son."

Jake nodded. "I'm gonna call the detectives and get this scene roped off. You okay here with Matt?"

"Yeah. Thanks, Jake."

Her cop buddy smiled, nodded sharply, and left.

Matt inspected the line and ran his hand through his thick, wavy, light brown and gray hair. He raised a brow and met her gaze. "And here I thought the laxative thing was bad."

Her stomach tightening harder, she shook off the willies. "I knew they hated me, but not this much."

Dressed for their surveillance job, Matt wore a black T-shirt, black sweatshirt, and black jeans. The sweatshirt made his bulky shoulders appear bigger than normal. The jeans hugged his sturdy hips, enhancing his fireplug form. He actually looked cute. She was so used to seeing him in a blazer and slacks, it was nice to see him in casual wear. Made him more approachable somehow.

Matt stood. "Did you hear anything? See anything?"

She wrapped her arms around herself. "No. But I made a big-ass deal about the staff keeping quiet tonight so I could sleep, since those passive-aggressive assholes love waking me up so much. I made it a point to tell everyone personally to shut up from five this afternoon until eleven. That no one was to make any noise, or I'd hurt them. Has to be one of those creeps down there. I knew whomever had done it would show up to see if their little trick worked."

Matt carefully examined the top of the polished bannister. He put on his glasses, got down on his hands and knees, and closely checked out the fishing line, the concern lines on his weathered, square face deepening. "Knots were made by an experienced fisherman. This is a clinch knot. A well-made one."

"So our culprit is a twelve-year-old who loves fishing?"

He stood, rubbed his left knee—his bad one—and met her gaze. "We'll find out who it is. Don't worry." He climbed over the line and joined her. "We'll keep you safe."

The tension in her spine eased. "Good."

He held out his arms, his blue eyes sympathetic and warm. They hugged, and his musky cologne filled her senses. A calm came over her she'd rarely felt. Because she'd rarely had anyone this solid in her corner.

When he pulled away, he sent her a half smile. "Well, if nothing else, this should prove your case to BC. For sure he'll fire the entire staff now. Even though I have zero idea why the cook is still working here and isn't in jail after she poisoned your food."

Hell coughed and pretended that the gun wasn't quite settled yet in her pocket. She adjusted it several times, hoping Matt would allow the subject to pass.

Matt frowned and turned all his focus on her. "You *did* tell him about the cook, didn't you?"

"Uh." She concentrated on a loose thread on her pants.

"*You didn't tell him?*" Incredulous.

Hell's face flushed. "No. I was going to, but the day I got back the lab results was the day he found out that he can't play tennis for a year because of his thigh wound. He was devastated."

"But that was almost a month ago," he countered in a higher register.

"I kept waiting for the perfect time, but it never came. Then I was afraid he'd be mad at me for not telling him sooner. Or worse, he wouldn't believe me."

"Of course he'll believe you."

She faced him. "You didn't believe me at first, if you will recall. First thing out of your mouth was something about food poisoning. Or a food allergy."

He made a dismissive gesture. "Yeah, but—"

Pointing at him, she said, "You didn't believe me until I showed you the photo of the package of pills in the kitchen garbage, the pill residue on the counter, and the lab results from my dinner showing the high concentration of the same laxatives."

His face fell. "Sorry about that. Shouldn't have doubted you. But I was convinced after you showed me the evidence. You didn't even mention it or show him the proof, did you?"

She shifted her attention to her hurt shoulder. "No. After you didn't believe me, I was worried he wouldn't. Even with the proof. I couldn't take him doubting me."

"Hell—"

"Look, Matt, even before the laxative thing, I tried to talk to Brad about my issues with the staff, and he made excuses for their behavior. Higgins and I got into it within an hour of meeting each other. Brad explained that Higgins was a snooty English butler and had always been brittle. He told me that I'll get used to Higgins' prickly ways, and I'll soon see that he doesn't mean any of it. *'Deep down, he's a gentle soul,'*" she said, imitating her fiancé. "Gentle soul, my ass. He's fucking gay Hitler."

Matt laughed, then got serious again. "Right, but when you told Brad that Higgins walking into your bedroom first thing in the morning to dress him upset you, he changed his routine immediately. He even remodeled his bedroom so he could have access to the next room and made it his changing room."

Hell made a puffing noise. "Right. I say one thing and this swarm of contractors descends on the property the next day. BC sounds the alarm!" She made a police siren noise and pantomimed a beacon by spinning her forefinger in the air. Cupping her nose and mouth, she imitated a police radio. *"'Emergency, emergency! All available personnel report to Collinswood!'"*

Matt laughed.

"Deploys the Army, Navy, and Marines. Like my needs are some *huge crisis.* Some giant emergency. I can't take it, Matt. These extremes are driving me insane. His staff is either torturing me or trying to help me in intrusive ways. I just want to be left alone."

He lifted his chin. "What about Toilet-Gate? Did you tell him about that? Or about Mario waking you up by banging two boards together underneath your window?"

Her heart rate rose higher, and she began to sweat again. "I made Josefina cry. I'm sure he would have loved to hear that," she said defensively.

Matt still wasn't convinced. "All you did was clean the toilet."

"Right, and the whole household acted like I'd disarmed a

nuclear weapon in a preschool classroom during nap time. I didn't want to tell Brad what I'd done. In his world, he's a king," she said with big wave of her unhurt arm. "He thinks I'm his goddamned queen. And queens don't clean toilets."

Matt sighed and shifted his weight to his other leg. "BC would not be upset that you cleaned the damned toilet, Hell. And what about Mario? Why not tell him about that?"

She threw up her hands. "I had no proof. By the time I grabbed my phone, the asshole was gone. There is no way Brad is going to believe that his maintenance man, who's worked for him for twenty years, would wake up his fiancée on purpose."

"Well, he must have at least noticed that you stopped eating here."

"He thinks I'm on a starvation diet."

His expression grew more urgent. "Hell, you aren't communicating with this guy at all."

Her shoulders drooped, sending a jolt through her wound. "Ow. Clearly. I tried to tell him the other night about Hatchet Face—Imelda—but he was all focused on this deal that could get him out from underneath his father's control. He's totally worried it won't go through. I didn't want to bug him when he's got so much other stuff on his mind. Besides, we've both been so busy we hardly see each other. I don't want to ruin the precious time we have together."

He looked at her like she was a complete idiot. "Hell. These people just tried to kill you. You don't think if you'd brought BC in on this conversation a little sooner, maybe this wouldn't have happened?"

Her stomach tightened to the point of pain. "Matt, I can't," she said with a wild gesture, hurting her shoulder yet again. "Ow. I can't tell him how bloody miserable I am here. This is his sanctuary. He keeps saying how happy he is to have me here. How happy he is to come home. How different the place feels to him. He'd be crushed if he found out how I really feel."

Amazing how much her upset didn't affect Matt. He was like this giant, unemotional boulder. "Hell—"

She began pacing. "My head's been all fucked up ever since I moved in here. I don't belong, Matt. Collinswood is this big, high-class machine, and I'm the low-class cog that doesn't fit. People waiting on me. I can't even clean a toilet without making people cry. It sucks. I wake up every morning wishing I were back in the Vortex. I love Brad with my whole heart, but I just want to go home."

Matt opened his mouth, then shut it. His posture and expression relaxed, and he sent her a fond smile. "I don't mean to be frustrated with you. We've just been talking about your problems here a lot, and you'd led me to believe that you'd talked to him."

"No. I think the truth is that I'm afraid to. Afraid I'll get blamed or he won't believe me. Even if I'd shown him the evidence about the laxatives, I can't see him buying it. Imelda's been with him as long as Mario has."

"Yes, he will. I did."

"You don't have a personal connection to these people. Brad and his staff are all like one giant family, and I'm the weird step-cousin once removed."

Matt sent her a slightly-less-than-patient look. "Hell, I have no idea why you're still arguing the point. She *poisoned* you. Not only is this a criminal offense, you can't tell me that BC wants his fiancée *poisoned* by his staff."

She held up her hands in surrender. "I know. You're right. Look, I'll tell him." Lowering her voice, she said under her breath, "Somehow. Someday. Someway." She made a face, sighed heavily, and waved her hand toward the fishing line. "Sooner rather than later because now there's no way to avoid the conversation."

Matt pursed his lips and shook his head, then broke into a smile. "Okay, so where are you going to stay until he gets back?"

"Duplex."

He furrowed his brow. "What duplex?"

"My duplex in San Mateo."

He looked at her like he didn't understand her. "You've lost me. Your apartment blew up."

"This is not my apartment. I'm talkin' about the duplex up the block from the Vortex. The place I put the down payment on two months ago."

Matt's head snapped back, and alarm crossed his weathered features. "*You're moving out*? Since when?"

The floor underneath her feet got shaky. She quickly tried to shore up the validity of her plan. "I always planned to have my own place and—"

He made a dismissive noise. "That was before you were engaged. You haven't mentioned it to me so I know you haven't mentioned it to Brad."

She had to turn this around. If she could convince Matt this was a great idea, she'd be able to convince BC. "Look, I didn't tell you because it all happened this morning. I got a notice from the storage facility in Morgan Hill where I've got the contents of the three-bedroom house I shared with Josh. The storage place just got sold, and they're jacking up the rents by half. Minutes later, I got an email from Mary Frances, my friend the landlord, notifying me that my unit was ready. I was like, 'What? What unit?' I'd totally forgotten about it," she lied, practicing for her performance for BC later. "So I called my favorite movers, they just happened to have a last-minute cancellation, and everything fell into place. And now that I've almost been *killed* here, I think living somewhere else for the time being is a pretty goddamned prudent idea."

Matt seemed both shocked and unnerved. Probably picturing his wife, Patty, getting a place without telling him. Completely different circumstances. Probably. "Not the point. The point is that you haven't talked to him about it."

"I, uh, was going to last night, but I was tired and his leg hurt and uh..." She worked on a snag on her fingernail.

"He's gonna think you dumped him."

A shot of adrenaline went through her, sending her heart rate higher. Worst possible outcome. *Stick to your guns!* "I'm not dumping him, nor am I completely moving out. I'm going to live between the two places. Like I'd be doing right now if my apartment hadn't been blown up *by his wife*. I would have never moved in with Brad this quickly."

"I agree you moved in together a little soon, but—"

If she acted like what she was doing was right, then it would be right. "I'll stay at the duplex when Brad's traveling for work, and somehow try to convince him to stay with me there a couple times a week when I want to eat and sleep and live without people attacking me."

"Hell—"

"Matt, I need normalcy," she said, trying to sound confident and not defensive or desperate. "I need my own place. I'm losing my mind here. Not to mention starving to death."

His expression remained firm. "You have forgotten a major point. You *did* move in with him. For the last two months. As far as he's concerned, it's all a done deal. He doesn't know anything about your problems here or the duplex. If you don't talk to him before you move your stuff, all he's going to know is that you had some issues here, and rather than discuss them with him, you chose to escape. You'll screw his trust."

Goddamn it, he'd completely nuked her foundation of logic. She stared at her Converse high-tops, tears threatening. She had to escape Brad's home. She had to. But no way did Brad want her to have her own place. She'd spent the last month trying to come up with a good argument for having her own home other than her pure hatred for Collinswood but had come up with zilch.

She heaved a huge sigh, gave herself an inner shake, and vanquished the tears. No more defense. No more worry. This was the right course of action for her.

Besides, asking for Brad's forgiveness would work much better than asking for his permission. If she sold the idea right, he wouldn't worry that she was dumping him.

Hopefully. She shook her head, and let out a long breath, doubt consuming her once more.

Matt's expression softened. Understanding came over his face, along with deep affection in his eyes. He put his hand on her shoulder. "Listen, let's just work on the case. Let's save your life first. Then you can deal with your future with Brad. First, you need a future. Priorities." He let go.

It was like Hell walked into a wall. *Priorities.* Darkness overtook her mind once more, and her stomach hardened. She slowly lifted her gaze to her partner's. "Please tell me I'm not sabotaging this relationship."

Matt sighed, his expression turning compassionate. "Not intentionally. I think you're reacting to the problems here at Collinswood like you reacted to the shit in your childhood. Take the abuse, slap a smile on your face, and pretend none of it is happening. Then, eventually, crack under the pressure and run away. Plus you're still overwhelmed from almost getting killed a bunch of times, having your life splashed all over the Internet, getting engaged, and moving in here to find yourself surrounded by new enemies. You haven't had a peaceful moment since you almost took a bullet in front of Starbucks back in March. But you do need to find some way to tell him what's going on with you. Aside from the duplex thing, he needs to know what's going on in his home."

Hell shook her head, dread coursing through her. Matt was right. She had to find a way to communicate with BC. "I sure as hell didn't miss this part of relationships. Crap. But you're right. I'm falling back into my old patterns. The self-aware dog thing. And I don't want to do that. I just don't know how to destroy his dreams of Collinswood when he's suffered so many other losses."

Matt's expression didn't change. "That's what marriage is about, Hell: the good and the bad. Crises never happen at convenient times. You have to be able to handle shit storms on top of more shit storms if you're going to make it as a couple."

Hell rubbed her forehead, then her eyes. "Damn it. As usual, and as irritating as it's become, you are right."

He turned up one side of his mouth, and rested his hands on his hips. "You could probably just move your stuff here to Collinswood for now. They must have some storage somewhere. Basement?"

She pictured her cheap, old crap surrounded by the expensive antiques and priceless artwork of Collinswood and grimaced. "Yeah, great plan. Like taking a load of garbage and dumping it in the middle of the Louvre."

"Hell—"

"Don't worry about it, Matt. I'll figure it out. I always do." She leaned against the bannister and frowned. "Confronting him will not be easy," she admitted in a dismal tone. Her stomach knotted. "We've only had one open argument and he was take-no-prisoners."

"The 'Cargument?'"

She rolled her eyes. "Yes."

Matt smiled. "Oh, come on, let him buy you the fully armored Humvee." His blue eyes twinkled.

Hell made a noise at the back of her throat. "Christ. All he talks about is how *dangerous* the Malibu is. I've never seen anyone hate an inanimate object more."

"Right, and you still stood up to him."

"Right, and it took screaming at him to shut him up. Shocked the hell out of him. But it didn't stop him. Three days later, he starts showing me pictures of cars again. Dude does not understand the word no."

Matt sent her a half smile. "Well, I don't know anyone more qualified to teach him than you. You need to stand up to that guy, Hell, and not let him railroad you. You won't lose him if that's what you're worried about."

She sighed and scratched the side of her thigh where some shrapnel was working its way out. "No, I'm not worried about losing him. I just hate arguing, and he seems to like it."

"So tell him that."

She let out an even bigger sigh.

Great. Now, in order to survive—and in order for their relationship to survive—she had to suddenly acquire negotiation skills she didn't have, and blanket bomb BC with two month's of truths and all her hidden needs. Basically, restart the entire relationship while he freaked out.

Hopping a plane to Africa sounded really good. Or maybe a rocket ship to Mars.

She pursed her lips. "God, I hate my life. Again. Still. I thought this part would be easier. Like, I solve the case, and he and I live happily ever after."

He shrugged. "Unfortunately, life is not a fairy tale."

"No shit. Especially mine. More like a goddamned horror story."

Lieutenant Jake Anderson stalked in the front door below, a grave look on his face. "Hell?"

She got queasy. "That doesn't look good."

"Assholes cut your brake lines."

Her heart thumped hard, and a chill went over her. "Great."

"Then it looks like they put a bit of tape around the cuts so they'd hold for a few miles then let go. But their tape fell off, and my guys found the fluid leaking out."

Hell shook off the willies. "Great. So when I hit the 101 freeway, my brakes would fail."

Matt muttered, "Christ." He gripped her shoulder.

Jake nodded, and his expression turned even darker. "Yeah, and that's not all of it. Looks like they might have rigged the accelerator to stick when you pressed it down hard enough. One of my guys is a car guy. He said he thinks the assailant was trying to rig the car so that when you merged onto 101, your car would have shot off like a rocket with no way to stop it."

A stronger wave of nausea hit her. She swallowed hard, and hugged herself. Matt put his arm around her. The 101 freeway through the Bay Area—and especially the Peninsula— was already super dangerous, overly crowded, and challenging to navigate. She definitely would have died, and probably taken out a bunch of people with her. "Damn."

"But nothing's for sure yet. That's just between us," Jake said. "I ordered a second team of detectives, and one's a car expert. We're gonna turn the car—and this place—upside down and make sure we find everything."

"Thanks, Jake."

He shook his head. "Sorry, kid."

Hell forced a bright smile. "It's okay. With you and Matt on my team, I'll be fine."

"World wouldn't be the same without ya, Hell." Jake winked at her and turned to a uniformed officer next to him.

Matt brought her close in a side hug. "We'll keep you safe. We'll find out who's behind this, and put the bastard—or bastards—behind bars."

His warmth and strength reassured her. "Thanks, hon. So I guess now we're looking for a twelve-year-old who likes to fish, work on cars, and kill people."

He grinned and pulled away, his eyes sparkling.

At least her partnership with Matt was working well. The only thing in her life that was.

She'd known the transition from her old life to the new one with Brad would be difficult, but she'd never expected it to be lethal.

Hell House will be released as soon as Janet finishes it